国家出版基金项目
NATIONAL PUBLICATION FOUNDATION

国学经典外译丛书（第一辑）

屈原诗选英译
Selected Poems of Chu Yuan

孙大雨 ◎ 译

上海三联书店

"十三五"国家重点图书出版规划项目

国家出版基金资助项目

目　录

屈原诗选　Selected Poems of Chü Yuan

增补篇

INTRODUCTION

导　论

INTRODUCTION[*]

1   Exordium

When Chü Yuan (*circa* 345 −286 B. C.)^① was born, the extensive feudal fabric of ancient China founded by King Wuh (武王, Ch'ih Fah by name, 姬发) of the Tsur Dynasty (周, 1122 −249 B. C.) and his brother the Duke of Tsur (周公, Ch'ih Tan 姬旦)^② had already past its first stage of disintegration in the Spring and Autumn Period (春秋, 722 −481 B. C.) . ^③ The undermining process in its details was critically, tersely and implicitly recorded by Confucius in his chronicle entitled *Spring and Autumn*. His work came to an abrupt end as he put in his last entry after a premonishing omen, so it seemed to him, of the irretrievableness of the order and glory of early Tsur was made manifest to him. The structure continued to crumble apace. Some four score years later, with the division of the state Ts'in (晋) by its three lords into portions of Wei (魏), Ts'ao (赵)

---

* The Chinese proper names such as personal names and place names in the text are basically spelled according to the Wade system in conformity with the English style.

① *Vide* § 1 and § 22 of section Ⅶ *Chü Yuan and His Works*, on the dates of his birth and death, *pp.* 84 −93,115.

② Henceforth we call him Duke Tsur to simplify the title.

③ The Spring and Autumn Period is generally known in Chinese history to have begun in 722 and ended in 481 B. C., the epoch Confucius wrote his renowned *Annals* on, which first took this name as its title. There was an intermediate stage of seventy-eight years from its end to the inception of the Warring States Period. For convenience's sake in relating historical events, it seems suitable to append these years to it as its continuation.

and Hang(韩), each becoming an independent state, in 403 B. C., the epoch of Warring States(战国) was formally initiated. During this, each of these fought incessantly with some others till predatory Tsing(秦) seized Tsur in 256 B. C. and preyed on the last of the six powers Tsih(齐) in 221 B. C., toppling the old suzerainty to its very base and wiping out the last trace of its order, to set up its own gigantic tyranny — only to be turned into ashes fifteen years later.

Living in such a world of political pressure and turmoil, our poet, a thinker, a statesman and a great soul withal, bore with him towering thoughts of the resplendent past, remembrances of the origin of his race and the part his own house had played in it, day and night. From two of the ancient *t'ih*(帝), he was lineally descended, and with Yao(尧), Suen(舜), Yu(禹) and Taung(汤), he was to a certain extent all collaterally related. What was more, in him, he felt quite sure, was lodged the vital stock of the righteous tradition — *Wang Dao*(王道) or the Kingly Way. Laid in with such a spiritual heritage together with his physical descent, he was keenly alive to the duty incurred. Yet reality doused him hard on the face. Closely connected with King Hwai of Ts'ou(楚怀王), as he was a member of the triad of families Ts'au, Chü① and Chin(昭, 屈, 景), he was denied the audience of his sovereign at first and then even expelled from the capital. His full confidence that in him was invested the mission as well as the capacity to revive the heydays of the two *t'ih* and three

---

① *The Yuan-ho Genealogy of Surnames*《元和姓纂》by Ling Pao(林宝) of Tdaung(李唐) says: Prince Ya(王子瑕) of King Wuh of Ts'ou(楚武王) was assigned the fief of Chü, so he adopted the name of his feud as his surname, and his descendants Chü Tson(屈重), Chü Daun(屈荡), Chü Jien(屈建) and Chü Ping(屈平) all followed his suit.

kings(二帝三王) for the benefit of the people had now become a burning feeling to him. The enemy, in the person of King Wei(秦惠王) and afterwards of King Ts'au of Tsing(昭王), with Tsang Yih (张仪) as their common henchman, intent upon despotic and totalitarian power for its own sake in domestic affairs, together with wanton aggression in foreign policy, and storing up the villany of their house for four reigns from Viscount Shao(秦孝公) and Wei Yang (卫鞅) till now, had cast its wide net of darkness around the royal house and the court of Ts'ou, so that, what with their open diplomacy and underhand espionage, the latter strengthened with saturating bribes, Chü Yuan had proved to be the only insuperable stumbling block — the one personage of note in the Ts'ou court who stood erect and dared to oppose openly the pro-Tsing force.

II Three *Hwang*, Five *T'ih* and Three Kings

In order to fully understand Chü Yuan and appreciate his personality and poetry, especially *Lee Sao*, one should have a clear notion of what the poet, thinker, statesman and spirit of eternity that he was, held dearest and felt most keenly at his heart. The commonweal of the people and so the beneficent rules of such sovereigns in the past as to have had conduced to it, formed the very stuff of his thoughts. A lineal offspring, though distant, of Hwang-*t'ih*(黄帝) and *T'ih* Kao-yang(帝高阳) and a collateral descendant, however removed, of *T'ih* Yao(帝尧) and *T'ih* Suen(帝舜), he was beset by caitiffs all around, hirelings and hellhounds of the state Tsing (秦). King Hwai of Ts'ou(楚怀王), his sovereign lord, was a wretched dupe; his successor, King Hsiang(襄王), a worse gawk. Distraught and tormented, he sang his songs of sorrow, wrath and despair; stricken again and again by repulse, expulsion and exiles and seeing the world had gone to the dogs, he finally ended his own life in protest and remonstrance with Hsiang on his father's and his folly and forewarning the impendent calamity to Ts'ou and the humanity of Tsur and the seven states. What follows is a sketchy account of the earliest rulers of the people, among whom were the poet's illustrious forefathers.

In ancient times, the Middle Empire① was called "Hsia"(夏) or "Hwa Hsia"(华夏), meaning the land that is beautiful and great, i. e., the Middle Empire has the greatness of culture, glory, rites and justice(文章光华,礼义之大).

The gray dawn of Chinese history was illumined by the rules of ten odd legendary patriarchs, emperors and kings. There were the three *hwang*, five *t'ih* and three kings.

First of all, the three *hwang* or two emperors and an empress are, viz., Fwu-shih(伏羲), Tseng-noon(神农) and Neü-ua(女娲). Fwu-shih(伏羲,variants of his name have 伏戏,虙戏,宓牺,包牺 and 庖牺), also called T'ai-hao(太昊,太皞) and surnamed Feng(风), was said to be endowed with sage virtues. He originated in his reign the Eight Symbols(八卦) to embrace all phenomena from the heavens to the earth and innovated the written script (notched on wooden boards), thus giving rise to recorded tablets. He also taught his people hunting, fishing, domesticating animals and tending herds.

----

① The land has been called 中国 since earliest antiquity, which means the Middle Country, to be distinguished from the surrounding barbarian states, the Yih in the east(东夷), the Mann in the south(南蛮), the Zone in the west(西戎) and the Di in the north(北狄). It has been often called the Middle Kingdom in modern publications in the West. Precisely, it should be the Middle Empire, the country of the three *hwang* and five *t'ih*. the emperors. not kings, of the remote past.

His domain was at Tsen(陈), the country now lying east of Kai-feng *hsien*(开封县), Ho-nan(河南), to the region north of Pûh *hsien*(亳县), An-whei(安徽), — formerly known as the Remains of T'ai-hao(太昊之墟). He reigned 115 years and was succeeded by fifteen sovereigns, lasting in all 1260 years.

Tseng-noon, surnamed Chiang(姜) because he was born at the Chiang Stream(姜水), also called the Emperor of Fieriness(炎帝) for he "ruled by virtue of the Virtue of Fire"(以火德王), was the sovereign who began to fashion farming implements and taught his people agriculture, tasted hundreds of herbs for curing diseases and set up markets to induce the flow of goods and chattels. His name, meaning the godly farmer, must have been a title given him by his subjects. Also ruling his territory at Tsen, he later moved his capital to Luh(鲁), the present San-tung Province(山东). He reigned 120 years and was buried at Tsang-sah(长沙), now the provincial capital of Hu-nan(湖南).

Neü-ua was the younger sister of Fwu-shih. She devised wind instruments and set down the rites of marriage, affirming that men and women with the same surname should not unite in wedlock. But according to a fresco in the excavated stone hall of Wuh-liang Temple (武梁祠) of Han(汉), Fwu-shih and Neü-ua, brother and sister, were the world's first man and his wife, with snakelike, scaly nether bodies and tails intertwined and a child between them. It was said that during the late years of her reign, K'ung K'ung(共工)[1], when beaten by Tsuo Yung(祝融) in their struggle to rule the world, butted

---

[1] The character 共 of the name 共工, according to a note by Yen Sze-k'uh(颜师古) of Tdaung(唐) in *The Table of Notables, Ancient and Modern*(《古今人物表》) of *The Fore-Han Chronicle*(《前汉书》), is pronounced K'ung(龚).

Mount Pûh-tsur（不周山）with his head so as to have broken the Pillars of Sky asunder and torn across the four corners of the earth; there-upon, she forged five-coloured stones to patch up cracks in the sky and tore off the legs of the celestial tortoise to prop up the four extremities. But that has gone into pure mythical fictions.

Legends differ as regards the identity of the third *hwang* as well as the order of the three. Instead of an empress, in two other traditions there were the emperors Tsuo Yung（祝融）, whose achievements are not recorded, and Suey-ren（燧人）, who was said to ignite fire, by means of a concave metal disc or a drill for boring wood, to teach his people to eat cooked food.

Next, the five *t'ih*（五帝）or emperors are as follows: First, there was Hsien-yuan（轩辕）, so called because he lived on the Highlands of Hsien-yuan（轩辕之丘）, surnamed Kung-sun（公孙）and also Ch'ih（姬）, as he was brought up by the Ch'ih Stream（姬水）, and generally called Hwang-*t'ih*（黄帝）or the Luteous Emperor, for he "ruled by virtue of the Virtue of Soil"（以土德王）which was taken to be yellowish brown or of the colour of clay. The eighth emperor after Tseng-noon, called Yih-moun（榆罔）, tyrannical and disorderly in his rule, was fought and beaten by Hsien-yuan at Pan-tsuen（阪泉）. Tze-yer（蚩尤）, a tribal chief, rising in revolt, was defeated and killed by him. He was then raised by common agreement of tribal heads to be their emperor. In his reign he instructed Tai Nau（大挠）to combine two sets of primordial signs（作甲子）, the heavenly *kan*（天干）and the earthly *tse*（地支） — the former, ten in number（甲、乙、丙、丁、戊、己、庚、辛、壬、癸）and the latter, twelve （子、丑、寅、卯、辰、巳、午、未、申、酉、戌、亥）, also called stems and branches（干支）, said to be contrived by the first sovereign of the race T'ien-*hwang*（天皇氏）— for indicating the days of months. The process of combining the ten *kan* with the twelve *tse* began from *ja-tse*（甲子）, *ih-tser*（乙丑）, *pin-yin*（丙寅）, *t'ing-mao*（丁卯）, *wuh-tsen*（戊辰）, *jih-tze*（己巳）, etc. till a cycle of sixty combinations was completed and then another cycle continued, and so on. Combinations of *kan* and *tse* were also often used to indicate the cycles of years, of the months of the year, and of the time periods of the day. But these, it is known, were later developments. He also ordered Tsoung Chi（仓颉）to originate the six ingredients of character writing（作六书）, Lin Lun（伶伦）to fix the twelve elemental tunes of musical sounds（定律吕）and Lih Sur（隶首）to set the laws of numbers（定算数）. Besides, he asked Gieh Pêh（岐伯）to note down *The Primal Questions*（《素问》）asked and answered between themselves, in which are recorded the recipes to various diseases. Hwang-*t'ih*'s queen Luai-tsou（嫘祖）bred silk-worms and cultivated silk; she also devised dresses. Hwang-*t'ih* reigned 100 years (2698 −2598 B. C.). His tomb, called the Bridge Mausoleum（桥陵）, is on the Bridge Mountain（桥山, also named Tsoon-buh Mountain, 中部山）in Suen-sih（陕西）today.

Second, there was Sao-hao（少昊）, the former's son, Tzeh（挚）by name and surnamed Jih（己）; he was called Sao-hao because he went after T'ai-hao's measures. He "ruled by virtue of the Virtue of Metal"（以金德王）and was therefore called the Emperor of the Golden Sky（金天氏）. He built his capital at Chü-ver（曲阜）, reigned 84 years (2598 −2514 B. C.) and was buried at Yün-yang（云阳）; his mausoleum is in the north-west of the present Chü-ver *hsien*, San-tung（山东）.

Third, there was Tsuan-shiuh（颛顼）, Emperor Kao-yang（高阳

氏). He was Hwang-*t'ih*'s grandson and the distant ancestor mentioned by Chü Yuan in the first line of *Lee Sao* (*Suffering Throes*). Being counsellor to his uncle Sao-hao at the age of ten (?), he succeeded him at twenty. He built his capital first at Kao-yang, hence his imperial title; its site is in the west of the present Chih *hsien*(杞县), Ho-nan(河南). He reigned 78 years (2519 −2436 B. C.).

Fourth, there was *T'ih* Ko(帝喾), also called Tsüen(夋), who succeeded Tsuan-shiuh. He aided the latter, his uncle, at the age of fifteen and was alloted his fief at Sing(辛), hence called Emperor Kao-sing(高辛氏). He built his capital at West Pûh(西亳), the site of which is now at Yien-sze *hsien*(偃师县), Ho-nan(河南). He reigned 70 years (2436 −2366 B. C.) and was succeeded by *T'ih* Tzeh(帝挚), who, having ruled only nine years, was forsaken by other tribal chiefs for his weakness and supplanted by Yao of Tdaung (唐尧), his brother, by common assent.

Legends vary as to the exact identities of the five *t'ih*. Some put two of the *hwang*, Fwu-shih and Tseng-noon, among the five *t'ih*; others put Yao and Suen among them.

And then, there were the two *t'ih* or emperors and the three kings(二帝三王). Emperor Yao(帝尧) of Dau Tdaung(陶唐), named Foun-shün(放勋) and surnamed Ih-chih(伊耆), was *T'ih* Ko's son; he reigned 99 years (2357 −2258 B. C.). Both the names Yao and Suen were, according to Tuan Yü-tsai(段玉裁), titles of respect and love given them by their subjects as tributes when they were still living. Yao was renowned for his beneficent rule. During his reign, he instituted the leap month. The Luteous River(黄河) overflowed in 2297 B. C.; he ordered Q'uen(鲧) to drain the flood. He elected Suen(舜), a common farmer, "untitled and humble"(侧

微), but "quick-witted", from the fields, who recommended to him the banishment of the Four Wicked Ones(四凶) from the court. He gathered at his court, with Suen's aid, the Eight Capable and Eight Virtuous Ones(八元八恺), well-known for their wise, kindly measures to the people. The empire attained wonderful peace and prosperity. His son Tan-tsu(丹朱) being wayward, Suen was promoted to act for himself as Protector(摄政) for twenty-seven years and appointed as his successor. He gave his two daughters Oerhwang(娥皇) and Neü-ying(女英) to marry Suen as his wife and concubine.

Emperor Suen(帝舜) of Neü(虞), surnamed Yau(姚) and named Tsoon-hwah(重华, *vide* Chü Yuan's address to him, lines 147－182 of *Lee Sao*), was a fifth generation grandson of Tsuan-shi-uh, Emperor Kao-yang. He reigned 47 years (2255－2208 B. C.) as a great beneficent sovereign of his people. When he was Protector at Yao's court, he gave the order that Q'uen(鲧), one of the Four Wicked Ones and Yü's father, be exiled for his criminal failure to drain the flood, then putting Yü in his place. He elected Ih, Kwei, Ji, Siue, Kao Yau(益,夔,稷,契,皋陶) and others, twenty-two of them, all virtuous and capable, to the court. When Yao died, although Suen had been formally nominated as the successor, he did not ascend the throne for three years to give chance to Tan-tsu in case the court and people might prefer him to himself. Like his late master, he made his premier Yü, who had already succeeded in drawing off the flood years ago, the Protector of his state to govern in his stead in 2224 B. C. His son Saung-chün(商均) was perverse; so he decreed Yü to succeed himself. Yü was at his post of protectorship to Suen for sixteen years before the latter died. Through Yao's, Suen's own and Yü's reigns which lasted over a century and a half, people lived in union, plenty and jubilee, except for the calamitous flood which ravaged the latter middle part of Yao's years. Suen died in the Wilds of Tsoung-ngou(苍梧之野) while leading his troops to subdue the revolting Miao tribesmen(有苗) (*vide* line 187 of *Lee Sao*) near the Nine-Doubt Mounts(九嶷山), in the south of the highest one of which, called Suen-yuan(舜源), he was buried and there was a temple there to his memory.

During Yao and Suen's times, as memorized in *The Canon of Yao* of *The Classic of History*(《尚书·尧典》), the four sons of Shih(羲) and Hoh(和) were decreed to ordain the calendarial year for the people according to astronomy, ... Yü(禹) was made the Lord of Excavation(司空), in charge of the scooping of clay to make dens for human habitation and the drainage of water(平水土); Chih(弃) was made the Lord of Grain(后稷), to oversee the planting of corn(播百谷); Siue(离) was made the Lord of Public Instruction(司徒), for teaching people the five ways of behaving properly between the members of a family(敷五教); Kao Yau(咎繇,皋陶) was made the Lord of the Judiciary(士), for ministering justice to men and setting up the five bodily(五刑) and the capital(大辟) punishments; Swei(垂) was made the Lord of All Sorts of Works or K'ung-K'ung(共工,理百工之事); Ih(益) was made the Lord Superintendent(朕虞) of herbs and trees, beasts and fowls on mountains and lowlands; Pêh-yih(伯夷) was made the Master of Ritual Ceremonies(秩宗), to institute the rites of homage to Heaven, Earth, the gods and ghosts(典三礼); Kwei(夔) was made the Master of Music(典乐), to accord with gods and men(和神人); and Loon(龙) was made the Imperial Secretary(纳言), to record *T'ih's* words and orders(出入帝命).

King Yü(后禹) of Hsia(夏), named Wen-ming(文命) and surnamed Szeh(姒), Tsuan-shiuh's progeny, reigned eight years (2205 −2197 B. C.). In the words of Fuh Yüen(傅玄, *fl.* 217 − 278) of the dynasty Ts'in(晋), "Yü became the Lord of Excavation (司空)(to *T'ih* Yao) at the age of twelve." He made his capital at An-ih(安邑), the site of which is in the north of the present Hsia *hsien*(夏县), San-sih(山西). Intrusted by Suen to rid the Nine States(九州) of the deluge, Yü excavated mountains and dredged rivers and streams all over the land like a god. The Herculean task took him eight years to accomplish and he did it excellently well. Hs is generally called Great Yü for his titanic labour to save the race from extinction. Like his master Suen in giving a chance to Yao's son, he waited for three years before he took his crown for the sake of Saung-chün, Suen's son. At his coronation at Mount Twu(涂山, in the south-east of the present Hwai-yüan *hsien*, 怀远县, An-whei, 安徽) when hundreds of tribal chieftains gathered to celebrate the occasion, he ordained the Hsia lunar calendar(夏历) which is still in partial use in China today. It was said that he laboured so hard in pursuing his work that there were no hairs on his hams and forefeet, his hands and feet (one of which at least was crippled) were covered with corns and his face was sunburnt and weather-beaten to a fulvous brown. Three times he passed his home doors, but he found no time to enter. Mencius said of him, as recorded in his analects *Mencius*(《孟子》), that when Yü heard good words spoken, he would do obeisance to the speaker(禹闻善言则拜). By good words, of course not words of praise or flattery were meant, but those that were beneficial to the people. He died during his inspecting tour of the country at Kuay-chih(会稽), Tsê-kiang(浙江), where his temple is situated.

Tseng Taung(成汤), named Leü(履), also called T'ien-ih(天乙) and surnamed Tse(子), was the 14th generation grandson of *T'ih* Ko's(帝喾, Emperor Kao-sing, 高辛氏) son Siue(卨 or 契, who was alloted the fief of Saung, 商, by Emperor Yao for his great merits in assisting Yü to draw off the deluge). He was the first revolutionary leader in China's history and the founder of the Saung(商), later called Yin(殷) Dynasty (1766 −1122 B. C.). Ghi, the last king of Hsia(夏桀), crazed with the woman Mei-shih(妹喜)① whom he got from the Sze tribe(有施氏) and made his queen (any one offending her would be instantly put to death), dug ponds for holding liquor, heapt hills of dregs(控酒池, 积糟丘) and habitually indulged in nocturnal orgies. According to Liu Shan's(刘向) *New Relatings*(《新序》), Ghi's liquor ponds were big enough to row boats in and atop his hills of dregs, one could command a view seven *lih* off. All state affairs turned awry and out of joint. His debauchery and ebriosity became intolerable to all sane people at court. When Kwan Loong-voon(关龙逢), a courtier of rectitude, insisted upon his stopping the folly, he was imprisoned and inflicted with capital punishment. Taung himself was once confined in prison by the autocrat at Hsia-dai(夏台). It was said that Ghi once saw a subject of his wading a stream full of floating ice. Being surprised that the man was not afraid of the cold, he ordered to have the man's legs cut through to see what was in their bones that made him so fearless of the cold. The cry of the age (as that of Zer's) was: "Why do the times and days not decline quickly? We people would perish the sooner with thee!" — meaning Ghi(桀).

---

① Variants of her name have Mê-shih(妹嬉) and Mê-shih(末喜).

So, in the name of Heaven and the people, Tseng Taung drew his sword against this dashing slaughterer and dealt him a crushing defeat at Ming-tiao(鸣条), banishing him to Nantsiao(南巢). The title Tseng Taung(成汤), given to him after his death, means "the one who eradicates tyranny and atrocity and is like the clouds and rain that give plenty." It is said of Taung, in his *Life* in Sze-ma Tsien's (司马迁) *The Chronicle*(《史记》), that once he came out from a house and saw nets being spread on all sides for snaring games, while some one was praying, "From all the four sides of the sky and earth, let them come into my nets." Whereas Taung said, "Ha! that would finish them!" Then he opened all the three sides and prayed, "Go to the right or go to the left as you will; if you do not follow what I tell you, you would get into my net." Hearing of this, his vassals said, "Taung's benevolence is far-reaching; it falls even on wild birds and beasts." He reigned for thirteen years (1766 −1753 B. C.).

The story of Ih Yün(伊尹), Taung's great counsellor and prime minister, should be told here, for his signal relation with the dynasty Saung(商) and its founder cannot be too much stressed; Chü Yuan speaks of it again and again in his poetry (*ll.* 289 −290, *Suffering Throse*; *ll.* 205 −212,239 −250,325—328, *Sky-vaulting Queries* and *l.* 34, *Pining My Past Days*) in regard to his notion of a sage sovereign relying on a sagacious minister. According to *The Spring and Autumn Annals of Leü*(《吕氏春秋》), Ih Yün's pregnant mother, living by the Stream of Ih(伊水), was told by the god of dreams one night that when she saw the cavity in the ground for thrashing rice oozing with water, she should run away to the east in great haste regardless of all. The next morning, she saw water in the cavity and told her neighbours to flee. After she had run ten *lih*, looking backward, she saw her village engulfed in flood. She herself was turned into a hollow trunk of a mulberry tree. A woman of the Sing tribe(有莘氏) plucking mulberry leaves picked up the infant from the hollow trunk and offered it to her clan chieftain or king, who ordered his cook to bring it up. Another version of the story from *The Great Commentary on the Classic of History*(《尚书大传》) has it, that Ih Yün's pregnant mother, going to draw water from the Stream of Ih, was turned into a hollow trunk of a mulberry tree. Her husband looking for her at the water-side found the infant in the tree hollow and took it back to breed it. The infant till it grew up to manhood was disliked for its and his condition of birth. The earliest anonymous *Genealogies of Ancient "T'ih"* (《世本》) says, Taung dreamt of some one holding a two-eared tripodal caldron(鼎俎) in his arms and smiling at him. Waking up the next morning, he sent messengers to find out that man, who proved to be Ih Yün on the plain of Sing(有莘之野). The king of Sing forbade Ih Yün to leave. Whereupon, Taung dispatched a match-maker to ask suit of the Sing clan. This was granted; a daughter was given in matrimony to him, and Ih Yün was sent as a follower in the bride's train. Conversing with the kitchen menial, Taung found him very much to his liking and made him his counsellor. At that time, however, things at the court of Ghi of Hsia were badly ruffled. It is said that Ih Yün went to Ghi five times to offer his services in putting state affairs into order, before he finally embarked upon the campaign under Taung as advised by him against Ghi that was to seal the latter's doom, but he was persistently rejected by the stubborn despot.

The earliest progenitor of the Tsur Dynasty was *Her* Ji(后稷, *Her* meaning "lord" or "high official"), elected to Yao's court by

Suen's counsel. The legend is told of him that his mother Chiang Yuan(姜嫄), stepping on the footprints of a giant, became pregnant and gave birth to him. When born, regarded as inauspicious, he was at first thrown away to a busy, narrow street, but oxen and horses refrained from treading on him. Then, the infant was cast on ice, but birds incubated on it to give warmth. So, he was taken back to be bred up and named Chih(弃, meaning "Castaway"). When fully grown up, Yao put him on the post of the Lord of Grain(稷官) to supervise the culture of cereals and alloted him the fief of Tair(邰). His progenies continued in the post for fifteen generations till King Wuh of Tsur.

Ch'ih Tsoun(姬昌), the spiritual founder of the great Tsur Dynasty(周,1122 − 256 B. C.), was formerly Count West(西伯) at the court of King Sing(辛) of Yin(殷). As governor of Yung Tsur (雍州,which was in the west, hence the official title), one of the ancient Nine States(九州), he was invested with the authority to launch campaigns against dependencies and subordinate states. A story is told of him in Liu Shan's(刘向) *New Relatings*(《新序》). While building foundations were being laid for his Observatory for Meteoromancy(灵台), a human skeleton was dug out from the soil. The future King Wen(文王) said, "Buriest it again." The overseer in charge of the work replied, "It is without a master, my lord." Whereat Count West said, "The world hath its master in the King, and a state hath its master in its chief. I am its master. Why seekest for him elsewhere?" So the skeleton was interred again. The world hearing of the incident said the count was kindly indeed, his favours were even extended to putrid bones, to say nothing of men.

He rode out hunting in a car one day and came across Leü Soun

(吕尚), a statesman, a strategist and a man of his like calibre at the hoary age of over eighty, angling by the waterside of the Wei Stream (渭水). At the time, he had hired himself at a butchery in his bare poverty at Tsau-ge(朝歌). He said to the Count, "An abject butcher slaughtereth bulls; a valiant one slaughtereth a state." Ch'ih Tsoun was cheerily struck. Conversing with him, he found him much to his heart's bent; "My father had long expected thee," said he to him, and thus called him Father Wang(太公望), meaning the one "my father expected"; so he brought him home in his dennet as his Teacher and the counsellor to his state. Ch'ih Fah(姬发), later to become King Wuh of Tsur(周武王), succeeding his father as Count West after his death, called Leü Teacher and Father Soun(师尚父). Later, he was to owe him much for his counsels in the revolution to overthrow the despot Zer(纣). He left to posterity his famous *Six Strategies and Tactics*(《六韬》) which had been lost during the earlier centuries of Tsur and was substituted by a surreptitious treatise of the same title in the Warring States Period.

Now Zer(纣), the name given to him after his fall, means the ruthless and malfeasant one. The last ruler of his dynasty, he was vigorous and full of sophisms, a habitual drunkard and a lecher, violent as well as atrocious. His royal concubine Ta Ch'ih(妲己) abetted him in his crimes. He also dug ponds for holding liquor, hung up meat to make a semblance of a forest and make nude men and women chase one another therein to amuse himself during his night-long carousals. He minced and parched the flesh of two of his chief courtiers, Marquises Quai and Ngo(鬼侯,鄂侯). The third one, Count West Tsoun(西伯昌), he put into prison at Yer-li(羑里, at present in the north of Taung-ying *hsien*,汤阴县,Ho-nan,河南) for heaving a sigh at the tidings that two of his fellow courtiers were treated like hogs. He was sentenced by the king to be executed after 100 days.[1] Zer put one of his tutors and uncles Prince Ch'ieh-tse(箕子)into prison for his admonition and cut out the heart of another, Prince Pih-kan(王子比干), to see whether it had "seven apertures", for he remonstrated with him in good earnest on his torturing punishments, lewdness and constant inebriety.

The future King Wen was only set free after his friend San Nie-sen(散宜生)and others had sent in bribing gifts of pretty women, gems and silk goods as ransom. The count became more amiable than ever after his release. Then he met Leü Soun on the northern bank of the Wei Stream(渭水之阳). And before long two thirds of the chiefs of petty states flocked to him to pay their tributes rather than to the King.

King Wuh, Ch'ih Fah, with Leü Soun as aid and a little force of only three thousand strong, strengthened with three hundred war chariots, led his revolutionary troops against the tyrant and battered his forces at Mo-yeh(牧野), the southern suburbs 30 *lih* from Yin's capital Tsau-ge(朝歌). Most of the tyrant's vassals were on his side; they aided him one and all. Badly beaten, Zer burnt himself to death[2] and ended his regime.

---

[1]　*Vide Ts'ao Strips* of *The Warring States Strips*(《战国策·赵策》).

[2]　*The Bamboo Book Annals*(《竹书纪年》) and Sze-ma Tsien's *The Chronicle* (《史记》) both say that when King Wuh came to the palace where Zer died (by hanging himself), he shot the dead tyrant with three shafts, struck him with his sword Chin-leü(轻吕), cut off his head with a bronze battle-axe(黄钺) and used the rod of his axe as the pole of his white Banner(大白), the flag of the Yin regime, to wave to its vassals. For *The Bamboo Book Annals*, see footnote on *p.* 33.

To show what a man of good faith Ch'ih Fah was, this anecdote of his is not out of place here. Jiau Ke(胶鬲), a Yin recluse, was recommended by Count West Tsoun(西伯昌) to the court of Zer. When King Wuh led his revolutionary force against Yin, Zer sent Jiau Kê to meet Tsur troops on the way. At the sight of Ch'ih Fah, he asked, "Whither is Count West heading for?" King Wuh said, "For Yin." "When wouldst thou arrive there?" "On the day of *ja-tse* (甲子), I would reach the outskirts of Yin's capital." Jiau Kê returned. Then it began to rain. But King Wuh hurried on in his march. The troop counsellor(军师) asked for a pause and rest. Ch'ih Fah said, "Jiau Kê must have reported the date of *ja-tse* to his king. If I could not make the date in time, Jiau Kê would appear untruthful to his master, who would certainly kill him. I have to march quickly to save Jiau Kê's life." And he reached the suburbs of Yin's capital just on the day of *ja-tse*.

As the founder of the Tsur Dynasty, King Wuh reigned only seven years(1122 −1115 B. C.). He gave the title King Wen(文王) to his departed father, who and Leü Wang had verily infused their spirits into his work to build up the new rule. In electing virtuous and capable men to offices, he was known to have three thousand friends!

Besides, Duke Tsur(周公旦), his brother, played a splendid role in promoting the Way and virtues, propagating fraternity and its proper means. He was the greatest statesman of ancient Cathay, perhaps next in fame only to Yao and Suen, but in actual achievements second to none. It is no wonder that Confucius dreamt of him every night in his yearning for the glory and concord of the happy, peaceful days of early Tsur. He set forth music and poetry, gave shape to education, instituted rites and laws, delineated government organs and formulated the official system of Tsur, served as Protector(摄政) and Prime Chancellor(冢宰) to his puerile and adolescent nephew King Tseng(成王), put down a rebellion and built up the eastern capital Lor-ih(洛邑). The political, economic and cultural measures of early Tsur were mainly his exploits.

Ⅲ Early Tsur (1122 − 1052 B. C.)

In the halcyon days of early Tsur, during the reigns of Kings Tseng and Kong(成王, 1115 − 1078 B. C. ; 康王, 1078 − 1052 B. C.), as a result of King Wuh and Duke Tsur's efforts to build concord and peace just touched upon above, life was easeful and happy. The wolf was kept away from people's doors. Disturbance and anxiety, with one sole exception, were signally absent. There was no war except the quelling of the revolt started by Wuh-kêng(武庚), Zer's son, and countenanced by Quan Swu(管叔) and two other uncles of the king out of jealousy, unfortunately in the first year of King Tseng's reign. But it was finally subdued in the third year. Grain, the staple food of the people, had become fabulously cheap and for forty odd years, prisons throughout the kingdom were empty of convicts. It seemed sorrow and fear had been banished from the world forever.

It was believed① that such union and public tranquillity were made possible, now as in the times of Yao, Suen, Yü and Taung, primarily because of the agrarian system distributing lands fairly

---

① *Vide* Erh-yang Siu's(欧阳修) *An Essay on Fundumentals*(《本论》) and Suh Süin's(苏洵) essay *On the Agrarian System*(《田制》). The former piece was written to stress the fundamental standpoints of the nation as against those of Buddhism which are undoubtedly not without their drawbacks.

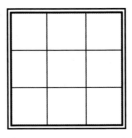

among all able-bodied tillers. Every nine hundred *mou*(亩) of fields[①] were equally divided between eight farming households round about and one public portion in the centre like this：Embracing the unit of nine farms，there were creeks all around. All the eight families helped to work on the public farm，and there were no more taxes. This was called the "Well-farm" System(井田制)，for the lines dividing the whole unit into nine portions resemble the character 井，meaning a well，and there was besides actually a well in the public lot for common irrigation and household uses.

But that was only the beginning of the story. There were then the cultural measures taken in the fields of music and poetry to bear on the individual. According to the chapter *On Heavenly Destiny* in *Tsaung-tse*(《庄子·天运篇》)，Confucius once said to Lao-dan(老聃，Lao-tse，老子) when he visited him to seek instruction of him about rites："I think I have worked long enough on the *Six Classics* (《六经》) *of Poetry*(《诗》)，*History*(《书》)，*Rites*(《礼》)，*Music* (《乐》)，*Mutability*(《易》) and *Spring and Autumn*(《春秋》)."

---

① This was Tsur's system，according to which each of the eight families was entitled to own 100 *mou*. Saung's(商) system，the same as those of the three preceding dynasties of Dau Tdaung(陶唐)，Neü(虞) and Hsia(夏)，allotted seventy *mou* to each family，with the public farm in the centre same in size，making the whole unit 630 *mou* in all.

The Classic of Music(《乐经》), compiled by Confucius, together with the others except that of *Mutability* was burnt by that monstrous tyrant Ying Tsen(嬴政) at the proposal of his black second Lih Sze (李斯) in 213 B. C. Those others were more or less partially restored, but *Music* was not. Anyway, we know, music, sometimes alone but often conjoined with dancing and or poetry, was made use of to beautify and enrich life in early Tsur. There are the names of seven dances, all said to be with musical accompaniments and songs, recorded in the *Tsur Rites*(《周礼》) (supposedly imputed to Duke Tsur himself at first, but now finally attributed by scholars of East Han(东汉) and Tsing(清), Ho Sher(何休) and Bih Si-ruey(皮锡瑞), to the Six States(六国) only) under the heading *Spring Officials*(《春官》), *Master of Music*(《大司乐》): viz., *Cloud Gate* (《云门》), *Great Rolling*(《大卷》), *Great Harmony*(《大咸》), *Great Continuance*(《大韶》,《大磬》), *Great Hsia*(《大夏》), *Great Aid*(大濩) and *Great Wuh*(《大武》) — the first two being dance-sonata-songs of Hwang-*t'ih* and the rest, those of Yao, Suen, Yü, Taung and Wuh respectively. And there are pieces of music known only by names today, such as *Sustaining Clouds*(《承云》) of Hwang-*t'ih*, *Nine Depths*(《九渊》) of Sao-hao(少昊), *Five Stems* (《五茎》) of Tsuan-shiuh(颛顼), *Six Elites*(《六英》) of *T'ih* Ko (帝喾), *Glorious Clouds*(《卿云》) of Suen (the verse recitative of which is suppositively extant but most probably surreptitious), *Nine Counts*(《九辩》) and *Nine Songs*(《九歌》) of Yü(禹) and *Morning Dew*(《晨露》) of Taung(汤).

As regards poetry, we know ballads, songs and odes were collected in early Tsur by the king's vassals, officials and messengers (太师,遒人) of his special governmental organs all over the land and submitted to him to acquaint him of the folklore and customs as well as the faults and discontents of the states. Over three thousand pieces were gathered from the country-side and the king's and his vassals' courts and ancestral temples, according to Sze-ma Tsien(司马迁) in *The Chronicle*(《史记》), from which Confucius made his edited selection of 311 poems known as *The Classic of Poetry*(《诗经》). But scholars like Kung Yin-dah(孔颖达) of Tdaung(唐), Tsu Hsih(朱熹) and Yi Sê(叶适) of Soong(宋) and Tsu Yie-tsen(朱彝尊) and Tsuai Tzê(崔述) of Tsing(清) all contended that Confucius did not ever delete a large number of collected poems as said by the Grand Curator of History. The anthology of Saung-Yin and early Tsur poetry as we have it, consisting of 305 pieces and called by this title, is however not the whole of Confucius' legacy to us. The original text and its copies which, carved or painted on bamboo strips, could not be a great many altogether, were obliterated by that enormous monster and his henchman Lih Sze. The criminal "law" of prohibiting the possession of books("挟书律") was upheld as valid for fifteen years after the extinction of the Tsing Dynasty(秦) in 206 B. C., throughout the reign of Kao-*t'ih* Liu Paun(高祖刘邦), the scoundrel founder of Han(汉), till 191 B. C., late in his son Wei-*t'ih*'s(惠帝) reign when it was publicly abolished. Thenceforth the renowned collection, restored by dictation from memory, began to be commented upon and taught by Sun Bêh, a native of Luh(鲁人申倍), Yuan Kuh a native of Tsih(齐人辕固) and Hang Yin, a native of Yen(燕人韩婴). But these commentaries were then all lost one after another since East Han. In the late years of West Han, Liu Shin(刘歆), son of Liu Shan(刘向), the scholar, said that he had discovered a commentary 《毛诗故训传》 left by the Venerable Mao(毛公), a scholar of the

Six States. Later, in East Han and the Three States(三国), Ts'eng Yüen(郑玄) and Loh Ch'ih(陆玑) said that the Venerable Mao was named Mao Heng(毛亨) and that this Mao Heng of Luh, the elder Mao, who was a pupil of Süin Whon(荀况), left the book as a bequest to his pupil Mao Tsang(毛苌) of the state Ts'so(赵国人), the younger Mao. The Tsing(清) scholar Bih Si-ruey(皮锡瑞) dismissed with keen analysis Liu Shin's *Commentary* of Mao as blank imposture in his *A General Comment upon "the Classic of Poetry"* (《诗经通论》). As to the number of poems, there are six of them lost to the extant collection of 305 pieces. For instance, the poem with the following two lines in it is not to be found in the present anthology:

Those who win people's hearts will flourish;(得人者兴)
Those who lose them will come to wrack.(失人者崩)

Next, the educational institutions of the Grand Colleges of the King(太学:辟雍,成均,上庠,东序,瞽宗), his vassals' schools(泮宫) and the country schools(庠序) played their telling parts too. In the primary schools of the country, pupils were taught the "six arts" (六艺) — rites, music, archery, chariot driving, reading and arithmetic(礼,乐,射,御,书,数). Although the specific subjects taught in the intermediate schools of the king's vassals and the royal colleges of the king are not explicitly mentioned in extant historical records and, strictly speaking, unknown to us, yet it may be generally presumed that the "six arts" were repeatedly taught, only in more and more advanced degrees and with additional subjects, in the higher schools and the king's colleges. It is known, however, that the schools of the king's vassals were surrounded with streams on the south flanks and south of the east and west gates. And of the king's colleges mentioned above, Pi Youn(辟雍), meaning "Bright and Concordant", was Tsur's own institution in the centre; Tseng Chün (成均) was a college after the manner of those of the five *t'ih*(五帝) in the south; Soun Ts'ian(上庠) was a college after the manner of that of the dynasty Neü(虞) in the north; Tung Seü(东序) was a college after the manner of that of the dynasty Hsia(夏) in the east and Kuh Tsoon(瞽宗) was a collage after the manner of that of the dynasty Saung-Yin(商殷) in the west — of a large stream some fifty *lih* north of the capital Hao-ching(镐京). This cluster of five Grand Colleges of the King with spacious thatched roofs and wholly surrounded or partially bordered with water was the centre where the Way and the arts were taught to have the king's world bright and harmonious.

Thirdly, there were the five categories of rites(五礼): the sacrificial rites(吉礼, twelve in number), the inauspicious ones(凶礼, five), those of greetings(宾礼, eight), the military ones(军礼, five) and the auspicious ones(嘉礼, six). For specific instance, among the last rubric there were rites of drinking and repast(饮食), rites of coming of age and nuptials(冠婚), rites of country archery gatherings(乡射), rites of banquetings and feastings(飨宴), rites of sharing sacrificial meat of the state and the ancestral temples(脹膰) and rites of congratulations and celebrations(庆贺). Even hunting, in spring, autumn and winter(蒐狩), was not without its rites. Thus, people were taught, when they were not occupied with farm work, how to behave on almost all occasions. They were pleased in their ears and eyes, modulated in mind and feelings and occupied in doing something beautiful and imbued with meaning when at leisure. Moreover, their being occupied with things of interest would prevent them from getting into mischief and trouble.

In 1111 B. C. , the Yin inhabitants(殷氏) of Tsau-ge(朝歌) were moved by Duke Tsur to the southern bank of the Lor Stream(洛水, 雒), two years after the suppression of the revolt. Another two years later, in 1109 B. C. , the domicile, much enlarged, was surrounded with city walls to be built into Tsur's eastern capital. The work of construction, overseen by the duke himself, was finished after seven years, a year after his death. The nine *t'ing*(九鼎), massive, two-eared, tripodal bronze vessels — developed out of bronze meat-broilers of the same shape but much smaller in size, for sacrificial and banqueting uses — cast by Great Yü to symbolize state sovereignty and preserved by the Saung-Yin Dynasty as such, were moved to the city, now simultaneously called Lor-ih(洛邑) or Jia-ruh(郏鄏), from the former Yin capital. In 1091 B. C. , King Tseng summoned his vassals to the eastern capital for a great jubilant celebration, to which all tribal chieftains of distant states came to pay homage. Thus, the gracious rules of Kings Wen, Wuh, Tseng and Kong, a stretch of some ninety years, have ever been regarded in China's history as the most benignant age since the illustrious reigns of Yao, Suen, Yü and Taung.

But spring and summer, in human affairs as in nature, could not last perpetually. From King Ts'au(昭王, 1052 − 1002 B. C.) till King Yih(夷王, 894 −878 B. C.), a lapse of over a hundred and seventy years, the royal house of Tsur shrunk weaker and weaker, so that the dignity and feudal ceremony the liege lord had used to hold in his reception of vassals had to be laid aside by the latter — he was obliged to go down the hall of audience to greet his feudatories.

Then, it was Kings Lih and You(厉王,878 −828 B. C.; 幽王, 781 − 771 B. C.), both despotic and debauched, who bedraggled their splendid lineage in the mire, splashing muddy water on the cinders of past glory. King Lih hired witches to fish out those who criticized him for his misdeeds behind his back as guilty of "slandering" and had them killed. His misdeeds must have been plenty and glaring, though not recorded and unknown to us, else he would not have taken such a step. In the end, he was expelled from the capital in a riot by his subjects to a small town called Tze(彘) where he died later. From his exile till his death, two dukes of his court declared a stage of Republic (共和) and governed in his stead for fourteen years.

King You, infatuated with his royal concubine Pau-szieh(褒姒), gave a summons to his vassals, by lighting signal alarm fires, to defend the capital from a non-existent imminent foreign attack just to provoke a smile of his favourite. Moreover, he deposed his formal queen and crown prince in favour of her and her son. It was the same old story: liquor and lechery sealed his doom, as he made a mess of his state affairs. He was killed in a sudden inroad of the Ch'eüan-zone(犬戎) tribesmen at the foot of the Lih Mountains (骊山), south-east of the present Ling-tung *hsien*(临潼县), Sen-sih(陕西).

However, King Lih's son and King You's father Hsuang *Wang* (宣王,827 −781 B. C.), the only reviver king in the long annals of the Tsur Dynasty, put to shame both his father and his son in a reign of nearly half a century. Beating the West Zone(西戎) of the north-west and the Shean-yüen tribes(猃狁, later in the Warring States Period and afterwards called Hwu, 胡, and Shiung-nou, 匈奴, i. e.,

the Huns） of the north in the first year, and conquering the Chin-man
（荆蛮）, Hwai-yih（淮夷） and Hsü Zone（徐戎） of the south and
south-west in the second year of his reign, King Hsuan restored the
domain of Kings Wuh and Tseng.

Bing *Wang*（平王, 770 −714 B. C.）, King You's son, frightened out of his wits by Ch'eüan-zone's killing his father, moved to
the eastern capital Lor-ih（洛邑） to get farther away from the invaders. Lor-ih was built by Duke Tsur for depositing the nine *t'ing*, not
as a retreat of safety for a descendant king to move to and hide himself from the enemy. In fact, not such place could ever exist, for
wherever you could run away from him, he could always get at you
by running to you. This folly of King Bing was the root of the
dynasty's being reduced to a mere shadow of itself, existing in name
only, but vanished in reality, as well said by Suh Sêh（苏轼） of
Soong（宋） in his essay *On Bing "Wang"*（《平王论》）. Thereafter,
the dynasty, ever in decline, is called East Tsur, to be distinguished
from the West Tsur from King Wuh downward till King You, with its
capital at Hao-ching（镐京）, the site of which is in the south-west of
Sih-an *hsien*（西安县）, Sen-sih（陕西） today.

It could be seen from the above account that the feudal dome of
early Tsur, weakened during the six reigns from King Ts'au to King
Yih, was jolted to the point of cracking by Kings Lih and You in
their reckless misdemeanours. Now, the cracks occurred again and
again, and widened and joined one another in the Spring and Autumn
Period, which commenced with the fourth year from the end of King
Bing's reign.

Ⅳ The Spring and Autumn Period （722 −481 B. C.）

The Spring and Autumn Annals（《春秋》） was written by Confucius, beginning with the first year of the reign of Marquis Yin of Luh (鲁隐公), the ninth generation grandson of Duke Tsur(周公)①, to sustain the feudal order built up by King Wuh(武王) and the duke. It was written, according to Mencius(孟子), when "the times had declined and the Way was getting low; besides, heresies and acts of violence became rampant. There were liege vassals who murdered their lords-superior and there were sons who murdered their fathers. ② Confucius grew apprehensive; so he wrote *The Spring and Autumn Annals*, which should have been the work of Heaven's son, His Royal Majesty. " Again: "When the exploits of beneficent kings had ceased to appear, poetry③ turned up no more; since poetry had ceased to be gathered, then *The Spring and Autumn Annals* came to be written. Ts'in's(晋) *History*(《乘》), Ts'ou's(楚) *Taur Wûh*(《梼杌》) and Luh's(鲁) *Annals* are of the same nature. The events recorded are those of (Marquis) Hwan of Tsih(齐桓) and (Marquis) Wen of Ts'in(晋文), the literature is history and 'the moral', as Confucius said, 'I have set down. '" The chronicle, from which is derived the name of the historical period, relates happenings for 242 years during the rules of twelve marquises. The last entry dated in the spring of the 14th year of Marquis Ai's(哀公) reign, after a *chi-lin*(麒麟, unicorn) was caught as game spoil in his hunting trip.

---

① A variant pedigree regards him as the eighth generation grandson of King Wen (文王).

② "During the Spring and Autumn Period, regicides were thirty-six, the extinction of states numbered fifty-two and vassal lords running for life. unable to keep their feuds, were innumerable," so says P'an K'uh(班固) in *The Lift of Sze-ma Tsien of The Han Chronicle*(《汉书·司马迁传》).

③ That is, ballads, songs and odes as formerly collected by the king's vassals and his special officials to be offered to the King of Tsur.

It was said, according to the *Kung-yang Commentary* on the *Annals* (《春秋·公羊传》), that thereupon Confucius exclaimed, "My Way is forlorn!" (吾道穷矣) on the incident, three years after he had put in his first entry. Wang Tsoon (王充), of East Han (东汉), quotes the *Annals* in his essay *Steelyard* (《论衡》) as saying, "the marquis' in his westward hunting trip picked up a dead unicorn', which people showed to Confucius." The earliest block-print edition texts of the three *Commentaries* of Tso, Kung-yang and Ko-liang (左氏、公羊、谷梁三"传") without the character "死" (dead), all date back only to the Soong Dynasty (宋). It is almost certain, I think, they were all based upon some mis-copied Han strips (汉简) or Swei (隋) or Tdaung (唐) scrolls (卷轴) lost during the Five Dynasties (五代). Now, the appearance of the *chi-lin* or the phoenix was generally regarded from time immemorial as the happy augury of an epoch of peace and union. The *Annals*, on the other hand, was obviously written by Confucius to record untoward and wicked incidents in censure, as explained by Mencius in the two quotations above. For example, there is the entry about Tsur Yü (州吁), prince of the state Wei (卫), murdering his father the Marquis of Wei and usurping his place in the fourth year of Marquis Yin of Luh (鲁隐公). That is the first mishap noted in the *Annals*. Then, in the eleventh year of Yin, Prince Whei of Luh (鲁公子翚) murdered the marquis. The exclamation of Confucius about the *chi-lin* noted in the *Kung-yang Commentary* obviously means his despair in expecting the recovery of the order of Duke Tsur's days. That is the reason why he put an end to his record of censure. Two years later, he died. Yet Tso-chur Ming (左丘明) and a host of Confucian scholars such as the annotator Fan Nien (范宁) of the *Ko-liang Commentary*, the annotator Kung Yieh

(孔衍) of the *Kung-yang Commentary*, etc., strangely hold that the appearance of the *chi-lin* was an auspicious omen of the advent of the sage Confucius on the scene, that it was to be congratulated and that therefore Confucius did not keep on his record of censure any more, for his mission was accomplished! That is decidedly mistaken, it seems to me, since it is just contrary to the sage's own opinion. It is downright confusion confounded: here we have Confucius' forlornness and sense of futility set at naught, or, what is worse, rather twisted to mean just the opposite of what he thought in spite of his expressed opinion.

Luh was a large state allotted by King Wuh to his brother Duke Tsur as his fief, with its capital at Chü-ver(曲阜). By a large state is meant one which was 400 square *lih* in area, and Luh(鲁), Wei (卫) and Tsih(齐) were the only three of such size.[1] In the first year of King Tseng's reign, since the duke, as the Protector and Prime Chancellor to the kingling, had to remain in the capital Hao-ching, the feud was settled on Pêh-jin(伯禽), the ducal prince, who was entitled the Marquis of Luh(鲁侯). It is therefore with particular significance that the *Annals* was inaugurated by Confucius with the reign of Marquis Yin of Luh, the lineal offspring of Duke Tsur, who was to pay out his life in the eleventh year of his reign, as stated above. After this unnatural event, a host of ghastly and disorderly happenings cropt up here and there and everywhere.

It was said that when the dynasty Saung was first founded, King Taung held in fealty as many as three thousand vassals and at the be-

---

[1] *Preface* to his *Chronology of Vassals Since the Rise of Han*(《汉兴以来将相名臣年表·序》) in Sze-ma Tsien's *The Chronicle*(《史记》).

ginning of Tsur, King Wuh had some eight hundred. [1] These were mostly tribal heads who had taken part in the wars of revolution against Ghi of Hsia(夏桀) and Zer of Yin(殷纣). The tributary heads of Tsur were divided into five orders as in mediaeval Europe: dukes(公), marquises(侯), counts(伯), viscounts(子), and barons(男). Before Confucius proceeded with the *Annals*, he had visited, we learn from Sze-ma Tsien[2], seventy odd states to convince their chiefs of the necessity of the Kingly Way, but he failed in his endeavour. A considerable number of the states he had not visited, such as Tsing(秦), Wuh(吴) and Yüeh(越). But it may be inferred that, during the intervening time since King Wuh till 722 B. C., the beginning of the Spring and Autumn Period, the total must have shrunk to a fraction of the original, though much more than seventy odd. In the period, the main vassals were twelve in number, or rather thirteen, including the "barbarian" state Wuh(吴), according to *The Chronicle*. [3] With the house of Tsur in a feeble plight, warfare

---

[1] *Vide* Liu Tsoon-yuan's(柳宗元) *An Essay on Feudalism*(《封建论》). But according to Hwang-fuh Tze(皇甫谧, *fl.* in the reign of Wuh-t'ih of Ts'in, 晋武帝, who reigned from 265 to 289) in his *Genealogies of "T'ih"* and Kings(《帝王世纪》), "When Yü was crowned at Mount Twu(涂山), vassals holding fealty to him numbered ten thousand. Taung's lieges were over three thousand. Tsur overcoming Saung, a thousand seven hundred and seventy-three states were allotted their fiefs. Durig the Spring and Autumn Period, there were twelve hundred states. In the Warring States Period, remaining states numbered ten odd. "

[2] *Preface* to his *Chronology of Twelve Vassals*(《十二诸侯年表·序》) in *The Chronicle*(《史记》).

[3] They were Luh(鲁), Tsih(齐), Ts'in(晋). Tsing(秦), Ts'ou(楚), Soong(宋), Wei(卫), Tsen(陈), Tsai(蔡), Tsaur(曹), Ts'eng(郑), Yen(燕) and Wuh(吴).

broke out intermittingly between its vassal states. The strong picked on the weak, as a rule without royal sanction. The king's authority was openly flouted. In 717 B. C., King Hwan of Tsur(周桓王) sent his officer Van-pêh(凡伯) to visit the marquisate of Luh. On his way back, the envoy was kidnapped by the Wei(卫) satrap. In 707 B. C., the king led his troops in person in a punitive expedition against his vassal state Ts'eng(郑). He was shot on the shoulder by a shaft of the soldiery of Count Tsoun of Ts'eng(郑庄公). Regal dignity was utterly disgraced.

As unruliness popped up rife, there was an obvious tendency to counteract the disorder in the rise of the Five Magnificent Princes(五霸) to seek hegemony. But the ultimate effect and result of their conferences and chartered alliances, though in the name of the royal house and for its defense, yet always generated from the ulterior motive of enhancing the prestige of the chief protagonists themselves, turned out to be just the opposite of their declared intentions. It was well said by Mencius in his censure: "the Five Magnificent Princes were culprits of the Three Kindly Kings."

In 715 B. C., the Duke of Soong(宋) and Wei(卫) and Marquises of Tsih(齐) met at Woa-o(瓦屋) to draw up an alliance. That was the first of such unions by league. Thereafter, many others followed.

Marquis Hwan of Tsih(齐桓公), the most eminent prince of the Five, came to power in 685 B. C., after his brother Marquis Hsiang(襄公) was murdered by someone else. Making the well-known statesman Quan Zong(管仲) his premier, he extended his rule of Tsih over four decades, when he gathered the chiefs of his brother states into confederacy nine times, led and induced them to declare their fidelity to the house of Tsur, defended it from foreign intrusions and brought general uprightness to the political scene. He married a daughter of his named Tsih Chiang(齐姜) to Prince Tsoon-erl(公子重耳) of Ts'in(晋) when he, fleeing from his own state, sought asylum in Tsih. Now, this Tsih Chiang, the future Marquise Wen of Ts'in(晋文公夫人), had a good deal to do with the making of the marquis, who was later to become the senior prince of the Five after the death of Duke Hsiang of Soong(宋襄公).

Marquis Wen of Ts'in(晋文公), a progeny of King Tseng's(成王) brother Swuo-neü, Marquis of Daung(唐侯叔虞), and the latter's son Si-fuh, Marquis of Ts'in(晋侯燮父), wore his coronet in 636 B.C. with the aid of Viscount Mo of Tsing(秦穆公). Prince Tai(王子带) of King Hsiang of Tsur(周襄王) led the foreign Di tribesmen(狄) of the north to menace the capital Lorih; so the king had to flee for safety westward to Ts'eng(郑). The marquis managed to have the prince killed; then he guarded the king back to his capital in 635 B.C. He elected statesmen like Hwu Yen and Ts'ao Tsuai(狐偃, 赵衰) to high stations, succoured the state Soong(宋), badly beaten by Ts'ou(楚) in 638 B.C., and later, in 632 B.C., won a victory in coalition with Tsing, Tsih and Soong over Ts'ou in the Battle of Tsen-pu(城濮之战, in the state Wei, 卫).

Chiêh Tuai(介推), generally known as Chiêh Tse-tuai(介之推), was a devoted follower of Marquis Wen of Ts'in, before the latter came to power, when he was forced to flee from his own state for nineteen years. On the way of his flight to Tsih, the young prince Tsoon-erl became very much famished for lack of food. Chiêh at first secretly cut his own flesh on the ham to feed him; later, the thing was made known to him. After his return to Ts'in years afterwards, he wore his coronet and rewarded his followers with high posts, but forgot to recompense Chiêh. Neither did Chiêh speak to Wen reminding him of the matter. Indignant at the marquis' ingratitude, Chiêh left the court to become a hermit on the Mien Mountain(绵山) with his old mother. The marquis remembered the affair and sought Chiêh in earnest to make amends to him, but he refused to come down. Wen ordered to set wild fire on the mountain to force him down. In ire, Chiêh hugged a tree trunk to let himself burnt to death. The marquis, deeply stricken in conscience, had the mountain named Chiêh Mountain, forbade hewing firewood from it, provided obituary service to Chiêh and clad himself in sables for grief. The day Chiêh Tuai perished on the mountain side clasping the tree trunk was remembered for twenty-six centuries by the nation with the memorial days of Cold Repast(寒食); for three days beginning from the third day of the third moon, people were supposed not to cook meals, but to eat cold food prepared in advance.

Viscount Mo of Tsing(秦穆公), succeeding his brother Viscount Tseng(成公), appointed to premiership and other high posts Yur Yü, Pêh-lih Yih, Chien So(由余,百里奚,蹇叔) and others who were virtuous and capable. The state of Tsing was in good shape under his able rule; its people were much benefitted by his magnanimous measures. During the reign of King Hsiang of Tsur(周襄王), in 624 B. C. , the viscount launched campaigns to the far west against the Zone tribes, where he annexed twenty states and expanded his territory by a thousand *lih*. He was endowed with the title the Chief of West Zone tribes(西方诸侯伯) by the king, and thus he became their Prince.

Pêh-lih Yih, the noted "Courtier of Five Black Sheepskins"(五

殺大夫）, had been previously a courtier of the state Neü（虞）. When Neü was blotted out of existence, he was taken captive with the king of Neü to Ts'in（晋）, and then was to be sent as a follower in the train of a Ts'in princess in her marriage to Viscount Mo of Tsing. Ashamed of his station as a portion train attendant, he ran away to Ts'ou, where he was held by the suburbans of Wuen（宛）. The viscount heard that Pêh-lih Yih was virtuous and intended to ransom him heavily. But fearing Ts'ou people would not consent, he sent messengers to say to Ts'ou that his portion train follower Pêh-lih Yih was held by them, and he asked to redeem him with five sheepskins of black rams. Pêh-lih Yih's captors agreed. Viscount Mo set him free and conversed with him, finding him very much to his heart's liking. He made him his premier there-upon. In seven years, the viscount became one of the Five Magnificent Princes（五霸） on account of Pêh-lih Yih's statecraft.

And then there was Duke Hsiang of Soong（宋襄公）, the progeny of Wei-tse（微子） of Yin（殷）, on whom King Tseng donned the title Duke Soong（宋公） to commemorate King Taung of Saung（商汤）. it was said that he liked to speak of the benevolence and justice of ancient *t'ih* and kings. His state was strong. In 643 B. C., after the death of Marquis Hwan of Tsih, his five princes broke out in internal strife for succession. Duke Hsiang of Soong sent troops to Tsih to uphold Marquis Shao（孝公） against his brothers. He died of a wound later in the Battle of Hoon（泓） fought with Ts'ou.

Finally, there was King Tsaung of Ts'ou（楚庄王）. It was said of him that when he commanded his troops to fight the tribesmen of Lon-wen（陆浑） in 606 B. C., he ordered an inspection of his battle array in the domain of King Ding of Tsur（周定王） to vaunt his prowess. The king sent a deputy to make cheer of his men. He took occasion to inquire the king's messenger how heavy was each one of these nine *t'ing*(九鼎) deposited in the ancestral temple of Tsur in the capital. The incident signifies that he had a mind to put an end to the old regime and set up his own in its stead.

In short, with the rise of the Five Magnificent Princes, expeditions were often dispatched in consort with their meeting at conferences and forming alliances, and then the direction of interstate politics as a rule rested with the dominant figures. In consequence, recklessness and licence became rife among the heads of states, including the kings and princes of Tsur; seditious courtiers and usurping stewards rose one and all in uproar.

A word should be said of the origins of Ts'ou(楚), its potential enemy Tsing(秦) and its latent antagonist-ally Tsih(齐). Descended from Hwang-*t'ih*(黄帝)(also called Yeou-hsiung, 有熊氏, for the country he ruled was so called, hence some of his descendants were sumamed Hsiung, 熊), *T'ih* Kao-yang, Hsiung Yih(熊绎), great grandson of King Wen's teacher Yuh Hsiung(鬻熊), was allotted the fief Ts'ou(楚) as viscount by King Tseng(成王) in early Tsur. His state capital was at Tan-yang(丹阳), the site of which is in the south-east of the present Tzi-kwei hsien(秭归县)[1], Hu-pei(湖北). Since viscountcy ranked fourth in the order of Tsur nobilities, his feud must therefore be quite small in size; a smallest feud was only fifty square *lih* in extent, and his was probably 100 square *lih*. That was the beginning of Ts'ou and its ruling house. Some four centuries

---

[1] Chü Yuan's ancestral home was here, in the north-west of Tan-yang, where he resided for some time at the beginning of his banishment to the south of the River(江南). See note 52 on "My sister", line 131 of *Lee Sao*.

later, in 704 B. C., Hsiung Tung(熊通) proclaimed himself King of Ts'ou. During the Spring and Autumn Period, Ts'ou had waxed to be the second great power, only next to Tsing, of the thirteen large vassal states of Tsur, with Tsih as a close third. In 690 B. C., its capital was moved to Ying(郢, the present Ch'ih-nan City, 纪南城, north of Kiang-Iing *hsien*, 江陵县, Hu-pei, 湖北) by King Wen of Ts'ou(楚文王). In 613 B. C., King Tsaung who ventured to ask the weight of Tsur's *t'ing* came to power. Then Prince Chih-tzi(弃疾) proclaimed himself King Bing of Ts'ou(楚平王) in 529 B. C. and moved his capital a little south-eastward to the Ying of Chü Yuan's time. The big "barbarian" state Wuh(吴) attacked Ts'ou in 506 B. C. and occupied its capital Ying so that King *Ts'au*(昭王) had to flee in exile to Swei(隋). The next year, Ts'ou's courtier Sun Pao-seü(申包胥) went to the court of Tsing to ask for relieving troops; he "leaning against the court wall, cried aloud for seven days and nights without respite and without swallowing a ladle of drinks" to win Viscount Ai's(哀公) consent to his suing. All through this period till about the middle of the Warring States, Ts'ou annexed T'eng(邓), Suh(舒), Liau(蓼), Tsen(陈), Tsai(蔡), Chih(杞), Leü(莒) and Yüeh (越), all comparatively small states except Tsai which was one of the big thirteen and Yüeh which had swallowed Wuh(吴) in 473 B. C. And of course there were some other smaller states than these taken by it.

The tragic stories of Oo Yuan(伍员, Tse-süe, 子胥) and his father and brother should be related here. Oo Sür(伍奢) was tutor to the prince royal of Ts'ou(太子太傅) in the Spring and Autumn Period. The prince was traduced by the courtier Fei Wu-gieh(费无忌). King Bing summoned Oo Sür to question him about the hearsay, who said, "Why do Your Majesty repudiate the kindred of flesh and bones to lay trust in a slandering, mischief-making little courtier?" The king in ire got his son Oo Soun(伍尚) and killed them both. Oo Tse-süe fled to the state Wuh(吴) where he got up and served its king Hê-leü (吴王阖闾) as his general to attack Ts'ou. After five battles, he penetrated into Ts'ou's capital Ying. King Bing was already dead then. Oo Tse-süe dug out the king's corpse from his grave, hung it up and whipped it three hundred times to avenge his father and brother's death. King Hê-leü of Wuh died of a wound he sustained in a battle with the state Yüeh(越). He was succeeded by his son Fuh-tsah(夫差). In a battle with Yüeh, he dealt it a crushing defeat. Gur-zien, the king of Yüeh(越王勾践), sued for peace, to which Fuh-tsah agreed against Oo Tse-süe's counsels. Afterwards, he counseled many times to fight Yüeh without success. The prime chancellor (太宰) Pih(嚭) of Wuh, being bribed by Yüeh, vilified Oo Tse-süe to the king, who ordered to give a sword to Oo for him to commit suicide with. Oo said to a follower of his, "Pick out my eyes from their sockets with a poniard and hang them up at the eastern gate of Wuh. I am sure they shall see Yüeh people come to extirpate Wuh." Then he cut his own throat. Nine years later, King Gur-zien of Yüeh indeed had Wuh extirpated.

The origin of the state Tsing was later than that of Ts'ou by almost a century. Fei-tse(非子, 飞子), surnamed Ying(嬴), the progeny of Pêh Ih(伯益, 柏翳) who kept beasts and fowls for Suen and assisted Great Yü to drain the flood with merits, was commissioned by King Shao of Tsur(周孝王) to take care of his stables and allotted the fief of Tsing, the site of which is in T'ien-sui *hsien*(天水县), Kang-suo(甘肃) today. His baronial holdings were quite small at first. Over a century later, when Marquis Sun（申侯）, the father of the deposed queen, led the Ch'eüan-zone（犬戎）tribesmen to make an inroad upon Tsur's capital Hao-chin and kill King You（幽王）, Lord Hsiang of Tsing（秦襄公）was powerful enough to beat off the barbarian invaders and in company with Tsur's other vassals put Prince Yie-jer（宜臼）on the throne as King Bing（平王）. He was then assigned the feud west of the Gieh Mountains（岐西）as a viscount for his pains and thenceforth formally regarded as one of the king's vassals. Three years later, Viscount Wen of Tsing（秦文公）won a smashing victory over the Zone invaders and cleared them off his fee. And then, there was Viscount Mo of Tsing（秦穆公）, one of the Five Magnificent Princes whose achievements have been briefly accounted for above.

Tsih was a large state next to Luh and Wei（卫, which was apportioned to Kong Swu, 康叔）, the fief assigned to Leü Soun（吕尚, or Leü Wang, 吕望）by King Wuh, with its capital at Yin-cher（营丘）, the present Lin-tzi *hsien*（临淄县）, San-tung（山东）. Marquis Hwan（桓公）, its powerful chief, was most active in the early years of the Spring and Autumn Period as the first leader of the Five Magnificent Princes. However, after the death of his highly capable premier Quan Zong, he gave ear to three eunuchs and sycophants who threw the state into wild tumult after his own decease. In consequence, Tsih fell into a low ebb of prestige for over two and a half centuries till its usurpation by its steward Dian Oo（田午）in 379 B. C. It absorbed the two small states Ch'ih（纪）and Suei（遂）early in the period, but was forced to disgorge its spoils to the states Luh and Wei（卫）in 589 B. C.

Though the Spring and Autumn and the Warring States Periods

were noted as epochs of stress, chaos and war, yet they gave nativity to a great luminary, two glorious stars of the first magnitude and many school-founders in ethics, philosophy and other fields of intellectual pursuits as well as to atrocious scoundrels and a blatant monster in practical politics. Senior to Confucius by some ten to sixteen years, Lao-tse(老子), named Lih Erh(李耳) and nicknamed Lao-dan(老聃), meaning the long-eared old man (another explanation of the character 聃 denotes flap-eared, that is, the ears of the man were two flat, unmoulded pieces), was a native of the state Ts'ou. Born in the village Lih(厉乡) of K'ou *hsien* (苦县), he was a scholar scribe of the Royal Hall of History of Tsur(周守藏室史)①. In Sze-ma Tsien's *The Chronicle*, it is said that "Confucius went to Tsur to inquire of Lao-tse about the rites." We are also told that he had a great respect for the Tsur official. According to the chapter *On Heavenly Destiny* in *Tsaung-tse*(《庄子·天运篇》), Confucius made his interview when he was fifty-one, which was in the year 502 B. C. In the chapter *Tseng-tse Asked*(《曾子问》) of *Notes of Rites*(《礼记》), Lao-tse is four times noted for what he said and did that are plainly contradictory to and incompatible with the positive assertions in *The* "*Dao-Têh*" *Classic*(《道德经》) or *Lao-tse*(《老子》) that "the rites mean fidelity and troth running thin and are the beginnings of confusion" and that "if the sages perish not, the big brigands will not

---

① According to the *Tsur Rites*(《周礼》), under the heading *Heavenly Officials* (《天官》), *Prime Chancellor*(《冢宰》), there were twelve scholar scribes (史官) whose office it was to keep record of important events and sayings. As early as in the times of Hwang-t'ih, there were the official historians Tsü Soon (沮诵) and Tsoung Chi(仓颉), notable for originating character writing. In the dynasties Hsia Saung and Tsur, the Grand Curators of History (and Astronomy)(大史，太史) also took charge of education in their official duties.

stop. " Thus, in the opinion of the Tsing(清) scholar Waung Ts'oon (汪中), in his *Novelties in Researches into Lao-tse the Man and "Lao-tse" the Book* of his *Studies Related*(《述学·老子考异》), the book *Lao-tse* (《老子》), for centuries ascribed to Lao-tse, was proved to be definitely not his work, but that of the grand curator of history and astronomy Dan of Tsur(周太史儋), who is said in the *Life of The Chronicle* to have had interviewed Viscount Hsien of Tsing(秦献公) 129 years after Confucius' death[①]. Judging from the *Life of The Chronicle*, we can see that Sze-ma Tsien in West Han was not quite sure whether the two men were two persons or the same person. And there was a third man called Lao-lai-tse(老莱子), also a native of Ts'ou and a thinker of the *Dao Têh* shool, whom the Grand Curator of History likewise suspects to be just this Lao-tse.

With the authorship of *Lao-tse* delayed more than a century till about 370 B.C., or a little earlier, the eldest as well as the greatest philosopher of the two periods was no doubt Confucius. He was born in the state Luh(鲁) of Soong(宋) progenitors in the 22nd year of Marquis Hsiang(襄公) (21st year of King Ling of Tsur,周灵王,551 B.C.) and died in the 16th year of Marquis Ai of Luh(鲁哀公) (41st year of King Jing of Tsur,周敬王,479 B.C.). Entitled the Consummate Successor, Prime Sage and Teacher of All Time(大成至圣先师), he was verily one of the very few great enlighteners of

---

① There is a slip of the brush in Sze-ma Tsien's date. Confucius died in 479 B. C. If it were 129 years after his death, that is, in 350 B.C., the curator of history Dan could not see Viscount Hsien of Tsing(秦献公), for the viscount was already dead by then (he died in 361 B.C.) and his son Viscount Shao (秦孝公) had succeeded him. Therefore, 109 years after Confucius' death, 370 B.C., was probably the correct year.

the world when his own age was plunging headlong to ward the darkest decade and a half humanity would ever see the next twenty-four
centuries. The age was an astounding epoch of human existence,
nevertheless. Solon(639? −559 B. C.), the sage, lawgiver and father of Western democracy, Pericles(495? −429 B. C.), the statesman and fosterer of Hellenic culture, and Socrates (469? − 399 B.
C.), the philosopher and dauntless teacher of truth, all Athenians,
were his contemporaries all, beaming abroad their splendour on the
Greek Peninsula while he was radiating his glory in the night air of
the haggled states of east Asia. Gautama, Sakyamuni (557? − *circa*
480? B. C.)① of India, the philosopher and founder of Buddhism,
lived his days almost identical with Confucius', being born six years
earlier and dead a year earlier than he. To be sure, his renouncement
of the family and the state is against the grain of human nature and
highly impractical, but his non-violence and salvation of all living beings are replete with benediction. His total negation of life's desires
on account of the anxieties and pains ensuing from them leads in consequence to the nihilistic ideal of nirvana, which cuts at the root of
life itself that is but a bundle of multifarious desires. Without admitting himself to be a Confucian in his extant writings, Chü Yuan was
yet decidedly in the illustrious tradition of *Dao* or the Way(道统) of
the Five *T'ih* and Three Kings, all of whom with King Wuh and
Duke Tsur were predecessors in principle of Confucius. Living about
134 years after the sage and being a contemporary of his greatest dis-

---

① The dates of his birth and death, as those of other eminent ancient thinkers,
vary according to different computations. Another chronology of Buddha gives
them out as 565 − 487 B. C. Still another sets them as early as 1016 − 949
B. C.

ciple Mencius, who was twenty seven years his senior, our poet was bound to be tremendously influenced by Confucius both directly and indirectly. Therefore, it behooves us to have some general knowledge of his teachings — his political ideal and ethical principles or means of attaining it.

It is said of Confucius that born with sage wisdom and virtues, he sought instruction not of any particular teacher for long, but of many a one from time to time. Besides learning from Dan-tse(郯子) and Lao-dan, he was taught music by Tsang Hohn(苌弘) and the hepta-chord(琴) by Sze Hsiang(师襄). He was made the Lord of Construction(司空,anciently known as "of Excavation") by Marquis Ding of Luh(鲁定公), then promoted to be the Lord of Judiciary(大司寇) and in the 14th year of Ding's reign (497 B. C.), made concurrently the Prime Minister when he was fifty-six. During his term of office, he executed the courtier Sao-tsen Mao(少正卯), the leader of the anarchical faction, for hatching conspiracies, because "his heart is rebellious and treacherous, his conduct wicked and resolute, his words are wily and packed with sophistries, his memory is vicious and fully loaded with evil instances and the trend he follows is pernicious and glossy." When Confucius was at his premiership for three months, Luh enjoyed a span of great welfare and tranquillity. Tidings of the effectual results of his statecraft were soon spread to the court of the neighbouring state Tsih(齐), which grew apprehensive. Eighty pretty maidens of Tsih were chosen from the state, taught fancy dancing steps and all dressed in fine silk; riding thirty quadrigae properly decked out, they were sent to the Marquis of Luh. His chief steward accepted the gladsome gift. For three days, the marquis did not attend his court, nor did he appear at the sacrificial rites to Heaven to offer roast meat. Confucius then resigned and left Luh. A friend by the name of Sze Ch'ih(师己) saw him off. Confucius sang a song at his departure to forewarn the ills that would ensue. We are also told that he travelled through more than seventy states for fourteen years, trying to find a master worthy of his high policy but in vain. Disappointed, he returned to Luh to write his *Annals*. While paying transcient visits to the states, he earned his meagre living by giving tuition to pupils whose number had grown to some three thousand. Among them, those who were virtuous and had mastered the six arts numbered seventy-two.

Now, the motive spirit of his political ideal, to which his ethical principles contribute as their ultimate end, as well as the harmony of the rules of the Five *T'ih* and Three Kings as summed up by him, could perhaps be best shadowed forth in the chapter *The Drift of Rites* of *The Notes of Rites*(《礼记·礼运篇》). Since it is the goal of his principles and highly significant, the passage should be presented here in rendition. "When the Great Way bears sway, the world's affairs would be conducted for the public benefit only. The virtuous and capable would be duly elected to office, and troth and concord are the aims of everybody. Then, filial piety would redound to the aged in general, the young are not just beloved by their own fathers. Thus, the old could have their days well ended, the able-bodied could be fitly employed, the juvenile meetly bred up and the widowed, the orphaned, the solitary, the disabled and the sickly could all have their sustentation. Men have their proper occupations and women are suitably married. People are loath that things are left on the ground (or in the earth) as naught, but they do not mean that these should be hoarded as private chattel; and they are loath that they have not made their own efforts for the community, but these, if they do make them, should not be only for themselves. Therefore, all plottings are given up and dissolved; robberies, thefts, disorders and heinous crimes do not arise; and outer portals are left open day and night. That is called Universal Union. "

This means to say that in that visionary state, selfishness is purged away from human relations and self-interest is molten in commonweal, that waste is insufferable to one and acquisition is no more a craving desire, that labour becomes a self-imposed duty and remuneration leaves much to spare, that brute power is no more the object of blind worship, the vainglory to predominate over others or to rule is wholly disarmed and tricks and fetches cease to be people's easy expedients and that the thousand and one black deeds will vanish forever and aye. This is the kernel of Confucian ideals as succinctly put as they could be.

It may be asked why Duke Tsur put rites first in his "six arts" to be taught and learnt in the royal colleges and state and country schools and why Confucius thought the drift of rites would ultimately result in Universal Union — both of them setting such a high value on rites. Why is the breaking up of rites, again, spoken of first by reputable historians and scholars alike with the ruin of music as the first of signals of the deterioration of the moral, social and political order of the Tsur world? That is because government by rites(礼治) was the keystone of the Tsur arch as well as those of the patriarchal polities of Yao, Suen, Yü and Taung. In the remote past of the *Hwang* and *T'ih*, rulers of states were always the most prescient, benevolent and capable elders of the nation selected by the reigning groups usually from among themselves and approved by the general public. The heads thus chosen could not but be the wisest, most selfless and conscientious elements of the whole people. Welfare, protection and service to all as well as sharing the good things of life with the multitude were the sum total of their concern and study. Duty was their motto.

While government by rites in its institution by Yao, Suen, Yü, Taung, Wen and Wuh was so much extolled by Confucius, it must be admitted that, throughout the centuries since his time till the modern age, there were hypocritical or blind sticklers to rites, parasites of the society, who, devoid of any vision of the original Confucian ideal, held a fetish of mere formalities, called themselves orthodox Confucians and fed on their profession by serving atrocious despots, shark courtiers or influential families to ravage the people. In fact , these were petty, sham and microbic Confucians, not scarce through the centuries.

In the pearly dawn of history, the common moral code of Yao, Suen and Yü was mild cordiality and civil self-effacement. Great Yü, meaning to hand over the state to Pêh Ih(伯益,伯翳,柏翳), his premier, when he was suddenly caught in fatal illness at Kuay-chih (会稽) during his inspection tour of the Nine States, did not live to see his wish realized. Pêh Ih, following the suit of Suen and Yü, retired to the south of Mount Chieh(箕山之阳) in favour of his master's son Chih(启). Partly because the liege vassals of Yü were overwhelmed by his glowing exploits and there was probably nothing positively faulty in his son up to that time comparable to Yao's son Tan-tsu(丹朱) or Suen's son Saung-chün(商均), and partly because Pêh Ih's fair repute was of rather short standing in contrast with Suen's and Yü's when they had been appointed as Protectors by their

Introduction

masters for already twenty-seven and sixteen years before they succeeded Yao and Suen respectively, the lords and courtiers of Yü crowned
Chih very soon after Yü's death. Most unfortunately, this created a
precedent of hereditary monarchy for all successions to follow suit
hereafter. ①

In the cases of Tsen Taung and King Wuh, they were certainly

---

① This follows in general Mencius' reference to the succession, though it is also
said there people were of the opinion that Yü was not so virtuous as Yao and
Suen, for he did not hand on his kingdom to the virtuous, but inherited it to
his son. *The Bamboo Book Annals*(《竹书纪年》) gives a quite different version to this part of our early history: "Appointed to succeed Yü. Ih took his
sceptre and imprisoned Chih, who broke loose his restraint, killed Ih and suc-
ceedad Yü." In *The Life of S'uo Tsê*(《束皙传》) of *The Ts'in Chronicle*(《晋
书》), it is said that "In the second year of T'ai-kong of Ts'in(晋太康二年,
281 A. D.), a Chi County(汲郡) man named Pûh-tsun(不准) plundered the
tomb of King Hsiang of Gwei(魏襄王). He took with him several tens of cart-
loads of bamboo strip books. Their thirteen chapters of annals keep a record
from the Hsia(夏) Dynasty till the time when King You of Tsur(周幽王) was
killed by Ch'eüan-zone(犬戎) tribesmen. And then the thread of relation is
connected with the panition of Ts'in(晋) by its three lords, which is continued
to the twentieth year of King Anlih of Gwei(魏安厘王). It is the state history
of Gwei. generally in accord with what is noted in *The Spring and Autumn Annals.*" *The Bamboo Book Annals* is also called *The Chi Mausoleum History*
(《汲冢书》). It was actually dug out by plunder in the fifth year of Yen Nien
(咸宁五年,279 A. D.) of Wuh *T'ih* of Ts'in(晋武帝). The *Annals* was written with the juice of *Rhus vernicifera*(漆) on bamboo strips in the polliwig type
of script(蝌蚪文), which antedated even the *Zur* script(籀书) or great *tsuan*
(大篆). The modern Chü Yuan scholar Yer Koh-en(游国恩) gives a detailed
account of Ih succeeding Yü according to Yü's decree and in despite of Chih's
attempt to wrest the power for himself but Chih breaking out from his place of
confinement to kill Ih and succeed Yü, from the historians and commentators of
the relevant passage of Chü Yuan's *Sky-vaulting Queries*, in his book *Studies
into the Superexcellence of "Sao"*, first series(《读骚论微》初集), *pp.* 193 –
202.

as meek and suave as Yao, Suen and Yü. The story of Taung's nets being let open on three sides is well known, as has been related above. When he had beaten the tyrant Ghi of Hsia and captured him, he did not kill him, but only banished him to Nan-ts'iao (南巢). When the cannibal Zer of Yin was beaten, he hanged or burnt himself to death, but his son Wuh-kêng (武庚) was still given a fief by King Wuh as the formal descendant of the Saung Dynasty. After the rebellion headed by him and Quan Swu was put down, they were killed by the order of King Tseng, but Vei-tse (微子), as a progeny of Saung of Taung, was made a duke and granted the feud Soong (宋). This was, by the way, the work of Duke Tsur in the spirit of King Wen. So, Taung and Wuh rose up in revolution against the tyrants Ghi and Zer primarily to purge away their atrocities and save the people.

In the times of the Three Kings and Five *T'ih*, it is understood, of course, not the whole warp and woof of society were in an ideal state. Neither Confucius nor Mencius held such an illusion. No. That would be a fool's paradise. Far from it, the society, emerging not very long from barbarism and stark ignorance, was bound to be full of mishaps and troubles. Living conditions were miserable, to be sure, and human relations were still terribly unstable, to mention just two obvious phases. Culture and education, habit and custom, laws and statecraft, all still in their primitive forms, had not begun to do their offices yet. For instance, Suen's own father, Kuh-sur (瞽叟), wicked to the extreme, tried several times to kill Suen without success. Nevertheless, the political make-up of the state under the fatherly rules of the patriarchs, though rough-hewn, pitifully simple and highly irregular, was yet permeated with love. The general tone and tendency of those ancient governments were peaceful and amiable, the patriarchal chiefs were tenderly solicitous about the well-being of the individual as that of a member of a big family.

And what Confucius brought forth in *The Drift of Rites* was just a broad outline of this general tendency of goodwill and felicity of patriarchism. The rites were the multiplicate ways by which one was led to a happier state of intellectual and emotive existence; they were positive in function for the well-being of the individual. Whereas laws told people: thou shouldst not do this, thou shouldst not overstep that; they were negative in function, prohibitive of certain misdeeds after these were already committed and it was too late to retract them, by means of belated punishments. Speaking of policy (statecraft), punishments (laws) and rites, Confucius said, as recorded in *The Analects*(《论语》): "Conducting policy with virtue, (the ruler) is like the Dipper, remaining unmoved while all other stars revolve around it." Again: "(When a ruler) directeth his subjects with policy and disciplineth them with laws, they would avoid punishments but have no sense of shame. When he directeth them with virtue and disciplineth them with rites, they would not only avoid crimes, but have a fine sense of shame."

Now, as means to an end, the rites, which were visible, pertinent measures, were to be carried out ostensibly for the realization of the state of mind called *ren*(仁), which was invisible. The Chinese character 仁 consists of two radicals, 人(men) and 二(two), meaning two men living together in peace, from which is issued the ideal of beneficence(仁政) and the pair of quadruple concepts: filial piety (孝), brotherliness(悌), loyalty(忠) and faithfulness(信), and good manners (or rites, 礼), justice (or righteousness, 义), purity (廉) and the sense of shame(耻). The character 仁 is thus best rendered into the English word *humanity*. In Confucian ideology, the highest attainment of virtue is this humanity. In response to questions on it by his disciples, Confucius made various answers. To Yen Yüen (颜渊), his wisest, most virtuous and greatest disciple during his lifetime, he said, "Humanity consisteth in restraining oneself and restoring the rites (of Tsur). The day when these things are done, the world would follow such a man's humanity without respite." To the virtuous Tsoon-koon(仲弓), he said, "Be in a mood of seeing great guests when thou steppest forth from thy doors. Be in a mood of high seriousness in performing solemn rituals when thou art ordering about the people. Dost not do unto others what thou dost not wish to be done to thee by others." To easy-going Tse-tsang(子张), he said, "Humanity consisteth in doing these five things to the world, namely: solemnity, magnanimity, faithfulness, swiftness in practice and beneficence. If thou wert solemn, people would not slight or insult thee. If thou wert magnanimous, thou mayest win the public the better. If thou wert faithful, people would believe thee. If thou wert swift in practice, thou wouldst gain the result quickly. If thou wert beneficent, thou wouldst order people about the more quickly." To Van Tze(樊迟), he said, "Humanity meaneth to love people."

To sum up, the principal concepts of Confucian thought closely connected with statecraft and ethics may perhaps be described in four catchwords as defined by Hang Yüe(韩愈) of Tdaung(唐) in his essay *On the Origin of "Dao"*(《原道》): "Charity towards all(博爱) is called humanity(仁); to perform it fitly is called justice(义); the Way to it is called *Dao*(道) and for one to be self-sufficient in its practice without relying on outside aid is called virtue(德)." Or, the moral philosophy of Confucius may be summarized in the Five Con-

stants(五常), which are humanity, justice, rites, wisdom and troth
(仁,义,礼,智,信). But over and above all the aforesaid ethical val-
ues, there are the three constant virtues of all ages: wisdom, humanity and bravery(智、仁、勇三达德), as set forth in *The Medium* of
The Notes of Rites(《礼记·中庸》). These three in combination
surely form the best credo and acid test of a perfect man in all climes,
just like truth, goodness and beauty stand for the ancient Hellenes.
And our trio is certainly superior to the ancient Greek one.

Synchronous with the dwindling of the king's suzerainty and the
riotous disorders in the uprisings of his vassals and their stewards as
well as the unceasing aggressions and conflicts between them, the
Well-farm was broken up into smithereens by the rich and powerful
farmers gulping down the ownings of the weak, poor ones. As a result, loafing and laziness stalked abroad, and crimes and atrocities
became rampant. The rites of hunting, nuptials, funerals, country
archery gatherings, etc. all fell into disuse one after another. Music
was undone and education ruined. That means the multiplex familiar
ways leading to the orderly and peaceful life of early Tsur were all
dug up and choked with rocks and rubbles. Codes of civil conduct
were blotted out; barbarity had come to stay. Chaos ran amuck
against society in broad daylight.

Thus, bordering on the beginning of the Warring States Period
and seeming to announce its approach, in the year 441 B. C., calamity erupted from the royal house of Tsur itself. After King Tsen-ding's
(贞定王) death, his prince royal Ch'ü-tsi(去疾) succeeded him as
King Ai(哀王). Then, his brother Swu(叔) murdered him and appointed himself to succeed as King Sze(思王). But another brother
of theirs named Wei(嵬) said "No!", murdered King Sze outright

and ascended the throne as King Cor(考王). So, one fratricide followed on the heels of another in quick succession, as if to echo the din of patricides and fratricides among their vassals.

V The Warring States Period (403 −221 B. C.)

When the partition of the state Ts'in(晋) by its three lords Gwei Sze(魏斯), Ts'ao Tsi(赵籍) and Hang Jien(韩虔) was formally recognized by King W'ai-li of Tsur(周威烈王) in 403 B. C. with his royal grant of admitting them to his vassalage, the epoch of the Warring States came in full blast. Warfare between states was intensified. Splits in the periphery of the feudal dome of Tsur became lengthened and widened ever more from now on. Moral deterioration in politics both worsened and quickened. In 386 B. C., Dien Huer(田和), a steward of Marquis Kong of Tsih(齐康公), was made a vassal of the king after he had banished the marquis. Seven years later, when the marquis died, Dien Huer's son Dien Oo(田午) seized the marquisate as his own feud. He encountered neither punishment nor denunciation from the king of Tsur, of course, nor resistance nor protest from the legitimate successor of the marquis or his fellow vassals, and was known as Marquis Hwan(桓公) of the state thenceforth called Dien Tsih(田齐). The prince of this Marquis Hwan proclaimed himself King W'ai(威王) on his succession to the marquisate, and henceforth Tsih was known as a kingdom.

Through annexation, splitting up and usurpation, the number of main struggling powers was now reduced to seven. They were Tsing (秦), Ts'ou(楚), Tsih(齐), Yen(燕), Ts'ao(赵), Hang(韩) and Gwei(魏). While the ruling house of Tsur was palsied or in fainting fits, the seven powers assailed one another with increasing fierceness and frequency. Intrigues, deceits, fabrications, blottings, slanders, distortions, frauds, open threats, blackmails, briberies, etc. were freely resorted to. With ferocious Tsing rearing its tall might in the wide west, massive Ts'ou sprawling along the Han, Yang-tse and Hwai Rivers'(汉水, 长江, 淮河) valleys in the south; rich Tsih marshalling its strength on the seaboard in the east; the Three Ts'in (Ts'ao, Hang and Gwei being so called), rather densely populated, filling up the wide gap, the expanse of the Luteous River basin shaped by the first three powers; and Yen somewhat out of the way further up in the north-east of Ts'ao; the scene was duly set for the belligerent forces. Crass degradation of morality on a large scale in such big states as Ts'in and Tsih opened up a new prospect of anarchy. The ancient illustrious examples of *Wang Dao*, the Kingly Way of the Two *T'ih* and Three Kings, were now utterly defaced in the minds of rulers. Worship of brute power or the cowering fear of it was the order of the day. There was no fair authority, none whatsoever. Gross ambition, battening on greed and zest and puffed up with vainglory, sallied forth in grandiose progress with sly deceit, seditious machination and brazen sophistry in his train. Infernal furies were let loose on the streets; terror in the name of government and the law was instilled into people's minds and dreams in one of the states at first.

　　That state was the Tsing of Viscount Shao(孝公) and the felon Wei Yang(卫鞅, *circa* 394—338 B. C.)[1], whom he made his Left

---

[1]　He was "one of the several collateral or concubine born princes of the state Wei(卫), bearing the name Yang(鞅) and the original surname Kung-sun(公孙)", but now more often called Wei Yang after he was rewarded with the fief of fifteen boroughs of Wuh and Saung(於商十五邑) and the title Lord of Saung(商君) for his wresting Gwei's domain west of the River. Thenceforth, he was better known as Saung Yang(商鞅).

Chief Steward(左庶长) in 358 B. C. to change the old statutes. The new laws instituted by him may be sampled by a quotation of two sentences from *The Life of Lord Saung*(《商君列传》) in Sze-ma Tsien's(司马迁) *The Chronicle*(《史记》): "The population was organized into adjoining groups of ten households and five; every household had the bounden duty to accuse and expose any other among the ten of a misdeed; if it were not done, all of them would be punished for hiding or conniving at the crime. Those that refrained from accusation were to be cut asunder at the waist(腰斩); those that accused properly would be rewarded with state distinction as killing a state foe who was a commissioned officer by chopping off his head; hiding a criminal was punished like yielding to the enemy, the person guilty of this to be punished accordingly and his whole family becoming slaves male and female. " As a "legalist", thus, the man was impregnate with savage cruelty.

Before the new laws were promulgated, to initiate his dominion of absolute power by means of foolery and instill fear into the populace, he published proclamations in the name of the viscount in the thoroughfares of the capital that whoever moved a piece of timber log thirty feet long from the south gate to the north gate would be rewarded with ten pieces of gold (increased to fifty pieces when nobody attempted because of puzzlement) and whoever left ashes or refuse on streets would be heavily punished with imprisonment. He then put these into practice. In this way, he implanted the sense of his dreadfulness, irrationality and "good faith"(威信) in people's minds. And after that, his statutes were unleashed and executed with fire and fury.

Wei Yang was not only frightfully ruthless and inhuman, and not to be questioned or reasoned with in what he did; he was also prolific in beastly cunning as a politician and commander of troops. After the state Gwei had suffered a crushing defeat from Tsih the previous year, Wei Yang advised Viscount Shao to attack it in 339 B. C. to snatch its lands west of the Luteous River. The viscount approved of his plan and appointed him to head an army for assaulting Gwei. "Gwei sent Prince A'ng(公子卬) as commander of its forces to ward off the attack. When the two armies were in sight of each other, Kung-sun sent a message to Prince A'ng, saying, 'I have been most kindly disposed towards Your Honour for ever so long. Now that we are both generals of our respective state armies, I fell very much against my bent to launch an attack. Please let me propose to meet Your Honour face to face and convene for an alliance instead, and we shall drink health to each other and then both draw our men backward, to make the affair a peaceful one to Tsing as well as to Gwei.' Prince A'ng thought well of the proposal. So, after the convening, they drank. But Kung-sun had laid an ambuscade in advance. He signaled his hidden warriors to fall on and capture the prince, and then ordered a massed attack on the Gwei army, overwhelmed it and had it surrender totally to Tsing. Now, King Wei of Gwei(魏惠王)[1] had his troops smashed once and again by Tsih and Tsing, the defense of his state becoming almost vacant and its territory shrinking day by day; being struck with fear, he sent an envoy to cut and offer his lands west of the River to Tsing to sue for peace."

Between the years of the two incidents just related in the quota-

---

[1] He was actually Marquis of Gwei then. After he had ceded An-*ih* and his domain west of the River to Tsing and moved to Ta-liang(大梁), he proclaimed himself King Wei of Liang(梁惠王).

tions above, in 349 B. C., Viscount Shao moved his capital from Yung *Tsur*(雍州) far up in the north-west where his state made its capital since more than three centuries before, early in 667 B. C., south-eastward to Yen-yang(咸阳). Yen-yang, Tsing's new capital, was built by Wei Yang, after he was promoted to be the Ta-Iiang-ts'ao(大良造, equivalent to the premier, but concurrently the commander-in-chief of troops) and had taken An-*ih*(安邑), the capital of Gwei. According to Wei Yang's plan of building up a totalitarian state of aggression, farming and warfare (the former being simply a means to the latter) were the two principal things that could not be too much stressed. The agrarian system of Well-farm was therefore formally abolished in Tsing. In 342 B. C., the viscount was promoted by King Hsien of Tsur(周显王) to be a count. All his fellow vassals congratulated him. And then, when Prince A'ng was captured as a result of the nasty trick, his troops were all seized as captives and Gwei's terrain west of the River was ceded to Tsing, the scoundrel-adventurer, who wormed his way up first through the mediacy of an eunuch, was rewarded with the fief of fifteen boroughs of Wuh and Saung(於商十五邑) and the title Lord of Saung(商君). Thoroughly unscrupulous, he was ready to do any mean, vicious or horrible thing if he was sure of success. Profit or gain at any price which he did not have to pay was his doctrine. The count died two years later. His successor proclaimed himself King Wei of Tsing(秦惠王). Lord Saung was pulled to pieces publicly by ox-carts tied to his head and limbs for a charge of high treason laid by the followers of Prince Jien (公子虔) of the ruling house, whose nose had been cut off by Wei Yang some nine years before for infringing his laws. But the policy of this arch-Machiavellian and his laws and ways of conducting state affairs had come to stay in Tsing; they underwent no change. This was the formal inception of the world's first hegemonism in history to my knowledge.

To illustrate how hard the seven powers were trying to cut one another's throats, a bare enumeration of hostile events during forty odd years would suffice. In 375 B. C., Hang(韩) absorbed Ts'eng (郑). Seven years later, Tsih attacked Gwei. In 353 B. C., Tsing beat Gwei and took Sao-liang(少梁). Gwei beseiged Ts'ao's capital Hang-tan(邯郸) the same year. The next year, Tsih laid siege to Gwei to relieve Ts'ao. In 340 B. C., Gwei fell on Hang, and Ts'ih assaulted Gwei, giving its troops a crushing defeat. The next year, Tsing overcame Gwei and captured its forces as related above. In 334 B. C., Ts'ou swallowed Yüeh(越) which had annexed Wuh(吴) a century and two score years before. In 333 B. C., the six states Yen, Ts'ao, Hang, Gwei, Tsih and Ts'ou combined in "united coalition" (合纵) to resist Tsing under the general command of Suh Tsing (苏秦).

The philosophers, school-founders, politicians, etc. of the pre-Tsing period, especially the Warring States, were many and diverse. A short account of Lao-dan and Confucius during the Spring and Autumn Period has been given above. Here, a cursory glance is to be made of some other prominent figures and their doctrines.

The earliest founder of a school in the Warring States Period was the writer of The "*Dao Têh*" *Classic*(《道德经》) or *Lao-tse*(《老子》), the latter a misnomer, perhaps by mistake in transmission, but more probably purposely put out by the grand curator of history Dan of Tsur(周太史儋, *circa* 420 −350 B. C.) as his counterfeit work in the name of Confucius' teacher Lao-dan, the best authority on Tsur rites, to confuse the Confucians and make fun of the world. Such a way of hoaxing the public and especially the disciples and followers of Confucius, of joking at and perplexing them with one of his mischievous pranks, to raise an uproarious laughter among the ranks of his fellow anti-Confucians, was in keeping with the temper of the real writer of this tract as well as with the spirit of the age. All things were turned topsy-turvy; so, why not people's thoughts too? The rites of early Tsur were shattered beyond recognition and its music was ruined; poetry and dance were dead and gone; education was broken up into tatters and shreds; the Well-farm system was uprooted by rapacious landlords; riotous peers and usurping reeves were all the rage now, giving rise to incessant warfare, political chaos and social upheaval. It was well then to have the confusion further confounded by calling some of the chief causes of the original feudal order, the rites especially, the very cause of all the disorder and chaos. What a clever and bold stroke! And at the same time, it was equally well to cry down the originators and upholders of rites, the Two *T'ih* and Three Kings and King Wuh, Duke Tsur and Confucius — the sages, or builders and promoters, of concord and order — by blaming them for at least giving rise to big brigandage if not advocating it. What another magnificent stroke! By calling the consequences of irrelevant causes the causes of causes, that is, by putting the wrong carts before the right horses, the grand curator of history Dan of Tsur, the huge joker, had made his roaring laughters resound through the centuries. But had he laughed off the drift of calamities and his own tears? No, decidedly not!

If rites were indeed "loyalty and faithfulness running thin and the beginning of chaos", as said by him, then the total absence of rites （the proper ways of conducting things and leading a civilized life）at the start would strangely bring forth loyalty and faithfulness, and is thus the mysterious beginning of good order. So, according to his occult, irrational logic, good order as an end is desirable, but to attain it, it is necessary to forego any kind of endeavours or efforts at first. In another word, inaction is the way to it. And he said, "If the sages die not, the big brigands would not stop"; which means to say that the sages（who worked hard to build up a good social order）were actually the occasions if not the causes of banditry. That implies that if there were no one who ever tried to build up good order, the world would be happy and peaceful by itself. Whereas in fact, if there were no sages like Suen（舜）, Tseng Taung（成汤）, King Wuh（武王）and Confucius but only tyrants, felons and scoundrels like Ghi（桀）, Zer（纣）, Lih（厉）, You（幽）and Count Shao（秦孝公）, King Ts'au（秦昭王）and Ying Tsen（嬴政）of Tsing, Wei Yang（卫鞅）, Tsang Yih（张仪）and Lih Sze（李斯）and their active underlings and millions of obedient subjects, dolts, dupes and willing tools, the world would be a great empire of hell enveloped in utter darkness lasting unto perpetuity, as Ying Tsen planned his.

In the chapter *Tse Travels to the North* of *Tsaung-tse*（《庄子·知北游》）, Tung-quo-tse（东郭子）asked Tsaung-tse, "The so-called *Dao*（Way）, where is it?" Tsaung-tse said, "It is omnipresent." Tung-quo-tse said, "Be more explicit." Tsaung-tse said, "It is among the gryllotalpas and the ants（蝼蚁）." "How low!" "In the millet-grass and panic-grass（稊稗）." "How even lower!" "In the tiles and bricks（瓦甓）." "How even more so!" "In the dungs and urines（屎溺）." Tung-quo-tse then kept mum. Such burlesque treatment of highly serious and tragic social and political havoc might serve as an effective narcotic to lull the sensibility of those afflicted with intellectual and emotional throes, even the writers of *Lao-tse* and *Tsaung-tse* themselves perhaps too, and that very well indeed, as it did to their readers of that age and all posterity; for the grand curator of history Dan of Tsur and his young contemporary Tsaung Tsur(庄周,368 - 320 B. C.) were certainly in mock earnest at least, else they would not have written their works at all. But that does not mean that their writings could solve the tormenting questions or subdue the tumultuous anarchy. They did not entertain any such vain hope, nor did or do their readers have this illusion. In fact, taking the calamities of the times so jocosely and offering to dissolve them by poking fun at them with a mere nonentity, they should not be taken seriously at all by the readers of their works.

In a way, the *Dao Têh* school appeared to afford some sort of re-lief — a semblance of it, though, not real alleviation — to the tense situation of distress, fear and affliction due to the crumbling of the whole feudal fabric. The decided manners of Lao-tse and Tsaung-tse in sweeping away the rubbles of the past seemed to be the right thing. Tsaung-tse's wild abandon of fancy in his metaphors of the fish Quen (鲲,a fabulous leviathan nobody knows how many thousands of *lih* long it is) and the bird Bun(鹏,a fabulous roc nobody knows how many thousands of *lih* long its back is) in the first chapter *Care-free Peregrination*(《逍遥游》) of his book likewise captures people's wonderstruck imagination; his crushing contrast between these and the cicada and the treron(莺鸠) impels the moral that, if left to them-selves, things no matter how great or small they be, would be at their ease according to their own respective natures. So, it is proposed to get rid of rites, culture, education, morality and all other institutions of man, since these are much ado for no good of the society, to restore the primitive state of the "noble savage". The obscurantism and bold-faced makebelieve of the whole thesis are simply ridiculous. How can all these mountainous negations be put into practice to rescind the stress and chaos and restore primeval peace? The answer is a huge, yawning puzzle.

And as a positive principle set forth by the founder of this school and further expounded by his followers, they offered the occult mysticism of quietude and inertness(清静无为) as a cordial of salvation. But this may be regarded as a soothing balm only, a temporary unguent at its best; it could not cure the root evil, nor heal the excruciating diseases. And besides, it led its way to the escapism of Hwang-Lao(黄老), the imaginary flight into the fairyland and the cult of Daoism(道教)[1] with its manifold superstitions and occult arts. The doctrine of quietude and inertness is in truth a midway hostel to that of Buddhism's nirvana, which aims at the total extinction of existence as agitated by desire and the attainment of self-centred composure of being. The latter, when divested of its mystic verbiage, is materially but the termination of both body and consciousness, or death pure and

---

[1] Daoists regard Hwang-*t'ih* and Lao-tse as the earliest progenitors of their cult, which was started by Tsang Dao-ling(张道陵) and his son and grandson in East Han(东汉) and formally established by Kur Chien-tse(寇谦之) of North Gwei(北魏) during the North Dynasties(北朝). Superstitions and occult arts connected with Daoism include divination of oracles through drawing lots(卜筮), oneiromancy(梦卜), fortune-telling(算命), the occult art of drawing the magic symbol(符箓), disciplining oneself through metamorphosis into a fairy(修仙), chastening the elixir(炼丹), choosing the auspicious location where to bury one's parents(堪舆,风水), analyzing the character drawn by lot (起课:六壬,太一,遁甲), etc.

simple, as witnessed by Buddha's nirvana, his lifeless and deathless eternity.

The imaginary flight into the fairy world had once given a transient relief to Chü Yuan, as described in his poem *Distant Wanderings* (《远游》)[①], where

> Seeing the fairy prince to pay respect,
> I inquire of him how the "airs" would come to zest.
> "The way could be had," quoth he, "but not shown;
> Minute'tis, without an in, grand sans bound;
> Confuse thy soul naught, it mayeth grow natural;
> Fill it with 'airs', some night their union would come

---

① This poem is said by Kuo Mê-ruo(郭沫若) to be suspected by some modern scholars as not Chü Yuan's authentic work and attributed by him to Sze-ma Hsiang-rue(司马相如) "for its construction bears much resemblance to *A 'Fuh' on the Magister*(《大人赋》) and certain piquant expressions are common to both pieces." But I have reasons to think his arguments quite flimsy and fallible. It appears to me that *The Magister* is an imitation of Chü Yuan's much earlier, original piece. The poet's feelings from the beginning of *Distant Wanderings* are genuinely Chü Yuan's own, while the Magister has no occasion to leave "his great mansions and lands ten thousand *lih* in extent." The emotional tone of Sze-ma's piece, written for show of the writer's agility in thetorical flourishes is a falsetto. The diction of *The Magister* is tortuous, laboured and decorative, not to be compared to the simple purity of *Distant Wanderings*. As to the similarity of construction and certain expressions, that is no argument in favour of Hsiang-rue either. Yau Nai(姚鼐), the editor of *A Compilation of Types of Old Prose and "Tze"*(《古文辞类纂》) has told us of the difference between the similarities of their conclusions. And readers of Soong Yu's(宋玉) *Nine Strains*(《九辩》) and Pan Ngo's(潘岳) *A "Fuh" on Autumn Feelings*(《秋兴赋》) could all see that there are piquant expressions common to both pieces, but it was Pan Ngo who imitated Soong Yü the better poet. See my other arguments in §11 of section Ⅶ *Chü Yuan and His Works*.

round;

Keep vacant, wait for it, inertness would ensue;

All lives prosper because of this primal spring. "

And at the end of the poem:

Then I ramble all around the four extremes,

And wander about the six spaces immense,

Up to where lightning swift its zigzags whippeth,

And down to overlook the unfathomed deep.

Below, it is bottomless and sans the ground;

Above, it is far-away and sans the sky;

To look out, it is fleetingly without sight;

To listen, it is emptily without sound.

Superseding inertness and arriving

At utter purity,

I come to inhere very next neighbouring

To Primitive Prime.

But this is merely a soaring poetic fantasy for the temporary soothing of the poet's distracted feelings; it is of no avail to get him out of his sufferings. For the cynicism, anarchism and nihilism, clothed in the vesture of magniloquence, exaggeration, sham, irony, mockery, burlesque, jocoseness, laughter and mysticism in *The "Dao Têh" Classic*, *Tsaung-tse* and *Li-tse* (《列子》)[1], to make

---

[1]   Li Yüh-kur(列御寇) was an earlier contemporary of Tsaung Tsur. *Li-tse*(《列子》), the surreptitious work falsely attributed to him, is a patched-up adulteration of his admirers forged after *Tsaung-tse*.

them appear like paradoxes and truisms could serve no end at all as philosophy and metaphysics. [1] They are none such in spite of the guise. They give no intellectual resolution worthy to be spoken of, but offer impenetrable puzzlement in plenty. In truth, the tranquillity and inaction, or emptiness and nothingness (虚无), prescribed to cure the maladies of the age proved to be no better than quack medicines or magic symbols. Astounded, bewildered and captivated especially by Tsaung-tse's flight of imagination in his literary properties, some of our easy thinkers and facile writers[2] mistake the mysticism and quackery of the *Dao Têh* school for wisdom, profundity and "transcendentalism". The refutation of the fundamental standpoint of *Dao Têh* is wittily and pithily put in a little quatrain of twenty-eight

---

[1] Obviously it is bootless, fallacious reasoning to say that "the Southern, or Transcendental School of Lao Tzŭ aimed at a complete revolution by means of paradoxical enunciations of apparent truisms. It undoubtedly contains the germs of truth magnificently conceived; but as history has conclusively proved, its gems cast before the multitudes have received no better treatment than the pearls did at the feet of the swine in the farnous parable of Jesus. ... ," as pronounced by Lim Boon-keng, in *The Historical Background*, introducing his version of the poem *Suffering Throes* (p. 19, *The Li Sao*, Commercial Press, Shanghai, 1935). I pay my liberal compliment to Lim's high admiration for Chü Yuan, but I must take exception to his opinion on this point, his enthusiasm for aristocratic politics and the British Empire, and his vulgar exaltation of Napoleon and Mussolini. Though his perseverance in doing this arduous piece of work is to be praised, I regret to say that his rendering is not without grave errors here and there and his sense of poetic diction is grievously lacking.

[2] Such as Lin Yü-tang(林语堂), whose confounding conglomeration of the excellences of Tsaung-tse, Chü Yuan and Shakespeare has shown him to be a wiseacre unstudied in all the three, but a smatterer of arts, letters and philosophies both Chinese and Western, and an ignoramus of the highest flights of poetry. *Vide* my short critique of his views in section IX *Chü Yuan's Position in China's History and the World's*; *His Adorers, Imitators and Critics*.

characters by the Tdaung(唐) poet Bêh Ch'üeh-yi(白居易) entitled *Reading "Lao-tse"*(《读老子》)：

> Speakers are unwise；the wise are mum：
> This I hear from the sage Lao-tse.
> If Lao-tse were a thinker wise，
> Why did he write these five thousand works？

Another quatrain of Bêh on the equalization of things of *Dao Têh* entitled *Reading "Tsaung-tse"*(《读庄子》) reads thus：

> Tsaung-tse equalizes all things as one；
> I say all is diverse not quite the same.
> To be carefree，you deem things alike；
> But phoenixes must excel snakes and worms.

Therefore，to clinch the whole question of *Dao Têh* as a system，in fine，it is an abject philosophy of self-deception，originated from an overwhelming sense of futility and blank despair.

When all these have been said to disparage the *Dao Têh* school or Hwang-Lao，however，a word of commendation is also due to its positive merits. First of all，those who are initiated in its occultness would acquire a tact and a skill of weathering adversity and defeat，and gain a perseverance of overcoming them at long last. It could endow one with a sustaining power and a coolness of mind to see what is unusual，unexpected and contradictory. Second，it broadens the imagination and affords a sense of detachment. Running counter to the obvious，the conventional and the vulgar，it gives another pair of wings, so to speak, to one's flight of literary vision. Third, sayings such as these in The "Dao Têh" Classic and Tsaung-tse are timely for all ages: "The people are famished for their rulers are too ravenous in exacting revenues." "The way of Heaven is to straiten the plenty to make up for the deficient; the way of man is not so; it straitens the deficient to make the plentiful overabounding." "The violent and ruthless could not die a natural death." "Nature giveth me form, laboureth me with life, calmeth me with age and resteth me with death." And this: "One who stealeth a hook is executed as a crook. One who stealeth a state is entitled a marquisate. At the house of a marquis, humanity and justice cannot go amiss." Such caustic criticism is justifiable and wholesome to most, I think, if not all ages.

What is a thousand times more deplorable is that, as well said by Suh Sêh (苏轼) of Soong (宋) in his essay On Hang Fei (《韩非论》), the school of Dao Têh gave birth to the school of legalists, viz., Shen Puh-hai (申不害), Saung Yang (商鞅), Hang Fei (韩非) and Lih Sze (李斯), which brought the catastrophe of Tsing (秦) to our people and, I must add, we are still being racked by it today. And Suh Sêh's well-founded opinion was preceded in a concise statement by Sze-ma Tsien in The Lives of Lao, Tsaung, Shen and Hang (《老庄申韩列传》) of The Chronicle (《史记》): "Shen-tse, endeavouring hard, brings exactitude to names and realities, and Hang-tse, applying strict rules to things and conditions, makes clear what is right and what is wrong — their utmost acridity and ruthlessness are rooted in the idea of Dao Têh." The moral code that one should do nothing, which sprouts from the cosmology that the world is nothing, cannot but be a doctrine of sheer negation, by which "one's father is not to be held in love, nor one's sovereign held in awe"; thus, "humanity is not to be cherished at heart, the sense of duty or justice not to be exerted in one's efforts, and rites and music are not being made use of to mould people's personalities. " Now, is this principle of nonentity capable of helping the man in power to govern the state? "Saung Yang and Hang Fei did not know how to put that puzzle into practice, but they had found out artifices to belittle the world and e-qualize life and death. " Since benevolence does not lead to humanity according to the asserted law of *Dao Têh*, and humanity is not to be distinguished from cruelty and acerbity any way, so the slaughtering of people is regarded as good as beneficence or even better than that because of its effectiveness. Therefore though the works of "Lao", Tsaung and "Li" may serve for literary reading and as diversion at times, they are of questionable worth, to say the least, as serious philosophical writings. For proof of my point in controversy, one has only to dwell on the calamitous consequences of the imbecile devotion to "Lao", Tsaung and Daoism of Whei-*tsoon* of Soong(宋徽宗), an emperor of unusually high talents in literature, art and calligraphy, whose wild abandon to "Lao"-Tsaung's philosophy and Daoist prac-tices resulted in his and his son's captivity by Chin(金). And as per-sonal practices, it is no hidden secret that through the centuries, many people have died unnatural deaths in their craze to chasten the elixir out of cinnabar and numerous ones have been cheated to do all sorts of absurdities in Daoist superstitions.

The school of legalists consisted of Saung Yang, Shen Puh-hai, Zuen T'ao(慎到), Süin Whon(荀况), Hang Fei(韩非) and Lih Sze. They were those known to be well studied in punishments that were relevant to the crimes in civil life, that is, the theoretics of law. For elevating the sovereigns above their liege inferiors and subjects, those punishments and their pertinent names were scrutinized in relation to the realities of guilts to make the metings out or sentences effectual in their purposes. Thus, the focuses of studying this branch of knowledge were fixed upon the interests of the rulers, in sharp contrast to the ideal of humanity and beneficence of Confucius and his disciples for the general benefit of the ruled. With a common aim in their pursuits, they were, however, widely different in giving expression to their personal traits in their individual activities under different circumstances.

In the state Tsing, to fabricate a fascisdom, Wei Yang set up his government of terrorism under the viscount by means of abolishing whatever old statutes that existed and old customs that prevailed, and installing his new laws that made farming and state warfare (the former for the sake of the latter) the only two things allowed and encouraged in his regime. Even the feudal priviledges of the state head's family members were shorn off and the number of these members was curtailed. Violence in the name of government and law was lavishly employed to infuse fear and enforce submission among the populace. The people were nothing but the fighting beasts of the viscount who was a figure-head by himself but had his unconditional power fully embodied in his steward or premier. The Confucian *Classics of Rites*, *Music*, *Poetry* and *History* and the virtues such as kindliness, filial piety, brotherliness, troth, integrity and humanity, together with the two "vices" — non-soldiery and shyness at warfare, were called a cell of lice(六虱) to be exterminated. With such a monster, whose character has been pictured in a quotation above, at the helm of the ship of state, Tsing had become a completely Nazified country in ten years.

Though Ghi of Hsia(夏桀), Zer of Yin(殷纣), Lih and You of Tsur(周厉,周幽) and Yang-*t'ih* of Swei(隋炀帝) in Chinese history, to name a few, were all tyrants atrocious and inhuman in their crimes, as were Herod, King of the Jews(40 −4 B. C.), and Nero, the Roman emperor (54 −68), yet they still had a limit in their heinousness. But Wei Yang, Tsang Yih, Ying Tsen(嬴政) and Lih Sze were pestilential and flagitious to a very much higher degree and bigger scale.

Sun Puh-hai, a contemporary of Wei Yang, was made the premier of Marquis Ts'au of Hang(韩昭侯) in 351 B. C., eight years after Wei Yang's appointment to his stewardship. It was said of him that during the fifteen years when he aided his master in governing the state, it was free from warfare except once when Gwei attacked it. He has been regarded together with Hang Fei as the orthodox progenitors of the legalist school. His speculations on the theories of law had their origin in Hwang-Lao(黄老).

And Zuen T'ao, according to *The Roll of Arts and Letters of The Han Chronicle* (《汉书·艺文志》), "in his book *Zuen-tse* (《慎子》), maintaining that the laws should neither out-do themselves beyond their proper spheres, nor be flaccid as to allow of plastic stringency, holds that, when administered in due time as disciplinary measures, they could lessen the efforts of governing and achieve tranquillity in rule. This is how *Dao Têh* unsheathes itself and turns into legalism. So, both Sun and Hang praise him in their writings."

Of Süin Whon and Hang Fei, not much would be said here of their thoughts, for when their writings were published in the form of bamboo strips, Chü Yuan had already died. Süin is traditionally regarded as a Confucian, for he apparently promoted the Kingly Way and rites and music after the great sage. Yet he disavowed very strongly Tse-sze(子思) and Mencius, who were most certainly Confucians if there be Confucians at all, and maintained that human nature is wicked and Yao and Suen were but artificialities and, as a self-evident proof of which school he should belong to, his pupils Hang Fei and Lih Sze were both legalists to the marrow.

Lih Sze was Ying Tsen's(嬴政) fellow culprit in their hellish crimes of burning the books and burying alive 460 odd scholars at Yen-yang. It should be said of him here that when Hang Fei (his fellow student under the tutorship of Süin Whon) went to see Ying Tsen, king of Tsing, as the envoy of the state Hang sent to Tsing, Lih Sze, knowing his master Ying Tsen's keen eagerness to see Hang after reading his writings and Ying's intention to elevate Hang to a high position in the Tsing court, concocted stories to traduce him, out of black envy, to have him imprisoned first, and then sent poison to him to make him commit suicide.

Meng Kuh(孟轲,372 − 289 B. C.), commonly known as Mencius(孟子), the greatest disciple and exponent of Confucius and a pupil of his grandson Tse-sze(子思,who, a pupil of Confucius' disciple Tsen Sun, 曾参, wrote *The Medium*《中庸》, by the way, expounding the golden mean or moderation in ethics), loomed bright in the early horizon of this period. He propagated with warm eloquence his master's teachings of the Kingly Way in his itinerary through the states and developed them. He tried to convince the heads of states in power, such as Liang-wei Wang of Gwei(魏梁惠王) and King Hsuan of Tsih(齐宣王), of the significance of humanity and eternal justice, righteousness and beneficence, high morals and the people's welfare, instead of their prepossession with the wealth and power of the state. He castigated the worship of Mammon and materialism. But in the first case, the king had just lost his capital An-ih (安邑) and his domains west of the River to Tsing. Inevitably, his exhortation fell on deaf ears. He upheld just revolution in very high esteem. King Hsuan of Tsih asked him on his visit to Tsih, "Was it true Taung exiled Ghi and King Wuh assailed Zer?" He replied, "These are recorded in chronicles." "Is it allowed for lieges inferior to kill their sovereign lords?" "Those who violated humanity are called evildoers; those who ravished justice are called vicious wretches. Evildoers and vicious wretches are depraved and lorn. It is known that Zer the lorn and depraved was put to justice, but that was not regicide." In Gwei, Tsih and Soong, Meng Kuh failed equally sadly of his purpose, for the simple reason that the occasions were invariably adverse and those whom he sought were all the wrong parties. But his faith, courage and stoicism in upholding humanity and justice (仁义) and preaching the beneficent rule of the Two *T'ih* and Three Kings were made manifest by his statement "I am well able to nourish my sublime animation, which wealth and high station cannot debase, poverty and humbleness cannot prevail on, and force and might cannot subjugate." His credo was, "the people are of the highest in import, the domain of a state stands next, the king is the lightest of the three." The Spring and Autumn Period had given our nation and the world the great luminary Confucius. This age of the Warring States was to give nativity to two illuminating stars Mencius and Chü Yuan that would last with humanity. However, under the circumstances, it may be definitely affirmed, as the age was crashing to its catastrophe, no human effort could save the situation.

While the Confucian ideal of the Great Way, based upon the

germinal practices of the very remote patriarchal state, prescribes that the world should be for the public, crass reality had it plainly that it was for the private interests of the hereditary monarchs only. In the cases of Taung of Saung and Wuh, Tseng and Kong of Tsur, the notion of public interests indeed prevailed somewhat for a number of years, but in the reigns of their successors easeful life sooner or later got the upper hand of caution and uprightness, and gradually degeneracy crept in, dominated the situation and in the end gave place to vice and tyranny. Thus, it is obvious when things had come to such a pass as the Spring and Autumn and the Warring States Periods, the mere sticking to rites and their ramifications here and there could not calm down a roaring, tossing sea of troubles. It was much too late to work for salvage. It is plain as daylight, by diagnosis, that absolute power invested in one person and its inheritance in his family (this latter is an extension of the former, meaning its monopoly in his family, the ruling house) were the root evils of all chaos, oppression and misrule, even if there were no foreign invasion or infestation to complicate the matter.

But for over forty centuries, no one dared to point out this simple truth! And even Confucius only promoted the general principle of "the world ... for the public" and lauded the illustrious examples of Yao, Suen and Yü in their appointments of successors outside of their families; it did not occur to him to oppose absolute power in one man and its hereditary succession in his family, or to advocate limited power in the chief of a state and its non-hereditary succession as the golden rule. For though it may be granted that the idea of limited power in the chief of a state was unthinkable at that time, for there was no precedent, yet succession by appointment instead of by inheritance was doubtless an exampled and excelling, therefore feasible and superior system. Of this, he signified his preference by insinuation.

In fact, during the forty centuries since King Chih of Hsia(夏启) succeeded Great Yü (most unfortunately, I must repeat), no one in China except the founders of dynasties and their successors, or else the rebel chiefs and the usurpers, was in a position or at liberty to broach the idea of opposing hereditary or advocating non-hereditary succession unless he was ready to pay the price with his own neck, and those of his family members, relatives and friends to boot. And the dynasty-founders and their successors, as well as the rebel chiefs and usurpers, were without an exception not public-spirited or selfless enough to bring up the topic.

Since Confucius set forth his doctrine of "the world ... for the public", none of the Confucians, including Mencius, had developed their master's teachings as to declare explicitly that the Great Way, beneficence and "the world ... for the public" were incompatible with hereditary monarchical government which, as a system, therefore, must go. To stand for royalism and its inheritance in a family and to expect beneficence at the same time are to leave commonweal to mere chance, and hope for the best. As long as the crucial question of absolute power and its succession was not settled, the best of wishes was unavailing and all ado vain. That is how and why Confucius and Mencius failed grievously in their efforts. Great Yü's line ending in Ghi, Tseng Taung's ending in Zer, and Wen and Wuh's ending in Lih and You(厉,幽) had given people plenty of lessons already.

Now I should turn to mention a few minor schoolmen other than the *Dao Têh* company and the legalists whom I have already touched above. Mê Di（墨翟）or Mê-tse（墨子）, an elder contemporary of Mencius, like him also a native of Luh（another tradition has it that he was a native of Soong,宋）, promoted universal love as his principle, and assiduity and frugality as its practices. He stood for election of the virtuous to public posts, advancement of filial piety and pacifism, and disbelief in heavenly destiny. He was against Confucius and the Confucians in thinking of their rites as a great waste and again unlike them who kept silent on the subject, was interested in talking of ghosts. Traveling through the states to find a king, he gathered a number of disciples and followers around him and became a courtier of Soong（宋）.

The school of military science（兵家）had its advocates in Sun Wuh（孙武）of the Spring and Autumn, and Wuh Chih（吴起）of the Warring States Periods, both of whom left after them works on the art of warfare. They were well-known generals, the former being that of the state Wuh（吴）and the latter those of Luh（鲁）, Gwei（魏）and Ts'ou（楚）. Sun Wuh's descendant Sun P'ing（孙膑）was a general of Tsih. As Chü Yuan's writings show no sign of his interest in warfare, it was unlikely that these men had any effect upon his mind.

And there was a freak of a philosopher Yang Tsu（杨朱）, a native of the state Wei（卫）, whose writings, though lost, were known in scraps through *Li-tse* and *Mencius* to contain the main idea of extreme egoism, summarized in the statement that he would not pluck a hair of his to benefit the whole world.

The school of "logicians" was noted for its hair-splitting distinctions and sophistries, the most outstanding of whom K'ung-sun Loon（公孙龙,*circa* 320 −250 B. C.）was a junior contemporary of Chü

Yuan. He tried to prove with brain-teasing arguments that a white horse is not a horse because it is a combination of the quality whiteness with the conception horse. The logical conclusion of his sophistical premise is that there is no such thing as a horse in itself, since it must be one of some colour, nor is there any such thing as whiteness, since it must be the visible quality of something. These people were friends and assistants to the legalists in giving good names and reasons to their dark deeds and discrediting virtues as senseless practices backward and out of mode.

And there was Quai-ko-tse(鬼谷子), the Sire of Ghost Valley, said to be "a true fairy... with disciples more than a hundred, the only two of whom not willing to be fairies learned the art of coalition, and conjunction(纵横术) of him. " Of course, this was a hilarious joke. His supposedly real name Wang Lih(王利) must be a mere fetch, meaning "for the benefit of kings". *The Roll of Arts and Letters of The Han Chronicle*(《汉书·艺文志》) does not list *Quai-ko-tse*(《鬼谷子》). It is said that someone in East Han(东汉) mixed up the supposedly posthumous writings of Suh Tsing(苏秦) and Tsang Yih(张仪), which were concoctions of their admirers in the last years of the Warring States and in West Han(西汉), to forge the book *Quai-ko-tse*. From this it can be seen how devilishly crafty and mischievous these two politicians (or rather one of them only, see below) must have been during their lifetimes to elicit such curiosity in them as to have produced these brewages. However, it was probable that Suh and Tsang were verily fellow pupils of a common master for, it was said, when the former had become the General Commander of the Pact of United Coalition(从约长) and concurrent premiers of all the six powers in 333 B. C., Tsang Yih went to see him to offer his diligence, but was refused; only the real identity of their common master was not divulged for reasons unknown but not hard to understand and he was purposely given these pseudonym and appellative to keep the public in the dark.

The traveling speakers(说客) or itinerant disputers(辩士) of that age were free-lance politicians of two sorts, antipodal in their difference. The fair ones included Tsen Ts'en(陈轸), Suh Tsing(苏秦) and his brothers Dai(代) and Lih(厉), Tsen-yü Quen(淳于髡), etc.; they were for united coalition(合纵) of the six powers to resist Tsing as their common enemy, for taken singly, none of the six was strong Tsing's equal match, but bound together, they could easily overpower it which was certainly the most aggressive vicious and dangerous of them all. The foul ones consisted of Tsang Yih(张仪) and Fan Tsui(范雎); the former advocated cross conjunction(连横) of the six powers separately with Tsing, each for its own safety against the menace of the other five, expressly to break up their united coalition, and the latter held the policy of conciliating distant states and attacking near neighbours(远交近攻).

Suh Tsing, a native of Lor-yang(洛阳) and a pupil of the Sire of Ghost Valley, as mentioned above, went to see King Wei of Tsing (秦惠王) first, it was said, trying to be of service to him in manoeuvring cross conjunction for Tsing, but was rejected. So he went to Yen, Ts'ao, Hang, Gwei, Tsih and Ts'ou one by one and succeeded in uniting them in a pact of combined military power against Tsing, with himself as the General Commander, two years later in 333 B. C. For twenty-nine years, according to Liu Shan[1], the Tsing peo-

---

[1] *Vide* his *Preface* to *The Warring States Strips*(刘向:《战国策·序》).

ple, overcome with fear, dared not display their battle array inside the Hehn-ko Pass (函谷关) to challenge the six powers.

Tsang Yih, a subject of Gwei, went to Tsing to interview King Wei, after his repulse by Suh Tsing, and succeeded in getting the premiership from the king in 328 B. C., presumably because of Suh's sweeping success in uniting the forces of the six powers under his standard. Now, Tsang sold his scheme of cross conjunction with a vengeance, and the train of events showed him to be an insidious and deadly schemer. By hook and by crook, he pushed on his intrigues and artifices to undermine Suh's coalition and grasp his own fist holds. With the house of Tsing Ying Tsen as his arsenal of espionage and trickery stratagems which was first established by Wei Yang, Tsang Yih wove an inter-state spy network, hatched assassination plots, employed crossbiting artifices, bought up and instructed gesta-pos, devised vilifications and flatteries, tendered bribes and gifts, etc. — in another word, this Vulcan of black arts became feverishly busy in pushing on his underhand enterprise. In 323 B. C., he left Tsing for Gwei, his native state, to become its premier. One of the stunning blows he dealt united coalition was to make Gwei take part in a coalite expedition against Tsing, while he was Gwei's premier, and then break it up and defeat it from within in 318 B. C., without anybody discovering the wrecking role he played. The next year, he returned as a triumphant secret agent from Gwei to Tsing to become its premier again. In the same year, Suh Tsing was assassinated in Tsih by a Tsih lord whose name was unknown. Neither was the cause of the murder made public, but it would be explainable to attribute its first author to Tsang Yih for reasons of political enmity and personal grudge.

As Tsang Yih was devilishly crafty and mischievous, full of treacherous trickeries and adept in spreading rumours and calumniations, it was most likely that the story of Suh Tsing having visited Tsing to see King Wei and offer his service in manoeuvring cross conjunction before he himself did, but being refused by the king, etc. was sheer fiction of Tsang. In a discourse of his with the king of Ts'ou[1], he is recorded for saying that "Suh Tsing, as premier to the king of Yen(燕), conspired with the king to overthrow Tsih and divide its lands between them, and then he pretended to flee to Tsih as a political runaway from Yen, whereas the king of Tsih made him his premier, only to find out two years later that he was the secret agent of Yen, so the king of Tsih in great ire ordered to have him, this treacherous, traitorous Suh Tsing, pulled to pieces publicly by tying his head and limbs to ox-carts." But history tells us that Suh Tsing was assassinated by a Tsih lord, not killed with ox-cards. So, very probably that Tsih lord perpetrated the assassination under Tsang Yih's instruction. Meanwhile, the feat of overthrowing, or rather of wrecking the coalite battle from within, was exactly done by himself, the secret agent of King Wei of Tsing, in Gwei; only the King of

---

[1] This discourse is erroneously entitled *Tsang Yih 's Address to King Hwai of Ts'ou*(《张仪说楚怀王》). The writer intended it to be an address to Hwai's successor King Ching-hsiang(顷襄王), for it contains the statement "The King of Ts'ou in great ire sent his tropps to attack Tsing again, and the two armies fought at Landien(蓝田)", etc., after mentioning Ts'ou's smashing defeat at Han-tsoon(汉中). But then, there is another incongruity at the end of the discourse where the king speaks of backing the East Sea, which could only be spoken after Ts'ou had moved its capital to Zur-tsen(寿春). The writer of this discourse had not taken into consideration that Tsang Yih did not live to that time.

Gwei, after Tsang was premier to Gwei for six years, was stupid enough as not to have discovered his crime, but let him go scot-free back to Tsing to become its premier once more.

At that time, four of the six states, bestowing feuds severally upon four of their princes, gave them titles which they made sweet with their fair deeds. They were Princes Meng Tsang（孟尝君）of Tsih, Bing Yuan（平原君）of Ts'ao, Sing Ling（信陵君）of Gwei and Tsen Sun（春申君）of Ts'ou. Each of these Princes of rectitude gathered several thousand friends, guests and followers around himself and under his patronage. They were all junior contemporaries of Chü Yuan, younger than he by more than thirty-five years.

Prince Sing Ling, youngest son of King Ts'au of Gwei（魏昭王）, named Wuh-gieh（无忌）, was noble-minded, kindly and hospitable by nature. He was renowned for his heroic exploits in beating Tsing forces twice to save Ts'ao and Gwei. When Ts'ao's capital Hang-tan（邯郸）was besieged by hosts of Tsing, Prince Bing Yuan of Ts'ao, whose wife was Prince Sing Ling's sister, sought help from King An-lih of Gwei（魏安厘王）and Prince Wuh-gieh. The king ordered his general Ts'in Pih（晋鄙）to succour Ts'ao with 100,000 troops, and then, daunted by Tsing's might, he stopped the general in his vacillation to wait and see. Prince Sing Ling, taking the counsel of his guest Her Ying（侯嬴）, wrested the troops from their general's command, led them to Ts'ao's aid in time and gave the invaders an unexpected menace and setback. And later, when Tsing phalanxes penetrated deep into Gwei, he commanded troops of five states back to put them to rout and flight, pressing hot pursuit as far as to the Hehn-ko Pass（函谷关）. Tsing then started a whispering campaign of calumniation against him. The king of Gwei, befooled by the slander, distrusted and repelled him. Disheartened and despairing, he spent his days in wine and women and died of illness due to inebriety. What he very aptly said of the state Tsing is well worth quoting: "Tsing shares its custom with the western Zone and northern Di barbarians(戎翟). It has the heart of tigers and wolves, greedy and perverse, ravenous of gain and devoid of troth, adverse to rites, justice and virtues. If there is profit to be gained, it would dash forward to grab it in despite of kins and brothers like wild fowls and brutes. "

Once stopped by Suh Dai(苏代) from entering Tsing for the reason that "it is like a tiger's mouth", after thousands of friends and well-wishers failed to stop him, Prince Meng Tsang eventually went to Tsing out of mere curiosity and trying to probe its haunting secrets somehow. He was even made the premier of Tsing in 299 B. C., but King Ts'au(秦昭王) found out finally the next year he was none of his own kind. Ts'au *Wang* was just on the point of trapping him for slaughter, when he escaped by a hair's breadth with the aid of a follower in his *entourage* imitating the crowing of a cock before the peep of dawn.

Prince Bing Yuan, premier to his brother King Wei-wen(惠文王), dispatched his emissary Mao Suei(毛遂) to Ts'ou to draw up a pact of coalition when Tsing beleaguered Ts'ao's capital Hang-tan(邯郸) hard, and meantime got relieving troops from Prince Sing Ling of Gwei, to ward off the impending menace of the enemy. Hospitable to guests and friends by thousands always, he was called "the swift-flying, fine prince of the disjointed times" by the Grand Curator of History.

Prince Tsen Sun of Ts'ou flourished much later after Chü Yuan's death; his activities, by no means prominent and of little interest to us, are skipped here.

And there was a plain subject of Tsih named Luh Lien(鲁连), noted for his brave opposition to violent, ravenous Tsing. A scorner of position and wealth, he had a ready tongue, was free in his actions and liked to offer unasked-for opinions that saved difficult situations. When he paid a visit to Hang-tan, the capital of Ts'ao, it was just beleaguered by the hosts of Tsing, and the Gwei emissary Sing Yuan-yien(辛垣衍) was there for counseling Prince Bing Yuan to ask the King of Ts'ao to recognize King Ts'au of Tsing as "the West Emperor", for in the opinion of King An-Iih of Gwei(魏安厘王), if Tsing were pleased by Ts'ao's recognition of its imperial title, it would soon withdraw its troops and leave Ts'ao alone. Luh Lien saw the Prince, blamed him for his readiness to accede to the Gwei envoy's advice, and then saw the Gwei envoy and convinced him of the danger and folly of enhancing the prestige of Tsing. He said that if Tsing, the state which tramples on rites and justice and regards decapitating the greatest number of people as the greatest merit, would become an empire to rule the world some day, the King of Tsing would most certainly mince the flesh of General Sing's master, the King of Gwei, and cook it, and then he would make his own sons, daughters, and concubines occupy the palaces of Liang of Gwei. By then, where and how would the General curry favour with his old master? As for himself, he would surely have jumped into the sea, were such catastrophe to befall to the world. When the Tsing general heard that Luh Lien had prevented Sing Yuan-yien from his attempt, he withdrew his troops for fifty *lih*. Just then, Prince Sing Ling led the columns of Ts'in Pih to come to Ts'ao's aid, and the legions of Tsing went away. Prince Bing Yuan then offered to donate a fief on and entitle Luh Lien, which he declined again and again. The prince entertained him next at a banquet. When the party at feast was fully warmed up by drinks, Prince Bing Yuan rose up and offered Luh Lien ten hundred-weights of gold. Luh Lien smiled and said, "What is praiseworthy in a gentleman scholar of the world is the propensity in him to expel troubles, solve difficulties and disentangle confusion for others without taking remuneration. He who takes recompense is mercantile minded. I do not wish to behave so." He bade farewell to Prince Bing Yuan and went away, seen no more by the prince ever afterwards. So here, in Luh Lien, we find "a high intellectual of Tsih" indeed, as Sing Yuan-yien said he heard him, as a noble soul, worthy to be a friend of Chü Yuan! He was, however, a younger contemporary of the poet by some forty years.

A few words should be said here of the general political situation and the inter-state warfare of the time. The prince of Marquis S'uo of Ts'ao(赵肃侯), on his ascension to the marquisate in 326 B. C., declared himself King Wuh-ling of Ts'ao(赵武灵王). Father of Prince Bing Yuan and King Wei-wen, he adopted the curt dresses, horsemanship and archery of northern Hwu(胡) tribesmen for his soldiery, making Ts'ao's army the strongest of the three Ts'in. He fought in the north and northwest, making conquests, and absorbed the state Tsoon-san(中山). In 323 B. C., when Tsang Yih left Tsing for Gwei to be its premier in order to subvert the united coalition of the six powers, both Hang (韩) and Yen(燕) claimed themselves to be kingdoms. Thenceforth, all the seven powers were on a par with the kingdom of Tsur nominally, though in reality they had all superseded her long before. In 318 B. C., with Ts'ou leading and under the general command of Suh Tsing, Ts'ou, Ts'ao, Hang, Gwei and Yen sent a coalite expedition to attack Tsing at the Hehn-ko Pass ending in discomfiture. The defeat was most probably planned by Tsang Yih long in advance, since he had become Gwei's premier. The next year, Tsing crushed Hang troops at Siu-yü(脩鱼). In 316 B. C., Tsing conquered Z'uo(蜀), the leading western state, lying in the central part of the modern Sze-tsuan Province(四川). It became a rich granary and an abundant source of pressed enlistment for Tsing's aggressive warfare. In 298 B. C., when Prince Meng Tsang fled back from Tsing, the joint expeditionary force of Tsih, Hang and Gwei beat Tsing columns at the Hehn-ko Pass.

The dialogues between the itinerant politicians and state chiefs said to be true records, as collected by Liu Shan(刘向) in *The Warring States Strips*(《战国策》) and Sze-ma Tsien in *The Chronicle*, are actually the imagined reconstructions made from reliable sources by Quai Tung(蒯通) early in West Han, according to the modern scholar Lo Ken-zê(罗根泽). The contents of these discourses are full of geo-politics and strategical arguments, punctuated in some cases with threats now and then. While Tsen Ts'en, the three Suh brothers and Tsen-yü Quen(淳于髡) stressed the necessity of mutual help and common resistance against Tsing among the six powers, Tsang Yih usually dwelt on the impending perils of not satisfying the demands of Tsing and at times resorted to distortion of facts, rumour mongering, impudent deception, malicious blotting and blank vilification.

As the legitimate successor to Wei Yang in the diabolical game of warfare mixed up with intrigues and clandestine politics, Tsang Yih innovated and manipulated his black arts and added them to the armoury of hegemony that was embodied in the state of Tsing. And he had his genuine offspring in Lih Sze(李斯), the Mephistophelian henchman of Ying Tsen(嬴政), who called himself the "Beginning Hwang-*t'ih*" (Emperor-emperor) of his dynasty of "tens of thousands of generations" — the two, master and varlet, who burnt the *Six Classics* as well as the philosophical and other works of antiquity and current times and buried alive 460 odd scholars at Yen-yang(咸阳)in 213 −212 B. C. [①] As evidenced by facts related above and below, Tsang ordered his tools and agents to traduce Chü Yuan and Prince Sing Ling, and succeeded in knocking them down and out. Once more, after Tsing's army had suffered smashing defeats in the hands of the great general Lih Mo(李牧) of Ts'ao, Lih Sze bought up Kuo Kai(郭开), a favourite minion of the Ts'ao court, to have

---

① He called himself, in 221 B. C., "shortly after he had annexed the world"(初并天下), by the titles of both the *hwang*(皇) and *t'ih*(帝) of ancient times who were kindly patriarchs noted for their beneficence. He decreed in 213 B. C., at the proposal of Lih Sze, to burn all the books. In 219 B. C., he sent a practitioner of occult arts(方士) Hsü Fu(徐福) to take along with him 3000 virgin boys and 3000 virgin maids on a fleet of galleons to sail on the Eastern Seas for seeking ambrosia, elixir or herbs giving perpetual life! In 212 B. C., he ordered the 460 odd scholars and magicians to give up their secrets or their ghosts. As they were unable to give him a satisfactory answer, he, in great ire, had them all buried alive. He also planned to build for himself an immense city of palaces of over 300 *lih* square in extent, with bowered two – layered ways leading to the Lih Mountains(骊山) over 80 *lih* long, the front hall of the main structure of which, called Oo Vaun Palace(阿房宫). And he built a huge mausoleum for himself on the Lih Mountains where he was said to be buried after his death in 210 B. C. with hundreds of living persons for immolation, his imperial concubines, palace waiting maids and eunuchs, to keep him company and a large number of masons, carpenters and other workers on the tomb.

him vilify the general with high treason and get Lih Mo executed! In the same year, the state of Ts'ao was absorbed by Tsing.

For the calamitous failures of the six states ending ultimately in their annexation one after another by Tsing, there were endless regrets among our students of history throughout the centuries. But the flash of victory of persistent evils of a house for six reigns[1] manifest in the conquest of all Cathay by Ying Tsen ran counter to the wishes of humanity all over the land, and indeed, it could not last for more than a span of fifteen years. Of the cause of defeat and overthrow of the six states, Suh Dai(苏代), in his discourse with King An-lih of Gwei (魏安厘王) to stop him from cutting lands to pacify Tsing, says pithily thus: "All wicked people wish to serve Tsing with lands. To do this is like embracing firewood to quench fire. As long as the firewood lasts, the fire would not stop. "

And he was supported and supplemented with detailed arguments by Suh Süin(苏洵) and his son Suh Tsê(苏辙) of Soong(宋) in their essays *The Six States*(《六国》) and *On the Six States*(《六国论》). To sum up their views, the underlying causes why the six states with their territories five times and their populations ten times greater than Tsing's were all undone and eradicated in the end were to be attributed: first, to their policies of conciliating Tsing with lands freely offered to it, not as results of defeats in wars, but as results of defeats in wars of nerves — the latter a hundred times greater than the

---

① Viscount (later, Count) Shao,孝公,361 – 337 B. C.; King Wei,惠王,337 – 310 B. C.; King Wuh,武王,310 – 306 B. C.; King Ts'au,昭王,306 – 250 B. C.; King Shao,孝王,3 days only; King Tsaung,庄王,250 – 246 B. C.; and Ying Tsen,嬴政,246 – 210 B. C. — six reigns, that of King Shao being not counted for its shortness.

former, — for while Tsih did not offer any part of its domain to Tsing, Tsih committed the grave mistake of befriending Tsing and not helping the other five states, and when the five were lost, Tsih of course could not stand alone; and second, to the geographical and strategical locations of Hang and Gwei just on the "heart" (or rather, the breast) and belly of Tsing — its eastward path, shielding their fellow vassals east of the Tsing Mountains(秦岭) — and their lack of support from the other four states, so that they, much weaker and smaller than Tsing, had to yield to it again and again, and finally open the way to Tsing's aggression of the other four.

Besides these, I have three specific points to complement them. First, Gwei, a small power, strategically vulnerable, was too bellicose at the very start; it was beaten by powerful Tsih three times in 386, 353 and 341 B. C., twice because it assaulted Ts'ao and Hang first, and when strong Tsing attacked it in 353, 339 and 275 B. C., it fell and lost its city Sao-liang(少梁) and capitals An-ih(安邑) and Ta-liang(大梁) without putting up a hardy struggle. Second, Ts'ou was to blame for its fickleness in not sticking to united coalition; King Hwai vacillated again and again by changing sides from the five states to Tsing back and forth, so that in 303 B. C., Tsih, Hang and Gwei fell on it for its disloyalty and in 301 B. C., they, in company with Tsing, assailed it again. The ruling house of Ts'ou and its court were utterly corrupt; the chief officials and King Hwai's favourite royal concubine were all thoroughly bribed, with the exception of Chü Yuan, Ts'au Tsui and a few others. Third, Tsih was not interested in taking part in the coalition pact, for it had fought Gwei many times, Ts'ou was faithless and Tsing's policies in the hands of Tsang Yih and Fan Tsui attracted and flattered its rulers.

And over and above the causes just analyzed, there was the politico-economic-military totalitarian structure of Tsing with its techniques, inherited from Viscount Shao(孝公) through Kings Wei(惠王) and Ts'au (昭王) to Ying Tsen(嬴政), and from Wei Yang through Tsang Yih and Fan Tsui(范雎) to Lih Sze, that the six states had to pit against. In comparison, they were like six tiny mites. Finally, kings like Hwai(怀王) and Hsiang(襄王) of Ts'ou and Anlih of Gwei(魏安厘王), the apexes of stupidity, with their houses and courts rotten to the core — what did they look like but scarecrows in the wind? Therefore, the six states were doomed to defeat and extinction, to be gulped down by voracious Tsing. Only, in the case of Tsing, like a massive carbuncle collecting all the poison of its brute force to a head, it burst by itself into collapse before very long.

Ⅵ   Ts'ou and Chü Yuan

In its plan to annihilate all the six states, Tsing had to defeat and overthrow Ts'ou and Tsih, the two strong ones of the six, first and foremost. Tsih lay far away in the east, separated from Tsing by Ts'ao, Gwei and Hang. Ts'ou, adjoining to Tsing, with its ruler and court quite easy to victimize, was thus the less hard nut to crack. But in Ts'ou, there was its prominent lord Chü Yuan, Left Counsellor to the king, who advocated alliance with Tsih and united coalition and was highly antagonistic to Tsing. Therefore, it was imperative on Tsing to remove this main rub in Ts'ou for destroying its chief force of opposition; if this were not done, not only Tsing's strategy could not be pushed forward, but its own security was menaced.

According to *The Annals of the State Ts'ou*(《楚世家 》) and *The Life of Tsang Yih*(《张仪列传》) of *The Chronicle*, as early as in

323 B. C. (the sixth year of King Hwai's reign, 怀王六年), Tsing sent Tsang Yih to Niêh-soun (啮桑) to league for alliance with Ts'ou, Tsih and Gwei; how could it be known, asks the Tsing(清) scholar Tsiang Ch'ih(蒋骥) in his *San-tai Pavilion Commentary on Ts'ou "Tze"*(《山带阁注楚辞》), it was not then that Tsang Yih got hooked up with the Saun-quan courtier, Jin Soun and others(上官大夫,靳尚等) of Ts'ou as a first step to expel Chü Yuan from court? After his return from the league, Tsang left Tsing for Gwei to be its premier, as we have related above, and then he wrought steadily to give a tottering blow to united coalition by discomfitting the joint expedition of the six states, headed by Ts'ou and under the general command of Suh Tsing, at the Hehn-ko Pass in 318 B. C.

In 313 B. C., the sixteenth year of King Hwai of Ts'ou, King Wei of Tsing(秦惠王), declaring his intention to attack Tsih and meaning to break up Ts'ou's coalition with Tsih, which he feared most now, pretended that he had ended the term of office of Tsang Yih as his premier. Tsang was then sent to Ts'ou to urge King Hwai to end his coalition pact with Tsih; for recompense, Tsing promised to slice off its Saung and Wuh terrain(商於之地) 600 square *lih* to Ts'ou. Now, Tsen Ts'en(陈轸) the disputer opposed the transaction very strongly, with a discourse of his addressed to King Hwai left to us to his credit, as Chü Yuan was certainly dead against it too, for in severing relations of alliance with Tsih, as pointed out by Tsen, it would leave Ts'ou in the lurch, and besides, cutting the Saung-Wuh region was only a promise — Tsing would not do it before Ts'ou's abolition of its pact with Tsih. And it should be noted that by then Chü Yuan was already repulsed("屈平既绌") by his master; he did not have a chance to see his sovereign. King Hwai listened not to their counsels, of course, either before or after his decision. He was overjoyed with the promise, gave the premier's seal to Tsang Yih and daily entertained him with banquets. So the pact between Ts'ou and Tsih was flippantly annulled.

Tsang Yih, in his open diplomatic mission to sever Ts'ou's coalition with Tsih, carried on simultaneously a secret espionage campaign of permeating Ts'ou with spies and tools. He had made his first contacts with the Saun-quan courtier, Jin Soun and others years before; now he personally came to Ying-*t'uh* to spin his web. The royal house, consisting of the triple branch families Ts'au(昭), Chü(屈) and Chin(景), and its court were thoroughly corrupted with bribes and gifts to saturation point. The Lord of War Tze-tsiao(司马子椒), certainly the Saun-quan courtier and Jin Soun(上官大夫,靳尚) his old friends, and the favourite royal concubine Ts'eng Sieü(郑袖) were all amply bought up in Tsing's favour. King Hwai alone remained a fool by himself. Against heavy odds of the pro-Tsing faction, Chü Yuan stood alone. His pupils Soong Yü(宋玉), Daung Le(唐勒) and Chin Tsa(景差), all poets, were much younger men having no voice on state affairs. Besides, they were timid men and not politically turned, as their later lives during Hsiang's reign had proved, though Soong Yü had written *Nine Strains*(《九辩》) to justify his master. Tsang Yih did not attempt to bribe Chü Yuan; he knew that had he tried, he would be publicly exposed, for the poet was incorruptible and was in sober earnest for joining Tsih to counteract Tsing.

As Lord of the Three (Family Lane) Portals (三闾大夫), which was something like the Earl-marshal of Ts'ou, the chief officer of arms at the Heralds' College, it was Chü Yuan's duty to lead the choice elements of his clan to act as examples to the flowers of the state. As Left Counsellor(左徒), the confidential exhortator to the king, he had the right and bounden duty to advice his sovereign on grave matters of state and diplomacy. History and current inter-state events had long taught him the inevitable need of united coalition against Tsing. A matchless patriot, a ringing poet and a scholar of the very first order, he reared his moral height pat to the occasion. He was dauntless and inflexible.

Years before, Tsang Yih had instructed Saun-quan and Jin Soun, who later formed the pro-Tsing ring and headed it, to eliminate Chü Yuan by working on the king. Surrounded by "herons and hernshaws", spies, King Hwai, foolish and self-sufficient, was easily pliable. Slanders were plentifully employed to blot their common opposer. The Saun-quan courtier, envying Chü Yuan's ability and the king's trust in him at first, had once paid him a visit at his home. Chü Yuan was just then drafting some royal decree for the king. Whereon Saun-quan asked to have his manuscript, but was blandly denied for it was not yet finished. Saun-quan then said to the king that everybody knew His Majesty had requisitioned Chü Yuan to do the drafting and that whenever a regal order was out, Chü Yuan always boasted that without him the thing could not be done. This was one of the lightest false reports made by Saun-quan and his clique. Others much more serious were to be sure not stinted by them. Of course, the king, a weakling, was offended and alienated from Chü Yuan by such mean tricks without trying to find out whether the charges were true or not. Hwai *Wang* had consequently been made to repulse him by denying audience to him("王怒而疏屈平"), as that was the surest way of denying access to his counsels. That was early in the sixteenth year of the king's reign, 313 B. C. Being repelled by his king and blockaded by the glozing caballers from news, Chü Yuan, though he might get some information afterwards, could do nothing to prevent the king from falling into the trap of Tsang Yih's brazen imposture. When he had learnt the whole story of Tsang Yih's visit and mission to Ts'ou and the king's decision, which leaked out through Ts'au Tsui（昭睢）, a high courtier and his clansman, he moved heaven and earth to see the king, to prevent him from committing Ts'ou to perdition, but in vain. He submitted written implorations and expostulations which were simply ignored. What was most intolerable to Chü Yuan was that this malicious imposter had now become the premier of Ts'ou!

Having gathered all the intelligence he needed, Tsang Yih returned to Tsing in a few months. King Hwai sent a special envoy with a number of subordinates and followers in the company of Tsang to Tsing to officiate in the ceremony of receiving the 600 square *lih* of the Saung-Wuh region. At Yen-yang, Tsang told the Ts'ou envoy he had only promised King Hwai six square *lih*, the six hundred square *lih* were unheard of! The indignant envoy reported the matter to the king on his return. In towering rage, King Hwai ordered a massed offensive engagement against Tsing from Han-tsoon（汉中）where Tsing and Ts'ou were contiguous. The outcome was a smashing defeat for Ts'ou, for Tsang Yih, all ready for the attack, had set a heavy pincers ambush in advance: over 80000 infantry-men of Ts'ou were decapitated and over seventy titled officers were slaughtered in the Battle of Han-tsoon, its general Chu Gai（屈匄）was captured and the entire county of Han-tsoon（汉中郡）, comprising the southern portion of Sen-sih（陕西）and the north-western part of Hu-pei（湖北）

today, was lost to Tsing. Madly enraged, King Hwai gathered all the troops he could lay hands on to attack Tsing once more, penetrating into the depth of Tsing but suffering another heavy bruise at Lan-dien (蓝田). Hang and Gwei hearing of Ts'ou's precarious position, thrusted at T'eng(邓), forcing its troops to hurry back. Ts'ou then had to cut two cities to indemnify Tsing. Tsang Yih's going back to Tsing and Ts'ou's two smashing defeats by Tsing all happened in the seventeenth year of King Hwai's reign, 312 B. C.

The king, after his army was badly pommeled twice, a large tract of his lands were lost and a great many of his commissioned officers were slaughtered, came to senses a little. Chü Yuan was called back to the court by him and sent to Tsih("使於齐") as his ambassador extraordinary and plenipotentiary to revive the coalition in 311 B. C. (怀王十八年). But meanwhile, Tsang Yih propagated his cross conjunction with a flourish of trumpets. And just then, Tsing asked to barter the lands outside of its Wuh Pass(武关外) for Ts'ou's Jen-tsoon(黔中) region[1], which was at its left flank, west of the modern Yuan-ling *hsien*(沅陵), Hu-nan(湖南). Certainly, Jen-tsoon was strategically more mortal to Ts'ou than the stretch of outlying lands south of the Wuh Pass to Tsing. The king said to the Tsing emissary that he would wish to get Tsang Yih in his clasp instead of

---

[1] This is according to *The Life of Tsang Yih*(《张仪列传》) of *The Chronicle* (《史记》). In *The Life of Chü Yuan* and *The Annals of the State Ts'ou*(《楚世家》), the anecdote is different. Instead of asking to barter outlying lands of the Wuh Pass for Ts'ou's Jen-tsoon region, Tsing proposed to return a half of Han-tsoon to make up with Ts'ou. King Hwai said to the Tsing emissary that he would wish to get Tsang Yih in his clasp without the Han-tsoon County. Hearing of this, Tsang asked to come to Ts'ou, since a Tsang Yih was worth the whole county of Hant-tsoon. So he came.

the Wuh Pass outlying lands, and would offer Jen-tsoon free to Ts-ing. Tsang came; the king had him confined and was ready to kill him. Then Jin Soun(靳尚) spoke to Ts'eng Sieu(郑袖) who begged mercy of the king to set him free. When forgiven, Tsang Yih urged the king to conjoin Tsing with the provision that Ts'ou would not have to offer Jen-tsoon. The king, glad that he could keep it intact, promised. Tsang Yih went away.

Coming back from Tsih, Chü Yuan("是时屈平既疏,不复在位,使于齐,顾返") said, "Your Majesty had been most meanly deceived by Tsang Yih. When he came, he should be cooked in a cal-dron. Your gracious clemency should not be again cheated by his atrocious nonsense." The king said it was profitable to promise him and save Jen-tsoon for Ts'ou. Tsang Yih was at that moment still within the border of Ts'ou. Hwai wavered and hesitated for half a day and a night, and then recanted his previous decision and sent men to chase Tsang Yih. But it was too late. Thus, the coalition resuscitated with great endeavour by Chü Yuan, to whom Tsih was favourably disposed, was again put to naught.

Chü Yuan, now that he had come back to the court, spoke for himself to the King against the malicious falsehoods and vile defama-tion heaped on his head in the past. This maddened the pro-Tsing toadeaters. No efforts were spared by his enemies, Tsing's tools, di-rect and indirect, all, to estrange the king from him. The riffraff, with the active cooperation of Ts'eng Sieü, now fabricated the story, together with other slimes, that Chü Yuan tried to make love to her (*vide ll.* 80 −90 of *Lee Sao*). Eventually, they succeeded once more to have King Hwai reject him.

The poet was now, late in the eighteenth year of King Hwai's reign, that is, 311 B. C., or early the next year, ordered by the king to be formally dismissed from his office, to pack and leave the capital (斥逐) for going to the north of the Han Stream(汉北), though not, strictly speaking, banished, for he was a member of the three branches of the royal family. To come back to Ying-*t'uh* was strictly forbidden of him. There he lived for some eleven years, roaming over the lands full of streams and lakes, till 300 B. C. (怀王二十九年), after Tsing had assaulted Ts'ou again in a campaign killing 20,000 of its soldiers[①] and their general Chin Chü(景缺), and the king had, in panic, sent his crown prince at pawn to Tsih once more to ask for coalition. Hwai *Wang* needed Chü Yuan's counsels now on diplomatic relations with Tsih, and so he was recalled. When he was first repulsed early in 313 B. C. (怀王十六年), Chü Yuan composed his *Bitter Declarations*(《惜诵》) to affirm his purity and fidelity. During those desolate years in Han Pei(汉北), he wrote *Drawing My Thoughts*(《抽思》)[②], *Musing on the Beauteous One*(《思美人》)[③], *Divining to Know Where I Should Stay*(《卜居》)[④], *Distant Wanderings*(《远游》)[⑤], *Lee Sao: Suffering Throes*(《离骚》)[⑥], the greatest lyric poem and ode ever written by man, and others.

In 309 B. C., King Min of Tsih(齐湣王), wishing to rejuvenate united coalition and being offended by Ts'ou's conjunction with Ts-

---

① *The Chronology of the Six States*(《六国年表》) of *The Chronicle*(《史记》) has the number of the killed 30,000.

② In the autumn of 310 B. C. (怀王十九年后秋).

③ In the spring of 309 B. C. (逾年春).

④ In 308 B. C. ("其三年"). The dates of composition of these three poems are according to Tsiang Ch'ih.

⑤⑥ The dates of *Distant Wanderings* and *Lee Sao: Suffering Throes* are discussed below in §11 and §12 of section Ⅶ *Chü Yuan and His Works*.

ing, wrote to King Hwai. At Ts'au Tsui's(昭睢) proposal, Ts'ou conjoined with Tsih again. Four years later, King Ts'au of Tsing(秦昭王), on his coming to power, donated dowries and gifts richly to Ts'ou for the marriage of a Tsing princess to a Ts'ou prince. The groom with a gaily bedecked nuptial party went to Tsing to welcome and bring back the bride. The occasion was greeted with acclaim by the pro-Tsing wheedlers. The propitious air of the conjugal union was made boot of by them to cry up Tsing's new king for healing Ts'ou's old wound. Thus, the coalition with Tsih and through Tsih with other states was once more battered.

In 304 B. C., Tsing and Ts'ou leagued at Hwang-chieh(黄棘), the former giving the latter Saun-yoon(上庸). The next year, Tsih, Hang and Gwei sent joint columns to punish Ts'ou for its lack of faith. Ts'ou despatched its crown prince to Tsing in hostage for relief troops. When Tsing legions arrived, the joint forces withdrew. Ts'ou's prince dueled with a Tsing lord, killed him and fled back the next year. In 301 B. C., Tsih, Hang and Gwei, together with Tsing, attacked Ts'ou, thumped its soldiery and killed the general Tdaung Mei(唐昧). And then, in 300 B. C., Tsing mauled Ts'ou forces once more as related above.

The next year, Tsing assailed Ts'ou again, seizing eight cities. King Ts'au of Tsing wrote to King Hwai that he would like to confer with him in person at the Wuh Pass(武关) for a new league. Chü Yuan and Ts'au Tsui(昭睢) admonished the king from going. They spoke of Wei Yang capturing Prince A'ng(公子卬) of Gwei; Tsing was a state of tiger and wolf, they said, not to be trusted. But the young prince Tse-Ian(子兰) said it was inadvisable to snub Tsing with a refusal. King Hwai took the counsel of his young prince supported by the adulators. They triumphantly saw their sovereign off, departing from Ying-*t'uh* in great state. As soon as the king and his gorgeous train entered the Wuh Pass on the border of Tsing, full-armed Tsing legions, tens of them, closed in upon the royal Ts'ou party. Thus, King Hwai was knavishly trapped. He was conducted to Yen-yang and given an audience of King Ts'au at the Tsaun Terrace (章台), like a vassal. He was asked to cede Wuh (巫) and Jen-tsoon(黔中) to Tsing. He refused in anger, and was detained. The prince royal came back to Ts'ou from Tsih and ascended the throne.

Chü Yuan was distracted by the filthy kidnaping. He had warned his sovereign of this eventuality in his strong remonstrance against his going. He saw the young king before his coronation, during which he attacked the traitorous rabble furiously. The pro-Tsing clique men, frightened by what they could not dream of, tried to minimize their guilts by tightening their hold on the green successor King Ching-hsiang(顷襄王). They induced him to make his young brother Tse-lan, their puppet now, his premier. Incensed with Chü Yuan for his charge of treachery, Tse-Ian worked hand in glove with the adulatory junto to undo him and get him away. In the second moon of Ching-hsiang's year of ascension to the throne, Chü Yuan was banished ("放流","顷襄王怒而迁之","放","放逐","弃逐",贬谪) to Lin-yang(陵阳), south of the River(江南) like a common criminal subject. In that year, 298 B. C., Tsing marshaled a series of campaigns against Ts'ou and wrested away fifteen cities, slaughtering 50000.

King Hwai tried to flee back from Tsing the next year. His attempt was found out and foiled in time. Troops were despatched to block up all passages leading to Ts'ou. He went through a by-path to

Ts'ao(赵). Ts'ao denied him admittance. Wanting to run to Gwei, he was forced to turn back when pursuing guards of Tsing neared. He fell ill, and then died in the coming year, 296 B. C. His remains were sent back to be interred. All relations between Ts'ou and Tsing were severed now.

In 293 B. C., Tsing sent a formal note to Ts'ou asking for a decisive battle to settle the difference between the two states. Unable to accede to the demand, Hsiang yielded by drawing up a league with Tsing. In 292 B. C., there was another nuptial affair between the two houses. This time, Hsiang himself became the son-in-law of Ts'au of Tsing. The conjunction pact was renewed again and again in 285 and 283 B. C. But in 281 B. C., the king sent envoys to Tsih and other states for leaguing coalition with them. Tsing attacked again and beat Ts'ou the next year, taking Saun-yoon(上庸) and the region north of the Han Stream(汉北), where the poet had been forced to live for over ten years. In 279 B. C., the Tsing general Bai Chih(白起) stormed Yiêh(鄢), T'eng(邓) and Yih-ling(夷陵), and the next year, captured Ying-*t'uh*(郢都), Ts'ou's capital, and set fire to the ancestral mausoleums and temples at Yih-Iing. Hsiang, with his royal family and courtiers, fled to Tsen(陈) in the north-east. Ts'ou soldiers fought no more and scattered. In 277 B. C., Tsing took Wuh (巫) and Jen-tsoon County(黔中郡). This latter is where the Stream of Tsaung-loung(沧浪) in the song of *The Fisherman*(《渔父》) flows and the region of Tsen-yang(辰阳) and Tsü-puh(溆浦) journeyed through and written on in *Over the Streams*(《涉江》). Ts'ou could put up no more resistance now. *The Warring States Strips*(《战国策》) quotes the Tsing general Bai Chih's(白起) words thus: "The king of Ts'ou, relying on the size of his state, pays no heed to his policies. His courtiers are eaten up with envy of one another; flattery and fawning form the order of things; good lords are repulsed and spurned; the people are disaffected. These are the reasons why we can penetrate deep into the country, capture so many cities and boroughs, and fulfil our exploits."

After a shadowy existence of fifty-four more years, Ts'ou, bulky but weak, was at last obliterated by Tsing in 223 B. C., Its enfeebling and ultimate effacement were mainly due to the repulse and spurn of Chü Yuan by Hwai and Hsiang, as evidenced by Bai Chih's words. If Chü Yuan's policy of alliance with Tsih and coalition with the other four states were adopted and consistently maintained from the start, history would have taken a quite different course. But the defeat and overthrow of the six states were certainly not a simple matter, which an analysis above has readily shown. They were just one of the results of the crash of the feudal edifice of Tsur. And it should be said of that Tsing general Bai Chih, by the way, that true to its tradition, he committed in 206 B. C. the heinous crime of burying alive 400,000 Ts'ao's soldiers that had just surrendered! And then, three years later, he himself was ordered to commit suicide for his feud with Fan Tsui(范雎), the premier. Thus, the history of Tsing was filled with intrigues and treacheries, murders and butcheries, frauds and pillage, which last couple was fully exemplified by Lin Hsiang-rue's(蔺相如) dashing feat of foiling King Ts'au of Tsing's(秦昭王) mean trick to rob Ts'ao of its priceless gem and getting it intact back to Ts'ao(完璧归赵), and Sze-ma Tsien's *The Life of Lih Sze*(《李斯列传》). Looking back today from the critical viewpoint of intrinsic value in human existence, that is, with respect to its culture, ethos and civilization, Chü Yuan has made his glorious, immortal contributions in poetry, state craft and morality. But what are Kings Hwai and Hsiang of Ts'ou and Kings Wei, Ts'au and Ying Tsen of Tsing? They have proved themselves to be nothing but fools and morons, rattlesnakes and sharks.

Since his banishment by Ching-hsiang to the south of the River, in the first nine years Chü Yuan stayed at Ling-yang(陵阳), far away in the east of Ying-*t'uh*, near the modern Hsuantsen *hsien*(宣城), An-whei(安徽). When King Hwai's remains were sent back from Tsing to be interred in the third year of Ching-hsiang, our poet wrote the elegy first entitled *Summoning the Soul*(《招魂》), later changed to *Great Summoning*(《大招》). At Ling-yang, he wrote, in the ninth year of his exile, *Plaint on Ying*(《哀郢》). The last part of the poem had stung the premier Tse-Ian and the pro-Tsing gang to the quick. Chü Yuan was thereupon exiled, the second time now, to Tsen-yang(辰阳) way down in the south-west early next year, that is, 289 B.C. On his way from Ling-yang to the basin regions of Tsen and Süe(辰, 溆), two streams south of Jen-tsoon, he wrote *Over the Streams*(《涉江》). From Waung-tsu(枉陼) to Tsen, he passed Wuh-ling(武陵), where he met the fisherman. The episode is described in *The Fisherman*(《渔父》). On his way to Tsang-sah(长沙), he wrote *Thinking of Sah*(《怀沙》), and in that city, staying for more than two years, he wrote *Lamenting on Whirlblasts*(《悲回风》) and *Pining My Past Days*(《惜往日》), his last poem before his death. Rambling for months in the regions Yuan and Hsiang(沅, 湘) and their tributaries, Chü Yuan saw as a poet, a thinker, a statesman and a patriot that Ts'ou, the world and himself were wrapped in utter darkness. There was absolutely no hope, not the least shaft of light! So he jumped into the Mi-Io River(汨罗江) one day "to seek Peng

Yen in his abode". And that was the fifth day of the fifth moon. Of the year of his death, there are various estimates, said to be in the tenth year (289 B. C.), or eleventh (288 B. C.), ... or twenty-first (278 B. C.) of Hsiang's reign. Tsiang Ch'ih's (蒋骥) estimates set it in the 13th or 14th year, or the 15th or 16th. The first guess would be 286 B. C., which appraises his departure from Ling-yang, the time spent on the way and his sojourn at Tsang-sah to be in all over three years.

The reason why there are so little detailed accounts of Chü Yuan's life in Sze-ma Tsien's *The Life of Chü Yuan* (《屈原列传》) is that the poet is a fearless opposer of Tsing in his lifetime. When Ying-*t'uh* (郢都), Ts'ou's capital, and Tsing-yang (青阳, that is, Tsang-sah, 长沙, where the poet lived his last two years or more) were taken by Tsing in 278 B. C. and later when Ts'ou was finally blotted off by Tsing in 223 B. C., its hellhounds spared no efforts to dislimn the poet's records from official sources. The miracle that *Lee Sao* and his other extant works survived the burning of books was due to their hidden existence in the private possession of Ts'ou's subjects, his adorers.

Ever since his death, ever more and more people, not only in Ts'ou, but in all the other states too, mourned the tragic death of this great poet of theirs, who in his life was so pure, brave and selfless. He died a martyr to beneficence for the commonweal of the people and a dauntless opponent to Tsing's satanic power politics. As time passed, the whole Han majority (汉族) of the Chinese people that has inherited the old culture, has come to have known and mourned the tragic life and death of this noble soul. The people commemorate him on the day of his death by rowing dragon boats and eating tri-conical sticky rice dumplings (stuffed with pork or mashed red beans, wrapped in a species of water plant leaves and well boiled). Dragons and phoenixes were from time immemorial in our history believed in folklore and set down in literature, long before Chü Yuan, as the only divine animal and bird capable of bearing and guarding the metamorphosed virtuous to Heaven, and the tri-conical sticky rice dumplings were supposed to be thrown into Mi-lo River to prevent fishes and turtles from nibbling our poet's corpse. The "Duan Wu Day" (the 5th day of the 5th moon by the Chinese calendar) has been an occasion to commemorate the death of Chü Yuan in China's traditions for thousands of years, on which people would eat dumplings and hold dragon boat races.

Ⅶ   Chü Yuan and His Works

In the above, I have dwelt on Chü Yuan as a giant political figure and patriot in his relations with the Ts'ou court and clashes with Tsing's satanic power politics and secret, espionage and diplomacy. Now, let us have a closer survey of his life and works which, though not copious as we have them, are yet effulgent, with *Suffering Throes* as their apex. In my narrative, there are unavoidable repetitions of certain foregoing details.

The years of the poet's birth and death are to this day not yet settled and so too the dates of his works, not excepting *Lee Sao*, are still being disputed by his students. Under the circumstances, we cannot expect any one to do a precise and thorough piece of work about the poet's biography in the near future. In the following, I would arrange a chronological list of the poet's birth and death years and his works dated, verified as far as possible by internal evidences in the poems and external ones, direct or indirect.

§1. Chü Yuan was born in the twenty-fourth year of King Hsien of Tsur(周显王二十四年), 345 B. C. This is suppositive, founded on §5, which is based on the first eight lines of *Pining My Past Days*(《惜往日》), his last work.

Since the above has been written, I have the chance to have borrowed these books for reference: *Studies into the Superexcellence of "Sao"*, first series(《读骚论微》初集), by Yer Koh-en(游国恩), 1936; *Studies in Chü Yuan*(《屈原研究》), by Kuo Mê-ruo(郭沫若), 1942; and *Studies in the Poet Chü Yuan and His Works*(《诗人屈原及其作品研究》), by Ling Kêng(林庚), 1952. These three modern students of the poet set the dates of his birth and death at 343 −277 B. C. (sixty-seven), 340 − 278 B. C. (sixty-two) and 335 −296 B. C. (forty) respectively. Before them, Liang Chih-tsao (梁启超) has given in his studies of the poet and his works the dates 338 − 288 B. C. (fifty). Liang's dates I obtain from Lim Boon-keng's(林文庆) *The Li Sao: An Elegy on Encountering Sorrows by Chü Yuan*. Here, let us deal with these surmised dates of the poet's birth first, and then I shall scrutinize Wang Yi's(王逸) confusing mistake and propose my conjectured date.

In establishing verity in such a disputatious matter as Chü Yuan's birth date which happened over twenty-three centuries ago, we have to depend on positive evidences spoken of above for ascertainment as well as negative ones for check, by which I mean disproofs obtainable from external sources and internal ones of the poems. I do not know how or why Liang Chih-tsao sets the poet's birth year on 338 B. C., which was the thirty-first of King Hsien of Tsur's reign. As the poet was Left Counsellor to Hwai in 319 B. C., according to *The*

Warring States Strips(《战国策》) and the poem *Pining My Past Days*(《惜往日》), he was, if born in 338 B. C., only nineteen years old (counted on the solar calendar) or twenty-one (on the lunar) when he was at that post, which evidently too young an age. It is true Tsuan-shiuh(颛顼), Emperor Kao-yang(高阳氏), is said to be the counsellor to his uncle Sao-hao(少昊) at the puerile age of ten, *T'ih* Ko(帝喾) is known to have aided Tsuan-shiuh when a lad of fifteen and great Yü is reputed to be the Lord of Excavation(司空) to Yao(尧) at twelve. But these cases were all legendary in nature, happening some twenty-two to nineteen and a half centuries before Chü Yuan. In reality, it behooves us to consider our poet in his early or middle twenties still too young to hold such a responsible post. And moreover, as Yer has well shown, Left Counsellor was the same as the curator of history(史官), requiring ample erudition and mature judgment on policies, to which he affords plentiful proofs as the poem *Sky-vaulting Queries*(《天问》) has also given eloquent evidences. Chü Yuan in that early age was obviously not yet qualified for such a task, however brilliant he might be. Now, Yer and Kuo both establish their birth years of the poet on the first two characters of the third line of *Lee Sao* after Wang Yi(王逸), they admit, which runs thus:

摄提贞于孟陬兮。

Here, the interpretation of 摄提 is open to question. Wang Yi, the East Han commentator, heartily supported by Hoon Hsintsou(洪兴祖) of Soong(宋), explains the expression as an abbreviated form of 摄提格, by which he means the year of the poet's birth is nominated in *kan* and *tse*(干支) with its latter symbol fixed by the earthly *tse* of *yin*(寅). Thus, he says, "the *yin* year", together with "the *yin* month"（孟陬）and the *yin* day（庚寅），"struck the very middle of the negative and positive laws"（得阴阳之正中）: "the three *yin*" formed the highly auspicious nature of the poet's birth. Tsu Hsih（朱熹）, the Soong commentator, maintains that 摄提 is none of such an abbreviation, but the year star, or, specifically, the name of a constellation of six stars, through which, with three on each side, the poet means to say in the line, the stem of the Dipper pointed just in the direction of the *yin* position of the year's first moon（lunar month）（寅位月）, i. e., the（north-）north-east, in the evening. If a *yin* year is meant, Tsu says, the character 格 should not be missing, for it could not be abbreviated, and besides, the words 贞于 become superfluous; that is to say, the line's wording should be 摄提格之孟陬兮. Ling, in his apt elucidation of 摄提 of his spirited treatise, quotes five illustrations from *The Calendar Book* of *The Chronicle* （《史记·历书》）to show that 摄提格 was the equivalent of a *yin* year, which is not to be abbreviated into 摄提, as Tsu-tse has contended. He further quotes two more instances from *The Heavenly Official Book of The Chronicle*（《史记·天官书》）, one more from *Êrl Ya* （《尔雅》）and one more from *Hwai-nan-tse*（《淮南子》）, all to show that 摄提格 was a year named with the earthly *tse*（地支）of *yin* （寅）, but it is not to be shortened into 摄提 for brevity. The two are clearly distinguished from each other; they should not be confused. And besides, the poet has no reason or necessity to abbreviate here, since his verse is not isosyllabic in structure. So, he rightly concludes that Wang Yi is erroneous and Tsu-tse is correct in their commentaries. Yer, following Wang Yi in setting the poet's birth in the twenty-seventh year of King Hsuan of Ts'ou's（楚宣王二十七年，or the twenty-sixth of King Hsien of Tsur, 周显王二十六年）reign, now

traceable back to be 戊寅, i. e., 343 B. C., is further gravely questioned by my computation of Chü Yuan's Left Counsellorship in 319
B. C., for if he is correct, in that year the poet was only twenty-four
years old(solar) or twenty-six(lunar), not yet a proper age to be the
curator of history(and astronomy). Kuo, who sets the poet's birth
year on 341 or 340 B. C. (twenty-eighth or -ninth year of King Hsien
of Tsur), which he calls a *yin* year(寅年), must have made a mistake in his calculation in the first place, as these two years, when
traced back in *kan* and *tse*, prove to be 庚辰 and 辛巳, having nothing to do with *yin*. When checked by the poet's Left Counsellorship,
it turns out that he was only twenty-one or -two years old (solar) or
twenty-three or -four (lunar) then, much too young to hold such a
high post. Ling, who sets the poet's birth in 335 B. C., has him
holding such a key position at the adolescent age of sixteen (solar) or
eighteen (lunar), which is plainly incredible.

Now, about Wang Yi's confusing mistake, I have to clarify the
origins of calling years, months, days and time periods of the day by
the heavenly *kan* and earthly *tse*, and calling the time periods of the
day and the positions of the lunar months merely by the earthly *tse*, in
order to show how he arrived at his erroneous conclusion.

On Designating Years, Months, Days and Time Periods of the Day with *Kan* and *Tse*, and Designating Time Periods of the Day and Positions of Lunar Months, Pointed at by the Dipper Stem through Sê-tih, with *Tse*

(1) To name years by combining heavenly *kan* and earthly *tse*,
the process is started from *ja-tse*(甲子), *ih-tser*(乙丑), *p'in-yin*(丙

寅）, *t'ing-mao*（丁卯）, *wuh-tsen*（戊辰）, *jih-tze*（己巳）, *kêng-oo*
（庚午）, *sing-vei*（辛未）, etc. till a cycle of sixty years is completed. Then, another cycle is begun and finished, and so on, unto infinity.

（2）To name months by combining *kan* and *tse*, the process is
undergone just in the same way, beginning from *ja-tse*（甲子）and
ending in *kuaihai*（癸亥）to complete a cycle of sixty months. Then,
another cycle is started and finished and still another in endless progression.

（3）（4）Days and time periods of the day are designated by
combinations of *kan* and *tse* exactly the same as the years and
months. So, a man's birth year, month, day and time period of the
day could be represented with eight characters, four *kan* and four *tse*,
properly combined, called the eight characters of one's birth time（生
辰八字）.

As I have stated at the start of this preamble（*vide pp.* 6 −7）,
combinations of *kan* and *tse* were first used to indicate the days of
months only in remote ancient times, and later on they were also employed for naming years, months and time periods of the day. This
"later on" was in East Han, during the reign of Kwang-wuh-*t'ih*（光
武帝）, his Jien-wuh（建武）years, i. e., 25 −57 A. D. But though
not in current use till Jien-wuh, the combinations of *kan* and *tse*
were, I believe, much earlier（over three centuries before）employed
for naming years, months and time periods of the day together with
kan and *tse* dates, by the School of Negative and Positive Laws（阴阳
家）, the calendar computers, in their studies. There were twenty-one
of them during the Warring States period, according to *The Roll of
Arts and Letters* of *The Han Chronicle*（《汉书·艺文志》）, the most

prominent of whom were Sze-sing Tse-wei（司星子韦）of Soong
（宋）, Kung-sun Fa（公孙发）, Tser Yien and Tser Si（邹衍,邹奭）
of Tsih（齐）. The two Tsers were junior contemporaries of Chü Yuan
by about twenty years. These schoolmen not only calculated years,
months, days and time periods of the day with cycles of *kan* and *tse*,
but also gave fanciful names to every one of the ten *kan* and twelve
tse in naming years. Thus, a *ja*（甲）year, an *ih*（乙）year, a *p'in*
（丙）year, etc. were called by them respectively *Eh-voon*（阏逢）,
Tsan-moon（旃蒙）, *Reur-tsor*（柔兆）, etc., and a *tse*（子）year, a
tser（丑）year, a *yin*（寅）year, etc. were called by them respectively *Quen-tun*（困敦）, *Tsê-fun-ruo*（赤奋若）, *Sê-tih-kê*（摄提格）,
etc. A *ja-tse* year was called *Eh-voon Quen-tun*, a *ja-yin* year *Eh-
voon Sê-tih-kê*, etc. A *yin* year was named *Sê-tih-kê*, because the *yin*
position of the first moon（lunar month）, north-north-east, when
pointed at by the star Sê-tih（or rather, specifically, by the Dipper
stem through the pair of triple stars of the constellation Sê-tih）,
marks the beginning of spring. In another word, the star Sê-tih following the Dipper stem and（or rather, specifically, the Dipper stem
through the two triplet stars of the Sê-tih constellation）pointing at the
yin position of the first lunar month, north-north-east, initiates
spring. The character kê（格）means beginning or commencing.
Spring commences with（is initiated by）the star Sê-tih pointing at
（specifically, the Dipper stem pointing through the constellation Se-
tih at）the first moon（lunar month）, north-north-east, the *yin* position. Therefore, *Sê-tih-kê* as a *yin* year means "the year is so called
just as the first month of spring is initiated by（or commences with）
its *yin* position". This is certainly an awkwardly tortuous way of naming a year with a fanciful substitute of its *kan* and *tse* combinations.

It is a great pity that the writings of these calendar computers had all vanished even in Wang Yi's time (due to Ying Tsen's and Lih Sze's crimes again, I believe), and now we have to base our statements on very scanty, shadowy evidences. Hence the puzzle and confusion of Wang Yi's *Sê-tih-kê*, a *yin* year, with Sê-tih, the year star. There was once current an unfounded surmise that these twenty-two obscure fanciful names given to *kan* and *tse* were all transliterations of epithets of the Babylonian cuneiform language. That is definitely disproved by the instance of *Sê-tih-kê*, whose meaning and application is within our grasp.

(5) The time periods of a day and a night, twelve in number, are called by the twelve earthly *tse*, each occupying two hours on the clock. They commence at eleven o'clock in the night. The first one is called the *tse* time period(子时), lasting from eleven P. M. to the end of twelve past midnight. The *tser* time period(丑时) is from one to the end of two o'clock after midnight. Three to four A. M. is called *yin*(寅时). Five to six A. M. is the time period named *mao*(卯时). Seven to eight A. M., *tsen*(辰时); nine to ten A. M., *tze*(巳时); eleven A. M. to twelve past noon, oo(午时); etc.

(6) The fixed positions of lunar months pointed at by the Dipper stem through the pair of triple stars of the Se-tih constellation in the sky are twelve in number. They are named with the twelve earthly *tse* symbols(地支), begun from the first moon (lunar month), the earliest spring moon, which is in the position of *yin*(寅位月), north-north-east. This is according to the Hsia calendar. In the Saung-Yin calendar, the first moon of a year started from the position of *tser*(丑位月), straight north. In the Tsur calendar, the first moon of a year started from the position of *tse*(子位月), north-north-west. In the

latter part of the Warring States Period, the Hsia calendar was in common use. For convenience sake, let us make use of the face of a clock or watch to expedite our description. When the Dipper stem points at one o'clock, north-north-east, it is the *yin* position of the first lunar month（寅位月） of the Hsia calendar; at two o'clock, north-east-east, the *mao* position of the second lunar month（卯位月）; at three o'clock, directly eastward, the *tsen* position of the third lunar month（辰位月）; … at eleven o' clock, north-north-west, the *tse* position of the eleventh lunar month（子位月） （or of the first moon of the Tsur calendar）; finally, at twelve o'clock, directly northward, the *tser* position of the twelfth lunar month（丑位月） （or of the first moon of the Saung-Yin calendar）. And then, the Dipper stem reverts to one o'clock. ①

In the above, （1）, （2）, （3） and （4） form a concerted system; they have each a separate existence, related in consecutive order, but not to be indiscriminately connected. It should be emphatically pointed out here, they have been so related in common usage from the reign of Kwang-wuh of late Han（后汉光武）, more than

---

① Tsing（秦）, after its annexation of the six states, had its first calendarial lunar month at ten o'clock （north-west-west）, the *hai* position of the tenth moon（亥位月）. Han followed Tsing's suit in its almanac of the Tsuan-shiuh calendar （颛顼历）, at the recommendation of Tsang Tsoung（张苍）, for a century and two years till the seventh year of Wuh-*t'ih*'s reign Yuan-foon（武帝元封七年）, when Kung-sun Ching（公孙卿）, Hwu Tsui（壶遂）, Sze-ma Tsien（司马迁） and others, seeing that there had been moons in the first nights of lunar months, proposed the change of the Tsing almanac. After many trials and errors in computation, verification and checking up, the almanac of Dun Bing's （邓平） planning and Lor-sha Hoon's（落下闳） equivalent calculation was finally adopted as the T'ai-ts'ou calendar（太初历） and the seventh year of Yuan-foon was renamed the first year of T'ai-ts'ou（太初元年）.

three centuries after Chü Yuan's death. In another word, in our poet's time, there was no such relation in practical use; only the days of the months were then indicated by combinations of *kan* and *tse*, the other three time periods being not yet so named in daily usage. Next, (5) and (6) are each an independent system, having nothing to do with each other, nor with the first four or any one of them. These rules must be strictly observed in application, for the natures of the three systems are distinct from one another. To assort any two or all three systems at haphazard is not allowed, as that would breed confusion.

*　　*　　*　　*　　*　　*　　*　　*

Now, Wang Yi's commentary on lines 3 and 4 of *Lee Sao* arbitrarily and mistakenly connects first, the designation of the poet's birth year (that is, (1), as intended by him only, not real) which he actually did not know but pretended to have known by wrongly making use of the entirely irrelevant term 摄提格 (which has one extra character and unfortunately means a *yin* year) as a makeshift and then boldly said that 摄提 in line 3 is the same as or an abbreviation of 摄提格; second, the designation of the *yin* position of the first lunar month of the poet's birth pointed at by the Dipper stem (that is, (6)); and third, the designation of the *yin* date of birth explicitly mentioned by the poet in line 4 (that is, (3)). And then, Wang's commentary whips together the three unrelated designations with the fiction (purely invented by himself to meet his demand, just like the other fiction he has fabricated that Chien-sieu(骞脩) was Fwu-shih's (伏羲) courtier) that "these three *yin* — the year, moon and date of the poet's birth", "struck the very middle of the negative and positive laws"（得阴阳之正中）and therefore augured high auspiciousness. From the above classification and analysis, it is plain that even the *yin* position of Chü Yuan's lunar month of birth, belonging to（6）, is not to be identified with a *yin* month which should be（2）. Next, of course, to say 掇提 is the same as 摄提格 or is its abbreviation, is far-fetched reasoning. But even worse than that, it is also a blunder of anarchronism. For when Chü Yuan wrote this ode, employing such combinations of *kan* and *tse* to indicate a year, whether its earthly *tse* be plainly called *yin* or fancifully called *Sê-tih-kê*, was not yet innovated by Tser Yien（he was only eighteen or nineteen years old then）and his schoolmen; even in the late years of Chü Yuan's lifetime, such practice was at least not yet current in common usage, although the nomenclature might be prevalent among discussions of the Negative and Positive schoolmen. It has been shown in the classified divisions and analysis above that only（1）,（2）and（3）could go together in successive order to indicate the year, month and day of a man's birth in their designations by *kan* and *tse*, that（6）, calling the positions of the lunar months, pointed at by the Dipper stem through Sê-tih, by the earthly *tse* only, could not go along with（1）and（3）, nor could it substitute（2）, for the simple reason that（6）is different in nature from（1）,（2）and（3）, and that "x", an unknown entity（the poet's birth year in Wang Yi's mind）, could not or should not be supplanted by n, an altogether irrelevant factor（掇提 is not 摄提格）, for expediency or convenience. So, the "three *yin*", forcedly put together by Wang Yi, prove to have nothing whatsoever to do with one another, but have proved to be a claptrap hindrance to the discovery of the actual birth year of the poet. In thus dissecting Wang Yi's error and how he arrived at it, I am confident his fiction is

forced to explode at last. The gross mistake of the "*yin* year",
though pricked by Tsu-tse when he says "the year was not necessarily
a *yin* one", is supported by the less obvious but equally misleading
mistake of calling the *yin* position of the lunar month, pointed at by
the Dipper stem, "the *yin* month", which Tsu-tse lightly passed over
as acceptable (the bare fact is that the *yin* position of the lunar
month, (6), is not equivalent to the *yin* lunar month, (2), as classified above): these two blunders, in company with the correct date
of *yin*, contribute mainly to the founding of the fiction "three *yin*".
This bloated error, taken over by the early Tsing(清初) scholar Tsiang Ch'ih, is handed down to Yer and Kuo in modern times intact,
because for more than eighteen centuries since Wang Yi, no one has
dissected his blunder, at the same time a hoax, and told how he
formed it. It is true Tsu-tse in the middle of Soong has first discredited the fiction of "three *yin*", but it continued to eke out its harmful
existence to our modern days. Ling, in support of Tsu-tse, has given
it a good blow on the head; he has done well, but his efforts are not
yet adequate to put an end to it. Now, I have smashed to smithereens
this stumbling block to our finding out the real birth year of our poet.

When all the above has been said, all students of Chü Yuan
could and should get out of the maze of this "three *yin*" conceit. I
hereby propose my conjecture that the poet was born in 345 B. C., in
the first moon (lunar month) of spring when all living beings, men,
birds, animals, flowers and trees, were jubilant and earth herself was
waking up from her winter sleep with its verdant plain, fountains,
rills and streams, and on a *yin* day (this was *Kêng-yin*, 庚寅, as distinguished from another one or two *yin* days in the month). Since *yin*
(寅) marked the first birth of man in this world, according to *Lien-*

san(《连山》), the first of the *Three Mutabilities*(《三易》), attributed to Hsia, to be born on a *yin* day in early spring was fairly auspicious. His late illustrious sire, "Seeing and weighing how I bore myself erstwhile", gave him names fair, formal as well as informal. As we know, the poet's first ceremonious name is Bing(平), not mentioned in this ode, which means he should be fair and equitable(均正公平) with heaven as his master, and his second ceremonious name is Ts'en-tsê(正则), expressly stated in line 7, bestowed on him to mean that he should observe the righteous and selfless law(正直无私之法则) under heaven. And then, his first informal name for daily use Yuan(原) was given him to match Bing, not mentioned in the poem, meaning he should go after earth, the plain(原), in giving sustenance to and bearing up all things(育载万物). In accordance with *The Tsur Officials*(《周官》), when he had grown up to manhood at the age of twenty, at the ceremony of formally wearing hat (冠礼), he was given this informal name Yuan together with a second, Ling-chün(灵均), given in line 8, an estimate of his carriage during his boyhood years, which means he was endowed with an intelligent and clear-sighted character, conforming with justice and uprightness(灵明均正之性格), in short, inspired harmony. When we ponder on his noble, illustrious ancestry and the relations of the meanings of these two pairs of names, how pertinent they are each to each respectively and how they are confluent with the circumstances of his birth, we can perhaps better grasp the full meaning of the first twelve lines of this ode. *Vide* notes 3,4,5 and 6 on *Lee Sao*, in *Notes and Comments*.

　　§ 2. In the thirty-sixth year of King Hsien of Γsur(周显王三十六年), 333 B. C., Yen, Ts'ao, Hang, Gwei, Tsih and Ts'ou(燕,

赵,韩,魏,齐,楚) signed the *Pact of United Coalition* (合纵约) against Tsing (秦), with Suh Tsing (苏秦) as its General Commander (从约长).

§ 3. In the first year of King Hwai of Ts'ou (楚怀王元年), 328 B.C., Tsang Yih (张仪) began his premiership under King Wei of Tsing (秦惠王).

§ 4. In the sixth year of King Hwai of Ts'ou (楚怀王六年), 323 B.C., according to *The Annals of the State Ts'ou* (《楚世家》) of *The Chronicle* (《史记》), Ts'ou sent its "State Pillar" (equivalent to the Great General) Ts'au Yang (柱国昭阳) to attack Gwei, defeating it at Hsiang Ling (襄陵) and taking eight boroughs. And then, the same general led his troops to attack Tsih, whose king, in panic, bade the itinerant politician Tsen Ts'en (陈轸) to persuade Ts'au Yang to withdraw his force and go back home. Later in the year, Tsing sent Tsang Yih to the town Niêh-soun (啮桑) to draw up a pact of peace with envoys of Ts'ou, Tsih and Gwei. In *The Life of Tsang Yih* (《张仪列传》) of *The Chronicle*, it is said that when he returned to Tsing after his signature of the pact, he was relieved of the duties of his premiership and subsequently went to Gwei to become its premier.

Chü Yuan's earliest extant poem *Ode to the Orange* (《橘颂》), the eighth piece of the *Sylva of Nine Pieces* (《九章》), collected and probably entitled by Liu Shan (刘向) of West Han in the anthology *Ts'ou "Tze"* (《楚辞》), was written in his middle or early late twenties, before he became King Hwai's Left Counsellor (when he was twenty-six or -seven from the lunar calendar). The mark of its early date is shown in the piece's four-charactered lines throughout (a few chanting particles 兮 excepted), a trait of his being still entirely in the tradition of *The Classic of Poetry* (or *The Book of Songs*)(《诗经》) and having not yet established his metrical innovation. The ode, like a mountain spring in its freshness and purity, announces at the start the firm personality and resolute ardour for what is fair of the young poet, together with his love for the homeland, most decidedly. It is going to develop into *Lee Sao* ultimately and the poet was to stick to his words unto his death.

§ 5. In the tenth year of King Hwai(楚怀王十年), 319 B. C., according to *The Warring States Strips* (《战国策》), Tsih helped Ts'ou to attack Tsing taking Chü Wau(曲沃). What Chü Yuan's last poem *Pining My Past Days*(《惜往日》) says in line 5

The state was rich and strong then, laws were well set up,

must refer to this, when he was Left Counsellor to the Crown, well intrusted by the king. His fine relations with Hwai *Wang* are alluded to in the other seven lines at the beginning of the poem. It is presumed that the poet was some twenty-six years old then from the solar calendar or twenty-eight from the lunar, for Left Counsellorship, a confidential high post next only to the premiership, would not likely be intrusted to a young man, however brilliant, less than that. From this, I make my supposition of § 1. To be exact, *The Warring States Strips* does not explicitly say Ts'ou's wresting Chu Wau from Tsing was done in the tenth year of Hwai, but it is my deduction from the vague general statement that the conquest happened around the eleventh year of Hwai, i. e., in the 10th, Ilth or 12th year. Since the expeditional force of United Coalition headed by Ts'ou sustained a reverse in the Ilth year of Hwai at the Hehn-ko Pass, as a result of

Tsang Yih's wrecking efforts, in his capacity as Gwei's premier, to give Suh Tsing's Coalition a tottering blow, and Chü Yuan was a determined anti-Tsing political figure of Ts'ou, I am perforce inclined to deduce thus from the *Warring States Strips* statement.

§ 6. In the eleventh year of King Hwai(楚怀王十一年), 318 B. C., with Suh Tsing as General Commander, the expeditionary force of United Coalition of the six states led by Ts'ou marched to the Hehn-ko Pass (at Lin-pao *hsien*,灵宝县, Ho-nan,河南, today). Tsing legions intrenched before attacked the combined columns of the six states. The latter all beat a retreat back home.

§ 7. In the sixteenth year of King Hwai(楚怀王十六年), 313 B. C., Tsang Yih came to Ts'ou to break up the Coalition Pact between Ts'ou and Tsih. Chü Yuan was thirty-two years old (solar calendar) or thirty-four (lunar) then. For details, see my account from the beginning of the last section *Ts'ou and Chü Yuan*. When Tsang Yih arrived at Ying-*t'uh*, Chü Yuan was already repelled by his sovereign for some time. After he was dismissed from his offices as the Lord of Three Portals and Left Counsellor to the king, he wrote *Bitter Declarations*(《惜诵》) to affirm his purity and loyalty, early in this year or late in the last.

§ 8. In the seventeenth year of King Hwai(楚怀王十七年), 312 B. C., Ts'ou fought a big battle with Tsing at Tan-yang(丹阳, the capital of Ts'ou's earliest fief, according to *The Chronicle*, in the south-east of Kwei-tsur,归州, or Tzi-kwei,秭归, Chü Yuan's ancestral home), suffering a smashing defeat, lost her Han-tsoon County (汉中郡) and then fought another one with Tsing at Lan-dien(蓝田), meeting a battering blow once more, with two of her cities cut as indemnity to her enemy. Chü Yuan was called back to the court probably late in this year, or early the next. He was thirty-three years old (solar calendar) or thirty-five (lunar).

§ 9. In the eighteenth year of King Hwai(楚怀王十八年), 311 B. C., the poet went to Tsih as the king's special envoy to revivify the Coalition Pact; he was thirty-four (solar) or thirty-six (lunar) then. When he came back from Tsih, he was restored to his former offices at the court. In a few months, late in this year or early the next, he was expelled to Han-pei(汉北); the details of his conflicts with the pro-Tsing junta and his falling into disgrace the second time with his king, as the background of this item and the next, have been accounted for in the previous section.

§ 10. In the nineteenth year of King Hwai(楚怀王十九年), 310 B. C., Chü Yuan wrote *Drawing My Thoughts*(《抽思》) in the autumn. *Musing on the Beauteous One*(《思美人》) was composed in the spring next year. These two dates are well traced from internal evidences of the poems by the Tsing scholars Ling Yün-ming(林云铭) and Tsiang Ch'ih. Late in the twenty-first year of Hwai(楚怀王二十一年), 308 B. C., *Divining to Know Where I Should Stay*(《卜居》) was written, for in it the first sentence of the prose preamble says, "Chü Yuan, being rejected, for three years could not see his king." Loh Kan-rue(陆侃如) and Yer Koh-en(游国恩), two modern students of the poet, say that like *Distant Wanderings*(《远游》) and *The Fisherman*(《渔父》), this poem is not an authentic work of the poet, and they are unconditionally supported by Kuo Mê-ruo(郭沫若). I have not seen Loh and Yer's arguments, but their assertions seem to me unconvincing. About the authenticity of *Distant Wanderings*, I would give my detailed reasons below. Here, suffice it to say that the other two pieces are without doubt both genuine works of the poet in conformity to the tradition from Wang Yi, Hoon Hsin-tsou and Tsu Hsih down. Our ancient poets and scholars usually would not call a celebrated poet or scholar whom they admired or revered brusquely by his name without any accompanying expression of esteem and respect in their literary works or miscellanies of a not very formal nature, cases of methodic, historical record or scholarly, critical discussion such as Sze-ma Tsien's *Life* of the poet and Liu Shye's （刘勰） literary essay on *Lee Sao*（《辨骚》） being excepted. Thus, for instance, in Chia Yieh's（贾谊） *Elegy on Chü Yuan*（《吊屈原》）, the West Han poet says,

> Bowing sadly, I heard of Chü Yuan
>
> Drowning himself in the stream Mi-Io;
>
> Going down to the river Hsiang,
>
> I mourn with dole our revered sire.

The tones of *Divining to Know Where I Should Stay* and *The Fisherman* in speaking of the poet are too blunt and unmannerly to be taken by Soong Yü, Chin Tsa or the poet's other pupils or admirers. Only the poet speaking of himself could assume such bare tones. Besides, Tsu Hsih has very fitly observed that the "woman" in the following lines is a satirical allusion to Ts'eng Sieü（郑袖）:

> Shall I wheedle by putting on a cautious air,
>
> Smile forcedly, affect and blindly follow,
>
> To attend upon a woman at her conceits?

And Tsiang Ch'ih points out that the first two lines form a most suit-

able thrust at the Saun-quan courtier (上官大夫) and Jin Soun
(靳尚).

§ 11. § 12. And then *Distant Wanderings*(《远游》), a longer
poem of about 180 lines was composed in the twenty-first to twenty-
second years of King Hwai(楚怀王二十一、二十二年), 308—307
B. C. Tsiang Ch'ih admits in his *San-tai Pavilion Commentary on
Ts'ou "Tze"*(《山带阁注楚辞》) that he could find no clue in the poem to its date. In his *Remaining Comments on Ts'ou "Tze"*(《楚辞余
论》), he suspects it might be written during the poet's banishment at
Ling-yang. His supposition, based upon the poet's mentioning in the
poem his riding the south zephyr to go to Nan-ts'iao(南巢), for seeing the fairy prince Jao(王子乔), which "is a few hundred *lih* north
of Ling-yang, yet near", is, I dare say, misguided. Loh Kan-rue
(陆侃如) and Yer, whose arguments I have not read, both denied
the poem Chü Yuan's authorship, according to Kuo. But in Yer's
book just coming to my hand, he does not maintain his views in *General Comments on Ts'ou "Tze"*(《楚辞通论》). I notice he explicitly
corrects his former views on two points (*p.* 131) in his discussions in
the book, and says generally that there are many mistakes in his former volume (*p.* 216); it is evident he has already changed his opinion on the spuriousness of *Distant Wanderings* (*p.* 148). Anyway,
Loh and Yer's first views are strongly maintained by Kuo, who definitely asserts that the poem, not written by the poet, is a first draft or
Sze-ma Hsiang-rue's(司马相如) *A "Fuh" on the Magister*(《大人
赋》). I am sure he is grossly mistaken in his opinion.

The clue to the poem's date could be found, I believe, in lines
98 −99 of the original：

By chariots ten thousand, fore, aft, abreast,

Preceded, followed, flanked on the way am I.

Toward the end of *Suffering Throes*, there are the lines 359 −360:

Spreading my chariots of state a full thousand,

I wave the jade axes to proceed together.

The state of ten thousand chariots(万乘之国) meant originally, before the Spring and Autumn Period, the state of Heaven's Son(天子
之国), the kingdom of Tsur, and a state of a thousand chariots(千乘
之国), one of its vassals. As the house of Tsur grew weaker and
weaker, its vassals proclaimed themselves kings and their own states
kingdoms one after another. Then, the former title came to be applied
to a big, strong state and the latter to a weaker, smaller one during
the Spring and Autumn and Warring States Periods. Thus, Liu Shan
in his *Preface to The Warring States Strips*(刘向:《战国策·序》)
says of the Spring and Autumn Period, "There were seven states of
ten thousand chariots and five of one thousand. " These chariots were
bronze fighting vehicles trimmed with leather(革车, acccording to
Yau Nai's(姚鼐) *Supplementat Commentary on Tso's "Commentary"*
《左传补注》). In *Distant Wanderings*, a poetic fantasia describing
his journey in the empyrean region and metamorphosis into a fairy,
Chü Yuan fancies that he could or should be the king of a big state,
in order to bring Yao and Suen's blissful reigns down to his imagined
country or world. This innermost thought or highest intent of his occurred to him quite properly, I think, after he had written *Divining to
Know Where I Should Stay*, when he, though already expelled from

Introduction

Ying-*t'uh* by Hwai for three years and full of bitter sorrow and hot wrath, was yet in a mental suspense, still entertaining the hope that the king would discover his own mistake and come to senses some day, as he did after repulsing his faithful servant for about two years in the past. In this state of mind, he wrote *Distant Wanderings*[①] after his *Divining*, to give some psychic relief to his heavily laden tribulations. He wrote it for his own consolation and emotional release, not to be shown to others, or at most to be read by his pupils if they came to see him. It could not be written after he was banished as a common subject by young Ching-hsiang(顷襄王) and his brother Prince Tse-lan, the premier(令尹子兰), to Ling-yang(陵阳), south of the River(江南), as spoken of in *Plaint on Ying*(《哀郢》) when he was an exile for already nine years. It could not be written then because his previous afflictions, once put to a stop for about two years from the twenty-ninth year of Hwai(楚怀王二十九年), 300 B. C., to the first of Ching-hsiang(顷襄王元年), 298 B. C., when he was called back to the court from his expulsion, were very much aggravated by the shocking formal exile. The mood of the poem, its emotional temper, does not agree with his more heavily struck state of mind at Ling-yang. And from the ten thousand chariots of *Distant Wanderings*, a poetic fantasia, to the one thousand of *Suffering Throes*, which mixes fantasies with realities, one can see the natural sequence of their dates of composition. I conclude, therefore, *Suffering Throes* was composed after *Distant Wanderings* in the twenty-sec-

---

[①] However, according to Professor Hu Xiao-shi(胡小石,1888—1962) in his tract *Distant Wanderings Analvsed and Discredited*(《远游疏证》,见《胡小石论文集》,上海古籍出版社,1982), it is a fabricated piece written by someone in the dynasty Han.

ond year of Hwai(楚怀王二十二年) to perhaps the earlier part of the
next year(二十三年), 307 –306 B. C. After deliberation, the poet
altered the ten thousand chariots of the former piece to the one thousand of the latter as a more plausible flight of imagination presentable
to Hwai to whom he would give a copy. I disagree with Tsiang Ch'ih
from his attribution of *Lee Sao* to later than *Bitter Declarations*(《惜
诵》) and earlier than *Drawing My Thoughts*(《抽思》) and *Musing
on the Beauteous One* (《思美人》). Tsiang notices quite a few
thoughts and expressions common to the last two poems on the one
hand and *Lee Sao* on the other. He does not say but we can see clearly that there are thoughts and expressions common to *Distant Wanderings* and *Suffering Throes* too. The gist of my arguments is that *Lee
Sao* was composed by the poet as a great cathedral with its own giant
central cupola and a host of spires, towers, turrets, flying arches and
colonnades, some isolated parts of which are in common with certain
details of his former and later minor works, but the whole edifice
bears a grand harmonious unity of its own. Hence these common
thoughts and expressions between it and his previous minor works. In
another word, *Suffering Throes* is somehow in feelings and thoughts
concluding in nature, but those three shorter pieces are not just slight
repetitions of its separate studies amplified and variegated.

A highly cultured reader somewhat familiar with Chü Yuan's life
and with a fine sense of originality and poetic diction can readily see
the genuine feelings of the poet clearly expressed in the first ten lines
of *Distant Wanderings*：

> Sad for the wringing and blockade of the crowd,
> I wish to rise aloft and wander afar.

Weak in agility and without the means,

What shall I ride, for uplifting, as my car?

Suffering from the taint of mud and slime,

Depressed and lorn, to whom could I tell the matter?

Awake and restless through the livejong night,

I mope about till dawn my nerves doth shatter.

Seeing the boundlessness of the heaven and earth,

I grieve that life is full of sorrow and pain.

In fact, the two initial lines give in their chaste simplicity the whole theme like a bubbling fount. In them, as well said by Tsiang, are condensed the deepest sorrows and bitterest pains of the poet. The entire piece, though not long in the eyes of a Western reader, is replete with originality and shining with the essence of purity. A "*Fuh*" *on the Magister*(《大人赋》) by Sze-ma Hsiang-rue(司马相如) of Han, on the other hand, is evidently an inferior, bungling imitation of *Distant Wanderings*. In the four incipient lines, we are told the grandiose magister dwells in his stately mansion commanding lands ten thousand (square) *lih* in extent in the central state(中州), yet he is discontent with his affluence. In the next two lines, he takes over Chü Yuan's idea in his two topical lines, altering three words:

Sad for the wringing and closeness of the world,

I wish to rise aloft and wander afar.

And then, before his readers are exhibited the thetorical somersaults of the Han *fuh* writer. After the line 横厉飞泉以正东, the magister goes through the four quarters, east, south, west and north, of the sky, to seek the fairy's habitation. Whereas in *Distant Wanderings*, Chü Yuan sets out first to seek the fairy prince Jao(仙人王子乔) at Nan-ts'iao(南巢) and then he ascends,

> And entering His Supremacy's palace,
> I hold an interview with Tsin-sze the God.

Coming out, he rambles round the sky and over the earth after arriving at Mount Ee-vei-Iü(于微闾, 医元闾, 医巫闾), to go through the four quarters, east, west, south and north. Finally, Hsiang-rue's Magister finds heaven too lonely for him where he sees nothing, hears nothing, has no friends and is cheerless. In a word, he is disappointed, and the sequel, though not written, must be his return to his great mansion and landed property of ten thousand *lih*. But to console himself with an emotive release, Chü Yuan, at the end of his poem, says,

> Superseding inertness and arriving
> At utter purity,
> I come to inhere very neighbouring
> To primitive Prime.

So, we see Chü Yuan's fantasia is motivated by his condemnation of the polluted air of the Ts'ou court, while Sze-ma's *fuh* is a vindication of Mammon and a rebutting of *Distant Wanderings*. To me, Hsiang-rue's botched-up work of rhetorical flourishes in contrast with Chü Yuan's original piece of ringing purity is like a Romanesque structure compared to the Parthenon of Athene. The Han *fuh* writer, a worshipper of power and wealth, has also written an elegiac piece on the "Emperor-emperor" Ⅱ of Tsing(《哀二世赋》) and another one *A "Fuh" on the Long Portal Palace*(《长门赋》). In the former, he compassionates Hwu-hay(胡亥), Ying Tsen's second son, who plotted with Ts'ao Kao(赵高), a devilish eunuch, and lih Sze(李斯), Ying Tsen's premier, to forge a false testament of the dead tyrant for inheriting his throne by himself and killing his elder brother Wuh-suh (扶苏), who had been strongly against his father's burying alive the scholars, and then, three years later, was murdered by the eunuch after Lih Sze was publicly pulled to pieces with ox-carts. Sze-ma Hsiang-rue commiserates the viper, who was as flagitious and ruthless as his father, for being murdered and having his Satanic dynasty extirpated because he laid trust in Ts'ao Kao's vilification! In this *fuh*, Hsiang-rue means to hint timidly that Wuh-*tih* should not lay too much trust in an eunuch surnamed Saung(商监) by pointing to the case of Ts'ao Kao as an example for warning; but his ingratiating sycophancy made him incapable of driving home his point. In the case of the latter *fuh*, according to Ts'au-ming's *Literary Selections* (《昭明文选》), Sze-ma let himself hired by Empress Tsen of Wuh-*tih* of Han(汉武陈皇后) to plead with the emperor for taking pity and refreshing his former favour on her; for that frivolous pursuit, which attained its effect, the mercenary literatus was rewarded with a hundred catties(百斤) of "gold"(bronze)! One can see plainly that neither his sympathy for one scoundrel against another among a pack of them equally vicious, nor his bawd-like gallantry in court enamouring affairs could reflect credit or honour on him. Now, this sorry piece of *fuh* on the Magister, with its laboured, showy splendour, is highly regarded to be such a masterpiece that Chü Yuan's excellent

Distant Wanderings could only be its first draft!

While students have been silent, as far as I know, on the ten thousand chariots and one thousand of these two poems and have not committed themselves about the fixed date of *Distant Wonderings*, Yer thinks *Suffering Throes* was composed later than the third year of Ching-hsiang's reign, for lines 19 −20 say,

> Reflecting on the trees and herbage that fall sear,
> I fear the Beauteous One would grow old one day.

and lines 65 −66 say,

> As old age is gradually gaining on me,
> I am anxious at the absence of a fair name.

And Kuo's conjecture of the date is even much later on the second evidence; he puts it before *Plaint on Ying*(《哀郢》), which, according to Wang Fuh-tse(王夫之) and him, "was written in the twenty-first year of Ching-hsiang", 278 B.C., when Ying-*t'uh* was taken by the Tsing general Bai Chih(秦将白起). I am first acquainted with Yer's points from Rao Tsoon-yieh's(饶宗颐) book *Geographical Studies of Ts'ou "Tze"*(《楚辞地理考》). In the third year of Ching-hsiang's reign, we know, Hwai died in Tsing as a kidnapped captive. Yer evidently thinks *Lee Sao's* date later than Hwai's death. Contrary to both Yer's and Kuo's conjectures, *Lee Sao* is signally silent on Hwai's death as a kidnapped captive. There is not the slightest trace of an allusion to that calamity in the ode. How could such a momentous event be ignored by the poet, if the poem were composed after it happened, in the first place? Next, the poet should not "fear the Beauteous One would grow old one day," for he was already dead. But in Yer's book which has just come to my hand, I see he regards "the Beauteous One" and "the wise Hng" (line 256) as Hsiang, and Ling-sieu as King Hwai. It seems to me altogether unthinkable for the poet to hold such a high opinion of Hsiang. And besides, during his Han-pei years, how could he, so passionate in nature, be so slothful as not to have written *Lee Sao*? Thirdly, the second evidence claimed by Yer becomes immaterial, for though the poet was eleven years older in the third year of Ching-hsiang than in the twenty-second to-third year of Hwai, he was still far from seventy, as he had never lived to that age, in case seventy was taken as old[1]. Moreover, it must be pointed out, in both these evidences, the poet only fears "the Beauteous One would grow old one day" and is afraid of "the absence of a fair name", "as old age is gradually gaining on me". In another word, these lines neither say his sovereign nor mean he himself is already old. Now, my contention that *Suffering Throes* was written in the twenty-second to -third year of Hwai(307 −306 B. C.) during his expulsion at Han-pei (further, this is in perfect accord with Sze-ma Tsien's *The Life of Chü Yuan*), when he was thirty-eight to thirty-nine years old (solar) or forty to forty-one (lunar), is quite proper. At forty-one, nine years from half a hundred, to think one's old age will gradually come is not at all unnatural. Chia Yieh（贾

---

[1] *Chü Lih of Notes of Rites*(《礼·曲礼》), says, seventy is called old. But that is not a fixed natural law, but a matter of opinion. Thus, although Hsueh Tsun (许慎) in his *A Book of Etymology*(《说文解字》) follows *Chü Lih*, Hwang Kan(皇侃), for instance in his annotation on the character to *The Anatects* (《论语》), says, over fifty is called old.

谊), the best *fuh* poet among Chü Yuan's Han disciples and adorers, whom Tsu-tse rightly holds in very high esteem, begins his *A Lament on Sworn Devotions*(《惜誓》)① with these two lines:

> I lament my growing old and weaker daily;
> Away the years fleet off, returning not.

Written as a monologue of Chü Yuan by Chia Yieh, who was sure to have known that his master did not live to seventy, Chü Yuan is made to say here in this plaint that he is old. Yer, seeing an incongruity in his second evidence with the poet's age in Hwai's reign, followed by Kuo and Rao, is therefore altogether untenable in my eyes. See my comments on Pih(阰) and Pih(沘), note 10 on *Lee Sao* in *Notes and Comments*. The poet, having meetly expressed his bitter sorrow for himself and to his king some four years after his expulsion from Ying-*t'uh* in the great ode, and now that his searing tears had gone dry long before while blank despair was staring him in the face, from the third year of Ching-hsiang downward, could not key up his imagination and emotional tune to a level as that of those exhibited in *Lee Sao*, no matter how. Finally, Kuo's comparison of the date of the ode, in his contention that it was composed in the year of the poet's death, with Goethe's finishing the second part of *Faust* when he was about eighty, seems to me totally out of joint. Chü Yuan was

---

① In Wang Yi's *Textual Critical Studies of Ts'ou "Tze"*(《楚辞章句》), this poem is said to be anonymous or, as some said, by Chia Yieh. Hoon Hsin-tsou (洪兴祖) and Tsu Hsih(朱熹) of Soong and Wang Fuh-tse(王夫之) of Tsing are firm in their opinions that it is by Chia. The title《惜誓》means, according to Wang Fuh-tse, a lament on Chü Yuan's swom devotions.

a man of mighty passion, perhaps comparable to Beethoven, but not to Goethe, who was calmly Olympian in temperament, and *Lee Sao* is the intensest ode, highly lyrical, ever written by man, to be contradistinguished from the drama *Faust*, which is a subjective-objective representation of the medieval-Renaissance Teutonic legend.

§ 13. After *Lee Sao*, *Nine Hymns*(《九歌》) and *Sky-vaulting Queries*(《天问》) were also written at Han-pei during his expulsion from Ying-*t'uh* before the twenty-ninth year of Hwai, when he was once more called back to the court. This is my conjecture, although Tsiang Ch'ih says he could not determine their dates. I make this surmise on the ground that the poet, though miserable and forlorn, was still in a mental suspense spoken of above which is in harmony with the temper of these poems.

Nine Hymns(《九歌》) the title given by the poet himself to this collection of hymns, means a group of many songs, not exactly nine, for they are eleven or rather ten in number. For distinguishing them from Yü's cantata of the selfsame name, I call them *Nine Hymns*. I disagree with Tsiang who says *On the Major God* and *On the Minor God of Life-ruling* form a class and *On the King of Hsiang* and *On the Lady of Hsiang* form another, therefore there are nine kinds of gods and goddesses addressed to, hence the group is called by this title. Nine, in the ancient Chinese language, bears the sense "many" as well as the utmost positive digit beginning from one. Thus, in line 86 of *Suffering Throes*, we have:

> Though being nine times dead, I regret not at all.

There, "nine" also means "many", not just nine. The last piece《礼

魂》, consisting of only five lines, as Wang Fuh-tse has it, is an epode, a tail piece, common to all the nine hymns above, not an independent hymn to spirits of deceased fair intellectuals, as taken by Tsiang Ch'ih and others. This bouquet of ten short pieces was in a sense gathered in his rambling over the Han-pei region visiting cities, towns and villages and making not infrequent excursions to the south by sailing on the Han Stream and going down the water. At the mouth where the Han converges with the River(长江), he visited the three cities and boroughs Hsia-puh(夏浦,later named Hsia-ker,夏口,today called Han-ker,汉口), T'uh-ker(堵口,now called Han-yang,汉阳) and Ngo-tsu(鄂渚,now known as Wuh-tsoun,武昌). Although he was expelled from the capital and supposed to reside in Han-pei, he was free to take trips to the south, provided he did not enter Ying-t'uh. So he boated upstream on the River and roved in the Hoon Lake (洪湖) and Doong-ding Lake(洞庭湖) regions. *Nine Hymns* was composed in his pensive solitude. It is distinguished from the *Sylva of Nine Pieces*(《九章》), another collection of short poems personally lyrical in nature, most of which (five) were in a bitterer sorrowful and a hotter wrathful mood, since his formal exile to Ling-yang till his self-drowning in Mi-lo River. Wang Yi says of these hymns like this: "In the past, in the boroughs south of Ying of Ts'ou and by the streams Yuan(沅) and Hsiang(湘), the custom believed in spirits and was fond of songs, which were in the form of mirthful hymns, accompanied by music and dancing, to gladden the gods, goddesses and spirits. Chü Yuan, being expelled, frequented the district. With bitter sorrow in his heart and mournful thoughts fuming and choking his mind, he saw the commonalty paying homage to the deities with rituals, songs and dances in jollity. The wording of those hymns was boorish and paltry. So he composed the verses of *Nine Hymns* for the rude folks, to express their devout affection as well as convey his own pensiveness as a sort of remonstrance. "

The titles of these sacrificial songs are given in the table of contents. Details about them are specified in the *Notes and Comments*. The subject, emotional tone, diction and thythmical form of these pieces are homogeneous. Tsu Hsih, who gives his own views correcting his predecessors in his comments on the individual hymns, is taken exception to by Tsiang Ch'ih on the major point of the supernatural agents not making response compared to King Hwai's ignoring the poet as well as on many minor points. It is too lengthy to go into these particulars here. But the two students are common in opinion as regards the poems' feelings of loyalty to the king and patriotism for the state, showing the poet's clinging remembrance for his master. It is plain these songs were works of the same period, not excepting *On the Mountain Sprite* (《山鬼》), which is attributed by Tsiang to a date after *Over the Streams* (《涉江》) and the *Sylva of Nine Pieces* (《九章》).

§ 14. After *Nine Hymns*, in utter isolation and loneliness, Chü Yuan wrote his *Sky-vaulting Queries* (《天问》). This strange poem of a hundred and seventy odd questions, some of which concerned with the early dawn of the nation's history are still unanswerable even today, is without its match in the world. Wang Yi's foreword to it says: "*Sky-vaulting Queries* was written by Chü Yuan. (After his expulsion from the capital,) the poet, grieving while rambling the mountains and lowlands, wailing with pain and heaving sighs at heaven, saw, during his wanderings over hill and dale, in the ancestral temples of Ts'ou's regal forefathers and their nobilities, the frescoes of the divinities of heaven and earth, strange and odd, also ancient sages, monsters and legendary tales. Tired of his roaming, he rested under them; looking up, he saw the pictures and wrote on the walls his questions to give vent to his distemper and wrath and spend his sorrowful thoughts. The Ts'ou people, commiserating Chü Yuan, put together the questions into a collection; so their senses are not quite relevant. " Wang Yi is mainly correct in his account of the poem, but is mistaken in his judgment in the last two statements, for which, see the criticism by Wang Fuh-tse(王夫之) of Tsing(清) quoted in the following section Ⅷ *Chü Yuan's Thought and Poetry*. The poem asks a series of concerted questions about the sky, the earth, inexplicable wonders of the world, the rise and fall of the dynasty Hsia (also King Yih, 后羿, and the origins of the Ts'ou and Wuh, 吴, peoples), the rise and fall of the dynasty Saung-Yin(商殷), the rise and fall of the house of Tsur, the war between Wuh(吴) and Ts'ou and the rise of the Tsing(秦) people, and finally, affairs of Ts'ou.

These two poems seem to me to occupy a part of Chü Yuan's time from the twenty-third year of Hwai to the twenty-ninth, 306 − 300 B. C., when he was recalled back to the court from his expulsion of some eleven years.

§ 15. The political events of Ts'ou and its battles with Tsih, Hang, Gwei and Tsing before and after Chü Yuan's recall to the court from Han-pei have been given in the last section, as well as the poet's conflicts with Tse-lan, the new king's brother, and his banishment to Ling-yang, south of the River. Some bamboo strips of *The Chronicle* (《史记》) must have been lost before the printing of its earliest block print Soong edition, for a sentence or two is surely missing before "hearing it, the premier Tse-Ian fell into a passion." In the third year of Ching-hsiang, 296 B. C., King Hwai died as a kidnapped captive in Tsing; his remains were sent back to be buried. News of the late king's death reached the poet in his exile; he wrote his elegiac piece at first entitled *Summoning the Soul*(《招魂》). Chü Yuan was fifty-one then in lunar years. This poem was later renamed with the new title *Great Summoning*(《大招》) instead at Tsang-sah(长沙), in my opinion, to distinguish it from the new piece written there given this first title then. Wang Yi was not quite sure, for he was very much confused by the two pieces of *Summoning*, whether this poem was composed by Chü Yuan or Chin Tsa(景差), Zau P'uh-tse(晁补之) of Soong, who had a very keen sense of diction, says: *Great Summoning* is primitive in diction and deep in import; it could not but be written by Chü Yuan. Hoon Hsin-tsou(洪兴祖) says: *The Roll of Arts and Letters* of *The Han Chronicle*(《汉书·艺文志》) mentions Chü Yuan's works as numbering twenty-five; *The Fisherman* has already fulfilled that limit; *Great Summoning* is probably not Chü Yuan's work. Tsu Hsih opines that Chin Tsa's words are said to be plain and primitive; it is obvious, he thinks, that *Great Summoning* must be Chin Tsa's work. Hwang Wen-pin(黄文炳) of Ming(明) and Ling Yün-ming(林云铭) and Tsiang Ch'ih of Tsing finally determine the authorship of both pieces of *Summoning* to be authentically Chü Yuan's. According to Ling fully supported by Tsiang, after his exile by young Ching-hsiang, for our poet, thinking of Hwai and clinging to the hope of his return, to climb up to his housetop in banishment to halloo for the coming back of his old master's soul was quite natural and so the poem is (finally) entitled *Great Summoning*, to be distinguished from his later work *Summoning the Soul*(《招

魂》), in which he describes how Sibyl Yang(巫阳), at the bidding
of God of Heaven, summons his own soul to come back from flight
into remote expanses of terror of the four quarters, in wry jest. As to
Hoon's statement about *The Fisherman* having already fulfilled the
number of twenty-five pieces, Tsiang points out in his *Remaining
Comments on Ts'ou "Tze"*(《楚辞余论》) that *Nine Hymns*, though
consisting of "eleven" pieces, is entitled with *Nine* and regarded as
nine in number in *The Roll of Arts and Letters*, so the inclusion of the
two pieces of *Summoning* just makes that number. Furthermore, asks
Tsiang, the last fifty odd lines speak of certain policies, institutions
and the general commonweal of early Tsur with allusions to Kings
Wen and Wuh and duke Tsur as recorded in *The Classic of History*,
Notes of Rites and some poems of *The Classic of Poetry*; how could
Soong Yü and Ch'in Tsa, mere poets as they were, without Chü
Yuan's majestic statesmanship, write *Great Summoning*?

§ 16. In the ninth year of Hsiang(襄), 290 B. C., *Plaint on
Ying*(《哀郢》) was composed at Ling-yang(陵阳) in reminisence of
the poet's departure from Ying-*t'uh*. The last portion of the poem reflecting on Tse-Ian the premier very strongly and even the king himself pointedly and attacking the pro-Tsing ring for its malicious libels
and toadeating must have given acute offense to the court from the
very top down. So, he was exiled, the second time, from Ling-yang
to the basin regions of the streams Tsen(辰) and Süe(溆) early next
year, 289 B. C. Ling-yang was far away from Ying in the wide
stretch of Ts'ou's eastern domain. The regions of Tsen and Sue way
down in the south-west were a very much worse, wild and barbarian
country. Wang Fuh-tse(王夫之) of early Tsing(清初) and Kuo
among modern students maintain that the poem was written after Ying

was captured by Bai Chih to describe the flight of its inhabitants eastward when Hsiang with his court was fleeing to Tsen(陈). The glaring mistake of this explanation of *Plaint on Ying* has been specifically criticized and set to right by Tsiang Ch'ih, and Yer Koh-en in recent times clarifies the progress of the poet in his exile from Ying-*t'uh* to Ling-yang in connection with the poet's feelings then, the way he took and the circumstances of the journey, in a detailed analysis that is not to be easily gainsaid.

§ 17. Next, in the ninth to tenth year of Hsiang, 290 −289 B. C., the poet wrote *Over the Streams*(《涉江》) when he was fifty-seven to fifty-eight in lunar years. It is a foregoing account of his exile trip off Ling-yang via the River, from the north-east to the south-west of Ts'ou, starting from Ngo-tsu(鄂渚,the present city of Wuh-tsoun,武昌), riding on horseback in the first stretch, taking to chaise riding next and then boating on the Hsiang(湘), the Doong-ding Lake. Crossing the wide expanse of water of the great lake tortuously, he sailed upstream on the Yuan(沅水). Then, setting forth south-westward from where the Waung Stream(枉水) flows into Yuan, he put up at night in the south of the river-mouth where the Tsen Stream(辰水) pours into the Yuan. On the way from Waung to Tsen, not long after he left the former, he wended his way on foot past Wuh-Iing(武陵) where he met the fisherman, which incident is memorized in *The Fisherman*(《渔父》). This short piece, together with *Divining to Know Where I Should Stay*(《卜居》), is said by certain modem students to be not the work of the poet, but I uphold the old tradition of taking them both to be the poet's authentic works. From Tsen-yang(辰阳), the water route continued south-westward upstream till at the converging point of the Sue Stream(溆水) and the

Yuan, the poet's boat turned south-eastward into the Süe and he landed at Süe-puh(溆浦). The regions he traversed through were mostly wild and scantily inhabited by rude tribesmen of the Miao(苗) and Yau(瑶) minorities; the time was early spring, with snow and sleet still falling, and high mountains and dense forests ("inhabited by hymadryas and acthiops", 乃猨狄之所居) greeted him all the way.

§ 18. Chü Yuan composed his *Thinking of Sah*(《怀沙》), at the beginning of summer in the same year, when he set out not long from Loon-yang(龙阳) after leaving the Waung Stream. He was fifty-eight then in lunar years. Sah means Tsang-sah(长沙), the earliest fief of Hsiung Yih(熊绎) of Ts'ou, according to the *Memorial Tablet of Tsang-sah's Folklore*(《长沙风土碑》) by Tsang Wei(张谓) of Tdaung(唐). He meant at first to live in the basin regions of Tsen and Süe among the Miao and Yau tribesmen to end his natural years, but after deliberation, he made up his mind to die by self-drowning at Tsang-sah. The city was a big one in the south-east of Ying and not very far from it. Since his first banishment, the poet did not venture to go north of the River. Now that he had decided to die at the burial-place of his earliest Ts'ou ancestors, as

> Birds will fly back to their old nests howe'er far;
> Foxes must die on the knolls where they were born.

he is thoughtful of the place with bitterness and anger, yet in firm resolution, in the poem. Death was forced on him by his utter despair at the state of affairs of Ts'ou in the hands of Hsiang and Tse-lan as well as that of the "world" under the menace of Tsing's dark forces.

§ 19. Chü Yuan was now preoccupied with death day and

night, since he had made up his mind to die at Tsang-sah. He imagined himself as already dead and composed *Summoning the Soul*, taking the title from his former piece of elegy written for his late king, giving that the new title *Great Summoning* and naming his new piece with this. Confused by the two pieces of *Summoning* and P'an K'uh's mentioning the number of twenty-five poems as the poet's extant works in *The Roll of Arts and Letters*, Wang Yi attributes *Summoning the Soul* to Soong Yü, Hoon Hsin-tsou questions its authenticity and Tsu Hsih follows Wang's suit, though Sze-ma Tsien lists it unmistakably among the poet's works in his *Life*. The poem begins its relation in the first person (朕) and soon goes on to call and urge the poet's soul, in the words of Sibyl Yang (巫阳), at the bidding of God of Heaven, to come back to Ts'ou from its possible flight into vastly distant regions of terror of the four quarters, back here where it could live in a great mansion of his own of wonderful, splendid beauty and enjoyment. This sumptuous descriptive elegy of summoning one's own soul back to safety, contentment and happiness at home, the utmost one could desire in the opulence of life, in wrested jocoseness while one was actually in the abyss of misery, is without its like in the world's history of poetry. The last line says:

> Come back, oh soul, to the south of River Ai!

"Ai" in the original means "sorrow". River Sorrow is the section of Hsiang Stream confluent with Mi-lo River, flowing northward into the Doong-ding Lake. It has two islets called Great Sorrow and Small Sorrow (大、小哀洲). Legend has it that Suen's two queens following in pursuit of, but failing to catch up with, him in his southern campaign cried on these two islets, hence their names. South of River Sorrow means Tsang-sah, whereabout he was to die.

§ 20. *Lamenting* on *Whirlblasts*(《悲回风》) was composed at Tsang-sah in the autumn of the year previous to that of his death, when he was sixty in lunar years. While *Suffering Throes* has its overarching prospects of things, past and present, that would make one, especially the sovereign of a state, sad and wise, to give, the poet's sublime devotion to virtues and goodness to depict and the boundless flight of imagination to go through in a broad compass, and the short pieces such as *Plaint on Ying* and *Thinking of Sah* each has its own particular feelings to embody with respect to their individual circumstances, peculiar or general, in trenchant bitterness, *Lamenting on Whirlblasts*, containing the passion of deep sorrow of one of the noblest of souls aspiring heaven-ward first, then coming down for his lingering love for the home-land and, finally, following the course of the River(江) into the sea before tracing the Ho(河, the Luteous River) from the sea upstream for seeing the spirits of Oo Tse-süe(伍子胥) and Sun-tuh Di(申徒狄), his predecessors, whose deaths could not save Wuh(吴) and Yin(殷) — the poem ends in despairing helplessness. For the pure contemplation of profound sorrow and wild despair of the immaculate intellectual distraught by the slimy realities of this world, *Lamenting on Whirlblasts* is without its equal throughout history. In it, the poet's reiterative wishings to go after Peng Yen are announced that were going to seal his tragic fate before long at last.

§ 21. And the last poem Chü Yuan wrote, in the spring of Hsiang's thirteenth year, 286 B. C., before he jumped into the river Mi-lo(汨罗江), was *Pining My Past Days*(《惜往日》). In this harrowing retrospect of the past from his youthful halcyon days as the trusted Left Counsellor to Hwai, the poet speaks three times of "the duped King"(雍君) and dupery with acrid repining, intent to point his finger at Hsiang no less poignantly as Hwai's successor. But at heart, he thinks very slightly of this despicable nephew of his. To say most favourably of the dolt, Hsiang is to him only comparable to the wayward sons of Yao and Suen, Tan-tsu(丹朱) and Saung-chün (商均), as he has insinuated at the end of *Plaint on Ying*, together with his utter contempt of the fawning wretches feeding on the sight of the weakling, that caused his second exile from Ling-yang to Tsen and Süe. He had fondly entertained a vain hope in the past that Hwai might be transformed into a virtuous sovereign:

> Riding a chariot drawn by coursers to speed,
> Come, let me hold the bridle and guide Thee for Thy day.

He was now totally disillusioned. As regards Hsiang, he did not even deserve to succeed Hwai, in his undisguised opinion. However, although the poet holds such a mean estimate of the present ruler, yet he expected him to read this poem after his death, with the hope that it might give him a timely alarm. His death was going to be a warning protest to the tomnoddy and his brother, for the sake of the state and its people. But it soon proved that this only fell on the deaf ears of the wretches. As I have pointed out above, it is to be doubted whether Chü Yuan himself and historians and literary critics after him were fully aware of the geo-political, traitorous nature of the traducings leveled at him by Tsing's tyranny. And of course it should be understood that Hwai and Hsiang, imbeciles as they were, fell as easy victims to the devilish duperies of Tsang Yih and his successor.

§ 22. Finally, the date of Chü Yuan's death fell on the fifth day of the fifth moon of that same year, the thirteenth of Hsiang's reign, 286 B. C., when he had resided at Tsang-sah for more than two years. He was sixty-one in lunar years, in full age fifty-nine. His death was not at all just a cowardly suicide out of despair at his own future. Far from that, it was a noble protest and a resounding expostulation with Hsiang on his father's and his own stupid dupery at the mercy of the wheedling junto and Tsing's totalitarian power politics, as evidenced by his declaration in his last poem *Pining My Past Days* (《惜往日》). Thus, the End of all his mortal coil, and Eternity to his lofty, effulgent spirit! His deathless soul has become a sublime ode resounding through all time of humanity, of which his life and works are indelible, irradiant symbols.

VIII   Chü Yuan's Thought and Poetry

To affirm the existence of slavery in ancient Chinese society, Kuo Mêruo, in his *Studies in Chü Yuan*, has brought forward the proposition, with divining scripts carved on tortoise shells and ox bones unearthed from the Yin Remains at An-yang(安阳殷墟甲骨卜辞) and inscriptions from cast bronze *t'ing* and other vessels of Saung-Yin and Tsur(商周金文) as evidences, that the Spring and Autumn and the Warring States Periods formed a transitional stage from the society of slavery, which lasted from Saung through early Tsur, to the epoch of feudalism of Tsing(秦), that the subjects of the conquered tribes and the overthrown dynasty were partially turned into slaves of the conquerors, bartered with live stock, silk-bundles and sheaves of grain or bought and sold with money, attached to the soil as peasants, employed for household labour, enlisted as soldiers, etc., but mainly driven to the states Soong(宋), Hsü(徐) and Ts'ou in the south and south-east of old Cathay. There is no doubt slavery was the order of things in Saung-Yin and early Tsur, only greatly ameliorated under the rules of Taung of Saung(商汤) and Wen, Wuh, Tseng and Kong(文,武,成,康) of Tsur, but certainly it did not cease to be and give prace to feudalism in its stead after Ying Tsen's annexation of the six states. The slaves were war captives and criminals in civil life and their family members. The two types of society most often co-existed synchronously and inextricably; they were not mutually excluding. In Ying Tsen and his son's reigns, feudalism actually vanished, while slavery deepened and oppression became more ferocious than ever, hence arose the rebellion of Tsen Sun(陈胜) and Wuh Kwan(吴广) in 209 B. C. The large number of labouring slaves employed in building Ying Tsen's mammoth mausolem on the Lih Mountains for years (and hundreds of imperial concubines, palace waiting maids and eunuchs as well as hundreds of workers on the tomb were sealed alive in it), paving the bowered two-layered way over eighty *lih* long leading to it from the Oo City(阿城) more than three hundred *lih* square in extent, building the luxurious Oo Vaun Palace(阿房宫), the front hall of a main structure which was not yet named, that took about thirty-four years to be built since the tyrant ascended his throne, raising the well-known Great Wall on the mountain ranges, constructing the imperial highways(驿道) from Yen-yang(咸阳) in modern Sen-sih(陕西) to Yen(燕) and Tsih (齐) in the east and Wuh(吴) and Ts'ou(楚) in the south, fifty paces wide all along, planted with pines on both sides every thirty feet, six thousand virgin boys and maidens sent to the Eastern Sea as

human sacrifice to seek ambrosia, elixir immortal herb for the historical "revolutionary hero" and last but not the least, the four hundred
and sixty odd scholars and practitioners of occult arts(方士) buried
alive at Yen-yang in 212 B. C.: what were all these human worms but
absolute slaves of the "heroic" Ying Tsen? ! In the dynasties following Tsing(秦), with a few exceptions of benevolent reigns like those
of Wen-*t'ih* and Ching-*t'ih* of Han(汉文帝,景帝), T'ai-*tsoon* of
Tdaung(唐太宗) and Ren-*tsoon* of Soong(宋仁宗), helotism and
feudalism continued to bear sway hand in hand till 1949 on the wide
expanses of the land, under the emperors, their courtiers and lords,
and the landlords. ①

It took tens of centuries to sweep away darkness and slavery
mainly in the West. The medieval age of Europe, lasting almost a
thousand years, was principally nothing but a series of orgies of
butchery and pillage, as well said by Gibbon in *The Decline and Fall*

---

① The dynasty Han is considered by perhaps most modern Chinese historians to
be a centralized rule of counties and *hsien*(中央集权郡县制), with feudalism
firmly established and slavery definitely abolished. But after the benevolent
Wen and Ching rules. in Wuh-*t'ih's* reign, for instance, there is sure proof of
the existence of slavery in reliable historical records. In *The Life of Sze-ma
Hsiang-rue*(《司马相如列传》) common to *The Chronicle*(《史记》) and *The
Han Chronicle*(《汉书》), there is the statement that "Tso Wang-sun(卓王
孙) could not deny her any more, so he apportioned to Wen-chün(文君,his
widowed daughter. who eloped with Sze-ma Hsiang-rue), a hundred waiting
men(僮百人) and a million cash(钱百万). " In *The Lives of Capitalists*(《货
殖列传》) of both these chronicles, it is said that Tso had eight hundred waiting men. What were those hundred and eight hundred men and their families
but slaves? In *The Dream of the Red-storeyed Chamber*(《红楼梦》), the well-
known novel of early Tsing by Zaur Süi-jin(曹雪芹), some of the old servants
and waiting maids openly admit they were slaves.

of the Roman Empire. In China, Confucianism had been chiefly a civilizing influence, though there were petty, hypocritical and microbian Confucians who did considerable harm. In Europe, Christianity had been such an influence too at times, but had often been an havoc in long stretches of time in the form of Catholicism. Religious wars, the inquisition and the persecution of Jews and Protestants are notoriously known in history. To come back to our ancient society, the Saung dynasty was commonly reputed to have as many as three thousand feudal vassals at the beginning, and Tsur eight hundred.

On account of the stewards killing their superior lords and sons killing their fathers to usurp their places, the feudal fabric of early Tsur fell to pieces in the Spring and Autumn and the Warring States Periods. It was only natural that the first glimpse of democratic ideas came to flash upon the minds of the slaves and abject subjects of those states where tyranny was not so high-tensioned as in the state Tsing (秦). The renowned patriarchs and a few beneficent rulers often remotely interspersed in the long past had lightened the yoke of servitude under their mild reigns. Duke Tsur and Confucius had advocated kindliness in human relations between the rulers and the ruled during early and late middle Tsur. Now, the crumbling of the feudal order bespoken by the downfall of oldtime authorities had taught the helots or people that the kings, marquises, counts and viscounts were not divine; the days of the common man would ultimately come some time later. The faithful spokesmen of their forefathers, Mencius and Chü Yuan, were already propheticly true to their thought and cause, as early as twenty-three centuries ago!

Chü Yuan was a nobility of the truest blue blood, since his ancestry was traceable to *T'ih* Kao-yang, but his heart and soul were de-

屈原诗选英译

cidedly for the people of Ts'ou and the humanity of all the other six states. His life ideal and political credo were beneficence of a sagacious sovereign assisted by a number of excellent, virtuous aids, the chief of whom was to succeed him in pushing forward his fine policies and achieve continuous concord and happiness among the people. The three *hwang* and five *t'ih*, Yao, Suen, Yü, Taung, Wen and Wuh, together with Kao Yau(皋陶), Kwan Lung-boon(关龙逢), Ih Yün(伊尹), Peng Yen(彭咸), Fuh Yüeh(傅说), Chi-tse(箕子), Pih-kan(比干), Pêh-yih(伯夷), Count Mei(梅伯), Leü Wang(吕望) and Duke Tsur(周公), extolled so highly by him in his works, were almost all the exemplars of sovereigns and their ministers upheld by Confucius and Mencius in their ethical and political teachings. Though we would not say Chü Yuan was a Confucian, there was only little difference between him and the sage's greatest disciple in their major standpoints. Highly illustrative of what he cherished of whom he admired or esteemed are the following lines in *Suffering Throes*:

> The glory and greatness of *T'ih* Yao and *T'ih* Suen
> Are due to their straight roads leading to upright ways.
>
> *ll*. 29 −30
>
> Going southward, I sail on the streams Yuan and Hsiang
> To present to divine Tsoon-hwah mine observings.
>
> *ll*. 145 −146
>
> Taung and Yü were Heaven-fearing and virtue-respecting,
> And early Tsur ruled by the Way without error,
> Raising the virtuous and intrusting the capable,

They all the good rule followed and the straight road trod.

ll. 163 −166

In "early Tsur", the tribute is paid to Wen and Wuh, as well as to Leü Wang and Duke Tsur.

Taung and Yü, austere with themselves, sought for concord;
Holding virtuous aids, they achieved harmony.

ll. 289 −290

In these two lines, the first revolutionary leader of the nation as of the world and the great savior of the race are exalted in company with their excellent aids Ih Yün and Kao Yau. (See the account of Ih Yün on *pp.* 11 −12 above and note 121 in *Notes and Comments on Suffering Throes.*)

Fuh Yüeh, who wrought at laying mud walls at Fuh-yan,
Was trusted by Wuh-t'ing when he was found by quest.
Leü Wang, a butcher hired at Yin's capital town,
Was elected to premiership by Count West;
Lord Hwan of Tsih made of Nien Ts'i a counsellor,
When he heard him a song chant while feeding his cow.

ll. 293 −298

These are instances of sagacious sovereigns seeking and finding virtuous, capable ministers. At the end of this plaint, the poet makes up his mind to put an end to his own being that is to be resounded again and again in *Lamenting on Whirlblasts*(《悲回风》):

Since none is worthy to hand fine policies with,

I will go for Peng Yen in his watery grave.

ll. 374 −375

By "fine policies" (美政), those of a virtuous sovereign's beneficent rule are generally meant, but here perhaps with specific emphasis on the state policy of United Coalition.

The beau-ideal of beneficence with an amiable and wise king as supreme ruler assisted by a circle of virtuous, capable ministers pervades all the minor works of the poet. In his earliest extant poem *Ode to the Orange*(《橘颂》), the concluding lines —

Although youthful thou dost appear.

Yet thou art fit my teacher to be;

Thy practices are like Pêh-yih's[①];

[①] There were two notables known by the names Pêh-yih(伯夷) in our early history. The first man xvas Suen's Master of Ritual Ceremonies(秩宗) mentioned in section Ⅱ of *Introduction* (see *p.* 9). The second Pêh-yih(伯夷), named here, was the elder prince of the king Ku-tso(孤竹君), a vassal state of Yin (殷). The king made his younger son Swuo-tsi(叔齐) his prince royal to succeed himself his deathbed, who begged his elder brother to take his place afier the king's death. But Pêh-yih declined to accept the position. They ran away together from their home state to Tsur. When King Wu rose in revolution against Zer Sing of Yin(殷后纣辛), the two brothers stopped his march and admonished him not to do so. Some of Chi Fa's followers wanted to kill them. But Leii Wang said that should not be done, and they were turned away. So they ceased from eating grains of Tsur and starved themselves to death. To take kingship not as a duty to the people for their benefit, but as a vested property in a family, even though the occupant had proved to be a cannibal, was certainly obstinate folly, but not wickedness in their case.

As mine image I would take thee.

declare in no uncertain language at the start his firm purpose of conducting public affairs in the best tradition. Surely, Pêh-yih is questionable in his wisdom when viewed today, but his austere purity is beyond criticism forever. It is persistence in what seems right to him that Chü Yuan vouches here. To revive the golden rules of the two *t'ih* and three kings was his prepossession. In reality, we could believe he was already resolutely decided for United Coalition against Tsing in his early or middle twenties, for Suh Tsing was by some thirty years his senior contemporary. In *Bitter Declarations* (《惜诵》), lines 7 and 8 go like this:

> Making the gods of mounts and streams to wait by,
> I ask Kao Yau to hear and pass his judgment.

Kao Yau was Lord of High Justice to Suen and Yü's chief minister. It was he who stood for genuine justice, not the socalled "legalist" Saung Yang who stole the title to perpetrate the black crimes of terroristic violence, official murder and wanton aggression. In *Drawing My Thoughts*(《抽思》), lines 33 and 34 have

> Holding the three and five as models to my king,
> I vow to look to Peng Yen for my law.

By the three and five are meant the three *hwang* and five *t'ih*, the legendary benevolent sovereigns of antiquity.

See how Yao and Suen touch the celestial blue,

With their noble great deeds exalted and sublime;

Yet envious traducers execrate them

With foul unnatural faults for muck and slime.

ll. 53 −56, *Plaint on Ying*(《哀郢》)

Both Yao and Suen did not bequeath their thrones to their sons who were wayward, but handed these to their virtuous aids. The intimation and open censure contained in these lines caused Chü Yuan's second exile from Ling-yang to Tsen(辰) and Süe(溆). In the following two lines, his kindred spirit Suen is said to keep him company in roving the fairy regions:

Bridling blue dragonets two, white dragons three,

I and Tson-hwa range the land of the fairy.

ll. 8 −9, *Over the Streams*(《涉江》)

Upholding kindness and its deeds apt,

I cherish caution and earnestness.

Tson-hwa cannot be met with today;

Who kenneth what noble law I caress?

Virtuous aids rarely met sage kings;

How could it be known why it is such?

Taung and Yü are far remote from now;

They are too far to be yearned for much.

ll. 45 −52, *Thinking of Sah*(《怀沙》)

Lo, how I made up my mind to follow Peng Yen,

My firm resolve was fixt; I have never forgot.

ll. 5 −6, *Lamenting on Whirlblasts*(《悲回风》)

The reason was that he had given his soul to the resolution; how could he forget it?

> The orphaned one moaneth his plaint, wiping his tears;
> The exiled one is gone out to return no more.
> Who can muse on these and be not stricken with pangs,
> So as to do what Peng Yen had anciently done?
>
> > *ll.* 49 −52, *ibid.*

"The orphaned one" means himself (Tsiang Ch'ih says it alludes to Hwai's death), and so too does "the exiled one", for he was at that time banished the second time by Hsiang.

> As anguishing maketh me lamentable always,
> Sinking into oblivion is my sure doom;
> Plunging over huge waves and following wind gusts,
> I would abide at Peng Yen's deep water abode.
>
> > *ll.* 67 −70, *ibid.*
>
> I pay visit to Chiêh-tse's famed spot of remains,
> And see the relics hallowed of Pêh-yih's scape days.
>
> > *ll.* 97 −98, *ibid.*

Chiêh-tse(介子) here means Chiêh Tuai(介推), a faithful follower of Marquis Wen of Ts'in. (His tragic story is accounted for above on *pp.* 24 −25.)

> It is well known that Pê-Ii had been a captive,
> And Ih Yun cooked as a humble kitchen menial.

Leü Wang was hired at a butchery in Tsau-ge,

And Nien Ts'i was singing a song feeding his cow:

If they met not their chiefs Taung and Wu, Hwan and Mo,

Is the world to know of their eminent deeds, how?

ll. 33 −38, *Pining My Past*(《惜往日》)

For Pêh-Iih Yih(百里奚), see his account on *pp.* 25 −26 above. The stories of Ih Yün(伊尹) and Leu Wang(吕望) are related above on *pp.* 11 −12 and 13 respectively. The anecdote of Nien Ts'i, 宁戚, is given in note 126 in *Notes and Comments* on *Suffering Throes*.

Chü Yuan's ideal of beneficence was early set forth by Confucius, we can candidly say, in the chapter *The Drift of Rites*(《礼运篇》) of *Notes of Rites*(《礼记》), though, as a poet, he does not lay so much emphasis on rites in his poetry as the sage and his great exponent in their ethical teachings; yet they stood on common ground as statesmen inherently. When the Great Way holds sway, there would be Universal Union: all endeavours, strivings and activities are for the public, the people, not for a dozen or half a dozen autocrats and their ministers, retainers and parasites. Therein, one can sense the earliest palpitation of democracy and socialism, the humane, fair-minded and honourable live-and-let-live kind of commonwealth. With beneficence as direct object and Universal Union as ultimate end, electing the virtuous and the capable to proper offices is naturally the incipient program. While there were in reality, during the Spring and Autumn Period, twelve (or thirteen) major states and many minor ones, and during the Warring States, seven major and several minor states, in addition to the shadowy supreme kingdom of Tsur, it was the fond aim of these visionary statesmen that all these states should be unified into one by the peaceful means of troth (veracity) and concord. It was the common wish of the times, ever since the enfeebling of the house of Tsur during King Yih's (周夷王) reign, that there should be a strong supreme ruling power to which all its vassal states were to pay fealty. King Hsuan (宣王), for forty-six years, fulfilled this popular will to some extent with his iron hand. But from the Spring and Autumn Period down to the Warring States, internecine warfare and disintegration of the feudal order and social turmoil became worse and worse every day. The public cry for grand unification was surging in the epoch atmosphere. The two main streams of thought regarding this political union, first voiced and practised by Confucius, with troth and concord as his watchwords, and then, about a century and a half later, claimed and pursued with deception, treachery, terrorism and aggression as the only right means in Tsing by Wei (alias Saung) Yang, are strongly antithetic in nature. Confucius travelled through seventy odd states for fourteen years to find a pivotal base of his nascent activities, but in vain. Mencius, living about two centuries later and having fully learnt his master's lesson of disillusion, also visited a number of kingdoms in high spirits, when the political, social and cultural arena had become much more chaotic than during Confucius' time, but his efforts ended likewise in failure. They both avoided Tsing (秦) in the west, for in Confucius' days, it was still too barbaric, and during Mencius' active years, it was already turned into a fortress of hegemonism. In Chü Yuan's time, itinerant politicians frequented all the royal courts with the exception of that of feeble Tsur perhaps, each trying to serve his chosen master in overcoming his rivals. In *Lee Sao*, we see the sibyls Ling-fung and Yen, speaking for their divinations, both urge the poet to leave his native state quickly and assure him "your two parties fair would finally unite" abroad. But he was dazed and failed to take action; or rather, after a brief circuit in the western sky, he stopped short and came down fatally to his old homeland of misery. The plain reason of his procrastination and inertness was his love of the native state and its people. As a base of his eminent policies, Tsing was decidedly ruled out. Weighing all the pros and cons, his decision was inalterably fixed on Ts'ou. Since he was a prominent member of its royal house, Ts'ou was best suited to his purpose because of its geographical size and adjacency to Hang(韩), Gwei(魏) and Luh(鲁) and of his personal understanding and cordial connections with Tsih and its court. Next to Ts'ou in size among the six states, Tsih was rich and powerful withal on account of its sea salt and fishery resources. Had Chü Yuan left Ts'ou for Tsih, a favourable personal career would certainly fall to his lot, but he would drop pitifully into no avail in trying to wield his influence in shaping a beneficent rule. Historians and scholars have said that he could not very well leave his native state, for he was a member of the royal house. Both Hang and Gwei were too small and strategically too vulnerable; Yen and Ts'ao were out of the way far up in the north, where he was not well known; and furthermore, conditions in Tsih were not very much better than in Ts'ou, as Suh Tsing was assasinated there and the criminal intrigue had not been officially probed or publicly exposed.

With beneficent rule as his ideal polity and Yao and Suen as peaks of civil expectations, Chü Yuan stood logically for succession of regal power by virtuous aids of excellent kings, instead of unconditionally by inheritance in a family. His views on this subject, though not expressly made in his poetry, is yet clearly insinuated in the phrases "chariots ten thousand" and "my chariots of state a full thousand" in *Distant Wanderings* and *Suffering Throes* respectively and in lines 53－56 of *Plaint on Ying*(《哀郢》), as discussed above in § 11, § 12 and § 16 in section Ⅷ *Chü Yuan and His Works*. Only the virtuous should govern, for the benefit of the governed, he opines in lines 167－170 of *Suffering Throes*:

> Heaven high above doth not incline with preference,
> Aiding but beneficence to rule on the earth;
> Only the sagacious, with their deeds excellent,
> Were empowered to reign by their intrinsic worth.

His devotion to Hwai was due to the latter's

> Keeping precedent usance to lighten the people,
> I clarified obscurities of statutes blear.
> The state was rich and strong then, laws were well set up,
> Affairs in trustworthy hands, the crown free from care.
>
> *ll.* 3－6, *Pining My Past Days*(《惜往日》)

At the beginning of his Left-counsellorship, as well as to his own

> Fond wish that a corus might fairness attain.
>
> *l.* 32, *Drawing My Thoughts*(《抽思》)

But when conditions had proved utterly hopeless, he did not hesitate to call Hwai "the duped king" (雍君). His moral code in passing judgment on a rule and practising statecraft on the part of its ministers is bracingly congruous and heartfelt:

> In life, one taketh delight in what one loveth;
> I alone crave virtue for its own sake unbent.
>
> *ll.* 127 −128, *Suffering Throes*(《离骚》)
>
> Looking to the past and pondering on results,
> I have examined the people's welfare ultimate.
> Of the depraved, who should be intrusted to rule?
> Of the wicked, who should bedeck a goodly, state?
>
> *ll.* 171 −174, *ibid.*

From these are reflected his deeply affecting integrity and candour. And he is not the least bashful in speaking to Tsoon-hwah of the well-graced radiance of righteousness that crowns his heart:

> Kneeling, I spread them out to free my mind to Suen,
> And flushed, fee anon this inner glory of mine.
>
> *ll.* 183 −184, *ibid.*

The sibyl Yen encourages him to seek his fair maid abroad in person:

> If both sides truly virtue love for its own sake,
> What need of the mediacy could there e'er be?
>
> *ll.* 291 −292, *ibid.*

In fact, the whole elegiac piece of *Lee Sao* is a sad song of his love of goodness and virtues and of how and why he suffers throes because of it. Readers are referred to the close analysis of the motive of the poem by Tsiang Ch'ih at the beginning of the notes on *Lee Sao* in *Notes and Comments*.

Chü Yuan's moral code of veracity and uprightness, fairness and sincerity, in holding himself and conducting public affairs, showing his intrinsic love of virtues and goodness, is no less exemplified in his lesser works.

> To be independent, unmoved,
> Is it delighting or the reverse?
> Steadfast and withal immovable,
> Immeasurably unconstrained,
> Awaking the world and unbound,
> Free and easy, but self-contained,
> Thou holdest thy heart with staid prudence,
> Without falling into default,
> Keeping to thy virtues public
> Which peer earth's expanse and heaven's vault.
>> *ll.* 19 −28, *Ode to the Orange*(《橘颂》)

How pithily true do these lines ring:

> Goodness doth not come unto one from without;
> Repute fair could not be upholstered to daub.
>> *ll.* 37 −38, *Drawing My Thoughts*(《抽思》)
> How earnestly straightforward my soul is!
> But other people's hearts do all from mine differ.
>>> *ll.* 63 −64, *ibid.*
> Fragrant and lustrous things are mixed herein;

Radiant, sweet florescence issues hence.

Luxuriantly is the scent far spread;

Having suffused within, it flushes forth.

When faith and quality are veracious,

Though in station shadowed, one bears renown aglow.

 ll. 47 −52, *Musing on the Beauteous One*(《思美人》)

Let mine heart be but upright and of honour;

What is the harm though I be exiled far and long?

  ll. 25 −26, *Over the Streams*(《涉江》)

To swerve from one's pristine wholesome faith

Is scoffed by the upright without haw.

Keeping to the good first plan and rules,

I conserve precedent codes of worth.

To hold integrity in esteem

Is priced by the sagacious with dearth.

  ll. 13 −18, *Thinking of Sah*(《怀沙》)

With mine intrinsic core and feelings

I cannot find in any one my peer.

Pêh-Ioh① was departed long ago;

How is the steed to show its powers sheer?

---

① Pêh-loh(伯乐), originally the name of a star, said to be the driver of heaven's horses, was the title given to Sun Yang(孙阳), a subject of Viscount Mo of Tsing(秦穆公), noted for his discretion of excellent coursers. The story is told of him that once he passed a craggy ridge of Mount Neü(虞山), coming across a draught horse of a salt-cart. At the sight of him, the nag snorted and neighed. Pêh-loh alighted from his cabriolet to weep before the maltreated courser, which lowered its head to snort and raised its neck to whinny aloud heavenward. Here, the courser alludes to the poet himself and Pêh-loh to Taung and Yü.

Introduction

Men's lives are each by fortune ordained;

They are all severally destined.

With heart fixed and intents wide focussed,

What do I fear, for what am chagrined?

ll. 65 −72, *ibid.*

From his political ideal of beneficence and moral aspirations for humanity, justice, veracity and righteousness, we can see Chü Yuan must have learnt profoundly from the north in Tsih and Luh(齐,鲁), the homeland of Leü Wang, Duke Tsur, Confucius and his disciples. Leü is twice named in the above quotations. The duke is explicitly mentioned as "uncle Tan"(叔旦) and also alluded to at the end of *Sky-vaulting Queries*(《天问》). There is an almost certain allusion to Confucius and his grandson Tse-sze(子思) in lines 143 −144 of *Lee Sao*,

I always tread the middle course of sages of yore;

Alas! at this, mine heart is so choked with anger.

with regard to Tse-sze's teaching in *The Medium*(《中庸》) expounding the sage's exaltation of the golden mean. Confucius was, however, not always consistent in practice with his eulogy of moderation; yet all honours and respects to him for his breach of his own avouching. A thorough-going orthodox Confucian — in my opinion, rather a petty or microbian one, a pusillanimous doctrinaire — would not get angry or bitterly sorrowful no matter how; he would stick to his rule of temperance at all costs. But our poet, being what he was and having met with what befell him, was definitely full of wrath and agony in his life and poetry. To be sure, Confucius was in ire when he had Sao-tsen Mao(少正卯) executed for his anarchical agitations and ringleader activities. Above all, he would not have written *The Spring and Autumn Annals* to register his utter contempt and horror of sons killing their fathers and subordinate lieges killing their lords superior, if he had not hated their heinous crimes to the extreme. And Mencius bluntly said, "Once King Wen grew wroth, the world was settled in peace!"(文王一怒而天下平) The clear-cut distinction between just revolution and disorderly rebellion in his apt reply to King Hsuan of Tsih's(齐宣王) question confusing the two (*vide* the account of Meng Kuh in section V *The Warring States Period*, *pp.* 49 − 50 above) shows what he praises and what he condemns with no nonsense. So, neither of them was strictly dispassionate in the matter of righteous indignation, as conventional Confucians want to have intellectuals hold themselves in their life and poetry. *The Classic of Poetry* was lauded by Confucius because its poems are "all fair and sweet in thoughts"(思无邪) and its ballads headed by "'Kwan Kwan' the ospreys sing by twain" are sometimes "joyous but not wanton"(乐而不淫) and at times "sad but not bitterly sorrowful"(哀而不伤). The greater part of Chü Yuan's poetry, we find, is now and then laden with anger and often vehement in throes. That is the moral tone of his works, as markedly distinguished from the standard of traditional or professional Confucians.

The other characteristic of the poet's thought is his attitude toward supernatural beings. Confucius is said "to mum on monstrosities, brute forces, rebellious violence and supernatural powers"(子不语怪、力、乱、神), for these are not conducive to cultivating the people, and besides, he could not stand them. His disciple Chi-Iuh

（季路）once asked him "how one should serve gods and spirits"（问事鬼神）; he said, "being not yet able to serve men, how is one to serve spirits?"（未能事人,焉能事鬼?）He is again asked "how one should serve the dead"（敢问事死）; his answer was, "when the living is not yet fully known, how could one know the dead?"（未知生,焉知死?）As a good, truthful philosopher, he did not talk of things he had no knowledge of. His silence on gods and spirits proceeded from his attitude towards knowledge. "If thou knowest a thing, thou dost know it; if thou knowest it not, thou dost not know it; that is knowing"（知之为知之,不知为不知,是知也）— this was how he taught his disciple Tse-luh（子路）. As a poet, Chü Yuan takes for granted a large number of supernatural agents in *Suffering Throes*, *Nine Hymns*, *Distant Wanderings*, *Summoning the Soul*, *Great Summoning* and the *Sylva of Nine Pieces*, but questions their origins, causes, outcomes and their hows and whys in *Sky-vaulting Queries*. He proves himself to be a pantheist and an inquirer of a great many natural phenomena and legendary and historical events at the same time. *Nine Hymns* is a nosegay of sacred songs on sundry deities and spirits. In lines 92 −93 of *Distant Wanderings*, he speaks of seeing Tsin Sze（旬始）, the supreme God of Heaven:

> Coming through the azure to twice bright Heaven
> And entering His Supremacy's palace,
> I hold an interview with Tsin-sze the God,
> Then take a round about the sacred place.

But this God seems to be not almighty in *Suffering Throes*:

I call to Heaven's Porter to open his portal;

He leaneth on the Gates, staring me fore the sill.

ll. 209 −210

for He does not even know His gate-keeper refusing to admit the poet without His knowledge or sanction, nor could He prevent the misdeed beforehand. Yet in *ll.* 167 − 168, it is assured that "Heaven high above doth not incline with preference, Aiding but beneficence to rule on the earth. " There, Heaven appears more like the inflexible physico-moral law, the *Dao*(道) or Way, governing the world than a personal deity bearing resemblance to Zeus or Jehovah. In *Summoning the Soul*, Heaven is described as having nine arched passes kept by tigers and leopards and a nine-headed porter with eyes like those of hyenas and wolves, who could uproot nine thousand trees at a time, and the god of the nether world is said to be a man-devouring devil, with three eyes, sharp horns on his tigerish head, a bull-like body, nine tails and bloody claws. To be brief, the supernatural world in Chü Yuan's poetry is derived partially from mythological legendary lores and partially from his own prolific imaginations which harmonizes whatever incongruities or conflicts that may arise out of them. His gods, goddesses, King of Clouds, Lord of Thunder, fauns and spirits, etc., on the whole contrary to Confucius' agnostic silence on such subjects, serve his purpose well as a poet's for giving to "airy nothings a local habitation and a name".

There have been rife disputes about whether or not Confucius actually "expunged" the mass of well over three thousand poems into three hundred odd, as affirmed by Sze-ma Tsien in *The Chronicle*, to form *The Classic of Poetry*. More probably, the Grand Curator of

History is mistaken than he is right in that statement. But it is certain the existence of a large body of poems, three hundred odd at least, mostly collected from the central Tsur court and domain and its vassal states commenced only with early Tsur, with a handful of odes taken from Saung-Yin. About the origins of these poems, Kung Yin-dah（孔颖达）of Tdaung（唐）and Ts'eng Tsiao（郑樵）and Tsu Hsih （朱熹）of Soong（宋）, among the scores of their students, attribute the first twenty-five pieces of Tsur-Nan（周南）and Sao-Nan（召南）, for instance, to as early as King Wen's（文王）time, while Tsuai Tsê （崔述）of Tsing（清）contends that they were definitely gathered during Kings Tseng's and Kong's（成王，康王）reigns and even much later. About the lowest time limit of the poems, it is commonly agreed on that when poems ceased to be collected, Confucius started his writing of *The Spring and Autumn Annals*.

According to *The Tsur Officials*（《周官》）[①], the instruction of the six properties of the collected poems（六诗）in the Grand Colleges of the King（太学）began not long after their gathering. These are afterwards called the six elements of *Poetry*（"诗"之六义）: viz., *feng*, *ya*, *zoon*, *fuh*, *p'ih* and *shin*（风，雅，颂，赋，比，兴）. "*Feng* is meant by folk songs or ballads from village and hamlet lanes of the states. Young men and women sang their strains severally to express their feelings for each other, whose words are ardently loving but not lascivious, sad sometimes but not bitterly sorrowful, often sweet and touching, gentle and not barefaced. Those who spake their say, for

---

① It was written by some anonymous historian to record the early Tsur official system, probably during the Warring States Period. It was called by Liu Shin（刘歆）of late West Han *The Tsur Rites*（《周礼》）and thereafter known by this title.

there were complaints and censures in plenty, were not blameworthy, but their hearers should take warning therefrom. *Ya* sings of things at the courts of the king and his vassals, being elevated poems of courtiers and lords. Words are bandied with admonishment and exhortation, grieving affections of loyalty and filial piety, aims of offering good and preventing mischief, earnestly presented and plainly spoken to make the listeners hear with apprehension. *Zoon* are the odes composed for sacrificial offering in the ancestral temples of kings and their vassals, to pay tribute to and impress deities and departed spirits. They extol consummate virtues, relate exploits and express devotional and reverential thoughts. Their words are harmonious and grand in diction, their meanings broad yet compact, being capable of making people awestruck and meditative. *Fuh* is the spreading out of the event and the description of it. *P'ih* compares one thing to another and *shin* sings of it with sentiments. *P'ih* serves as comparison (i. e., metaphor, simile, metonymy), while *shin* conveys emotional resonance. The former, though closely fitted in sense to what is compared, is yet rather shallow; the latter, broad but full of meanings. In short, *feng*, *ya* and *zoon* are types of poetry; *fuh*, *p'ih* and *shin* are their applications. " These six types or elements of *Poetry* defined by scholars from Han down to our days diverge considerably; the above close delineation appears to be most appropriate in describing their nature.

The subject matter of these poems could be generally classified into six orders: the family, the court, political matters, military events, customs and folklore, and miscellaneous. To reiterate what has been said before, the *feng* poems are all sorts of folk love songs and popular lyrical strains on a variety of subjects. The *ya* poems are commonly political in substance, in which are sung, for instance, the origins of the Tsur house — Chiang Yuan(姜嫄) and her son Huer Ji (后稷, *vide* section Ⅱ *Three "Hwang", Five "T'ih" and Three Kings* above, *p.* 12), K'ung Liu (公刘, Ji's great grandson) and Dan-wuh(古公亶父, King Wen's grandfather) — and reproved Kings Lih and You, the black sheep of Tsur's rulers, for their misdemeanours. The *zoon* poems are odes about Kings Wen, Wuh, Tseng and Kong of Tsur, Taung and Wuh-ting of Saung-Yin and God of Heaven. Being the primeval outbursts of the nation's utterances, these ballads, lyrics and odes are as a rule gentle in tone, soft in emotions and simple in rhythm. Terse and pithy in expression, the pieces are on the whole short in compass. It is said by most scholars that they were all matched with accompanying airs in their own time; only their melodic counterparts were destroyed, lost and forgotten in war and fire. In *Mê-tse*(《墨子》), it is attested that all the poems were chanted, sung, set to music and matched with dances.

With *The Classic of Poetry* as the starting point of divergence, Chü Yuan's works form a supereminent development. While the anonymous strains of *Sze-ching* are in the main mild and urbane in tune, the effulgent outpourings of our poet are principally intense and passionate in temper. In regard to the blandness of these poems headed by the two *Nan*(二南), Confucius has highly recommended their cultural influence thus: "*Poetry* could be studied for the benefit of learning by comparison, for seeing the thriving or decline of a state in its folklore and customs, for helping one another to live virtuous gregarious lives severally and for complaining of and criticizing the policies of a state. It could adapt one to serve well one's parents at home and one's sovereign abroad and, besides, help one to acquire a wide knowledge of the names of birds, beasts, herbs and trees."(诗可以

兴,可以观,可以群,可以怨,迩之事父,远之事君;多识于鸟兽草木之名。)[1] But Chü Yuan has made a superb advance over and above that: he has shown in his poetry what he, as a poet of the first magnitude, a profound thinker and a valiant martyr, has heroicly done, despite of failure and his personal defeat, to forward the cause of humanity and justice and fight against the dark fascistic power of Tsing （秦） and its appendages — Hwai and Hsiang's stupidities and the corruption of their courtiers. Chü Yuan stood up against them by taking valiant actions in his lifetime, and continues to declare his radiant faith and denounce them amuck to posterity in his poetry. So first and foremost of all is this righteous cause or motive of his flaming poetry.

Next but not second in splendour is the glorious personality of the poet: he is not an incognito like the anonymous singers of *Poetry* or a sheer disaffected courtier, but, he declares at the beginning of his career as a poet and statesman,

> Thou holdest thy heart with prudence stead,
> Without e'er falling into default;
> Keeping close to thy virtues public
> Which peer earth's expanse and heaven's vault.
>
> *ll.* 25 −28, *Ode to the Orange*(《橘颂》)

He paid out his life in putting his words into practice. There was no retreat, no trepidation. "Poetry speaketh of one's highest intents; songs chant these speakings; tunes cling to such chantings; melody accordeth with the tunes"(诗言志,歌永言,声依永,律和声), so

---

[1] This quotation from *The Analects*(《论语》) of Confucius is rendered according to the *Commentaries*(《集解》) of Kung An-kuo(孔安国) of West Han and Ts'eng Yüen(郑玄) of East Han, collected by Ho Ien(何晏).

Introduction

quoth *The Canon of Suen* of *The Classic of History*(《书·舜典》)①.

_____

① According to Kung An-kuo(孔安国) of West Han and Kung Yin-dah(孔颖达) of Tdaung, the title of the tome known as *Saung-suh*(《尚书》) means a bundle of strips "handed down from ancient times". The book is also called *The Onssic of History*(《书经》) or simply *History*(《书》) after Confucius. as evidenced by what he once said to Lao-tse. "I have worked on the *Six Classics of Poetry*, *History*, *Rites. Music. Mutability* and *Spring and Autumn*, I think myself, long enough." which is memorized in the chapter *On Heavenly Destiny* of *Tsaung-tse* (《庄子·天运篇》). The volume consists of imperial rescripts, royal edicts, official directions. exhortatory epistles, etc. in the name of "canons, projects. precepts, enjoinments, injunctions and mandates"(典,谟,训,诰,誓,命), one hundred pieces in all, from Yao and Suen to Viscount Mo of Tsing, compiled and edited by Confucius with a preface by him. The book, that is, all the obtainable copies of it, bumt by Ying Tsen at the proposal of his varlet Lih Sze, was eradicated out of existence in 213 B. C. However, a Tsing doctor(秦博士) named Fwu Sun(伏胜) managed to have hidden a copy of it in his walls before the devastating fire. Then ravaging war broke out that was to dislimn Tsing and put an end to the Ts'ou(楚) of Shiang Yeü(项羽), and the greater part of Fwu's hoarded treasure was scattered and lost. When the dynasty Han had settled down on its own over twenty years later, Fwu Sun found to his distraction only twenty-nine pieces or chapters remaining intact. In the reign of Wen-*t'ih* (文帝), the scholar courtier Zau Ts'ou(晁错) was ordered to visit Fwu, who, already ninety odd years old and incapable of walking, could not leave his home, to instruct him to have the text which had been written in the not easily legible *Zür* script(籀文), rendered into the then current dih hand(隶书). But the piece *The Canon of Suen*(《舜典》), said to have been written by Suen himself, was missing in Fwu Sun's twenty-nine chapters of the *dih* hand text《今文尚书》. Then, some eighty years later, late in Wuh-*t'ih's* reign, a quantity of the ancient polliwig script(蝌蚪文)《古文尚书》 text strips was discovered in the walls of Confucius'lifetime residence at Chü-ver(曲阜). The scholar Kung An-kuo(孔安国), the twelfth generation grandson of Confucius, was entrusted by Wuh-*t'ih* to render the indecipherable text into the current *dih* hand and write a *Commentary*(《书传》) on the find. Among the restored texts of the book, Kung found there were sixteen extra chapters over and above the twenty-nine of Fwu Sun, and *The Canon of Suen*(《舜典》) was one of them. Unfortunately, the uproar of the witchery(巫蛊) incident raged furiously at the court very soon after, and all the polliwig script text strips, together with Kung An-kuo's rendering and *Commentary*, were lost. So, the recovered sixteen chapters plunged once more into oblivion. Over two centuries later, in East Ts'in(东晋), a scholar courtier Mei Tser(梅赜) said he had discovered Kung's *Commentary* and offered it to his emperor Yuan-*t'ih*(东晋元帝). More than three centuries later, in the reign of Tai-*tsoon* of Tdaung(唐太宗), the scholar Kung Yin-dah(孔颖达) was commissioned by the emperor to write *The Critique of the Five Oassics* (《五经正义》), in which Mei Tser's *Kung Commentary* forms a constituent part of *Saung-suh's* text. During the centuries since then, Mei's *Kung Commentary* was suspected to be a surreptitious work by students of South Soong(南宋) and Ming(明), and at last definitely proved by the Tsing(清) scholar Yen Ruo-chü (阎若璩) to be a fraudulent fabrication. But ever since Kung Yin-dah of Tdaung wrote *The Critique of "Saung-suh"*(《尚书正义》), adopting the text of Mei, the sixteen chapters, including *The Canon of Suen*, have been accepted as an indispensable substitute for the pieces recovered and second time lost.

Chü Yuan has uttered his highest intents indeed in his fiery poetry and has truly matched himself with heaven and earth. He was conscious of his self-appointed duty and brave deeds all the time, for although he entertains the highest esteem and admiration for the ancient benefi-cent *hwang*, *t'ih* and kings and their eminent ministers in history, he always calls them by their names in his poetry, as if they were his intimate friends. Poverty, exile, "pickling and mincing", death itself — nothing could daunt him or make him cower. In short, the mission and the personality of the poet form the two prime prerequi-sites of immortality in his poetry; fine frenzy and masterly verbal art are the two necessary conditions to follow in natural course.

Confucius' encomium "of moderation as perhaps the supreme one of all virtues since it was no longer in sway for long stretches of time"(中庸之为德也,其至矣乎? 民鲜久矣) was pronounced by him to mean that the mild, benevolent rules of the illustrious ancient sovereigns were so far away in the past, the world around him had become tumultuous so long and was getting worse every day, so that it was high time that kings, marquises, counts, viscounts and their ministers and reeves should restrain themselves a little to restore to some extent the salutary order of early Tsur. *The Classic of Poetry* was commended by him for its bland, educative functions in the same spirit. The fascistdom of Tsing laid foundation to by Viscount Shao and Wei Yang was not yet begun at his time. In one word, his lauda-tion in either case was based upon his vain hope that the world might be restored to humanity and justice by the common resort of all rulers and their lords inferior to the golden mean. The doctrine of the medi-um formulated by Tse-sze(子思) on the basis of the sage's panegyric of moderation ultimately formed a component part of Confucianism which truly produced wholesome effects upon certain monarchs of posterity. But in the last century or so of the Spring and Autumn epoch and throughout the Warring States Period, the dynasty Tsing and incipient Han till Emperors Wen and Chin (汉文帝, 景帝), both Confucius' high praise and Tse-sze's principle proved to be flat failures. Chü Yuan, seeing the world's salvation in the practice of the ideal of Universal Union eye to eye with Confucius, departs widely from the mild and sedate manners of _The Classic of Poetry_. That is because he had been the stricken victim of Tsing's hegemony permeation of Ts'ou through Tsang Yih's (张仪) intrigues in espionage diplomacy, though he had not fully realized his own situation. On this account, intense and passionate in substance, his works have become in the main inflamed with passion and throbbing ryhthm and vocalized with a superior resonant quality, when compared to the primitive, rather archaic movements and forms of the pieces in _The Classic of Poetry_.

His earliest extant poem _Ode on the Orange_, in manner and form still in the tradition of _Poetry_, is chastely serene and resolute in feelings, but already sounds a quite different note from the latter's mildness and urbanity. It reveals in no uncertain language the inviolable personality of the poet that is absent from the early Tsur anthology. The note of individuality rings more conspicuously by gradation in _Bitter Declarations_ (《惜诵》), _Drawing My Thoughts_ (《抽思》) and _Musing on the Beauteous One_ (《思美人》). Their lyrical timbre becomes finer and more chastened as the descriptive, _fuh_ qualities are played upon by his acute personal feelings of sad pensiveness.

In _Divining to Know Where I Should Stay_ (《卜居》), there are certainly thunderbolts of wrath and whippings of lightning zigzags of contempt in these lines toward the close of the poem:

> Confused and muddled, the world is topsy-turvy:
> Thirty thousand catties are regarded light,
> A wing of the cicada is deemed weighty;
> The golden bell is smashed quite and scrapped,
> While the earthen *phu* doth roar like thunder-claps;
> The man of virtue is roundly bullied down;
> The calumniator is donning the crown!

ll. 42 −48

The note of Chü Yuan's fulmination resounds unmistakably here. It is inconceivable that either one of his two pupils Soong Yü (宋玉), timid in temperament, or Chin Tsa (景差), more so, or any one else could have written these lines.

Then, in *Distant Wanderings* (《远游》), the poet composes a poetical fantasia of rising aloft and journeying in the sky to seek the fairy prince Jao (仙人王子乔) first and hear from him of the Supreme Vis so as to pursue it, and after that,

> Drinking the elixir of Jetting Vale,
> I keep in my bosom nonpareil gems twain.
> The lustre pink of the gems fuseth my face;
> My spirit beginneth to be pure amain.
> My stuff molten becometh soft and frail;
> My soul, refined and blown, profound and vibrant.

ll. 75 −80

Thus, he is transformed into an ethereal being to continue his aerial excursion far up in the empyrean.

> By chariots ten thousand, fore, aft, abreast,
> Preceded, followed, flanked on the way.
> I drive eight dragons that speed winding about,
> With cloud ensigns waving alongside, that fly,
> And the he-rainbow decked with feather pennants
> Flourishing its variegated glory.
> Holding the comet as my streaming banner,
> I raise for waving pennant the stem of the Dipper.
> I rove in the currents of the shaken mist,
> Cleaving the pearly waves to range high and low.
>
> *ll.* 95 −100,115 −118

And finally, he has reached such a rarefied or spiritual state:

> Below, it is bottomless and sans the ground;
> Above, it is far-away and sans the sky;
> To look out, it is fleetingly without sight;
> To listen, it is emptily without sound.
>
> *ll.* 167 −170

"Arriving at utter purity" (至清) and coming to "inhere the very next neighbouring to Primitive Prime" (太初) in the end. An escape from spiritual duress and emotional repression, a far-removed flight into a transfiguring vacuity, the work serves as an æsthetic balsamic for the poet's frustrated ideal and scorched personality. This it a remarkable leaping forward from the nascent clarity and firmness of *Ode on the Orange*, a brave new world altogether different from the sedate, pedestrian matter and manner of *The Classic of Poetry*. The poet's stage of apprenticeship is hereby thrown a long way back into the past.

He is now all ready for plunging into the intellectual depth, imaginative breadth and massiveness of passion of his great life work. His political vision of beneficence, his prepossession with humanity and justice, his noble descent, excellent education and perfect breeding, the mean vilification and throttling expulsion from Ying-*t'uh* inflicted on him, and above all, his indomitable will, resplendent personality and peerless genius as a poet, all fuse together to mould this resounding masterpiece *Lee Sao*. It is without a match in Chinese poetry, nor could one, I am sure, find an ode or a lyrical poem in the world's poetry to equal its greatness of soul, intensity in thought, magnificent flight of imagination and mighty emotional power. The meditation and devoted pursuit of beneficent rule for the good of the people, the profound sorrow and afflicting throes undergone and reprehended, the wealth of historical instances named and alluded to, the imaginative sweep encompassed and detailed imageries pictured, the beauty of symbolism inherent in the fair flowers, aromatic herbs and auspicious birds, the splendour of diction animated with ballad qualities and the richness of vocabulary seasoned with dialectic words of Ts'ou, and last but not the least, the elastic metrical form employed and the rhythmical resonance ensuing: all these have whirled together their incandescent flames to contribute to the conflagrant pillar of fire that *Suffering Throes* is. True to its title, the ode's texture becomes a labyrinth of grieving objects, names, thoughts and associations, so that its 375 lines seem to be of inordinate length, with intricate curves, windings and inmost recesses, because of its high tension. The effect of profound sorrow and afflicting throes thus produced under contemplation cannot but revert to the subject of beneficence and its catastrophe in Ts'ou and the Tsur world. Here, therefore, as modern readers, we should sense the full significance of this greatest ode ever written by man for mankind of all time.

In *Nine Hymns*, written during his expulsion at Han-pei in a mood of pensive solitude after the purgation of great sorrow and agony in *Suffering Throes*, the motive is uniquely idyllic and quivering with enchantment. Our poet is now a perfect master of the descriptive lyric in these flawless sacrificial songs of piping and singing qualities, in which he is so congenial with the gods, goddesses and spirits addressed to. The deities and spirits are so lofty or commanding, yet so elusive, so sprightly and betwitching, so evanescent. His bearings toward them are reverential and solemn, or adoring and full of greetings. In these holy strains are pictured druidical priests in ritual apparels, singing words of homage and praise to the celebrated divinities with rattles of drums, the ringing and tinkling of bells, flutings and pipings, strikings on tabours and tabourines, pluckings on the cithara and zithern, clinking of cymbals, blowing of pandean pipes and mallet beats on gongs. An assortment of fragrant flowers and odorous herbs is used to garnish the weird rituals; incense of aloes and sandalwood is burnt; pearls, precious gems — rubies, sapphires, topazes, turquoises, garnets and emeralds — and jades are used to decorate the divine apparitions and enrich the ceremonial festivities. The superhuman presences appear in irradiant glory and then vanish all of a sudden unexpectedly, on chariots drawn by dragons or on barges on the

Doong-ding Lake.

About *Sky-vaulting Queries*(《天问》) the strangest poem ever written by poets, Wang Fuh-tse（王夫之）of Tsing（清）has well said, in his *Common Explications of Ts'ou "Tze"*(《楚辞通释》), that it is not just a work composed by the poet "to give vent to his distemper and wrath and spend his sorrowful thoughts", as assumed by Wang Yi(王逸) of Han. Although there seems to be a welter of events questioned, the things queried range from heaven, earth, mountains and rivers, to human affairs, of which those of remote ancient times are named first and finally Tsou's ancesters are spoken of. There is pertinent order in the poem. Clearly the subject is constructed by the poet himself. To say that the queries were scribbled on the walls is therefore not correct. Wang Yi says, the title does not say *Questioning Heaven*（问天）, but *Heaven's Questions*（天问）, because heaven so high above cannot be questioned: this is also a mistaken notion. Chü Yuan thinks that nature changes and human affairs prosper or droop, all because Heaven's just law determines them. So, he names the inscrutable but inflexible instances decreed by Heaven to question the foolhardy self-sufficient kings and thoughtless ministers. In this sense, this poem should be entitled *Heaven's Questions*, not *Questioning Heaven*. Although words said in the poem are extensive in scope, the quintessence consists in this: to be of the Way would thrive, to outlaw it would perish. Aggression and violence, repulse of exhortation and remonstrance, indulgence in lust and profligacy, distrust of the virtuous and credit in villainy — these afford crucial tests to decline or prosperity, extinction or durance. Chü Yuan's caution and expostulation to the king of Ts'ou have done their utmost. He urges his sovereign to interrogate the ancient instances in order to inquire his own doings, to follow in the footsteps of the Three Kings and Five Princes to do their beauteous and valorous deeds, and avoid the forewarning pitfalls of Ghi, Zer, Lih and You. Basing upon the inceptive and fructifying hinge and spring of things, Chü Yuan has done what is humanly possible in his relation with his liege and offered what is of practicable adoption. The extremity of counsel and caution is reached here in this poem.

Taking this explication as the veritable one, the title *Sky-vaulting Queries* in translation conveys the sense that Heaven or the sky predominates all spiritually, morally and physically as it arches over all existence, and the queries are questions of the hows and whys. There are certain obscure passages in the poem still not yet clarified by its students. Recently, some fifty years ago, Wang Ko-wei(王国维) in his *Collected Works*(《观堂集林》) has unravelled some intricate difficulties in the blank history of Saung-Yin with his studies in divining scripts carved on emyd shells and ox bones unearthed from the Yin Remains at An-yang(安阳小屯殷墟甲骨卜辞), by casting light on the names 该,季 and 恒. Written probably after *Nine Hymns*, the poem, principally intellectual instead of being imbued with sentiments, begins with questions about cosmogony, goes on to the physical structure of sky and its relation with earth, the sun, moon and stars, mythology and legends, mountains and rivers, historical tales and records, lives of illustrious sovereigns and their ministers, notorious tyrants and villains, finally to questions about Ts'ou affecting the poet himself. The lines, often in quatrains and couplets, are a medley of dimetric and trimetric periods; each foot is dissyllabic or trisyllabic in structure.

The two pieces of *Summoning*, although mainly reverting in metrical form to the four-charactered line of *The Classic of Poetry*, are in temper, subject matter and diction a great departure from the chaste purity of *Ode on the Orange*. The descriptive, *fuh* quality pervades their texture. Anciently, when a person was dead, it is said in *The Drift of Rites* of *Notes of Rites*(《礼记·礼运》), some one would be sent up aloft the housetop, with the upper garment of the departed to face northward and halloo in a long-drawn voice his or her name thrice, waving the clothe meanwhile, "So-and-so, come back to thyself!" Then the crier would go down and cover the corpse with the dress. If the dead one did not come to, funeral rites would be performed. Such were the measures to be taken, according to what is meant by "Long halloo, So-and-so, recover"(皋,某,复) as recorded in *Notes of Rites* some twenty-five centuries ago. Of course, this is sheer superstitious nonsense to us moderns. But the original purpose of this customary practice in ancient primitive times was, besides trying to evocate and revive the dead one, basically motivated by the love of his or her family. Now, these two pieces of *Summoning* were written by Chü Yuan supposedly to be read aloud after the prolonged hallooing. *Great Summoning*(《大招》), the evocator of which is the poet himself, warns his master's soul of the fearful dangers of the distant expanses of the four points of the compass first, and then goes on to urge it to return to Ts'ou to its mortal vesture, where he could live peaceably, contentedly and happily unto longevity without having resort to flight as in Tsing from kidnapped captivity. Here, as the sovereign of his own state, he could enjoy his fill of whatever that is best in life of his exalted station: victuals and delicacies rich and rare, cultural amelioration and entertainment from poetry, music and dancing, bewitchery and enamouring of graceful beauties, attraction and diversion offered by the amenities of a legitimate royal life, and last and above all, the bounteous rule of his people, through the aid of virtuous ministers, with wisdom and justice, concord and benevolence.

In *Summoning the Soul*(《招魂》), composed after *Thinking of Sah*(《怀沙》) and supposed to record the words of Sibyl Yang(巫阳) to call the poet's own ghost back to the south of River Ai(哀江), while he was in the very depth of despair, in inverted jocoseness, the whole evocation of the divine soceress is in mood and tone an enhancement of *Great Summoning*. The four distant quarters are said to be infested with frightful monstrosities (soul-devouring giants eight thousand feet tall, savages of tattooed foreheads and blackened teeth having butchered human victims for sacrificial offerings, trigonalheaded vipers that squirm and wriggle by millions, giant foxes assuming weird shapes to bewitch that speed a thousand *lih* in an instant, nine-headed adders flitting swiftly to and fro, scarlet ants as big as elephants, large wasps like bottlegourds), beset with fatal climes and overlaid with natural calamities (ten suns rising in succession to melt metal and burn rocks and stones, drifting sands a thousand *lih* in extent, waterless immense lands of rotting earth and boundless terrain of frozen mountains and icebergs with incessant falling of snow). The approach of heaven's gates is pictured to be guarded by tigers, panthers and a nine-headed monster, while hell is under the horrible rule of a devil, as given above in the discursus on the poet's thought. His soul is now conducted by an apt wizard[1] to have entered the city gates of Ying-*t'uh* to his fairly located beautiful residence, which is

---

[1] The wizard is described here to be walking backward while holding with his hands a spiritous streamer and a bamboo-strip trellis-work case wound with multi-colour threads for the soul to nestle in.

richly furnished with equipages of comfort and ease and decorated with artistic embellishments. His painted portrait① is hung up on the wall, looking down composedly in a quiet, high, spacious hall. Across the balustrade round the profile of the stately mansions topped by upward curving eaves, that enclose on three sides a high platform, could be seen through the windows a mountain stream falling down a valley distantly② that meanders its way to half embrace the garden mansion-house. Mellow orange draperies, clasped with jade hooks, are hung in the hall, which is paved with fine grindstone slabs on the floor covered with plaited bamboo-strip mats stained to a deep crimson. Kingfisher's tail feathers crest the bed hangings. Pearls and red and blue bird's plumes garnish the bed coverlets. The walls are covered with a braided texture of fine typha; balzarine valances are suspended from them. On scarlet and variegated bands, against coloured and white satin fabrics, are hung banded rings of chalcedony and la-

---

① This is based on Tsiang Ch'ih's commentary, taking the portrait to be that of the poet when he was still alive. Tsu Hsih's note gives out that it is the likeness of Chü Yuan drawn after his decease; but in his prefatory remarks to the poem, its authorship is attributed to Soong Yü as for summoning the soul of his master while he was still living. Wang Fuh-tse interprets' the original 像设 as "It is imagined that…"; so, to him, there is no portrait at all. Since the evocation is said to be hallooed by Sibyl Yang to the vagrant spirit. she must have known clearly all the detailed things described in this elegiac *fuh* without having to imagine them.

② This is my interpretation. Both Tsu-tse and Tsiang Ch'ih take the original 临高山些 as meaning the residence is on a high mountain, which seems to me not enough imaginative as well as not true to the original. It is unreasonable to picture the poet as a mountain hermit in the first place. Besides, for Chü Yuan to imagine himself living in a set of mansions on a highly ejevated terrace in Ying-t'uh facing a mountain at a distance instead of dwelling inaccessibly on the mountain itself, it is better poetry and truer to his character.

pis lazuli. Precious curios and articles of virtu are exhibited. Tall tallow-candles of frankincense illumine the halls at night. Sixteen gentle, fair maidens, matchlessly graceful and *spirituelle*, are to attend him in the mansion-house, or when he is going to loiter in the garden... The victuals and delicacies richer and more luscious than in *Great Summoning*, songs, music and dancing more delightful, friends and banqueting parties full of gentlemen and ladies, amusements in chess, backgammon, surrounding petit multi-checkers and other games, the composing of poetry and chanting of *fuh* after drinking bouts: all these form a crescendo, an intensification, an aggrandizement of those in *Great Summoning*. Then, his journey of banishment from Ling-yang to Tsang-sah is briskly touched upon in narrative in the first person. And the evocatory long apostrophe is concluded with five lengthy lines ending in "Come back, oh soul, to the south of River Ai!" So, in this gorgeous web, we find the poet's emotive compensation for his years of extreme poverty and misery in exile life before he dislimmed it at last.

Like most of his other works, *Plaint on Ying*(《哀郢》), composed at Ling-yang in the ninth year after his banishment by Hsiang (襄) from the capital and causing his second exile to the basin regions of Tsen(辰), Süe(溆) and Ai(哀), and *Over the Streams* (《涉江》), written in anticipation of his exile trip from Ling-yang on Luh Kiang(卢江), the Great River(江) and Doong-ding Lake, to the streams Yuan(沅水), Waung(枉水), Tsen(辰水), Süe(溆水) and Yuan again, are both models of memorable lyrical sorrow. In the former piece, "the feelings cherished are plaintive with sobs, meaning to go on yet lingering, for impelled by severe degradation, the poet is weighed down by the grief of banishment", while in the latter one, "the drift of emotions is a powerful drive of antipathic sorrow, because incensed by indignation, he has made up his mind to sever his all from the world," so says Tsiang Ch'ih.

The prevalent use of the chanting exclamatory word 兮 taken from ballads and popular songs is a remarkable feature of Chü Yuan's works with few exceptions. In *The Classic of Poetry*, this choral particle is not found in the *ya*(雅) and *zoon*(颂) poems of elevated diction, but is commonly employed in the *feng*(风) poems or ballads and folk songs. For example:

1. 螽斯羽,诜诜兮! 宜尔子孙,振振兮!   (《国风·周南》)
2. 手如柔荑;肤如凝脂;领如蝤蛴;齿如瓠犀;螓首蛾眉;巧笑倩兮,美目盼兮!   (《卫风·硕人》)
3. 彼狡童兮,不与我言兮! 维子之故,使我不能餐兮!

                                    (《郑风·狡童》)
4. 野有蔓草,零露漙兮。有美一人,清扬婉兮。邂逅相遇,适我愿兮。   (《郑风·野有蔓草》)
5. 陟彼岵兮,瞻望父兮。父曰:"嗟予子! 行役夙夜无已。上慎旃哉! 犹来无止!"   (《魏风·陟岵》)
6. 月出皎兮。佼人僚兮。舒窈纠兮。劳心悄兮!

                                    (《陈风·月出》)
7. 匪风发兮,匪车偈兮。顾瞻周道,中心怛兮!

                                    (《桧风·匪风》)

This character 兮, pronounced "shih" or "yih" in modern Chinese, is said by Kung Kwang-sun(孔广森) of Tsing(清) to have been pronounced "ah"(阿) in ancient times, the same as 猗. Its pervasive use in Chü Yuan's poetry taking its origin from ballads is further evidenced by the quotation of this folk song in *The Fisherman*(渔父)：

> When the water of Tsoung-loung is limpid,
> I could wash mine hat cords with it;
> When the water of Tsoung-loung is turbid,
> I could wash my twain feet with it.

The same strain is also cited in *Mencius*(《孟子》).

Thinking of Sah(《怀沙》) was written on his way by water route to Tsen-yang(辰阳) and Süe-puh(溆浦) after he had met the fisherman and set out from Loon-yang(龙阳) for Tsang-sah to die there. In his *Life* of the poet, Sze-ma Tsien quotes the whole poem (with considerable variants from the generally accepted text) in *The Chronicle* after a passage from *The Fisherman*, which contains the sentence "I would rather go to the Tsang stream(常流) and bury myself in the bellies of the River fishes." As Tsiang Ch'ih has pointed out, even such an authority as the Grand Curator of History, when he wrote the poet's *Life* less than two centuries after his death, has mistaken the title as meaning his intention of clasping sand and stone in his bosom to drown himself in a river (which is followed by Tsu Hsih in his *Variorum Commentary*); so, it is no wonder that Chü Yuan's poetry has been so often and variously misunderstood through the centuries. The emotional tone of the poem, though nearer death than those of *Plaint on Ying* and *Over the Streams*, is still "fixed but not tense, straight but not dashing"(纡而未郁,直而未激), and yet preceding the stressing note of *Lamenting on Whirlblasts* and *Pining My Past Days*.

Lamenting on Whirlblasts(《悲回风》) was written by the poet to reiterate his resolution of self-drowning by following Peng Yen, as I have said before. It is an everlasting memento to the world of the noble, altruistic intellectual for his abysmal sorrow and tempestuous despair. In a world like ours today, Chü Yuan's life and poetry cannot but be fraught with meanings.

In *Pining My Past Days*(《惜往日》), the last poem before his death, Chü Yuan strives to awaken, after his death, the present king Hsiang to the impending dangers of the state, since he could not bestir him in his lifetime, by recounting the glaring folly of the late king and his mislaid trust in the cringing, pro-Tsing junto at the court. The foreign policy of the government, the suicidal pursuance of Cross Conjunction with Ts'ing instead of betaking to United Coalition with Tsih and Ts'ou's other four natural allies, was the crucial question at the time having all in all to do with the extinction or existence of Ts'ou itself and "the world" in general, which is laid bare to Hsiang in this testament poem for him to wake up to senses and make this discretion. And all this was to be determined whether or not the crass dolt was to continue to be led with his nose by the fawning cabal. But alas! Chü Yuan's alarm in this poem was of no avail to turn the tide of the inevitable. The nincompoops Hsiang and his brother Tse-lan were firmly determined to send Ts'ou to perdition as an inevitable prelude to reduce "the world" to a holocaust for Tsing's gormandism.

In our discussion of *Suffering Throes* before, we have spoken of the ballad qualities and dialectic words of Ts'ou in Chü Yuan's poetry. The pervasive use of the exclamatory particle 兮 has been dealt with above. In *Great Summoning*, the particle 只, pronounced "tse" and carrying the sense of definiteness or connoting emphasis (exclamatory), is adopted from *The Classic of Poetry*. In *Summoning the Soul*, the particle 些, pronounced "suh", is a word taken from

charms of witchery to end a sentence, current in the western portion
of Ts'ou at the time. As for the dialectic expressions such as 汩,搴,
莽,羌,佗,傺, etc., there are some two scores of them; an enumeration and discussion of them would be of no interest to our readers, on
account of the linguistic barriers.

Last but not the least, a short discourse is due on the verse form
of Chü Yuan's works. Being evolved from that of *The Classic of Poetry*, it is a natural outgrowth of it. The norm of verse lines ("periods") of that garland of early Tsur poetry is a dimeter of four characters, with two to each measure, which may be illustrated by the first
stanza of the first poem:

关关	雎鸠,
在河	之洲;
窈窕	淑女,
君子	好逑。

The obvious fact that there are four characters in a line here is not so
important when compared to the less obvious one, though more important because it is structural in nature, that each line is a dimeter,
for our classical verse is intrinsically metrical, not isosyllabic[1].
While the regular lines are measured with two-charactered feet, varia-

---

[1] lsosyllabic verse is peculiar to Avesta, the sacred book of Zoroaster of the Gue-
bres or Parsees in Persia (Iran), and the French Alexandrine of the twelfth
century. With sixteen syllables and twelve respectively in a line cut in the mid-
dle by a silence or caesura, they may be symbolized by |00000000| |00000000
| and |000000| |000000|. *Vide* E. A. Sonnenschein: *What Is Rhythm?*, *pp.*
41 –46, Oxford, 1925.

tions or irregular lines are partially made up of feet with only one character or with three characters. Such lines are occasional, not at all common occurrences in all the *feng*, *ya* and *zoon* poems. And there are a very few lines of trimeters or even tetrameters in that ancient anthology. In the scansions below, this symbol ～～ denotes the protraction of the previous character or mute "rest". That character is lengthened in pronunciation to produce the equivalence in time duration of that particular measure which contains it with other feet of two component characters. In case there is a "rest" or break in the flow of characters, the protraction or pause sign after the "rest" signifies its lengthening to produce a soundless measure of similar duration. When there are three characters to a foot, the length of each character is shortened in pronunciation to approximate the time duration of that foot to that of a two-charactered foot. Here, we most often see two characters forming an integer to shape a foot, and the integration is due to their meanings having affiliation with each other or they are grammatically closely related.

It is a universal phenomenon of common knowledge that poetry, from primitive folk songs and ballads to its most elevated expressions by the world's few great poets of the first order, was and is chanted or composed with measured language. As the proper vehicle of poetry, verse is the thythmically recurrent or continuous, rippling flow of syllables or word sounds having unitary time durations in the form of metre in time. And metre is fashioned by the folk song or ballad singer or poet with the aid of certain prominent characteristics of the language in which a particular song, ballad or poem is made, to produce a fine sense of proportion between the syllables or word sounds in a foot, between the progressing feet in a line, between the running lines of a stanza and between the successive stanzas of a song, ballad or poem. This process of the formation of metrical units and their progress in the flow of a line is just in accord with the original meaning of metre in Sanscrit that it is measure. [1]

In the ancient Indo-European languages of classical Greek and Latin, the sound patterns of feet in verse, with variations now and then, are formed by making use of the long and short syllables of these two tongues in placing them in proper positions or time sequence to fashion the primary rhythms and produce the auditory sense of uniformity and proportion. When the inner structure of the feet in a line is well set, the relative time durations of one to one between the various feet of a line are established as a matter of course. This is the secondary rhythm. Next, the tertiary one between proportionate lengths of lines is likewise the subject of study of poets and prosodists. Thus, the typical line of Homer's *Iliad* is a dactylic hexameter, with its fifth foot a dactyl and last foot a spondee definitely, the first four feet, generally dactylic, capable of being substituted with equivalence. In modern French verse since Corneille, the classical Alexandrine, for instance, is a line of twelve syllables divided into two hemistichs in the middle by a *coupe or césura* and each hemistich is again divided into two feet of from one to five syllables each, the aggregate remaining six in number, and the four feet thus formed are each pronounced with its last syllable lengthened in time, heightened in pitch and stressed in tone. In Anglo-Saxon verse, which is accentual in nature, metre is fashioned by means of alliteration and accent, and the

---

[1] This and the following two paragraphs are a brief extract with additions, taken from my treatise *The Metrical Law of Poetry*(《诗歌底格律》) in Chinese, published in 1956—1957, Shanghai.

stressed syllables are as a rule longer in duration when compared with the unstressed ones, according to Henry Bradley as quoted by Robert Bridges in his *Milton's Prosody*[1]; the feet thus formed, though giving readers a clear unitary feeling as regards their relation with the make of the whole line, are in sensible time duration not so finely proportionate to one another as the feet of the same rhythm in classical verse. In modern English and German verse, both of which are accentual in nature, metre is formed with the aid of stressed syllables as its pivots, so that a distinct sense of proportion (one to one) is produced between the various feet of the lines. Chaucer, the father of English poetry, learning his art of decasyllabic normal lines (with fluctuations, from occasional novena-syllabic ones to not infrequent lines of thirteen syllables) from Dante's norm of hendecasyllables and early French Alexandrines and ten-syllable lines, is however basically syllabic in his verse. Shakespeare in his earlier plays is syllabic, but in his later, mature works has become decidedly accentual, shedding syllabism in his lines. Milton in *Paradise Lost* is accentual as well as syllabic (decasyllabic).

Now, classical Chinese verse from *The Classic of Poetry* down to the five- and seven-charactered verses of our "old poetry" of Tdaung(五、七古,唐五、七言) and of their later progenies or imitations is, as I have signified above, inherently metrical in formation, though seemingly numbered in characters in appearance. Tze(词) or "the long and short periods" of Soong(宋人长短句) and *chü bai*(曲牌) of the Yuan drama(元曲) are verse forms relying on the melodic

---

① *Vide Milton's Prosody, with a chapter on Accentual Verse, p.* 102, Oxford, 1921.

tunes of music, during those two dynasties, now lost and forgotten, though their notations in *bing*(平) and *tsê*(仄) are known and could be "filled in"(填) today; therefore, they have no independent metrical structures of their own to speak of. About the verse of *The Classic of Poetry*, I have spoken of its Han characters forming integers to modulate its measures, which is quite different from the way verses of Aryan languages, ancient or modern, shape their metrical units or feet. This is done by coalescence of characters due to their affinity of sense or mutually attractive grammatical functions.

To emphasize the salient features of verse I have spoken above, especially with regard to the element of time in metre and prosody, I beg pardon of my readers for repeating my understanding of the matter like this. Poetry is (or should be) written in verse, which is measured or metrical language in time. What is measured, to be precise, is a series of syllable or character sounds in lines of verse. The standard of measure, which is called metre, is formed by character or syllable sounds (generally in twos or threes, occasionally in ones or fours and rarely in a mute "rest") having time durations in a way handled by poets by making use of the prominent characteristics peculiar to each particular language, so as to produce an aesthetically pleasurable rhythmical effect. Any such unitary measure may be called a foot. The effect thus produced is a regular sequence of time durations filled with character or syllable sounds, with varieties in the arrangement of these sounds now and then to break monotony. A sense of proportion of time durations psychological in nature rather than strictly physical or mechanical, exists between the sounds within the feet, between the feet, between the lines and between the stanzas. ① In classical Chinese verse, especially in Chü Yuan's verse with which we are concerned here, we commonly find two or three characters forming an integer to shape a foot, the integration being due to their meanings having affiliation with each other or they are grammatically more closely related. So, the metrical ties here are quite different from those of ancient Greek or Latin verse, which makes use of the long and short syllables to shape a foot, and English or German verse, which makes use of the stressed and unstressed syllables to do so, and French verse, which makes use of the lengthened, stressed, higher-pitched and ordinarily pronounced syllables to do so, though in the verses of these ancient and modern Indo-European tongues, prosody is also not entirely alienated from sense and grammatical structures.

In the above, I speak of the regular lines measured with standard metrical units in the verse of all languages and I also speak of the urgent need of variety. This second requisite is complemental to the first and thus should not be belittled, nor be allowed to run to excess either, for when the first condition exists, as often in the verse of eighteenth century English poets like Pope and Johnson often times, we have a tedious feeling of stilted formality, and of course, if the second condition prevails, too much freedom would beget lines of prose instead in the end. As aptly said by Bridges, "It is a natural

---

① The best authoritative studies in the principle of metre and comparative prosody I know of are: T. S. Omond: *A Study of Metre*, London, 1920; Omond: *English Metrists*, Oxford, 1921; Robert Bridges: *Milton's Prosody, with a chapter on Accentual Verse*, Oxford, 1921; Egerton Smith: *The Principles of English Metre*, Oxford, 1923; George Saintsbury: *History of English Prosody*, 3 vols., London, 1923; E. A. Sonnenschein: *What Is Rhythm?*, Oxford, 1925; Sidney Lanier: *The Science of English Verse*, New York, 1927.

condition of rhythm, that the common rhythms should be familiar and popular, and they are probably fundamental, but after familiarity with them the ear soon grows dissatisfied and wishes them to be broken; it is only those who have no natural ear for rhythm, who can be charmed and contented with regularity, and they will resent any infraction of it; but those who love rhythm for its own sake know that it is not worth calling rhythm unless it is freely varied, and that rhythm truly begins to be beautiful only when the regularity is broken. "

While the regular lines of *The Classic of Poetry* are measured, with feet of two characters, as are exemplified above by "Kwan, kwan", the osprey's cry by twain, variations or irregular lines, made up of regular feet and feet of only one character or of three characters, are not uncommon in all the *feng*, *ya* and *zoon* poems. Here are some examples:

> 1. | 谁谓 | 雀无角, |
> | 何以 | 穿我屋? |
> | 谁谓 | 女无家, |
> | 何以 | 速我狱? |
> | 虽速 | 我狱, |
> | 室家 | 不足。 |　　　　　　(《召南·行露》)
> 2. | 溱与洧 | 方涣涣 | 兮,〰〰|
> | 士与女 | 方秉蕑 | 兮,〰〰|
> | 女曰, | "观乎?" |
> | 士曰, | "既且。" |
> | "且往 | 观乎! |
> | 洧之外 | 洵訏 | 且乐。" |
> | 维士 | 与女, |

| 伊其 | 相谑，|
| 赠之以 | 芍药。|　　　　　　　　　　（《郑风·溱洧》）

The first two lines of this stanza are known to be trimeters, for those
of the next stanza | 溱与洧 | 浏其 | 清矣 | and | 士与女 | 殷其 |
盈矣 | are no doubt trimeters.

3.　| 毋教 | 猱升木，|
　　　| 如涂 | 涂附；|
　　　| 君子 | 有徽猷，|
　　　| 小人 | 与属。|　　　　　　　　（《小雅·角弓》）
4.　| 虞芮 | 质厥成，|
文王	蹶蹶生。
予曰	有疏附；
予曰	有先后；
予曰	有奔奏；
予曰	有御侮。|　　　　　　　（《大雅·緜》）
5.	笃 V	公刘！
匪居	匪康。
乃场	乃疆；
乃积	乃仓。|　　　　　　　（《大雅·公刘》）

The symbol V used above indicates a catalectic foot, a mute "rest" or
break in the flow of character sounds.

6.　| 昊天 | 有成命，|
　　　| 二后 | 受之。|
　　　| 成王 | 不敢康，|

｜夙夜 ｜基命 ｜宥密。｜

｜於 〰〰 ｜缉熙，｜

｜单 〰〰 ｜厥心，｜

｜肆其 ｜靖之。｜

(《周颂·昊天有成命》)

And finally, let us quote this stanza from a satirical folk song to show how often the exclamatory particles 兮 and 猗 are protracted to fill in the measures at the end of lines：

7. ｜坎坎 ｜伐檀 ｜兮，〰〰 ｜

　｜置之 ｜河之干 ｜兮，〰〰 ｜

　｜河水 ｜清且涟 ｜猗。〰〰 ｜

　｜不稼 ｜不穑，｜V 〰〰 ｜

　｜胡取禾 ｜三百廛 ｜兮? 〰〰 ｜

　｜不狩 ｜不猎，｜V 〰〰 ｜

　｜胡瞻尔庭 ｜有县狟 ｜兮? 〰〰 ｜

　｜彼君子 ｜兮，〰〰 ｜

　｜不素餐 ｜兮。〰〰 ｜

Here, these 兮 and 猗 at the end of seven lines are all aspirated and protracted in chanting. Lines four and six are both ended probably with a prolonged "rest"or catalectic foot. The characters 檀, 干, 涟, 廛, 狟 and 餐 are rhymes. The first seven lines are the last two dimeters. We find, on the whole, two-charactered feet are preponderant in all the measures of these poems.

In Chü Yuan's works — let us take some lines of *Lee Sao* as examples — the verse is more prominently than that of *The Classic of*

Poetry not character counting, but metrical in structure. The least number of characters in a line is five, such as line 8:

字余日灵均。

and the most number is ten, such as line 69:

苟余情其信姱以练要兮。

The lines are generally dimeters and trimeters, with occasional tetrameters. In this respect, *Suffering Throes* is an ode sometimes and somewhat Pindaric in metrical make-up. Three-charactered feet predominate the measures in the main. The ode proceeds in quatrains, with the possible exception of lines 45 - 50, the first two of which have been suspected to be an interpolation: The first seven stanzas of the poem are scanned as follows:

帝高阳	之苗裔	兮, ～～
朕皇考	曰伯庸。
摄提	贞于	孟陬兮,
惟庚寅	吾以降。

| 皇览揆 | 余于 | 初度兮,
肇锡余	以嘉名:
名余	曰正则	兮,～～
字余	曰灵均。

| 纷吾 | 既有此 | 内美兮, |
| 又重之 | 以修能; |

| 扈江离 | 与辟芷 | 兮，〰〰 |
| 纫秋兰 | 以为佩。|

汩余	若将	不及兮，
恐年岁	之不吾与；
朝搴阰	之木兰	兮，〰〰
夕揽洲	之宿莽。

日月	忽其	不淹兮，
春与秋	其代序；
惟草木	之零落	兮，〰〰
恐美人	之迟暮。

不抚壮	而弃秽	兮，〰〰
何不	改乎	此度？
乘骐骥	以驰骋	兮，〰〰
来！V	吾道夫	先路。

昔三后	之纯粹	兮，〰〰
固众芳	之所在；
杂申椒	与菌桂	兮，〰〰
岂维	纫夫	蕙茝？

The predominance of three-charactered feet over two-charactered ones, the frequent use of the protracted 兮 at the end of lines, the alteration of trimeter with dimeter lines in a stanza, the shifting of this pattern to one trimeter, one dimeter and two trimeter lines and then to three trimeter and one dimeter lines, the occasional appearance of a four-charactered foot and of a tetrameter line, etc.; and the whole piece being regulated by the particle 兮 ending every other line — give the ode a metrical flow of vivacity, surprise and swiftness entirely novel and undreamt of in the tame, staid rhythms of *The Classic of Poetry*. When such elastic, tensile measures, as I call them, fuse together with the rich imageries and glowing symbolism, the bitter sorrow and acrid wrath of the poem flare up in incandescence, we have wonders.

The idea of expounding Chü Yuan's prosody and scanning his verse was first broached by me in my tract in Chinese *The Metrical Law of Poetry* published twenty years ago. No one before has ever attempted the thing during the centuries after Chü Yuan, though studies in his thyme commenced from Soong are not lacking. However, it is said in *The life of Wang Pau*(《王褒传》) of *The Han Chronicle* that a scholar surnamed Bie from Chur-kiang(九江被公) was summoned by Hsuan-*t'ih*(宣帝) to chant(诵读) Ts'ou "*Tze*"; *The Roll of Classics of The Swei Chronicle*(《隋书·经籍志》) says that the Buddhist bonze Dao-chien(僧道骞) was noted for reading the poet's works with Ts'ou voice, by which I understand he could chant the verse properly with Ts'ou tunes of the original. But their art of chanting has become long lost and unknown, as witnessed by Tsu Hsih in the *Preface to his Variorum Commentary*. Under the heading *Spring Officials*(《春官》), *Master of Music*(《大司乐》) of *The Tsur Rites* (《周礼》), there were six particular ways of instructing the sons of nobles and courtiers about the cantata, one of which was chanting. The East Han scholar Ts'eng Yüen(郑玄) says in a note to that book, to intone metrically(以声节之) the verse is called chanting. It is possible, I think, my scansion has restored the rhythmical way of chanting the poet's verse by the scholar Bie and the monk Dao-chien.

IX   Chü Yuan's Position in China's History and the
      World's; His Adorers, Imitators and Critics

As a flaming spirit of eternity, Chü Yuan is extolled as a thinker, personality, statesman and poet of the first magnitude in his native
land. His conception of beneficence for the commonwealth of the
people as the beau-ideal of his political philosophy in close connection
with ethics, and his deeds of fortitude through tribulation and martyri-
zing suicide cannot but give universality and permanence to him when
immortalized by his superexcellent, fiery poetry. His hatred of tyranny and aggression was in his life as is in his poetry on a par with his
love of humanity and justice. His valiant, selfless opposition to totalitarian power politics — the regal and legalized terrorism of Tsing and
its insidious spy trickeries — in consequence of his whole-hearted
support of united coalition in Ts'ou's foreign policy against cross conjunction, has won him an everlasting renown. So, in China's history, he keeps good company with the three *hwang*, five *t'ih*, three
kings and their excellent ministers and Confucius and Mencius, as he
has openly avouched his place in these lines:

> The world is in a muddle, kenning me not,
>
> Heedless of it, I fleetly ride aloft;
>
> Bridling blue dragonets two, white dragons three;
>
> I and Tsoon-hwah range the land of the fairy.
>
> Ascending the heights of the Mountains Quen-lung,
>
> I eat gem sprouts that give life immortal;
>
> Enjoying longevity with Heaven and Earth,
>
> I vie in glory with the moon and sun.
>
> *ll.*6 −12, *Over the Streams*(《涉江》)

So too, in the world's history, his compeers are benefactors of mankind such as Solon, Sakyamuni, Confucius, Pericles, Socrates, Plato, Mencius, Jesus, Washington, Jefferson, Lincoln, Sun Wen, M. Gandhi, F. Roosevelt and Churchill. In evaluating his greatness in China's as well as the world's history, the places of thinker, personality, statesman and poet are properly ranged in sequence, when we consider that "poetry speaketh of one's highest intents". The style is the man: in his poetry, we find Chü Yuan's effulgent personality.

Among his admirers and imitators, his pupils Soong Yü(宋玉), Tdaung Le(唐勒) and Chin Tsa(景差) were "well known for their love of *tze*(辞) and compositions of *fuh*(赋)," as said by Sze-ma Tsien in his *Life*(《屈原列传》). In *The Roll of Arts and Letters* of *The Han Chronicle*(《汉书·艺文志》), it is recorded that Tdaung has left after him four pieces of *fuh* and Soong sixteen, but Chin is not mentioned. Of Chin Tsa's *fuh*, it is probable that even at the time when the Grand Curator of History wrote *The Chronicle*(《史记》), only empty titles were left, for Liu Shan's anthology *Ts'ou "Tze"* (《楚辞》) contained naught of them, as evidenced by Wang Yi's *Textual Critical Studies of Ts'ou "Tze"*(《楚辞章句》). *Great Summoning* is erroneously attributed to Chin Tsa by Wang Yi with the support of Tsu Hsih of Soong and Wang Fuh-tse(王夫之) of Tsing; it is correctly proved by Ling Yün-ming(林云铭), confirmed by Tsiang Ch'ih(蒋骥), to be the authentic work of Chü Yuan himself, not by Chin, as I have shown above (*vide pp.* 96 −97,122 −123). Soong Yü's well known *Nine Strains*(《九辩》), composed by him to justify and commiserate his master, is noted for being the coursing channel for Chü Yuan's *fuh* qualities in his *tze* to run through to the *fuh* type of poetry(赋) of posterity, while his other pieces A *"Fuh" on the Wind*(《风赋》), *A "Fuh" on Kao-tdaung*(《高唐赋》), *A "Fuh" on the Divine Lady*(《神女赋》) and *A "Fuh" on T'ung-duh-tse Loving the Other Sex*(《登徒子好色赋》) mark the first uses of this term to name such a type of *belle-lettres* of the nature of descriptive lyric poetry. In Soong Yü's *fuh*, however, one does not find such tenseness of emotional power and solemnity of mood ("high seriousness") as are found in Chü Yuan's writings. A fine poet, without daring to adjure his king with gravity, Soong was a much lesser personality than his master.

Admirers and imitators of the poet were rife after his disciples, but without his thought, personality and statesmanship, nor gifted with his rare poetic genius, none of them could ever hope to approach him. In *The Song of the Blast*(《大风歌》), for instance, the founder of the Han Dynasty, Liu Paun(汉高祖刘邦), has attained the blindly forceful, grandiose manner with these three lines:

> The blasts are risen and clouds are tost amain.
> I'm back home when the land is swayed by my main.
> Let warriors fierce be found to guard my domain!

Although this is a personal air after the mode of the Ts'ou folk song, yet, as Zau P'uh-tse(晁补之) has fitly quoted *Wen-tsoon-tse*(《文中子》) to point out in his *Ts'ou "Tze" Continued*(《续楚辞》), incorporated in Tsu Hsih's *Hinder Words of Ts'ou "Tze"*(《楚辞后语》): "'does it partake of the character of the Machiavelian prince somehow?'(其伯之存乎?), so that Han, ruling the world, could not attain the beneficence of the Three Kings because of it perchance." In truth, Liu Paun was an unredeemable scoundrel not at all to be compared to Chü Yuan — to whom the beneficent rules of the Three Kings were nothing but so much nonsensical trash and whose sole ambition was to swallow in one huge gulp the Tsing(秦) world which he succeeded in doing with satisfaction; how could he come near our poet, though he did not intentionally attempt to imitate him in this noted song of brute force?

Chia Yieh(贾谊), the best *fuh* composer among Chü Yuan's admirers and followers in Han, was notable for his poetical gifts and high intents in statecraft during his late twenties. Wen-*t'ih* of Han(汉文帝) elevated him as a Doctor on account of his fame. He was "promoted to be a Grand Councillor"(太中大夫), esteemed and intrusted by his sovereign and about to be further raised to a higher station when the Marquises of Joun, Tsur Buh(绛侯,周勃), of Yin-yin, Quan Yin(颍阴侯,灌婴) and of Tung-yang, Ferng Jin(东阳侯,冯敬), all attacked him for "his youth and greenness in learning, his ambition and lust for power, and his confusion of state affairs"[1]. Chia Yieh's advisory epistles(奏疏) to Wen-*t'ih* are well known; his magnificent triple essays *On Tsing Condemned*(《过秦论》) are of great celebrity. On account of his youthful brilliance and daring spirits being strongly opposed by the titled elders, he was delegated by Wen-*t'ih* to be the royal tutor, first to the Prince (King) of Tsang-sah and then to the Prince (King) of Liang-hwai(长沙王,梁怀王太傅). At Tsang-sah, he composed his elegiac piece *Mourning Chü Yuan*(《吊屈原》), throwing a copy of the manuscript into the Mi-lo River, and his *A "Fuh", on the Buzzardet*(《服赋》), when a bird of

---

[1]　*Vide The Life of Chia Yieh*(《贾谊传》) in *The Han Chronicle* by P'an K'uh(班固).

that feather flied into his study and alighted on his settee, to note his musings on life and mutability. His *A Lament on Sworn Devotions* (《惜誓》), assuming the soliloquy of Chü Yuan but speaking for himself meanwhile, composed at his office at Liang, remained in anonymity till authenticated by Hoon Hsin-tsou(洪兴祖) of Soong; it is a masterpiece of the grand manner in Ts'ou *tze*, with Chü Yuan's *Distant Wanderings* as its gangway to fly aloft. Prince Liang-hwai died of a fall from his horse. Chia Yieh blaming himself for being unable to prevent the accident, wept for over a year and died in grief, when he was only thirty-three in lunar years.

Liu An, Prince (King) of Hwai-nan(淮南王刘安), was an ardent adorer of Chü Yuan. He wrote eighty-two pieces of *fuh*, of which only one is left to us, entitled *Convoking Recluses*(《招隐士》), and an occult mystical tome of *dao*(道), *Hwai-nan-tse*(《淮南子》). He was reputed to be an adept in the art of metamorphosis into a fairy and to be so transformed. His extant *fuh* is weird in feelings and atmosphere. In his *A "Fuh" on Lee Sao*(《离骚赋》), composed at the bidding of Wuh-*t'ih*, now lost, with two commenting sentences of its poem quoted and preserved in Liu Shye's(刘勰) *Carving Dragons in the Heart of Literature*(《文心雕龙》), it is said that "*The State's Folk-songs*(《国风》) are amorous but not lustful, and *The Small 'Ya'*(《小雅》) poems are complaining and critical but not rebellious, whereas *Lee Sao* could be said to have in common both these qualities. Like the cicada shedding its chrysalis in mud and slime and then flying up above beyond the dusty earth, *Lee Sao* beams forth from its throes immaculate and radiant to vie its brilliance with the sun and moon".

And then, Sze-ma Tsien, the Grand Curator of History (and Astronomy)（太史公司马迁）of Wuh-_t'ih_, wrote his _Lives of Chü Yuan and Chia Yieh_(《屈原贾生列传》) of _The Chronicle_(《史记》), to which we have referred many a time. Of _Lee Sao_ and its author, the eminent historian says, "It was written by him to repine at his misfortune. It speaks of _T'ih_ Ko(帝喾) above, of Hwan of Tsih(齐桓) below and of Taung and Wuh(汤,武) in the middle, in censuring contemporary events. He makes evident the extent and scope of the Way and virtues, and sets forth the order and sequence of peace and confusion of the times. His language is concise, his words are superexcellent, his intents pure and his deeds spotless. His phrasing is small, but its inference is very great; his pointing at is near, but its application is far beyond. His intents are pure, so the things he speaks about are fragrant; his deeds are immaculate, so after his death, he is understood and revered by all..." After Sze-ma Tsien, the noted scholar Liu Shan(刘向) affords us some details of the poet's life in his _New Relatings_(《新序》) that cast beams of necessary light on his political tribulations and personality.

Since Chia Yieh and Liu An, admirers and imitators of Chü Yuan in West and East Han amounted to some seventy _fuh_ writers, the better known of whom were Mei Zuen(枚乘), Yen Jih(严忌), Sze-ma Hsiang-rue(司马相如), Liu Tsê, Wuh-_t'ih_ of Han(汉武帝刘彻), Tung-faun Suo(东方朔), Wang Pau(王褒), Liu Shan(刘向), Yang Hsiung(扬雄), P'an K'uh(班固), Tsang Heng(张衡), Wang Yi(王逸) and Tsai Yean(蔡琰). No one in this list could come near Chü Yuan in spirit, personality and poetry, of course, though in feelings of sadness, the _fuh_ poetess Tsai Yean's _Eighteen Stanzas on the Hwu Hautboy_(《胡笳十八拍》) is transcendent for its rare acuteness of pitch. Captived by the invading Hwu tribesmen (the

South Huns) at the end of Han and being forcibly made their queen for twelve years, she gave birth to two Hwu princes. Zaur Tsao(曹操) of Han, a good friend of her deceased father Tsai Yong(蔡邕), compassionating on his having no son, ransomed her with a heavy price pf gold and gems from her Hwu captor-king. Her keen and penetrating grief for her captivity and enforced separation from her two sons embodied in *Eighteen Stanzas* and *Bitter Sorrow*(《悲愤诗》) is personal in temper and therefore slender in volume, breadth and depth, not comparable to Chü Yuan's profound throes for the people of Ts'ou and the whole humanity of Tsur and the seven states. But Tsai Yean's two poems are decidedly intense and heartfelt in pathos when contrasted with the shallow, false or even maleficent sentiments of her predecessors Sze-ma Hsiang-rue and Yang Hsiung.

Hsiang-rue was an abject sycophant of Wuh-*t'ih*, his *fuh* are generally games of flatulent rhetorical somersaults or flushes of gaudy descriptions, hollow in passion or real sentiments, sometimes decked with a little admonition after a long string of flatteries. I have criticized his decorative *A "Fuh" on the Magister*(《大人赋》) above in comparison with Chü Yuan's *Distant Wanderings* (*vide pp.* 87 −88). Chia Yieh and Liu An, even Liu Tsê, are animated and vivacious in feelings, lithesome and agile in diction. With Hsiang-rue, verbosity and flamboyance set in in the decadent Han *fuh*; his turgid fabrications *A "Fuh" on Saun-Iin and A "Fuh" on Tse-sheü*(《上林赋》,《子虚赋》) are sodden and vapid in spirit and choked with masses of grandiloquent depictions. Finally, his brazen adulatory piece *Homage to Heaven and Earth*(《封禅文》) has set a shameful example for Yang Hsiung and P'an K'uh to follow suit. In short, picking Chü Yuan's phrases and vocabulary and imitating his diction with flaunting excesses, Hsiang-rue at his heart must have thought his master was an impractical fool, a mere poet incapable of taking care of his own interests.

A zealous admirer of Sze-ma Hsiang-rue, Yang Hsiung was a blackguard of utter degradation. What was uppermost in his mind was to be a big official, a magnate of the first rank, at any price. While his master Sze-ma was ashamed to cast open disapproval or contempt at our poet, Yang wrote a *fuh* entitled Anti *"Lee Sao"* (《反离骚》) to give public counsel to Chü Yuan's spirit and show him the folly of drowning himself. Also as a mouthpiece of Hsiang-rue perhaps, Yang says in his *fuh* that when a gentleman meets with favourable hap, he could perform his utmost to his heart's content, if otherwise, he should retire and be a hermit, meeting with an intrusting sovereign or not is a matter of destiny and so, why was there the need of drowning himself? To insult Chü Yuan and smear muck on his fair memory, Yang threw a copy of his mock *fuh* with distortions and twistings of certain lines of Chü Yuan's great ode into the River from Mount Min(嵋山). At the courts of three emperors of Han, Yang got no promotion in his official career. He did not retire to become a hermit, however. When the hypocrite and scoundrel Wang Maun(王莽) was hot in power before his usurpation of the imperial throne, Yang already fawned on him in his foul writings by comparing him to Ih Yün (伊尹) and Duke Tsur(周公). When Wang snatched the crown, the stuttering cringeling wrote a sycophanting address and became a favourite of the usurper. His other brewages are but torpid imitations and developments of Sze-ma Hsiang-rue by a literary court politician devoid of intellectual light and moral sheen.

P'an K'uh(班固) of East Han, co-writer with his father P'an Pi-ao(班彪) of *The Han Chronicle*(《汉书》) and a composer of the obese Han *fuh*, criticized Chü Yuan for "vaunting his talents to elevate himself and giving vent to his wrath in reviling his king and self-drowning". To be fair to P'an, one has to admit that his father's and his *The Han Chronicle* is an arduous and monumental work in Chinese history, only second in excellence to Sze-ma Tsien's *The Chronicle*. But when Literary *talents* are spoken of, P'an showed *his* by singing a pæan of Han's virtues to profit himself with his *The Constant Law Drawn Out*(《典引》). His unscrupulous worship of power led to his close affiliation with Der Hsien(窦宪), brother of the mother empress of Her-*t'ih*(汉和帝), a victorious general and a cabal leader of his family members at the court. When the emperor grew up in age and came to senses about Der's dark intrigues and grasping for power, he was ordered by imperial decree to commit suicide. As a member of Der Hsien's junto, P'an was imprisoned and died in jail. His ostentatious *A "Fuh" on the Two Capitals*(《两都赋》) is a showy display of ornamental delineations of Han's western capital Tsang-an(长安) and a complimentary recounting of the virtues and glory of Kwang-wuh-*t'ih*(光武帝), the reviver of Han, and Ming-*t'ih*(明帝), who and whose successors founded their eastern capital at Lor-yang(洛阳). The fabric is skillfully done, but uninspired and flat.

After P'an K'uh, Yen Tse-tuai(颜之推) of the South and North Dynasties(南北朝) blamed Chü Yuan for "making conspicuous his sovereign's faults". Yen is well known as a Confucian moralist. but he served consecutively as lords and high officials at the courts of four dynasties. No doubt, he got along nobly with all his sovereigns, which is, however, contrary to the traditional ethics of Confucianism.

Sze-ma Hsiang-rue, Yang Hsiung, P'an K'uh and Yen Tse-tuai are all prominent literati and scholars in China's history; they all professed themselves to be Confucians in some sort. The trouble with them is that they thought one's poetry could be divorced from one's personality, for while they all more or less admired and imitated Chü Yuan's *tze*, his poetry (Yen excepted), they, as pseudo-Confucians in thought and practice, became undisguised in their disavowal of Chü Yuan's ideals and deeds. The root of their disparagement of our poet is due to the antipodal difference between their outlook of life and Chü Yuan's. Supreme political power was their fetish, jungle law their ethics and personal gain their credo. They thought and believed that "the world" (天下) was the private property of their emperors, the "Sons of Heaven" (天子), in conformity with the concept of the divine right of kings of medieval Europe, and that they themselves and their fellow beings were but his absolute helots and chattels. Being changelings of opportunism and material realism in their individual lives, they thought Mencius' dictum that "the people are of the highest in import; the domain of a state stands next; the king is the lightest of the three" is a truism not to be taken seriously, but they dared not oppose or deny it openly. Now, here came a poor poet, a sad failure during his life, who avowed the motto in his practice and poetry in good earnest. It is no wonder then that they spoke their mind of him in naked censure. On the other hand, if Chü Yuan had his ghost leading an immortal existence, he would certainly abhor such admirers and imitators of his poetry who were such defilers of his thought and personality.

In the dynasties Gwei (魏) and Ts'in (晋), followers of Chü

Introduction

Yuan included Wang Tsai(王粲, he is also known as one of the seven men of letters of Jien-an of East Han, 东汉建安七子之一）, Tsaur Tsê(曹植）, Pan Yue（潘岳）and Dao Ts'ien（陶潜）. Dao's *A "Tze" on Retracing My Way Home*（《归去来辞》) is celebrated for its composer's bland and transcendent personality and the poem's serene tone and pellucid diction. During the South Dynasties, Bao Tsao（鲍照）of Soong（宋）and Kiang An（江淹）of Liang（梁）excelled in their *tze* and *fuh*. Bao's *A "Fuh" on the Desolate City*（《芜城赋》) is an orient pearl of a poem, worthy to be esteemed the excelsior model for Goldsmith's *The Deserted Village*. Liu Shye（刘勰）of Liang, the great critic and author of *Carving Dragons in the Heart of Literature*（《文心雕龙》), devotes a chapter of glowing praise in his classic of literary criticism on the *genre sao*, with which he calls Ts'ou tze, commenting on Chü Yuan's works with the highest of tributes and touching on Soong Yü, Chia Yieh and others. The Buddhist bonze Dao-chien（僧道骞）of Swei（隋）is said to be an adept in the art of chanting our poet's works with Ts'ou tunes of the original.

In the Tdaung Dynasty（唐）, the great poets Wang Wei（王维）, Lih Bêh（李白）, Yuan Ch'i（元结）, Hang Yüe（韩愈）, and Liu Tsoon-yuan（柳宗元）were all followers of Chü Yuan. Lih's sole poem in the manner of Ts'ou *tze* but in his own aerial diction entitled *The Song of Long Howl*（《鸣皋歌》) is a miniature symphony of heavenly tunes with a single whirl of mundane air, which, it must be said, stands on a level with Chü Yuan's minor poems. In Soong（宋）, Suh Sêh（苏轼）and Hwang Ding-jian（黄庭坚）took up the tradition of Ts'ou *tze* and *fuh* of our poet and Soong Yü. After Suh's celebrated *Fore and Hind Pieces of a "Fuh" on the Red Cliffs*（《前后赤壁赋》), there were no more eminent writers of this type of verse.

One of the last imitators of our poet, Wang Fuh-tse(王夫之) of early Tsing(清初) is an outstanding name, as he is also a noted student of Chü Yuan.

Of the early commentators and scholars of Chü Yuan's works, a brief account has been given on Wang Yi, Hoon Hsin-tsou, Tsu Hsih and Tsiang Ch'ih at the beginning of my annotations on *Lee Sao* in *Notes and Comments* after the poems. Since there are more than a hundred of them from East Han to today and I have quoted in details scores of their interpretations in the notes, nothing more of them will be dwelt on here. But in the case of the great Soong editor Tsu Hsih, a word must be said about his critical estimate of Chü Yuan the man and the poet. As a renowned Confucian philosopher and scholar, Tsu-tse, a warm adorer of our poet, apologizes more than once in his three books for Chü Yuan's lack of moderation in his life and poetry, although it is admitted that he "was one man in a thousand years". Now, the doctrine of moderation was formulated by Tse-sze(子思), Confucius' grandson, in his tract *The Medium*(《中庸》), from the sage's eulogy that moderation is "perhaps the supreme one of all virtues since it was no longer in sway for long stretches of time!" I have discussed it above in section Ⅷ *Chü Yuan s Thought and Poetry*. I have also said that our poet was not a Confucian, still less a traditional one — he was far greater a personality than that. When a society was comparatively normal even under a government of absolute monarchy, while its political air was more or less temperate, moderation could or should be its prevalent moral code. But in a society of political and social stress and chaos such as the Warring States, when the feudal fabric of Tsur was falling to pieces and the fascistdom of accipitrine Tsing was casting abroad its furies and vicious trickeries in all the states, to expect and demand moderation in such a thinker, personality, statesman and poet as Chü Yuan is, to say the least, lack of discretion and judgment. Tsu-tse is therefore plainly wrong in his critical estimate of Chü Yuan, though he has done a greater service to the poet than any other of his students in the textual criticism of his works.

In modern China, the late popular scholar Hwu Seh（胡适, Hu Shih）, in his article *Reading Ts'ou "Tze"*（《读楚辞》）, puts forth the surprising assertion, in company with another writer Liao Jih-bin（廖季平）, the author of *New Explanations of Ts'ou "Tze"*（《楚辞新解》）, that Chü Yuan as a man and a poet was non-existent in history. Without having read their writings, I know their arguments from Kuo Mê-ruo's（郭沫若） *Studies in Chü Yuan*（《屈原研究》）which quotes Hsieh Wuh-liang's（谢无量） *New Comments on Ts'ou "Tze"*（《楚辞新论》）about their points. Hwu and Liao's reasons of proof are based mainly on certain incongruities and defects of narration in Sze-ma Tsien's *Life* of the poet in *The Chronicle* and partially on their own irrational suspicions. Their absurd notions have been properly refused in Kuo's book; being not worth a pin, they are not to be specified here. While Liao's name is comparatively obscure, Hwu is well known both in China and in the West, especially the English-speaking countries. He was a pupil of John Dewey, an exponent of pragmatism of the school of William James and Dewey in China, and a popular interpreter of ancient Chinese philosophy to the American and British reading public. His delvings and studies in both Chinese and classical Western philosophies were, however, rather journalistic and superficial. Thus, he was incompetent to finish his *An Outline of the History of Chinese Phitosophy*（《中国哲学史大纲》）, of which his doctorate thesis, consisting of the Pre-Tsing(先秦) period, forms but the first of two or three volumes, for he was inconversant with the realms covered by the Han, Tdaung and Soong Dynasties(汉,唐, 宋), which demand a prerequisite knowledge of Buddhism in China. But we should not ask too much of a man perhaps. Hwu has, however, made a great contribution to modern China and a resounding name for himself by advocating the use of *bai hua*(白话文), the vernacular longuage, in place of *wen yien*(文言), the literary speech, for writing prose as well as poetry, in the company of Tsen Doh-siu(陈独秀), Luh Süin(鲁迅), Tsur Tso-ren(周作人), Tsien Yüen-doon (钱玄同), Liu Fu(刘复), Sun Yin-mu(沈尹默) and others, in the New Cultural Movement since 1917 to the twenties. Their common platform was the magazine *New Youth*(《新青年》). Previous to their promotion, our written literature, with the exception of certain volumes of analects(语录) of Soong philosophers, "related tales"(评话) from Soong(宋) down to Tsing(清) and the Republic(民国), and popular novels, short tales and musical dramas(曲,杂剧) of the dynasties Yuan, Ming and Tsing(元,明,清), was set down in the literary language only. Hwu Sêh published the first volume of vernacular poems of the movement in crude free verse entitled *Essaying Poems*(《尝试集》), his attempts being, however, but sorry stuff as poetry. The entire movement is the result of cultural contact with the modern Western world, but is sometimes called "the Chinese Renaissance", as by Hwu Sêh. The Renaissance in the West means Re-birth and New Birth: the revival of learning — studies in arts, letters, philosophies, sciences and political, civic and social systems of ancient Greece and Rome, first in Italy, then in France and England and last in Germany, and as a result of invigorating studies in the Classical legacies and the religious revolt of the Reformation headed by Martin Luther, against popery or Vaticantism, a new birth or vivification was brought about in arts, letters, sciences, politics, religion, social institutions and human life in general in Western Europe.

The New Cultural Movement(新文化运动) of China, flaring up with brilliance in the May 4th and June 3rd, patriotic demonstrations of students, closing up of shops and general strike of students and factory workers in Peking and Shanghai in 1919, succeeded by the boycotting of Japanese goods in great cities of the country, went on smoothly; in its promotion of democracy, science, the vernacular language in place of the old literary medium, and a rational revaluation of ancient institutions (such as the family and marriage) and traditional thoughts (such as Confucianism), among the literate circle. Soon, internecine warfare between the warlords got the better of everything and not much is put up. Yet, the prevalent use of *bai hua* as our written vehicle of expression has come to stay and radical, lasting changes are gradually wrought in the family and in marriage as well as in realms of the thought. In his flourishing years, Hwu Sêh was chiefly interested in the popular novels *Water Margin Tales*(《水浒传》), *Western Travels*(《西游记》), *The Dream of the Red-storeyed Chamber*(《红楼梦》), *Anecdotes of Scholars*(《儒林外史》), *Flower Fairies Seen in the Mirror*(《镜花缘》), etc. … He wrote critical studies of these works serving as introductions to their modern reprints of his time. His understanding and appreciation of the more elevated, deeper sort of *belles-lettres*, especially hign flights of poetry, both Chinese and Western, were unfortunately skimming and sciolous, just as his knowledge of Chinese and classical Western philosophies was superficial and fragmentary, and his acquaintance with Chinese and

European art was pitiably destitute. With a smattering understanding and shallow appreciation of poetry, he could not love the master pieces of Chü Yuan, Lih Bêh and Duh Fuh of China or poets of the first order of the outside world. About the intercourse and interfusion of western culture with Chinese, he opined that China "should be completely westernized". Yet he once told me in all frankness in the autumn of 1931, I remember, at his home in Peking, that he could see nothing excellent or admirable in Duh Fuh's(杜甫) *Eight Poems on Autumn Feelings*(《秋兴八首》) and Shakespeare's *Hamlet*. Now, *Hamlet*, in common knowledge in English speaking countries, is decidedly an excellent portrait of the model Renaissance man of Elizebethan England. To the modern cultured public of Britain and America, the play *Hamlet*, together with Shakespeare's other somber tragedies and resplendent comedies, is a priceless heritage of their past still bearing scintillating significance to their present democratic outlook of life. Yet Hwu, professing himself to be an interpreter of the West to China, admitted that he could see nothing remarkable in this marvelous creation! So, perhaps one should not be surprised after all that he could have denied the existence of Chü Yuan in his sensational or rather absurd article[1] to court vulgar favour by mimicking the Vandalic agitators in England in raising the Shakespeare-Bacon controversy.

A well-known example of a man crouching on all fours before the "unimpeachable" wisdom of Tsaung-tse(庄子) may be found in Lin Yü-tang(林语堂), a popular Chinese writer and sinologue in the United States in recent years. In his *My Country and My People*, he

---

[1] See Hwu Sêh's *Reading Chu Chi* (in *Literary Works by Hwu Sêh*, second series, Volumn I) — the editor.

says, "All good Chinese literature, all Chinese literature that is worthwhile, that is readable, and that pleases the human mind and soothes the human heart is essentially imbued with this Taoistic spirit. " He speaks further of his *Herbert Giles in Heaven*, in which he makes the delirious assertion that "whatever is best even in Western literature is in line with Taoism", and he compares the churchyard scene in *Hamlet* with Tsaung-tse's meditation on an hollow, bleached skull. Lin recommends to Chü Yuan, whom he condescends to compliment as having "some rhetorical genius", in the guise of God's counsel, that our poet "should acquire the philosophy of Tsaung-tse" in order to match Shakespeare in the judgment of Western literary criticism. Now, I have made a proper discursus of the philosophy of the *Dao Têh* school and Tsaung-tse's literary merits above (see *pp.* 41 – 47). The grave-diggers' dialogue in *Hamlet* is assuredly replete with life's philosophy of vicissitude, but it has long become a threadbare platitude for lack-lustre journalists to chatter about those ironical jests with glowing eulogy to vaunt their knowledge of Shakespeare. There are numerous high lights in Shakespeare's awe-commanding tragedies and glorious comedies — his sublimity, terror, wrath, pity, pathos, wonders and delights; but the churchyard scene is certainly NOT "the best of Shakespeare". And to say Chü Yuan has only "some thetorical genius" without feeling his mountainous personality, blazing passion, dolorous sorrows and lyrical profundity, is to betray a downright one-sidedness of his viewpoint.

In the above, we have dealt broadly with Chü Yuan's place as a thinker, a personality, a statesman and a poet, in one word, as a great spirit of eternity in China's and the world's history. Now, from the point of view of poetry's his extant works, though rather slender in volume, surely rank the highest over and above all other poets of our nation. In intensity of passion, depth of thought, range in imagination, richness of diction and force of metrical verve, he is peerless in Chinese poetry. Exceeding the primitive or archaic pieces of *The Classic of Poetry* by long stretches, Chü Yuan is almost neared by Lih Bêh(李白) and Duh Fuh(杜甫) of Tdaung(唐), and much less so by Suh Sêh(苏轼) and Sing Chih-zi(辛弃疾) of Soong(宋) in their *tze*(词). In the world's poetry, he is the fourth in chronology among its poets of the very first order, but second to none of the others in intrinsic qualities. These are Homer, Aeschylus, Sophocles, Chü Yuan, Virgil, Dante, Shakespeare, Milton and Goethe. Whitman's poetry, not written in metrical language, but in symphonic prose, stands apart from them all.

Pioneer sinologues like H. St. Denys and James Legge, followed by certain European critics, I understand[①], are of the opinion that not only *Lee Sao* is a mediocre work, but the genius of the whole Chinese nation is plainly inferior, when compared to the grandeur and excellence of *Iliad* and *Paradise Lost*. This is chiefly due to their inadequate knowledge of the classical Chinese language, in spite of their vain efforts at French and English versions of their own, and the lack of fair translations into Western tongues, as well as to their deplorable want of acquaintance with the ode's general historical background, including, of course, the poet's knowledge of ancient Chinese history, his political ideal, personality and heroic fight with the dark forces, which has great vital validity to our modern world, and the critics'

---

①   I learn this from Lim Boon-keng's(林文庆) introductory piece to his English version of *Lee Sao*.

lopsided view of the functions of poetry. The subject of solemn contemplation of our greatest lyric poet of political beneficence, commonwealth of the people and universal union of mankind is most decidedly not less interesting or meritorious than the diverting, pictorial, fresco-like qualities in the epic narratives of Homer, Dante and Milton. I have made a particular discussion of this point in my *Notes and Comments* on *Lee Sao*; a repetition here is not necessary. Homer is by no means all perfection to all his critics: *ali-quando bonus dormi-tat Homerus*. He had his Zoilus, *La Divina Commedia and Paradise Lost* are both highly religious in substance, but not all of their readers are Christians, Catholic or Protestant. As regards grandeur and excellence, the main rub of the lack of penetration and appreciation of *Suffering Throes* in the West lies in the barrier of language and the absence of fine foreign versions as well as the want of an all-embracing, penetrating introduction that should cast lights on the poet's ideals and personality, his thoughts and feelings, his historical heritage and political *milieu*, and his verbal allusions and poetical nuances. In another word, to be a fair judge of Chü Yuan in comparison with Homer, Dante, Milton and others, a critic must scan minutely Chü Yuan's external cosmos and his internal ego, and go back and forth many times between the two, for the simple reason that *Lee Sao* and his other works are an ode and lyric poetry of high subjective intensity, not epics and dramas of fresco-like objectivity. This, however, does not mean in the least a slight on the other great poets of the very first order, but only points out the difference between the natures of odes and lyrical poetry on the one hand and epics and dramas on the other.

In a preface of Herbert A. Giles to Lim's book, for instance, the late well-known sinologue praises the first quatrain of E. H. Parker's rendering,

> Born of the stock of our ancient Princes,
> (My father, Peh Yung by name,)
> The Spring-star twinkled with cheery omen
> On the lucky day I came.

thus: "the lilt of his first verse impressed me very favourably", though he regrets "the lilt did not last". The rhythm and tone of Parker in these four lines are obviously of a light, rippling and gay nature, and therefore quite shallow in substance of feelings and thought, altogether foreign, nay, directly antithetic to the highly grave, meditative and afflicted subject and temper of *Suffering Throes*. Lin Yütang ridiculously puts Giles in heaven (and he insultingly makes Chü Yuan sour on Shakespeare's magnificent achievements in contrast with his own trite, "rhetorical" successes) on a par with Chü Yuan for the former's version of the passage in *Tsaung-tse*, with which he adoringly compares the churchyard scene in *Hamlet* that he holds as "the best of Shakespeare". Lin's God, when stripped of the garb of his childish worship, proves to be nothing but the misguided though prevalent opinions of the common run of Western literary critics who are but scantily informed of, and therefore only rudely studied in, Chü Yuan's inner as well as outer worlds, plus Lin's own fetich of Tsaung-tse's philosophy. The lack of understanding and disparagement of sinologies and critics just spoken of may lie, as illustrated in this case of Giles, in their deficiency of a genuine sense of poetic diction and rhythmical flux even in their own mother tongues, French and English. When they are not competent judges of verse in their native tongues, how can they fitly criticize excellent poetry in ancient Chinese which they could neither thoroughly understand and appreciate, nor do so through the medium of a non-existent ideal rendition? And I find Lim's English translation, the latest, quite disappointing besides being fraught with verbal mistakes, just as even the only Chinese vernacular version of this greatest ode by China's modern poet and scholar Kuo is most wretchedly done and laden with unpardonable errors.

导　论[*]

一　引　言

屈原(约公元前 345—公元前 286)^①出生时,由周朝(公元前 1122—公元前 256)武王姬发及其兄弟周公姬旦^②所创建的中国古代庞大的封建体制,在春秋时期(公元前 722—公元前 481)^③的第一阶段的瓦解已经结束。其衰败的过程和细节由孔子记录在《春秋》这一编年体史书之中,笔触精练、含蓄,并带有批判性。当孔子把最后一则史料编写完毕,这部史书就戛然而止,因为他似乎已清楚地感觉到一种征兆:周朝早期的荣耀和秩序已无可挽回了。封建体制继续加速崩溃。大约又过了 80 年,于公元前 403 年,随着晋国的三个贵族分裂为魏、赵、韩三个独立的小国,终于正式引来了战国时代。在此期间,国与国之间战火频仍不断,直到公元前 256 年,掠夺成性的秦国并吞了周。接着在公元前 221 年,秦国又攻克了六国中最后的齐国,从根本上推倒了老的封建主权力,彻底消灭了旧秩序及其痕迹,并建立了自己一统天下的残暴专制政权——但它仅历时 15 年又化为灰烬。

生活在这种充满政治压力和动乱的时代,我们的诗人、思想家、政治家和具有非凡魄力的伟人屈原,本着崇高的信念,日夜思

---

*　此中译部分由吴起仞先生翻译。

①　参看本文"七 屈原和他的著作"第 1、22 节中有关他的生卒年月的叙述。

②　简称为周公。

③　中国历史一般认为春秋时期始于公元前 722 年,公元前 481 年结束。孔子所编写的著名史书就以这一段时期为事实基础,史书也因此而得名。从春秋时期结束到战国时期开始,还有一段长达 78 年的中间时期;在叙述史实时为方便起见,就把这段时间看成是春秋时期的延续。

念着往日的光辉灿烂,缅怀着他的氏族的来历以及他家族所作出的贡献。他是古代二帝的嫡系后裔,又与尧、舜、禹、汤多少都有点旁系关系。更重要的是,他自恃秉承了生气勃勃的正义的传统——王道。这种精神上的天赋,加上他的家世门第,使他深深地感到落在他肩上的重任。但是现实却似当头一盆凉水,十分无情和冷酷。由于他是昭、屈①、景这三位一体家族中的一员,理应与楚怀王有密切的亲戚关系,即便如此,起先他被拒绝朝觐,接着甚至被逐出京都。他总感到为了百姓,他既负有恢复二帝、三王盛世的重任,也拥有这种才能。他对这方面的充分的信心这时在胸中已燃起炽烈的火焰。可是,以秦惠王和其后的秦昭王为代表的敌对势力,有他们共同的走卒张仪为虎作伥,为了维护他们的权力,对内热衷于搞霸道的极权政治,对外实施肆无忌惮的侵略政策,还对从秦孝公和卫鞅四个朝代以来王室家族的罪恶暴行姑息养奸。这一切早在楚国朝野和王族周围编织成了无所不包的黑色网络。他们明里搞外交,暗中搞的却是间谍活动和捣乱,凭借达到饱和的贿赂行径,他们居然横行无阻。面对这一切,屈原成了黑暗势力唯一的不可逾越的障碍——在楚国朝野只有这样一位有威望的人士敢于站起来反对亲秦的恶势力。

二 三皇、五帝和三王

为全面了解屈原,景仰他的人格和欣赏他的诗篇,尤其是《离骚》,就应先弄清楚这位诗人、思想家、政治家——这位永垂不朽的人物,他所珍惜和渴望的是什么。他所念念不忘的就是黎民百姓的福祉以及以往那些君主为百姓造福的仁厚的政治。他是年代久远的黄帝和帝高阳的直系子孙,又是悠远的帝尧、帝舜的旁系后

---

① 按李唐林宝所著的《元和姓纂》:楚武王的王子瑕受封于屈,他就取采邑的名为姓。他的后人屈重、屈荡、屈建和屈平都沿用了这个姓。

代,所以秦国在他的周围布满了卑劣的小人、帮凶以及鹰犬式的人物。他的君主楚怀王是个不可救药的蠢材,继承楚怀王的楚襄王是个更糟的笨伯。屈原在饱受折磨、迫害之余,精神上出现了错乱,只能"引吭高歌"来抒发胸中的抑郁、愤怒和绝望。一次又一次的排斥、驱逐和流放把屈原逼到了绝境,眼看这天地已沉沦到无复有生还之望的地步,为了对楚襄王和其父亲那种敌友不分的倒行逆施表示反抗和抗争,为了警告针对楚国、周天下的臣民以及七国诸侯的迫在眉睫的灾难,他最终结束了自己的生命。诗歌的末尾部分描绘了早期的百姓的领袖,其中有诗人的功勋卓著的祖先。

古时候中国①称为"夏"或"华夏",意思是这片土地的美丽和伟大,即所谓"文章光华、礼义之大"。

中国历史的初期由于传说中的十多位族长、皇帝和国王的治理而显得光彩夺目。这十多位君主就是三皇、五帝和三王。

首先,三皇实际上是两位皇帝和一位女皇,即伏羲、神农和女娲。伏羲又名伏戏、虙戏、宓牺、包牺或庖牺,也称太昊、太皞,姓氏为风。相传他具有超人的智慧,当君主时创造了八卦,概括了天地之间的一切事物、现象,又发明了书写字符(刻在木板上),以后发展成为简。他教导人民狩猎、捕鱼、驯养畜类和照看牲口,他的领地在陈,即现今河南省开封县以东、安徽亳县以北的地区,古时称为太昊之墟。他在位 115 年,继承他的有 15 位君主,延续达 1260 年之久。

神农因出生于姜水,故姓姜,也叫炎帝,这是因为他"以火德王"。他当君主时开始制作农具,教育人民从事农业,尝辨数以百种计的药草,医治疾病,设立市场促使货物流通。他的名字"神农"估计是他的臣民对他的尊称。他的领地也在陈,之后他迁都至鲁,

---

① 这片土地最初就叫中国,以此区别于相邻的蛮帮,如东夷、南蛮、西戎和北狄。近代西方的刊物中也常称之谓中国。确切地说,应称之谓中帝国,即作为皇帝的三皇、五帝的国家,而并不是远古时期的小王国。

即今山东省。他在位 120 年,死后葬于今湖南省省会长沙。

女娲是伏羲的妹妹。她发明了管乐器,制订了婚姻的礼仪,确定同姓氏的男女不许通婚。但根据发掘的汉武梁祠石室中的壁画所载,伏羲和女娲虽为兄妹,却是世上第一个丈夫和第一个妻子。他们的下半身像带鳞片的蛇,尾部绕缠在一起,他们中间夹着一个小孩。相传女娲在位的后期,共工①在与祝融的争霸世界之战中败北,因而一头撞在不周山以致天柱折、地维绝。这时女娲便炼出五色之石以补天(上的罅隙),并拆下天龟的腿来支撑大地的四角。但这已是纯粹的神话虚构了。

关于三皇中第三位的本身以及三皇排列的次序,传说纷纭。有两种传说认为,第三位不是女皇而另有两位皇,即祝融和燧人。祝融的业绩无有记载,燧人在传说中用凹形的金属圆盘或钻头钻木取火,教导臣民熟食。

再说五帝,首先是轩辕帝。他因住在"轩辕之丘"故名轩辕,姓公孙,又因长于姬水也姓姬。轩辕"以土德王",土以黏土的棕黄为代表色,所以一般也称为黄帝。神农后的第八位皇帝叫榆罔,是个治国无方的暴君,在阪泉被轩辕打败。蚩尤是个部落头领,因反叛溃败后也为轩辕所杀。此后,部落的头领们一致拥戴轩辕为皇帝。他在位时命大挠把两套太古的符号合并作甲子,即天干和地支。天干共 10 个,甲、乙、丙、丁、戊、己、庚、辛、壬、癸;地支共 12 个,子、丑、寅、卯、辰、巳、午、未、申、酉、戌、亥,合称干支。相传这是天皇氏族的第一位君主发明用来表示月份和日期的。天干和地支的结合程序从甲子开始依次排列如乙丑、丙寅、丁卯、戊辰、己巳等,直到第六十对于支为一周,然后再从甲子开始为另一周,依此类推。干支相连经常用来表示年份、一年中的月份和一天中的时辰,但这是以后才发展起来的。他命仓颉作六书(汉字的六种条例),命伶

---

① 据唐颜师古《前汉书·古今人物表》注,共工的"共"应读如"龚"。

伦定律吕(音乐的 12 种基本声调),命隶首定算数。此外,他又命岐伯录《素问》(他们的问答语录),其中记录了治疗各种病症的处方。黄帝的皇后名嫘祖,她养蚕、缫丝并发明了衣裳。黄帝在位 100 年(公元前 2698—公元前 2598),他的坟墓称桥陵,在今陕西省的桥山,亦称中部山。

第二位是少昊,是轩辕的儿子,名挚,姓己。由于他继承了太昊的措施,所以叫少昊。他"以金德王",也称金天氏。他建都于曲阜,在位 84 年(公元前 2598—公元前 2514),葬于云阳。他的陵墓在今山东省曲阜县西北。

第三位是颛顼,高阳氏。他是黄帝的孙子,也是屈原的远祖(见屈原《离骚》第 1 行)。颛顼 10 岁(?)时就随叔父少昊参政,20 岁时继位。起先,他建都高阳,即其帝号。高阳地处今河南省杞县西面。颛顼在位 78 年(公元前 2519—公元前 2436)。

第四位是帝喾,也名夋,他接了他叔父颛顼的位。15 岁时,他就协助叔父理事,受封采邑于辛,故亦称高辛氏。他建都西亳,位于今河南偃师县。他在位 70 年(公元前 2436—公元前 2366),传位于帝挚。帝挚弩弱,在位 9 年后为各部落首领废黜而由其兄弟唐尧即位。

对五帝的身份也是传说纷纭。有的把伏羲和神农二皇放在五帝之中,有的把尧和舜置于五帝之中。

这样就成了二帝三王。陶唐帝尧名放勋,姓伊耆,是帝喾之子,在位 99 年(公元前 2357—公元前 2258)。按段玉裁所言,尧与舜这两个名字为二帝在世时臣民对他们赞颂以示尊敬和热爱的称号。尧以施仁政著称,在位时制订了闰月。公元前 2297 年,黄河泛滥,尧命鲧治水。他从田野中选拔了一位普通农民舜,舜"既无官衔又出身侧微",但"思路敏捷",由于舜的提议,尧从朝中驱逐了四凶;也由于舜的举荐,朝廷选拔了"八元八恺",这些都是以明智、对百姓仁慈为怀而称著的人物。因而当时国泰民安,非常繁荣昌盛。尧之子丹朱刚愎自用、反复无常,舜就被擢升摄政,代为治国,历时 27 年,最后被确定为继承人。尧又把两个女儿娥皇、女英嫁给舜为妻妾。

虞帝舜姓姚,名重华(见《离骚》第 147—182 行屈原对他的称呼),是高阳帝颛顼的第五代孙。他在位 47 年(公元前 2255—公元前 2208),是一位伟大又仁慈的君主。舜在帝尧的朝廷任摄政时,由于禹的父亲鲧未能治退洪水,他下令把鲧列为四凶之一,并放逐出京,又命鲧之子禹继父业。他选拔了益、夔、稷、契、皋陶等共 22 位德才兼备之士入朝任职。虽然舜已正式被提名为尧的接位人,但在尧死后长达 3 年的时间里,他一直没有接位登基;因为他想如果朝廷和民众拥戴丹朱,他应把皇位让给他。与他的前任君主一样,他于公元前 2224 年把以前疏浚洪水有功之臣禹提为摄政,代他治国。舜之子商均执拗乖戾,所以他命禹继位。禹为舜摄政 16 年后,舜去世。尧、舜二帝和禹为政前后共 150 年,民间同心同德,国强民富,一片喜气洋洋。只是,尧执政时的后半期有一次洪水泛滥成灾。舜为平定部落有苗的叛乱,率兵出征(见《离骚》第 187 行),在九嶷山附近的苍梧荒野去世,安葬在九嶷山的最高峰舜源以南,并建祠庙以备祭祀。

按《尚书·尧典》记载,尧舜之时,羲与和的四个儿子受命根据天象为民定年历,……禹任司空,负责挖洞穴居以及平水土;弃任后稷,播百谷,即播种管理;卨任司徒,敷五教,即教导臣民家庭成员之间的五种礼仪;咎繇任士(狱官之长),制五刑、极刑大辟,即为民执法、制定刑罚的法官;垂任共工,理百工之事;益任朕虞,主管高山和低地的草木、走兽、飞禽;伯夷任秩宗,典三礼,即立礼仪以敬天地鬼神;夔任典乐,以和神人,即主管音乐;龙任纳言,出入帝命,即记录皇帝的话和命令。

夏后氏部落长禹名文命,姓姒,颛顼的后代,在位 8 年(公元前 2205—公元前 2197)。按晋代傅玄(公元 217—278)所言,"禹 12

岁时即随帝尧任司空。"他建都安邑,即今山西夏县以北。禹受命于舜治九州的洪水,他到处开凿山丘,挖河川,指挥得心应手,决非凡人力所能及。工程浩大,耗时 8 年,结果是成绩辉煌。禹所付出的艰巨劳动使整个民族免遭没顶之灾,所以人们都尊称之为大禹。他继承了舜为帝尧之子等候 3 年才接位的传统,也为帝舜之子商均等了 3 年才登基。在涂山(今安徽怀远县东南)的加冕典礼上,数以百计的部落首领都来参加庆贺,就在这一场合,他宣布使用夏历。至今中国仍有些地方还沿用夏历。传说禹由于过度操劳,他的足和腿上的毛都摩擦殆尽,手足(四肢至少有一肢已伤残)皆重趼。长期的野外劳动和风吹日晒把他的脸染成了棕褐色。真所谓三过家门而不入。据《孟子》记载,禹闻善言则拜。这里的"善言"当指对人民大众有利的话,而决非拍马赞美之词。禹在视察今浙江会稽地区时逝世,他的祠庙至今还在。

成汤名履,也叫天乙,姓子,是帝喾(高辛氏)之子卨(或契)的第十四代孙。卨(或契)由于协助禹治退洪水立了大功,帝尧赐封地于商。他是中国历史上第一位革命领袖,也是商的创建人。商以后称殷(公元前 1766—公元前 1122)。夏的末代国王夏桀迷恋妹喜①,妹喜是有施氏之女,后来成了桀的王后,任何人得罪了她将立即处死。桀挖酒池,积糟丘,酗酒作乐,纵情欢宴,通宵达旦,习以为常。按刘向《新序》所言,桀的酒池之大足可划船其中,而登糟丘之巅可观望七里之遥。朝政失控混乱,处处脱节乱套。桀的放荡和纵酒使朝中所有头脑清醒的人感到难以容忍。大臣关龙逢秉性耿直,力谏夏桀停止其声色淫逸,却被投入大牢处以辟刑。汤本身曾在夏台被专横的君主囚于狱中。据说一次桀见到一个老百姓涉冰川而过,心想为什么他不怕冷,就命砍断他的腿,察看其骨髓,以弄清他不怕冷的原因。那个时期(正如纣王时代一般)的呼声

---

① 妹喜亦作妹嬉和末喜。

是:"时日害(同曷)丧,予及汝(指桀)偕亡!"

因此,成汤以天、人的名义拔剑起义,在鸣条(今河南封丘东)给了这个骄奢淫逸的屠夫以毁灭性的打击,把他放逐到南巢。成汤是他死后的谥号,意思是"为民铲除了专制和暴行,像云雨一样使世人富裕充足。"司马迁的《史记·成汤世家》载,一次汤从屋中走出来看到田野四角都撒开了捕猎的网,有人还在祝祷:"让它们从天地四方都到我的网中来吧!"但汤却说:"嘿,那它们不全灭种了吗?"于是,他就网开三面并念祷说:"往右往左随你走,如果你不听我的话,就将投入我的网中。"他的仆从听了之后说:"汤的仁慈既深又远,遍及到飞禽和走兽。"他在位 13 年(公元前 1766—公元前 1753)。

汤的大丞相和辅弼伊尹的故事也该讲一下,他与商朝及其创建者的显著关系是再强调也不会过分的。屈原在他的诗篇(《离骚》第 289—290 行,《天问》第 205—212、239—250、325—328 行,《惜往日》第 34 行)中再三提到他关于圣明的君主由一位睿智的宰相辅佐的思想。按《吕氏春秋》所言,伊尹的母亲怀孕时住在伊水,一天夜里梦中神告诉她:一旦她看到地上舂米的臼穴里渗出水来的时候,就应不顾一切地赶快往东逃走。次日早晨,她果然看到臼穴中渗水,就告诉邻居快跑。她跑出了 10 里路,回头一看,村子已为洪水淹没,而她自己则化作了一棵空心树干的桑树。结果,有莘氏的采桑叶的女子在桑树空洞中发现了婴儿,把他献给她的族长或国王,婴儿被交给厨师领养。《尚书大传》的另一种说法是,伊尹的母亲怀孕后到伊水去汲水时化作了空心树干的桑树,她的丈夫在伊水边四处找她,只在树洞里发现了孩子,就领回去抚养了。孩子虽然长大成人,然而他的出生情况始终遭人嫌弃。最早的《世本》(著者佚名)的说法是汤梦见一人捧双耳三足鼎俎而笑,次日清晨醒来,汤便差人寻访此人,结果在有莘之野发现了伊尹。但莘王不准伊尹离去,因此汤派遣了媒人去与有莘氏族说亲,获准后,有莘氏的一个女子便被送往汤处成婚,伊尹就作为新娘的随从一起去了。与这位厨子作了一席谈之后,汤非常喜欢他,便请他入朝辅佐。那时夏桀的朝政已经乱成一团,相传伊尹曾五次赴桀处表示愿意协助重振朝纲,但顽固的桀专断成性,屡加拒绝。之后,伊尹在汤的鼓动之下终于参加了由汤率领的伐桀战役,导致桀的覆灭。

周的最早祖先是后稷(后即领主或高官),由舜推荐入帝尧朝中为臣。传说后稷的母亲姜嫄因踩着巨人的脚印而怀孕生了他。他出生后被认为不祥而弃之于人烟嘈杂的小街之上,然而牛马都让道以免踩伤了孩子。后来孩子又被弃置在冰上,但众鸟都飞孵其上为孩子保暖。无奈,孩子才被领了回去养大,遂名弃(即遗弃之意)。成人后,尧命其为稷官,主理禾谷之事,封地于邰。稷的子孙承袭官职到周武王时已是第十五代后人了。

姬昌作为创建伟大的周王朝(公元前 1122—公元前 256)的精神领袖,以前是殷辛王朝的西伯,统领雍州(地处西域,故官衔为西伯,属古时的九州之一),有权对附属国或藩邦发动讨伐。刘向的《新序》中讲到他的故事是:为筑灵台奠基时,从土中挖出一具骷髅,这位未来的文王道:“把它再埋上。”督工答道:“大人,这遗骨已无主了。”西伯道:“天下以王为主,国有首领为主。我就是它的主,为什么还要去为它找主呢?”骷髅又被埋上了。听了这个故事,天下人都称道西伯之贤,说西伯的恩泽能遍及朽骨,更何况于人。

一天他驾车出猎,遇吕尚垂钓于渭水之滨。吕尚虽已年逾八十,白发苍苍,却是与他才智相当的政治家和战略家。那时吕尚在朝歌一贫如洗,只得受雇于某屠户。他对西伯说:“没出息的屠夫只能宰牛,果敢的屠夫可当宰相。”姬昌听后不禁为之动容,继而长谈,心更悦之。他对吕尚说:“吾父早就企盼着你哩。”因而称吕尚为太公望,意即他父亲所企盼的人。随后同车载吕尚而归,尊为太师并参与朝政。西伯死后由姬发接位,就是后来的周武王,他尊称吕尚为师尚父。往后在推翻专制霸道的纣王的革命中,多亏吕尚为之运筹帷幄。吕尚留给后世的著作有《六韬》,在周早期时已失散,代之而问世的是战国时期的伪本,书名也叫《六韬》。

再来说纣王。这个称号是他被推翻后起的,意思是灭绝人性、劣迹斑斑的家伙。这个商朝的末代君主既精力旺盛又擅长诡辩,是个不可救药的酒徒和淫棍,其残忍绝不亚于暴桀。他身旁的王妃妲己更助长了他的暴行。他也凿池盛酒,把食肉悬吊起来像成排的树林,彻夜欢宴时命裸露的男女相互追逐其间作为他佐酒的娱乐。大臣鬼侯和鄂侯被他剁为肉泥并加以烤炙。第三名受害者是西伯昌,他在羑里(今河南汤阴县以北)被关进了牢房,罪名是因为听说他的两位同僚遭到像猪肉一样的对待而叹了一口气,纣王判定百日之后处决。① 纣王的老师和叔父箕子由于进忠告而被囚禁。王子比干因对纣王的酷刑、淫逸及成天纵酒进行苦谏而被剜心以视其"七窍"。

这位未来的文王后来由于其友散宜生等行贿送礼,以美女、宝石和绸缎当赎金后才被释放。此后西伯变得更为谦虚和蔼,之后又在渭水之阳(北岸)遇吕尚。不久,三分之二的小国首领都投奔西伯而不向纣王了。

武王姬发由吕尚辅佐,仅以3000名士兵、300辆战车的革命军队对这个暴君发起了进攻,并在殷都朝歌以南30里的郊外牧野粉碎了纣王的部队。绝大多数纣的仆从都掉转枪头,一致拥戴武王,于是纣溃不成军,自焚而死②,结束了他的罪恶统治。

为说明姬发的言而必信,恐怕还得叙述一段故事。殷隐士胶鬲由西伯昌推荐于纣,武王率兵伐殷时,纣遣胶鬲中途迎之。胶鬲

---

① 见《战国策·赵策》。

② 《竹书纪年》和司马迁的《史记》都记载,武王到达纣王身亡(悬梁自尽)的宫殿时,射之以矢者三,并用轻吕剑击之,以黄钺断其首级,并以钺柄作殷旗大白的旗杆舞召纣的臣属和仆从们。关于《竹书纪年》另见第182页注①。

见到姬发,问道:"西伯何去?"武王答曰:"去殷。""何时能抵达?"
"甲子之日,吾将抵殷都之郊外。"胶鬲即返回。接着天下雨了,但
武王仍催军前进,军师请求驻歇,姬发道:"胶鬲必向纣呈报吾将于
甲子之日至殷郊。吾若不按时抵达,纣当疑胶鬲之不忠而杀之,故
应加速行军以救之。"武王终于在甲子之日到达殷都郊外。

武王作为周朝的开国元勋只在位 7 年(公元前 1122—公元前
1115),谥其已故的父亲为文王。这时武王已充分地接受了他父亲
和吕尚的精神,并贯彻于他创建的新的大业之中。在选拔贤能的
人士任职之时,据说他所拥有的朋友达 3000 之多。

此外,武王的兄弟周公旦在施道行善、光大博爱以及所采取合
适的措施、方法上成绩卓著。在古代中国,他是最伟大的政治家,
声誉上恐怕仅次于尧、舜,但论实际功绩,无人能出其右。因此难
怪孔子冀求初周那种安居乐业、百姓欢腾、万众一心的辉煌日子时
要每夜梦见他了。他推行音乐和诗歌,建立了教育制度,制订了礼
法和刑律,布置了政府各职能部门,设立官吏任免制度。为了辅佐
将成年而又未臻成熟的侄儿周成王,他亲任摄政和冢宰,平定了叛
乱,建都于东部洛邑。初周的政治、经济和文化各方面的措施和业
绩都是周公旦的功劳。

三 初周(公元前 1122—公元前 1052)

如上所述,武王及周公旦下大力气开创了百姓安居乐业又同心
同德的局面,因而出现了成、康(成王,公元前 1115—公元前 1078;康
王,公元前 1078—公元前 1052)的太平盛世,日子既安逸又幸福;民
间丰衣足食,骚扰和忧虑几乎绝迹,也没有战争。只有一次例外,那
就是平定武庚叛乱之战。武庚,纣之子,在出于妒忌的管叔和成王的
其他两位叔父的庇护和纵容之下,在成王接位的第一年发动了叛变,
最后在成王三年平定。这对成康盛世来说是一大遗憾。那时民间主
食五谷的价格便宜得出奇,也没有罪犯,一连 40 多年狱中空空如也。

这世界似乎已把悲伤和恐惧都永远赶跑了。

有人认为①这种与尧、舜、禹、汤时代相仿的社会稳定和团结一致的局面之所以会出现,根本上是因为当时的土地制度把土地合理地分配给所有的耕者。每900亩地②按九宫格划分,周围八块分给八家农户,中间一块为公地(见下图)。在这九块一组的农田周围开有小溪渠。中间的公地由八户农家共同负责农务,国家就不再征税了。这就是所谓的"井田制",因为划分九块地的线条似汉字"井",再则在中间的公地里确实有口井作公共灌溉及家用。

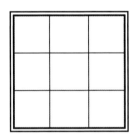

但是这不过是本篇的开场白而已。为了开导民众,在音乐和诗歌等文化方面也采取了措施。按《庄子·天运篇》载,一次,老子聃去拜访孔子请教关于礼的事,孔子说:"丘治《诗》、《书》、《礼》、《乐》、《易》、《春秋》六经,自以为久矣。"孔子所编《乐经》以及其他经典(《易经》除外)于公元前213年由于穷凶极恶的暴君嬴政听了他的罪恶的大臣李斯的建议被焚毁。有的经书事后多少或部分地得到恢复,但《乐经》的挽救却无影无踪。不过我们知道,音乐有时单独即可陶冶人性,但时常与舞蹈和诗歌合并在一起来美化和丰富初周的生活。《周礼》记载有7种舞蹈的名称,都是由乐器和歌

---

① 见欧阳修的《本论》和苏洵的论说文《田制》。《本论》强调国家民族的立场观点,反对佛教界的看法。佛教界的看法无疑是有缺点的。

② 这是周制,每农户分100亩。商制与以前陶唐、虞和夏三个朝代一致不变,但每户分地为70亩,地块的总面积为630亩,包括中间的公地(也是70亩)在内。

曲伴奏的。起先有人以为《周礼》是周公旦所作,但最后东汉和清的学者何休、皮锡瑞认为只是六国的产物,题目是《春官》、《大司乐》:包括《云门》、《大卷》、《大咸》、《大韶》(也作《大磬》)、《大夏》、《大濩》和《大武》——其中《云门》和《大卷》是关于黄帝的舞蹈—器乐曲—歌曲,其他都是分别关于尧、舜、禹、汤、武的。还有些乐曲我们现在只能闻其名了,如黄帝的《承云》、少昊的《九渊》、颛顼的《五茎》、帝喾的《六英》、舜的《卿云》(有人推测曲词还在,但恐是伪本而已)、禹的《九辩》和《九歌》以及汤的《晨露》。

　　说到诗,我们知道初周由太师、遒人(即诸侯、藩属、专职官吏和信使)从遍布各地的特别政府部门搜集民歌、诗歌和颂歌,目的是向朝廷反映各地的民俗、风尚以及行政弊端和民间的不满。根据司马迁的《史记》,当时从乡间、帝王和诸侯的朝廷以及宗庙中收罗的诗篇有3000多首,孔子从中选辑了311首汇编成《诗经》。但是唐朝学者孔颖达、宋代学者朱熹、叶适、清代学者朱彝尊、崔述对太史公认为孔子曾把一大批诗歌加以剔除的说法都持争议的态度。商殷和初周以《诗经》命名的诗歌选集有305篇,但这并不是孔子留给我们的全部遗产。诗篇的原文或抄本都刻绘在竹简上,数量上本来就不可能很多,却仍难逃被那个罪恶滔天的暴君秦始皇和他的心腹李斯焚毁于一旦的命运。秦朝于公元前206年覆灭之后,汉朝那个无赖开国皇帝高祖刘邦统治期间仍在实施着不准人们拥有书本的"挟书律",前后共达15年,直到公元前191年刘邦的儿子惠帝在位后才公开废除。以后,这部名闻遐迩的诗选单凭人们的记忆和复述才得以恢复。鲁人申倍、齐人辕固和燕人韩婴开始依新本对人施教,并加诠注。但东汉以来这些注疏也都先后失散。西汉后期,学者刘向之子刘歆说他发现了六国学者毛公所诠注的《毛诗故训传》。之后,在东汉和三国时代,郑玄和陆玑说毛公名毛亨(或称老毛),鲁国人,是荀况的学生,他把这本诠注传给了他的学生,赵国人毛苌(或称小毛)。清代学者皮锡瑞在他所著的《诗经通论》中以犀利的分析把刘歆对毛的说法斥之为纯粹的欺骗。至于诗选的诗篇总数,有 6 篇失散了,所以现在的诗选共305 篇。例如,有下列的两行诗在现在的诗选中是没有的:

得人者兴,
失人者崩。

其次,有关教育体制,如帝王的太学(分辟雍、成均、上庠、东序、瞽宗)、藩臣的学校(泮宫)及乡间的学校(庠序)都起到了显著的作用。乡间的初级学校对学生传习六艺,即礼、乐、射、御、书、数。虽然诸侯的中学和帝王的太学里施教什么科目,现在的史料里没有明确的记载,严格地说,我们不得而知,但可以大致推测,不过是程度要求上更高些地重复教授六艺,也可能另外加些什么科目而已。据了解,诸侯的学校在南边和东门、西门的南侧都有河流环绕。至于上述帝王的太学,辟雍(意思是光明和谐)是周王朝的学院,地处其他四座学院中间;成均是仿五帝制的学院,处于国都镐京以北 50 里左右的大河以南;上庠是仿虞制的学院,在大河以北;东序是仿夏制的学院,在大河以东;瞽宗是仿商殷制的学院,在大河以西。这五所帝王太学院一起形成一个建筑群,茅草屋顶,很宽敞,四面环水或部分有水围绕,其中间就是传道、授艺的所在。教育的目的是使帝王的天下更光明和谐。

第三,礼分五种类型:吉礼共十二部分;凶礼共五部分;宾礼共八部分;军礼共五部分;嘉礼共六部分。具体举例说,最后一种嘉礼分为饮食、冠潜(即入冠和婚姻)、乡射(即射箭集会)、飨宴、脤膰(太庙和宗祠祭品的分派)及庆贺。即使春、秋、冬季的蒐狩(打猎)也有礼节。其目的是教育人民在务农之外的其他各种场合里怎样才能行为得体。一旦合乎礼,人们所看到和听到的都会比较舒服。心理和感情上得到调节,做什么事都想做得更好些,即或空闲时生活也很充实有意义。这样把人们的兴趣引导到礼仪的轨道,于是捣蛋闯祸、扰乱社会的事自然就少了。

公元前 1111 年即平定叛乱后的第二年,周公旦把住在朝歌的殷民迁至洛水(雒)南岸。又隔了两年,即公元前 1109 年,这片居民区大大拓宽了,四周筑起了城墙,终于成为周的东都。整个建设工程由周公旦亲自过问,7 年后竣工,周公却于竣工前一年去世。由大禹铸就的象征国家主权、又由商殷作为国宝加以保存的九鼎也搬运过来了。这庞大的双耳三脚铜鼎的前身是小得多的、形状相同的铜铸煮肉容器,是古时候祭祀、宴会时的用具。东都从过去的殷都改称洛邑,也称郏鄏。公元前 1091 年,成王召集诸侯们去东都举行盛大欢宴,地处偏僻的所有的部落首领也都赶来敬贺。文、武、成、康四代施仁政的君主一起相沿约 90 年,在中国历史上成为自尧、舜、禹、汤的辉煌时代以来仁政的极盛时期。

但人事与大自然一样春去夏来,不可能永恒不变。从昭王(公元前 1052—公元前 1002)直到夷王(公元前 894—公元前 878)共 170 多年的时间里,周王室日趋衰落,甚至连接见臣从藩属时按上尊下卑的封建礼仪都被下属搁置一边——君主必须亲自走下朝堂去迎接他的诸侯们。

真正把周王朝名声显赫的宗族拉向泥潭、并在祖宗过去那种鼎盛荣耀的余晖上泼溅泥浆污水的是既暴虐霸道又骄奢淫逸的厉王(公元前 878—公元前 828)和幽王(公元前 781—公元前 771)。厉王为侦查在背后批评其劣迹的人竟雇佣了女巫,对批评者加罪名为"污蔑"并处死。有关厉王的罪行虽不见记载,我们无从洞悉,但估计为数一定不少且劣迹昭著,否则不会采取上述措施的。最后,厉王在人民起义作乱中被逐出京都,逃往名"彘"的小镇,并老死在那里。从厉王流放到死亡的 14 年里,朝中两位公侯宣布了共和制,并治理朝政。

幽王迷恋妃子褒姒。为了博她一笑,他竟然在并无外敌入侵的情况下点燃了烽火,召集各路诸侯领兵前来保卫京都。为了抬举褒姒和她的儿子,他又把皇后和太子废黜。有关他的情况还是老一套:纵酒、淫乱,把朝政弄得一团糟,最后导致覆灭。在犬戎的一次突然入侵中,在骊山脚下,即今陕西临潼县东南,幽王被杀。

但厉王之子、幽王之父宣王(公元前827—公元前781)在不到半个世纪的统治时期的政绩应叫他的父亲和儿子感到羞愧。在周朝漫长的历史中,宣王是唯一的一位中兴国王。在位第一年,他讨伐西戎于西北,北伐猃狁(战国及战国之后称胡、匈奴),次年在南方与西南部征服了荆蛮、淮夷和徐戎,恢复了武王和成王的势力范围。

幽王之子平王(公元前770—公元前714)由于其父为犬戎所杀而吓得魂飞魄散,遂迁都至洛邑以远避入侵之敌。周公旦当时建洛邑是为了安置九鼎,而不是为他的子孙躲避敌人而准备的安乐窝。事实上,避风港是不存在的,因为任你逃到什么地方,敌人总是会追踪而来。正如宋代苏轼在《平王论》中所说的,平王的驽钝、懦弱是周王朝落得名存实亡、削弱得像幻影的根本原因。以后,周朝更趋衰败,史称东周,以区别于自武王至幽王国都在镐京(位于今陕西西安县西南)的西周。

从上述可知,西周的封建天下自昭王到夷王的六代君主期间开始削弱,又由于厉王和幽王肆无忌惮、荒淫无道,终于把国家折腾到分裂的地步。到了春秋时期,分裂不断重复出现,蔓延扩大,一个分裂与另一个分裂又纠缠在一起,这是平王统治结束后第四个年头的事。

四　春秋时期(公元前722—公元前481)

《春秋》是孔子所编写的一部史书,记事从鲁隐公在位第一年开始。鲁隐公是周公第九代孙①,他想维持由武王和周公所创立的

---

① 　另一种家谱认为他是文王的第八代孙。

封建秩序。据孟子所言,当孔子编写《春秋》之时,"道衰微,邪说暴行有作,臣弑其君者有之,子弑其父者有之。① 孔子惧,作《春秋》。《春秋》,天子之事也。"又说:"王者之迹熄而诗②亡,诗亡,然后《春秋》作。晋之《乘》,楚之《梼杌》、鲁之《春秋》,一也;其事则齐桓、晋文,其文则史。孔子曰:'其义则丘窃取之矣。'"《春秋》所记述的是 12 位公侯统治前后达 242 年时期里所发生的事,这段历史时期也因书而得名。最后一则记事的编写时间是哀公十四年春,哀公出猎获一麒麟。据《春秋·公羊传》,孔子闻此事后惊呼,"吾道穷矣!"那是孔子编写第一则记事后的第三年。东汉王充在《论衡》中引《春秋》说:"哀公'西向出猎捡得死麒麟一具',仆从展视孔子。"宋代左氏、公羊、谷梁三"传"最早的木刻本中均无"死"字。我以为,这肯定是五代时失散的汉简或隋唐卷轴的版本讹误所致。从远古时期起,麒麟或凤凰的出现就通常被认为是一种吉祥之兆,预示和平友好。另一方面,正如上述两句孟子的话所述,孔子撰写《春秋》的目的很明显是用指责性的笔触记载那些背时和邪恶的事件。例如,有一则记事是关于卫公子州吁谋害了他的父亲并篡夺了公位,这是发生在鲁隐公四年的事,也是《春秋》中记载的第一次灾祸。接着,鲁隐公十一年时,鲁公子翚谋害了隐公。《公羊传》所记载的麒麟以及孔子为之惊呼一事明显地说明了孔子对希望恢复周公时代的社会秩序已经绝望了,这也是他停写指责性记事的理由。两年后,孔子去世。但奇怪的是,左丘明及另外一批关于孔子的学者如《谷梁传》评注者范宁、《公羊传》评注者孔衍等,都认为麒麟的出现固然是吉兆,但只是指圣人孔子的出现而已。这是值得庆贺的,因此,孔子才停止了他的指责性记事,因为他的任务已经完成了!我以为这是绝对错误的,因为这正与圣人自己的看法相

---

① 据班固所著《汉书·司马迁传》,春秋时期弑君事件有 36 起,诸侯国家覆灭的有 52 起,而领主不克维持其封地而亡命者无数。

② 指以前由诸侯藩国或专业官吏收集并呈报周王的民歌、诗和颂。

违背。这简直是乱七八糟的颠倒是非:这种看法不仅置孔子的灰心丧气和百事无成的心态于不顾,更糟糕的是对孔子所说的话强加歪曲,从反面去解释和领会。

鲁是个大国,是武王赐给兄弟周公的封地,国都在曲阜。所谓大国是说其疆域有 400 里方圆,当时只有鲁、卫、齐三国才堪称大国。① 成王登基第一年,周公为他年轻的侄儿担任了摄政和冢宰,所以只得留在国都镐京,他的封地就授予他的儿子伯禽,称鲁侯。因此孔子选择鲁隐公作为撰写《春秋》的起始记事时期是含有特殊意义的。这是由于如上所述,鲁隐公为周公的嫡系后人,并且在执政 11 年后丢了性命。自这次灭绝人性的事件之后,一连串骇人听闻和伤天害理的事件在各处相继发生。

商朝开国时汤王拥有的藩属达 3000 之多,初周时武王有 800。② 这些藩属绝大部分是参与了反夏桀或反殷纣的革命战争的部落首领。周时附属国头领的官衔正像中世纪欧洲一样分为公、侯、伯、子、男五等。如司马迁所说③,孔子在写《春秋》之前曾出访过 70 多国,对各国国君游说实施王道的必要性,但一事无成。当然还有许多如秦、吴、越等国他没有去访问。不过也许可以推测,从周武王到公元前 722 年春秋时期开始之前的那段时间,诸侯属国的数字已减少到了原数的一个零头,自然远远不止 70 多国。按《史记》记载,在此期间,大诸侯国有 12 个,如包括"蛮"邦吴则为 13 个。④ 由于周王室式微,诸侯各国之间战事频仍,强者置王命于不顾,对弱者横加侵吞,王权遭到公开蔑视。公元前 717 年,周恒

---

① 见司马迁《史记·汉兴以来将相名臣年表·序》。
② 见柳宗元《封建论》。但据皇甫谧(公元 265—289 晋武帝年间)的《帝王世纪》,禹在涂山加冕时拥有的藩属达 10000;汤王有 3000;周灭商后有 1773 国的属地;春秋时期有 1200 国;战国时期只剩 10 余国。
③ 见《史记·十二诸侯年表·序》。
④ 指鲁、齐、晋、秦、楚、宋、卫、陈、蔡、曹、郑、燕、吴。

王派使者凡伯访鲁，返回时为卫主所虏；公元前 707 年，周王御驾亲征讨伐郑国时，郑庄公的士卒射中王肩。王权沦丧殆尽，叹为观止。

尽管叛道忤逆一时猖獗，但随着五霸争雄局面的出现，恢复社会秩序的趋势已很明显。五霸时而大会诸侯，时而约法三章、歃血为盟，名义上都以保卫王室当招牌，而实际上却是以提高那些盟主们本身的威望为目的。因此，尽管说得漂亮、写得巧妙，但事实结果却总是适得其反。正如孟子的评语所说："五霸者，三王之罪人也。"

公元前 715 年，宋公、卫公与齐侯相会于瓦屋起草联盟，开联盟之先河。从此各式联盟此起彼伏。

五霸中的佼佼者齐桓公于公元前 685 年因其兄襄公被害而上台执政。他起用著名政治家管仲为相，使其政权维持了 40 多年之久。他九会诸侯结成联盟，引导大家共同效忠周室，保卫周室抵御外寇入侵，使政局一时恢复了正气。晋公子重耳逃离本国在齐国避难时，齐桓公把女儿齐姜嫁给了他，这位未来的晋文公夫人在宋襄公死后使晋文公成为五霸盟主的霸业中起了很大的作用。

晋文公系成王兄弟唐侯叔虞之子燮父的后代。晋侯燮父借助秦穆公于公元前 636 年接了位。当时周襄王的王子带率领北狄兵马直逼京都洛邑，襄王只得向西避难逃到了郑。晋文公设计杀了王子带，并于公元前 635 年卫护襄王返回京都。他提拔狐偃、赵衰为高官。公元前 638 年，当宋国被楚国攻击得溃不成军时，他挽救了宋，之后又于公元前 632 年与秦、齐、宋联盟，在卫国爆发的城濮之战中打败了楚国。

介推，通常叫介之推，是晋文公被迫在外流亡 19 年时的一位忠贞不渝的随从。在逃亡齐国的途中，因食物短缺，重耳饥饿难忍，介之推暗地里割下自己的腿肉，煮之而解重耳之饥。重耳后来也知道了这事。嗣后重耳返国复位，封官赐爵犒赏群臣，却忘掉了介之推。对重耳的忘恩不报,介之推大为愤懑,他一声不吭,带了老母离朝隐居于绵山。重耳终于想起了割股之恩,急于召回介之推以报恩,而介之推却拒绝下山。晋文公下令放火烧山以逼迫介之推下山,介之推怒不可遏,紧紧抱住树干,被焚烧而死。文公深感内疚,命名该山为介山,禁止上山伐木砍柴,并为他举丧,亲自缞服致哀。为了怀念介之推抱树焚死的事迹,他的死期被命名为"寒食"。这一纪念习俗在中国流传了 2600 年之久,农历三月初三起一连三日,人们停止举炊,只吃事先准备好的冷餐。

秦穆公继承他哥哥成公的大位后,即任命由余、百里奚、蹇叔等一批德才兼备的贤者为相国和其他官职。由于穆公善于治国,秦国日趋强盛;他宽厚的施政也使百姓大为受益。公元前 624 年周襄王在位时,穆公领兵远征西域伐戎,并吞了 20 国,把秦国疆域拓宽了 1000 里,襄王赐号西方诸侯伯,统领诸侯。

百里奚又以五羖大夫著称于世。他原是虞国的臣僚,虞灭后,他与虞王一起为晋所掳。晋公主嫁秦穆公时,他作为随从之一员被送走。他羞于为人妆奁随从和奴仆,逃亡到楚,在楚郊宛被扣。穆公久闻百里奚之贤,欲以重金赎之。又恐楚人不同意,就先派信使与楚人洽谈,云:有晋公主妆奁随从一名逃亡于楚,愿以黑色公羊皮五张以赎回。楚人同意放人,穆公即恢复了百里奚的自由。一席长谈,心甚悦之,即拜为相。百里奚所献的国策使穆公在 7 年之内变为五霸之一。

下一位是宋襄公。他是殷微子的后人,成王为纪念商汤王而赐封宋公。据说宋襄公好谈古代帝王的仁慈和正义,他的国度也很强盛。公元前 643 年,齐桓公死后,他的 5 位公子为争继承权而起了内讧。宋襄公即派军赴齐排斥众兄弟而扶孝公接位。日后襄公与楚战于泓,受伤而死。

最后是楚庄王。据说他于公元前 606 年领兵与陆浑部落交战时,以检阅为名,令部队在周定王的领地列队摆阵以炫耀其威武。

定王派代表去为他的将士欢呼喝彩,庄王乘机问来使周朝国都宗庙的九鼎各重多少。这预示着庄王已有心要结束旧的政权,兴建他自己的新王朝来取而代之。

简而言之,五霸兴起之后,在大会诸侯或誓盟之时,常常伴随着出兵远征,各国的政治就靠掌权人来操纵,这自然导致荒淫无道泛滥成灾,连周室的国王和王子都不例外。佞臣乘机鼓动如簧之舌,兴风作浪。宦官越职擅权肇事生非的现象屡见不鲜,一时甚嚣尘上。

还应谈一下关于楚的来源、其潜在的敌国秦及其隐伏的敌对盟国齐。熊绎系黄帝(也称有熊氏,有熊是当时的国名,因此黄帝的某些苗裔姓熊)和高阳帝的后人,文王之师鬻熊的重孙,初周时成王封地于楚,为子爵,国都在丹阳(今湖北秭归县①东南)。按周贵族次序,子爵排在第四位,所以其封地面积较小,最小的封地仅50里圆。他的封地约在100里方圆左右,这是楚及楚王室的起源。大约400年之后,即公元前704年,熊通自立为楚王。春秋时期,楚日益壮大,在13个周属大诸侯中仅次于秦,齐紧随于后位列第三。公元前690年,楚文王迁都至郢(今湖北江陵县北纪南城)。公元前613年,就是这位问周鼎有多重的楚庄王上台了。之后,公子弃疾于公元前529年自称楚平王,并在屈原的时代迁都于离郢稍偏东南一点的地方。公元前506年"蛮"邦大国吴进攻楚,占领楚都郢,楚昭王不得不逃亡至隋。次年,楚臣申包胥赴秦求救兵,他"身倚秦廷门墙,嚎啕大哭达七天七夜,既无休止,也不饮一勺水",秦哀公感其诚心,同意发兵。由此开始直到战国中期,楚先后并吞了邓、舒、蓼、陈、蔡、杞、莒和越。这些都是较小的国度,只有蔡属于13个大诸侯国。越也在公元前473年并吞了吴。当然楚还

---

① 屈原祖先的住宅就在此,即丹阳的西北。屈原被放逐江南的前期,曾在这里住过一些时候。见《离骚》第131行"女嬃"注52。

并吞了其他一些较小的国度。

伍员(子胥)和他父亲及兄弟的悲壮故事也该叙述一下。春秋时期,伍奢为楚太子太傅。朝臣费无忌诽谤太子,平王召伍奢追究此事,伍奢答道:"陛下为何置骨肉之亲于不顾而相信造谣中伤、惹是生非的小人?"平王怒,捕其子伍尚,把父子二人斩首,而伍子胥逃亡至吴国,后擢升为吴王阖闾攻楚的将军。经过5次战役,伍子胥攻陷楚都郢,那时平王早已死亡,伍子胥掘墓开棺,吊起平王尸体,鞭尸三百,以报父兄惨死之仇。吴王阖闾因与越开战时受伤,结果不治身死。其子夫差即位,并在对越战争中给予毁灭性的打击。越王勾践求和,夫差不顾伍子胥的谏议忠告同意议和。之后,伍子胥又再三启奏建议伐越,都未获准。楚太宰嚭受贿于越,在吴王面前进谗加害伍子胥,吴王授伍子胥剑赐死,伍子胥对随从说:"挖吾双目,悬挂于吴城墙之东南,定当见越人至而灭吴。"说罢拔剑自刎。9年后,越王勾践果然灭吴。

秦国的起源比楚国几乎晚了一个世纪。非子(飞子)姓嬴,是伯益(柏翳)的后人,伯益为舜饲养飞禽走兽,并助禹治水有功;周孝王时主管马厩,封地于秦(即今甘肃天水县)。作为男爵,他的封地当初是很小的。一个多世纪后,被废黜的王后之父申侯借犬戎部落的兵力入侵周都镐京并杀死幽王。当时秦襄公已很强大,终于击退了野蛮的入侵者,并与周的其他诸侯一起扶太子宜臼继位,是为平王。秦襄公因功升子爵,正式成为周王的诸侯,并加封岐西的地块。3年后,秦文公大胜戎军,把侵略成性的犬戎赶出其封地。之后,就是秦穆公,作为五霸之一,其业绩前已简略地叙述过了。

齐是大国,仅次于鲁、卫(卫分封给康叔),原是武王赐吕尚(或称吕望)的封地,建都营丘(今山东临淄县)。春秋初期,齐桓公作为实力雄厚的国君和五霸之主,是当时最活跃的人物。但在治国能手管仲相国逝世后,桓公宠信三个太监和谄媚小人,这些奸佞在桓公死后把齐国推向混乱的深渊。由此,在250年的时间里,齐国的威望降至低潮,最后在公元前 379 年,由宦官田午篡位。春秋早期,齐曾并吞了纪、遂两个小国,但在公元前 589 年又拱手交给了鲁和卫。

春秋和战国两个时期虽然以紧张、混乱和战祸出名,但这时在伦理、哲学和其他学术等方面却诞生了一位超一流的杰出人物、两位光芒四射的巨星和许多学派的创始人;可是同样就在这时,在政治界也产生了一批凶残万恶的无赖恶棍和一个飞扬跋扈的暴君。老子名李耳,绰号老聃,因为他是个耳朵特别长的老人(聃的另一种解释是耳长垂肩,即耳朵像两片平平的不成型的皮肉)。他是楚国人,比孔子年长 10 到 16 岁,出生在苦县厉乡,是周守藏室史①的史官。司马迁的《史记》说:"孔子赴周问礼于老子。"我们也听说孔子对周的官吏万分敬佩。据《庄子·天运篇》,孔子问话时 51 岁,即公元前 502 年。在《礼记·曾子问》章节中有四处关于老子的言行,与《道德经》或《老子》中言之凿凿的论述完全是南辕而北辙,风马牛不相及的。例如,《道德经》上说:"夫礼者,忠信之薄而乱之首。"又说:"圣人不死,大盗不止。"故此,清学者汪中的《述学·老子考异》认为,几百年来都以为《老子》是老子的作品,但结果证实绝对不是,而是周太史儋所著。据《史记·列传》,儋曾谒见秦献公,那是孔子死后 129 年的事②。从《史记·列传》判断,司马迁在西汉还没能弄清这两个人究竟是同一个人还是不同的两人。另外,还有一个叫老莱子的人,也是楚国人,也是道德学派的思想家,太史公同样也猜想他是真正的老子。

---

① 按《周礼》"天官、冢宰"条,史官共 12 位,其职责为记录重要事件和讲话。早在黄帝时代就设有正式史官沮诵和仓颉,仓颉以发明汉字称著于世。夏、商、周时,主管历史、天象的官员大史(或称太史)的职责还包括教育。

② 这是司马迁在日期上的笔误。孔子死于公元前 479 年。照此推算他死后的 129 年应为公元前 350 年,那么太史儋不可能见到秦献公,因为那时献公已死(死于公元前 361 年),其子秦孝公接位。可见孔子死后的 109 年,即公元前 370 年可能是正确的日期。

Introduction

　《老子》一书的作者属谁的问题拖延不决达 100 多年之久,直到公元前 370 年或稍早些。从春秋、战国两个时期看,年岁最长、最伟大的哲学家无疑应该是孔子。他生于宋的祖先襄公二十二年(周灵王二十一年,公元前 551 年)的鲁国,殁于鲁哀公十六年(周敬王四十一年,公元前 479 年)。孔子被尊为大成至圣先师,真正是世界上为数不多的伟大启蒙者之一。他所处的时代一连 15 个年头江河日下,堕落到在日后 2400 年的历史中人们罕见的最黑暗的深渊,那是个骇人听闻的时代。梭伦(公元前 639?—公元前 559,圣人、法典制订人和西方民主之父)、伯里克利(公元前 495?—公元前 429,政治家、希腊文化的哺育人)和苏格拉底(公元前 469?—公元前 399,哲学家、勇敢地宣扬真理的大师),以上三位都是雅典人,也都是孔子的同时代人。正当这三位巨人以他们光芒四射的智慧之星从希腊半岛照耀到国外时,身在东亚的孔子在被各国战火糟蹋得乌烟瘴气、漆黑一团里吐露出光耀夺目的异彩。印度的释迦牟尼(公元前 557?—公元前 480?[①],哲学家、佛教创始人)比孔子早出世 6 年,早去世 1 年,几乎是孔子的同龄人。可以肯定,他放弃家庭和国家的主张违背了人类的天性,是很不实际的,但他坚持非暴力和拯救众生的主张却洋溢着对人类的同情的恩泽。他认为人的欲望是产生并引起苦难和痛楚的根源,所以应该摈弃一切贪欲;这种主张自然导致虚无主义的理想——涅槃。这种主张也像刀子一样切到了生命的根子本身,因为生命原就是一团各式各样欲望的综合体。屈原在现有的著作中虽不承认是儒者,但他的思想肯定是属于道统的范畴。而道统以三王、五帝以及武王、周公为代表,这恰恰是孔子儒学原则的先驱。屈原生在孔圣人之后 134 年,是孔子最出色的门徒孟子的同时代人,比孟子小 27

---

① 　他的生死日期正如古时其他杰出的思想家一样,根据不同的推算方法有不同的说法。有一种佛教年表认为他生于公元前 565 年,卒于公元前 487 年;另一种说法则认为是公元前 1016—公元前 949 年。

岁。不论直接或间接,我们的诗人必定会大大地受到孔子的影响,所以我们有必要对孔子的学说、政治理想、伦理道德原则及其付诸实施有关方式有个概括的认识。

传说孔子天生赋有圣人的睿智和德性,他并不长期师从某一位大师,而是一时一事地个别向众多的老师探求学识。他除了向郯子和老聃求学之外,又向苌弘学音乐,向师襄学琴。鲁定公时他任司空(古时"空"作开挖解,司空即专管建设的大臣),鲁定公十四年(公元前497年)升任大司寇(司法大臣),56岁时兼任相国。他在职期间,臣僚少正卯为无政府主义派领袖,"心达而险"、"行僻而坚"、"言诡而辩"、"记丑而博"、"顺非而泽",因策划阴谋而被正法。孔子任相历时三月,鲁国升平,民间富庶。孔子治国有方的消息很快传播到邻国,使齐国朝廷大为震慑。齐即选美女80名,教以舞步,以优质丝绸衣着,分乘三十辆饰彩四轮马车送呈鲁公。宦官收下了这令人兴奋的厚礼,于是鲁公一连三天不上朝,也不出席祭天大礼奉献烤肉。孔子遂辞官离鲁,老朋友师己一人送行而已,分手时孔子高歌一曲,讽喻鲁国即将大祸临头。据说孔子曾周游70多个国家,觅访贤主以图实施其德政,历时14年,但却一事无成。失望之余,他回归鲁国,编撰《春秋》。时而仍作短期出访,平时就收薄酬授徒谋生。孔子学生3000人,其中谙练六艺、有德行的有72人。

孔子的道德原则形成他政治思想的动机和精神,政治是道德的最终目的。他总结了三王、五帝协调一致的规章制度,《礼记·礼运篇》似乎把上述意思表达得最为完整了。这里选择代表其道德准则的目的、也是最有意义的一节:"大道之行也,天下为公,选贤与能,讲信修。故人不独亲其亲,不独子其子,使老有所终,壮有所用,幼有所长,鳏寡孤独废疾者皆有所养。男有分,女有归。货恶其弃于地也,不必藏于己;力恶其不出于身也,不必为己。是故谋闭而不兴,盗窃乱贼而不作;故外户而不闭,是谓大同。"

这就是说,在这种理想的社会里人际关系中的自私性已经消除,个人利益已与社会公益融为一体;人们不能容忍浪费,也不会无理地贪求有所获得;劳动成了自身的要求和职责而酬报又绰绰有余;人们不再盲目崇拜残暴专权,骑在别人头上统治人的虚荣已完全消失,人们不再以诈骗和猎取作为致富的捷径;数不清的肮脏交易永不再出现。这就是孔子理想的最概括的简述。

有人可能要问当初在王家、诸侯和乡间学校实施六艺教学时,周公为什么把礼放在第一位?为什么孔子认为礼运会最终导致世界大同?——为什么他们两人都那么重视礼?在谈及周朝的道德、社会和政治秩序败乱时,为什么著名的历史学家及学者都首先提到礼的解体并指出最早出现的征兆是音乐的败坏?那是因为周帝国也好,尧、舜、禹、汤的家长式政体也好,他们治国的基石是礼治。在远古的皇与帝的时代,国家的领袖一般是统治集团内部选拔出来,并由民众认可的,因此,他总是最有预见、最仁慈和最有本领的人。通过这种方式选举出来的首领肯定是全体民众中最明智、毫不自私且责任心最强的人。这种人所关心和研究的是大众的福利、如何保护好民众、为民众服务以及与民同乐;恪尽职守是他们的座右铭。

虽然尧、舜、禹、汤、文、武制订礼治受到孔子如此的颂赞,我们必须承认,从孔子一直到近代的千百年以来,确实有过虚伪的或盲目追随礼的人。他们是社会的寄生虫,他们丝毫没有孔子那种独到的远见,只是狂热地追逐形式或仪式,却自封为正宗的儒学家。他们从事的专业是助纣为虐,为凶残的霸头作帮讨、为贪得无厌的官僚和权贵家族们装潢门面和鱼肉人民。事实上,几千年来确有卑微、假冒、渺小、猥琐的所谓儒学家,为数还不少哩。

在历史的黎明时期,尧、舜、禹共同的道德准则是温和、真诚、礼让和不愿突出个人。大禹原来就想让位于他的宰相伯益(伯翳,柏翳),却在他视察九国的途中病倒在会稽,随即去世,终于没有实现他的理想。伯益效法舜和禹,隐避于箕山之阳,好让禹之子启继位。当时可能由于禹的功勋过于显赫,使藩属、从臣们佩服得五体投地,又可能由于与尧之子丹朱和舜之子商均相比,当时尚未发现禹之子有什么大的差错,也可能因为舜、禹在接大位之前都曾被委任摄政之职(舜任摄政 27 年、禹任 16 年),相形之下,伯益的声望过于短暂。总之,禹死后不久,大臣、官僚们就拥启登了基。这为此后帝国王位世袭接替的传统开创了先例,真是不幸之至!①

以成汤和周武为例,他们肯定与尧、舜、禹一样是谦恭、温和的。上面已讲过汤的网开三面的著名的故事。当他打败并俘获了夏桀时,并没有杀他,只是把他放逐到南巢。暴君殷纣兵败时,他是悬梁自尽的;即使如此,他的儿子武庚仍作为商王朝的正式后裔而得到武王的封地。武庚和管叔的叛乱被平定以后,成王才下令处决他们,但微子仍然作为商汤的后人贵为公并封地于宋。这也就是周公秉承文王的精神而办下的业绩。所以汤和武分别对桀和纣的革命,其目的只是消灭残暴,拯救黎民。

当然,我们都了解到,三皇五帝时代的社会结构并非已达理想境界。孔子与孟子也从来没有这种幻想。是的,否则那就成了白

---

① 这大致根据孟子对王位继承的著述,当然也有人说由于禹未能让位于贤者,而叫儿子继承,所以不及尧、舜贤德。《竹书纪年》对我们的早期历史却有与众不同的记载:"伯益受命接禹位,取得了权柄并监禁了启,但启摆脱了监禁,杀益而继禹位。"《晋书·束皙传》说:"晋太康二年(公元 281年),汲郡人不准盗了魏襄王的墓,得竹籍数十车,其中第十三章记载了自夏起至周幽王为犬戎部落杀死的历史。由此,历史的线索就连贯到晋国被三贵族瓜分并维持到魏安厘王二十年,这就是大致与《春秋》记载相符的魏国历史。"《竹书纪年》又名《汲冢书》,实际上是盗墓贼在晋武帝咸宁五年(公元 279 年)发掘出来的。《竹书纪年》系用漆以蝌蚪文写在竹简上的,蝌蚪文比籀书、大篆还早。近代屈原学者游国恩在所著的《读骚论微》初集中(第 193—202 页)据历史学家和诠注家对屈原《天问》的有关章节的论述,详尽地叙述了伯益受命继禹位,置启企图篡夺王权于不顾,但启终于逃脱了监禁,杀益而登大位。

痴的天堂。刚从野蛮和毫无教化的状态脱胎而来的社会离理想境界太远了,相反倒是充满着灾难和困苦。生活条件肯定糟得令人叹息,人际关系又极不稳定,以这两个较为显著的方面为例就足够了。文化和教育、风俗和习尚、法律和治国政策还处于原始状态,尚未发挥应有的效应。例如,舜的父亲瞽叟是个坏透的家伙,他竟几次三番要杀害舜,但均未得逞。慈父般家长制国家的政体组成虽然极为粗糙,简陋得可怜,且很不规范,但却充满着爱。这些古代的政体就其总的风尚和趋势而言是平和可亲的,那些家长式的首领把社会个人作为大家庭的一员,对大家的福利予以亲切的关怀。

孔子在《礼运篇》中所阐述的正是概括了家长政治那种总的来说是友善和其乐融融的态势。礼其实是各种各样的方式方法,使人们在生活中、在理智和感受上达到更惬意的状态,所以礼对人们的幸福起着积极的作用。但法告诉人们:不许做这个,不许逾越那个界限,起的是消极作用,虽能禁止某些错误罪行,但毕竟木已成舟,事后的刑罚无法消除前愆。按《论语》记载,孔子谈到(治国)政策、刑罚(法)及礼时说:"为政以德,譬如北辰居其所而众星拱之。"又说:"道之以政,齐之以刑,民免而无耻;道之以德,齐之以礼,有耻且格。"

礼作为达到目的手段是有形和适当的,礼可以使人们的心灵达到仁的境界,这种境界是无形的。中文的"仁"字由"人"和"二"两个部首组成,意即二人和平共处,由此演变到理想的仁政以及一对四字组的概念:孝、悌、忠、信和礼、义、廉、耻。中文的"仁"字因此只能用英文的 humanity 才能最全面贴切地译出其含义。儒学的思想体系认为,德的最高境界就是仁。关于仁,孔子的弟子提出过问题,孔子给予了不同的答复。对他生前最聪明、最贤德、最伟大的弟子颜渊的提问,孔子答道:"克己复(周之)礼为仁。一日克己复礼,天下归仁焉。"对有德行的仲弓的提问,他答道:"出门如见大宾,使民如承大祭。己所不欲,勿施于人。"对随和的子张的提问,他答道:"能行五者于天下为仁矣。……曰:恭、宽、信、敏、惠。恭则不侮,宽则得众,信则人任焉,敏则有功,惠则足以使人。"对樊迟问仁的答复是:"爱人。"

总之,孔子的主导思想与政策和伦理密切相关,也许可用唐代韩愈在他的论说文《原道》中众所周知的四组词来加以注释:"博爱之谓仁,行而宜之谓义,由是而之焉之谓道,足乎己而无待于外之谓德。"孔子的道德哲学可以总结为五常:即仁、义、礼、智、信。上述道德标准之外,《礼记·中庸》还提出三种永恒的德行,即智、仁、勇三达德。三达德合在一起肯定是最佳的信条,也是在任何情况下考验一个人是否达到完美境界的最完备的标准。这与古希腊所提出的真、善、美相似,不同的是我们的三达德的涵义比古希腊人的提法更完美。

随着周王朝的宗主权日益衰退,诸侯各国及宦官乘机犯上作乱,他们之间相互侵犯、冲突永无休止。与此同时,井田制彻底崩溃,富裕的、有权势的农户侵吞了无权势、贫困农民的耕地产业。于是,混日子、懒散便应运而生,犯罪与暴力事件开始猖獗。狩猎、婚嫁、殡丧、乡郊射箭聚会等礼节逐项被废除。音乐被搁置,教育遭破坏。就是说,造成初周秩序井然、友善安乐、为大家所熟悉的生活方式被连根拔起,再用石块、瓦砾加以封闭。讲礼貌的规则被铲除,代之而起的是蛮横不讲理。扰乱社会的作案竟在光天化日之下公开逞强肆虐。

就在战国时代即将开始之际,似乎为了宣告时代的变迁,周王室内部于公元前 441 年发生了惨祸。贞定王死后,太子去疾即位为哀王。王兄叔弑哀王篡位,自立为思王。但另一个王兄嵬说"不行!",当即杀思王,再擅登大位为考王。就这样,兄弟相残的事件在短时期内接连爆发,好像在与诸侯各国的频繁谋父弑兄事件遥相呼应。

五　战国时期(公元前403—公元前221)

晋国被三家贵族魏斯、赵籍、韩虔瓜分的局面于公元前403年终于正式得到了周威烈王的承认,三人都被加封为诸侯。从此战国时期便汹涌地展开了。诸侯各国之间的战事愈演愈烈,周王朝的封建宗主权力大厦的穹顶周围的裂缝从此越裂越长,并日益加宽。政治道德加速堕落,不断败坏。公元前386年,齐康公的宦官田和因康公被放逐而承袭了王家诸侯的公位。7年后,这位公侯去世,田和之子田午便夺得了公位和封地。周王对这种倒行逆施居然听之任之;齐康公的合法继承人以及其他诸侯方面当然更加没有什么反应。这个田午后称齐桓公,他的封国称为田齐。齐桓公之子接位时自封为威王,此后齐便成了王国。

通过不断的兼并、分裂和篡夺,争斗各方终于形成了七国的局面;它们是秦、楚、齐、燕、赵、韩、魏。由于周王朝已处于瘫痪或昏厥状态,七国之间不断相互攻打,次数愈见频繁,手段也日益残酷。阴谋、诡计、捏造、玷污、诋毁、歪曲、诈骗、悍然威胁、敲诈勒索、行贿等等无所不用其极。凶猛的秦国在辽阔的西方养精蓄锐;幅员广大的楚国在南面盘踞汉水、长江和淮河流域;富庶的齐国在东部海滨调理国力;赵、韩、魏三国合称三晋,人口众多,填补了以上三个大国的疆域所留下的宽广空隙,即黄河流域的大片土地;燕国坐落在较远的地点,在赵的东北方向;这就是穷兵黩武的七国所面临的地理形势。晋和齐两国的道德普遍极度败坏,汇合成无政府状态的前奏。古时二帝、三王实施王道的丰功伟绩在统治者心中的印象已消蚀殆尽,时兴的是对野蛮暴力的崇拜或屈服和畏惧;而公平合理的当权者是没有的,绝对不会有的。十足粗俗的野心家,得力于贪得无厌和无休止追求的欲望,再加上好卖弄炫耀为之鼓气助威,居然就装腔作势大肆招摇过市,他们的手法当然是狡猾的欺诈、蛊惑人心的阴谋诡计以及恬不知耻的巧言诡辩。该死的暴力行径公开在街上横行;用政令或法律作招牌的恐怖已首先灌输到一个国家人民的心灵和梦境之中。

这个国家就是秦。当时执政的是秦孝公和孝公于公元前358年任命为左庶长进行变法的首恶分子卫鞅(约公元前394—公元前338)①。他所制订的新法可从司马迁《史记·商君列传》中的一段话而见其一斑:"令民为什伍,而相司连坐,不告奸者腰斩,告奸者与斩敌首同赏。匿奸者与降敌同罚(其一家老小不分男女全部沦为奴隶)。"可见作为"法家",充斥他心头的全是兽性和凶残。

新法颁布之前,为了在国内树立绝对权威,他用愚弄百姓和在民间制造恐怖的办法,以秦孝公的名义在国都的通衢大街上张贴告示:谁把一根30尺长的木料从南门搬往北门就奖赏10金(200两黄铜)。一时由于疑惑不解无人尝试,奖赏遂加至50金(1000两黄铜);谁把灰渣和垃圾遗留在街上将被监禁重罚。他按告示付诸实施,以此树立人们对他的恐惧和荒唐的威信。此后,他的新法就如火如荼地推行开了。

卫鞅不仅毫无人性和凶残得令人发指,且他的所作所为不允许别人提问、质疑或据理分辩。作为政府主管和军队统领,他那残暴的诡诈更是花式繁多、层出不穷。公元前340年魏大败于齐,公元前339年卫鞅便纵容孝公乘机攻之,以掠取魏国黄河以西的领土;孝公对他的献计大加赞赏,即派他领兵伐魏。"魏使公子卬将而击之。军既相距,卫鞅遣魏将公子卬书曰:吾始与公子欢,今俱为两国将,不忍相攻;可与公子面相见盟,乐饮而罢兵,以安秦魏。魏公子卬以为然。会盟已饮,而卫鞅伏甲士而袭,虏魏公子卬。因攻其军,尽破之,以归秦。魏惠王②

---

① 他是"卫国的庶出或旁系的公子之一,名鞅,原姓公孙",但常称卫鞅。由于他攫取了河西魏国的领地,被赐封于商十五邑,并尊为商君,之后人们便称他为商鞅。

② 事实上他那时是魏侯。他把安邑和河西的领土割让给秦之后,就迁都至大梁自立称王,是为梁惠王。

兵数破于齐、秦,国内空日以削,恐,乃使割河西之地献于秦以和。"

在以上引号中所述两宗事件之间的时期里,即公元前349年,秦孝公把国都从远在西北的雍州迁至东南方向的咸阳。雍州是秦300多年之前、早在公元前667年建立的京都。新都咸阳系由卫鞅建造,当时他已擢升为大良造(相当于宰相的官职,但又兼任军队司令官),并已取得了魏国国都安邑。按照卫鞅要建立侵略性的极权主义国家的计划,农事与战事(事实上农事只作为战事的工具)是两件头等大事,对其重要性的强调不受任何限制。秦国从此正式取消了井田制。公元前342年,周显王把秦孝公的子爵升封为伯爵,诸侯同僚都来祝贺。再说公子印中了奸计被俘,他的军队也悉数降秦;尔后魏又把河西土地割让于秦,卫鞅被加封于商十五邑并赐号商君。当初这个流氓恶棍式的冒险家只是由太监的引荐才蹑手蹑脚地爬上去的;所以他只要能成事,不论什么卑鄙、骇人听闻的罪恶勾当都会不择手段去干。他的宗旨是:只要有利可图或有所猎获的,不管其代价如何他都要,只要他自己不付出什么就行。两年以后,秦孝公死去;继承人即自立为王,称秦惠王。后来卫鞅因叛逆大罪被五牛分尸,告发他的是王室成员公子虔的随从;大约9年前,虔因触犯新法被卫鞅割去鼻子。卫鞅死后,这个无所顾忌的大阴谋家所制订的治国法律和方式方法依然保留在秦国,毫无改变。据我所知,秦是有史以来世界上正式诞生的第一个霸权主义国家。

至于七国之间相互想置对方于死地的争斗发展到何种疯狂的程度,只要看看这40年里他们的敌对事件的数目,就可想而知了。公元前375年,韩并吞了郑;7年后齐伐魏;公元前353年,秦伐魏取少梁;同年,魏围困赵都城邯郸;次年,齐围魏救赵;公元前340年,魏攻韩,齐又击魏并大败魏军;又次年,如上述,秦克魏并掳其军队;公元前334年,楚灭越(越于140年前并吞了吴);公元前333年,燕、赵、韩、魏、齐、楚六国以苏秦为总指挥合纵抗秦。

先秦,尤其是战国时期,哲学家、学说(派)创始人、政治家等为数众多,流派纷呈。上面我们已谈到过春秋时期老聃和孔子的简短故事,这里再浏览一下其他一些杰出人物及其学说。

战国时期最早的一种学说的缔造者是《道德经》或《老子》的作者。"老子"的名称是谬误的,这可能是由于传播时引起的错误,但更可能是周太史儋(约公元前 420—公元前 350)故意的造作。他冒用周礼的最高权威、孔子老师老聃的名义推出他自己的作品,以混淆儒家的视听和取笑于世。以如此方式哄骗各界,尤其是孔子的门生和信徒,用他那玩世不恭的鬼把戏来与他们开玩笑,弄得他们感到似是而非,纠缠不清,最后在他的反儒同道之间引发一阵嚣闹的欢笑——这与这部著作的真正作者的品性以及当时的时代精神是相吻合的。这世界上的一切原本已经给糟蹋得乾坤颠倒了,那么为什么人们的思想不可以也倒个个儿呢? 这时,初周的礼已被践踏得难以辨认,音乐几乎毁灭,诗歌和舞蹈已经消亡得无影无踪,教育也被破坏得支离破碎,井田制被贪婪凶狠的地主连根铲除。眼前猖狂一时的是贵族之间的争斗不歇,臣从弒君篡位此起彼伏,以致战火连绵不绝,政局变化无常,社会动荡不安。时至今日,不妨乱上加乱,把原来封建秩序的起因,尤其是礼,说成是眼下这一切纷扰、混乱的起因,这真是既聪明又有胆识的一招啊! 同样,我们何不把礼的创始人和维护者,二帝、三王、武王、周公和孔子——那些社会秩序、和睦协调的缔造者、发扬光大者和圣人们——一起拉下神坛呢? 即使不说他们倡导了盗贼,至少可以斥责他们引起了盗贼的横行,这又是多么漂亮的一招啊! 把不相关的起因的结果说成是起因的因由,既错位又颠倒,这位周太史儋真是个玩笑大家。他那爽朗的笑声千百年来一直回荡在人们耳际,但他的笑声有没有笑掉那一阵又一阵的灾难人祸? 有没有笑掉他眼中的泪水呢? 没有,绝对没有!

如果真的像他所说"夫礼者,忠信之薄而乱之首也",那么一开始就没有礼(处世处事和过文明生活的合适的方式方法)即会离奇地带来忠和信,因而会不可思议地产生良好的社会秩序。根据他那神秘莫测又荒谬悖理的逻辑,虽然良好的社会秩序是人们期待达到的目标,但开始时必须放弃任何为此所作的尝试和努力才行。换言之,清静无为才是达到目的的方法,所以他说:"圣人不死,大盗不止。"这就是说,圣人(即为创建良好的社会秩序而努力工作的人)即使不是引起盗贼的原因,实际上也是为盗贼的兴起提供了场合。这意味着如果从未有人想为创建良好的社会秩序而努力,那么世界本来就会是和平幸福的。但事实上,如果没有像舜、成汤、武王和孔子那些圣人,而只有桀、纣、厉、幽、秦孝公、秦昭王、秦嬴政、卫鞅、张仪、李斯那班暴君、首恶和流氓以及他们那些为虎作伥的下手、成百上千万顺民、笨蛋、受人操纵的傀儡和驯服的人体工具,那么这世界该是个被黑暗吞没的人间地狱式的大帝国,直到永远。这也就是嬴政为他的王朝所作的计划。

《庄子·知北游》中,东郭子问庄子:"所谓道,恶乎在?"庄子答道:"无所不在。"东郭子又说:"期而后可。"庄子道:"在蝼蚁。"曰:"何其下邪?"曰:"在稊稗。"曰:"何其愈下邪?"曰:"在瓦甓。"曰:"何其愈甚邪?"曰:"在屎溺。"东郭子不应。对这种高度严肃的、悲剧性的社会和政治动乱作如此戏谑性的处理,正可作为一帖高效麻醉剂用来缓解人们理智和感情上的创痛。这对于《老子》和《庄子》的作者本身、对于那个时代的读者以及后代,恐怕也都起到了同样的效应,这还正是件大好事哩。因为周太史儋和他的年轻的同时代人庄周(公元前368—公元前320)至少是肯定想对时代竭力地进行一番挖苦和嘲弄,否则根本不会去撰写这些著作了。但这并不意味着他们的著作能解决好揪人心肺的社会问题和抑制汹涌喧嚣、无法无天的现象;当然,他们本身也许并不抱这种虚无缥缈的希望。同样,那时的读者以及后世的读者也都不会有此幻觉的。实际上,作者用这种滑稽的口吻对待时代的灾难,又想借助虚构和玩世不恭的办法来解决问题,读者就没有理由以认真的态度去理会和对待了。

"道德"学派在一定意义上对当时整个封建制度的崩溃所产生的忧虑、恐惧、苦楚和紧张的局势似乎提供了一些解脱——当然只是"似乎"而已,不是真正的缓解。老子和庄子想把过去的碎砖、瓦砾一扫而光的斩钉截铁的态度应该说是对的。庄子在《逍遥游》第一章中比拟鲲(一种大得出奇的鱼,究竟有多少千里高无人得知)和鹏(一种难以想象的大怪鸟,它的背到底有多少千里长也无人知晓)时所用的狂放不羁的想象力不禁令人惊讶,也把人们深深地吸引住了。他把鲲、鹏与蝉、莺鸠两类巨、细截然不同的动物作强烈的对照,迫使人们把他的寓意理解成为东西不论大小,只要让其按各自的天性去生活,他们就会安然自得。因此他建议撤除礼、文化、教育、道德和所有其他的制度规定,他认为这些煞费苦心的名堂对于社会并不能起什么好的作用,而不如返璞归真到"神圣的野蛮人"的原始状态为好。文章的蒙昧主义和放肆的假托真令人发噱,文章中堆积如山的否定又怎能付诸社会实践来解除压力和混乱,并恢复所谓原始的太平呢? 答复只能是令人张口结舌的大谜底。

这个流派的创始人提出一种明确的教义,其后人又进一步加以演绎。他们所提出的是玄妙而又神秘的清静无为,其目的不过是聊作解救用的强心剂。所以这至多只是一种一时镇痛的镇静药膏,绝不可能从根本上割除弊端和治愈令人苦恼的病痛。此外,这也导致了黄老的逃避人世的幻想,用许多迷信和玄妙的法术以求飘向想象中的仙境,并对道教①顶礼膜拜。清静一说实质上是通向佛教涅槃的中继站,涅槃的主张是:由于生存激起了欲念,故生存

---

① 道家认为黄帝和老子是他们礼拜的始祖。此说由东汉时张道陵和他的儿孙所创导,北朝北魏的寇谦之正式建立。道家的迷信和法术有卜筮、梦卜、算命、符箓、修仙、炼丹、堪舆(或称风水)、起课(六壬、太一、遁甲)等。

应该完全消灭而达到以自我为中心的存在的平静。所以如果别除其神秘莫测的冗词赘句，涅槃实际是肉体和知觉的终止，或者干脆说是死亡，正如佛教所谓的不生不灭的永恒。

飘向仙界的想象是曾给屈原带来过解脱的，见其诗《远游》①：

> 见王子而宿之兮，
> 审壹气之和德。
> 曰，"道可受而不可传，
> 其小无内兮，其大无垠。
> 毋滑而魂兮，彼将自然，
> 壹气孔神兮，于中夜存。
> 虚以待之兮，无为之先；
> 庶类以成兮，此德之门。"

在这首诗的结尾，又说：

> 经营四方兮，
> 周流六漠，

---

① 郭沫若说近代学者怀疑这首诗不是屈原的真作。由于其遣词用语与司马相如的《大人赋》特别相似，某些妙语隽句也颇类同，郭认为这是司马相如的作品。但我有理由相信他的看法是错误的。我认为《大人赋》是对屈原更早些的原作的模仿篇章。《远游》篇开头时诗人所表达的感情是真正的屈原的感情，而"大人"也没有理由离开其巨宅及广达万里的土地。司马的篇章不过是卖弄作者在华丽辞藻堆砌方面游刃有余的手法，从感情格调看来是虚浮不实在的。《大人赋》的用词拐弯抹角、刻意求工，不可与《远游》的简洁、纯正同日而语。至于遣词用语或某些妙语的类同，对司马相如也未必有利。《古文辞类纂》的编者姚鼐已把它们归结为类似之间的区别告诉了我们。读过宋玉的《九辩》和潘岳的《秋兴赋》的人都可看到这两篇的妙语有类同之处，但实际是潘岳对宋玉的模仿，宋玉作为诗人更胜一筹。见本文"七 屈原和他的著作"第11节中的论述。

上至列缺兮，

降望大壑。

下峥嵘而无地兮；

上寥廓而无天；

视倏忽而无见兮；

听惝恍而无闻。

超无为以至清兮，

与泰初而为邻。

但这仅仅是充满诗意的想象在遨游飞翔，对诗人忧愤得几乎发狂的情感只能给予一时的安抚镇静而已。至于充斥于《道德经》、《庄子》和《列子》①的玩世不恭、无政府主义和虚无主义，即使披上了大言不惭、浮夸、假冒、讥刺、嘲弄、夸大戏谑、滑稽幽默、喧笑和神秘奥妙的外衣，想打扮成似是而非和一目了然的真理，从哲学和形而上学看都是于事无补的②；外装再好也掩饰不了本质上的不同。他们提不出什么理性上解决的办法，然而捉摸不透的谜底却不少。把清静无为或虚无作为治疗时代痼疾的处方，其效果未

---

① 列御寇是庄周较早的同时代人。《列子》是列御寇的作品一说是有问题的。《列子》是部伪作，风格上模仿《庄子》，其中糅合了列御寇的崇拜者的说法东拼西凑而成。

② 林文庆在《历史背景》一节中介绍他的《离骚》诗篇英译本（1935 年上海商务印书馆版《离骚》第 19 页）时说："老子的南方或超然学派把一目了然的真理说成似是而非，其目的是想彻底的革命。无疑，其中包含着出于崇高的追求而悟出的真理的萌芽，但历史下的结论是这些宝贵的真理一旦置于群众面前，其遭遇恐怕未必会比有名的耶稣基督的寓言中所说的珍珠掉在猪的脚爪跟前好些……"这种说法显然在理性上是无根据和靠不住的。我盛赞林先生对屈原的高度推崇，但对他上述的看法、他对贵族政治和大英帝国的热衷、对拿破仑和墨索里尼的庸俗的吹捧，我是绝不敢苟同的。他能坚持把这么艰巨的工作做成固然值得称道，遗憾的是其译作通篇不无较大的误译，同时他对诗歌词汇用语的意识也缺乏得可怜。

必比江湖郎中的假药和符箓好些。尤其是出于对庄子的飞扬不羁的想象以及独特的文才感到惊奇、稀罕和迷恋,我们某些得心应手的思想家和下笔千言的作家①把道德流派的神秘莫测和故弄玄虚理解成为无限的智慧、深奥和"超脱尘寰"。对道德一派的基本观点,唐代诗人白居易的一首七绝《读老子》作了机智诙谐又简洁有力的否定:

> 言者不知知者默,
> 此语吾闻于老君。
> 若道老君是知者,
> 缘何自著五千文?

对道德一派的齐物归一说,白居易另有一首七绝《读庄子》:

> 庄生齐物同归一,
> 我道同中有不同。
> 遂性逍遥虽一致,
> 鸾凰终校胜蛇虫。

所以,把道德一派的问题归结为一种思想体系的话,可以简单地说这不过是可怜巴巴、自欺欺人的哲学,是沉溺于无可奈何、希望彻底破灭的深渊而不能自拔的产物。

但是,在我们把对道德派或黄老的批判性的话讲完之后,对于他们正面的功绩也得表扬一番。首先,一旦入了道家的玄妙、奥秘

---

① 如林语堂,他把庄子、屈原和莎士比亚的精粹糅合成一团,对这三位大家并不熟悉,对中国和西方的人文科学、文学、哲学似乎缺乏精深的理解,而对诗的崇高的奔放并不熟悉。详见本文"九 屈原在中国和世界历史上的地位;他的崇拜者、模仿者和评论者",其中有我批评他的观点的文字。

的门道,就等于学会了经历逆境和失败的本领和技巧,从而坚持下去,最后克服之。其次,可以拓宽想象的境界,培养超脱自得的意识。与明明白白的、传统的、世俗的现象背道而驰之后,就等于插上了一双所谓的翅膀,你的文学遐想即能自由地翱翔了。第三,《道德经》或《庄子》中像下列所摘录的一些章句,不管在什么年代将都是合时和中肯的:"民之饥,以其上食税之多,是以饥。""天之道,损有余而补不足。人之道,则不然,损不足以奉有余。""强梁者不得其死。""夫大块载我以形,劳我以生,佚我以老,息我以死。"还有一句:"彼窃钩者诛,窃国者为诸侯。诸侯之门而仁义存焉。"像这类批评挖苦,如果不说在任何年代,至少在绝大多数年代里将是无可非议、并对人们有所启迪的。

宋代苏轼在《韩非论》中说得好,比这更糟一千倍的是,道德派导致了像申不害、商鞅、韩非、李斯等一批所谓法家派的诞生。这批人把当时出现在秦国的灾难加以扩散,贻害全体老百姓,我还认为直到今天恐怕仍不无影响。苏轼的看法是有根据的,在此之前司马迁在《史记·老庄申韩列传》中有一段简洁的论述:"申子卑卑,施之于名实。韩子为引绳墨,切事情,明是非,其极惨礉少恩,皆原于道德之意。"他们的道德准则是人不需要去做什么,其根源来自宇宙论的所谓世界本来是微不足道的说法。这必然导致不折不扣全盘否定的教条,因此"对父亲不必敬爱;对君主不必敬畏";"心中不必怀有人道,不必努力实施责任感或正义感,不必以礼与乐来塑造人的性格。"像这种"虚无、不存在"的原则难道能帮助那些掌权者来治理国家吗?"商鞅和韩非不懂得如何把这个谜付诸实施,但却掌握了蔑视世界和把生与死等同的伎俩。"由于道德的教条法则确认仁慈并不导致人道,所以人道与残暴和刻毒之间并不存在任何差别;屠杀平民百姓与仁慈是一致的,并且从效果看比仁慈更优越。所以,老、庄、列的著作只可以时而作为文学的消遣去阅读,但作为严肃的哲学来对待,其价值是有问题的。为证实我的观点,只要看一下宋徽宗由于对老、庄和道教愚蠢的崇拜而引起的灾难性结局就够了。徽宗在文学、艺术和书法上的才能非同一般,却由于对老、庄哲学和道教的教义和做法的无限的热衷,结果使他们父子俩一起为金所掳。从个人角度来看,千百年来许多人疯狂地追求朱砂炼丹而死于非命,又有许多人因为上了道教迷信法术的当而做了各式各样荒唐的行为,这已经不是什么秘密了。

法家一派的代表人物包括商鞅、申不害、慎到、荀况、韩非和李斯。据说这些人对有关社会生活的犯罪的刑律,即法律的理论研究得很精到。为了把君主的地位提得高于其臣民,各种刑罚的名称根据犯罪的实际情况都经过严格审查,以求在处罚和判刑时达到效果。因此,这门学问的研究宗旨在于维持统治者的利益,而孔子及其门徒所倡导的人道和仁慈的理想乃是出于对被统治者的关怀,与之截然相反。这批人虽然追求着一个目标,但在不同情况下,他们各自在政务活动中所表现的个人特点却不太一样。

卫鞅在秦国为了组成法西斯政权,在秦孝公的名义下建立了他的恐怖政府;其手段是废除一切现行的法制和习俗,实行他的新法。在他的国度里只允许,也只鼓励做两件事,即农事和为国家而进行的战事(农业为战争服务)。君主家族成员的封建特权甚至也受到限制或免除,同时王室家族人员也有所减少。卫鞅又用政府和法律的名义大量施暴,制造恐怖气氛,迫使民众顺从。秦孝公本身只是傀儡,他那无限的权力只是通过他的左庶长或丞相才得以充分地体现;老百姓则成了他指挥下的半兽。儒学的经典礼、乐、诗、史、儒学的美德厚道、孝、悌、信、正直、仁以及被称之为二"恶"的非兵和厌战被统称为六虱,一律加以破除。这位暴君的形象在上述的引语中已描摹过了;秦国在他的把持下,在 10 年里已成为一个地道的纳粹式国家。

从中国历史的几个统治者,如夏桀、殷纣、周厉、周幽和隋炀帝看,他们正像犹太国王希律(公元前 40—公元前 4)和罗马皇帝尼禄(公元54—68)一样,都是暴君。虽然他们的罪行极其残忍、灭绝人性,但他们的穷凶极恶终究还有局限性。而卫鞅、张仪、嬴政、李斯之流,他们的无法无天、狂暴残虐像瘟疫似地在程度上更为骇人听闻,范围也广得多。

申不害是卫鞅的同时代人,公元前351年韩昭侯拜他为相,比卫鞅任左庶长晚了8年。据说他协助韩侯治国的15年里,除魏侵犯过一次以外没有发生战事。他和韩非一起被认为是法家的正宗先驱人物。他对法律理论的研究,其思想根源也来自黄老。

据《汉书·艺文志》,慎到在所著的《慎子》一书中说,法律执行既不应超出一定范围,也不能软弱无力而在严厉性上有伸缩余地。他认为法律作为处罚的措施如果执行及时,可减少治国的困难,使国家平安无事。这也就是道德蜕变成法家学派的过程。所以申不害和韩非著书时都对他表示赞赏。

关于荀况和韩非的思想,这里不多谈了,因为他们的著述用竹简记录成册时,屈原已经去世。荀况从传统习惯上一直被认为是儒家,因为他表面上像孔圣人一样也主张王道和推广礼、乐。但他竭力反对子思和孟子,而如果说有儒家的话,这二位却正是最地道的儒家。荀况的论点是人性本恶,尧和舜不过是矫揉造作而已。他究竟应属于哪一派的最明白的证明就是他的两个学生韩非和李斯,此二人恰恰是十足的法家。

李斯是嬴政在咸阳焚书坑儒460余人这一令人憎恶的滔天罪行中的同谋犯。有件事应该提一下,有一次韩非(是李斯向荀况学艺时的同学)作为韩国的使臣赴秦朝见嬴政。李斯知悉嬴政已读过韩非的著作,急于想与韩会面,并有意请他在朝廷任要职;出于极度的嫉妒,李斯就在嬴政面前造谣生非,对韩中伤。结果韩被投入大牢,之后又赐毒令其自尽。

孟轲(公元前372—公元前289)通常称为孟子,是孔子最杰出的弟子,又是孔学的代表人物。他是孔子的孙子子思的学生。子思是孔子的弟子曾参的学生。附带说一下,他的作品《中庸》阐述了中庸之道或温和的道德伦理。孟子在战国初期名声显赫。他周游列国的时候,以热烈、雄辩的口才传播和发展了他的老师孔子提出的关于王道的教导。他力图说服一些在位的国君,像魏梁惠王和齐宣王,使其相信仁、永恒的公道、正义、仁慈、高尚的道德和人民的福利比拥有财富和国家权力更为重要。他抨击了对金钱的崇拜和唯物主义。但此时魏王刚被秦掠去国都安邑和河西的土地,与这种头等大事相比,孟子的游说不可避免地遭到了置若罔闻的待遇。他竭力推崇正义的革命。在齐国时,齐宣王问道:"汤放桀,武王伐纣,有诸?"孟子对曰:"于传有之。"曰:"臣弑其君可乎?"曰:"贼仁者谓之贼,贼义者谓之残。残贼之人,谓之一夫。闻诛一夫纣矣,未闻弑君也。"在魏、齐、宋,孟轲的游说同样没有得到什么效果,令人遗憾。道理很简单,时机和场合似乎有点不合时宜,同时他找的人也不对。但是他拥护仁义,宣传二帝、三王的仁政,他在这方面的信念、勇气、淡泊和坚韧可用他自己的话来说明:"……独行其道;富贵不能淫,贫贱不能移,威武不能屈……"他的信条是:"民为贵,社稷次之,君为轻。"春秋时期为我国和全世界引来了最伟大、最杰出的人物——孔子。战国时期也诞生了两位光芒四射的巨星——孟子和屈原,他们将与人类一起共存不朽。但是就当时的形势看,可以非常肯定地说,那个时代正在坠向灾难,却是任何人力所无法挽回的。

虽然孔子在远古家长式统治那种不成熟的、萌芽式的社会实践基础上提出了天下应以民众为主的理想——大道,但冷酷的现实却明摆着:世界只是为世袭的专制统治者的私人利益服务的。在商汤和周武、成、康的年代里,群众利益至上的主张确实流行和实施多年;但到他们的继承者时,舒适的生活终于熔化了他们谨慎和保持正直的戒心,腐化堕落潜移默化地渗透了进来,左右了整个局势,最后邪恶和暴政便成了他们新的准则。所以,很明显,事态发展到像春秋和战国时期这种地步,单单主张推行礼或在与礼有关的其他方面的枝节问题上东抓一把、西打一锤,这种被动乱搅得似汹涌咆哮的海涛般的局面是绝不可能平静下来的。做挽救工作为时已晚。只要稍加分析和判断,便可得知个人拥有绝对权力、并由其家族(实际上家族就是掌权人的延伸,即他家族或统治者家族对权力的垄断)世袭继承就是这全部混乱、压迫和苛政的病根;即使没有外来入侵或天灾人祸发生,也无法避免这种恶果,个中道理是再明白不过的。

但是4000多年以来,却从未有人提出这个简单的真理!即使孔子也只是主张推行他"天下为公"的总原则和赞扬尧、舜、禹禅位的卓越先例,他并没有想到要去反对个人拥有绝对权力并让其家族世袭罔替,或者主张国家首领的权力应受到制约和不允许其家族世袭继承的准则。虽然我们可以理解在那个时代因缺乏先例,要限制国家领袖的权力似乎不可想象;但以禅位代替世袭无疑是有过先例并已证明其效果超过世袭,因而是可行和优越的体制。在这个问题上,孔子只是把他的想法用讽喻的手法表示而已。

事实上,从夏启继承大禹而登基(我得重复一遍:这是最不幸的事)以来的4000多年中,中国除了王朝的创建人和其继承人,或造反、篡位的头头,有权或敢于提议反对世袭或主张禅位的思想,其他人对此都一律讳莫如深;否则他就要付出掉脑袋的代价,还要搭上他的家庭成员、亲戚朋友们的脑袋。而王朝的创建人、他的继承人、造反和篡位的头头都决不会为民众着想和不顾个人安危去提这种建议。

自从孔子提出他的"天下为公"的主张以来,所有的儒学人物,包括孟子在内,没有一位曾发展过他们老师的教导而明确宣称大道、仁政和"天下为公"是与君主世袭政体水火不相容的,因而君主世袭制必须见鬼去!维护忠君主义和君主世袭制,同时又祈求实施仁政,这只能是把民众的幸福寄托在听天由命上而去作无限期的企盼。个人一掌握绝对权力和世袭制这个关键问题如果得不到解决，人们的希望再虔诚也永远不会实现；所作的努力最终也不过是徒劳而已。这就是孔子、孟子的辛勤操劳一律以凄凄惨惨的失败告终的原因。大禹的一脉以桀告终，成汤至纣结束，文、武又落得厉、幽的下场，这给人们的教训已够多的了。

再来谈一谈上述道德派和法家派之外的一些次要的流派及其有关人物。墨翟（或称墨子）是孟子的同时代人，只是年岁较长。墨子与孟子是同乡，也是鲁国人（也有传说认为他是宋国人）。他崇尚博爱，并以此为学说的原则，操行刻苦、节俭，力主选贤与能，推广孝顺、消极的和平，不信天命。他反对孔子和儒教的礼，认为这是莫大的浪费。他还好谈鬼魅，不像儒家在这个问题上缄口不语。为了选择明主，他也周游列国，聚集了大批门徒和从者，最后成了宋国的臣僚。

兵家学派的创始人、春秋时期的孙武和战国时期的吴起都给后世留下了关于战术的著作。他们都是著名的大将；孙武是吴国的将领，吴起先后在鲁、魏、楚三国担任军职。孙武的后人孙膑是齐国的将领。遍览屈原的著作，我们找不到任何他对战事有兴趣的迹象，可见这些人对屈原似乎没什么影响。

还有个哲学家杨朱，卫国人，是个怪人。他的著作都失散了，只能从《列子》和《孟子》中找到一些零星片断。他的中心思想是极端的利己主义，总结性地表现在他的名句：拔一毛而利天下，不为也。

逻辑学派以其格物穷究、毫发不爽及诡辩称著于世。该派的杰出人物公孙龙（约公元前320—公元前250）是屈原的同时代人，年龄较轻。他试验论证的一个煞费苦心的命题是：白马非马，而是白色的质地和马的概念的结合。从这个诡辩式的前提引出的逻辑结论是：世界上没有马这样的东西，因为是马必然有一定的颜色，同样也无所谓什么白色，因为它必然又是某种可见的形状。这批人属法家的朋友和帮手，为法家狠毒的作为正名、提供根据和理由；他们对德行表示怀疑,认为这是毫无意义的行为,是落后和过时的。

鬼谷子这位先生据说是"真正的仙家,门徒百余人,其中有两人不愿成仙的就向他学了纵横术。"这自然只是有趣的说笑而已。有人以为鬼谷子的真名叫王利,意即"为王者利益服务",这也只不过是一种附会。《汉书·艺文志》没有列入《鬼谷子》。据说东汉时有人把苏秦和张仪死后的所谓遗著综合成文,这实际上是战国末年和西汉时苏秦和张仪的崇拜者的做作,最后拼凑成《鬼谷子》一书。这两位政治家(或者只是其中一位,见下述)生前非同寻常的狡诈和鬼把戏由此可见一斑。他们炮制了这些名堂,令人好奇不已,又难以捉摸。但有一点是可能的,苏、张都是某位大师的学生,因为据说苏秦于公元前 333 年由六国拜相成为从约长时,张仪去求见欲谋个差使而未得同意。只是他俩的师父的庐山真面目始终没有暴露;什么道理不清楚,不过也不难猜测。他们故意在师父头上加上这种假名或称呼,令外界无从探知其真相。

那个时代的说客和辩士是一种自由职业的政治工作者,分为本质截然相反的两种类别。正派的人物有陈轸、苏秦及其兄弟代和厉、淳于髡等,都是为合纵工作的,即联合六国共同抗秦。因秦国侵略成性,是最凶恶和危险的敌人,六国中任何一国论国力均非秦之对手,但如果团结起来是完全可以制服它的。反派人物有张仪和范雎,张仪主张连横,即六国分别与秦结成联盟以防止其他五国的威胁,其目的显然是为了破坏他们合纵的联盟;范雎力主远交近攻的政策。

苏秦,洛阳人,如上述是鬼谷子的学生。他曾先游说秦惠王,试图献上他为秦制订的连横策略,但遭到拒绝。之后,他又分赴燕、赵、韩、魏、齐、楚。两年后,于公元前 333 年终于成功地使六国结成军事同盟共同抗秦,由他本人担任从约长。按刘向所说[1],在其后的 29 年

---

① 见刘向:《战国策·序》。

中,因慑于六国的联合军威,秦国不敢到函谷关来列阵入侵。

张仪,魏国人,在遭到苏秦的拒绝之后,也到秦惠王处游说,于公元前 328 年得到了相国的职位。也许是因为苏秦把六国联合在他的旗帜下取得了非凡的成功,张仪是带着报复的心情来推行他的连横计划的,以后的一连串事件证明他是个阴险毒辣的阴谋家。他千方百计地推出一出又一出的阴谋诡计来破坏苏秦的合纵联盟,以巩固他自己的权力。张仪以秦嬴政王朝作为他搞间谍活动、害人圈套和阴谋诡计的基地(秦王朝这种特殊环境原来是卫鞅所创建的),在国与国之间编织了一张奸细网,用作制造凶杀、设计相互攻讦、收买和指使盖世太保式活动、炮制污蔑诽谤与奉承捧场、行贿送礼等行径;一言以蔽之,这个可恶至极的奸计大师就此热热闹闹地干起了他那肮脏的勾当。公元前 323 年,张仪离秦返回他的故乡魏国,并成了魏的相国。他给予合纵联盟的致命打击之一是在他任魏相时,唆使魏参与合纵联盟对秦的征讨,然后他却从中破坏,使出征于公元前 318 年从内部溃败,并且成功地掩饰了他所扮演的拆台角色。次年,作为大功告成的奸细,他又回到秦国再度当他的相国。同年,苏秦在齐国为一不知名的官僚所刺杀。谋杀的动机也未公布,但从政治上的敌对以及个人的恩怨看,把这次谋杀的首要发起人归诸于张仪名下是可以说得通的。

由于张仪的狡诈和玩弄权术过人,举手投足都是欺骗和害人的圈套,又擅长散布谣言和污蔑中伤,说苏秦曾在他之前游说秦惠王兜售其连横策略遭到拒绝等等完全有可能纯粹是张仪的捏造。他在与楚王的一次谈话①的记录中说:"苏秦封武安君相燕,即阴与

---

① 这次谈话的题目《张仪说楚怀王》是谬误的。谈话编写者的真正意思是张仪说顷襄王,即怀王的后任。因为谈话中记载了"楚王大怒,出兵再度攻秦,二军战于蓝田"等,这之前又提及楚军大败于汉中。但在谈话的结尾还有一处有出入:楚王谈过背靠东海,这只有在楚迁都寿春之后才有可能。编写者没有考虑到张仪并没有活到那个时候。

燕王谋伐破齐而分其地。乃详有罪出走入齐,齐王因受而相之,居二年而觉。齐王大怒,车裂苏秦于市。"但历史告诉我们,苏秦是被齐的臣僚刺杀而不是五牛分尸的,所以,实际情况很可能是齐国的臣僚在张仪的指使下谋杀了苏秦。同时,那次从内部颠覆或破坏合纵联盟战事的行动是张仪本人作为秦派往魏的奸细所干的。只是魏王在张任魏相长达6年之久的时间里竟然会没有发现他的罪恶行径而听任其自由自在地再返回秦国当相国,这实在是太愚蠢了。

那时六国中有四国分别为其王子封采邑并赐以封号,这四位又各自以其业绩而名闻遐迩,他们是齐国的孟尝君、赵国的平原君、魏国的信陵君和楚国的春申君。这四位德行公正的王子各自供养和庇护着几千个朋友、食客和随从。他们都是屈原的同时代人,比屈原年轻35岁以上。

魏昭王最小的儿子信陵,名无忌,生性仁慈、好客,心境高尚、宽宏。他曾两次英勇地打退秦兵,挽救了赵和魏被困的危机,为此名噪一时。赵都邯郸为秦兵所困,赵平原君之妻系信陵君之姊,因而向魏安厘王及公子无忌求援。魏王命其将晋鄙领兵十万救赵,后又怕不敌秦兵力强大,犹豫不决,令晋鄙驻军以观望。信陵君听从食客侯嬴的计议,强索晋鄙的部队麾师及时救赵,出其不意直逼侵略者并击退了他们。之后,秦军深入魏国腹地,信陵君又统率五国部队击退了秦军,打得他们狼狈逃窜,并穷追不舍直到函谷关。秦于是煽风点火,对信陵君进行造谣中伤。魏王听信谗言,对他表示怀疑并最终驱逐了他。信陵君心灰意懒,失望之余成天沉溺酒色,结果酗酒过度得病而死。他对秦国的评价可谓一语中的,值得一读:"秦之风俗习惯与西戎北翟等同,心如虎狼,既贪得无厌,又乖张暴戾,掳掠无度,毫无信义,与礼、义及德实背道而驰。只要有利可图就会一跃而上,不顾是否会伤及自己的亲属或兄弟,恰似禽兽。"

苏代曾以"此乃虎口"一语劝阻了孟尝君想去秦的念头。但后来尽管有数以千计的朋友好心的劝说都无法阻止他去秦,他终于到了秦国;目的不过出于好奇,总想设法去探索一下老是萦绕在心头的不解之谜。公元前299年秦王拜他为相,但次年秦昭王终于发现孟尝君绝非他的同流之辈。昭王正要捕杀他的千钧一发之际,他借助随从在天明之前学鸡鸣的掩护才逃离了秦国。

平原君为其兄长惠文王的相国。秦围困赵都邯郸危急之时,他遣使毛遂至楚都起草合纵条约,同时又从魏信陵君处求得援兵以解燃眉之急。他招待的食客、朋友总是数以千计,所以太史公称他为"翩翩浊世佳公子也"。

楚国春申君的得意兴盛在时间上要晚得多,是屈原死后的事了。他的活动毫无突出之处,也与我们感兴趣的无甚干系,这里就从略了。

齐国有一位名叫鲁连的平民,由于他对残暴、贪婪的秦国的无畏反抗而称著于当时。他藐视地位、财富,善于辞令,行为狂放不羁;人或遇困境时,他能主动为他人提出意见和解救办法。他到赵都邯郸时恰逢秦军围困,那时魏使者辛垣衍也正在与平原君商量请赵王同意承认秦昭王为"西方皇帝"。因为按魏安厘王之见,赵王一旦承认秦国的皇帝称号,秦必会欣然撤军放赵一条生路。鲁连求见平原君,指责他不该过早地同意魏使的建议,并随后去魏使处说服他无端提高秦国威望是愚蠢和危险的。他指出:秦作为一个国家却践踏礼、义,以杀戮大量无辜为最高功勋。如果让其有朝一日统治世界,秦王必然会把辛垣衍将军的主子魏王剁成肉酱而烹之,还会让他的子女及嫔妃们来占领魏梁的宫室。到那时试问辛将军用什么方法、到何处去求老主子的欢宠? 至于他自身,他说万一这种灾难真要降临世界,他就肯定会跳海的。秦将得悉鲁连阻止了辛垣衍的提议后,便把军队后撤50里。正在这时信陵君率晋鄙赶来救赵,秦只得撤军。于是平原君要为鲁连赐地封官,而鲁连再三推辞。尔后平原君设宴款待鲁连,酒酣耳热之际,平原君起立赐鲁连百金。鲁连笑道:"天下有学之士所以值得称道是由于他愿为人排忧解难、摆脱混乱困境而不取报酬。收取酬报者不啻市侩,我所不愿为也。"即向平原君道别而去,从此再未与公子会面。正如辛垣衍所言鲁连心地高尚,我们说他真是"齐之高士",不愧为屈原的同道! 他虽然也算屈原的同时代人,但却比他年轻约40 岁。

对那个时代总的政治形势和国与国之间的战事也应稍稍提一下。赵肃侯在公元前 326 年接侯位后,即自称赵武灵王。他是平原君和惠文王的父亲,他的军队一律采用北方胡族的短式戎装,骑、射均按胡族方式训练,所以赵国的军队在三晋中最为剽悍。他转战北方、西北,多有征服,且并吞了中山国。公元前 323 年,正当张仪离秦赴魏为相、颠覆六国合纵联盟时,韩、燕都先后称王。此后,名义上的七国与周已不分高下,实际上他们把周王朝置于无足轻重的地位为时已很久了。公元前 318 年,周王朝带头,由苏秦任总指挥,楚、赵、韩、魏、燕合纵联兵伐秦于函谷关,以大败告终。这次兵败极有可能是张仪当了魏相之后预先谋划的结果。次年,秦在脩鱼克韩军。公元前 316 年,秦征服蜀;蜀为西部的首富之国,地处今四川省中部。蜀终于成了秦侵略战争的富足粮仓,并为秦强制兵役提供了充沛的人力资源。公元前 298 年,正当孟尝君逃离秦国之时,齐、韩、魏联军在函谷关大破秦军。

据近代学者罗根泽称,刘向的《战国策》和司马迁的《史记》中所搜集的当时说客和辩士与各国首领之间的谈话虽然传说都是真实的记录,但实际上是西汉初期蒯通按可靠的资料,加上作者的想象撰写而成的。这些谈话的内容充斥着地理政治学说和战略论点,有些还夹杂着威胁。如陈轸、苏氏三兄弟和淳于髡强调的是六国必须相互帮助,共同抵御秦国;而张仪则老是着重谈如不满足秦的要求必将遭到不测,时而还扭曲事实、搬弄是非、无耻欺骗、恶毒玷污和进行纯粹的诽谤。

张仪在秦国那穷凶极恶的战争把戏中掺杂了阴谋诡计和见不得人的政治交易,他正是卫鞅最合适不过的继承人。他把自己发明的邪恶勾当加以充分地运用、发挥,大大地丰富了在秦国得以体现的霸权武库。张仪的真正的传人可数李斯,他是嬴政的亲信和恶棍。嬴政把自己尊为他那"千秋万代"王朝的"始皇帝"——主子和臣仆俩于公元前213—公元前212年间在咸阳焚毁了《六经》和古代及当代的其他哲学书籍,活埋了460多位学者。① 张仪还命他的傀儡和走狗对屈原和信陵君横加诋毁,并成功地搞垮了他们,使之潦倒不堪;这有上述及以下的事例为证。其后,秦军遭到赵国大将李牧的粉碎性打击;于是李斯收买了赵国朝中的宠儿郭开对李牧进行诽谤,污蔑他叛国,结果李牧被杀!同年,秦灭赵。

六国横遭覆灭、最终被秦国先后并吞的惨祸,千百年来的历史学者为之扼腕长叹,遗憾无穷。秦王国六代君主②,积恶如山,攻城略地的胜利光芒虽也显赫一时,并由嬴政侵吞六国,但由于毕竟与

---

① 公元前221年,嬴政并吞六国("初并天下")之后,竟把古时候"皇"与"帝"两顶桂冠都套上了自己的脑袋。但古时的皇和帝作为元老的领袖却是以仁慈和蔼著称的。公元前213年在李斯的建议下,他悍然下令焚烧所有的书籍。公元前219年,他派遣方士徐福带领3000名童男和3000名童女乘帆船出航东海以求长生不老的仙果、灵丹或妙药。公元前212年,他召集460多名学者和方士,命令他们交代这一切奥秘,否则便献上他们的脑袋。由于他们无法提供满意的答复,他便勃然大怒,下令活埋。他又制订计划为自己建造广300里方圆庞大无比的宫殿区,另有长80里的林荫大道直达骊山。主建筑的正厅叫阿房宫。他还在骊山为自己建造宏伟的陵墓,据说公元前210年他死后就葬在那里,陪葬的活人有数以百计的王室嫔妃、宫女、太监和一大批石匠、木工和其他筑墓工人。

② 子爵(后受封为伯爵)秦孝公,公元前361—公元前337年在位;秦惠王,公元前337—公元前310年在位;秦武王,公元前310—公元前306年在位;秦昭王,公元前306—公元前250年在位;秦孝王,只在位3天;秦庄王,公元前250—公元前246年在位;秦嬴政,公元前246—公元前210年在位。秦孝王在位时间太短,略而不计,故称六代君主。

人民的愿望背道而驰,故其霸权只能维持短短的 15 年。苏代在规劝魏安厘王不可对秦割地求和时,曾精辟地归纳了六国溃败和覆灭的原因,他是这样说的:"以地事秦,譬犹抱薪而救火也,薪不尽则火不止。"

宋代苏洵与其子苏辙在《六国》和《六国论》中作了详细的论述,对苏代的说法予以支持,并作了应有的补充。总结他们的观点,六国版图比秦大五倍,人口十倍于秦,为什么最终都被解体和消灭,其主要原因在于:第一,是由于六国对秦大量割地求和的政策。问题是这种割地并非由于战争败绩所致,而是心理战上的败退。这种心理上败退的严重性与真正的战败相比其危害要大一百倍。齐国虽未对秦让出领土,但齐所犯的严重错误是不帮助其他五国,而对秦一味友好苟安。这样,在五国丧失主权之后,齐又何以能单独存在? 第二,是由于地理和战略位置上的特殊情况。韩和魏的位置正好处于秦的心脏和腹地,秦东向的道路包抄着这两个地处秦岭以东的国家,使他们难以求得其他四国的援助。这两个国家又比秦弱小得多,只有对秦一再退让,并最终为秦入侵其他四国铺开了道路。

此外,我还想补充三点具体看法:第一,魏是个小国,从战略上看极易攻破,而起先却又特别好战。魏于公元前 368、353、341 年曾三次为齐国打败,其中有两次是魏先对赵、韩出击所致。所以强大的秦国在公元前 353、339、275 年攻魏时,魏并未作什么艰苦的搏斗就垮了下来,失去了少梁、国都安邑和大梁。第二,楚的罪责是反复无常,不能坚持合纵联盟。楚怀王一会儿靠拢秦,一会儿又倒向五国,来回不断地摇摆变卦,以致于公元前 303 年,齐、韩、魏因为楚不信守合纵联盟而对它发动征讨。公元前 301 年,齐、韩、魏竟然伙同秦一起再度攻楚。楚王室统治集团及其朝廷腐败透顶,朝中主要官员及楚怀王的嫔妃等都被贿赂彻底买通,只剩下屈原、昭睢和其他少数几个不受贿的人。第三,齐无意参加合纵联盟,因为齐曾多次与魏交锋,楚又不守信义。而秦的政策在张仪和范雎操纵之下,不断对齐国的统治者进行奉承,这对他们又很有吸引力。

在分析了上述原因之后,还应看到秦在政治—经济—军事上的极权主义结构和手段。君主一方是从孝公到惠王、昭王传给嬴政,臣僚一方是从卫鞅到张仪、范雎传给李斯。在秦与六国的抗衡之中,这一点是很有分量的。这方面如果把六国与秦对比的话,可谓小巫见大巫了。原因的最后一点是楚怀王、楚襄王及魏安厘王除了愚蠢到无以复加的地步以外,其统治集团王室和朝廷都已腐败到骨子里去了,所以他们的地位只像是劲风中的稻草人而已。六国的覆灭和为贪婪成性的秦所吞并的命运就此注定了。不过就秦国而论,也像一处巨大的痈疮,野蛮、暴力的毒汁都已聚集其中化脓并出脓头了,所以为时不久也就不攻自破了。

六 楚国和屈原

秦计划消灭六国,必须首先击溃和推翻六国中最强大的楚和齐。齐地处东方边陲,距离远,中间隔着赵、魏、韩。楚与秦边界相接壤,由于楚的统治者及朝廷较易摆布,故问题不大。但楚王的左徒、杰出的屈原大夫却力主与齐结成合纵联盟以抗秦,态度坚决。因此秦急于除去楚国的这个障碍,摧毁其主要的反秦力量;否则不单是秦的政策无法推行,且本身的安全也会受到莫大的威胁。

据《史记·楚世家》和《史记·张仪列传》记载,早在公元前323年(楚怀王六年)秦派张仪赴啮桑与楚、齐、魏结盟。清代学者蒋骥在《山带阁注楚辞》中发问:谁能知道是不是在那时张仪就与楚国的上官大夫和靳尚等勾结了起来,谋划把屈原逐出朝廷的第一步行动? 张仪在那次结盟返秦后即如上述赴魏任相国,接着他便一步步地着手准备于公元前318年在函谷关击退苏秦任总指挥、由楚国牵头组织的六国联合讨秦,给予合纵联盟致命打击。

公元前313年,即楚怀王十六年,秦惠王声称欲攻齐,而意在破坏他最害怕的楚齐联盟。他托辞张仪已罢相，并随即送张去楚以催促楚怀王终止与齐的合纵条约。秦答应割"商於之地"600里方圆给楚以资补偿。和屈原对此极力反对一样，楚国辩士陈轸也表示反对，他所著《说楚怀王辞》一书中的记载流传至今，为世人所称颂。陈轸指出：一旦与齐脱离了关系，楚将处于孤立无援的困境。此外，秦所谓割"商於之地"，只不过是一句空话；楚如不先取消与齐的和约，秦是决不会履约的。这儿还应指出，那时屈原已被楚王驱逐（"屈平既绌"），没有机会再入朝面君了。楚怀王在作决定之前或事后根本不听忠臣们的谏议，却为秦的虚假诺言欣喜若狂，而把宰相大印授予张仪，每天宴请。就这样，楚、齐的条约被轻率地废除了。

张仪在执行公开的外交任务以破坏楚齐团结的同时，又开展秘密的间谍活动，在楚国布满了他的奸细和爪牙。他在几年前已与上官大夫、靳尚及其他人有所联系，而现在又亲自出马到郢都来编织他的特务网络。楚王室的昭、屈和景三家支脉以及朝廷已彻底腐败，受贿、收礼已达饱和程度。司马子椒、当然还有上官大夫、他的老朋友靳尚和楚王的宠妃郑袖全都被秦国收买。他们欺瞒愚弄的只是楚怀王一人。面对占绝对优势的亲秦派，屈原一个人硬撑着。他的学生宋玉、唐勒和景差都是诗人，年龄也轻得多，对国家大事没有什么发言权；再说他们都是谨慎怕事的人，没有政治抱负。后来襄王接位时，虽然宋玉曾写《九辩》为老师申辩是非，但与其他几位学生一样终究没什么作为。张仪未曾向屈原行贿，他知道如果这么干会被公开揭发。屈原作为诗人是不可腐蚀的；他很清醒，也急切地要联齐抗秦。

屈原的官衔是三闾大夫，具体职务有点像是楚王室典礼大臣和宗谱纹章院的负责官员，所以他感到有责任领导他族中的精英身体力行，为国家的优秀分子作出榜样。作为楚王的左徒，是国王亲信的谏议官，对国家大事及外交事务给楚王提供忠告是他的权利,也是应尽的职责。历史和国与国之间的现状使他深深感到合纵抗秦是不可避免的必要举措。屈原作为爱国主义者是无与伦比的,作为诗人是毫不含糊的,作为学者又是第一流的。他为自己树立的形象从道义高度说来,与当时的场合正好匹配。他是无畏的,又是不屈不挠的。

多年前,张仪早就对上官和靳尚作了布置,之后他们两人组成了亲秦帮派,并成为其头领,不断地在楚王面前进谗言以驱逐屈原。楚怀王处在"鸱鹰"、奸细的包围之中,显得既愚昧无知又自负,所以不难摆布。上官和靳尚对他们共同的对手蓄意大加诽谤。上官大夫起初一直妒忌屈原的能力和楚王对他的信任。有一次他去拜访屈原,屈原正在为楚王起草一项王命,上官要看底稿,屈原婉拒,谓尚未起草完毕。于是上官对楚王说,人人皆知陛下令屈原代为起草,但每当王命公布后,屈原总是自吹自擂,说没有他王命是出不来的。这不过是上官及其帮派所进谗言中最轻微的例子。当然,他们对屈原作更为严重的造谣中伤是决不会手软的。楚王则驽钝不堪,从不去追究这些指控是否属实,相反在听了这些卑鄙的鬼话后却对屈原感到愤怒,并疏远他。结果怀王不准屈原朝见("王怒而疏屈平"),这是不听他的谏议的最好办法——这事发生在公元前313年,即怀王十六年。屈原一方面遭到楚王的排斥,又被那些吹捧拍马的阴谋家封锁了朝廷的消息,虽然事后能了解一些情况,但终究无法阻止楚王跌进张仪那肆无忌惮的骗局之中。他从同宗大臣昭睢口中得悉张仪访楚的任务以及楚王的决定之后,竭尽全力设法见到了楚王,对他的决定进行劝阻,想使楚国免遭覆灭之灾,然而结果徒劳。他又书写了请求和劝诫的奏章,楚王也不屑一顾。更使屈原受不了的是张仪这个居心叵测的骗子竟然摇身一变成了楚相!

张仪把他所需要的一切情报搜集完毕,便在几个月之后回到了秦国。临行时,楚怀王派了一名特使和许多下属及随从人员,旨在陪同张仪一起返秦,主持商於 600 里方圆土地的交接仪式。张仪到达咸阳后却对楚使说,他只答允楚怀王 6 里方圆的土地,而 600 里方圆的地块则闻所未闻! 使者大怒,返楚后如实禀报楚王。楚王一腔怒火直冲霄汉,即下令召集军队,在两国领土的交界处汉中伐秦。结果楚军大败,因为张仪早有准备,预先遣重兵设下掎角之势的埋伏。楚兵 8 万人马丢了脑袋,70 多位将领也在这次汉中战役中丧生,楚军主将屈匄被俘,整个汉中郡(今陕西南部和湖北西北部)均为秦所占。这使楚王气愤得几乎发狂,他把国内所能集结起来的军队全部集中起来,再度伐秦,虽然深入秦境内,但仍在蓝田遭到重创。韩、魏闻及楚局势危若累卵,即驱兵直插楚地邓,逼得楚军首尾难顾,只得催军返回。万般无奈,楚又割让两座城池作为对秦的赔偿。上述张仪返秦及楚两次惨败都发生在公元前 312 年,即怀王十七年。

　　楚军两次兵败,失地一大片,大批将领牺牲,这些事实总算使楚王稍稍清醒了些。公元前 311 年,即怀王十八年,屈原被召回朝,并作为楚的特命全权大使赴齐为合纵条约复盟。同时,张仪则为推行其连横而大肆宣传。是时,秦正图以其武关外土地与楚的黔中地区①交易。黔中地区左侧即今湖南沅陵县。从战略角度看,黔中比秦武关外的土地重要得多。楚王对秦使说愿把黔中给秦,但不要武关外的土地而宁要张仪。张仪来楚后,楚王即予关押而欲斩之。于是靳尚便向郑袖吹风,郑袖再在楚王面前为张仪求赦。张仪得赦后,又怂恿楚王与秦联合,条件是不必再交出黔中。楚王眼看可以不再让出土地,便欣然允诺。事成后张仪便离楚了。

----

① 　这里出于《史记·张仪列传》所载。如果按《屈原列传》和《楚世家》的说法就不同了:不是秦要以武关外土地与楚的黔中地区互易,而是秦提议把汉中的一半地区归还给楚,以修好。楚怀王对秦使节说,宁愿放弃汉中而要张仪。张仪听说后,即请求入楚,因为他认为既然一个张仪能值一个汉中郡,他就来楚。

屈原出使齐国后返楚("是时屈平既疏,不复在位,使於齐,顾返"),对楚王说:"陛下为最卑鄙的小人所骗。他来了,就应置于釜中烹之。陛下决不可再为他可恶的胡说八道所蒙蔽而错绝仁慈。"楚王说能保住黔中对楚是有利的。此时,张仪尚未越过楚的边界。楚怀王拿不定主意,犹豫不决,一夜半天过去之后才终于决定撤销与秦的条约,派人追张仪,但为时已晚。屈原与齐国关系一直很好,通过他的努力挽回的合纵条约就这样又一次遭到破坏。

屈原被召回朝廷之后,自然为过去堆在自己头上的恶意造谣中伤和诋毁作申辩。这可把那批亲秦的谄媚者急慌了,于是秦安插在楚的傀儡走狗们便不遗余力直接或间接地离间屈原和楚王之间的关系。这批流氓恶棍在郑袖的积极配合之下,除继续对屈原进行污蔑外,又别出新招制造了屈原企图调戏郑袖的谣言(见《离骚》第 89—90 行),终于又一次成功地使楚王拒见屈原。

楚怀王十八年,即公元前 311 年末或次年初,诗人被正式解职,离开京都(斥逐)去汉北。由于屈原属于王室三支脉中的一员,严格地说,这还不算是放逐,但王命却规定不得再返郢都。诗人在汉北待了约 11 年,游荡于水乡的河川与湖泊之间。至公元前 300 年,即怀王二十九年,秦又一次对楚发动战役,杀楚军 2 万①及其将军景缺。楚王惊慌失措之余把太子送齐作人质,再次请求恢复合纵条约。与齐重建外交关系,屈原的角色是少不了的,于是楚王再召他入京。公元前 313 年,即怀王十六年,屈原初次遭贬时写了《惜诵》以表白诗人的清白、忠贞。在汉北的那些孤独的年代里,诗人创作了《抽思》②、《思美人》③、《卜居》④、

①　按《史记·六国年表》记载,被杀楚军的数目是 3 万。
②　于公元前 310 年秋,即怀王十九年后秋。
③　于公元前 309 年春(逾年春)。
④　于公元前 308 年("其三年")。这三首诗的创作日期系根据蒋骥的注释。

《远游》①、《离骚》②（人类抒情诗和诗歌中最伟大的杰作）以及其他一些篇章。

公元前 309 年,齐滑王想恢复合纵联盟,由于对楚与秦的结盟不悦而致函怀王。在昭睢的建议下,楚、齐才又恢复了结盟。4 年后,秦公主嫁楚公子,秦昭王继位后赐赠大量妆奁、礼品。楚公子组成一支迎秦队伍,盛装赴秦迎亲。亲秦派的谄媚之辈对这次吉期大为欢呼。楚、秦这次联姻的祥和气氛被用来大力褒扬新登基的秦王,说这是昭王为弥合秦对楚所造成的创痛之举。于是,楚、齐以及楚通过齐与其他四国的合纵联盟再次遭到破坏。

公元前 304 年,秦、楚在黄棘结盟,秦把上庸交给楚。次年,齐、韩、魏责楚无信义,联军伐楚。楚把太子送秦当人质以求救兵。秦军一到,三国联军退兵。楚太子与秦某大夫决斗,杀之,并于次年逃回楚国。公元前 301 年,齐、韩、魏与秦联军攻楚,重创楚军,杀其将领唐昧。之后,在公元前 300 年,如上所述,秦再次大破楚军。

翌年,秦又攻楚,攫去 8 座城市。秦昭王又致函楚怀王,说要在武关和他亲自协商结成新的联盟。屈原和昭睢劝诫怀王不能去,他们提及卫鞅拐掳魏公子卬之事,说明秦乃虎狼之邦不可置信。但楚国年轻的公子子兰认为对秦的提议置之不理不妥,拍马奉承之辈即乘机大肆赞扬,于是怀王接纳了他们的建议。他们举行了隆重的礼节,在郢都喜气洋洋地为怀王送行。怀王与洋洋大观的随从一进武关到达秦的边境后,数以十计的军团把他们团团围住,怀王就此入了圈套,落进了陷阱。他被带到咸阳,秦昭王把他当作附属国君对待,在章台召见了他,要他让出巫与黔中;楚王怒拒,即被扣押。从齐返楚的太子继承了王位。

---

① 《远游》和《离骚》的写作日期将在本文"七 屈原和他的著作"第 11、12 节中讨论。

② 同上。

秦对楚王实施的肮脏绑架使屈原气疯了。楚王行前,他曾强烈谏诤,表示反对,并警告楚王可能产生的后果。屈原在新国王加冕前见到了年轻的新国王,并痛斥那些叛逆的乌合之众。亲秦派慑于难以预料的后果,为掩饰他们的罪恶只有加紧对顷襄王这位稚嫩的继位者加以笼络和控制。由于公子子兰已成为他们的傀儡,所以他们怂恿顷襄王拜子兰为相。子兰因听说屈原指控他叛逆而大为恼火,就与拍马奉承那伙人紧密合作,对屈原进行陷害,设法除掉他。顷襄王接位后第二个月,屈原被作为普通臣民犯法一般流放到江南陵阳。公元前298年,秦对楚发动一系列战役,攫去15座城池,杀戮5万人。

次年,怀王企图逃离秦,但是事机不密,计划失败。秦在所有通往楚的道路都设兵把守。怀王从小道逃亡到赵,但赵不予接纳;又想去魏,但必须再折回改道,而秦军却步步逼近。他终于病倒了,于一年后,即公元前296年死去,遗体被送回本国安葬。至此,楚、秦之间所有关系彻底破裂。

公元前293年,秦正式照会楚,愿以决战方式解决历年来两国之间的纷争。楚无法应战,顷襄王只得让步,低声下气地与秦签盟约。公元前292年,秦、楚王室之间又有联姻,这次顷襄王成了秦昭王的女婿。公元前285年和公元前283年,两国之间的盟约一再续签。但公元前281年,顷襄王又遣使至齐及其他四国,准备再搞合纵盟约。秦听说后即于来年攻楚,取上庸及汉北之地。诗人屈原遭贬后曾在汉北居住10多年。公元前279年,秦将白起大举袭击鄢、邓、夷陵,第二年攻陷楚都郢都,并在夷陵放火焚毁楚王陵及宗庙。顷襄王带了王室和群臣逃亡到东北部的陈,楚军不战而溃。公元前277年,秦军又攻下巫及黔中郡。黔中就是屈原在《渔父》中提到的沧浪江所流经的地方,辰阳和溆浦地区是《涉江》中所描述的诗人步履曾到达过的地方。一言以蔽之,楚军已无法抵御外侮了。《战国策》记载了秦将白起的一段话:"楚王自恃疆域广袤而不重政策。群臣只顾彼此嫉妒,拍马谄媚成了正经事,忠臣遭排斥冷落,老百姓则愤愤不平。此所以我军能深入其国掠取众多城池、郡县,建立军功。"

　　庞大却孱弱的楚国又经过了 54 年名存实亡的时代,于公元前 223 年最终为秦所灭。秦将白起上面这段话可以证明,楚国的衰落及最终被消灭主要是由于怀王与顷襄王排斥和冷落屈原之故。如果屈原联齐并与其他四国结成合纵联盟的策略被采纳,并从一开始就坚持下去的话,历史可能会因此而改写。正如以上所述,打败和消灭六国绝不是一件简单的事,这也是周王室封建大厦倾覆的必然后果之一。顺便说说秦将白起,他也所谓"名不虚传",在公元前 206 年竟把赵国已经投降的兵将 40 万人活埋,犯下了骇人听闻的罪孽! 而 3 年后,他本人又因与秦相范雎争斗而被赐死。所以,一部秦史充斥着阴谋诡计和背信弃义、谋害和杀戮、欺诈和掠夺。欺诈和掠夺的典型事例就是蔺相如智勇双全挫败秦昭王想夺取赵璧的卑鄙阴谋而使完璧归赵的业绩以及司马迁《李斯列传》的记载。今天,从人类生存的内在价值的批判性观点出发,即就社会文化、精神面貌和文明方面回顾,屈原在诗歌创作、治国策略及道德上作出了辉煌的、不朽的贡献。但楚怀王、顷襄王和秦惠王、昭王、嬴政他们作了些什么? 历史证明,他们只不过是笨蛋、低能儿、响尾蛇和鲨鱼。

　　屈原被顷襄王放逐江南后,前 9 年留在郢都以东偏远的陵阳,靠近今安徽宣城县。顷襄王三年,当楚怀王的遗体从秦国送回安葬时,诗人写了名为《招魂》的挽歌,之后又改名为《大招》。流放的第九年,诗人在陵阳写成了《哀郢》,诗篇的最后部分刺痛了当时任相国的子兰和亲秦派的要害。于是第二年,即公元前 289 年年初,诗人又一次被放逐到西南的辰阳。从陵阳到辰、溆盆地,路经黔中南面的两条河流,诗人又写下了《涉江》。从枉陼到辰,路经武陵时,他遇上了渔夫,诗篇《渔父》的内容即取自这段经历。赴长沙途中,诗人写了《怀沙》。他在长沙待了 2 年多,创作了《悲回风》和《惜往日》。《惜往日》是他生前的最后诗篇。漫游于沅、湘地区及其支流旁川之间,作为诗人、思想家、政治家和爱国主义者,屈原感到整个世界和他本人都笼罩在黑暗之中。毫无希望,连一丝光明也看不到,他终于投入了汨罗江,"托彭咸之所居"。这时刚好是农历五月初五。至于诗人去世的年份,众说纷纭,有说是顷襄王十年,即公元前 289 年,或顷襄王十一年,即公元前 288 年,……或顷襄王二十一年,即公元前 278 年。蒋骥的估计是顷襄王十三四年,也可能是顷襄王十五六年。最近似的估测是公元前 286 年,这种说法的依据是把诗人离陵阳到长沙路程所需的时间以及在长沙小住的日子加起来算大约是 3 年多。

司马迁的《屈原列传》中关于屈原生平的记载如此之少,这是因为诗人生前是无畏的抗秦者。楚都郢都和青阳(即长沙,诗人的最后 2 年多的时间就在这里度过)在公元前 278 年为秦所占。后来,在公元前 223 年秦最终灭楚时,那些凶神恶煞似的鹰犬曾不遗余力地把官方的有关记载加以歪曲。至于《离骚》以及目前留下的其他著作之所以未被毁坏,是因为这些典籍都由诗人的崇拜者们秘密收藏才得以保存下来的。

屈原死后,不仅在楚国,而且在其他各国也有越来越多的人鉴于诗人一生的清白、勇敢和大公无私而对他表示哀悼。他是为黎民百姓的公益做好事和对秦国魔鬼式大国政治作英勇反抗的牺牲者。随着时间的推移,中国的大族——汉族继承了古老的文化传统,同时也终于明白了这位诗人的崇高品质以及他那凄楚的生与死。在他逝世之日,人们划龙船和食粽子以示纪念。所谓粽子是用苇叶包裹糯米成三角锥形、以猪肉或豆沙作馅的食品,煮熟。龙与凤在中国历史上从远古时候起,早在屈原之前的民间传说和文学作品中,都被认为是有灵性的鸟兽,他们能把有德行的人的灵魂在解脱躯壳以后带到天上去。为防止诗人遗体在汨罗江中为鱼龟所啮食,人们便把三角粽投入江中喂鱼龟。为纪念屈原而定下的端午节(农历五月初五)以及在这天吃粽子、赛龙舟,千百年来已成为中国人民的一个传统习俗。

七　屈原和他的著作

上面我们谈到屈原是一位伟大的政治人物,他与楚朝廷的关系以及对秦国魔鬼式大国政治和见不得人的阴谋外交活动的反抗,证明他又是一位爱国主义者。现在让我们对他的生活和著作作详细的探讨。他的著作留下来的不多,但都辉煌灿烂,尤以《离骚》为最。谈这个问题不可避免地会重复上面某些已涉及的情节。

诗人的生卒年迄无定论,他的著作日期当然也无法确定,包括《离骚》在内仍是目下学者们争论的问题。在目前情况下,我们很难指望有人能在近期内写出一部精确和彻底的屈原传记。下面我要排列一份诗人生卒年及著作的编年表,尽量用诗篇内的资料和直接或间接的外部资料作为佐证。

§1.屈原生于周显王二十四年,即公元前 345 年。这个假设的根据见§5,即以他最后的诗篇《惜往日》的起始 8 行为基础估计的。

走笔至此,我有机会借得下列参考书:游国恩的《读骚论微》初集,1936 年版;郭沫若的《屈原研究》,1942 年版;林庚的《诗人屈原及其作品研究》,1952 年版。这三位研究诗人的近代学者把他的生卒年各自定为公元前 343—公元前 277 年(67 岁)、公元前 340—公元前 278 年(62 岁)和公元前 335—公元前 296 年(40 岁)。在他们之前,梁启超在研究诗人及其著作中把他的生卒年定为公元前 338—公元前 288 年(50 岁)。梁启超所估计的日期载于林文庆所著《屈原的离骚:一曲遭受痛苦的悲歌》中。先讨论以上各家对诗人生卒年的估计,然后仔细地弄清王逸的混淆视听的错误,再提出我个人估计的日期。

屈原生日的话题始于 23 个世纪之前,为这样一个争议不休的问题追查有真实性的答案,必须要有以上所谈到的正面的论据方可查究,也要搜集反面的例证来核对;这指的是从外部可能求得的或从诗篇内部发现的反证。我不明白梁启超为什么和凭什么把诗人的生日定为公元前 338 年,即周显王三十一年。公元前 319 年,诗人任楚怀王的左徒大夫。据《战国策》和《惜往日》诗篇的记述,如果诗人生于公元前 338 年,他任左徒时按阳历算年仅 19 岁,按阴历算是 21 岁,很明显年龄过于轻了些。诚然,据说高阳氏颛顼作为 10 岁的孩子就在他叔父少昊跟前当辅佐大臣,传说帝喾辅佐颛顼时也只有 15 岁,大禹在尧时当司空年仅 12 岁。但这些都是传说,他们的时代比屈原又要早 2200 到 1950 年。从实际出发,认为诗人在担任这样责任重大的官职时,如果只有 20 岁左右似乎在年龄上轻了些的说法是合适的。并且游国恩已说得很清楚,左徒和史官一样需要有渊博的学识和成熟的判断力来制定政策,在这一点上他从《天问》诗篇中找到了大量雄辩的证据。很明显,即使诗人聪明过人,要在那个年龄来担当这样的工作恐怕还是不够格的。游国恩和郭沫若都按王逸所说,从《离骚》第 3 行:

摄提贞于孟陬兮。

的头两个字设定诗人的出生年份。首先,"摄提"这两个字的解释尚待讨论。宋代洪兴祖十分支持东汉诠注家王逸的说法,把"摄提"解释为"摄提格"的缩略语。由此他解释道,诗人的出生年份由干支决定,而第二个字符地支为寅,所以寅年与寅月(孟陬)和寅日(庚寅)正得阴阳之正中,"三寅"组成了诗人诞生的十分吉祥的特征。宋代诠注家朱熹却认为"摄提"并非缩略语,而是年份的星象,或具体地说是六星星座的名称。诗人在这行诗中说的是通过这三颗星一排的星座,北斗星的星柄正指向该阴历年第一个月的寅的方位(寅位月),即傍晚时分东北北方向。朱熹说如果是指寅年,那么必须带有格字,这个字是不可略去的。同时,这样一来"贞于"又显得多余的了,也就是说,这行诗应该写成"摄提格之孟陬兮"。林庚在他那生气勃勃的文章中对"摄提"作了恰当的阐述。他从《史记·历书》中摘出五处论述证明摄提格是寅年,正如朱子的看法决不可缩略成"摄提";他又从《史记·天官书》中摘出两处例证,再从《尔雅》《淮南子》中各引出一个例子,都证明摄提格是指以地支寅命名的年份,但决不可为简便起见缩略成"摄提"。这两个词组意义完全不同,决不应混淆等同,这一点是非常清楚的。再说诗人在诗行中也没有理由去用缩略语,因为他的诗并不是同音节格律的结构。所以,他的结论是王逸错了,而朱子的评注是正确的。游国恩按王逸的说法,把诗人的出生设定在楚宣王二十七年或周显王二十六年。按此标准推算是公元前 343 年,戊寅年,那么据我的算法屈原任左徒时是公元前 319 年,问题就更大了。因为如果游国恩一说正确的话,那年按阳历诗人是 24 岁,按阴历是 26 岁,这似乎仍不是担任史官(和天文)的官职合适的年龄。郭沫若把诗人的出生年说成是公元前 341 或 340 年,即周显王二十八或二十九年。他说这年是寅年,这说明首先他在推算上有了失误,因为这两个年头照干支来算的话应是庚辰和辛巳,与寅毫不相干。如果从诗人担任左徒这一高级官职的情况来核对,他那时按阳历算只有 21 或 22 岁,按阴历算是 23 或 24 岁,年龄太轻。林庚说诗人生于公元前 335 年,那么诗人担任这个重要职位时按阳历算只有 16 岁,按阴历算只是个 18 岁的青年;很清楚,这是不可信的。

  说到王逸的一笔糊涂账的错误,必须把如何以天干、地支命名年、月、日和时辰以及单以地支命名的时辰和阴历月份的方位的来龙去脉弄清楚,才能说明王逸所得出的结论错在什么地方。

以干支的编排来命名年、月、日和时辰
以及以支命名时辰和阴历月份的方位
（即北斗星星柄通过摄提所指的方向）

（1）以天干和地支的排列组合命名年份。其次序从甲子开始，接着是乙丑、丙寅、丁卯、戊辰、己巳、庚午、辛未等，一周刚好是60个年头。于是再从头开始直到第60年为另一个周期，依此类推。

（2）以干支编排命名月份，其过程也是一样。从甲子开始到癸亥结束，一周期是60个月。于是再开始另一个周期，依此类推。

（3）（4）日期与时辰也可用干支的编排命名，其方法与命名年、月一样。所以说，人的出生年、月、日和时辰可以用八个字来表示，即由四个干和四个支编排组合而成，称为生辰八字。

我在这篇导论开始时谈到，起先只是在远古时把干支编排组合起来表示月份中的日期而已；在随后的时期，干支就又用来命名年、月及时辰了。这里所说的随后指的是东汉时期光武帝建武年间（公元25—57）。我相信，用干支的排列组合来命名年、月、时辰以及日期虽到建武年间才流行开来，但在更早的时候（约300多年前）阴阳家和历本演算专家在研究时已用上了。据《汉书·艺文志》记载，在战国时期，阴阳家就有21位之多，其中最有名的有宋国的司星子韦和齐国的公孙发、邹衍、邹奭。这二邹是屈原的同时代人，年轻约20岁。这些阴阳家不光用干支来推算年、月、日、时辰，还为十个天干和十二个地支组合后代表的年份又加上了各式各样的名称。譬如，他们把甲年、乙年、丙年等又分别命名为阏逢、旃蒙、柔兆等，子年、丑年、寅年等分别命名为困敦、赤奋若、摄提格等。这样甲子年就又叫阏逢困敦、甲寅年叫阏逢摄提格等。寅年之所以叫摄提格是因为第一个月（阴历月）的方位是东北北，即摄提星所指的方向（或者，具体地说是北斗星星柄通过摄提格星座的两组三星群所指的方向）标志着春季的开始。换言之，是摄提星随

着北斗星星柄(或者,具体地说是北斗星星柄通过摄提格星座的两组三星群所指的方向)指向第一个阴历月东北北的方位时是春季的开始。格字的意思是开始或起始。就是说,摄提随北斗星星柄指向(具体说,是北斗星星柄通过摄提星座)第一个月(阴历月)东北北寅的方位时,春季开始了或引来了春季。因此,摄提格之所以代表寅年是由于"寅年春季的第一个月是从寅的方位引来或开始的"。当然,用干支编排成花式众多的代名词来命名年份的做法是太啰唆和转弯抹角了。令人抱憾的是,那些历本演算家的著作都消失了,即使连王逸也未见到过(相信又该归罪于嬴政和李斯)。所以,现在我们能借鉴的证明资料数量既少又模糊不可靠;也因此才出现了王逸在摄提格代表寅年和摄提代表年份星象之间的迷惑或混淆不清。有一种论据不足的猜测曾经流行一时,说是给二十二个干支所起的各式各样难以理解的名称原都是巴比伦楔形文字中有关形容词或称谓的音译或直译。从我们所掌握的关于摄提格的含义和具体应用看,上述臆测绝对经不起驳斥。

(5) 一日一夜的时刻共十二个时辰,由十二个地支命名,一个时辰即现在钟表上的两个小时。从夜间十一点开始第一个时辰名子时,从夜间十一时开始到午夜十二时结束;丑时从一时开始到午夜后二时结束;凌晨三时到四时末是寅时;早晨五时到六时末为卯时;七时到八时末为辰时;九时到十时末为巳时;中午十一时到十二时末为午时,以此类推。

(6) 由北斗星星柄通过两组各由三颗星形成的摄提星座指向阴历月份的固定方位有十二处,也以十二个地支命名。春季最早的一个月,即第一个阴历月是寅位月,在东北北方向,这是根据夏历的说法。按商殷的历本,一年中第一个月从丑位月开始,即在正北方向。按周历,一年的第一个月从子位月开始,即西北北方向。战国后期得到广泛应用的是夏历。为简便起见,拟用钟表的表面来更好地说明问题:北斗星柄指向一时,即东北北方向,是夏历的寅位月,第一阴历月;指向二时,即东东北方向,为卯位月,第二阴历月;指向三时,即正东方向,为辰位月,第三阴历月;……指向十一时,即西北北方向,为子位月,第十一阴历月(或者是周历的第一个月);最后,指向十二时,即正北方向,为丑位月,第十二阴历月(或者是商殷历的第一个月)。此后北斗星柄又再回到一时。①

以上(1)、(2)、(3)、(4)形成一个统一的系统,虽然可以独立存在,但彼此关系是连贯的、有先后次序的,不可颠倒次序胡乱拼凑。要强调指出的是,这种排列组合及广泛应用起始于屈原死后300多年的后汉光武时期。换言之,诗人在世时实际使用中还没有出现上述的相连贯的关系。干支只是用来表示月份中的日期,至于年、月和时辰在日常生活中还未用干支加以命名。其次,(5)与(6)是独立的系统,彼此无关,与以上四项也没有什么关系。在实际应用中,必须遵循以上规则。这是因为这三个系统的性质彼此不同,不可任意把两个系统或三个系统一起相配,这样会产生混乱。

＊　　＊　　＊　　＊　　＊　　＊　　＊　　＊

王逸在评注《离骚》的第3、4行时武断、错误地把下列以干支排列组合命名年、月、日的三个系统连在一起了。首先是关于诗人出生年份的干支关系,即(1)所述,他只是随个人意图,并不根据事实;他本人实际上根本不知道,但硬是冒充内行,错误地把不相干的摄提格(不幸的是其意思是寅年,只多了一个额外的字)拿来生

---

① 秦并吞六国以后,其年历的第一个阴历月份是处在钟表表面的十时位置(西西北方向),即第十个月份的亥位月。汉听从张苍的推荐,沿用秦时的颛顼历书达102年。至武帝元封七年,公孙卿、壶遂、司马迁及其他人发现阴历月份的头几个夜晚都有月亮出现,才建议修改秦历书。经过多次测试、计算上的错误以及核实检验,最后才采用邓平设计的历书及落下闳的等同计算法,名为太初历。又改元封七年为太初元年。

搬硬套,且贸然声称第3行中的摄提与摄提格相同,是其缩略语。其次是诗人出生时第一个阴历月的寅位月的干支关系,即北斗星星柄所指的方向,如(6)所述。第三是诗人在第4行中清楚地提出的出生寅日的干支关系,如(3)所述。而王逸把这三种根本不相关联的干支排列组合硬凑在一起,创造出他的子虚乌有(纯粹为了迎合自己的需要的"发明",他另一个性质相似的虚构和"发明"说骞脩是伏羲的大臣)的论调,即所谓"诗人出生年、月、日为三寅"而"得阴阳之正中",因此征兆十分吉祥。从以上的归类和分析,即使屈原出生的阴历月的寅位月也应属(6)的范畴,而决不可与由(2)推算的寅月等量齐观,这一点是一目了然的。再说,把摄提等同于摄提格的缩略语固然属牵强附会,更糟的是在时代上也出了差错。屈原写这首诗歌时,邹衍(那时才十八九岁)和他的阴阳家们还没有来得及发明用干支的排列组合来表示年份,所以地支究竟是简单的寅或者叫花式名称的摄提格就不成其为问题了。在屈原的后期,有关的术语在阴阳家们讨论问题时可能已很流行,但在日常生活中,这种方法至少是不大可能被广泛运用的。从以上归类和分析可知,(1)、(2)、(3)可以循序结合以干支的排列组合来表示出生的年、月、日。(6)是依北斗星星柄通过摄提所指的方向,以地支来命名阴历月份的方位,因而不能与(1)、(3)连同运用,也不能代替(2)。理由很简单,因为(6)在本质上与(1)、(2)、(3)不同。未知物体 X(在王逸心中是诗人的出生年份)不可、也不应该为应急或方便起见而用一个毫不相干的 n 因子(摄提不是摄提格)来代替。所以,王逸把所谓"三寅"生搬硬套地凑在一起,并未改变这三者之间毫不相干的实际情况,而只是一种哗众取宠的把戏,对于了解诗人真正的出生年月反而起到阻碍的作用。对王逸的错误作了如上的剖析并探讨了怎样造成他失误的原因之后,我相信他虚构的创造必将最终倒台。所谓"寅年"是个大错,朱子在批评时说过:"这一年未必是寅年"。支持这个大错的另一个错误虽然不太明显,也同样会使人迷失方向,那就是把北斗星星柄指向的寅位月说成"寅月"。这一点连朱子竟也轻描淡写地认可了(明摆着的事实是寅位月(如(6)所述)与寅月(如(2)所述)是截然不同的)。这两处谬误与正确的寅日一起便产生了子虚乌有的"三寅"。这个大纰漏由清初学者蒋骥接受了下来,再完完整整地传授给近代的游国恩和郭沫若。从王逸以来至今 1800 余年,还没有人对他的错误,同时也可算是一种欺蒙,以及铸成这种错误的原因进行过分析。诚然,宋朝中期的朱子首先对这种缺乏根据的"三寅"表示过异议,但"三寅"却依然一直存在到近代,且为害匪浅。林庚是支持朱子的,给了"三寅"说当头一棒。他做得很对,但他所作的努力还不够,未能制止"三寅"说。而现在我则把探求诗人出生真正年月的绊脚石捣成了碎片。

行文至此,研究屈原的学者可以并应该从附和"三寅"的迷津中走出来了。这里,我对诗人的出生年月提出我的估测。我以为诗人生于公元前 345 年,在春季的第一个月(阴历月),正值一切生物、人、鸟、动物、花草、树木都欣欣向荣,而大地本身也正从隆冬的沉睡中苏醒过来。原野一片嫩绿,山泉、河川、小溪流水潺潺,一派勃勃生机。诗人出生的日子是寅日(这是庚寅日,与该月中其他的一个或两个寅日不同)。根据《三易》(其创作时期为夏)的第一部《连山》所述,"寅"标志世界上人的最初的诞生,因此诞生在早春的寅日是很吉祥的征兆。他的显赫的先辈"皇览揆余于初度兮",给了他嘉名,包括名和字。就我们所知,诗人第一个正式的名是"平"(诗中并未提到),意思是他应该均正公平,以天为主宰。诗歌第 7 行则说得清楚,他的第二个正式的名是"正则",起这个名字的用意是在世界上应遵守正直无私之法则。诗人日常用的第一个字是"原",与"平"相匹配,意即应像大地平原一般育载万物。按《周官》记载,当他长到 20 岁成人行冠礼时,起字原,又字灵均(见诗歌第 8 行)。从这个字可对诗人童年时期的行为有个估价,灵均指灵明均正之性格,总之他的性格是融洽又匀称的统一体。如果考虑诗人高贵、显赫的祖先与这两对名字的意义之间的关系,他们之间彼此匹配得何等贴切,同时与诗人出生的环境又显得异常协调相宜,那么我们也许可以更好地掌握诗篇开头 12 行的全部意思了。参阅《离骚》注释第 3、4、5、6 条。

§2. 周显王三十六年,即公元前 333 年,燕、赵、韩、魏、齐、楚签订了一致抗秦的"合纵约",由苏秦任从约长。

§3. 楚怀王元年,即公元前 328 年,张仪出任秦惠王相国。

§4. 楚怀王六年,即公元前 323 年,据《史记·楚世家》记载,楚派柱国(相当于大将军)昭阳伐魏,大败魏军于襄陵,取其郡县 8 处。接着昭阳又统兵伐齐,齐王大惊,遣说客陈轸劝说他班师回朝。同年稍后,秦派张仪出使啮桑,与楚、齐、魏订立和约。据《史记·张仪列传》记载,张仪签约返秦后即被解除相国职务,后来又去魏任相国。

屈原现存的最早诗篇《橘颂》,即《九章》第八篇是他在担任楚怀王左徒(按阴历算,约二十六七岁)之前的 25 岁或稍早些时候写成的。诗篇由西汉刘向搜集,可能由刘向起的题名而归入《楚辞》文集。说诗篇的创作时期较早,是因为除了少数吟咏的小品词兮之外,通篇都是四字句。这说明诗人还未完全摆脱《诗经》的传统,即尚未建立起他自己的格律。诗篇有如山中的泉水,清新、纯洁,一开始就道明了年轻的诗人已定型的性格以及对公平的坚定不移的热爱,当然也包括他对家乡最执著的爱。这已为诗人的创作最终发展到《离骚》,并恪守他的创作信念,至死不渝,定下了基调。

§5. 楚怀王十年,即公元前 319 年,据《战国策》所载,齐助楚攻秦,取其曲沃。屈原在他最后的诗章《惜往日》第 5 行所说

国富强而法立兮,

就是指的这件事。当时他任怀王的左徒,深得怀王信任。诗篇开始时的另外 7 行诗句中,诗人提及他与怀王之间良好的君臣关系。可以推测,诗人当时按阳历计算约 26 岁,按阴历计算 28 岁,这是因为左徒是仅次于相国的级别很高的机密官职,尽管诗人聪明过人,如果年龄再小的话恐怕不会得到委任。由此,我得出了§1 的假设。说得精确些,《战国策》并未明确地说楚攻秦并取其曲沃之地这件事发生在楚怀王十年,而我则是从总的、泛泛的记叙中推断出事发的时间在楚怀王十一年左右,即十年、十一年或十二年。因为张仪任魏相国时为了给苏秦的合纵条约以致命的打击,乘由楚牵头的合纵联盟长征军攻秦之机,从中破坏、捣乱,致使联军在函谷关败退。这件事发生在楚怀王十一年,而屈原是楚国坚定的反秦政治人物,这些前提促使我在《战国策》的基础上作出以上的推断。

§6.楚怀王十一年,即公元前 318 年,由楚领头、以苏秦任总司令的合纵六国联盟的长征军开至函谷关(即今河南灵宝县)。秦军先筑垒固守阵地,然后对六国联军出击。六国联军鸣金收兵,撤军返回。

§7.楚怀王十六年,即公元前 313 年,张仪赴楚,破坏楚、齐之间的合纵约。时屈原按阳历 32 岁或按阴历 34 岁。详见本文"六楚国和屈原"开头的叙述。张仪至郢都时,屈原已被君王排斥有些时候了。诗人被免去三闾大夫及左徒的职务后,便在同年或前一年末写下了《惜诵》,以表白自己的清白和忠贞。

§8.楚怀王十七年,即公元前 312 年,楚、秦大战于丹阳(按《史记》所言,这是楚最早的封地的首府,地处归州东南或秭归,即屈原故乡),以楚大败告终,楚失去汉中郡。接着楚、秦又战于蓝田,楚再度损兵折将,且割两座城池作为赔偿。大约就在这年晚些时候或翌年初,屈原奉召回朝,时屈原按阳历 33 岁或按阴历 35 岁。

§9.楚怀王十八年,即公元前 311 年,诗人作为楚怀王的特使赴齐重修合纵约,时屈原按阳历 34 岁或按阴历 36 岁。自齐返楚后,诗人恢复了朝中原有职务;仅几个月后,同年末或次年初,诗人又被放逐至汉北。他与亲秦派的冲突以及再次在国王跟前被整下台的细节在前一节已谈过了,这也是本段和以下一段的背景。

§10.楚怀王十九年,即公元前 310 年秋,屈原写了《抽思》,《思美人》则是来年春写成的。这两首诗歌的写作日期已由清代学者林云铭、蒋骥从诗歌内部找出了可靠的证据。楚怀王二十一年末,即公元前 308 年,诗人创作了《卜居》。诗中的散文序的首句说:"屈原既放,三年不得复见(怀王)。"近代研究诗人的两位学者陆侃如、游国恩说,正如《远游》和《渔父》一样,《卜居》不是诗人的真作。此说深得郭沫若赞同。我未读过陆、游两位的论点,但我以为未必令人信服。至于《远游》是否是诗人的真作,我将在下面细说我的论点。我与王逸、洪兴祖、朱熹以来的传统看法一致,《远游》和《渔父》无疑是诗人的真作,这里只想提这一点就够了:古时的诗人或学者在他们的文学著作或性质并不十分正经的杂记中,凡是提到他们钦佩或推崇的知名诗人或学者时,不会唐突地直呼其名而定会带上些崇敬之词;系统条理性的、历史性的记载,如司马迁的《屈原列传》和刘勰关于《离骚》的文学评论等学术著作或评论文章就不属此例了。如西汉诗人贾谊的《吊屈原》诗句:

> 仄闻屈原兮,
> 自湛汨罗;
> 造托湘流兮,
> 敬吊先生。

在《卜居》和《渔父》的诗篇中提到诗人时,其语气十分直截了当,不讲究什么礼节尊敬,因此绝不是宋玉、景差或诗人的其他学生和推崇者会采用的笔法;只能是诗人写自身时才会用的语气。此外,朱熹的看法很得当,他指出在下列诗行中的"妇人"是对郑袖的一种嘲笑性的讽喻：

> 将呢訾栗斯，
>
> 喔咿嚅睨，
>
> 以事妇人乎？

同时蒋骥也指出，头两行矛头直指上官大夫和靳尚，是对他俩最合适不过的讽刺。

    §11. §12.《远游》是较长的诗篇，共约 180 行，其创作日期大概在楚怀王二十一、二十二年，即公元前 308—公元前 307 年。蒋骥在所著《山带阁注楚辞》中承认，他找不出诗篇创作日期的任何线索。他在《楚辞余论》中估摸可能是诗人被放逐到陵阳时期的作品。他的根据是诗人在诗中提到乘南风去南巢见仙家王子乔，"南巢在陵阳以北约数百里，但不远"。这种说法的来源我以为是有问题的。郭沫若说陆侃如和游国恩都不承认《远游》是屈原的作品。他俩的论点我没有读到过，但我刚得到的游国恩的书中说他并不坚持《楚辞通论》中的观点。我注意到他在书中（第 131 页）明确地修正了以前的两个观点，然后又说，一般地讲他以前的本子中差错不少（第 216 页）；他已经改变了认为《远游》是伪作的看法了（第148 页），这一点是明白的。可是郭沫若强烈为陆、游以前的观点辩护，他肯定地说诗篇决非出于屈原而是司马相如《大人赋》的初稿。我则也肯定地说郭的看法是大错而特错的。

    该诗创作日期的线索，我认为可以从原文的第 98—99 行中找到：

> 屯余车之万乘兮，
>
> 纷溶与而并驰。

诗篇《离骚》的结尾处第 359—360 行：

屯余车其千乘兮，
齐玉轪而并驰。

所谓万乘之国在春秋时期之前指的是天子之国，即周王国，而千乘之国指的是诸侯之国。由于周王室式微，诸侯纷纷称王，于是在春秋、战国时期万乘之国便用来指强大的国家，而千乘之国指弱小的国家。因此，刘向在《战国策·序》中说，春秋时期"万乘之国凡七而千乘之国五。"乘指的是铜制的战车饰以皮革（姚鼐的《左传补注》中称为"革车"）。《远游》是充满诗意的幻想曲，描述诗人遨游苍穹变成了仙家。屈原想象他可以也应该成为大国的国王，以便把尧、舜式的万民欢腾的日子搬回到他臆想中的国家或世界上来。诗人在写完了《卜居》之后，产生这种发自内心的意念或崇高的向往是完全顺理成章的。当时他被楚怀王逐出郢都已 3 年，虽然他有满腔苦涩的忧愁和炽热的愤懑，但尚处在恍惚而未定型的精神状态，心底里仍然期望着有朝一日楚王会像过去那样，在把他这位忠臣斥逐约 2 年之后，认识到自己的错误而恢复理性。《卜居》之后，就在这种心态下他写了《远游》①，其目的无非是被接二连三的沉重苦难折磨得不堪负荷以后，在心理上和精神上求得一些解脱。写这篇诗章的用意是自我安慰或寻求吐出一点心中的苦水，而不是为了给别人看的，至多是在他的学生去拜望他时读一读罢了。其写作日期也不可能在诗人被年轻的顷襄王与令尹子兰有如普通百姓一般被放逐到江南陵阳之后。他在《哀郢》中提及这次流放，那时他被放逐已达 9 年了。之所以说诗人不可能在那个时候写

---

① 根据胡小石教授（1888—1962）《胡小石论文集》中《远游疏证》（上海古籍出版社，1982 年版）所述，他认为这是一部汉代某人的伪作。

《远游》,是因为自楚怀王二十九年(公元前 300 年)至顷襄王元年
(公元前 298 年)止他召回朝中才约 2 年,这就是说在以前的痛苦
刚刚要结束之际,顷襄王对他的正式放逐令又给他苦上加苦。遭
受如此严重打击来到陵阳之后诗人的沉重心境与诗篇总的情调和
感情色彩是绝对无法衔接起来的。从作为诗意幻想曲的《远游》中
的万乘到由幻想与现实相混杂的《离骚》中的千乘,就不难看出其
创作日期的自然次序。因此我得出的结论是:《离骚》的写作时间
在《远游》之后,在楚怀王二十二年或可能是二十三年初,即公元前
307—公元前 306 年。诗人把万乘改为千乘是经过考虑的,因为他
可能准备呈送一份稿件给楚怀王;在怀王面前,把诗人的想象力从
万乘压缩成千乘较为合适,也容易得到认可。蒋骥认为《离骚》的
创作日期晚于《惜诵》,但早于《抽思》和《思美人》,这一点我无法
同意。蒋注意到了《抽思》和《思美人》为一方,《离骚》为另一方,
有不少概念和用语是有共同点的。他虽然没有明说,但我们可以
清楚地看到,在《远游》和《离骚》之间也有概念及遣词用语上的共
同之处。我要说的是,诗人写《离骚》好比建造一座天主教堂,它有
自己巨大的中央圆顶,也有一大群尖顶塔、楼塔、角塔、吊碴、廊柱,
其中有些局部可能与建造者以前或以后的小建筑物在某些细节上
是有共同之处的,而教堂的整体建筑乃是一个与众不同的、庞大又
和谐的统一体。这就是诗人的《离骚》与他以前的小作品在概念及
用语上有共同点的由来。换言之,《离骚》在感情上和思想上不论
从哪方面看都已经有了定型的性质,但是那 3 篇较短的诗章却并
不是在作另一种"离骚"式的思索而仅仅加以引申、改头换面和再
作信手拈来的重复而已。

有修养的读者如果对屈原的身世比较熟悉,具备独创的见解
和对诗歌的知识,从《远游》开头 10 行中便可清楚地看出诗人真正
的情感:

悲时俗之迫阨兮，
愿轻举而远游。
质菲薄而无因兮，
焉托乘而上浮？
遭沉浊而污秽兮，
独郁结其谁语？
夜耿耿而不寐兮，
魂营营而至曙。
惟天地之无穷兮，
哀人生之长勤。

事实上，诗篇开头几行既朴素又简洁地勾勒了整个主题，犹如汩汩冒水的泉源，娓娓道来。正如蒋骥说得好，诗行中凝结着诗人内心极其深刻的忧伤和激烈的痛苦。对于西方人来说，诗篇不算太长，但却充满了诗人的创造性，其清白、贞洁作为诗篇的精髓更是光彩照人。回过头来看汉代司马相如的《大人赋》，就明显地使人感到差劲；其摹仿《远游》的笔法还真有点笨手笨脚哩。我们从该诗开始 4 行看到，这位大人在中州的住宅堂皇宏大，所拥有的土地广袤万里；他虽然如此富裕，却仍不满足。接着的 2 行就把屈原的原诗拿了过去作为他的主题，总共只改了 3 个字：

悲世俗之迫隘兮，
揭轻举而远游。

此后，展示在读者面前的只是这位汉赋作者不断地翻腾词藻而已。在"横厉飞泉以正东"一行之后，那位大人走遍了天上东、南、西、北四个方位去寻找仙人的居处。反之，屈原出发后，先去南巢寻觅仙人王子乔，然后才飞升，

集重阳入帝宫兮,
造旬始而观清都。

走出宫来,到达于微间(或称医元间、医巫间)山以后,即在天上和地上游荡,走遍了东、西、南、北,最后相如的那位大人因为在天上见不到什么,听不到什么,又没有朋友,就感到天上太冷清、无趣。一句话,他失望了,结果虽未写明,却肯定是回到他的宏大的邸宅和广袤万里的领地去了。而屈原则是为了求得放松感情来安慰自己才在诗篇的结尾写道:

超无为以至清兮,
与太初而为邻。

可见,屈原写幻想曲的目的是对楚王朝的乌烟瘴气进行谴责,而司马相如的赋却为崇拜和追求财富辩解开脱,唱的是《远游》的反调。在我看来,司马相如不过是玩弄词藻的胡乱堆砌,而屈原的作品其清白和纯洁实在感人肺腑。如果作个对比,司马相如犹如罗马式的建筑,而屈原的作品才是雅典的巴台农神庙。这位汉赋作者是权力和财富的崇拜者,他为秦"皇+帝"二世写了《哀二世赋》,又写了《长门赋》。《哀二世赋》对秦二世表示哀悼。秦二世名胡亥,为嬴政次子,他与恶魔太监赵高及嬴政的相国李斯合谋,伪造已故暴君的遗诏篡位,并杀死他的兄长扶苏。当初嬴政坑儒时扶苏曾强烈地反对。3年后,李斯的结局是五牛分尸,而胡亥本身又为太监所害。胡亥是毒蛇式人物,与其亡父一般罪大恶极又残忍无比,而司马相如对他却哀悯倍加,认为他的被害及其魔鬼王朝的覆灭只是缘于对赵高的诋毁、污蔑之辞过于相信所致! 司马相如写此赋的目的是想借古讽今,用赵高的前车之鉴来战战兢兢地暗示武帝不可太信任商监,可惜他讨好、巴结、谄媚之心过于急切,反而词不

达意。据《昭明文选》,写《长门赋》的背景是他受雇于汉武陈皇后,
对武帝摇尾乞怜、苦苦哀求,以谋重温往日的恩宠;《长门赋》果然
达到了这种轻佻、猥琐的目的,这位雇佣文人因此得赐百金(黄
铜)! 在一群一丘之貉的流氓、恶棍中,这位文人不管同情谁或反
对谁,其后果都不可能在他脸上贴金;同样,为宫闱求爱式的风流
韵事献殷勤,充当皮条客的角色,也不会为他带来什么荣誉,这一
点是很清楚的。对这篇令人抱憾的《大人赋》,也许由于这位文人
竭尽了刻意求工、卖弄炫耀之能事,现在居然有人大加推崇,认为
是一篇稀世杰作,而屈原优秀的《远游》竟然只是它的初稿!

就我所知,对于《远游》和《离骚》中万乘和千乘的演变,有关学
者迄今未发表任何看法,也未下工夫查找《远游》确切的写作日期。
而游国恩认为《离骚》的第19、20行写道:

> 惟草木之零落兮,
> 恐美人之迟暮。

第65、66行写道:

> 老冉冉其将至兮,
> 恐脩名之不立。

因此其创作日期应晚于顷襄王三年。郭沫若根据第65、66行推测
其写作日期应该还要晚得多,可能在《哀郢》之前。王夫之和郭都
以为是在秦将白起掠取郢都时,即顷襄王二十一年(公元前278
年)。我是在饶宗颐所著《楚辞地理考》中了解到游国恩的观点的。
我们知道,顷襄王三年,怀王被扣于秦且死于秦。很清楚,游以为
《离骚》的写作日期在怀王死后。与游与郭的设想相反,怀王被扣
于秦且死于秦的一节在《离骚》中一点反映也没有。如果说诗歌是

写在怀王死后，首先对于这样一件大事诗人怎能熟视无睹，毫不理会？其次，怀王既死，诗人就没有必要"恐美人之迟暮"了。但在我刚得到的游国恩的书中，他说："美人"和"明君"（第 256 行）是指顷襄王，"灵秀"是指怀王。诗人竟然会对顷襄王如此推崇吗？我看这是完全不可思议的。再说，诗人秉性热情奔放，在汉北的流放年代里怎么可能懒懒散散、不去动笔写《离骚》呢？第三，虽然顷襄王三年的屈原要比怀王二年至三年时要增长 11 岁，但如果 70 岁算老的话①，他还未到老境，所以游国恩所持的第二个论据就化为乌有了。实际上，诗人也没有活到 70 岁。此外，还必须指出，在这两处证据里，诗人只是"恐美人之迟暮"和"老冉冉其将至兮，恐脩名之不立"。换言之，在这些诗行里决未提及君王或诗人已经老了。所以，我认为《离骚》写于怀王二十二至二十三年，即公元前 307—公元前 306 年，那时诗人放逐在汉北（这与司马迁的《屈原列传》记载也是完全吻合的），年龄按阳历是 38 至 39 岁，按阴历是 40 至 41 岁。我相信我的论点是颇为恰当的。41 岁离半百还有 9 年，在这个年龄上人们还感到老冉冉其将至是很正常的。汉时屈原的门生和崇拜者之中最优秀的写赋的诗人是贾谊，朱子对他非常赏识，他在《惜誓》②的开头 2 行中写道：

> 惜余日年老而日衰兮，
> 岁忽忽而不返。

---

① 《礼·曲礼》说七十为老。但是这并非固定不变的自然规律，只是一种看法。故此，虽然许慎在《说文解字》中赞同《曲礼》的说法，皇侃却在《论语》注释中说五十以上可谓老。

② 在王逸的《楚辞章句》中，这首诗作者是无名的。有人认为这是贾谊所作。宋代洪兴祖、朱熹及清代王夫之都坚定地认为是贾谊的作品。据王夫之说，"惜誓"的意思是屈原的宣誓和奉献的悲歌。

这是贾谊假托屈原独白而写成的,他当然明白他的老师并未活到
70岁,但他依然在悲歌中写屈原叹息说老了。游国恩所持关于怀
王时屈原年龄的第二个证据虽然得到了郭沫若和饶宗颐的拥护,
但由于其中确有不符之处,所以我看是站不住脚的。详见《离骚》
注解中我关于"陑"和"泚"的第10条注释。在这篇伟大的诗章中,
在被逐出郢都约4年之后,诗人向君王恰如其分地表达了自己激
烈的痛苦。自顷襄王三年以来,诗人面临的是彻底的绝望,而此时
他灼热的眼泪早已枯竭。在这种情况下,诗人的灵感和感情是无
论如何也不可能活跃到像《离骚》中所表达的那种程度。最后,郭
沫若认为《离骚》是诗人临死那年写成的,又说《浮士德》的第二部
分是歌德在80岁左右完成的,最后还把两者的创作日期进行比
拟。我看这完全是风马牛不相及的事。屈原的感情非常炽热奔
放,恐怕可与贝多芬相比;但歌德的秉性安静得像奥林匹亚山上的
仙人,两者决不可同日而语。同样,《离骚》是人类写作史上感情最
强烈、抒情味最浓厚的诗篇;而《浮士德》是歌德对中世纪文艺复兴
时期条顿民族的传说从主客观的角度加以描写而成的剧本,这也
难以相提并论。

　§13. 楚怀王二十九年之前,放逐中的诗人在汉北完成了《离
骚》之后又写了《九歌》和《天问》,此时他又一次被召回朝廷。这
是我的猜测,蒋骥说他无法把日期定下来。我作为臆测的理由是
诗人虽然悲痛、孤独、绝望,但如上所述尚在游移未定的状态之中,
我设想这些与诗篇的内涵是协调的。

　《九歌》是一部赞歌集,名字是诗人自己起的。所谓九歌是一
组歌,有一定数量,但并不一定刚好是9首,实际上是11首或者说
10首更合适。由于大禹的合唱也名"九歌",所以我把《九歌》译成
《九首赞歌》,以资区别。蒋骥说以主宰生命的大神和小神为一类,
又以顷襄王和顷襄王夫人为另一类,所以称颂的神和女神有九种
之多,"九歌"因而得名。我不同意这种看法。古汉语中,"九"有许

多意思,可以是从"一"数起的最高的整数。因此,《离骚》第86行:

虽九死其犹未悔。

这里"九"的意思也是"许多",而不是刚好是九。最后一首叫《礼魂》,只有5行。如王夫之所说,这是诗歌的末节或结尾歌,与以上的9首是一样的,并不像蒋骥或其他人所说,是对已故正直的有识之士的灵魂所作的独立的赞歌。这10首短诗为一集的诗篇在一定意义上可说是诗人游历汉北时访问各城镇乡村,不时扬帆于汉水南下小游时凭所得的灵感写成的。在汉水与长江交汇处,诗人访问了夏浦(后称夏口,今称汉口)、堵口(今称汉阳)和鄂渚(今称武昌)等县城。虽然诗人已从京都放逐,汉北是他的定居之地,但只要他不进入郢都,还是可以自由地南下远足的。所以他乘舟沿长江而上,漫游于洪湖及洞庭湖地区。写《九歌》时诗人的情绪既凄凉又孤独,与《九章》的背景又有不同。《九章》作为另一组短诗集,其特色是抒发个人的情怀,大部分(约有5首)的内容是指诗人从正式被放逐陵阳直到投汨罗江自尽为止,所以其悲痛和愤愤不平的心情在程度上要激烈得多。王逸谈《九歌》时说:"昔楚国南郢之邑,沅湘之间,其俗信巫而好祠,其祠必作歌乐鼓舞以乐诸神。屈原放逐,窜伏其域,怀忧苦毒,愁思沸郁。出见俗人祭祀之礼,歌舞之乐,其词鄙陋,因为作《九歌》之曲。上陈事神之敬,下见己之冤结,托之以风谏……"

　这些祭祀歌的题目见目录表,评述详见本书注释部分。其所表现的主题、感情色彩、措辞及格律形式都有共同的特色。朱熹对赞歌分别评注时,为了修正前人的观点,表达了他自己的见解。但蒋骥却表示反对,意见不同之处主要在把鬼神之不予应验比之楚怀王对诗人的不予理会,另外还有些次要的地方。这方面如果要细细查考恐怕太费篇幅了。但上述两位学者有一点看法是一致的,那就是诗歌所表达的感情对楚怀王是忠贞不渝的,对楚国的热爱是无限的,诗人对君主的怀念是坚定不移。虽然蒋骥认为《九歌》的创作日期应排在《九章》《涉江》之后,但这些诗篇,包括《山鬼》在内都应是同时期的作品,这一点是再清楚不过的。

§14.《九歌》写作之后,处于孤苦伶仃的绝境之中的屈原又写了《天问》。这首与众不同的诗歌一连提出了170多个疑问,其中有些关系到中国历史早期的起源问题,直到今日仍是无法解答,实属举世无双的第一奇文。王逸在《天问》的前言中写道:"《天问》者,屈原之所作也。屈原放逐,忧心愁悴。彷徨山泽,经历陵陆。嗟号昊旻,仰天叹息。见楚有先王之庙及公卿祠堂,图画天地山川神灵,琦玮僪佹,乃古贤圣怪物行事。周流罢倦,休息其下,仰见图画,因书其壁,呵而问之,以渫愤懑,舒泻愁思。楚人哀惜屈原,因共论述,故其文义不次序云尔。"王逸对诗篇的说法基本正确,但在最后两点陈述中暴露了判断上的错误。清代王夫之曾对此提出批评,详述见本文"八 屈原的思想和诗歌"。诗篇提出了一连串相互关联的问题,问天、问地、问天地间无法解释的奇异现象;又问夏朝的兴衰(包括后羿与楚、吴民众百姓的来源)、商殷的兴衰、周室的兴衰、吴楚之战、秦人的兴起、最后楚国的政局等等。

这两首诗依我看占据了屈原在楚怀王二十三至二十九年(公元前306—公元前300)之间的时间,也就是诗人被逐约11年后又被召回的时候。

§15.上一节里谈到楚国的政治事件、屈原从汉北被召回朝廷前后楚与齐、韩、魏、秦之间的战争以及诗人与顷襄王兄弟子兰之间的矛盾,从而被放逐到江南陵阳。宋代最早的《史记》木刻本印刷之前,有些竹简可能遗失,因为在"令尹子兰闻之大怒"之前肯定缺少了一二句。顷襄王三年,即公元前296年,怀王被扣于秦并死于秦,其遗体被送回国安葬。诗人在放逐中得到怀王死讯,便写了挽歌,起先题名为《招魂》,时屈原按阴历计算为 51 岁。事后诗人在长沙把挽歌改名为《大招》,依我之见,这是因为那时诗人又写了一首诗歌并以"招魂"命题,改名是为了加以区别。王逸不明白这一点,见到两首"招魂"就完全糊涂了,他弄不清这是屈原还是景差的作品。宋代晁补之精于辨析字义,说:《大招》用辞古朴,寓意深沉,必为屈原所作。洪兴祖说:《汉书·艺文志》提到屈原的作品共计 25 篇,至《渔父》已满此数,《大招》恐未必系屈原所作。朱熹的意见是景差用词既朴实无华又颇具古风,所以《大招》必为景差所作。明代黄文炳和清代林云铭、蒋骥最终认定这两篇"招魂"的真正作者就是屈原。按林云铭所说,诗人被年轻的顷襄王驱逐之后,仍然怀念着怀王,心中依然萦绕着被召回的向往。在这种情况之下,他爬上流放地的屋顶大声呼唤,招回他君主的亡灵,显得很自然正常。之后,屈原又写了《招魂》,描写巫阳奉天帝之命,把他自己的游魂从四个方向的既遥远又空旷恐怖的地方招回来。这当然是嘲讽式的打趣而已。所以,把前一首《招魂》改名为《大招》只是想借以区别于后一首《招魂》。对于这种说法,蒋骥表示完全赞同。对于洪兴祖的《渔父》已凑满 25 篇的说法,蒋骥在《楚辞余论》中指出,《九歌》虽然共 11 篇,却仍以九命名,并且在《汉书·艺文志》中也以《九歌》命名,所以把两篇"招魂"包括进去也并不矛盾。蒋骥还进一步问道:诗篇的最后 50 多行中涉及与《书经》和《礼记》中记载的文王、武王、周公事迹有关的周初某些政治、制度和公众福利的问题以及《诗经》中有些诗的问题;而宋玉和景差只是单纯的诗人而已,他们没有屈原那种崇高的施政本领,怎么能写得出《大招》这类诗篇呢?

　　§16. 顷襄王九年,即公元前 290 年,流放在陵阳的诗人回忆离别郢都的情景写成了《哀郢》。诗的最后部分尖锐地提到了令尹子兰和顷襄王本人,并对亲秦派的恶意中伤和拍马谄媚给予无情的指责。这必然引起当时楚国朝廷上下强烈的不满。于是来年年初,即公元前 289 年初,诗人又从陵阳被放逐到辰水和溆水流域盆地。陵阳在楚东部的大片疆域之中,离郢都已很远了;辰、溆地区则处于更远、更糟糕的西南部,是个未开化的野蛮地区。清初王夫之和近代学者郭沫若都坚持诗歌的写作在秦将白起克郢之后,描写楚民向东部逃难,顷襄王带着满朝文武奔陈的情景。这种说法显而易见是错误的,蒋骥已很具体地加以批驳并改正。近来游国恩又讲清楚了诗人从郢都流放到陵阳的路程以及诗人当时的心情、诗人取道所经过的地方、沿途的境遇,分析极为详尽,是不容否定的。

§17. 顷襄王九至十年,即公元前 290—公元前 289 年,诗人写了《涉江》,时年按阴历为 57 至 58 岁。流放的路途前面已谈过了。即自陵阳渡江,从楚的东北部到西南部,从鄂渚(今武昌)开始的第一段路程骑马,之后坐马车;在湘的洞庭湖上再坐船。在洞庭湖辽阔的水域里,诗人迂回前进,先沿沅水而上,再从枉水流入沅水的入口处转向西南。诗人在辰水注入沅水的入口处南面歇了夜。从枉水到辰水途中,离枉水不远,诗人便步行到武陵,得遇渔父;为纪念此事,诗人写了《渔父》。《渔父》是个短篇,与《卜居》一样在某些近代学者眼里不是诗人的作品。但是我赞同传统的看法,这两篇都是诗人的真作。自辰阳起,诗人沿水路继续向西南上行至溆水与沅水交汇处,再向西南折入溆水,在溆浦靠岸。经过的地区绝大部分都属蛮荒之地,只栖息着粗陋未驯的苗、瑶少数民族。那时正值春季,天下着雪,有时是雨夹雪,迎面而来的是崇山峻岭和浓荫蔽日的丛林,“乃猨狖之所居”。

§18. 同年初夏,诗人自枉水启程,在离龙阳不远处创作了《怀沙》。按阴历算,时年 58 岁。沙是指长沙,按唐代张谓的《长沙风土碑》所记,长沙是楚熊绎最早的封地。起先,他打算就在辰、溆二水流域盆地,在苗、瑶族居住的地方了此一生;经过考虑之后,他下决心还是在长沙自溺而死。长沙是东南地区的一座相当大的城

池,离郢都也不太远。自遭流放后,诗人从不想渡江北上,现在他终于决定死在楚国最早的老祖宗的葬地,正如:

> 鸟飞返故乡;
> 狐死必首丘。

从诗中可以看出,诗人想到这块地方时心中的痛苦和悲愤,但是他的决心是坚定不移的。他是被迫去死的,迫使他死的原因是楚国的政局在顷襄王及子兰的手中已到了使他彻底绝望的地步,整个"天下"都已处于秦国罪大恶极的军事力量的胁迫之下。

§19. 自从屈原决心死在长沙之后,他就日夜思念着去死。他想象自己已经死去,就写下了《招魂》,把他以前为招楚怀王的亡灵的《招魂》篇改名为《大招》。班固被这两篇"招魂"搞糊涂了,在《汉书·艺文志》中提出诗人作品的数目为 25 篇。王逸说《招魂》是宋玉所作,洪兴祖对诗篇的真伪提出了疑问,朱熹对王逸的看法表示附和,只有司马迁在《屈原列传》中毫不含糊地将该诗列为诗人的作品。诗篇以第一人称"朕"开始描述,接着很快就以巫阳奉了天帝之命的口吻来催促和招回诗人的游魂。诗中想象诗人的游魂可能流放到了四方的遥远又茫无涯际的可怖地区,而巫阳要把诗人的游魂招回来,因为这里有诗人自己的奇妙而又堂皇、宏丽的宅第供他享用。《招魂》是招诗人自己的魂,应是一曲挽歌;而招回之后写来又是那么豪华奢侈,享尽人间的荣华富贵,生活得万分安乐幸福。读来叫人感到别扭又滑稽,因为实际上诗人正掉在无底的痛苦深渊之中。这种笔法在世界诗歌史上也是独一无二的。诗歌的最后一行写道:

> 魂兮归来哀江南

"哀"原来的意思是"悲痛"。湘江与汨罗江交汇合流的一段就是哀江,向北注入洞庭湖,中有大、小哀洲两座小岛。相传舜帝南下征战,他的两位皇妻随后赶来却未能追上他,就哭泣于两岛上,故名哀洲。哀江以南即长沙,也是诗人将去世的地点。

§20. 屈原60岁(按阴历),即死前一年秋在长沙写了《悲回风》。《离骚》高屋建瓴检视着过去和现在,使人,尤其是一国之主感到不好受,但却可以使其变得明智。诗人凭着为美德和善良献身的精神而描写,他的创造和想象在广袤无垠的领域里狂放不羁地飞翔。《哀郢》和《怀沙》都是短篇,根据各个不同的一般环境或细节表达了两者各自独特的感情。《悲回风》是在严酷的痛苦之中写的,包含着一位心灵最崇高的诗人所抒发的沉痛的激情。他起先想上天,接着又下得地来对他的祖国表示依依不舍的眷恋,最后随江直下而入海,再从海中溯流而上,想去见见伍子胥和申徒狄的灵魂。这两位前辈也曾为国捐躯而未能挽回败局;一位为了吴国,另一位为了殷朝——诗歌在孤立无援的绝望之中结束。一位纯洁无瑕的有识之士被污泥浊水和现实世界糟蹋得发狂之后表达了深沉的痛苦、狂怒和绝望。有良知的人如想细细揣摩个中感受,《悲回风》是举世无双的杰作。其中诗人一再地宣称要追随彭咸的愿望,这最终注定了他不久就实现的命运安排的悲惨结局。

§21. 顷襄王十三年,即公元前286年,诗人在投汨罗江之前所写的最后一首诗歌是《惜往日》。诗人对自己多灾多难的过去作了回顾,从安乐幸福的青少年时代起到担任深得怀王信任的左徒止;诗人用辛辣、牢骚的笔调三次谈到容易受骗上当的国王(雍君)及其受人愚弄之处,意在同样尖锐地指责怀王的继承者顷襄王。但是从内心讲,诗人对他这位可鄙的王亲可说是不屑一顾的。说句最好听的,在诗人心目中,这个傻瓜顷襄王至多不过像是尧、舜他们的恣意妄为又反复无常的儿子丹朱和商均。这一点,诗人在《哀郢》中已有所讽示,同时对那些死死缠住那个半痴不呆的王亲拍马

溜须的可怜虫们也表示了极端的鄙夷。就是这批阿谀奸佞之徒造
成了他从陵阳再次流放到辰、溆。诗人过去一直梦想有朝一日能
把怀王改变成一位明君：

乘骐骥以驰骋兮，
来，吾道夫先路。

但是，现在他的希望已经彻底破灭了。至于顷襄王，诗人毫不掩饰
地认为不应让他继承王位。尽管诗人对顷襄王绝对看不起，但是
他仍然期望在自己身后顷襄王会读读他写下的诗篇，让他的诗歌
对这个年轻的统治者能起到及时的警戒作用。为了楚和楚国的子
民，诗人之死对于这个傻瓜及其兄弟将是一声响亮的警钟和抗议。
但是事实很快证明这两个可怜虫对此犹如风吹过耳，听而不闻。
如我在上面已经指出过的，屈原本人及他之后的史学家、文学评论
家究竟是否清楚秦国的专制暴政强加在诗人头上的各种诽谤是带
有阴谋奸诈的地理和政治的特殊性质的？我看这个问题是值得考
虑的。当然，怀王和顷襄王由于都是低能儿，他们会很容易跌入张
仪及其继承者所设置的恶毒卑劣的圈套中，这也是完全可以理
解的。

　§22. 最终，屈原的逝世日期是他在长沙住了 2 年多之后，顷
襄王十三年，即公元前 286 年的阴历五月五日，按阴历计算他是 61
岁，或 59 足岁。他的死并非由于对未来绝望而怯懦自尽，绝不是
如此。诗人舍命的行为乃是对顷襄王和其父怀王在秦王朝的极权
和霸道政治以及那批阿谀奸邪的亲秦帮派的支配下，酿成的昏庸
的丧权辱国的现状的反对和其声铮铮的谏诤。这一点诗人在《惜
往日》中的表白可以作证。因此，尽管诗人的躯体已终止了存在，
但他那崇高、辉煌、灿烂的精神将永垂千古！诗人不朽的灵魂将像
一首人皆尊崇的颂歌响彻云霄，永远回荡，感动整个人类。他的生

平和著作是永不消逝、光芒万丈的丰碑。

八 屈原的思想和诗歌

为了证实在古代中国社会曾经有过奴隶存在,郭沫若在《屈原研究》中提出看法,并以安阳殷墟出土的甲骨卜辞和商周金文为佐证。春秋、战国时期形成了奴隶社会的过渡时期,从商、初周直到秦的封建时代,被征服的部族或王朝的臣民部分都成了征服者的奴隶,他们可用牲畜、绢绸、谷类交易或以金钱买卖。奴隶将终身与土地连成一体而耕作、成为奴隶主的家奴或送去当兵等,但大部分都送往古老中国南部和东南部的宋国、徐国和楚国。无疑,奴隶制是商殷和初周时代社会结构的一个部分,在商汤及周文、武、成、康统治时期大大得到改善,但在嬴政并吞六国之后决没有消失或由封建主义来代替。所以战俘、罪犯及其家属都是奴隶。两种模式的社会制度常常相互渗透而同时存在,两者并不互相排斥。在嬴政和他儿子在位时,封建主义其实已经不存在了,而奴隶制反而进一步深化,压迫也愈见残忍,因而引发了公元前 209 年陈胜、吴广的起义。大批苦力奴隶为建造嬴政在骊山上的宏大陵寝服苦役多年,完工以后数以百计的嫔妃、宫娥、太监及数以百计的筑墓劳工都被活埋在墓中。无数奴隶又被驱使去修铺从广 300 里见方的阿城通向陵寝的林荫花木通道,长达 80 多里。自从那个暴君坐上大位之后,奴隶们又为他建造豪华奢侈的阿房宫建筑群,其主建筑的前厅未及命名,建造期共 34 年。此外,又在连绵不断的千山万岭上修筑了举世闻名的长城,铺设了从今陕西咸阳直达东面的燕、齐及南面的吴、楚的驿道,宽 50 步,每 30 英尺间隔都植以松柏。为了替这位历史上的"革命英雄"去寻觅长生不老的灵丹妙药,6000名童男童女作为活生生的牺牲品被赶往东海。最终的暴行是在公元前 212 年 460 多名学者和方士在咸阳被活埋。这些可怜的人们难道不是这位"英雄"人物嬴政的无可争议的奴隶吗?秦之后的各个王朝,除少数仁慈的明君像汉文帝、景帝、唐太宗和宋仁宗外,奴隶主和封建主在 1949 年以前一直联手统治着这片辽阔的土地,统治者是皇帝们及其官僚大臣和地主。①

在西方基本扫除奴隶制及黑暗花了数以千年计的时间。欧洲的中世纪时期延续了几乎 1000 年之久,吉本(公元 1737—1794,英国历史学家)在《罗马帝国衰亡史》中说得好,这大抵不过是一连串屠杀和抢劫的惨祸。在中国,儒教一直是一种主要的文明教化势力,但难免也有作恶多端的卑微的、伪善的、寄生虫式的儒派人物。在欧洲,基督教在大多数时间里也是一种文明教化的势力,但天主教的形式在较长的时间里曾时常带来灾祸。宗教战争、审判异教徒的宗教法庭及其对犹太人和新教徒的迫害在历史上是臭名昭著的。回过头来看我们的古代社会,商代初期一般都认为有 3000 个封建诸侯或藩属,周代有 800 个。

到了春秋、战国时期,官僚场中下级杀上级,为了篡夺王位儿子害父亲等现象层出不穷,初周的封建结构因此而瓦解。在专制政治不如秦国那样严酷、紧张的国家中,民主思想的曙光会首次照耀到奴隶和百姓们的心中,这是自然而然的事。远古以来断断续续出现过的家喻户晓的元老领袖和一些仁慈君主曾经使百姓头上奴役枷锁的负担减轻了些。周公和孔子在周朝初期和中后期提倡在统治与被统治之间建立仁慈友好的关系。封建制秩序的崩溃,其具体表现是过去的权势人物纷纷下马。这一事实教育

---

① 绝大部分的中国史家认为汉朝是中央集权的郡县制,封建制度已牢固地建立,而奴隶制已绝对消灭了。但在文、景二帝之后,如汉武帝时,据可靠的资料记载,奴隶制的存在是确定无疑的。《司马相如列传》(《史记》和《汉书》都一样)中有如下叙述:"卓王孙不得已,分予文君(卓王孙的新寡女儿,后来随司马相如私奔)僮百人,钱百万。"在上述两部书的《货殖列传》中,说卓有家僮 800 人。这 100 名家僮和 800 名家僮以及他们的家属不是奴隶又是什么呢? 在清初曹雪芹所写的著名小说《红楼梦》中,那些老家人和丫环使女们都公开承认自己是奴隶。

了奴隶和人民,使他们懂得,王、侯、伯、子并非天生的人上人,普通人的日子今后终究要到来的。他们祖先的忠实代言人孟子和屈原在 2300 年之前早已预见到了这一点并且都忠实地推行其思想和事业!

　　屈原可算是真正的贵族。他的祖先可以追溯到高阳帝,但他的心灵倒是坚定地为楚和六国的老百姓着想的。他生平的理想和政治信念乃是睿智仁慈的君主由一群优秀的有德行的臣僚辅佐,群臣为首的人物当遵照他的英明政策加以推广,为子民的长期和睦平安和幸福建功立业。三皇、五帝、尧、舜、禹、汤、文、武以及皋陶、关龙逄、伊尹、彭咸、傅说、箕子、比干、伯夷、梅伯、吕望、周公这几位在屈原著作中受到高度颂扬的人物,几乎也都是孔子、孟子在道德伦理和政治学说中极为推崇的君主及辅佐大臣的典范。虽然我们不能说屈原是个儒派人物,但就主要观点看,他和孔圣人最伟大的门徒之间的分歧恐怕是几乎没有的。诗人向往的是什么,推崇的又是什么,可从下列《离骚》的诗行中得到最佳的说明:

彼尧舜之耿介兮,

既遵道而得路。　　　　　　（第 29—30 行）

济沅湘以南征兮,

就重华而陈辞。　　　　　　（第 145—146 行）

汤禹俨而祇敬兮,

周论道而莫差;

举贤才而授能兮,

循绳墨而不颇。　　　　　　（第 163—166 行）

对初周时期文、武以及吕望、周公都给予赞扬:

汤禹俨而求合兮，

挚咎繇而能调。　　　　（第 289—290 行）

在这两行诗中,国家和天下的第一个革命领袖和民族的伟大的拯
救者以及出类拔萃的辅佐大臣伊尹和皋陶(即咎繇)都得到了颂
扬。(见本书关于伊尹的故事及《离骚》注释第 121 条)

说操筑于傅岩兮，

武丁用而不疑。

吕望之鼓刀兮

遭周文而得举。

宁戚之讴歌兮，

齐桓闻以该辅。　　　　（第 293—298 行）

这些都是明主寻访贤能并任之以辅弼大臣的事例。哀歌结束时,
诗人决心终止自己的性命。这在《悲回风》中又一再有所呼应:

既莫足与为美政兮，

吾将从彭咸之所居。　　（第 374—375 行）

"美政"一般作贤明的君主新推行的仁政解,但在这里特别强调的
恐怕是合纵约的国策。

　　诗人其他所有的较次要的著作中也都渗透着这种仁智君主由
一群贤能的大臣辅佐而施仁政的优美思想。在他最早的《橘颂》
中,结束的诗行——

年岁虽少，

可师长兮。

行比伯夷①,

置以为象兮。

就以毫不含糊的语言宣告了他想按前人最优越的模式来领导和执行国家大事的初衷。当然,伯夷的所谓明智在今天看来是有问题的,但他那种严肃、清廉的作风在任何时代都是无可非议的。屈原想引以为证的是他将坚持自己认为是正确的思想和行为。恢复二帝、三王统治的黄金时代是他朝思暮想的头等大事。事实上,我们可以相信他在二十五六岁或更早些时候就已决心支持合纵约以抗秦的策略了,因为苏秦作为他的同时代人大约比他年长 30 岁。见《惜诵》的第 7、8 行:

俾山川以备御兮,

命咎繇使听直。

皋陶(即咎繇)是舜的大法官,是禹的主要大臣,他主张真正的正义和法制,而并非商鞅的所谓"法家"。商鞅是盗用了法的名义来进行恶劣的犯罪活动的,他推行的是恐怖和暴力,动用官方力量进行谋杀及滥施侵略他国。《抽思》的第 33、34 行:

---

① 在我国早期历史上有两个著名人物都叫伯夷。第一个伯夷是舜的秩宗,见导论第二节。这里讲的第二个伯夷是殷的藩属国国王孤竹君的长子。孤竹君临终前封次子叔齐为太子,在他死后继承王位。但叔齐不愿接位,兄弟两人一起离开了故国逃亡到周。武王举事反殷后纣辛时,兄弟两人拦住了武王坐骑,劝他不要革命。姬发的随从要把他俩杀死,但吕望认为不应如此,便把他们赶走了。于是他们便不食周粟而死。他们认为接承王位并不是对老百姓的福利的一种责任,而认为即使王者已变成食人兽时,王位依然是王室的固有财产。这显然是既固执又愚蠢的想法,但从他俩本身看却并非恶劣。

望三五以为象兮，

指彭咸以为仪。

其中"三五"指的是三皇、五帝，即古代传说中的仁慈君主。

彼尧舜之抗行兮，

瞭杳杳其薄天。

众谗人之嫉妒兮，

被以不慈之伪名。（《哀郢》第53—56行）

尧、舜眼见他俩的儿子刚愎任性就没有让他们继承王位，而让他们贤德的辅佐接了大位。诗行中的暗喻及公开谴责导致屈原第二次从陵阳放逐到辰、溆。以下两行说的是与诗人一脉相承的舜的灵魂陪伴着他遨游仙境。

驾青虬兮骖白螭，

吾与重华游兮瑶之圃。（《涉江》第8—9行）

重仁袭义兮，

谨厚以为丰；

重华不可遌兮，

孰知余之从容？

古固有不并兮；

岂知其何故？

汤禹文远兮；

邈而不可慕。　　（《怀沙》第45—52行）

夫何彭咸之造思兮，

暨志介而不忘？　　（《悲回风》第5—6行）

原因是他已把自己的灵魂倾注于决心之中,怎能忘却?

> 孤子吟而抆泪兮,
> 放子出而不还。
> 孰能思而不隐兮,
> 昭彭咸之所闻? （《悲回风》第 49—52 行）

诗中"孤子"指的是诗人本身(蒋骥说这暗示楚怀王之死)。"放子"指的也是诗人,因为他当时第二次遭到顷襄王的放逐。

> 愁悄悄之常悲兮,
> 翩冥冥之不可娱;
> 凌大波而流风兮,
> 托彭咸之所居。 （《悲回风》第 67—70 行）
> 求介子之所存兮,
> 见伯夷之放迹。 （《悲回风》第 97—98 行）

这里"介子"即介推,是晋文公的忠实随从。关于他的悲惨故事见本文第 172 –173 页。

> 闻百里之为虏兮,
> 伊尹烹于庖厨,
> 吕望屠于朝歌兮,
> 宁戚歌而饭牛:
> 不逢汤武与桓缪兮,
> 世孰云而知之? （《惜往日》第 33—38 行）

百里奚的故事见本文第 173 页。伊尹和吕望的事迹见本文第 159 –

161 页。宁戚的轶事见《离骚》注释第 126 条。

坦率地说,屈原关于仁慈的概念,孔夫子在《礼记·礼运篇》中早就提出了。作为诗人,屈原不能在诗歌中像孔圣人和他的伟大的代表人物那样,在他们的伦理学说中对礼做过多地强调。但如果把他们一并看作是内在的政治家的话,他们的立场是相同的。一旦大道得以推行,天下就会大同。正如孔子早先宣称的,要保证一切努力、竞争和所作所为都是为了大众、为了人民,而不是为了那么几个独裁者以及他们的官僚、跟班和寄生虫。这里我们可以感觉到最早的民主和社会主义的脉搏在跳动,是一种讲人道的、公正不偏、光明磊落又相互宽容的共和国。实施仁政是直接的目标,而大同则是最终目的,其启动方案自然是选贤能并任以合适的公职。春秋时期,大国有 12 个,小国有许多个,到了战国时代只剩了 7 个大国和几个小国,最高的周已成了影子王朝。几位有远见的政治家尽管觉得很难达到成功,但仍然想通过忠诚信义和协调一致的和平方法,把所有大大小小的国家联合起来。自从周夷王统治期间,周室开始衰落,大家都希望出现一个最高的、占统治地位的大国,所有的诸侯都为其效忠。周宣王在位 46 年,采用铁腕政策在一定程度上实现了这个愿望。但是从春秋时期开始到战国时期血腥的自相残杀、封建秩序的解体以及社会动乱正是江河日下,愈演愈烈。要求天下统一的呼声自然成为时代响亮的基调。在政治统一的概念下,产生了两种思潮:第一种是孔夫子提倡并加以推行的,主张忠诚信义和协调一致;第二种是在大约 100 到 150 年之后,由秦国的卫(又名商)鞅提出并追求的,认为欺诈、背信弃义、恐怖和侵略是唯一可靠的手段。两者在性质上是截然相反的。孔夫子开展他的萌芽状态的活动时,为了想找一个主要的根据地,游历了 70 多个国家,历时 14 年,结果落了空。大约 200 年之后出生的孟子接受了他老师失败的教训,也振作精神访问了许多国家,但那时的政治、社会和文化状况已变得比孔子的时代更加混乱不堪,他的努力最终也归于失败。孔子与孟子都未去位于西方的秦国，因为在孔子的时代，秦尚处于野蛮状态之中，而在孟子活跃的年代里，秦已成为霸权主义的堡垒。到了屈原的时代，辩士们和说客们访遍了所有的王朝，恐怕只丢下了衰落的周朝。他们都想选择一位合适的君主，借以克服敌方。《离骚》中的女巫灵氛和咸作预言时都催促诗人赶紧离开他的故国（"勉远逝而无狐疑兮"），并对他保证"何所独无芳草兮!"，不过地点在异国。但是诗人变得眼花缭乱，并未付诸行动；或者说，在西天兜了一圈之后便打住了，并且回到他那充满苦难的老家。他所以拖拖拉拉没有行动的原因，很明显是对故国和故国人民的热爱。实施他的杰出政策的基地绝对不可能是在秦国。经过正反面的再三斟酌，他的目标不可改变地仍定在楚国，因为他是楚王室一名杰出的成员。此外，由于楚与韩、魏、鲁相邻的地理条件以及他与齐国朝廷上下的交谊良好，双方又能以诚相待，所以楚仍然是最适合于他施展宏图的地方。六国中疆域略次于楚的是齐，齐由于其海盐及渔业资源充足，所以既富又强。倘若屈原能离楚赴齐，也许可使其个人的事业大大改观，但他却宁愿让以个人的影响来形成一个施仁政的王朝的努力落得前功尽弃的可悲下场。史家和学者们都说，他所以未能干脆走出故国是因为他毕竟是王族的一员。韩、魏地域太小，且从战略上讲经不起攻击；燕与赵在北方，又太远，再则他的名声怕也传不到那里；说到齐，当时的情况也未必比楚强到哪里去，苏秦被刺的罪恶阴谋始终未正式追查和公开曝光。

诗人认为施仁政是最理想的政体，尧、舜的治国方法是大众所能期望的最高境界。所以，从逻辑上看，屈原主张王权应由明君的贤臣来继承，无条件的王室继承权应予废除。他对这个问题的看法虽未在诗中明确交代，但在《远游》及《离骚》中的"万乘"和"吾千乘之国"等词句以及在本文"七 屈原和他的著作"第11、12、16节中讨论过的《哀郢》的第53—56行，都很清楚地讽示了这一点。

诗人在《离骚》的第 167—170 行中表示了他的看法,为了子民的利益,只有贤者才能担任官职:

> 皇天无私阿兮,
> 览民德焉错辅;
> 夫维圣哲以茂行兮,
> 苟得用此下土。

他对楚王的忠心是因为楚王

> 奉先功以照下兮,
> 明法度之嫌疑;
> 国富强而法立兮,
> 属贞臣而日竢。　　(《惜往日》第 3—6 行)

对他刚开始担任左徒以及对他自己

> 愿荪美之可完。　　(《抽思》第 32 行)

但是在情况证明已绝对无望时,他就直截了当地称楚王为"壅君"。他对朝政或大臣们政绩的判断恰如其分和情真意切,令人心悦诚服:

> 民生各有所乐兮,
> 余独好修以为常。(《离骚》第 127—128 行)
> 瞻前而顾后兮,
> 相观民之计极。
> 夫孰非义而可用兮,
> 孰非善而可服?　　(《离骚》第 171—174 行)

这些都反映了诗人的正直和坦率的品质,实在感人至深。他可以毫不含糊地在重华面前表明他闪烁着忠义之光辉的内心世界:

> 跪敷衽以陈辞兮,
>
> 耿吾既得此中正。 (《离骚》第 183—184 行)

巫咸鼓励他到异国去亲自找寻他的美人:

> 苟中情其好修兮,
>
> 又何必用夫行媒? (《离骚》第 291—292 行)

事实上,《离骚》通篇是一首哀歌,痛诉了诗人为了对善良与美德的热爱而遭受到各种灾难的历程和原由,读者可参阅《离骚》评注开头蒋骥对诗篇写作动机的详细分析。

诗人在律己和施政中所体现的真实、正直、公平和真诚的道德标准都充分说明他对美德和善良的热爱。这在他较次要的作品中也都有所反映:

> 独立不迁,
>
> 岂不可喜兮?
>
> 深固难徙,
>
> 廓其无求兮。
>
> 苏世独立,
>
> 横而不流兮。
>
> 闭心自慎,
>
> 终不失过兮。
>
> 秉德无私,
>
> 参天地兮。 (《橘颂》第 19—28 行)

下列诗行读来使人感到多么简洁又真切：

> 善不由外来兮，
> 名不可以虚作。　　（《抽思》第 37—38 行）
> 何灵魂之信直兮，
> 人之心不与吾心同。（《抽思》第 63—64 行）
> 芳与泽其杂糅兮，
> 羌芳华自中出；
> 纷郁郁其远蒸兮，
> 满内而外扬。
> 情与质信可保兮，
> 羌居蔽而闻章。　　（《思美人》第 47—52 行）
> 苟余心之端直兮，
> 虽僻远其何伤？　　（《涉江》第 25—26 行）
> 易初本迪兮，
> 君子所鄙。
> 章画志墨兮，
> 前图未改。
> 内厚质正兮，
> 大人所盛。　　　　（《怀沙》第 13—18 行）
> 怀质抱情，
> 独无匹合。
> 伯乐①既没，

---

① 伯乐原是星座的名称，相传是天上的赶马伕。秦穆公的子民孙阳因善于
　辨别骏马被赐予这个称号。关于孙阳的故事说，一次他路过虞山，山岗巉
　岩林立，山路崎岖。这时遇见一匹马拉着一车盐，这马一见孙阳就又是嘶
　鸣又是喷响鼻。伯乐便下了车，走到忍受着拉盐的屈辱的马跟前，放声大
　哭；这马就一会儿低头吹响鼻，一会儿抬头对天长嘶。这里马指的是诗
　人，伯乐指的是汤和禹。

骥焉程兮?
民生禀命,
各有所错兮。
定心广志,
余何畏惧兮。　　　　（《怀沙》第 65—72 行）

诗人的政治思想是施仁政,道德上追求人道、正义、真实和正直。
可见他一定在北方的齐、鲁,即吕望、周公、孔子和他的门徒们的故
地作过很深刻的研究。以上引文中两次提到了吕望的事;"叔旦"
明显即指周公,在《天问》结束时也提到了他;在《离骚》第 143—
144 行中也提到了孔子和他的孙子子思:

依前圣以节中兮,
喟凭心而历兹。

说的是子思在《中庸》的教导中阐述了孔圣人对中庸之道的宣扬。
孔子虽然颂扬节制,但是他本人在处理问题的实践中却未必恪守
节制的准则。然而,他虽有时违背了自己的准则,却仍获得了荣誉
及人们对他的尊敬。依我之见,一个彻底的、真正的儒家理所当然
不应是卑猥的、爬虫式的、怯懦的教条主义者,就是说不论发生什
么情况都不会激怒或异常悲伤,无论如何他都要恪守节制的准则。
但是我们的诗人,由于他的出身和遭际,他的一生或他的诗歌中绝
对是充满着愤怒和痛苦。可以肯定地说,由于少正卯的目无法纪
的骚动和充当叛乱头目的活动,孔子判以正法时肯定是动了怒的。
最突出的例子是,如果孔子对当时发生的子害父、臣弑君的现象不
是十分愤恨的话,他就不会动笔写《春秋》来记载这些为人极端蔑
视的恐怖事例。孟子的话更加直截了当:"文王一怒而天下平。"孟
轲在《答齐宣王问》中对正义的革命和叛乱作了明确的区分,对宣

王分不清两者含义的问题所作的恰当的回答(见本文"五 战国时期"中孟轲的故事)很严肃地表明了他赞美的是什么,谴责的又是什么。可见他们两人为了正义而不平、感到愤慨时,都没能做到绝对的无动于衷,没能像传统儒家所要求的知识分子在生活和诗歌写作上做到克制。孔子对《诗经》大为赞赏是因为其中的诗篇"思无邪",以《雉鸠》作篇首的民歌"乐而不淫,哀而不伤"。我们发现屈原的大部分诗作都壅塞着愤怒的激情,其痛苦的情状常常极为激烈;这已成为他作品的风格,与传统的或赖以为生的儒家的准则大异其趣。

诗人思想的另一个特色是对鬼神的态度。据说孔子是"子不语怪、力、乱、神",因为他觉得这对教化民众不利,并且他也不能容忍鬼神的说法。孔子的门徒季路有一次"问事鬼神",子曰:"未能事人,焉能事鬼?"又问道:"敢问事死",曰:"未知生,焉知死?"作为受人尊敬的、实事求是的哲人,他不谈及他不了解的事物。他闭口不谈鬼神源于他求知的态度,即"知之为知之,不知为不知,是知也",他就是这样教导他的门徒子路的。屈原作为诗人在《离骚》《九歌》《远游》《招魂》《大招》和《九章》中写到大量的鬼神,但又在《天问》中对这种超自然现象提出了其来源、起因、结果、怎么会以及为什么等的种种问题。在充当泛神论者的同时,他又对大量的自然现象、传说和历史事件来个刨根问底。《九歌》是对种种神灵的祭歌的集锦。在《远游》的第 92、93 行中,诗人谈及他见到了最高的天帝旬始:

> 集重阳入帝宫兮,
> 造旬始而观清都。

但在《离骚》中天帝似乎也并不显得那么法力无边:

> 吾令帝阍开关兮,
> 倚阊阖而望予。　　　　　(第 209—210 行)

看来门丁不让诗人进门之举并未得到天帝的应允,天帝不但根本不知道这件事,并且也未必能事先阻止这种错误行为。可是在《离骚》第 167—168 行中诗人又肯定地说:"皇天无私阿兮,览民德焉错辅。"这里皇天更像是主宰世界的永恒不变的自然法则或规律,即"道",而并不像西方的天神宙斯或耶和华那种赋有人性的神。诗人在《招魂》中写道,上天有 9 条拱形的通道,都由虎豹把守,守门神有 9 个头,眼如鬣狗和狼,力大无穷,可一次拔起 9000 棵树。冥界的帝君是个食人的恶魔,老虎似的头上长着尖角,有 3 只眼睛,身若公牛,尾巴有 9 条,爪蹄鲜血淋淋。一句话,屈原在诗歌中对仙界或冥界的描写都是根据神话或传说取材的,部分则来自他丰富的想象力。诗人独特的想象力能把任何无关或相互排斥甚至冲突的事物和谐地融合在一起。他笔下的神、女神、云神、雷神、半人半羊的农牧之神以及各种精灵等虚无缥缈的现象都有了"自己的住处和名字"。从总体来看,这与孔子对这些现象所保持的无神论式的缄默是背道而驰的。虽然如此,这对屈原的诗歌创作还是起了很大的作用。

司马迁在《史记》中说,孔子把留传下来的 3000 多首古诗大加砍伐,"删"成 300 多首,编成《诗经》一书。对于这个问题,学术界长期以来热烈争论。太史公在这一点上正确的可能性较小,失误的可能性更大些。但这为数至少 300 多首的大量诗歌,绝大部分肯定是初周时从周室王朝、其领地以及诸侯各国搜集来的,另有商殷遗留下来的不多的颂歌。关于这些诗歌的来历,唐代孔颖达和郑樵、宋代朱熹及其几十位学生代表了一家之言。例如,他们把《周南》《召南》的开始 25 首归结为周代早期文王时代的作品;而清代的崔述则断定是成王、康王时代或更晚的作品。对于这些诗歌产生的最晚的时间极限,则各家意见一致,认为搜集诗歌工作一经停顿,孔子就开始着笔写《春秋》了。

据《周官》①记载,诗歌搜集工作完毕后不久,在太学中即开始

① 《周官》是不知名的史家所作,记载的是初周的官吏制度,写作日期可能在战国时期。西汉刘歆称之为《周礼》,因此,该书即以此名留传后世。

关于六诗的讲授;后来称为"诗"之六义,即风、雅、颂、赋、比、兴。
"'风'是各国乡村(或农庄)小巷(或胡同)中的民歌或叙事诗歌。年
轻男女吟咏着歌调来表达对各自对象的感情,词句充满着热烈的爱,
却不淫秽;时而忧郁却无悲痛之感,他们通常给人的感觉是甜蜜、感
人、温存但又不露骨。其中包含许多申诉冤屈和谴责性的诗歌,都属
言者无罪、闻者足戒的性质。'雅'涉及的是周王室及其诸侯朝堂上
的事,是大臣、贵族们的格调较高的诗歌。内容大抵为规劝和告诫、
对忠孝的感怀之作;或以鼓励善行、防止祸乱为目的;陈词恳切,文笔
平直,使闻者足戒。'颂'是帝王和诸侯的宗庙进行祭祀活动时所作
的颂歌,用以祭祀神道和亡灵并引起感应。歌词赞颂完满的美德、记
叙功勋和业绩以及表达虔诚的敬意。措词庄重,一气呵成,词义既广
博却又精炼,读来使人感到敬畏,令人深思。'赋'是对事物的铺陈和
描述。'比'指的是相互比较或比拟。'兴'是带有感情的诗歌。
'比'即比较,即暗喻、明喻和转喻;而'兴'带有感情色彩。'比'所指
的事物之间的比喻在意义上虽然扣得紧而贴切,但还是浅了些;而
'兴'虽其含义不那么紧扣,却寓意十分丰富隽永。一句话,风、雅、颂
是诗歌的类型;赋、比、兴是诗的写法和运用。"从汉朝开始至今的学
者们对于诗歌的六种类型和因素的说法分歧很大,上面所述是采用
《周官》的说法,对"诗"之六义的阐述看来是最为中肯的。

诗歌的主题一般可依次分为六类:家庭、朝廷、政治事件、军事
事件、风俗和民间传说及其他。再重复一遍,"风"收集了各种民间
情歌及广为流传的抒情曲调,题材范围广泛。通常"雅"是政治性
质的诗,其典型的内容如周王室的起源——姜嫄和她的儿子后稷
(见本文"二 三皇、五帝和三王",第160页)、公刘(稷的重孙)和
古公亶父(文王的祖父)——还谴责厉王和幽王的倒行逆施,把他
们比作周室统治集团中的败类。"颂"诗颂扬的是周朝的文、武、
成、康,商殷的汤、沃丁和天帝。这可算是中华民族在诗歌方面所
喷发的最原始的心声。所以民歌、抒情诗或颂歌一律在音调上较

委婉,感情上含蓄有度,格律上简单。诗歌一般篇幅较短,文体简练有力。有关学者绝大多数都认为这与当时伴奏的曲调是相符合的,只是乐谱部分已毁于战火或散失和遗忘了。《墨子》证实,这些诗篇在当时都配乐吟咏和歌唱的,且还配合各种舞蹈。

屈原的诗作以与《诗经》的分化为起点,演化成一种卓绝的发展。《诗经》中无名氏的诗歌大部分读起来都是文绉绉的,而屈原的倾诉光辉灿烂,总体说来都慷慨激昂、感情激烈。对于以"二南"为首的、以温文尔雅为特色的诗风所造成的文化影响,孔子曾给予高度的评价:"研究诗可以学到'比'、'兴',可以从一国的民俗和风俗来观察到其兴盛或衰败,可以使人按道德标准分别合群共同生活,可以使人懂得对一国的政策如何进行批评或申说你的不满。诗可使人学会在家中善事父母,出外为君主效力,此外还可使人学到关于鸟、兽、花草、树木等名称方面的广博知识。"(诗可以兴,可以观,可以群,可以怨。迩之事父,远之事君;多识于鸟兽草木之名。①)但是,屈原所作的优越的贡献远远超过这些,他在诗歌中显示出为了推进人道和正义的事业,不顾屡屡失败和个人一再遭到挫折,对秦国狠毒的罪恶势力及其依附者——楚怀王、顷襄王的愚蠢及其朝臣们的腐败——展开不懈的斗争,显示出他作为第一流的诗人、目光深远的思想家和大无畏的牺牲者在斗争上所作出的英勇业绩。诗人不仅在生前以勇敢非凡的行为对他们加以反对,并且在他留传后世的诗歌中既播送了他的光耀照人的信念,又对秦、楚的行径愤怒地加以斥责。所以,他的充满着炽热情感的诗歌所表达的主题或目的首先就是为正义事业而奋斗。

其次,他的杰出人格与其辉煌的英勇行为相比也毫不逊色。他不是《诗经》中的佚名诗人,也不让自己隐姓埋名或单纯是个对朝廷不满的官僚,而在一开始就以诗人和政治家的面目宣称:

---

① 引语根据何晏收集的西汉孔安国和东汉郑玄关于孔子《论语》的《集解》。

Introduction

闭必自慎,

终不失过兮,

秉德无私,

参天地兮。　　(《橘颂》第 25—28 行)

为了言行一致,他终于献出了生命,不退缩,也不畏惧。正如《书·舜典》①所说:"诗言志,歌永言,声依永,律和声。"屈原在怒火中烧

---

① 据西汉孔安国和唐代孔颖达,这部《尚书》著作的意思是"从古时留传下来的"一捆竹简。《尚书》也称《书经》或《书》。这种说法来自孔子,有《庄子·天运篇》中的记载为证:一次孔子对老子说:"丘治《诗》、《书》、《礼》、《乐》、《易》、《春秋》六经,自以为久矣。"《尚书》由孔子编辑、校订,其中包含从尧、舜一直到秦穆公为止,以典、谟、训、诰、誓、命为名的诏书、敕令、政令以及谏议性的诗体书简共 100 篇,孔子还作了序。该书所有的版本都在公元前 213 年由嬴政听从其帮凶李斯的提议一并烧为灰烬。但有位名伏胜的秦博士却设法在焚书之前在墙壁里藏匿了一本。接着,爆发了毁灭性的战争,大大地削弱了秦的残暴和凶恶的统治,也叫楚霸王项羽完结了。伏胜所珍藏的大部分秘籍也随之散失殆尽。待汉朝建立 20 多年后,伏胜才发现只有 29 篇或章节免遭劫难,他差不多要气疯了。文帝时,文臣晁错受命访问伏胜,其时伏已九十有余,不能行走,也不能离家了。他通知伏胜整理那些用籀文写的令人难以辨认的文字,并叫老人以当时通用的隶书重新加以书写,但伏胜用隶书写的 29 章《今文尚书》中却没有传说中舜亲自撰写的《舜典》。大约又过了 80 年,到汉武帝后期时,在曲阜孔子生前居处的墙中发现了一批蝌蚪文的《古文尚书》竹简。孔子第十二代孙、学者孔安国受命把那些没法读懂的文字用隶书重新书写,并为这次发现写了《书传》。经孔安国挽救出来的书籍内容比伏胜的 29 章多出 16 章,其中就有《舜典》。不幸的是,不久朝中发生了巫蛊之灾,一时甚嚣尘上,所有的蝌蚪文竹简,包括孔安国重新书写的《古文尚书》及序都失散了,那新发现的 16 章也完了。又过了 200 多年,到东晋时,文臣梅赜说,他发现了孔安国的《书传》,并献呈晋元帝。再过了 300 多年,到唐太宗时,学者孔颖达受太宗命编著《五经正义》,其中梅赜发现的孔安国《书传》被引为《尚书》的一个组成部分。此后的几百年中,南宋和明代学者都怀疑梅赜所发现的《书传》是伪作。最后到了清代,有学者阎若璩证明这绝对是赝品。但自唐代孔颖达所作《尚书正义》采用了梅赜的《书传》后,这 16 个章节,包括《舜典》,一直被认为是得而复失的篇章的必不可少的替代之作了。

的诗篇中真正道出了他最崇高的意愿,并且真正地做到了"参天地兮"。对于为自己规定的职责及自己的英勇行为,他的心中一直是很清楚的。虽然他对古时仁慈为怀的皇、帝、王及其称著于世的辅佐一贯表示最高的尊敬和钦佩,可是在诗歌中他却像对待老朋友一样直呼其名。贫穷、潦倒、流放、"千刀万剐"、死亡,没有一样能把他吓唬住。总之,他之所以能创作出永垂不朽的诗章,他一生所执行的使命以及他个人的人格是两个重要的先决条件。愤怒的激情以及遣词用语上超凡脱俗的艺术应该说是自然而然随之而来的两个必要的条件。

孔子所说"中庸之为德也,其至矣乎?民鲜久矣!"这句赞语意思是古时显赫的君主们温和、仁慈的统治已过去很久了,而他所处的世界很长时间以来已变得动荡不安,并且局势还在不断恶化。因此,他觉得王、侯、伯、子等贵族以及他们的大臣、地方官吏们必须收敛一下自己胡作非为的时候已经到来了;只有这样做才能在一定程度上恢复初周时期那种顺天安民的社会秩序。他就是本着这种精神对《诗经》的淡雅的、有教化作用的篇章大加赞赏的。由秦孝公和卫鞅创始的强暴统治在孔子时代尚未开始。总之,孔子发出赞赏的根由在于他仍然希望,如果所有的统治者和贵族大臣都能共同按中庸之道行事,那么世界还会恢复人道和正义的。当然,他的希望不可能实现。由于圣人称颂节制,在此基础上子思制订了中庸之道的学说。这最终成为儒学的一个组成部分,对后世的某些君王倒也真正起到过一些好的作用。但在春秋时期最后100年左右直至整个战国时期、秦王朝以及汉朝初期,即汉文帝、景帝即位之前,孔夫子高度赞扬的大道以及子思的学说原则在现实面前都遭到了失败的下场。关于以大同的理想付诸实施来拯救世界这一点,屈原与孔夫子的看法是一致的,但是与《诗经》中所表达的那种温文尔雅、娴静安详的气度却相去甚远。这是因为张仪的间谍外交和阴谋诡计终于使秦国的霸权主义成功地渗透了楚国的机体,虽然屈原对于自己所处的境地可能不完全清楚,但是他确实是深受其害的牺牲者。所以与《诗经》那种早期的颇具古风的韵律流动及格式的诗篇相比较,屈原的作品在气质上显得言辞剧烈、情绪激昂。他的大部分作品给读者的感受是感情炽烈、炙手可热,格律的搏动雄浑有力,吟诵之间音调超逸、回荡隽永。

诗人留传至今的最早的诗篇《橘颂》,无论在诗风上或形式上均未脱离《诗经》的传统,读来朴实、淡雅安详,感情沉着、坚定。但是与《诗经》温文尔雅的特色相对照,他的诗已经表现出一种不同于一般的分歧。诗篇以明确无误的语言阐明了诗人不可亵渎的人格,这在初周时代的文选中是见不到的。在《惜诵》、《抽思》和《思美人》等诗篇中,个性的呼声分阶段地日益明显、突出。诗人在宣泄他深切的悲憾和凄凉之感时,采用了赋的手法,因而使得抒情的诗意愈加细腻、感人和精练。

诗篇《卜居》的结尾处表达对世态的蔑视和愤慨之情的诗句,犹如电光闪闪、霹雳轰鸣,气势压人。

> 世溷浊而不清:
>
> 蝉翼为重,
>
> 千钧为轻;
>
> 黄钟长弃,
>
> 瓦釜雷鸣;
>
> 谗人高张,
>
> 贤士无名! （第 42—48 行）

这里屈原的鞭笞声和怒喝声真是响彻耳际,毫不含糊。他的学生宋玉生性怯懦,另一位学生景差更不如宋玉,所以认为他们两位或其他什么人能写出这般诗句的说法实在难以令人想象。

《远游》篇中诗人创作了一首诗意盎然的幻想曲。他飞升翱翔

苍穹,先寻访仙人王子乔,探听最高权力,随即奋力追求,然后

吸飞泉之微液兮,
怀琬琰之华英。
玉色頩以晚颜兮,
精醇粹而始壮。
质销铄以汋约兮,
神要眇以淫放。　　　　（第 75—80 行）

这样,他成了仙客,继续进行太空遨游。

屯余车之万乘兮,
纷容与而并驰。
驾八龙之婉婉兮,
载云旗之委蛇,
建雄虹之采旄兮,
五色杂而炫耀。　　　　（第 95—100 行）
擎彗星以为旍兮,
举斗柄以为麾。
判陆离其上下兮,
游惊雾之流波。　　　　（第 115—118 行）

他终于升腾到了超凡脱俗、俨然神仙的境界：

下峥嵘而无地兮,
上寥阔而无天。
视儵忽而无见兮,
听倘悦而无闻。　　　　（第 167—170 行）

"抵达至清",最终"下一步将承袭太初"。诗篇描述了一次在隔绝人世、杳渺又空濛的宇宙之中的航行,诗人本身已脱胎换骨成了仙家。这正是他力图从精神的沉重压力以及痛苦的感情抑郁下求得解脱的写照;也可说是他在理想屡屡遭挫、人格被践踏到令人焦头烂额时,所制作的一帖美学上的镇痛剂。与他初期的作品《橘颂》那种清醒、感情沉着的诗风相比,这是一次不容忽视的飞跃。脱胎于《诗经》特有的娴雅和平庸的格调和主题,他勇敢地为诗歌创作开辟了一处截然不同的新天地。至此,诗人的写诗习作期已被他远远地甩到后面去了。

诗人投入他一生中的伟大创作所需要的条件,如思维智慧上的精到、想象的广博无垠以及感情上丰厚又深切等业已具备。在政治上他的理想是实行仁政;他执著地热爱人道与正义;他出身显贵,接受了优秀的教育,品行教养完美,但他却必须一再忍受卑劣的污蔑、攻击,甚至遭到逐出郢都的令人喘不过气来的下场。这一切在他心中留下了创痛。此外,更重要的是他那不可战胜的意志、光辉灿烂的人格以及作为诗人的无与伦比的天才,上述种种因素汇合在一起,最终形成了《离骚》这部名震尘寰的杰作。在中国诗歌史中没有任何篇章可以与之匹敌,我相信,通览全世界的诗歌作品同样也难以找到一首颂歌或抒情诗在气魄上、情操上、思维活动的紧凑和密集程度上、在想象力飞翔的恢宏幅度以及磅礴的感情气势上,能与之相比拟。为了实施有利于民众的仁政,他不停地思考和专心致志地追求。他忍受了深切的悲伤和经历了折磨人的苦难,也提出了谴责。为列举或比拟他提及的大量历史事迹,想象力扫描所及的博大的范围以及精心描绘的各种形象,按不同种类的悦目、芬芳的花卉和吉祥的鸟类各自的属性为准引发出来的美丽的象征性笔法;绚丽的词藻配上诗歌格律显得格外活跃而毫不刻板,流畅、丰富的词汇巧妙地掺和了一些楚国的方言土语;最后是他所采用的灵活又开合自如的格律形式以及随之而来的韵律和节奏上的回味无穷;屈原作诗的各种独特的手法犹如一股股金光闪闪的火苗,诗人如神之笔挥洒之际,各股火苗终于聚集一体,燃烧成一柱光焰炽烈的火炬——这就是《离骚》。就诗篇的题目而言,其内容正是名副其实。这是一座充斥着各种令人悲哀的事物、名称、思想和联想的大迷宫,虽然诗篇全长 375 行,读来却显得特别长。由于其高度紧凑的氛围,迷宫里的曲线显得格外头绪纷繁,回转令人目眩;其核心部分似乎更深邃、含蓄。对于诗歌所表达的深切悲哀和折磨人的苦难,如果我们静心凝神地加以思考,结果仍将回归到实施仁政以及楚国和周朝天下所面临的灾难的题目上。所以,作为现代的读者,我们应该意识到诗人献给人类的这部永远是最伟大的诗章的全部涵义。

《九歌》是屈原被流放在汉北时写的,作者心态忧愁、孤独。由于在《离骚》中他尽情地宣泄了巨大的悲伤和痛苦,《九歌》的主题则是一种独特的田园风光,跳动着迷人的节律。祭祀典礼时诵唱的完美曲调由笛子吹奏配乐,其内容是可以歌咏的抒情诗;诗人在这方面是十分到家的大师,他与祭歌所赞美的男、女神仙或鬼怪精灵彼此似乎非常融洽相宜。神仙、鬼怪都非常高深莫测、居高临下,但又稍纵即逝、灵气十足、蛊惑迷人、瞬息万变。诗人对他们的态度是崇敬、肃穆、景仰和礼拜有加。这种圣歌中描绘的是礼服盛装的祭司对祭神讴歌着致敬和赞美的诗句;伴奏的有击鼓、钟、铃齐鸣、长笛及管乐吹奏、单面小鼓及狭长小鼓的打击,有古筝和古琴的弦乐,有铙钹拍打、排箫吹奏和击锣。装点这种神奇仪式的有各式各样的香花、芳草;焚烧着沉香和檀香。为了增添典礼的节日气氛,在神像上饰以珍珠、宝石——有红宝石、蓝宝石、黄玉石、绿松石、石榴石、祖母绿和玉器。这些车载的神仙由龙舟或平底船牵拉着出现在洞庭湖上,真是光彩照人、气象万千,但突然间出人意料地却消失得无影无踪。

《天问》是诗人所撰写的最稀奇古怪的作品。清代王夫之在

《楚辞通释》中说得好,诗人在诗篇中并不如汉代王逸所说只是"发泄气愤和恼怒,倾诉忧伤和感受"。所提及的问题虽然有一大堆,从天、地、山、河到人间世事,远古时代的事在先,最后涉及楚国的祖先,诗歌通篇次序井然。很清楚,主题是诗人自己拟就的,因此认为这些问题是刻在墙上的说法是不正确的。王逸说,题目说的不是"问天"而是"天问",因为老天那么高,人是没法向它提问的,这种说法也不对。屈原认为自然界在变化着,人间世事有起有落,这都是天律决定的,公正不偏。他提出了由老天注定的、没法解释清楚却又不以人的主观意志而转移的世事变化,来责问那些鲁莽又妄自尊大的国王和头脑简单的大臣们。从这个意义上讲,诗章的命题似乎应该是"天问"而不是"问天"。诗章叙述的范围虽然极为广博,但就其精髓而言可归纳为:得道者昌,失道者亡。侵略与暴力、排斥忠告与谏议、纵情骄奢淫逸、抵制贤能、亲信奸佞——这为兴、衰或存、亡提供了极好的试金石。屈原对楚王所作的告诫和规劝可说已尽了最大的努力。他敦促国王对古代的世事实例进行调查,再回过头来检讨自身的所作所为;希望他能效法三王、五帝,多办善事、好事和有魄力有胆识的事,而不要重蹈桀、纣、厉、幽的覆辙。根据事物的起因和后果的关系看,在可供国王采取的切实可行的方案方面,屈原正是竭尽所能,他在规劝和告诫上的努力在诗篇中已达到了顶点。

姑且认为这种解释是切实可信的,《天问》的英译文的含义是笼罩世间万物的老天或苍天从精神上、道义上和实体上主宰着一切,提出的问题是怎么会和为什么? 其中有些隐晦的字句,学者们至今仍未能弄明白。近代约在 50 年前,王国维在《观堂集林》中根据他研究安阳小屯殷墟甲骨卜辞时对名词"该"、"季"、"恒"所作的解释,阐明了几乎是空白的商殷历史上的一些复杂疑难问题。《天问》可能写在《九歌》之后,内容并非纠缠于感情问题,而主要是智慧和知识性方面的问题。开始时提到关于宇宙的问题,接着问到天的结构、天与地、太阳、月亮、星星、神话传说、山河、历史故事和记载、明君贤臣们的生平、臭名昭著的暴君和奸佞等各种事物之间的关系,最后问的是影响到诗人本身的楚国的事。诗篇大抵是四行诗和对句,从格律上说是二音步和三音步的组合;两个或三个字(音节)构成一个音步。

《招魂》和《大招》虽然基本上恢复了《诗经》的四字一句诗行的格律形式,但就其特征、主题和措辞而言,与《橘颂》的精练纯洁的诗风相比仍有很大的区别,诗篇中充分运用了赋的手法。据《礼记·礼运》记载,古时候人死后得有人爬上屋顶手持死者上衣面北高声长呼死者名字三次,同时舞动衣衫喊道:"某某人回来吧!"叫魂人下来再把衣衫覆盖在死者身上。如果死者并未还魂,就举行葬礼。这种长呼死者名字的叫魂方式是根据《礼记》的记载而来的。大约2500年前《礼记》中的"皋!某复!"说的就是这个意思。从现代的眼光来看,这当然纯属迷信,毫无意义。但在古代和原始时候,这种习俗的本来目的除了想叫死者复活之外,基本上是出于表达死者家属的眷爱。屈原写的《招魂》和《大招》大概就是在长呼死者之后再高声朗读的。诗篇《大招》中招魂者正是诗人本身,他一开始就告诫其君主的亡灵在天地四方遥远又广袤无垠的原野上险境可怕,接着催促亡灵返归到楚国,回到他的真身上来。这样,楚王便可不必害怕被秦国强行掳去作人质,再逃亡、流离,而可以平安愉快地祈求永生。在楚国,以他九五之尊的地位,他可以尽情享受生活的一切,包括稀有而丰盛的美味佳肴;通过对诗歌、音乐和舞蹈的鉴赏又可提高文化修养;对富有魅力的佳丽的眷恋以及王室生活条件所能提供的各种合情合理的具有吸引力的娱乐;而最主要的还是由贤臣们辅佐对子民实施宽厚的仁政。大臣们个个智能过人,有正义感,办事同心协力,又都是仁慈为怀的贤德之士。

《招魂》写在《怀沙》之后,其中记载了巫阳召唤诗人自己的亡灵重返哀江以南的语言。当时诗人正处于极度绝望之中,巫阳召唤的口吻和情势比之于《大招》都是有过之而无不及,这正是个有趣的颠倒。四方密布着狰狞可怖和肆虐的妖怪(啮食亡灵的巨怪高 8000 尺;宰人以献祭的野人前额刺花、利齿漆黑;千百万条头形三角的毒蛇到处缠绕蠕动着;作祟于人的狐妖硕大无朋、形态怪异,疾行瞬息千里;九头蟒蛇来回游动迅速异常;红色蚁怪巨若大象;还有大如葫芦的黄蜂)。这里的气候非人所能忍受,而且自然灾害连绵不断(10 个太阳相继升起,白热化程度足可使金属熔化、烤枯岩石;流沙的飞动一泻千里;大片大片的土地由于缺水而枯槁龟裂;继而大雪绵绵永不休止,一望无际的山脉雪拥冰冻,遍地冰柱)。通向天堂的大门由虎、豹和九头怪物把守,而地狱又有恶魔可怕地统治着。这一点在以上讨论诗人的思想的题目中已叙述过了。他的魂魄现在由一个灵活敏捷的巫士①引路,进入郢都城门,回到了他那环境宜人的家园。这里备有大量舒适和方便的生活设施,还点缀着各式艺术性的装饰。他的画像②高悬在墙上,泰然地俯视着高大宽广的安静的厅堂。宏伟壮观的宅邸周围设有栏杆,房顶饰有飞檐,从三面怀抱着一处高高的平台。通过住宅的窗棂和栏杆可以眺望远处③溪谷中的山泉滚滚而下,绕着半个住宅花园

---

① 这里对巫师的描写是他正在走回去,一手执幡,飘飘忽忽;另一手提着只用竹篾编织、带花格子的箱笼,四周绕着各种颜色的线绳,用来收容亡灵。

② 这是根据蒋骥的评注,他认为这是诗人生前的画像。朱熹则认为这是屈原死后的画像,但是他在诗歌的序言中说,是宋玉在他老师还在世时要为他招魂而写成的。王夫之对原文的"像设"解释为"想象";所以,他认为根本没有什么画像的问题。由于是巫阳在长呼招游魂,故她应该非常清楚这首挽歌赋中所描述的一切细节,而决不需要作什么想象。

③ 这是我本人的理解。朱子和蒋骥都认为原文的"临高山些"意思是宅园坐落在高山之上。但我认为这并非原文的本意,也缺乏想象力。首先,把诗人描绘成高山上的隐士是不合乎道理的。此外,从屈原本人的想法看,说他的那套宅园坐落在郢都城中地势较高的地方,对面远远地可以见到高山,这比认为他住在山道崎岖难行的高山上更符合他的性格,也更有诗意。

蜿蜒流去。厅堂上橘红色的帷幕的挂钩是玉石制成的,地上铺着磨石板,覆盖着染成深红色的由竹篾编织的地席。床前帐幔顶部边沿上装饰着翠鸟的尾毛,床罩上点缀着珍珠并饰以红、蓝色的鸟羽。墙上满挂由精选的香蒲草编结镶缫带的织物,窗帘的顶部还悬挂着群青印花薄纱的短帷。背衬着彩色和白色锦缎,在绯红和杂色斑驳的绳索上挂有成串的玉髓和天青石制成的环。贵重的珍品和古董陈列在堂上。掌灯时分即燃起长长的乳香蜡烛,照耀得满堂通明。在宅邸或庭园闲步时,有 16 位文静、娟秀、娴雅、伶俐无比的使女奉侍左右……与《大招》相比,这里的美味佳肴更丰盛、更香甜,歌舞乐曲也更欢快悦耳。无论在宴会或来往友朋中都是大夫、绅士和贵夫人,可以下棋、玩十五子游戏、对弈围棋或其他的消遣,也可以饮酒作诗吟赋。所有这一切似乎是以《大招》的描述为基础发展而成的高潮,范围更大,气氛更紧凑,场面更壮观。于是,他以第一人称的口吻轻快地写到了他从陵阳流放到长沙一路上的景况。招魂的长呼由 5 行较长的诗句收尾,结束是“魂兮归来哀江南!”因此,在这张编织得绮丽异常的图案中,我们体会到诗人在长期流放中所经历的极端贫困和苦楚的生涯之后,努力寻求感情上的补偿。最后还是由他自己使这一切慢慢地自行消失。

　　《哀郢》像屈原的绝大部分诗作一样,是他被顷襄王从首都驱逐到陵阳后的第 9 年的作品;这又导致他再次被放逐到辰、溆、哀等流域地区。写《涉江》时,他已料到将被从卢江、大江和洞庭湖的陵阳放逐至沅水、枉水、辰水和溆水,然后再回到沅水。这两个篇章都是令人难忘的悲伤情调的抒情诗楷模。在《哀郢》中所表达的感情是“如泣似诉,将欲启程而难以举步,严厉的贬谪和流放的痛苦把诗人压垮了”。《涉江》的情调“已变为一股强有力的反悲痛情绪,因为诗人被激怒了,他决心使自己所有的一切与世界分离”。以上所引是蒋骥的说法。

　　现代民歌和通俗歌曲中常用的感叹词“兮”是屈原作品的特

色,极少例外。《诗经》中的"雅"和"颂"措辞高雅,这种便于吟唱的语助字是不用的,但在"风"、民谣或民歌中却是常用的。例如:

1. 螽斯羽,诜诜兮! 宜尔子孙,振振兮!　　（《国风·周南》）
2. 手如柔荑;肤如凝脂;领如蝤蛴;齿如瓠犀;螓首蛾眉;巧笑倩兮,美目盼兮!　　　　　　　　　　　（《卫风·硕人》）
3. 彼狡童兮,不与我言兮! 维子之故,使我不能餐兮!

（《郑风·狡童》）

4. 野有蔓草,零露溥兮。有美一人,清扬婉兮。邂逅相遇,适我愿兮。　　　　　　　　　　　　　（《郑风·野有蔓草》）
5. 陟彼岵兮,瞻望父兮。父曰:"嗟予子! 行役夙夜无已。上慎旃哉! 犹来无止!"　　　　　　　　　（《魏风·陟岵》）
6. 月出皎兮。佼人僚兮。舒窈纠兮。劳心悄兮!

（《陈风·月出》）

7. 匪风发兮,匪车偈兮。顾瞻周道,中心怛兮!

（《桧风·匪风》）

"兮"字现在读如"系"或"伊";清代孔广森说古代读如"阿"或"猗"。屈原诗作中常用的这个兮字来源于民歌,以下摘录的《渔父》这首民歌可以进一步证明这一点:

> 沧浪之水清兮,
> 可以濯我缨;
> 沧浪之水浊兮,
> 可以濯我足。

在《孟子》中也引用了这首曲调。

　　屈原写《怀沙》前已遇到了渔父,并从龙阳出发到长沙自尽。

这部诗篇就是他乘船赴辰阳、溆浦的途中完成的。《史记·屈原列传》中，司马迁引述了这首诗的整个原文（与常见的版本有较大的差异），诗前引了《渔父》中的一节，其中的一句是"宁赴常流而葬乎江鱼腹中耳。"蒋骥指出，像太史公这样的权威人物在屈原死后不到 200 年的时候撰写他的传记时，竟然会把《怀沙》的诗题意思误解为他要把沙和石子揣在怀里去投河自尽（朱熹在集注本注释中也同声附和），千百年来屈原的诗时常以不同的方式被错误地理解也就不足为奇了。诗篇的感情色彩虽比《哀郢》和《涉江》更接近临死的氛围，但仍是决断而不紧张，直率而不激烈（纡而未郁，直而未激）；也稍逊于《悲回风》和《惜往日》那种带强调性的语气，因为在时间上要比它们早一些。

在《悲回风》中，正如我以上已讲过的，诗人重新又表明他要效法彭咸自溺的决心。对于品性高尚和无私的知识界人士，他那极端深切的悲伤和激动人心的失望的诗篇乃是永垂不朽和有纪念价值的杰作。在我们所处的世界中，屈原的生平和诗作肯定是富有现实意义的。

《惜往日》是诗人自尽前最后一部作品。屈原想以死来唤醒当时的顷襄王，让他明白国家所面临的险境。由于作者生前未能使其警觉，所以在这篇遗诗中再次陈述了顷襄王令人触目惊心的愚蠢行为以及他犯下的信任朝中那班竭尽阿谀奉承之能事的亲秦帮派的错误。楚政府在外交政策上，不去致力于同齐国及其他四个自然的同盟者联成合纵势力范围，反而奉行追求与秦国联横的自杀性策略，在当时这是一个绝对与楚国及"天下"生死存亡攸关的关键问题。诗人在这篇遗诗中把问题剖析得一清二楚，想藉此使顷襄王恢复理智，以便作出明智的判断。决定的因素是仍得看这个十足的傻瓜是否还继续被那批拍马奉承的帮派牵着鼻子走；可惜的是屈原无法回避当时时代的潮流，在诗中敲响的警钟未能力挽狂澜。作为笨伯的顷襄王和子兰这一对难兄难弟似乎已经狠下

决心,定要把楚国置诸死地,成为秦帝国侵吞兼并"天下"的不可避
免的前奏。

在讨论《离骚》时,我们谈到了屈原诗歌的民歌特色和楚国方
言用语的手法。我们也谈到了感叹词"兮"。《大招》中的语助词
"只"读如"支",意思是肯定或加强语气(感叹),这种用法来自《诗
经》。《招魂》中的语助词"些"读如"叔",这是巫术和魔法用语中
句子的结尾字,当时盛行于楚国的西部。至于方言用语如"汩"、
"搴"、"莽"、"羌"、"侘"、"傺"等,大约有 40 来个。由于语言隔阂,
外国读者也许没有兴趣来做逐字研究。

最后,应该对屈原作品的诗体格式作简单的介绍。既然是从
《诗经》发展而来,也因此必然是《诗经》的产物。这部初周的诗歌
集锦,其诗行(格律群)的规范是二音步,四字一行,每音步两个字。
依第一首诗的第二节为例:

> |关关 |雎鸠, |
> |在河 |之洲; |
> |窈窕 |淑女, |
> |君子 |好逑。|

显然,每一诗行都有四个汉字。但从诗行结构看,另一个特色更重
要但却并不很明显,那就是中国的古典诗或韵文都是有格律的而
不是同音节①(相同重音)的,每一行都是二音步诗。正常的诗行均
为一个音步两个字,但有些有变化的非正规的诗行中一个音步只

---

① 同音节的韵文只见于阿维斯德,即波斯(今伊朗)伽巴尔和帕西人所供奉
的琐罗亚斯德教的圣典(为该教创始人琐罗亚斯德所著)和 12 世纪法国
的亚历山大诗。每诗行由 16 个或 12 个音节组成,中间有一处间歇,可用
符号表示为:|00000000|00000000|和|000000|0000000|。见《什么叫韵
律?》(E. A. Sonnenschein 著,1925 年,牛津版,第 41 – 46 页)。

有一个字或三个字。这种变化的诗行在风、雅、颂中偶尔出现,但绝不是普遍现象。古代诗集中还有极少数三音步甚至四音步的诗行。以下我们所作的音步划分的例举中,用"〰〰"符号表示前一个字声调的延长或无声的"休止"。也就是说前一个字的发音拖长些,使这一音步在节律上与其他由两个字组成的音步相对称。所谓"休止"或"稍歇"的情况是对汉字的发音而言的,休止符后的延长或稍歇意思是由无声的延长来构成一个相应的音步。如一个音步由三个字组成,那么这三个字的发音都得相对地缩短些,使这一音步在节律上大致与两个字构成的音步相同。当然,最常见的是两个字作为一个单元组成的音步,这两个字的结合则按照彼此之间在意义上的互相关联或者在文法上有紧密的联系而定。

凡诗歌,从原始的民歌和民谣到少数世界上第一流的伟大诗人的最高雅的诗作都是由格律文字语言书写和吟诵的,这是世界上的普遍现象,是常识。韵文作为诗歌的一种特有的表达形式,把音节或字的发音按一致的时间长度有节奏地排列成有起有伏、延续的波状流动,这就是时间意义上的格律。而格律的形成是民歌或民谣的歌手或诗人根据所用文字的某些主要特征在音步中的字与字之间、音节与音节之间,在每诗行中上一音步与下一音步之间以及民歌、民谣或诗歌的上一诗节与下一诗节之间经过精心安排而产生的一种美妙和细腻的轻重缓急有变、又恰到好处的感觉。在诗行进展的过程中形成的格律单元正与梵文中所说的节拍的意义是一致的。[①]

古代印欧语系的古典希腊和拉丁文中,音步的声调布局是由诗人根据这两种文字的长、短音节的特色,对诗文的文字在前后次序或发音时间的长短上进行调整,形成第一韵律,时而糅合一些变

---

① 本段以及随后的两个段落都是拙作中文本《诗歌底格律》(1956—1957年,上海版)中的简要摘录,作者稍作补充。

换,这样吟诵起来就很有规律、匀称和悦耳。诗行各音步的内部结构安排好之后,音步与音步之间的时间长短关系也自然而然地完成了,这就是第二韵律。接着是诗行与诗行之间在长、短上的安排或联系,这也是诗人和诗体学者要研究的课题。例如,荷马所著的《伊利亚特》长诗的典型诗行是六音步扬抑抑(长短短)格。其中第五音步为扬抑抑格,最后的音步为扬扬格,这是绝对不能变动的。第一至第四个音步一般也都是扬抑抑格,但可以相应地作变换。自高乃依(公元 1606—1684,法国古典主义悲剧奠基人)起的法国近代诗歌中,如亚历山大诗行,每行为十二个音节,中间由停顿或中断分割为两个半行,每半行又分为两个音步,每音步可由一个或五个音节构成,两个音步的总数仍为六个音节不变。这种由四个音步组成的诗行在朗读时必须把最后一个音节的声调延长、上升并读成重音。根据布里奇斯(公元 1844—1930,英国诗人)在《弥尔顿的诗体学》①中摘录布拉德利(公元 1845—1923,英国语言文学家)的著述,盎格鲁-撒克逊(古英语)诗歌的特色是以重音定节奏的,格律是由头韵和音节重读形成的,重读的音节一律在时间上比不重读的音节要稍长些。这样形成的音步在组成诗行时虽然可让读者得到明显的节拍一致的感觉,但敏感的听众会发现在时间长短上却不如古典式诗歌中同样韵律的音步那么细腻和匀称。近代的英国和德国诗歌都有以重音定节奏的特点,格律是以重读的音节作为关键的一环而形成的,这样在诗行中各个音步之间造成了极为清晰的节奏感。英国的诗歌之父乔叟的有规律的十音节的诗行(偶尔也出现九音节甚至为数不少的十三音节的诗行变换)是取自但丁(公元 1265—1321,意大利诗人,文艺复兴运动的先驱人物)的十一音节的规律诗行以及早期法国的亚历山大十音节诗行,但他的诗基本上是以音节形成格律的。莎士比亚的早期作品也用音

---

① 见《弥尔顿的诗体学及重音节格律韵文》,1921 年,牛津版,第 102 页。

节成格律,但他后期成熟的作品已摆脱了音节格律而一律用重音成格律了。弥尔顿(公元1608—1674,英国著名诗人)的《失乐园》同时运用了重音格律及音节格律(十音节)。

中国的古典诗歌从《诗经》到五、七古,唐代的五、七言,以及更晚些时候更进化的诗篇或模仿性的作品,虽然从表面上看是以字计数的,但都具有内在格律;这一点我在上面已提到过了。词或宋人长短句和元曲的曲牌作为诗歌的形式,主要是按宋、元时代音乐的旋律和曲调为基础而制定其诗律的,现已失传和被遗忘了。遗留下来的只有关于平、仄声的规律,现今也仍有人按平仄声填写诗词的,因此谈不上有什么它们自身独立的格律结构。关于《诗经》,我已说过是由汉字组成的单元而形成节律的,这与古代或近代印欧语系的诗歌形成格律单元或音步的规则完全不同。中国诗歌的格律是由汉字根据其意义上的相互联系以及文理上的相互连贯结合而形成的。

从格律和诗体学的时间因素上看诗歌的特色,虽然我已谈了一些,但如果要着重作解释的话,恐怕不得不把我的观点再重复一下,这一点我得向读者先致以歉意。诗歌(应该)是用韵文书写的,即在时间上有节律或格律的语言文字。说得确切些,所谓节律是由一组组音节或字(如汉字的单字)的发音在诗行中的调排而形成的。节律的标准单位是音步,由音节或字的发音组成(一般有两或三个,时而有单个或四个形成,无声或间歇较少出现)。诗人运用所书写的文字的特点在音节或字的发音上作精心的安排,使诗行在朗诵时产生优美悦耳的节奏感的效果。节律的单元称为音步,所产生的效果是一连串有节律又相互连贯的时间单元,在这些时间单元中填入了由诗人安排有度的字或音节(的发音)。为了防止节律上的单调一致,诗人时而又安排了某些变换。这样在音步中、音步与音步之间、诗行与诗行之间以及诗节与诗节之间的声调进展会使人从心理上体验到一种定时的节奏感,而不是严格的声调本身或机械性的节奏。① 中国的古典诗歌,尤其在我们所讨论的屈原的诗歌中,通常是两个或三个字形成音步中的一个单元,字与字的结合则依其在意义上或文理上相互关联而定。在下列印欧语系中,无论是古代或近代的诗歌,虽然它们在诗体学中也并不完全排除意义和文理(文法)结构的存在,但古代希腊或拉丁诗的音步是由长短音节组成的,英国或德国的诗歌用重读或不重读的音节来形成音步,法国诗歌则以延长声调、重读、提高声调和发音正常的音节来组成音步。总之,以上与我们现在所谈的中国诗的格律关系是很不相同的。

上面我说过,不论什么语言写成的诗歌,其正规的、工整的诗行必然由标准的格律单元有节奏地组成。我也提到了诗歌的格律必须要有变换,所谓变换是正规格律的辅助,但决不可以忽略不用,也不可用得过度。如果像 18 世纪英国诗人蒲柏和约翰逊的诗,只有格律没有变换,读者就会因过于矫揉造作、拘泥形式而感到腻烦;如果以变换为主,做得过火,诗行最后势必变为散文。布里奇斯说得好:"说到韵律就有一个自然而然的情况,那就是一般的韵律应该是人们所熟悉和热爱的,这可以说是基本规律,但一段时间之后,人们的听觉便会感到不满足而希望这种韵律应该要有所突破。如果有人会对单一的韵律产生迷恋或满足且不允许有变换的话,那只能说他们缺乏鉴赏韵律的天赋了。真正懂得并热爱韵律的人会觉得如果没有一定自由度的变换,就不能称为韵律,也就是说,只有在单一的韵律有所突破、有所变换时,韵律才能真正

---

① 我所了解的关于格律原则和比较诗体学方面的权威性文献有:T. S. Omond 著《格律研究》(1920 年,伦敦版)、Omond 著《英国韵律学家》(1921 年,牛津版)、Robert Bridges 著《弥尔顿的诗体学及重音节格律韵文》(1921 年,牛津版)、Egerton Smith 著《英文格律原理》(1923 年,牛津版)、George Saintsbury 著《英文诗体学史》三卷(1923 年,伦敦版)、E. A. Sonnenschein 著《什么叫韵律?》(1925 年,牛津版)、Sidney Lanier 著《英文韵文学》(1927 年,纽约版)。

地开始显示出内在的美。"

《诗经》中正规的诗行以上列"关关雎鸠"为例,都是由两个字组成音步形成诗行的节律。但是,在风、雅、颂等诗歌中,由正规音步和只含一字或多至三字的音步组成的变换性或非正规诗行也不少见,例如:

1. ｜谁谓｜雀无角,｜
 ｜何以｜穿我屋?｜
 ｜谁谓｜女无家,｜
 ｜何以｜速我狱?｜
 ｜虽速｜我狱,｜
 ｜室家｜不足。｜　　　　　　　　(《召南·行露》)

2. ｜溱与洧｜方涣涣｜兮,〜〜｜
 ｜士与女｜方秉蕑｜兮,〜〜｜
 ｜女曰,｜"观乎?"｜
 ｜士曰,｜"既且。"｜
 ｜"且往｜观乎!｜
 ｜洧之外｜洵訏｜且乐。"｜
 ｜维士｜与女,｜
 ｜伊其｜相谑,｜
 ｜赠之以｜芍药。｜　　　　　　　(《郑风·溱洧》)

这一节的头两行称为三音步诗行。随后的一节中的｜溱与洧｜浏其｜清矣｜和｜士与女｜殷其｜盈矣｜当然无疑是三音步诗行了。

3. ｜毋教｜猱升木,｜
 ｜如涂｜涂附;｜
 ｜君子｜有徽猷,｜

|小人 | 与属。| （《小雅·角弓》）

4. |虞芮 | 质厥成，|

 |文王 | 蹶蹶生。|

 |予曰 | 有疏附；|

 |予曰 | 有先后；|

 |予曰 | 有奔奏；|

 |予曰 | 有御侮。| （《大雅·緜》）

5. |笃 V | 公刘！|

 |匪居 | 匪康。|

 |乃场 | 乃疆；|

 |乃积 | 乃仓。| （《大雅·公刘》）

例 5 中的符号 V 指的是音节短缺音步，即在应该连续的字声中出现的无声、"间歇"或中断。

6. |昊天 | 有成命，|

 |二后 | 受之。|

 |成王 | 不敢康，|

 |夙夜 | 基命 | 宥密。|

 |於〰〰 | 缉熙，|

 |单〰〰 | 厥心，|

 |肆其 | 靖之。| （《周颂·昊天有成命》）

最后，我们从一首讽刺性的民歌中摘录一节，从中可以看出感叹词"兮"、"猗"经常延长发音来补满诗行结束时的节律：

7. |坎坎 | 伐檀 | 兮，〰〰 |

 |置之 | 河之干 | 兮，〰〰 |

| 河水 | 清且涟 | 猗。〰〰 |

| 不稼 | 不穑, | V 〰〰 |

| 胡取乐 | 三百廛 | 兮? 〰〰 |

| 不狩 | 不猎, | V 〰〰 |

| 胡瞻尔庭 | 有县狟 | 兮? 〰〰 |

| 彼君子 | 兮,〰〰 |

| 不素餐 | 兮。〰〰 |

在例 7 中有 7 行皆以"兮"和"猗"结尾,唱咏时都带送气音,并加以拖长些。第 4、6 行则以"间歇"的延长或音节短缺音步结束。"檀"、"干"、"涟"、"廛"、"狟"和"餐"是押韵词。头 7 行是三音步诗行,最后 2 行为二音步诗行。总的说来,这些诗的格律主要是以二字组的音步形成的。

从屈原的作品看,我们不妨也摘录几行《离骚》的诗句为例,比之于《诗经》,这些诗行更着重格律结构而不重字数这一特色显得更突出。诗行字数最少的只有 5 个字,如《离骚》第 8 行:

字余日灵均。

最多的有 10 个字,如第 69 行:

苟余情其信姱以练要兮。

诗行一般都是二音步和三音步,偶尔出现四音步诗行。就这方面来看,《离骚》作为颂诗有时在格律结构上有点像品达(公元前518? —公元前 438?,古希腊诗人)体诗。这些诗行主要由三字组音步形成格律。诗歌以四行诗为一节,可能第 45—50 行是例外。其中头 2 行一般认为是插入语。以下我们把《离骚》的开头七节诗行的格律作音步划分：

帝高阳	之苗裔	兮，⌇
朕皇考	曰伯庸。
摄提	贞于	孟陬兮，
惟庚寅	吾以降。

皇览揆	余于	初度兮，
肇锡余	以嘉名：
名余	曰正则	兮，⌇
字余	曰灵均。

纷吾	既有此	内美兮，
又重之	以修能；
扈江离	与辟芷	兮，⌇
纫秋兰	以为佩。

汩余	若将	不及兮，
恐年岁	之不吾与；
朝搴阰	之木兰	兮，⌇
夕揽洲	之宿莽。

日月	忽其	不淹兮，
春与秋	其代序；
惟草木	之零落	兮，⌇
恐美人	之迟暮。

不抚壮	而弃秽	兮，⌇
何不	改乎	此度？
乘骐骥	以驰骋	兮，⌇
来！∨	吾道夫	先路。

昔三后	之纯粹	兮,〰〰
固众芳	之所在;
杂申椒	与菌桂	兮,〰〰
岂维	纫夫	蕙茝?

诗行中三字组音步多于二字组音步;诗行末常用"兮"字长音结尾;四行诗节中三音步诗行与二音步诗行交替出现;再从这种格局转变为一行三音步、一行二音步和两行三音步诗,接着又转变为三行三音步和一行二音步;四字组音步和四音步诗行偶尔出现;诗歌整篇每隔一行由小品词"兮"结尾——所有这些使诗歌在格律进展上显得活跃动人,速度奇快且令人感到意外。这与《诗经》那种庄重和循规蹈矩的韵律相比,真可说是闻所未闻,也是不可想象的。这种我称之谓有弹性和可伸展的格律,配上诗歌所描述的丰富多彩的形象以及闪烁着智慧光芒的象征主义笔法,终于使诗歌要表达的悲惨的痛苦和火辣辣的愤怒升温到白热化的程度,在读者心中产生奇迹般的效应。

　　对屈原的诗体学进行解释并对他的诗歌进行音步分析,是我在20年前出版的《诗歌底格律》一文中首次提出的。从屈原至今的千百年里,虽然从宋代开始不乏研究他的诗韵的文献,却无人作过诗体学和音步分析。但据《汉书·王褒传》说,有九江学者被公曾经奉宣帝之召诵读楚辞。《隋书·经籍志》说,僧道骞以用楚音吟诵屈原的诗歌而称著当时。据我的理解,他大概能以楚国原来的音调来吟诵诗歌。但据朱熹的《"名家"集注》序中证明,上述吟诵的艺术已失传和被遗忘。在《周礼》的《春官》和《大司乐》题目下有六种方法来教导贵族和官家子弟进行大合唱,其中的一种方法就是吟诵。东汉学者郑玄在《周礼》的一项注释中说,按格律朗读诗歌(以声节之)就称为吟诵。我想我对屈原作品所作的音步分析可能恢复了被公和僧道骞对诗人作品的吟诵方式。

九 屈原在中国和世界历史上的地位；
他的崇拜者、模仿者和评论者

人们认为屈原是一种燃烧不尽、永放光芒的精神,赞美他是思想家、杰出人物、政治家以及中国第一流的诗人。出于对广大老百姓福利的关怀,他主张以仁爱为本。这种思想又体现为他最高的政治理想,并与伦理道德标准紧密地结合在一起。他身受百般磨难却坚韧不拔、最终献身殉国的事迹,通过出类拔萃、如火如荼的诗文,使他升华为万世敬仰的永生的形象。这一切必然使他为人类所共同景慕且名垂千古。他在诗歌中所表达的对专横暴政的憎恨以及他生前以实际行动与之抗争的激烈程度,正好与他对人道和正义的热爱相媲美。他全心全意的支持使楚国外交政策抵制连横,缔结合纵盟约;他英勇无私地反对高压统治,反对秦王朝合法化的暴行以及狡诈阴险的间谍密探的把戏。这为他赢得了永垂不朽的声誉。所以,在中国历史上,他完全可以与三皇、五帝、三王及其卓越贤能的大臣以及孔子、孟子齐名。他在诗文中对自己的地位公然断言如下:

> 世溷浊而莫余知兮,
> 吾方高驰而不顾。
> 驾青虬兮骖白螭,
> 吾与重华游兮瑶之圃。
> 登昆仑兮食玉英,
> 吾与天地兮比寿,
> 与日月兮齐光。　　（《涉江》第 6—12 行）

所以,在世界历史上与他并列为伍的都是对人类有过贡献或所谓施过恩泽的人物,如梭伦、释迦牟尼、孔子、伯里克利、苏格拉底、柏拉图、孟子、耶稣、华盛顿、杰斐逊、林肯、孙文、甘地、罗斯福和丘吉尔。我们估计屈原在中国历史和世界历史上所起的伟大影响时，对他的赞誉首先是思想家，然后按合适的次序则是：杰出人物、政治家、诗人，这是因为我们考虑到"诗言志"。文风即其人：打开他的诗文，屈原的光辉形象跃然纸上。

司马迁在《屈原列传》中说，屈原的崇拜者和模仿者之中，他的学生宋玉、唐勒和景差均以好辞作赋称著。《汉书·艺文志》记载，唐勒流传后世的赋有 4 首，宋玉有 16 首，却未提及景差。关于景差的赋，即使在太史公撰写《史记》时恐怕只留有缺乏内容的题目，再说刘向的《楚辞》中也没有什么记载，这一点可从王逸的《楚辞章句》中得到佐证。王逸错误地认为《大招》是景差所作，这一说法曾有宋代的朱熹和清代的王夫之予以支持；但终于由林云铭作出正确的论证，并由蒋骥加以确认：《大招》是屈原的真作而非景差手笔。关于这一点，我在上面已说过了。宋玉所著有名的《九辩》是他为表达对师长的同情并为他辨明是非的作品，一般认为这是他的辞作从屈原式赋的特色演化为后世的赋的转变渠道。宋玉的其他作品，如《风赋》、《高唐赋》、《神女赋》和《登徒子好色赋》标志着首次以赋来命名这种属于描述性抒情诗的纯文学。但是，宋玉的赋中却再也见不到屈原作品中那种使人觉得紧张的感情冲击力和肃穆（高度严肃认真）的语态。宋玉虽然也是优秀的诗人，但是由于他未曾敢于对王者提出严肃的要求，因而，就其人品而言，与他的老师相比差距是不小的。

继屈原的学生之后出现了大批崇拜者和模仿者，但却没有一个具备他杰出的思想、高尚的品格、政治家的素质，也不具备他那种稀世的诗歌天才；一句话，他们之中没有人赶得上他。例如，汉高祖刘邦的《大风歌》的下列 3 行诗确实达到了他本人并未自觉的雄浑有力和气势恢宏的效果：

大风起兮云飞扬。

威加海内兮归故乡，

安得猛士兮守四方！

虽然这只是模仿楚国民歌的一首表示个人意见的曲调，但正如晁补之在编入朱熹的《楚辞后语》的《续楚辞》中恰如其分地摘录《文中子》所指出的“'其伯心之存乎？'，或者就由于这个缘故，汉得天下没能实施三王的仁政。"事实上，刘邦是个不可救药的流氓，没有一点可与屈原相比的。在刘邦看来，什么三王的仁政都是些愚蠢的废话，他唯一的野心是想一口吞下秦王朝的天下，他终于志得意满地成功了。在这首歌颂野蛮暴力的曲调中，他虽然不自觉地模仿了诗人，但他怎么能与屈原比肩呢？

在汉代崇拜和模仿屈原的人中，贾谊的赋写得最为出色。贾谊25岁后就以他的诗才及政治上崇高的抱负称著于世。由于他声名卓著，汉文帝把他提为博士。贾谊被“超迁岁中至太中大夫”，深为君主推崇和信赖。正当他将再升高位时，绛侯周勃、颍阴侯灌婴和东阳侯冯敬群起而攻之，说他“雒阳之人，年少初学，专欲擅权，纷乱诸事，于是天子后亦疏之。"[1]他给文帝的奏疏都很有名，他的三篇一组的论文《过秦论》是非常出名的。由于他智慧过人、年轻和勇往直前，终于遭到有官衔的老家伙们的强烈反对。结果文帝先任他为长沙王太傅，之后又为梁怀王太傅。他在长沙写了挽歌《吊屈原》，并把一份诗歌投入汨罗江。他又撰写了《服赋》，据说服鸟竟真的飞进他的书房，停在他的卧榻上，注视着他对人生和无常的思考。他的《惜誓》是任梁怀王太傅时写成的，却一直默默无闻，直到宋代才被洪兴祖证明为贾谊的真作。作品借屈原独白的口吻，当然同时也写出了他自己所想说的话。这是一篇仿楚辞的

---

[1] 见班固《汉书·贾谊传》。

庄重风格的杰作,而屈原的《远游》则是他的作品起飞的跳板。梁怀王骑马摔死,贾谊因未能防止事故发生引咎自责,痛哭了一年多,之后在阳历计33岁时因悲伤过度而死。

淮南王刘安是屈原的热烈崇拜者。他作了82篇赋,但遗留下来的只有一篇,题为《招隐士》,另一部是神秘奥妙的"道"的书籍《淮南子》。相传他精于成仙之术,可以变成仙人。他留传下来的赋不论在感情上还是在气氛上都是稀奇古怪的。刘安奉武帝命写的《离骚赋》现已散佚了,只有刘勰的《文心雕龙》中还保留了他这篇赋中的评论的摘录:"《国风》好色而不淫,《小雅》怨诽而不乱,若《离骚》者可谓兼之。蝉蜕秽浊之中,浮游尘埃之外,皭然涅而不缁,虽与日月争光可也。"

我们再来看看武帝时的太史公司马迁是怎样评价屈原的。他写了《史记·屈原贾生列传》,前面我们曾多次提到这部书。这位卓越的史学家对《离骚》及其作者写道:"屈平之作《离骚》盖自怨生也。上称帝喾,下道齐桓,中叙汤武,以刺世事。明道德之广崇,治乱之条贯,靡不毕见。其文约,其辞微,其志洁,其行廉,其称文小,而其指极大。举类迩,而见义远。其志洁,故其称芳;其行廉,故死而不容自疏。……"继司马迁之后,著名学者刘向则在他的《新序》中披露了一些诗人所遭受的政治磨难以及他崇高的人格。

西汉和东汉期间,自贾谊和刘安开始,屈原的崇拜者及模仿者之中从事写赋的作者曾发展到70多位;他们之中较出名的有枚乘、严忌、司马相如、汉武帝刘彻、东方朔、王褒、刘向、扬雄、班固、张衡、王逸和蔡琰。从精神内涵、人格和诗的角度看,上列各位无人能与屈原相提并论,但如果就表达悲愤之情而论,女诗人蔡琰所作的《胡笳十八拍》则以其难能可贵的高亢曲调,凌驾于众人之上。汉末,胡族(南匈奴)入侵,蔡琰被俘,强迫为胡后12年,生育胡族王子二人。汉代曹操系蔡琰亡父蔡邕好友,有感于蔡邕无后,以大量金银珠宝高价把她从胡族王那里赎了回来。她的《胡笳十八拍》

和《悲愤诗》诉说了她的被俘以及被迫与二子分离的激烈的、撕心裂肺的悲痛之情。所以，这首诗就气质和情调而言，只是宣泄个人恩怨而已，内涵和气势失之乎纤弱；就深度和广度来看，也不能与屈原那种为楚国人民、为周王朝、为当时的诸侯七国的全体民众而产生的深沉的悲痛相比拟。但是蔡琰的这两首诗的感染力肯定是强烈的，感人肺腑的；相比之下，她的前辈如司马相如和扬雄的作品在感情上就显得肤浅、造作甚至有害。

司马相如只是武帝跟前一个蹩脚的谄媚者，他写的赋大致都是浮夸的、词藻翻滚的游戏，或者充斥着华而不实的描写；至于就真实感情或激情而言，只能说是苍白无力、空洞无物。有时，在一连串肉麻的吹捧之后，也会来一点小小的劝诫以资点缀。我在前面谈及《大人赋》与屈原的《远游》对比时，已提出批评，即这篇赋只能算是装饰品而已。贾谊、刘安甚至刘彻倒是感情活跃，生气勃勃，遣词用语也轻巧机敏，灵活自如。自司马相如起，日趋颓废的汉赋开始了冗长、啰唆、浮华、虚饰的文风。他的《上林赋》和《子虚赋》都是些虚张声势的杜撰，精神内涵上呆板迟钝、索然无味；大段大段的描写显得过于装腔作势，压得读者喘不过气来。最后是他的《封禅文》，文中吹拍奉承已到了令人汗颜的地步，成为文坛可耻的"范例"。然而，其后也自有扬雄、班固奉之为楷模。总之，司马相如专门从屈原的诗文中寻章摘句，模仿他的遣词用语，并加以夸张到不适当的程度；而他心底所想的必然是屈原乃是个不考虑现实的愚蠢的家伙，只不过会做诗而已，连自身利益都照顾不到。

扬雄作为司马相如的一名狂热的崇拜者，是个极端堕落的无赖。他内心最高的期望是不惜一切代价当个大官，当个第一流的大人物。他的老师司马相如还有点羞耻心，不敢对诗人表露任何反对和轻蔑之意；而扬雄却写了一篇题为《反离骚》的赋，公开对屈原的亡灵提出意见，指出他投汨罗江是不明智的。也许，他充当了司马相如的代言人角色。他在赋中说，君子如果得遇好运就该尽心尽力往好里去做;如果行运欠佳可以退出尘世去做隐士,至于是否能得遇明主的信任,那是命中注定的事,何必投江自尽呢?扬雄在他那首拙劣可笑的仿作中引述了屈原的伟大诗歌的若干诗行,加以歪曲附会,并把他的赋稿一份从嶓山投入江中,企图侮辱屈原,并玷污诗人留给后世的美好形象。扬雄在汉代是三朝元老,在官场上并未蒙恩受提拔,但他也并没有退居而为隐士。虚伪叵测的王莽在篡位之前权势蒸蒸日上之时,扬雄早就尾随,竭尽奉承之能事,在他那令人作呕的诗文中把王莽比作伊尹和周公。王莽篡位之后,这个结结巴巴、卑躬屈膝的扬雄终于因为写了一份谄媚奉承的奏章而得宠。他的其他作品也只是些作为御用文人对司马相如的麻木不仁、有气无力的模仿或相如文风的发展,毫无智慧和道德方面的光彩可言。

东汉的班固与他的父亲班彪合著了《汉书》。他在所作的臃肿的汉赋中批评屈原"炫耀个人的天赋,抬高自己以污蔑楚王,并以自溺来发泄他的愤怒。"说句公道话,班固与其父所撰的《汉书》实在是一部艰巨的典籍,是中国历史上仅逊于司马迁《史记》的不朽之作。但就文才而言,班固只不过以他的《典引》对汉朝进行歌功颂德以求个人有所得益而已。他对权力无原则的崇拜使他与汉和帝的舅舅窦宪结成党派。当时窦宪是得胜有功的将领,是他在朝为官的家族成员的首领。汉和帝成年之后,逐渐明白了窦宪企图夺权的阴谋,便下令赐死。作为窦党一员,班固被关入大牢,死于狱中。他的《两都赋》读来过于夸耀卖弄,在描述汉代西京长安的华丽场面以及为汉朝中兴的君主光武帝和明帝歌功颂德时也过于招摇。光武帝和明帝以及他们的后人建立了东都洛阳。《两都赋》技巧成熟,但缺乏生气、没精打采。

班固之后,南北朝的颜之推责怪屈原"过于扩大和突出了君主的过失"。颜之推作为儒家的伦理学家而称著,然而他是四朝元老,一直是朝中的贵族、高官显爵。无疑,他与四位君主的关系必然不错,而这一点却与传统的儒家伦理观点背道而驰。

司马相如、扬雄、班固和颜之推都是中国历史上有地位的文学家和学者,他们都自我标榜在一定程度上是儒家。问题出在他们都认为诗歌与作者的人格是没有关系的。当然,他们都或多或少地崇拜并学习屈原的辞与诗(颜之推除外),但是他们在思想观念上和实际行为上却只是冒充的儒家,因为他们毫不掩饰地不赞成屈原的理想和行事。他们藐视屈原的根本原因是他们对人生的看法与屈原截然不同。他们所崇拜的是政治上的最高权力;他们的伦理观念是弱肉强食;他们的信条是为个人攫取利益。他们所想的以及所持的信念是"天下"是皇帝"天子"的私有财产,这一点与中世纪欧洲的王权神授一说是一致的。他们本身及随从都是君王的绝对的奴隶和资产。他们在个人生活中总是在机会主义和物质至上的现实主义之间摇摆,所以他们认为对待孟子所说的"民为贵,社稷次之,君为轻"的至理名言不必过于认真,可是对此又不敢公然反对或者加以拒绝。在他们心目中,屈原虽然公开坚定地在诗文和实践中恪守孟子的箴言,但只不过是个可怜的诗人而已,一生凄苦潦倒。所以,他们对屈原表示内心的看法时,对他进行赤裸裸的批评,也就不足为怪了。从另一个角度来看,如果屈原的亡灵真的永生不灭,他定然会憎恶那些亵渎他的思想和人格的崇拜者和模仿者。

魏晋时,屈原的追随者又包括了王粲(东汉建安七子之一)、曹植、潘岳和陶潜。陶潜的《归去来辞》因作者的温和及出类拔萃的人格、诗文的宁静安详的声调和明白的措辞而名声卓著。南朝时,宋朝的鲍照和梁朝的江淹的辞和赋可称冠绝一时。鲍照的《芜城赋》是东方诗歌中的一颗明珠,堪与英国诗人、剧作家、小说家哥尔德斯密斯的《荒村》齐名,称得上文坛精益求精的范例。《文心雕龙》的作者,梁朝的刘勰是伟大的文学评论家,在他的文学评论的典籍中用了一个章节的篇幅热烈地赞扬了骚体。刘勰称之为"楚辞",同时在评价屈原的著作时一律冠以最高级的赞词。他也涉及宋玉、贾谊和其他一些人。隋代僧道骞据说精于用楚国原来的语气声调来朗诵屈原的诗歌。

唐代伟大的诗人王维、李白、元结、韩愈和柳宗元都是屈原的追随者。李白只有一首仿楚辞的诗,题为《鸣皋歌》。这首诗以其超逸缥缈的措词构成了天堂式圣曲的微型交响乐,其中虽略带一抹凡尘味,但应该说不失为可与屈原的较次的诗歌并驾齐驱的上乘之作。宋代的苏轼和黄庭坚继承了屈原和宋玉的楚辞和赋的传统。在苏轼名扬后世的《前后赤壁赋》之后,再也没出现过杰出的辞、赋名家。清初的王夫之可说是屈原的最后一个模仿者,也是一位研究屈原的著名学者。

在评注《离骚》的注脚中,我一开始就简略地提到早期研究屈原著作的学者和评论家,如王逸、洪兴祖、朱熹和蒋骥。东汉至今,研究屈原的学者不下百余名,我在所作的注脚中详细地摘录他们的心得体会足有数十条,关于他们的情况不再赘述了。但是关于宋代伟大的诠注家朱熹从个人和诗人的角度对屈原所作的批判性评价,我还得谈一点看法。朱熹是声名卓著的研究儒学的哲学家和学者,又是屈原的热烈崇拜者。虽然他承认屈原是"千年一遇的伟人",但在关于屈原的三部著述中却不止一次地因为屈原在生活和诗作中缺乏克己和中庸而露出抱憾之意。克己是孔子的孙子子思根据圣人的赞词"克己为德之最,废之者久矣!"而在《中庸》中提出的。这点我在本文"八 屈原的思想和诗歌"中已讨论过了。我也说过,屈原并不是儒家,更不是传统的儒家,他的人格要比儒家伟大得多。如果社会秩序相对地稳定和正规,即使在绝对的君主政体下,政治气氛比较温和克己可能也应成为普通老百姓的道德标准。但是在战国时期的社会中,到处充满着压力和动乱,周王朝的封建体制面临解体和崩溃,鹰隼似的秦国又以暴力和恶毒的阴谋不断施虐于各国;在这样的社会条件下,如果期待像屈原这样一位思想家和具有伟大的人格的政治家把克己奉为道德准则,至少是不慎重和缺乏判断的。所以,尽管朱熹在屈原著作的校勘和评注工作中有很大贡献,但是对屈原的批判性评价显然是错了。

近代中国颇有名气的学者胡适在他的《读楚辞》一文中竟然提出了一种令人吃惊的观点,说历史上的屈原作为人和诗人来说是子虚乌有的。另一位作者廖季平在《楚辞新解》中也提出了这一观点。我未曾有幸拜读他们两位的大作,只是从郭沫若的《屈原研究》里引录谢无量的《楚辞新论》的文章中才得悉他们的论点。胡和廖论证的根据主要是司马迁的《史记·屈原列传》中某些前言后语不相一致以及某些失误;另一方面,可能是他们自己无端的怀疑。对他们毫无价值的看法,郭在著作中已给予了恰当的驳斥,这里不详谈了。在中国,廖季平相对地说比较鲜为人知;而胡适则不然,尤其在通用英语的国家颇具声望。他是杜威的学生,又是詹姆斯和杜威实用主义学派在中国的倡导者。胡适同时是把中国古代哲学介绍给英美读者的著名翻译家。但是,他对中西方古典哲学的探索和钻研还只在报章杂志式的阶段,比较肤浅。因此,他未能写完《中国哲学史大纲》,该书的头二、三卷是他的博士论文,谈的是先秦时期。他未能写完是因为他对汉、唐、宋等朝代的史实还不够熟悉。这里所牵涉的一个先决条件是,必须掌握中国有关佛教方面的知识。不过,也许我们不该对人要求太高。从 1917 年至 20 年代的新文化运动中,胡适和陈独秀、鲁迅、周作人、钱玄同、刘复、沈尹默等人力主废除文言,提倡用白话文书写散文及诗歌。他在这方面对近代中国作出了伟大的贡献,也为自己树立了响亮的名声。他们共同的讲台是《新青年》杂志。在他们的创举之前,我国的文学作品,除了某些宋代哲学家的语录、始自宋代直至清代和民国时代的评话、一些通俗小说、小故事以及元、明、清的曲和杂剧之外,一律都是用文言文书写的。胡适首次用白话文出版了一本书,以粗糙的无格律的自由诗形式写新文化运动,题为《尝试集》。但是,这作为诗歌方面的一种尝试却不够成熟。整个新文化运动是由于在文化上接触了西方世界而引起的,然而胡适有时却称之为"中国文艺复兴"。这里的英文字"复兴"意思是"再生和新生",即学术上的复兴——指的是首先在意大利、之后在法国和英国、最后在德国兴起的对古代希腊和罗马的艺术、文学、哲学、科学、政治、公民和社会体系的研究。同时,由于重振对古典文化的学习和由马丁·路德为首的反对天主教或教皇至上(梵蒂冈主义)的宗教改革运动,为西欧的艺术、文学、科学、政治、宗教、社会习俗以及人的生活等方面重新带来了普遍的生机,使之活跃起来。

1919 年 5 月 4 日和 6 月 3 日,中国的新文化运动在北京和上海如火如荼地展开,学生发动爱国示威游行,商店停业,学生罢课,工人罢工,接着全国各大城市共同抵制日货。运动在促进民主、科学、提倡白话文、废除文言、对古代的习俗和制度(如家庭和婚姻)以及在文学界的思想(如儒学)重新作合理的评价等方面进展很顺利。不久,军阀混战的尘土埋没了一切,所以最终建树不多。所幸以白话文作为人们表达思想的工具这一点终于未被动摇,并在家庭、婚姻观念以及思想领域方面逐渐地促成了根本的、永久性的变革。胡适在他的极盛年代里,把兴趣主要集中在《水浒传》、《西游记》、《红楼梦》、《儒林外史》、《镜花缘》等小说上。他为这些书籍撰写了评价和研究,把它们介绍给他的同时代人,而当时的社会也只是这些书本中的故事的近代翻版而已。不幸的是,对于高层次和较深的文学,尤其是中国和西方诗意的迸发和奔放,他的了解和欣赏是浮光掠影和不求甚解的;他对于中国和西方古典哲学的知识也是浅尝辄止、东拼西凑的;他对于中国和欧洲的艺术鉴赏更是缺乏得可怜。由于对诗歌的一知半解、欣赏浅薄,他不可能热爱中国的屈原、李白、杜甫的诗歌,也不可能热爱世界各国第一流诗人的杰作。对于中国和西方的文化交流和相互渗透,他则希望中国"全盘西化"。我记得,在 1931 年有一次在北京他的家中,他很坦率地告诉我说,他认为杜甫的《秋兴八首》和莎士比亚的《罕秣莱德》没有什么特别好或值得钦佩的。莎翁的《罕秣莱德》是英国伊丽莎白时代文艺复兴的典型人物的绝妙写照,这绝对是英语通用国家的共识。对于近代英、美的文化界来说,《罕秣莱德》和莎翁的其他一些令人忧郁沉闷的悲剧以及斑驳灿烂的喜剧,作为他们的文化遗产,其价值是不可估量的。直到今日,莎剧焕发的智慧火花和一些真知灼见对于他们的民主的人生观仍然有令人注目的现实意义。然而,胡适一方面自我宣称是西方文化在中国的传播者,一方面却认为上述了不起的创作并没有什么突出之处。由此看来,他那篇有轰动效应、却颇带荒唐意味的著述中,为了哗众取宠竟然提出屈原此人并不存在一说①,也就不足为怪了。他是在东施效颦,仿效英国那批鼓吹拆毁文物之徒所提出的莎士比亚—培根争议案而已。

把庄子的智慧抬高到"无可指摘"的高度,又对他崇拜得五体投地的典型人物是林语堂。近年来,林语堂作为作家和汉学家在美国颇受人欢迎。他在《吾土吾民》一书中说,所有中国优秀的文学,有价值的、具有可读性的、能令人兴奋又使人平静的中国文学,都具有道教的精神。他又谈到他的《赫伯特·翟理思在天堂》一文,文中他异想天开地断言:即使西方文学中最优秀的作品也都与道教的教义是一致的。他又把《罕秣莱德》一剧中墓地的一景与庄子对着孔黑骨白的骷髅作禅思进行比较。蒙林先生屈尊称赞屈原"还有一点修辞的天赋"。林先生以上帝的劝导口吻说,屈原"应该学得一点庄子的哲学",这样便可在西方文坛的评论界中与莎士比亚媲美了。我对道教学派的哲学以及庄子在文学上的优点已作过一些论述。《罕秣莱德》剧中掘墓人的对话肯定是充满人世沧桑的哲学意味的,但是这早已成为老掉牙的老生常谈了,只有那些平庸

① 见胡适《读〈楚辞〉〈胡适文存〉二集卷一》——编者注

的人们在聊天时或许仍然会热烈地赞美那段讽刺性的俏皮话,以显示他们是莎士比亚的行家里手。莎士比亚的使人惊叹不已的悲剧和令人欢欣鼓舞的喜剧中的精彩部分多得不胜枚举——崇高庄严、恐怖、愤怒、同情怜悯、感人至深、稀奇古怪、愉悦欢乐;但是墓地这一场景肯定不是"莎翁的最动人之处"。说屈原只"有一点修辞上的天赋"而不去体会他雄伟的人格、炽热的激情、令人感伤的悲痛和引人入胜的抒情,是一种极其片面的见解。

上面概括地论述了屈原作为一位思想家、杰出人物、政治家和诗人的地位,一言以蔽之,他是中国和世界历史上一位永垂不朽的精神形象。至于他的诗歌,虽然留传下来的数量不多,但是论质量,他的作品是我国诗歌之最;或者说,比所有其他诗人都要高出一筹。在中国诗坛上,论诗歌激情的强烈、思想的深刻、想象力的高远、词汇量的丰富、格律神韵的力度,他的作品都是无与伦比的。屈原的著作比之于古老的《诗经》篇章确实高出一大截。唐代的李白、杜甫可说稍能与他接近,而宋代的苏轼和辛弃疾的词只能说等而下之了。在世界范围的诗坛上的第一流诗人,如果按时间顺序排列是:荷马、埃斯库罗斯、索福克勒斯、屈原、维吉尔、但丁、莎士比亚、弥尔顿和歌德。屈原名列第四位,但是就诗歌的内在神韵来看,他决不在任何人之下。惠特曼的诗没有格律,称为交响散文诗,属于另一个范畴。

据我了解①,前辈汉学家丹尼斯和莱克以及后来的某些欧洲评论家都认为,与《伊里亚德》(荷马著)和《失乐园》(弥尔顿著)的辉煌庄丽和优秀杰出相比,不单《离骚》是平庸之作,整个中华民族的天赋也极为低下。这主要是因为尽管这些专家们曾努力研究了法文版和英文版的有关译本,但是却无助于他们求得对中国古典文学充分的了解。历来中国古典诗歌很少有合格的外文翻译版本,

---

① 这是我从林文庆所译英文《离骚》的序言中得悉的。

同时他们更无法对《离骚》写作的总的历史背景具有稍稍清晰的概念;当然也不会很清楚屈原对中国古代历史理解的深度、屈原本身的政治理想、人格以及他对当时黑暗势力所作的英勇斗争,而这一切对于当今世界所产生的影响却是极其重要的。还有一点需要提出的是,这些评论家对诗歌的功能的观点本身就失之偏颇。我们的最伟大的抒情诗人严肃地思考的主题是政治上的德行、人民的福利和人类的团结,与荷马、但丁和弥尔顿所作的娱乐性的、形象生动的、壁画式的叙事史诗相比,无论在趣味性或价值、功绩上是决不会稍见逊色的。关于这一点,我在《离骚》的注释里作了讨论,这里不谈了。荷马在他所有的评论家中也绝不是十全十美的:*aliquando bonus dormi-tat Homerus*①,他有他的 Zoilus②。《神曲》和《失乐园》实质上宗教味极浓,但读者未必都是基督徒、天主教徒或新教徒。说到所谓"辉煌庄丽和优秀杰出",西方人之所以无法深入探讨和欣赏《离骚》,主要问题还在于语言障碍以及缺乏优质的外文翻译版本和全面、深刻的介绍。这使得西方人未能对诗人的理想和人格、他的思想感情、他的历史和政治背景、他使用的文字典故以及精妙的诗意加以辨别,有所了解。换言之,如果要把屈原与荷马、但丁、弥尔顿等人作比较,公正的评论者应该细致地研究他外部的世界和内心的自我,并在这两者之间作多次来回往复的体察思考。理由很简单,因为屈原的《离骚》和其他诗作是主观意识高度集中表现的颂歌和抒情诗,而不是表现客观的壁画式的叙事长诗和戏剧。但是,我丝毫没有贬低其他第一流的伟大诗人的意思,我无非是想指出颂歌和抒情诗作为一方与叙事史诗和戏剧作为另一方之间在性质上的差别而已。

　　例如已故著名汉学家翟理思在林文庆所著书的序言中赞美了

---

① 　拉丁文:荷马也有打瞌睡的时候。
② 　拉丁文:苛刻的批评者。

柏克所译《离骚》头 4 行的一节诗:

> Born of the stock of our ancient Princes,
> (My father, Peh Yung by name,)
> The Spring-star twinkled with cheery omen
> On the lucky day I came.

他说:"他(指柏克)的第一节译诗的韵律给我的印象很好",他又抱憾地说:"这种韵律却没有持续下去"。很明显,柏克这 4 行译文的韵律和格调是属于轻飘、波动和欢快的性质,因而从思想和感情性质上来说是比较浅薄的,与《离骚》那种非常严肃、思想深沉、苦难重重的主题和情调完全是格格不入的;不,是截然相反的!林语堂可笑地把翟理思捧上了天(他突出莎士比亚的伟大成就,然后又用他的老话说:屈原只有点"修辞"上的名堂,不无侮辱性地使诗人相形见绌),说他可与屈原齐名,说是因为翟理思英译了《庄子》中的一段——即林语堂恭恭敬敬地引用来与"莎士比亚最精彩的"《罕秣莱德》中墓地场景作比较的那一段。林语堂心目中的上帝,如果剥去他那种幼稚崇拜的外衣,只不过是西方文艺评论界的泛泛之辈中传播的、但又是方向有误的看法。说他们方向有误,乃是因为他们对屈原的内心和外部世界只作了些粗浅的研究,了解太少。另一个因素是林语堂自身对庄子哲学的盲目崇拜。我们以翟理思为例,谈了那批汉学家和评论家由于对屈原缺乏了解而贬低了他,他们这么做的另一原因可能是由于他们对自己的法语或英语等母语的诗歌、对诗歌的遣词用语和格律的流动变化的真正涵义恐怕也未必已经融会贯通。如果他们对本国语言的韵文都无法做出合格像样的评论,那么,在他们无法对中国诗歌彻底了解和欣赏又缺乏理想的翻译文本作媒介的情况下,又怎么能对优秀的中国古典诗歌作出中肯的评论呢? 我发觉林文庆最近的译本除了文字上的错误以外,是十分令人失望的,其情形与中国现代诗人和学者郭沫若对屈原的最伟大的颂歌作的唯一的白话文翻译不相上下。郭的译文有许多错误是不可原谅的。

屈原诗选

SELECTED POEMS OF CHÜ YUAN

离　骚

LEE SAO:
SUFFERING
THROES

离　骚

帝高阳之苗裔兮，
朕皇考曰伯庸。
摄提贞于孟陬兮，
惟庚寅吾以降。
皇览揆余初度兮，
肇锡余以嘉名：
名余曰正则兮，
字余曰灵均。
纷吾既有此内美兮，
又重之以修能。
扈江离与辟芷兮，
纫秋兰以为佩。
汨余若将不及兮，
恐年岁之不吾与。
朝搴阰之木兰兮，
夕揽洲之宿莽。
日月忽其不淹兮，
春与秋其代序。
惟草木之零落兮，
恐美人之迟暮。
不抚壮而弃秽兮，
何不改乎此度？
乘骐骥以驰骋兮，
来吾导夫先路！

Lee Sao: Suffering Throes

A scion far of Emperor Kao-yang[1] I am;

My sire illustrious deceased is hight Pêh-yung;[2]

On that propitious day *Kêng-yin*[3] I came down here,

When *Sê-tih*'s glow was pointing bright to that first moon. [4]

Seeing and weighing how I bore myself erstwhile,

My late parental lord bestowed on me names fine:

He gave me *Ts'en-tsê*, Upright Rule, the good name formal,[5]

And for easy use, *Ling chün*, Ethereal Poise, did assign. [6]

So, I am well endowed with inner virtues diverse,

Added to furthermore by nurture brave and daedal;

Endued thus with selineas and angelicas,[7]

I wear as pendant ruffle eupatories autumnal[8].

Swift time — meseems I could not catch up with its flight,

I fear the years would not detain for me the least while:

At morn, I pluck magnolia[9] sprays on the big knoll[10];

Before dusk falls, I pick herb evergreen[11] of th'isle.

As days and months away do haste without a pause,

So spring and autumn alternate by turns alway:

Reflecting on the trees and herbage falling sear,

I fear the Beauteous One would grow old too some day. [12]

"Not holding on Your prime and clearing off rank weeds,[13]

Why do You not from Your track turn to find a new way?

Riding a chariot drawn by coursers[14] fleet to speed,

Come, let me hold the bridle and guide You for Your day!"

昔三后之纯粹兮，
固众芳之所在。
杂申椒与菌桂兮，
岂维纫夫蕙茝？
彼尧舜之耿介兮，
既遵道而得路。
何桀纣之猖披兮，
夫唯捷径以窘步。
惟夫党人之偷乐兮，
路幽昧以险隘。
岂余身之惮殃兮，
恐皇舆之败绩！
忽奔走以先后兮，
及前王之踵武。
荃不察余之中情兮，
反信谗而齌怒。
余固知謇謇之为患兮，
忍而不能舍也。
指九天以为正兮，
夫唯灵修之故也。
曰黄昏以为期兮，
羌中道而改路。
初既与余成言兮，
后悔遁而有他。
余既不难夫离别兮，
伤灵修之数化。
余既滋兰之九畹兮，
又树蕙之百亩。

The Purity of the three renowned chiefs of old[15]

Had destined erst th' assemblage of sagacious aids;[16]

Having mixed up the peppers of Sun with cinnamons[17],

They drew not just coumarous and angelicas[18].

The gloriole of Emperors great Yao and Suen

Is due to their paths straight leading to upright ways;

Why were both Ghi and Zer[19], in ill repute, disordered

But for their taking to narrow straits the wrong short cut!

I see those junto men all take to pleasures ill;

Their paths are dark and hazardous in butt.

Am I afraid of meeting grave disaster myself?

I do but fear the royal state would fail to hold.

I bustle before and after sure to show sans blur

The long revered examples of exalted crowns of old;

Queen Acorus[20], heedless of my thoughtful deep concern,

To slander[21] gross doth credit give and vent to rage.

I have known all along fidelity is my trouble,[22]

But, bearing lt hard, I cannot at all it assuage.

I point to nine-compassed Heaven[23] as my witness, —

My strivings all are but for the sake of Ling-sieu![24]

The espousal time was whilom set at sundown;[25]

Alack, the course was altered midway then by Her!

Having Her word of good faith pledged with my humble self,

She yet recanted Her plighted troth and changed Her lieu;

The frequent shiftings of Her Sweetness I do deplore,

Although it is not hard for me to bid Her adieu!

I've planted full nine *woan*[26] of eupatories sweet,

And raised a hundred *mou* of fragrant coumarous,

畦留夷与揭车兮,
杂杜衡与芳芷。
冀枝叶之峻茂兮,
愿竢时乎吾将刈。
虽萎绝其亦何伤兮?
哀众芳之芜秽!
众皆竞进以贪婪兮,
凭不厌乎求索。
羌内恕己以量人兮,
各兴心而嫉妒。
忽驰骛以追逐兮,
非余心之所急。
老冉冉其将至兮,
恐修名之不立。
朝饮木兰之坠露兮,
夕餐秋菊之落英。
苟余情其信姱以练要兮,
长顑颔亦何伤。
揽木根以结茝兮,
贯薜荔之落蕊。
矫菌桂以纫蕙兮,
索胡绳之纚纚。
謇吾法夫前修兮,
非世俗之所服。
虽不周于今之人兮,
愿依彭咸之遗则。
长太息以掩涕兮,
哀民生之多艰。

Together with fifty of *liou-yih* and *chi-chü*[27] ,

And asarums[28] and angelicas fresh and new.

Expecting sore their foliage would then flourish fast,

I wish I could in due time reap an odorous crop.

What is mine harm, though they all perish withering?[29]

But I do grieve the scentful herbage rot and drop!

The rabble, greedy for gain and power, rusheth on,

Chock-full, yet still not content with what it hath got;

Each of them, self-condoning and doubting others,

Becometh bristling with envy rancid and hot.

But running like wild to vie with the madding mob

In what it contendeth for is to me a shame;

As now old age is gradually gaining on me,

I am anxious at the absence of a fair fame.

At morn, I drink the magnolia's dripping dews;

At nightfall, I on asters' fallen petals dine. [30]

If pure my feelings be and yet intently set forth,

What is the harm e'en though in hunger I long pine[31] ?

I pick root filaments to tie the angelicas,

And string up stamens dropt from pomelo figs'[32] vine;

I pluck off cassia barks[33] , hemp-agrimonies plait

And into odorous wreaths sweet ivies[34] entwine.

I follow nearly the virtuous modes of the past,

But such of course is not in use and wont to-day;

I wish to trace the long set example of Peng Yen[35] ,

Though not in accordance with the usual way!

Heaving a sigh prolonged and wiping off my tears,

I grieve our lives mundane with thorns and hardship laid:

余虽好修姱以靰羁兮，
謇朝谇而夕替。
既替余以蕙纕兮，
又申之以揽茞。
亦余心之所善兮，
虽九死其犹未悔。
怨灵修之浩荡兮，
终不察夫民心。
众女嫉余之蛾眉兮，
谣诼谓余以善淫。
固时俗之工巧兮，
偭规矩而改错。
背绳墨以追曲兮，
竞周容以为度。
忳郁邑余侘傺兮，
吾独穷困乎此时也。
宁溘死以流亡兮，
余不忍为此态也。
鸷鸟之不群兮，
自前世而固然。
何方圜之能周兮，
夫孰异道而相安？
屈心而抑志兮，
忍尤而攘诟。
伏清白以死直兮，
固前圣之所厚。

Although to goodness and honour I am bounden[36]

And thus cannot but by preceptive curbs be staid,[37]

Yet faithful counsels in the morning I submit,

La! I am relieved of my duties ere nightfall.[38]

My worth is flouted for wearing the fragrant herbs,

And the fault is aggravated for the same gall;

But that is the one thing I heartily care for, —

Though I'd be nine times dead, I regret not at all.

I repine at Ling-sieu's lack of penetration,

Her want of perspicacity into people's hearts:[39]

The calumny hath it that I am a wanton;

The riffraff is simply jealous of my fair parts.[40]

It is the depravity of the current times[41]

To violate equity and rebuff good rule;

People pursue the crook and trample principle and order,[42]

Heaping up together their common gambling pool.

I am far gone in doleful throes for my distress,

As to have sunk into this afflicted plight now;

I would rather die quickly to avoid their blot,

For I could not bear such disgrace, no matter how!

Fierce-spirited birds flock not with others e'er;

It always hath been their practise from times of old.

How could the square conform suitably with the round?

How could opposites one another in peace hold?

Bending my nature just and restraining my will,

I chew the cud of blame and the disgrace gulp down;

To stand on spotlessness and die an upright death, —

That was indeed esteemed by sages of renown![43]

悔相道之不察兮，
延伫乎吾将反。
回朕车以复路兮，
及行迷之未远。
步余马于兰皋兮，
驰椒丘且焉止息。
进不入以离尤兮，
退将复修吾初服。
制芰荷以为衣兮，
集芙蓉以为裳。
不吾知其亦已兮，
苟余情其信芳。
高余冠之岌岌兮，
长余佩之陆离。
芳与泽其杂糅兮，
唯昭质其犹未亏。
忽反顾以游目兮，
将往观乎四荒。
佩缤纷其繁饰兮，
芳菲菲其弥章。
民生各有所乐兮，
余独好修以为常。
虽体解吾犹未变兮，
岂余心之可惩！
女媭之婵媛兮，
申申其詈予。
曰："鲧婞直以亡身兮，
终然殀乎羽之野。

On tiptoe, straining my neck, ready to turn round,

I regret mine incaution in choosing this track;

While I have gone astray thus not very far yet,

I better retrace by the dennet my way back. [44]

I walk mine horse on the fen grown with eupatories,

And gallop to a hillock of peppers to rest; [45]

As I halt, because of the blame, in advancing,

In retreat, I shall don mine old clothes that seem best.

I make nelumbo and trapa [46] leaves mine upper,

And gather lotus flowers to make my nether garments:

Being not understood — let it be as it is,

So long as mine aims are fair, despite those incumbents'! [47]

Let my tall, tall hat be highly set on mine head, [48]

My bands of jade pendants be richly hung on me:

Things aromatic and lustrous are herein mixed; [49]

My bright, pure qualities are as they use to be. [50]

Abruptly, backward I turn and look all about,

Ready to command a grand sight the four wilds round:

My jades and adornments are rich and manifold;

Aroma potent spread about me doth abound.

In life, one taketh delight in what one loveth;

I alone crave virtue for its own sake unbent:

E'en though I be to pieces torn, I would change not;

How could I be afflicted to make me relent? [51]

My sister [52], deeply concerned for me, short of breath,

Blamed me with love in this wise again and again:

"Q'uen lost his life for being stubbornly headstrong;

He died before his time at last on the Yeü plain. [53]

汝何博謇而好修兮，

纷独有此姱节？

薋菉葹以盈室兮。

判独离而不服？

众不可户说兮，

孰云察余之中情？

世并举而好朋兮，

夫何茕独而不予听?"

依前圣以节中兮，

喟凭心而历兹。

济沅湘以南征兮，

就重华而陈辞：

"启《九辩》与《九歌》兮，

夏康娱以自纵。

不顾难以图后兮，

五子用失乎家巷。

羿淫游以佚畋兮，

又好射夫封狐。

固乱流其鲜终兮，

浞又贪夫厥家。

浇身被服强圉兮，

纵欲而不忍。

日康娱而自忘兮，

厥首用夫颠陨。

夏桀之常违兮，

乃遂焉而逢殃。

后辛之菹醢兮，

殷宗用而不长。

Why dost thou, learned, loyal too, on goodness dote,

Alone thou dost fidelity bear such a lot?

Behold, the court is filled with weeds and xanthiums rank; [54]

The wearings foul, to all so common, thou canst brook not.

It could not be explained to people from house to house;

Who mayeth be said to see mine heart's genuine aim?

The world with vines and tendrils climbeth to form factions;

Why art thou, all alone and forlorn, deaf to my blame?"

I always tread the middle course of sages of yore;

Alas! at this, mine heart is so choked sore with wroth; [55]

Going southward to sail on the streams Yuan and Hsiang,

I hail to Tsoon-hwah divine and heartily quoth: —[56]

Feeding on the cantatas *Nine Counts* and *Nine Songs*,

Chih of Hsia became pleasure soused and wild enow; [58]

Disregarding perils and disastrous results,

His prince Wuh-quan raised thereupon a royal row. [59]

Infatuated in ranging and hunting, Yih

Went crazed for endless trips of giant foxes' chase;

Reckless in conduct, he was bound to end in ill; [60]

So, Tso snatched his life, took his wife and grabbed his place.

Gnaw, violent in nature from his wild descent,

Gave unbridled license to his loosened appetites;

In lustful pleasures steeped and forgetting himself,

He wrought only to have his head to the ground fall. [61]

The constant depravity of King Ghi of Hsia

Resulted in calamity doomed after all; [62]

Atrocious Sing of pickle and human mince-meat fame

Cut short the Yin regime in his shocking terror. [63]

汤禹俨而祗敬兮，
周论道而莫差。
举贤才而授能兮，
循绳墨而不颇。
皇天无私阿兮，
览民德焉错辅。
夫维圣哲以茂行兮，
苟得用此下土。
瞻前而顾后兮，
相观民之计极。
夫孰非义而可用兮，
孰非善而可服？
阽余身而危死兮，
览余初其犹未悔。
不量凿而正枘兮，
固前修以菹醢。
曾歔欷余郁邑兮，
哀朕时之不当。
揽茹蕙以掩涕兮，
沾余襟之浪浪。
跪敷衽以陈辞兮，
耿吾既得此中正。
驷玉虬以乘鹥兮，
溘埃风余上征。
朝发轫于苍梧兮，
夕余至乎县圃。
欲少留此灵琐兮，
日忽忽其将暮。

离骚

Taung[64] and Yü[65] were Heaven-fearing and virtue-respecting,
And early Tsur[66] ruled by the Way without error;
Raising the virtuous and intrusting the capable,
They all the good rule followed and the straight road trod. [57][67]
Heaven high above doth not incline with preference,
Adding but beneficence to rule on the earth;
Only the sagacious, with their deeds excellent,
Were empowered to reign by their intrinsic worth.
Looking to the past and pondering on results,
I have examined the people's welfare ultimate;
Of the depraved, who should be intrusted to rule?
Of the wicked, who should bedeck a goodly state?[68]
With my body merely on the sheer brink of death,
I look back without regret to the beginning;
Minding not the square peg to fit in a round hole, —
That is why our fair precursors suffered mincing. [69]
Oftentimes I do sob, so deeply sunk in woe;
I lament my time doth not occur befitting:[70]
I pluck soft coumarous to wipe away my tears,
Which, streaming down, make my apparel folds dripping.
Kneeling, I spread them out to free my mind to Suen,
And flushed, feel anon the inner glory of mine;[71]
In a quadriga of jade-bitted dragonets[72], phoenix[73] —
Lifted, I rise fast in sand gusts in upward line. [74]
Setting forth early at morn from Tsoung-ngou Mountains[75],
Late after noon I reach the mid cliffs of Quen-lung[76];
I wish to loiter at these carved Heaven's gates[77] a little,
But the Sun hasteth away, the sky turning dun.

吾令羲和弭节兮，
望崦嵫而勿迫。
路漫漫其修远兮，
吾将上下而求索。
饮余马于咸池兮，
总余辔乎扶桑。
折若木以拂日兮，
聊逍遥以相羊。
前望舒使先驱兮，
后飞廉使奔属。
鸾皇为余先戒兮，
雷师告余以未具。
吾令凤鸟飞腾兮，
继之以日夜。
飘风屯其相离兮，
帅云霓而来御。
纷总总其离合兮，
斑陆离其上下。
吾令帝阍开关兮，
倚阊阖而望予。
时暧暧其将罢兮，
结幽兰而延伫。
世溷浊而不分兮，
好蔽美而嫉妒。
朝吾将济于白水兮，
登阆风而绁马。
忽反顾以流涕兮，
哀高丘之无女。

离骚

I make Shih-her[78], the Sun's car driver, to slow off,

Biding his time toward Yan-tze[79] in no hurry;

My way layeth remote and so far, far away;

I shall go up and down to make my long search aye. [80]

I let my coursers drink at Yen-tze[81], the Sun's bath,

And tie together their bridles on the tree Fwuh-soung[82];

Breaking off a *ruoh*-wood branch to withhold the Sun, [83]

I bid him to linger for some while not too long. [84]

I make Wang-suh[85], the Moon's chaise driver, mine herald,

And fleet-footed Fei-lian[86] to follow in my wake;

Phoenix is flying before as my van-courier

Thunder sayeth he's not ready the trip to make;

I let those sacred birds arise, soar and hover,

And do so continually by day and night;

Whirlblasts[87] collect around me and would not scatter,

Having rushed Rainbow and Cloud to greet me as drivers.

The variegated shapes disperse and assemble;

They heave up and down, multiversant, ultra-diverse;

I call to Heaven's Porter[88] to open his portal;

He leaneth on the Gates, staring me fore the sill.

The time is gloaming and I am growing weary;

I braid eupatories in my standing vigil; [89]

The world is so confused, muddled and promiscuous,

So apt to cover the fair and envy the brave.

Early at morn, on the White Stream I do embark, [90]

Mount Laun-feng[91] to ascend, my steed to bind;

Suddenly I look backward with mine eyes streaming,

Sad for there is on this plateau no Lady Divine[92].

溘吾游此春宫兮，
折琼枝以继佩。
及荣华之未落兮，
相下女之可诒。
吾令丰隆乘云兮，
求宓妃之所在。
解佩纕以结言兮，
吾令蹇修以为理。
纷总总其离合兮，
忽纬繣其难迁。
夕归次于穷石兮，
朝濯发乎洧盘。
保厥美以骄傲兮，
日康娱以淫游。
虽信美而无礼兮，
来违弃而改求。
览相观于四极兮，
周流乎天余乃下；
望瑶台之偃蹇兮，
见有娀之佚女。
吾令鸩为媒兮，
鸩告余以不好。
雄鸠之鸣逝兮，
余犹恶其佻巧。
心犹豫而狐疑兮，
欲自适而不可。
凤皇既受诒兮，
恐高辛之先我。

In haste I come to visit this Vernal Palace[93],

With a furcate gem-tree twig pendant on me laid;[94]

While its florescence is still in full-flushed blooming,

I think of giving Her it through Her earthly maid.[95]

I order Feng-loon the Chief to get on his Clouds,[96]

To find out for me the whereabouts of Fwu-fei[97];

Untying bands of pendants for pledging my troth,

I ask Chien-sieu to induce the courtship for me.[98]

Words in favour and traducings foul become rife;

Stiff and stubborn the suit soon turneth out to be:[99]

In the eve I retire to put up at Chun-sze[100];

The morn next, at Woei-pan[101] I go to wash mine hair.

Keeping her beauty but growing puffed up with pride,

Fwu-fei, a sybarite now, is caught in life's snare:[102]

With all her prettiness, she is unmannerly;

Come, I must forswear her and pay my suit elsewhere.

Having looked over the four extreme expanses[103]

And traversed heaven, I get down eventually;

I catch sight of the fair damsel of Yeou-soong[104],

While viewing her high steeple of lapis lazuli.

I bid Zun of deadly poison to guide the match;

Zun telleth me bluntly the thing should not be done.[105]

Treron then crieth to make it for me instead;

Yet I dislike his lubric, sly, chattering tongue.[106]

With mine heart hesitative and fluctuating,

I think of going myself, but that should not be:

Still, Phoenix hath conveyed Kao-sing's betrothal gifts;

I do fear *T'ih* Ko's Mystic Bird would precede me.[107]

欲远集而无所止兮，
聊浮游以逍遥。
及少康之未家兮，
留有虞之二姚。
理弱而媒拙兮，
恐导言之不固。
世溷浊而嫉贤兮，
好蔽美而称恶。
闺中既以邃远兮，
哲王又不寤。
怀朕情而不发兮，
余焉能忍与此终古！
索藑茅以筳篿兮，
命灵氛为余占之。
曰："两美其必合兮，
孰信修而慕之？
思九州之博大兮，
岂唯是其有女？"
曰："勉远逝而无狐疑兮，
孰求美而释女？
何所独无芳草兮，
尔何怀乎故宇？"
世幽昧以眩曜兮，
孰云察余之善恶？
民好恶其不同兮，
惟此党人其独异！

Meaning to fare far but being to go nowhere,

I could only wander about and ramble around;

So, before Sao-kong of Hsia hath become married,

There still remain the two sisters of Yau unbound. [108]

Knowing my match-makers to be dull and awkward,

I fear whate'er they say for me would be futile;

The times are muddled and jealous of the virtuous,

So apt to cover the fair and laud the evil. [109]

The maidens stay deep in their chambers and afar;

Moreover, the Wise King doth not read my good will; [110]

With the feelings I cherish at heart unexpressed,

How can I hold myself mute forever and aye?

Taking up holy inula and bamboo splints [111],

I ask Ling Fung [112] the sibyl to divine for me.

Thus she sayeth:

"Who would admire thy goodness and fine virtues here,

Though your two parties fair would finally unite? [113]

Think of the immensity of all these Nine States [114];

Could it be that only here there are damsels right?"

Again sayeth she:

"Try to go far away and be indubious;

Who could reject thee from her choice, among the fair? [115]

Where is it where there are no aromatic herbs? [116]

Why canst thou not ever thy native country spare!"

It is darkling here; people are confounded and blind;

Which of them could see I am a glare or a blot?

Mab's likes and dislikes are commonly not the same,

But the caballers are perverse at heart, I wot:

户服艾以盈要兮，

谓幽兰其不可佩。

览察草木其犹未得兮，

岂珵美之能当？

苏粪壤以充帏兮，

谓申椒其不芳。

欲从灵氛之吉占兮，

心犹豫而狐疑。

巫咸将夕降兮，

怀椒糈而要之。

百神翳其备降兮，

九疑缤其并迎。

皇剡剡其扬灵兮，

告余以吉故。

曰："勉升降以上下兮，

求榘矱之所同。

汤禹俨而求合兮，

挚咎繇而能调。

苟中情其好修兮，

又何必用夫行媒？

说操筑于傅岩兮，

武丁用而不疑。

吕望之鼓刀兮，

遭周文而得举。

宁戚之讴歌兮，

齐桓闻以该辅。

及年岁之未晏兮，

On their girdles hang white artemisias[117] to the full;

They vouch ohers should not eupatories append.

Incapable of observing and judging of plants,

How can they gems of surpassing beauty perpend?

Taking manured loam to fill their perfume sachets,

They warrant that pepper of Suen is not spicy![118]

Wishing to follow Ling Fung's happy augury,

I hesitate and waver with dubiety;

The sibyl Yen[119] would come down before twilight falls

To ask whom to divine, I put up spiced, choice rice.

The whole pantheon covereth heaven to descend;

Spirits of Nine Doubts greet me too in company:[120]

The godheads glowingly their deity beam forth,

Telling me the auspicious haps of history.

For them Yen sayeth:

"Go up and down as thou mayest rise or descend,

Trying to seek equivalent integrity:[121]

Taung and Yü, austere with themselves, sought for concord;

Holding virtuous aids, they achieved harmony. [122]

If both sides truly virtue love for its own sake,

What need of the mediacy could there e'er be![123]

Fuh Yüeh, who wrought at laying mud walls at Fuh-yan,

Was trusted by Wuh-ting when he ws found by quest;[124]

Leü Wang, a butcher hired at Yin's capital town,

Was elected to premiership by Count West;[125]

Lord Hwan of Tsih made of Nien Ts'i a counsellor,

When he heard him a song chant while feeding his cow. [126]

As thy tenure of years is not yet far advanced,

时亦犹其未央。
恐鹈鴂之先鸣兮，
使夫百草为之不芳。"
何琼佩之偃蹇兮，
众薆然而蔽之。
惟此党人之不谅兮，
恐嫉妒而折之。
时缤纷其变易兮，
又何可以淹留？
兰芷变而不芳兮，
荃蕙化而为茅。
何昔日之芳草兮，
今直为此萧艾也？
岂其有他故兮，
莫好修之害也？
余以兰为可恃兮，
羌无实而容长。
委厥美以从俗兮，
苟得列乎众芳。
椒专佞以慢慆兮，
樧又欲充夫佩帏。
既干进而务入兮，
又何芳之能祗！
固时俗之流从兮，
又孰能无变化？
览椒兰其若兹兮，
又况揭车与江离？
惟兹佩之可贵兮，

Thy time is still not drawing to its close just now.

But it is feared the shrike would cry before its time,

Making all plants, because of it, their verdure spend. " [127]

Proudly I wear these garnishings, yet wan they look,

How jealously the mob hideth them with disdain;

Thinking those clique maligners are so dishonest,

I fear they would damage them with envious stain. [128]

Since these times hard are troubled and sliding for the worse,

How could I in such difficult states long remain?

Eupatory and angelica spread sweets naught,

Acorus and coumarou have changed into reeds. [129]

Why is the odorous herbage of yesterdays

Turned directly into artemesias to-day?

Could it be that there were other reasons unknown

Than this mock of principle is the root of decay? [130]

I thought Eupatory could be relied upon,

But he, fine in looks, proveth vapid in effect;

Casting away his fairness, custom to follow,

He striveth yet to be classed amongst the elect. [131]

Sun Pepper, full in power and fawn, is swoln in pride; [132]

Cornus, but to stuff the perfume bag doth expect. [133]

As they dote on the court and feed on Her Presence,

So, what pure virtue can they possibly respect!

Surely, the run of people the currents followeth;

Which of them, then, would not have a change undergone?

I have seen Pepper and Eupatory changed thus;

How can Chi-chü and Selinea stay scentful long? [134]

But these wearings of mine have proved to be precious;

委厥美而历兹。
芳菲菲而难亏兮,
芬至今犹未沫。
和调度以自娱兮,
聊浮游而求女。
及余饰之方壮兮,
周流观乎上下。
灵氛既告余以吉占兮,
历吉日乎吾将行。
折琼枝以为羞兮,
精琼爢以为粮。
为余驾飞龙兮,
杂瑶象以为车。
何离心之可同兮?
吾将远逝以自疏。
遭吾道夫昆仑兮,
路修远以周流。
扬云霓之晻蔼兮,
鸣玉鸾之啾啾。
朝发轫于天津兮,
夕余至乎西极。
凤皇翼其承旂兮,
高翱翔之翼翼。
忽吾行此流沙兮,
遵赤水而容与。
麾蛟龙使梁津兮,
诏西皇使涉予。
路修远以多艰兮,

Traduced and slighted, they keep their worth to the last:

Their aromata, pure and rare, yield not a whit,

Smelling still odoriferous as in the past. [135]

Finding delight in union and harmony,

It behooveth me to ramble round to seek the Maid;

While mine adornments fair are quite lusty and full,

I wander up and down to conduct my survey. [136]

Since Ling Fung hath told me of her gracious omen,

I choose the propitious day to start my journey;

Plucking bloom buds of the gem tree[137] for provisions,

I take along its pearly fruits as my staple fare.

Flying dragons are bridled as my speeding coursers;

Jades and ivory, used to decorate my car.

How they do all oppose me in their unity;

I would get away hence and vanish e'er so far.

I turn my way forth toward the Quen-lung Mountains; [138]

They lie so remote, I go to them windingly.

As I start, the rainbow-cloud flags raise their shadows[139],

And tinkle the bells of the phoenix of chalcedony[140].

At morn, setting off from the Celestial Ferry[141],

Before dusk, I reach the western extremity.

Phoenixes, flying with unfurled colours behind

Rise high and hover to give me guard on the way.

Swiftly I range above over the Drifting Sands[142],

And along the course of the Red Stream[143] I rove and play.

I wave the dragons to bridge over the water,

And ask Sao-hao, god of West Sky[144], to help me cross.

The way is long drawn and fraught with difficulties,

腾众车使径待。

路不周以左转兮，

指西海以为期。

屯余车其千乘兮，

齐玉轪而并驰。

驾八龙之婉婉兮，

载云旗之委蛇。

抑志而弭节兮，

神高驰之邈邈。

奏《九歌》而舞《韶》兮，

聊假日以媮乐。

陟升皇之赫戏兮，

忽临睨夫旧乡。

仆夫悲余马怀兮，

蜷局顾而不行。

乱曰：

已矣哉！

国无人莫我知兮，

又何怀乎故都？

既莫足与为美政兮，

吾将从彭咸之所居！

I send the host of cars to go straight in advance;

I would wend round by Pu-tsur and turn to the left; [145]

To wait for me there, at West Sea they should gather.

Spreading my chariots of state a full thousand,

I wave the jade axes to proceed together;

I drive mine eight dragons that speed winding about,

With cloud ensigns waving long drawn out at backside.

I stop the cloud streamers by curbing the dragons;

My spirit, though, still high up and far off doth ride:

Nine Songs is being played and *Sao* [146] cantata danced;

By whiling away time, my sorrow thus I bide. [147]

Rising to th'upmost height into a galore of light,

I see suddenly in a squint the native land;

My retinue groweth sad and mine horses pine, —[148]

Curling up, gazing backward and dazed, they budge not. [149]

The epiphonema [150] goeth thus:

Let it be, then! [151]

There is no one in the state, none who knoweth me;

Why should I the old capital longingly crave?

Since none is worthy to hand fine policies with,

I will go for Peng Yen to my watery grave.

本书《九歌》列入十一篇。有《山鬼》、《国殇》、《礼魂》合一说（黄文焕:《楚辞听直》），故总九篇,符合一个九字;而按王夫之说,"《九歌》系袭用远古乐章的旧名,它之所以标名为'九',只是说由多数歌辞组合成一套完整的乐章而已,歌辞的实数,并不受到九的限制。"(《楚辞集注》p.118）

——编者

九 歌

NINE SONGS

一　东皇太一

吉日兮辰良，
穆将愉兮上皇。
抚长剑兮玉珥，
璆锵鸣兮琳琅。

瑶席兮玉瑱，
盍将把兮琼芳。
蕙肴蒸兮兰藉，
奠桂酒兮椒浆。

扬枹兮拊鼓，
（盈气度兮茂腔。）*
疏缓节兮安歌，
陈竽瑟兮浩倡。

---

* 此处遗佚一句 2000 余年，我姑且大胆补足——译者。

1 Hymn on East Emperor Tai-ih[①][(1)]

Auspicious day and tide of augury fine

Hail Your Divinity Tai-ih the Supreme.

Holding the jade-stuck handle ear of his tall sword,

He[②] cometh, his pendant gems hung clinking, agleam.

With saffron jades[(2)] to press the close knit mat,

In his grasp are blooming twigs and bunched sweet herb.

Meat wrapped with boneset, steamed and stuffed with orchid,

Is offered with cassia brew and spiced drinks superb.

Drum sticks are lifted and stricken down to lead,

(The thythmic flush with the heart-felt leading doth chime;) [*]

While lingering on pauses soft and rich,

The Pandean pipes and zithern[③][(3)] keep their time.

---

[*] This line in the original is missing for over twenty-two centuries, and is tentatively supplied by the present translator.

[①] East Emperor Tai-ih was the supreme god of the state Tsou(楚) during Chü Yuan's time in the Warring States Period(475 −221 B. C.) of ancient Cathay. Chü Yuan, the first poet known by name, as well as the greatest one of the Chinese people, as a patriot, statesman and great thinker, was a dauntless opponent to the world's first totalitarian, Fascistic state Tsing(秦). This poem is the first one of his *Nine Songs*. Before him, the poets of the Ya(雅) section of the *Classic of Poetry*(《诗经 》) were all anonymous.

[②] The chief wizard who performed the rite of paying homage to Tai-ih, the supreme god of Tsou. He was assisted by sorcerers as stated in line 13.

[③] The zither or zithern of remote ancient China was said to be innovated by the prehistoric legendary king Fu Shih which had fifty chords and was eight feet long. The legendary king *Tih* Yao. it was said, had a fairy lady play for him on the instrument; its tune was sorely sad. so he asked her to stop plucking, but in vain. Thereupon, he afterwards reduced the number of chords to twenty-five, and the size of the instrument was shortened to five and a half feet long.

灵偃蹇兮姣服，
芳菲菲兮满堂。
五音纷兮繁会，
君欣欣兮乐康！

九歌

All the enchantresses in vestures sheen
Dance in the sacred hall in scented air.
The multiple tunes are sounded in high accord;
Content and joy are wished to Your Godhead e'er!

二 云中君

浴兰汤兮沐芳，
华采衣兮若英。
灵连蜷兮既留，
烂昭昭兮未央。
謇将憺兮寿宫，
与日月兮齐光。

龙驾兮帝服，
聊翱游兮周章！
灵皇皇兮既降，
猋远举兮云中。
览冀州兮有余，
横四海兮焉穷。
思夫君兮太息，
极劳心兮忡忡。

2   Hymn on the King of Clouds

In eupatory-soused sweet water bathed,

With florid raiments blushing like fresh-blown flowers,

His Divinity, coming down tall and slant,

Glowing with incessantly dazzling splendours,

Would be pleased with the altar He poreth on,

As he glareth vying the sun and moon.

In a car by dragons drawn, in flowery gown,

He hath vanished so fleetingly and soon!

His Deity, flooding light while coming down,

In a twinkle is again far up in the clouds,

O'erseeing the Middle Empire fore'er more,

And speeding all o'er the seas beyond their shore.

Thinking of His Kingship we heave a sigh

And pulsate with warm adoration high.

三　湘夫人 *

君不行兮夷犹，
蹇谁留兮中洲？
美要眇兮宜修，
沛吾乘兮桂舟。
令沅、湘兮无波，
使江水兮安流。
望夫君兮未来，
吹参差兮谁思？

驾飞龙兮北征，
邅吾道兮洞庭。
薜荔柏兮蕙绸，
荪桡兮兰旌。
望涔阳兮极浦，
横大江兮扬灵。
扬灵兮未极！
女婵媛兮为余太息。
横流涕兮潺湲，
隐思君兮陫侧！
桂棹兮兰枻，

---

3   Hymn on the Lady of Hsiang[*]

Failing to come, by whom art Thou, beauteous

And brightest, on the isle detained, lingering?

With excellence fair by adornments graced,

In a cassia boat I ride the waves speeding.

I make the streams of Yuan and Hsiang calmly flow,

To let their waters tranquillizingly go.

In vain I expect Thee in time to appear;

Whom art Thou playing the Pandean pipes to cheer?

Thou pliest Thy dragon-winged boat to fleet north;

By way of Doong-ding, I guide Thee to turn forth.

In pomelo-fig's vine frock, coumarous-tied,

Thou hiest on thy sweet-flag skiff, eupatory-buntinged. [1]

Seen distantly at Jin-yang's[2] water margin,

Thy splendours daze me, on the River shining.

Ah, Thy blazing glow glareth boundlessly!

Even Thine handmaids sigh for me in pity;

For I shed tears that stream so drippingly down,

As I, pining for Thee, my forlornness mourn.

To pull cassia oars o'er magnolia planks

[*]   See note on *pp.* 639 −649 — the editor.

斫冰兮积雪。
采薜荔兮水中,
搴芙蓉兮木末;
心不同兮媒劳,
恩不甚兮轻绝。
石濑兮浅浅,
飞龙兮翩翩。
交不忠兮怨长,
期不信兮告余以不闲。

鼌骋骛兮江皋,
夕弭节兮北渚。
鸟次兮屋上,
水周兮堂下。
捐余玦兮江中,
遗余佩兮澧浦。
采芳洲兮杜若,
将以遗兮下女。
时不可兮再得,
聊逍遥兮容与。

To chase Thee is like chopping ice from snow-banks,

Or trying to pick, on streams, pomelo-figs

And to pluck lotus flowers from high tree twigs.

Thine heart is parted from mine; our tie is shorn:

The love-knot, loose at first, is easily torn.

The rapids I pass gurgle with a loud sound;

Thy flitting dragons are too far to be found.

When the troth is light, the complaint must be long;

Since the plight is remiss, the sad rue's foregone.

At morn, I rush and ride madly by the River;

Fore dusk, I pace on the north bank of the water[3].

Birds stop to perch on the thatched roofs over walls;

Currents of a rill wind along below the halls. [4]

I throw mine incised gem hoop near the water

And leave my jade pendant by the Lih River.

I cull pollia bouquets from the green isle,

To give as gifts to Her handmaids for the while.

The good occasion could not happen again;

I would take time to wait as Her bonny swain.

四 湘君*

帝子降兮北渚，
目眇眇兮愁予。
袅袅兮秋风，
洞庭波兮木叶下。

登白薠兮骋望，
与佳期兮夕张。
鸟何萃兮蘋中？
罾何为兮木上？

沅有芷兮澧有兰，
思公子兮未敢言。
荒忽兮远望，
观流水兮潺湲。
麋何食兮庭中？
蛟何为兮水裔？

朝驰余马兮江皋，
夕济兮西澨。
闻佳人兮召予，
将腾驾兮偕逝。

---

* 见第 514 −521 页英文注——编者。

4 Hymn on the King of Hsiang*

Oh, Prince Rare! on the stream's north bank descendeth;
His winsome eyen twinkling make me pine.
The autumn zephyr breatheth a long slim swing;
The waves of Doong-ding ripple and wood leaves decline.

I climb up the cyperus to view afar;
I look for the bower of tryst at sundown.
But how could birds on water plants alight?
Wherefore should fish nets, tops of trees be cast on?[1]

Yuan hath its angelicas and Lih, eupatories;
Musing on Him the Rare, I dare not speak out.
Dazed and confused, I gaze at the distance;
I see the current rapidly flush and spout.
What hath the elk to do in the courtyard?
How could a dragon, the waterside come about?[2]

At morn, along the river bund I gallop;
Fore eve, o'er the west water margin I row.
Wishing, if He the Rare summon me, to fleet,
I would bound to the trysting nook with joy.

---

* See note on *pp.* 514 −521 — the editor.

屈原诗选英译

筑室兮水中，
葺之兮荷盖；
荪壁兮紫坛，
播芳椒兮成堂；
桂栋兮兰橑，
辛夷楣兮药房；
罔薜荔兮为帷，
擗蕙櫋兮既张；
白玉兮为镇，
疏石兰兮为芳：
芷葺兮荷屋，
缭之兮杜衡。
合百草兮实庭，
建芳馨兮庑门。
九嶷缤兮并迎，
灵之来兮如云。

捐余袂兮江中，
遗余褋兮澧浦。
搴汀洲兮杜若，
将以遗兮远者。
时不可兮骤得，
聊逍遥兮容与。

The secluded spot is on the Lake islet:

The roofs are thatched with lotus leaves fresh and green;

Walls, laid with sweet-flags; the courtyard groweth purple grass[3];

The hall is plastered with limed, ground Sun pepper;

With cassia beam and rafters of magnolia[4],

Lintel of aloes and angelica flank,[5]

It is draped with pomelo-fig's vine for curtain,

Laid with mat eupatory-braided as floor plank;

Lustrous white gems are used for pressure stones,

And mountain orchids spread for their grateful odours:

This chamber weird o'erlaid with lotus leafage

Is bounded with asarums of sweet favours.[6]

Flowers multitudinous are planted in the court;

Scents fragrant are diffused all around the house.

Spirits of Nine Doubts greet away the One Rare;

Their godheads come in company like clouds.

I cast my sleeve to float it in the River,

And leave mine upper bodice by Lih Water;

I cull pollia bouquets from the level isle,

To give as gifts to His handmaids[7] for the while.

The good occasion could not recur very soon;

I better take time to wait for the chance boon.

五　大司命

广开兮天门，
纷吾乘兮玄云。
令飘风兮先驱，
使涷雨兮洒尘。
君回翔兮以下，
逾空桑兮从女。
纷总总兮九州，
何寿夭兮在予！

高飞兮安翔，
乘清气兮御阴阳。
吾与君兮齐速，
导帝之兮九坑。
灵衣兮被被，
玉佩兮陆离。
壹阴兮壹阳，
众莫知兮余所为。

折疏麻兮瑶华，
将以遗兮离居。
老冉冉兮既极，
不寖近兮愈疏。
乘龙兮辚辚，
高驰兮冲天。

5　Hymn on the Major God of Life-ruling[1]

Wide open are heaven's azure gates[2] vast.
I[3] drive multiplicate clouds dusky,
Command whirlblasts to be mine herald,
Splashing showers to wash ways dusty.
Low Thou descendest by whirling down;
I follow Thee via Mount Koon-soung[4];
Thou flittest all over the Nine States,
Giving people their lives or short or long. [5]

High fliest Thou, calmly hoverest,
Riding pure air, bridling Shade and Light.
I fleet in equal high speed with Thee
Transmitting *T'ih's* decree to Nine K'ong[6].
In sheen spiritous apparels long,
With pendants of gem sparklingly bright,
By turns Thou darkest and shinest.
People ken not whereunto I[7] have gone. [8]

Picking sacred hemp for its fair blooms,
Thou givest me them to think of Thee.
Mine old age would come about ere long;
If not bestowed, I would the loss dree. [9]
Driving a rumbling dragon-drawn car,
Aloft Thou rushest swiftly heavenward.

结桂枝兮延伫，
羌愈思兮愁人。
愁人兮奈何？
愿若今兮无亏。
固人命兮有当，
孰离合兮可为。

Knitting up cassia twigs to expect,

Missing Thee, I am much grieved inward.

What shall I do with the grief weighty?

I beg Thou'd come hence to Thy homage.

Our mundane ship is under Thy sway;

From sinking, we could resolve no salvage. (10)

六　少司命

秋兰兮麇芜，
罗生兮堂下。
绿叶兮素枝，
芳菲菲兮袭予。
夫人兮自有美子，
荪何以兮愁苦？

秋兰兮青青，
绿叶兮紫茎。
满堂兮美人，
忽独与余兮目成。

入不言兮出不辞，
乘回风兮载云旗。
悲莫悲兮生别离，
乐莫乐兮新相知。

荷衣兮蕙带，
倏而来兮忽而逝。
夕宿兮帝郊，
君谁须兮云之际？

6 Hymn on the Minor God of Life-ruling[1]

Autumn eupatories, selineas —
They grow side by side below the hall.
With leaves full verdant and branches white,
Their odours fragrantly on me fall.
There are good sorts among all the people;
How could worry possibly Thee mall?[2]

Luxuriant, the eupatories,
With green foliage and peduncles mauve.
The hall is full of boon adorers;
Thine eyen on mine, quick fixeth Thou. [3]

Thou comest and goest with no beck,
Riding whirlblasts, stepping on clouds'flue.
Nothing is sadder than live parting.
Or gladder than dearness formed new. [4]

In lotus clothes with coumarou bands,
Swiftly Thou comest, fleetly to flee.
At night, putting up in Heaven's suburbs,
Whom dost Thou wait in the clouds to see?[5]

与女沐兮咸池，
晞女发兮阳之阿。
望美人兮未来，
临风怳兮浩歌。

孔盖兮翠旍，
登九天兮抚彗星。
竦长剑兮拥幼艾，
荪独宜兮为民正。

九 歌

I wish to bathe with Thee in Yen-tze;

Couldst dry Thy locks in the first sunshine.

Waiting for my Beauty coming not,

Disheartened, I sing a sad song to pine. [6]

Riding a dennet with peacock plumes

For cover and alcedo streamers,

Thou mountest ninth Heaven to check the comet;

With Thy tall sword to guard the aged and young,

Thou alone art fit people's fortune to set. [7]

七　东君

暾将出兮东方，
照吾槛兮扶桑。
抚余马兮安驱，
夜皎皎兮既明。

驾龙辀兮乘雷，
载云旗兮委蛇。
长太息兮将上，
心低徊兮顾怀。
羌声色兮娱人，
观者憺兮忘归。

緪瑟兮交鼓，
箫钟兮瑶簴；
鸣篪兮吹竽，
思灵保兮贤姱。
翾飞兮翠曾，
展诗兮会舞。
应律兮合节，
灵之来兮蔽日。

7 Hymn on East King[①](1)

Dawn is arising in the east sky
From Fwuh-soung my balustrade to light.
Tapping mine ambler, I ride to greet it;
Ere long now night will turn to be bright. (2)

With a dragon-curved beam, birring wheels
And cloud ensigns flapping alongside,
His Deity, the altar to mount,
Cometh, puffing, content, and abide. (3)
Elysian sights and music Him please,
As onlookers throng to watch at ease.

Strung are the zitherns, peppered, the drums;
Bells hung from jade rods chime pipes Pandean;
Whistled are the flutes and circular reeds;
Sibyls all fare debonair and clean,
Like kingfishers rising to hover,
Diffusing poetry, concerting dance,
In glib affluence with tunes and rhythms.
Sprites crowd down, Him to Heaven to advance. (4)

---

① East King: the Sun God.

屈原诗选英译

青云衣兮白霓裳，
举长矢兮射天狼。
操余弧兮反沦降，
援北斗兮酌桂浆。
撰余辔兮高驰翔，
杳冥冥兮以东行。

九歌

Appareled in clouds azure and white,
At Heaven's Wolf I shoot mine arrow long;
I toast East King off with the Dipper's wine,
When my bow faileth to turn back sundown;
Holding my bridle I ride up aloft,
Flitting eastward in the night profound. [5]

八　河伯

与女游兮九河，
冲风起兮横波。
乘水车兮荷盖，
驾两龙兮骖螭。

登昆仑兮四望，
心飞扬兮浩荡。
日将暮兮怅忘归，
惟极浦兮寤怀。

鱼鳞屋兮龙堂，
紫贝阙兮朱宫。
灵何为兮水中？

乘白鼋兮逐文鱼，
与女游兮河之渚，
流澌纷兮将来下。

子交手兮东行，
送美人兮南浦。
波滔滔兮来迎，
鱼鳞鳞兮媵予。

8　Hymn on the Count of Ho①(1)

I would ride with Thee on the Nine Streams,

With winds dashing and waves heaving free,

In water cars with lotus covers,

Bridling two dragons, dragonets three. (2)

I mount Quen-Iung cliffs to look about;

Mine heart feeleth flighty and unsound;

Dusk falling, I feel like lost and lorn;

Thinking on water-sides far, I come round. (3)

Fish-scaled tiles o'er a dragon-scaled hall,

Cypraea port, cinnabar palace, —

What doest Thou down there (kennest my call)?(4)

Riding large white turtles after stript fish,

We sport along by a River isle,

When waves drift down in torrential swish. (5)

Thou graspest mine hand to fare eastward;

I see Thee off at the southern lee.

Waves multitudinous roll to greet Thee;

Fishes countless bid Thee adieu with me. (6)

---

① 　The Count of Ho: the God of Luteous River.

九　山鬼

若有人兮山之阿，
被薜荔兮带女萝。
既含睇兮又宜笑，
子慕予兮善窈窕。
乘赤豹兮从文狸，
辛夷车兮结桂旗。
被石兰兮带杜衡，
折芳馨兮遗所思。

余处幽篁兮终不见天，
路险难兮独后来。
表独立兮山之上，
云容容兮而在下。
杳冥冥兮羌昼晦，
东风飘兮神灵雨。
留灵修兮憺忘归，
岁既晏兮孰华予？

采三秀兮于山间，
石磊磊兮葛蔓蔓。
怨公子兮怅忘归，
君思我兮不得闲。

9 Hymn on the Mountain Sprite[1]

The manito from a retired mountain nook.

Robed in pomelo-figs vine, girdled with usnea,

Smiling and eyeing me with a charming look,

Thou, beaming with gleamy beauty, dost me leer.

Driving a red panther after brindled wild cats,

Riding an airy chaise of magnolia

And fluttering osmanthus-plaited pennants,

Thou, with Thy vehicle and pennons wound with orchids

And banded too with asarum blooms fragrant,

Dost pluck odorous flowers Thy love to present. [2]

Biding in bamboo groves, I see not the sky;

The way is difficult, hence I come so late.

I stand upright atop of a mountain high;

Clouds are floating about in the dale below.

The deep-set gloaming being dense for the nonce,

East winds sprinkle magic rains as Thou cometh down.

I detain Thee with joy, forgetting to home;

In mine eve of life, who else would make me glow?[3]

Thou, picking fairy fungi on mountain heights

Where rocks and stones abound and puerarias grow,

Hast vanished swift; I pine and homing forget.

Thou must yearn too, but have no time to come below. [4]

山中人兮芳杜若，
饮石泉兮荫松柏。
君思我兮然疑作。

雷填填兮雨冥冥，
猨啾啾兮又夜鸣。
风飒飒兮木萧萧，
思公子兮徒离忧。

九歌

The mountaineer, making bouquets of pollia,

Drinketh rock spring, taking shade from cypress and pine.

Why dost Thou, mindful of me, to descend, decline?[5]

Thunder clappeth and rain, darkening, falleth;

Gibbons screech and lemurs in the night cry;

Wind blasts blow and wood foliage rustleth.

Thinking of the fair one, I sadly retire. [6]

十　国殇

操吴戈兮被犀甲，
车错毂兮短兵接；
旌蔽日兮敌若云，
矢交坠兮士争先。

凌余阵兮躐余行，
左骖殪兮右刃伤。
霾两轮兮絷四马，
援玉枹兮击鸣鼓。
天时怼兮威灵怒，
严杀尽兮弃原壄。

出不入兮往不反，
平原忽兮路超远。
带长剑兮挟秦弓，
首身离兮心不惩。

诚既勇兮又以武，
终刚强兮不可凌。
身既死兮神以灵，
魂魄毅兮为鬼雄！

10 Hymn on Spirits of State Warriors Slayed in War

Warriors wielding Wuh tridents fierce

Are with rhinoceros hide armoured;

Chariots' axle-barrels clash one another;

Daggers and swords are stabbed, heads severed;

Pennons and streamers the sky cover;

Enemy hosts the sun shade like clouds;

Arrows and darts fly like hail to pierce;

Men on both sides attack in massed crowds. (1)

Foes our ranks and files trample and mow down;

My left side-horse killed, wounded the right one;

Two wheels are halted, four horses caught.

With jade-handled sticks I beat the battle drum.

Heaven above is wroth, His ires high run.

The scuffle over, corpses strew the plain. (2)

Those that have come out could not back draw;

The field having trod, they return not.

Tall swords they bear, and strong bows of Tsing;

Beheaded, they have yet no rest got. (3)

Indeed, they are brave and heroic,

Strong e'en after death, and inviolable.

Though dead, they have spirits that are quick;

Their souls firm are among ghosts admirable. (4)

十一　礼魂

成礼兮会鼓，
传芭兮代舞，
姱女倡兮容与。
春兰兮秋菊，
长无绝兮终古！

11　Epode to All the Hymns Above[(1)]

Rounded off the rite, drums rapidly beaten;

Exchanged the bouquets, dances again begun;

Fair chorus' songs and chantings gracefully done.

In spring, homage is paid with eupatoriams,

In autumn, 'tis paid with asters fresh and pure,

Forever and aye.

九　　章
（选六篇）
SYLVA OF NINE
PIECES
（SIX SELECTED）

一　涉江

余幼好此奇服兮，
年既老而不衰。
带长铗之陆离兮，
冠切云之崔嵬。
被明月兮佩宝璐。
世溷浊而莫余知兮，
吾方高驰而不顾。
驾青虬兮骖白螭，
吾与重华游兮瑶之圃。
登昆仑兮食玉英，
与天地兮同寿，
与日月兮齐光。

哀南夷之莫吾知兮，
旦余将济乎江湘。
乘鄂渚而反顾兮，
欸秋冬之绪风。
步余马兮山皋，
邸余车兮方林。
乘舲船余上沅兮，
齐吴榜以击汰。
船容与而不进兮，

1 Over the Streams[1]

From youthful days, I love this novel gown;

Now I am aging, but still do so as of auld;

I bear by my side a sword of sheen blade long,

And wear atop this tall, tall hat Cut-cloud.

With matchless Night Glow I my back impearl

And hang as pendant this gem nonpareil.

The world is in a muddle, kenning me not;

Heedless of it, I fleetly ride aloft;

Bridling blue dragonets two, white dragons three,

I and Tsoon-hwah range the land of the fairy.

Ascending heights of the Mountains Quen-lung,

I eat gem sprouts that give life immortal;

Enjoying longevity with Heaven and Earth,

I vie in glory with the moon and sun. [2]

Grieving the south barbarians not knowing me,

To-morrow I would sail the Hsiang and River,

Passing by Ngo-tsu therefrom to look back,

Ah, I would sighs heave in the last blasts of winter.

Walking mine horse by mounts and water-sides,

I would have my dennet reaching Foun-lin.

Rowing upstream in a windowed boat on Yuan,

Boatmen would raise their oars the waves to beat.

The vessel, pausing, would cease to advance,

淹回水而凝滞。
朝发枉陼兮，
夕宿辰阳。
苟余心其端直兮，
虽僻远之何伤？
入溆浦余儃徊兮，
迷不知吾所如。
深林杳以冥冥兮，
乃猿狖之所居，
山峻高以蔽日兮，
下幽晦以多雨。
霰雪纷其无垠兮，
云霏霏而承宇。

哀吾生之无乐兮，
幽独处乎山中。
吾不能变心以从俗兮，
固将愁苦而终穷。

- -

接舆髡首兮，桑扈裸行。
忠不必用兮，贤不必以。
伍子逢殃兮，比干菹醢。
与前世而皆然兮，
吾又何怨乎今之人！
余将董道而不豫兮，
固将重昏而终身！
乱曰：
鸾鸟凤凰，日以远兮。

Being dashed by quick whirlpools to retreat.

At morn I would set forth from the port Waung-tsu,

Putting up at Tsen-yang toward sundown.

Let mine heart be but upright and of honour;

What is the harm though I be exiled far and long?

Arriving at Süe-puh I would linger there,

Being at a loss whereunto I should drive.

The forest dense there is deep and darkly set;

It is where monkeys and aethiops hive.

Precipitous cliffs thereof cover the sun,

Below which it is gloomy and rainy.

Falling down sleet and snow thick boundlessly,

Clouds flutter which closely all over the sky. [3]

Lamenting mine life lorn is so cheerless,

Retired, I live on mountains an eremite.

I cannot change my mind to suit the crowd,

But will stay long afflicted in hapless plight.

Tsi-eü was shorn of hair; Soun-wuh stayed naked.

The faithful and virtuous were not chosen:

Oo Yuan met disaster; Pih-kan was minced.

Since I persist to do as my precursors,

Why should I complain of my strikers to-day?

I will ride on high unheedful of the world,

Keeping to my repulsion without dismay. [4]

The epiphonema goeth thus:

Phoenixes have flied away farther day by day;

屈原诗选英译

燕雀乌鹊,巢堂坛兮。

露申辛夷,死林薄兮。

腥臊并御,芳不得薄兮。

阴阳易位,时不当兮。

怀信侘傺,忽乎吾将行兮。

九章

Sparrows and ravens nest on altars and in halls;

Daphnes and magnolias die in the coppice;

Fishy, rancid things are savoured; fragrant, repelled;

Fair and foul ones change places; the times are awry:

With good faith and distress, puzzled, I would fleet away. (5)

二 哀郢

皇天之不纯命兮，
何百姓之震愆！
民离散而相失兮，
方仲春而东迁。
去故乡而就远兮，
遵江夏以流亡。
出国门而轸怀兮，
甲之鼂吾以行。

发郢都而去闾兮，
怊荒忽其焉极？
楫齐扬以容与兮，
哀见君而不再得。
望长楸而太息兮，
涕淫淫其若霰。
过夏首而西浮兮，
顾龙门而不见。
心婵媛而伤怀兮，
眇不知其所跖。
顺风波以从流兮，
焉洋洋而为客？
凌阳侯之泛滥兮，
忽翱翔之焉薄？
心絓结而不解兮，

2　Plaint on Ying[1]

Heaven hath miscarried from its constant law;

See, bow for their guilts the people are trembling!

Scattered are they, missing one another,

While wandering eastward early in mid-spring.

Leaving my homestall far-away to remove,

I float on the River and Shiah, straying along;

At morn of a *jea* day to ride on my boat,

Out from the state gate I go woebegone. [2]

I set out from Ying-*t'uh* and mine home portal,

Sad for my journey's end being so remote!

The oars are raised in unison with leisure;

I grieve I could see my sovereign no more.

Looking at the high tree tops I heave long sighs;

My tears stream flowingly like drippings of sleet.

Passing o'er Shiah's mouth and winding in its curve,

The Dragon Gate of Ying could not mine eye greet.

With mine heart pulsating and full of laments,

I, filled with anguish, know not where I would stand;

Following the stream currents to float onward,

I become a wayfarer on a strange strand.

Riding on Marquis Yang's big waves heaving high,

Like flying birds, I ken not where to alight.

Mine heart is hard compressed and closely knitted;

思蹇产而不释。

将运舟而下浮兮,
上洞庭而下江。
去终古之所居兮,
今逍遥而来东。
羌灵魂之欲归兮,
何须臾而忘反。
背夏浦而西思兮,
哀故都之日远。
登大坟以远望兮,
聊以舒吾忧心。
哀州土之平乐兮,
悲江介之遗风。

当陵阳之焉至兮,
淼南渡之焉如?
曾不知夏之为丘兮,
孰两东门之可芜?
心不怡之长久兮,
忧与愁其相接。
惟郢路之辽远兮,
江与夏之不可涉。
忽若去不信兮,
至今九年而不复。
惨郁郁而不通兮,
蹇侘傺而含戚。

九章

My crimpled thoughts are twined into knotted coils tight. [3]

I would employ my vessel to float downstream,
With Doong-ding up above, below, the River. [4]
Leaving where my forefathers lived for ages,
I am now forced eastward to drift and wander.
My spirit is yearning to Ying to return;
How for a while, it forgetteth to come back.
With my back against Shiah, I pine for the west;
Ruing the old town is far off doth me rack.
I climb up a big shoal to look far away,
To mitigate somewhat my dolorous heart;
Grieving the wide domain as rich habitat,
I mourn for the riverside left customs' part.

Where shall I fare after coming to Ling-yang?
Waves stretch to the sky; southward, where shall I stray?
I cannot conceive great mansions fallen to ruins,
How the two east gates levelled into decay.
Long hath mine heart been constringed by suffering,
Sore sorrows after sorrows sore I do dree;
I think of how far stretched the way is to Ying,
How Shiah and the River could not crossed be.
Vaguely I seem to have left, but am skeptic;
Being exiled nine years, I can return not!
So deeply woebegone, I fail to set up,
Distressed, disrupt in mind, I have anguished got. [5]

外承欢之汋约兮，
谌荏弱而难持。
忠湛湛而愿进兮，
妒被离而障之。
尧舜之抗行兮，
瞭杳杳而薄天。
众谗人之嫉妒兮，
被以不慈之伪名。
憎愠惀之修美兮，
好夫人之慷慨。
众踥蹀而日进兮，
美超远而逾迈。

乱曰：
曼余目以流观兮，
冀壹反之何时？
鸟飞反故乡兮，
狐死必首丘。
信非吾罪而弃逐兮；
何日夜而忘之？

Outwardly the rabble fawneth on to please him,

Who groweth indeed pliantly weak within.

The faithful, solemn, wish to loyally serve;

The jealous riffraff segregateth between.

See how Yao and Suen touch the celestial blue,

With their noble great deeds exalted and sublime;

Yet envious traducers execrate them

With foul unnatural faults for muck and slime.

The honest and integral are resented,

While outspoken servile cringelings win the day.

The crowd sycophantic rusheth on like mad,

As the pure and virtuous go their own way. [6]

The epiphonema runneth thus:

I cast my looks around to command a view,

Expecting when I could make my fit return.

Birds will fly back to their old nests howe'er far;

Foxes must die on the knolls where they were born.

Mine exile is verily none of my fault;

My remembrance of Ying setteth me e'er lorn! [7]

屈原诗选英译

三　怀沙

滔滔孟夏兮，
草木莽莽。
伤怀永哀兮，
汩徂南土。
眴兮杳杳，
孔静幽默。
郁结纡轸兮，
离愍而长鞠。
抚情效志兮，
冤屈而自抑。

刓方以为圜兮？
常度未替。
易初本迪兮，
君子所鄙。
章画志墨兮，
前图未改。
内厚质正兮，
大人所晟。
巧倕不斵兮，
孰察其揆正？
玄文处幽兮，
矇瞍谓之不章。
离娄微睇兮，

3 Thinking of Sah[1]

Rolling, the waves in foresummer are;

Luxuriant, the woods and herbage.

Woeful at heart, afflicted am I;

Fare to the south land doth my voyage.

Mine eyen twinkling catch sight of naught;

Utterly mute is mine inaudible tongue.

Woe-stressed, repressed, in agony deep,

Suffering pains, I am sore undone.

Palming my feelings and heart's intent,

Though ill used, I still myself refrain. [2]

Shall I the square chop to make it round?

Inalterable is the constant law.

To swerve from one's pristine wholesome faith

Is scoffed by the upright without haw.

Keeping to the good first plan and rules,

I conserve precedent codes of worth.

To hold integrity in esteem

Is priced by the sagacious with dearth.

If skilful Tsuai excel not in arts,

Who could appreciate his dexterous parts?[3]

Black tracery in twilight shadows

Is said by the blind to be not just blear.

Quick-sighted Lih-lur cast but a glance;

瞽以为无明。
变白以为黑兮,
倒上以为下。
凤皇在笯兮,
鸡鹜翔舞。
同糅玉石兮,
一概而相量。
夫惟党人之鄙固兮,
羌不知余之所臧。

任重载盛兮,
陷滞而不济。
怀瑾握瑜兮,
穷不知所示。
邑犬群吠兮,
吠所怪也。
非俊疑杰兮,
固庸态也。
文质疏内兮,
众不知余之异采。
材朴委积兮,
莫知余之所有。
重仁袭义兮,
谨厚以为丰。
重华不可遻兮,
孰知余之从容?
古固有不并兮,
岂知其何故?

The stone-blind take all things as not clear.

Thus, what is white is changed into black

And what is up is turned toppling down.

The phoenix is cooped up in a pen,

While cocks and ducks dance and hover round.

Jades and pebbles are mixed up together;

Content measures scraped with the same stave.

Since the caballers are doltish all,

They ken not what I prize to behave. (4)

Capable of bearing heavy burden,

I am debased low as of no use.

Holding jades and bosoming gems rare,

Forlorn, I am downtrod with abuse.

Borough dogs bark in an uproar high,

Yelping at what they take to be strange.

Defaming and suspecting the wise

Are usances of the common range.

With affluent art concealed within,

I hold wits sparkling unknown to men.

With my gifts hidden in equipoise,

Who hath hints of what sports in me den?

Upholding kindness and its deeds apt,

I cherish caution and earnestness.

Tsoon-hwah cannot be met with to-day;

Who kenneth what noble law I caress?

Virtuous aids rarely met sage kings:

How could it be known why it is such?

汤禹久远兮，
邈而不可慕。

惩违改忿兮，
抑心而自强。
离愍而不迁兮，
愿志之有像。
进路北次兮，
日昧昧其将暮。
舒忧娱哀兮，
限之以大故。

乱曰：
浩浩沅、湘，
分流汩兮。
修路幽蔽，
道远忽兮。
怀质抱情，
独无匹兮。
伯乐既没，
骥焉程兮？
民生禀命，
各有所错兮。
定心广志，
余何畏惧兮？
曾伤爰哀，
永叹喟兮。
世溷浊莫吾知，

Taung and Yü are far remote from now;
They are too far to be yearned for much. [5]

I dare not reason blot and people hate,
Restraining myself to be upright.
Suffering throes, I change not my stand,
But cling to my brave fortitude bright.
Winding my way up northward to Ying,
I see the sun doth set in the west.
To ease my dole and cheer my sorrow,
I could but expect my final rest. [6]

The epiphonema runneth thus:
Gush forth in expanse, the Yuan and Hsiang,
Flowing apart with turbulent dash;
Their deep streams silent are far off stretched
From winding sources of mighty swash.
With mine intrinsic core and feelings,
I cannot find in any one my peer.
Pêh-loh is departed long ago;
How is the steed to show its powers sheer?
Men's lives are each by fortune ordained;
They are all severally destined.
With heart fixed and intents wide focussed,
What do I fear, for what am chagrined?
Harbouring grief and distress ceaseless,
I do lament forever and aye.
The world confounded kenneth me not;

人心不可谓兮。
知死不可让,
愿勿爱兮。
明告君子:
吾将以为类兮!

九章

People could be spoken and told to nay.

I know inevitable to me is

Death now; this life I cherish no more.

Let me tell Thee in plain words, Peng Yen:

I would Thy trod way take for my lore. (7)

四　惜往日

惜往日之曾信兮，
受命诏以昭时。
奉先功以照下兮，
明法度之嫌疑。
国富强而法立兮，
属贞臣而日竢。
秘密事之载心兮，
虽过失犹弗治。

心纯庞而不泄兮，
遭谗人而嫉之。
君含怒而待臣兮，
不清澈其然否。
蔽晦君之聪明兮，
虚惑误又以欺。
弗参验以考实兮，
远迁臣而弗思。
信谗谀之溷浊兮，
盛气志而过之。

何贞臣之无辜兮！
被离谤而见尤。
惭光景之诚信兮，
身幽隐而备之。

4 Pining My Past Days[1]

I pine my being much intrusted in the past,

For having ta'en decrees to make policies clear.

Keeping precedent usance to lighten the people.

I clarified obscurities of statutes blear.

The state was rich and strong then, laws were well set up,

Affairs in trustworthy hands, the crown free from care;

State secrets were nearly hidden in my bosom;

Though I should be blamed sometimes, yet my lord did spare. [2]

With heart pure, nobly turned, and close in confidence,

I was by envious detractors backbitten;

My masters sovereign grew wroth at their liegeman,

Finding not out if the charge be by truth ridden.

Shading over my lords' wisdom and discretion,

They misgave, puzzled and cheated them, better to plot.

Without confirming facts to test out their falsehoods,

They their repelled liege vassal forsook and forgot.

Believing in aspersions and sawders muddling,

They, puffed up vehemently, persisted to sot. [3]

How faultlessly their faithful liege himself doth hold!

Yet he is vilified and then censured with blame.

Ashamed for being slandered inadvertently,

An eremite I become, but still guard my name.

临沅湘之玄渊兮，
遂自忍而沉流？
卒没身而绝名兮，
惜壅君之不昭。

君无度而弗察兮，
使芳草为薮幽。
焉舒情而抽信兮，
恬死亡而不聊！
独鄣壅而蔽隐兮，
使贞臣为无由。
闻百里之为虏兮，
伊尹烹于庖厨。
吕望屠于朝歌兮，
宁戚歌而饭牛。
不逢汤武与桓缪兮，
世孰云而知之？
吴信谗而弗味兮，
子胥死而后忧。
介子忠而立枯兮，
文君寤而追求。
封介山而为之禁兮，
报大德之优游。
思久故之亲身兮，
因缟素而哭之。
或忠信而死节兮，
或訑谩而不疑。
弗省察而按实兮，

九章

Facing the limpid depths of the streams Yuan and Hsiang,

I will depress myself to plunge into the waves.

Dead by drowning and putting my name to an end,

I sorely pine my duped kings kenning not their knaves. [4]

My lords aware not of how things stand about them,

Do make fair herbs darkened round the swamp tract evolve.

How I express my feelings and mine earnest show,

By going to my quietus with calm resolve!

Alone, in isolation and shadowed from light,

Their vassal loyal is denied access to them.

It is well known that pêh-lih had been a captive,

And Ih Yün cooked as a humble kitchen menial,

Leü Wang was hired at a butchery in Tsau-kuh,

And Nien Tsi was singing a song feeding his cow;

If they met not their chiefs Taung and Wuh, Hwan and Mo,

Is the world to know of their eminent deeds, how?

Wuh-tsa believed calumny and distinguished not;

When Tse-süe died, the state lacking him to grief came.

Chiêh-tse's loyalty forgot, he was burnt to death;

Marquis Wen regretting, himself did deeply blame:

He ordered Mount Chiêh exempt from firewood lopping,

To show his grateful thanks for Chiêh's devotion;

Thinking of his old-time follower's sacrifice,

He wore sackcloth and mourned with heartfelt emotion. [5]

There were those who with fidelity and troth died,

There were deceivers who beguiled with credit fine;

Without descrying clear truth and confirming facts,

听谗人之虚辞。
芳与泽其杂糅兮，
孰申旦而别之？
何芳草之早夭兮，
微霜降而下戒！
谅聪不明而蔽壅兮，
使谗谀而日得。

自前世之嫉贤兮，
谓蕙若其不可佩。
妒佳冶之芬芳兮，
嫫母姣而自好。
虽有西施之美容兮，
谗妒入以自代。
愿陈情以白行兮，
得罪过之不意。
情冤见之日明兮，
如列宿之错置。

乘骐骥而驰骋兮，
无辔衔而自载；
乘泛泭以下流兮，
无舟楫而自备。
背法度而心治兮，
辟与此其无异。
宁溘死而流亡兮，
恐祸殃之有再。
不毕辞以赴渊兮，
惜壅君之不识。

Liege masters oft listed defamers' lies malign.

The fair is confoundedly mixed up with the foul;

Who is to discriminate 'twixt them which is which?

How the green herbs do wither ere their timely end;

The early frost descendeth and they fall prickly!

In faith, kings' wisdom opaque shadowed and duped

Doth make traducings and cringings prevail daily. [6]

Since former days the virtuous are gibed with grudge;

Nor coumarous nor pollias deemed pendants meet.

Envious of the loveliness of damsels fair,

The ugly hag doth boast of her gracefulness feat.

Spiteful of See-sze's beauty superexcellent,

Scandal and jealousy are sure selves to commend.

Wishing to lay mine heart ope and mine acts make clear,

I got unexpectedly into fault instead.

The facts revealed and injuries sustained are plain

Like spangling stars o'erspread aloft above mine head. [7]

Driving their coursers fleeting to gallop forward,

They make no use of bridle and bit for their harness;

Riding log timbers hitched up to float down waters,

They take as their conveyance no boats nor barges.

Contrary to methodic ways, self-reliant, —

This is how they direct the state's perilous course.

I would prefer to perish swiftly and vanish,

Fearing calamities twain would my drear doom seal.

I finish not my words for hasting to the stream,

Lamenting my duped kings list not to mine appeal. [8]

五　橘颂

后皇嘉树，
橘徕服兮。
受命不迁，
生南国兮。
深固难徙，
更壹志兮。
绿叶素荣，
纷其可喜兮。
曾枝剡棘，
圆果抟兮。
青黄杂糅，
文章烂兮。
精色内白，
类任道兮。
纷缊宜修，
姱而不丑兮。

嗟尔幼志，
有以异兮。
独立不迁，
岂不可喜兮？
深固难徙，
廓其无求兮。
苏世独立，

5　Ode to the Orange

Orange, fair tree of Heaven and Earth,
Hail to thee, here habiteth thou!
Endowed the trait not to be moved,[1]
Thou dost in this southern land grow,
Steadfast and withal immovable,
In purpose and intent fixed through,
With verdant leaves and blossoms white,
Delightfully flourishing, ho!
Thickset in brambles, prickly in twigs,
With fruits globular and rotund;
Green when unripe, yellow, mellow,
They from the foliage peep out so,
Of triple snowlike interior,
Like unto those virtuous, pure;
To be pruned yearly, as if purged oft,
Being kept trim, chaste and demure.[2]

Heigh to thy fine youthful intents!
They are from others so diverse.
To be independent, unmoved,
Is it delighting or the reverse?
Steadfast and withal immovable,
Immeasurably unconstrained;
Awaking the world and unbound,

横而不流兮。
闭心自慎，
终不失过兮。
秉德无私，
参天地兮。
愿岁并谢，
与长友兮。
淑离不淫，
梗其有理兮。
年岁虽少，
可师长兮。
行比伯夷，
置以为像兮。

九章

Free and easy, but self-contained;

Thou holdest thy heart with staid prudence,

Without falling into default;

Keeping to thy virtues public

Which peer earth's expanse and heaven's vault.

I wish thou would last with the year

Livelong and deign to befriend me.

Thou art beautiful and temperate,

Both rigorous and versatile.

Although youthful thou dost appear,

Yet thou art fit my teacher to be.

Thy practices are like Pêh-yih's;

As mine image I would take thee. [3]

六　悲回风

悲回风之摇蕙兮，
心冤结而内伤。
物有微而陨性兮，
声有隐而先倡。

夫何彭咸之造思兮，
暨志介而不忘。
万变其情岂可盖兮？
孰虚伪之可长？
鸟兽鸣以号群兮，
草苴比而不芳。
鱼葺鳞以自别兮，
蛟龙隐其文章。
故荼荠不同亩兮，
兰茝幽而独芳。
惟佳人之永都兮，
更统世而自贶。
眇远志之所及兮，
怜浮云之相羊。
介眇志之所惑兮，
窃赋诗之所明。
惟佳人之独怀兮，
折若椒以自处。
曾歔欷之嗟嗟兮，

6 Lamenting on Whirlblasts[1]

Lamenting on whirlblasts shaking the coumarou,

Mine heart, unjustly injured, hath been wounded sore.

The thing marking the first signal would lose its life;

The incipient sound signeth its start to roar. [2]

Lo, how I made up my mind to follow Peng Yen;

My firm resolve was fixt; I have never forgot.

Through numerous changes, how could mine aim be concealed?

Were it fickle, how could it last to decide my lot?

Birds and beasts cry to gather up in flocks and herds;

Rushes and weeds waxing rank and fat are not sweet;

Fishes their scales fold to differ from one another;

Dragons and dragonets hide their elegance feat.

Sonchus and capsella grow not on the same plot;

Angelica and eupatory singly smell.

Thinking that Peng's example will remain fore'er fair,

Examine I these two reigns: no second I can tell.

Eyeing my distant aim of following his suit,

I pity mine own thoughts which are like fleeing clouds.

For fear of mine intents going astray the while,

I have set forth my purpose in several poems. [3]

Thinking but of the Beauteous One all along,

I pluck odorous peppers myself to dispose;

Ofttimes I heave long-drawn sighs again and again,

独隐伏而思虑。
涕泣交而凄凄兮,
思不眠以至曙。
终长夜之曼曼兮,
掩此哀而不去。
寤从容以周流兮,
聊逍遥以自恃。
伤太息之愍怜兮,
气于邑而不可止。
糺思心以为纕兮,
编愁苦以为膺。
折若木以蔽光兮,
随飘风之所仍。
存髣髴而不见兮,
心踊跃其若汤。
抚佩衽以案志兮,
超惘惘而遂行。
岁曶曶其若颓兮,
时亦冉冉而将至。
蘋蘅槁而节离兮,
芳已歇而不比。
怜思心之不可惩兮,
证此言之不可聊。
宁溘死而流亡兮,
不忍为此之常愁。
孤子吟而抆泪兮,
放子出而不还。
孰能思而不隐兮,

九章

Alone, crouching and cogitative, sans repose.

With tears streaming down and feeling wretched meantime,

I remain wide awake thinking till dawn doth break;

Lasting the whole livelong night through with repining,

I try without success my deep dole to forsake.

A little doze after dawn, and I would wander out,

In order to ramble along my grief to dispel;

But I break into sighs while thinking of these throes,

Being choked in breath and unable my sobs to quell.

I twist pensive thoughts of mine into wearing bands,

And twine miseries to braid my breast covercloth.

I lop off a *ruoh*-wood branch to shade me from sun,

And follow wherever the whirlblasts list to blow.

Keeping hazy images in mind but unseeing,

I feel mine heart pulsating like water boiling.

Stroking bandages and lapels to palm mine aims,

I expect to set out in airily roving.

The years seem to be slipping fast and sinking low;

Mine old age thus appeareth to approach soon now.

Cyperus and asarum are withered and fallen,

Their aromata have become spent, their joints rent.

I grieve my ruminations cannot be chastised

To be stopt, nor my set aim in poetry be annulled.

I would rather hasten to die and vanish off,

Than to let this bruised heart of mine clotted with gore.

The orphaned one moaneth his plaint, wiping his tears;

The exiled one is gone out to return no more.

Who can muse on these and be not stricken with pangs,

昭彭咸之所闻？

登石峦以远望兮，
路眇眇之默默。
入景响之无应兮，
闻省想而不可得。
愁郁郁之无快兮，
居戚戚而不可解。
心鞿羁而不开兮，
气缭转而自缔。
穆眇眇之无垠兮，
莽芒芒之无仪。
声有隐而相感兮，
物有纯而不可为。
邈蔓蔓之不可量兮，
缥绵绵之不可纡。
愁悄悄之常悲兮，
翩冥冥之不可娱。
凌大波而流风兮，
托彭咸之所居。
上高岩之峭岸兮，
处雌蜺之标颠。
据青冥而摅虹兮，
遂儵忽而扪天。
吸湛露之浮凉兮，
漱凝霜之雰雰。
依风穴以自息兮，
忽倾寤以婵媛。

So as to do what Peng Yen had anciently done?[4]

I mount a rocky mountain cliff to look afar;

The way to it is void of human shapes and sounds;

Into my sight no trace of influence doth come;

Nor voice e'er remembered or thought of could be heard.

Woes melancholic are depressing without cheer;

Dolorous moments suffer rues' writhing and gird;

Mine heart, harnessed and bridled, is restricted by bonds;

My breath twirleth and turneth itself to wreathe.

The silence deep seemeth o'erwhelming and profound;

The infinite expanse is boundlessly immense;

The signal sound inceptive respondeth to me;

My life thus signified would be at last undone.

So far remotely it would vanish away hence;

So fleetingly gone, ne'er to come back any time;

As anguishing maketh me lamentable always,

Sinking into oblivion is my sure doom;

Plunging over huge waves and following wind gusts,

I would abide at Peng Yen's deep water abode. [5]

I climb a precipice steep of a lofty peak,

To where the she-rainbow hath its curvature top;

Leaning 'gainst the blue to eject the he-rainbow,

I then do quickly heaven above with gentleness stroke.

Imbibing the light coolness of heavy dew drops,

I gargle the o'erspreading particles of frozen frost;

Reclining by the aperture of winds to rest,

I suddenly shift and wake, and am drawn by sights. [6]

冯昆仑以澂雾兮，
隐浸山以清江。
惮涌湍之礚礚兮，
听波声之汹汹。
纷容容之无经兮，
罔芒芒之无纪。
轧洋洋之无从兮，
驰委移之焉止。
漂翻翻其上下兮，
翼遥遥其左右。
氾潏潏其前后兮，
伴张弛之信期。
观炎气之相仍兮，
窥烟液之所积。
悲霜雪之俱下兮，
听潮水之相击。

借光景以往来兮，
施黄棘之枉策。
求介子之所存兮，
见伯夷之放迹。
心调度而弗去兮，
刻著志之无适。
曰：吾怨往昔之所冀兮，
悼来者之愁愁。

浮江淮而入海兮，
从子胥而自适。

On the Mountains Quen-lung I clear the mists opaque,

On the Ming Mountain I clear the Ming Stream luteous;

Wonder-struck at mad cataracts dashing at rocks,

I list to high waves torrential roar and resound.

Ultra-diverse and multifarious in forms,

I ken not how boundlessly, vastly the waves heave.

To and fro toss they one another forever;

Swiftly they hie from crest to crest without a pause.

Floating high top over high top never to stop,

Flanking from all sides towards the e'erchanging centre,

Streaming fluently back and forth with might and main,

They wax and wane in perpetual ebb and flow.

Seeing warm air doth alternately come and go,

I notice clouds and rains collect and then disperse;

Feeling depressed for frost and snow both falling down,

I hear tidal currents progress and then recede. [7]

Borrowing days and nights from nature to go and come,

I lash swift time with a pricked twig to speed its race;

I pay visit to Chiêh-tse's famed spot of remains,

And see the relics hallowed of Pêh-yih's scape days.

I yearn towards their modes and calibres with love,

And carve my mind with their memorial events,

Saying: "I cannot but at mine expectations past pine,

And feel lamentable over calamitous bents. " [8]

I float on the River and Hwai downstream to the sea,

And then on Tse-süeh's spirit make my doleful call;

望大河之洲渚兮，
悲申徒之抗迹。
骤谏君而不听兮，
任重石之何益？
心絓结而不解兮，
思蹇产而不释。

Tracing upstream while seeing the great Ho's islets,

I sorrow o'er Sun-duh's elevated deeds all.

Remonstrating oft with his king without avail,

What was the use of his bearing a stone to drown?

Mine heart, hampered and twinged, is tense with anxiety;

My thoughts with knotted coils are entwined, tightly drawn. (9)

远　游

DISTANT
WANDERINGS

远　游

悲时俗之迫阨兮，
愿轻举而远游。
质菲薄而无因兮，
焉托乘而上浮？
遭沉浊而污秽兮，
独郁结其谁语？
夜耿耿而不寐兮，
魂茕茕而至曙。
惟天地之无穷兮，
哀人生之长勤。
往者余弗及兮，
来者吾不闻。
步徙倚而遥思兮，
怊惝怳而永怀。
意荒忽而流荡兮，
心愁凄而增悲。
神儵忽而不反兮，
形枯槁而独留。
内惟省以端操兮，
求正气之所由。
漠虚静以恬愉兮，
澹无为而自得。
闻赤松之清尘兮，
愿承风乎遗则。

远游

Distant Wanderings

Sad for the wringing and blockade of the crowd,

I wish to rise aloft and wander afar.

Weak in agility and without the means,

What shall I ride, for uplifting, as my car?[1]

Suffering from the taint of mud and slime[2],

Depressed and lorn[3], to whom could I tell the matter?

Awake and restless[3] through the livelong night,

I mope about till dawn my nerves doth shatter.

Seeing the boundlessness of heaven and earth,

I grieve that life is full of sorrow and pain.

The bygones are no more within my reach;

What is coming I cannot as yet attain.

With hesitative steps and thoughts remote,

Dejected, untuned, I am burdened in mind.

As my mind is in a haze and shifting still,

Mine heart, afflicted, is with more sorrows lined.

My spirit flitteth off and returneth not;

My form, withering, is left alone indeed.

I probe myself for behaving rigidly,

Seeking only from loftiness[4] to proceed.

And placid, vacant, free from likes and dislikes,

I prefer to be quiescently inert. [5]

Hearing of the high sereneness of Tsê-soon[6],

I wish to trace his steps when he was alert.

贵真人之休德兮，
美往世之登仙。
与化去而不见兮，
名声著而日延。

奇傅说之托辰星兮，
羡韩众之得一。
形穆穆以浸远兮，
离人群而遁逸。
因气变而遂曾举兮，
忽神奔而鬼怪。
时髣髴以遥见兮，
精皎皎以往来。
超氛埃而淑邮兮，
终不反其故都。
免众患而不惧兮，
世莫知其所知。
恐天时之代序兮，
耀灵晔而西征。
微霜降而下沦兮，
悼芳草之先蘦。
聊仿佯而逍遥兮，
永历年而无成。
谁可与玩斯遗芳兮，
长乡风而舒情。
高阳邈以远兮，
余将焉所程。
重曰：

远游

Setting store by the supreme men's fine virtues[7],
I esteem those who turned fairies in the past.
Metamorphosed, having vanished and invisible,
They have become renowned with names that last.

Wondering at Fuh Yüeh who rideth the Tsen star[8],
I admire Hang Ts'oon[9] that hath gained purity.
With gracious shapes, still farther gone from earth,
They have left the crowd and escaped laity.
Being transformed and thus able to rise aloft,
They appear, like gods or sprites, abruptly to sight.
Often distantly seen but not quite visible,[10]
Along they speed, trackless, in flashes of light.
Without a whiff of dust, between dales of fay
They flit, but come not to the capital at all.
Free from all cares and devoid of any dread,
Unknown to the world is whither they would call.
For fear lest the seasons would alternate soon,
I hie west shined on by the great luminary.
Hoar frost beginneth to descend on the plain;
I mourn the herbage fresh declining early[11].
Wandering about and rambling round the while,
I dissipate my years having done nothing.
With whom may I gaze with love these residues green[11]?
Oft in breeze I free my feelings in the morning.
Old *T'ih* Kao-yang[12] hath too remotely gone;
For whom should I mine arduous efforts essay?[13]
Further, this is to be added:[14]

春秋忽其不淹兮，

奚久留此故居？

轩辕不可攀援兮，

吾将从王乔而娱戏。

餐六气而饮沆瀣兮，

漱正阳而含朝霞。

保神明之清澄兮，

精气入而粗秽除。

顺凯风以从游兮，

至南巢而壹息。

见王子而宿之兮，

审壹气之和德。

曰："道可受兮而不可传，

其小无内兮，其大无垠。

毋滑而魂兮，彼将自然；

壹气孔神兮，于中夜存。

虚以待之兮，无为之先；

庶类以成兮，此德之门。"

闻至贵而遂徂兮，

忽乎吾将行。

仍羽人于丹丘兮，

留不死之旧乡。

朝濯发于汤谷兮，

夕晞余身兮九阳。

吸飞泉之微液兮，

怀琬琰之华英。

玉色頩以脕颜兮，

精醇粹而始壮。

As the flight of time is swift and not to be held,

Why should I in this old town longer stay?

Incapable of being led aloft by Hsien-yuan[12],[15]

I shall go after Wang Jao[16] and be full gay.

I draw the "six airs"[17], — the midnight one of North drink,

The glow of dawn imbibe, South noon air gargle.

Thus, I would hold my soul in purity rare,

The pith of Shade and Light purging the dross out. [18]

Riding the southward zephyr I set forth,

Till I come to Nan-ts'iao[19] where I am to rest.

Seeing the fairy prince to pay respect,

I inquire of him how the "airs" would come to zest.

"The way could be had," quoth he, "but not shown;

Minute, 'tis without an in, grand sans bound;

Confuse they soul naught, it mayety grow natural;

Fill it with 'airs', some night their union would come round;

Keep vacant, wait for it, inertness would ensue;

All lives prosper because of this primal spring."[20]

Hearing of this verity, it to pursue,

In great dispatch now, I have to be going.

I visit flying fairies at nightless T'an-chiu[21],

And remain in that etherealized clime.

In the morn, in Taung Vale[22] I wash mine hair,

At dusk I bare myself in nine Suns' shine[22],

Drinking the vital elixir of Jetting Vale[23],

I keep in my bosom nonpareil gems twain[24]

The lustre pink of the gems fuseth my face;

My spirit beginneth to be pure amain.

质销铄以汋约兮，
神要眇以淫放。

嘉南州之炎德兮，
丽桂树之冬荣。
山萧条而无兽兮，
野寂漠其无人。
载营魄而登霞兮，
掩浮云而上征。
命天阍其开关兮，
排阊阖而望予。
召丰隆使先导兮，
问太微之所居。
集重阳入帝宫兮，
造旬始而观清都。
朝发轫于太仪兮，
夕始临乎于微闾。
屯余车之万乘兮，
纷容与而并驰。
驾八龙之婉婉兮，
载云旗之委蛇。
建雄虹之采旄兮，
五色杂而炫耀。
服偃蹇以低昂兮，
骖连蜷以骄骜。
骑胶葛以杂乱兮，
班漫衍而方行。
撰余辔而正策兮，

远游

My stuff molten becometh soft and frail;
My soul, refined and blown, profound and vibrant. (25)

I hail the fiery virtue of South State,
And laud the cinnamon in winter verdant. (26)
The mountains desolate are without wild beasts;
In the solitary wild there are no men.
Springing from earth up lightly for the distance, (27)
Above the white lumps I set out from a ben.
I call to Heaven's Porter to ope his portal,
To push apart Sky-gates (28) and wait for me. (29)
I summon Feng-loon (30) as my van-courier,
To lead me to where T'ai-wei's ten stars (30) be.
Coming through the azure to twice bright Heaven (31)
And entering His Supremacy's palace,
I hold an interview with Tsin-sze (32) the God,
Then take a round about the sacred place (33).
Starting from His palatial court (34) in the morn,
I arrive at Mount Ee-vei-lü (35) after noon.
By chariots ten thousand (36), fore, aft, abreast,
Preceeded, followed, flanked on the way am I.
I drive eight dragons that speed winding about,
With cloud ensigns waving alongside, that fly,
And the he-rainbow decked with feather pennants
Flourishing its variegated glory.
Two dragons in the middle prance up and down;
Two side ones curl their lengths and romp wildly.
The chariots by scores of batches gather;

吾将过乎句芒。

历太皓以右转兮，

前飞廉以启路。

阳杲杲其未光兮，

凌天地以径度。

风伯为余先驱兮，

氛埃辟而清凉。

凤凰翼其承旂兮，

遇蓐收乎西皇。

揽彗星以为烟兮，

举斗柄以为麾。

叛陆离其上下兮，

游惊雾之流波。

时暧曃其曊莽兮，

召玄武而奔属。

后文昌使掌行兮，

选署众神以并毂。

路漫漫其修远兮，

徐弭节而高厉。

左雨师使径侍兮，

右雷公而为卫。

欲度世以忘归兮，

意恣睢以担挢。

内欣欣而自美兮，

聊媮娱以淫乐。

涉青云以泛滥游兮，

远游

In ranks and rows they continue to rumble on.

Keeping my bridle in front and the whip straight up,

I first pass by the Lord of Wood, Kur-moun[37],

Then God T'ai-hao, the Great Light, and then turn right[38],

With fleet-footed Fei-lian[39] to open my path.

The blazing Sun hath not yet shown his full light.

To shine on heaven and earth with length and breadth.

The Principal of Winds, as mine harbinger,

Bloweth off gas and dust; all's clear and cool now.

Shielded and flanked by phoenixes on both sides,

I meet Ruo-sur, the Gold Lord, at Sao-hao's court. [40]

Holding the comet as my streaming banner,

I raise for waving pennant the stem of the Dipper,

I rove in the currents of the shaken mist,

Cleaving the pearly waves to range high and low.

Often there are the gloaming, murky shades,

For I call to my train the God of Shadow. [41]

I ordain many gods to ride in the march,

With Wen-tsoun[42] to oversee and bring up the rear.

The way of progress is long drawn and far-off;

The train ascendeth and goeth on in good cheer.

On the left the Chief of Rain[43] attendeth me,

On the right the Lord of Thunder[43] giveth guard.

Wishing to depart from this world for aye,

My mind is rampant on rising aloft hard.

I am full glad at heart and self-rejoicing,

Overwhelmed by and buoyant with delight.

Entering the blue, I look about; in a squint

忽临睨夫旧乡。

仆夫怀余心悲兮,

边马顾而不行。

思旧故以想象兮,

长太息而掩涕。

泛容与而遥举兮,

聊抑志而自弭。

指炎神而直驰兮,

吾将往乎南疑。

览方外之荒忽兮,

沛濛濊而自浮。

祝融戒而跸御兮,

腾告鸾鸟迎宓妃。

张《咸池》奏《承云》兮,

二女御《九韶》歌。

使湘灵鼓瑟兮,

令海若舞冯夷。

玄螭虫象并出进兮,

形蝹虬而逶蛇。

雌蜺便娟以增挠兮,

鸾鸟轩翥而翔飞。

音乐博衍无终极兮,

焉乃逝以徘徊。

舒并节以驰骛兮,

逴绝垠乎寒门。

轶迅风于清源兮,

从颛顼乎增冰。

历玄冥以邪径兮,

The homeland suddenly cometh into sight.

My driver longeth and mine heart groweth sad;

Two side horses, dazed, gaze back and fail to go.

Thinking of kins and friends and imagining,

I heave a sigh and shade my face as tears flow.

Since I have taken to roving high and far,

I might as well restrain myself and calm be.

Toward divine Yen, God of Fiery Virtue [44],

I to the sunny South now speed directly.

Seeing the fairy world in a radiant flux,

I soar above the expanse of the South Sea. [45]

Tsuo-yung the Lord of Fire [46] cometh to keep watch,

Sending off Phoenix to greet hither Fwu-fei [47].

Performing the pieces *Yen-tze* and *Tsen-yün* [48],

Two Genü fair also play *Jer-zau* and sing; [49]

I ask the Spirit of Hsiang to pluck the zithern, [50]

And have the Gods of Sea and the River [51] dance.

Dragonets, luteous, strange, turn in and out;

They wriggle, in flexures whirl and then advance.

The she-rainbow with comely grace doth arch;

The phoenixes arise to hover and fly;

The music is high-flushed and endlessly drawn out; [52]

Then I retire to fix my course by-and-by.

Loosing my reins to speed up the progress grand,

I have reached at the horizon the Arctic Gate. [53]

My car outstripping the swift blasts at Tsing-yuan [54]

I come to Tsuan-shiuh the old *t'ih* at Tsen-p'ing.

Having gone by Yuan-ming, now from the North

乘间维以反顾。

召黔嬴而见之兮，

为余先乎平路。

经营四方兮，

周流六漠。

上至列缺兮，

降望大壑。

下峥嵘而无地兮，

上寥廓而无天。

视倏忽而无见兮，

听惝恍而无闻。

超无为以至清兮，

与泰初而为邻。

远游

I look back through heaven's spaces, at earth's margins.

I summon Jê-lê, the God of Nature himself[55],

Asking him the broad way to spread for me.

Then I ramble all around the four extremes,

And wander about the six spaces immense,

Up to where lightning swift its zigzags whippeth,

And down to overlook the unfathomed deep[56].

Below, it is bottomless and sans the ground[57];

Above, it is far-away and sans the sky[57];

To look out, it is fleetingly without sight[58];

To listen, it is emptily without sound[58]

Superseding inertness and arriving

At utter purity,

I come to inhere very next neighbouring

To Primitive Prime. [59]

卜　居

DIVINING TO
KNOW WHERE
I SHOULD STAY

卜　居

　　屈原既放,三年不得复见。竭知尽忠,而蔽障于谗,心烦虑乱,不知所从。乃往见太卜郑詹尹,曰:"余有所疑,愿因先生决之。"詹尹乃端策拂龟,曰:"君将何以教之?"

　　屈原曰:

　　"吾宁悃悃款款

　　朴以忠乎?

　　将送往劳来

　　斯无穷乎?

　　宁诛锄草茅

　　以力耕乎?

　　将游大人

　　以成名乎?

　　宁正言不讳

　　以危身乎?

　　将从俗富贵

　　以媮生乎?

　　宁超然高举

　　以保真乎?

　　将呢訾栗斯

　　喔咿嚅唲

　　以事妇人乎?

卜居

Divining to Know Where I Should Stay

Chü yuan, being rejected, for three years[1] could not see his king. Striving his wits to devote his loyalty, he is yet insulated by calumny; confused and perplexed, he doth not know what to do. So he went to the Grand Soothsayer Ts'eng Tsan-yün[2] and said to him, "I am in a fix of doubt and wish to decide my course with Thy Honour's aid." Tsan-yün then adjusted his achilleas and rubbed his emyd shell[3] saying, "What dost thou have to teach me?"

Chü Yuan said,

"Would I be rather genuinely candid

And true at heart in my loyal devotion?

Shall I have much ado in pleasing people

And waiting on their whims with my supple notion?[4]

Would I prefer to clear off weeds and shrubs

And toil with labour[5] tilling the soil for grain?

Shall I keep company with magisters[6]

To make myself well-known with insipid main?

Would I rather speak out boldly what I think,

Though that would peril myself in the end?[7]

Shall I play the common in being rich and high,

To steal a vulgar life that could no worth lend?

Would I rather soar aloft and over all[8],

My pure integrity to uphold and defend?

Shall I wheedle by putting on a cautious air,

Smile forcedly, affect and blindly follow,

To attend upon a woman[9] at her conceits?

宁廉洁正直，

以自清乎？

将突梯滑稽，

如脂如韦，

以洁楹乎？

宁昂昂若千里之驹乎？

将泛泛若水中之凫，

与波上下，

偷以全吾躯乎？

宁与骐骥亢轭乎？

将随驽马之迹乎？

宁与黄鹄比翼乎？

将与鸡鹜争食乎？

此孰吉孰凶？

何去何从？

世溷浊而不清，

蝉翼为重，

千钧为轻；

黄钟毁弃，

瓦釜雷鸣；

谗人高张，

贤士无名。

吁嗟默默兮，

谁知吾之廉贞！"

詹尹乃释策而谢，曰：

"夫尺有所短，

寸有所长；

Would I rather be austere and strict with myself,

Earnestly upright and full of clear heart beats?[10]

Shall I be slippery and dubious

Like coagulant swine fat or tanned ox hide,

Ready to round a square for any with pay?

Would I rather uplift mine head in pride

Like a colt that runneth a thousand *lih* a day?

Shall I be like the mallards on the water,

Rising and falling with the waves they float on,

To steal a life and keep intact my body?

Would I rather the blooded horses rival?

Shall I pursue the tracks of jades old and skinny?

Would I rather with the yellow cygnus[11] fly?

Shall I vie with hens and ducks in picking feed?

Which of these are auspicious and which evil;

What should I leave out and what take in deed?

Confused and muddled, the world is topsy-turvy:[12]

Thirty thousand catties are regarded light,

A wing of the cicada is deemed weighty;[13]

The golden bell is smashed quite and scrapped,

While the earthen *phu* doth roar like thunder-claps;[14]

The man of virtue is roundly bullied down,

The calumniator is donning the crown![15]

Alack-a-day! As I keep silence the while,

Who kenneth my rectitude and integrity?"

Tsan-yün then laid down his achilleas and excused himself,

"A foot is sometimes inadequate in length;

An inch mayeth happen to be a little too long;

物有所不足，

智有所不明，

数有所不逮，

神有所不通。

用君之心，

行君之意，

龟策诚不能知事。"

卜居

Things natural may fall too short of their use;

The intellect of man canneth not always con;

My skill in piercing matters is unfit now;

The depth of wisdom I fail to fathom;

Make use of thy native quick wits;

Carry out thy wishes at will;

The emyd shell and the achilleas

Could really not know thy inquiry. " [16]

渔　父
THE FISHERMAN

渔 父

屈原既放,游于江潭,行吟泽畔,颜色憔悴,形容枯槁。渔父见而问之曰:"子非三闾大夫与? 何故至于斯?"

屈原曰:"举世皆浊我独清,

众人皆醉我独醒,

是以见放。"

渔父曰:"圣人不凝滞于物,

而能与世推移。

世人皆浊,

何不淈其泥而扬其波?

众人皆醉,

何不哺其糟而歠其醨?

何故深思高举,

自令放为?"

屈原曰:"吾闻之,

新沐者必弹冠,

新浴者必振衣。

渔父

The Fisherman

Chü Yuan, being rejected, wandered by the side of the River depths[1], sighing while roving along marshes, worn out in complexion and withered in looks. The fisherman saw and asked him, "Art thou not the Lord of the Tri-Lane Portals[2]? Wherefore hast thou come hither?"

Chü Yuan replied,

"People are all muddled but I alone am clear;

They are all drunk while I am sober and drear:

That is why I am rejected,"

The fisherman said,

"The sagacious are not stuck on things,

But could get along patly with the world

By fitting with their surroundings.

If the general run is muddled,

Why not confound the mud and raise the waves clear?

If all the people have gone dead drunk,

Why not eat the dregs and drink the dilution therefrom?

Why dost thou think so intently and fly thus aloft

To let thyself rejected?"

Chü Yuan replied,

"I have heard,

Those who have newly had taken their baths

Are sure to beat their hats and their clothes shake.

安能以身之察察，

受物之汶汶者乎？

宁赴湘流，

葬于江鱼之腹中。

安能以皓皓之白，

而蒙世俗之尘埃乎？"

渔父莞尔而笑，鼓枻而去，乃歌曰：

"沧浪之水清兮，

可以濯吾缨；

沧浪之水浊兮，

可以濯吾足。"

遂去，不复与言。

渔父

How could I stand, with all my purity,

All the blot and shame I am forced to take?

I would rather go to the Hsiang Stream

And bury myself in the bellies of the fishes.

How could I bear, with mine immaculateness,

All the filth and dirt of this nasty world?"

The fisherman showed a little smile, tapped the side of the

boat with his oar and rowed away, singing meanwhile,

"When the water of Tsoung-loung is limpid,

I could wash mine hat cords with it;

When the water of Tsoung-loung is turbid,

I could wash my twain feet with it. " [3]

He went away, speaking no more with the outcast.

增 补 篇

[说明]

　　《英译屈原诗选》是译者在 1974—1978 年历时四年多完稿的，迨至 1996 年才得以按照他生前的亲自定稿付排出版。此书目录中"《九章》（选六篇）"，说明当初有三篇未译。译者于 1997 年逝世，其后在整理遗物时，发现他在 1986—1987 年期间又译有《九章》中的其余三篇——《惜诵》、《抽思》、《思美人》，庶几《九章》终于译全。另外，他还译了《招魂》。现在把它们作为增补篇以飨读者。

——编者

惜　　诵
PINING　PLAINT

惜 诵

惜诵以致愍兮，
发愤以抒情。
所非忠而言之兮，
指苍天以为正。

令五帝*以折中兮
戒六神与响服；
俾山川以备御兮，
命咎繇使听直。

竭忠诚而事君兮，
反离群而赘肬。
望儇媚以背众兮，
待明君其知之。

言与行其可迹兮，
情与貌其不变，
故相臣莫若君兮，——
所以证之不远。

Pining Plaint

I grieve with pain to voice my heart-felt thoughts,
Express high complaint to show my feelings.
If what I say be not conformed to truth,
Let Heaven be the witness to my dealings.

I ask Gods of the Five Quarters* to hold the pith,
And Six primeval Deities th'umpires be;
I bid sprites of all the mounts and streams be th'jury,
And order Gao-yao to preside as judge.

I strive with fidelity to serve my king,
But am treated as a wen and ousted out lone.
I care not how to wield sly wiles with th'rabble,
Awaiting th'sovran wise for my faith to be known.

My words and deeds are traceable to their cause,
My heart and aspects would remain all the same, —
In knowing th'courtiers, none is apt as th'king,
For by his side, quite near at hand is his aim.

---

* Gods of the five quarters: God of the East, Tai Hoi(太皞), God of the
South, Yeh Ti(炎帝), God of the West, Sao Hoi(少昊), God of the
North, Tsuan Shuo(颛顼) and God of the Center, Hwang Ti(黄帝). Six
Primeval Deities: they are Heaven, Earth and the Seasons. Gao Yao(咎繇
or 皋陶): the legendary chief of an ancient eastern state elected by Ti Suen
(帝舜,2255 −2206 B. C.) to be his Chief of Justice.

吾谊先君而后身兮，
羌众人之所仇也。
专惟君而无他兮，
又众兆之所仇也。

一心而不豫兮，
羌不可保也；
疾亲君而无他兮，
有招祸之道也。

思君其莫我忠兮，
忽忘身之贱贫。
事君而不贰兮，
迷不知宠之门。

忠何罪以遇罚兮，
亦非余之所志也。
行不群以颠越兮，
又众兆之所咍也。

纷逢尤以离谤兮，
謇不可释也。
情沉抑而不达兮，
又蔽而莫之白也。

心郁邑余侘傺兮，
又莫察余之中情。
固烦言不可结而诒兮，

惜诵

My principle setteth on repal, fore private weal,
That raiseth th'ire of an interested clique.
I bear erst in mind the good of our lord supreme,
And so th'cabal its malice on me doth wreak.

I am all set in mind, unwavering;
Yet this devotion could avail me not.
Mine earnest upholding th'royal cause sans demand
Would give me along this path at last a swat.

Bearing my liege in mind in all good faith,
I forget the humbleness of my present state.
Serving him, I never once in thought waver,
But being confused, to favour I lose sight of the gate.

What is the guilt of punished loyalty?
'Tis not th' reward I set on in my thought.
My deeds so different from theirs cause my fall,
Thus I have reaped their jeers and abuse for sport.

Being condemned and slandered again and again,
Badly hurt, I aim to roid the blot, but in vain.
My feelings mortified, my heart depressed,
Facts are concealed, but foul is th'blotting bane.

How so despondent and depressed I am,
And none there be who feeleth as I do.
Indeed, innumerable words could not be tendered;

愿陈志而无路。

退静默而莫余知兮，
进号呼又莫余闻。
申侘傺之烦惑兮，
中闷瞀之忳忳。

昔余梦登天兮，
魂中道而无杭。
吾使厉神占之兮，
曰："有志极而无旁!"

"终危独以离异兮?"
曰，"君可思而不可恃。
故众口其铄金兮，
初若是而逢殆。

惩于羹而吹齑兮，
何不变此志也?
欲释阶而登天兮，
犹有曩之态也?

众骇遽以离心兮，
又何以为此伴也?
同极而异路兮，
又何以为此援也?

惜诵

I wish to loosen my heart, but th'path is taboo.

Receding, mute, by none I am understood;
Advancing, shouting, none would listen to me.
How so dejected, stunned, I have become!
I grow at heart confounded, dazed in esprit.

Once I embarked in a dream on ascending th'sky,
My soul, amidst the void, had no lifting barque;
I asked the Arch-wizard to divine the sequel,
He said, "With flushing wishes, an aide you lack stark."
Arch-wizard: the priest of the Supreme Deus and his sooth-sayer.

"Being periled, lone and lorn you are at last;
"T'is said, 'a sovran may be adored, not leant on',
"For in what the public hath mouthed, gold could be molten;
"Having undergone all this, you've suffered long.

"One burnt by broth would blow on salted chives;
"Why do you persevere in your wonted course?
"You think of foregoing th'means for rising aloft,
"Your bygone mode of acts why do you endorse?

"The rabble dazed, disjunct in heart and acts from you,
"What can you do, with such defiant ones round th'king?
"With end the same, but means divergent quite,
"What can you do, to break through such a ring?

晋申生之孝子兮，
父信谗而不好。
行婞直而不豫兮，
鲧功用而不就。

吾闻作忠以造怨兮，
勿谓之过言。
九折臂而成医兮，
吾至今乃知其信然。

矰弋机而在上兮，
罻罗张而在下。
设张辟以娱君兮，
愿侧身而无所。

欲儃佪以干傺兮，
恐重患而离尤。
欲高飞而远集兮，

惜诵

"Suen Suen[①], the filial prince of th'Duke of Tsin,

"His father believing in slander loved him not;

"Quen[②], being stiff and stubborn in demeanor,

"Failed to achieve any deed in his tragic lot. "

I've heard fidelity would give rise to grudge;

Slightingly I regarded that as to exaggerate;

Breaking one's arms too oft would make one a surgeon;

Now I believe it's true, 'tisn't to innovate.

With arrow shafts of tail tip ties up high,

And nets bespread so thickly on the ground,

They sprawl machines and traps to lull the king, *

While I could, to avail, seffle down nowhere around.

I think of loitering there to seek for chance,

But fear to incur his ire and risk harm sore;

I think of flying aloft and ranging far,

---

* This means that King Whai of Tsou(楚怀王) is surrounded by a circle of self-seeking sycophants fooling him for their own interests, while Chü Yuan himself, waiting to be of real service, could find no room to stand by his sovereign.

① Suen Suen(申生), filial son and prince elect of Duke Hsien of Tsin(晋献公), was slandered by his step-mother Li Chi(骊姬), whence, having lost the love of his father, he committed suicide.

② Quen(鲧,鮌), also called Taur-wuh or Daur-wuh(梼杌), was Great Yü's (大禹) father. He failed in his mission to turn the Grand Deluge(洪水) ravaging the banks of the Luteous River(黄河) from 2,297 to 2,278 B. C. to the Eastern Sea, and was banished by Suen(舜,2255 −2206 B. C.) to the Yi Mounts(羽山) and there, being imprisoned, died.

君罔谓汝何之？

欲横奔而失路兮，
盖志坚而不忍。
背膺牉而交痛兮，
心郁结而纡轸。

捣木兰以矫蕙兮，
凿申椒以为粮。
播江离与滋菊兮，
愿春日以为糗芳。

恐情质之不信兮，
故重著以自明。
矫兹媚以私处兮，
愿曾思而远身。

But fear to incite his query "Whither dost thou sora?"

I think of running rampant, wild, astray,
But firm in will, I could not to such resort;
My breast and back are breaking with aches,
My heart with sorrow and pathos is distraught.

Pounding magnolia and kneading coumarous
Petals, also thumping, as staple, peppers of Suen,
I take to grow chrysanthemums and selineas,
Ready as victuals for my spring hike run.

Anxious for this my troth being not ta'en true,
So do I compose this poem to show my heart.
I exalt those deep felt thoughts for mine own relief;
When I have done this well, I shall far depart.

抽　思

DRAWING MY THOUGHTS

抽　思

心郁郁之忧思兮，
独永叹乎增伤。
思蹇产之不释兮，
曼遭夜之方长。

悲秋风之动容兮，
何回极之浮浮？
数惟荪之多怒兮，
伤余心之忧忧。

愿遥赴而横奔兮，
览民尤以自镇。
结微情以陈词兮，
矫以遗乎美人。

昔君与我成言兮，
曰黄昏以为期。
羌中道而回畔兮，
反既有此他志。

憍吾以其美好兮，
览余以其修姱。
与余言而不信兮，
盖为余而造怒？

愿承间而自察兮，
心震悼而不敢。

抽思

Drawing My Thoughts

My heart is pursed with melancholic thoughts;
I heave long sighs to heighten my grieving strains,
With thoughts confused and twined with memory,
I come upon this long night's drawn out drains.

Sad at th'autumnal winds that touch our miens,
I wonder why the heavenly system doth move.
Time and again His wrothful mien is thought of,
When my heart is hurt to see him us reprove,

Wishing to hurry thither from afar,
I see our people's ill haps kept in mind.
With feelings of mine I'll tender my report,
To th'Beauteous One for his disposal kind.

In th'past my sovran reached his promise with me,
Laying his faith in me right till his life's eve.
But later on, he shifted from his promise,
His given words he blankly did retrieve.

You pride on those tricksters fair and worth your praise;
Your trust from me now withdrawn is in them all laid.
The promised words you reached with me are broke;
Why do you with blames unfair me hold and upbraid?

I think of taking a chance to state for myself,
But too much stunned, I dare not thus attempt.

悲夷犹而冀进兮，
心怛伤之憺憺。

历兹情以陈辞兮，
荪详聋而不闻。
固切人之不媚兮，
众固以我为患。

初吾所陈之耿著兮，
岂至今其庸亡？
何犹乐斯之謇謇兮？
愿荪美之可光。

望三五以为像兮，

抽思

Woe to me, hesitating, still do so I would,
My heart is torn, afflicted, from peace exempt.

I offered my strains for perusal to sovran mine,
Affecting deafness, he declined to list me.
Indeed, the frank and henest are straight and blunt;
Those wheedlers all my foes have proved to be.

What I did say at first is plain as daylight;
How could it be forgotten by you e'en now?
Why do I like to persist in fidelity thus?
I wish but th' glow to th' virtues of my king to endow.

Looking up to the Three and Five① for ideals,

---

① The Three and Five: there are two possible explanations to this expression ——
　(A) According to legendary lore, the Three Hwang (三皇) and Five Ti (五帝) at the beginning of the world's history:
　　(1) The Three Hwang:
　　　(a) Sui Rén Shi(燧人氏), the driller of wood to ignite fire,
　　　(b) Voh Shieh Shi(伏羲氏), that is, Tai Hao(太昊), also called Mi Shieh(宓牺), Pao Shieh(包牺), Pao Shieh(疱牺), Voh Shieh(伏戏), or Hwang Shieh(皇羲), and
　　　(c) Tsen Noon Shi, the Divine Farmer(神农氏), all of the primaeval times of human existence.
　　(2) The Five Ti: Luteous Emperor(黄帝), Tsuan Shuo(颛顼), Ti Kao(帝喾), Yao of Tdaung(唐尧) and Suen of Neü(虞舜),
　(B) The Three King (三王)
　　(1) Great Yü of Hsia(夏禹),
　　(2) Taung of Saung(商汤), and
　　(3) King Wen of Tsur(周文王), and
　　the Five Hegemonic Autocrats(五霸):
　　(1) Duke Huan of Tsih(齐桓公),
　　(2) Duke Wen of Tsin(晋文公),
　　(3) Duke Mo of Tsing(秦穆公),
　　(4) Duke Hsiang of Soong(宋襄公), and
　　(5) King Tsuan of Tsou(楚庄王).

指彭咸以为仪。
夫何极而不至兮?
故远闻而难亏。

善不由外来兮,
名不可以虚作。
孰无施而有报兮?
孰不实而有获?

少歌曰:
与美人之抽思兮,
并日夜而无正。
憍吾以其美好兮,
敖朕辞而不听。

倡曰:
有鸟自南兮,
来集汉北。
好姱佳丽兮,
胖独处此异域。
既惸独而不群兮,
又无良媒在其侧。
道卓远而日忘兮,

抽思

I point at Peng Yen[①] as my model boon.

For to what ulterior peaks have they not climbed?

So throughout th' ages their fair reputes attain lone.

One's goodness cometh not from the without,

One's fame cannot be made from nothing sheer.

Who canst reward obtain sans issue first?

Who canst a harvest reap void of planting mere?[*]

Bye-song:

I draw my deep felt thoughts the Beauteous to tell;

By day and night they are to none else proven.

My lord yet stresseth to me his favoured one's merits,

Ignoring my words as vain to him fast bounden.

Chanting:

A bird arising from the south,

Flieth to the north of the stream Han to abide.

Its plumage shineth fully fair;

Yet it hath to settle in foliage strange and reside.

Forlorn and solitary in daily life,

It hath no go-between to join me with my lord.

The way is far apart and I'm forgtten;

---

[*] These four lines of our poet show the poverty of his ingenuity to the communists, for they can easily obtain "goodness" and "fame" as well as reward and harvest by propaganda and through agitative deception.

[①] Peng Yen: according to Wang Yih(王逸), the East Han annotater of Lih Sao, Peng Yen was a vintuous courtier of the dynasty Yin(殷); his counsel to his King being rejected, he committed suicide by drowning himself.

愿自申而不得。
望北山而流涕兮,
临流水而太息。

望孟夏之短夜兮,
何晦明之若岁?
惟郢路之辽远兮,
魂一夕而九逝!

曾不知路之曲直兮,
南指月与列星。
愿径逝而未得兮,
魂识路之营营。

何灵魂之信直兮?
人之心不与吾心同!
理弱而媒不通兮,
尚不知余之从容!

乱曰:
长濑湍流,
溯江潭兮。
狂顾南行,
聊以娱心兮。

抽思

I wish to speak for myself, but to no avail.

Facing the northern range of mounts to shed tears,

By th' flushing stream I heave sighs drear and frail. *

Watching th' first summer moon's short night to pass,

I wonder why the dawn approacheth like th' year.

Thinking th' way back to the capital Ying is far off,

My spirit yet speedest it through oft one night mere.

I know not th' way be twisting or lie quite straight,

Pointing to th' south to guide me with th' stars and moon,

I wish to go straight to Ying, but fail so to do,

Only to my dreaming spirit th' way is known.

Why is it my soul is steadfast in its faith?

People's devotion differeth quite from mine!

My go-between is weak and th' ties are broken;

The world yet knoweth not how casually I opine!

Envoi:

By th' rapids' rocky bank,

　The current rushed on up headlonge;

Speedily I trod alongside

　Southwards to soothe my sadness strong.

---

* 　The metaphor in the first four lines is transfused into a simile from the fifth
　　line forth in the original. This transition is observed in the English version ac-
　　cordingly.

轸石崴嵬，
蹇吾愿兮。
超回志度，
行隐进兮。

低徊夷犹，
宿北姑兮。
烦冤瞀容，
实沛徂兮。

愁叹苦神，
灵遥思兮。
路远处幽，
又无行媒兮。

道思作颂，
聊以自救兮。
忧心不遂，
斯言谁告兮？

抽思

Crossing the ridges, tall, steep,
  Against my wish, I had oft to delay,
Passing th' twists, with th' trek in mind,
  I went on, unawares, yet on my way.

Delaying, hesitant,
  I lodged at an inn by night in North Ku.
With feelings lorn and jumbled,
  This trek to me hath proved to be rue.

Sighing with anguish and moans
  My soul afloat doth pine afar.
Distantly removed and withdrawn,
  It is like unto a fallen star.

For showing my thoughts in song,
  I ease the cherishings of my heart.
Deeply affected, I fail to do so;
  To whom these strains I effuse on my part?

July 18, 1986.

思 美 人

THINKING
OF THE
BEAUTEOUS ONE

思美人

思美人兮，
揽涕而伫眙。
媒绝路阻兮，
言不可结而诒。

蹇蹇之烦冤兮，
陷滞而不发。
申旦以舒中情兮，
志沉菀而莫达。

愿寄言于浮云兮，
遇丰隆而不将。
因归鸟而致辞兮，
羌迅高而难当。

高辛之灵盛兮，
遭玄鸟而致诒。
欲变节而从俗兮，
愧易初而屈志。

思美人

Thinking of the Beauteous One

While thinking of the Beauteous One my lord,

I hold my flush of tears to stand and gaze.

No me diator there is, th' way forbidding,

No words I could put forth and to him raise.

With folds of my anxieties and grievings twined,

My heart is wrung and strained with pangs pulsing.

Day after day I bide here mouthing my thoughts,

Mine in nermost intents are depressed, flagging.

I wish to ask the clouds to bring my words,

Meeting Feng-loon, the thunder god, who declineth.

I ask the homing birds to voice my request,

They all fly fast and high, out of reach of my breath.

Kao Sing＊ the pristine king of virtue divine,

Was bestowed by a phoenix with heaven sent rich boon.

With apstasy to follow vulgar practise,

I feel ashamed to be inconstant eftsoon.

＊ Kao Sing(高辛氏)：Tih Ku(帝喾), Sao Hoi(少昊)'s son, was on his throne for seventy years (2,436 −2,365 B. C.). He was Luteous Emperor (黄帝)'s great grandson. Old legendary saying has it that while Tih Ku's queen Jien Dih(简狄) was taking a bath, a phoenix flied past her and left its egg by her side; feeling fond of it, she swallowed it and afterward gave birth to Kao Sing.

独历年而离愍兮，
羌凭心犹未化。
宁隐闵而寿考兮，
何变易之可为？

知前辙之不遂兮，
未改此度。
车既覆而马颠兮，
蹇独怀此异路。

勒骐骥而更驾兮，
造父为我操之。
迁逡次而勿驱兮，
聊假日以须时。
指嶓冢之西隈兮，
与曛黄以为期。

开春发岁兮，
白日出之悠悠。
吾将荡志而愉乐兮，
遵江夏以娱忧。

揽大薄之芳茝兮，
搴长洲之宿莽。

思美人

For years many tribulations I have endured,
But all along to principle I've held fast.
I'd rather suffer through out my days till death;
How could I stand my playing false at ast?

I know full well my front track doth not avail,
Yet mine ideal sustaineth no whit of change.
Though th' chariot be upset and the horse be tripped up,
The unusual right path remaineth my right range.

Curbing my steed to bridle all o'er again,
I asked Tsao-wu① to hold the reins for me.
I go on troting slow to bide my time,
So as to lag, behind to wait and see.
I aim to reach the western flank of Bo-tsoon②,
By th' time when twilight falleth on the lea.

When spring arriveth to commence the year,
The radiant sun would rise up high aglow,
I shalt exalt my heart to gladden high,
Along th' streams Kiang and Hsia to soothe my sorrow.

I cull angelicas sweet from the lush wild,
And gather verdant herbs of the isle long.

---

① Tsao-wu(造父), noted driver of King Mo(穆王, reigning 1001 – 946 B. C.) of the dynasty Tser(周). Here, simply an excellent driver is Meant.
② Bo-tsoon: a mountain in the west of Tsen hsien(成县), in Kang-su Province (甘肃省) today.

惜吾不及古人兮，
吾谁与玩此众芳？

解篇薄与杂菜兮，
备以为交佩。
佩缤纷以缭转兮，
遂萎绝而离异。

吾且僤佪以娱忧兮，
观南人之变态。
窃快在中心兮，
扬厥凭而不竢。
芳与泽其杂糅兮，
羌芳华自中出。

纷郁郁其远蒸兮，
满内而外扬。
情与质信可保兮，
羌居蔽而闻章。

令薜荔以为理兮，
惮举趾而缘木。
因芙蓉以为媒兮，
惮褰裳而濡足。

思美人

A pity'tis, I lived not with th' fair of yore,
With whom could I these enjoy, since they are gone?

Weeding out bulrushes and cattails rank,
I braid the fair trim blooms as a flora sprig.
The sprig appeareth florid and lushly twined,
But withered out and shriveled as a bare twig.

Thereon I linger here my grief to soothe,
Observing how the southern lot[1] behave.
In their heart's secret there is filled that joy,
Issuing resentment gainst me to out brave.
Fragrance and rankness, blend though they are,
Yet scented blooms still blossom out therefrom.

Sweet virtue, thick set, spreading far and wide,
With beauty filled, is bound to flush outward.
Its pith and calibre, while kept intact,
Even though in hermitage, would spread abroad.

Bidding th' magnolia tall to mediate,
I hesitate to do the clam bering feat.
Asking the lotus fair to go between,
I waver to lift my gown and wet my feet.

---

[1] Our poet, being expelled to the north of the River Han, observed the courtiers of the capital Ying(郢都) of the south in their words and deeds with disapproval.

登高吾不说兮，
入下吾不能。
固朕形之不服兮，
然容与而狐疑。

广遂前画兮，
未改此度也。
命则处幽我将罢兮，
愿及白日之未暮也。
独茕茕而南行兮，
思彭咸之故也。

思美人

Scrambling up high, I take no pleasure in,

And throwing my self low, I could not so do.

Indeed, it countereth my bodily bent,

But also my mind forbearing, hesitates too.

To my plan of th' past I mean to give full shape;

This dream I've made up my mind to alter not.

If I am doomed to be overcast, be it so.

Yet that I'd have, ere night would come and me blot.

Thus, solitarily I southwards go,

As Beng Yen's * end is thought of to be my lot.

July 3rd., 1987.

---

* According to Wang Yih(王逸, cir. 89 −cir. 158)'s Textual Critical Studies
of Tsu Tze(《楚辞章句》), Peng Yen(彭咸) was a courties of the ancient
dynasty Yin(殷, 1600 − 1046 B. C.) who committed cuicide by drowning
himself when his counsel to his King was rejected.

招　　魂
HAIL HOME THE
（REGAL）SOUL

招　魂

朕幼清以廉洁兮，
身服义而未沫。
主此盛德兮，
牵于俗而芜秽。
上无所考此盛德兮，
长离殃而愁苦！

帝告巫阳曰：
"有人在下，
我欲辅之。
魂魄离散，
汝筮予之。"

巫阳对曰："掌梦……
上帝，其命难从！"
"若必筮予之！
恐后之谢，不能复周！"

巫阳焉乃下招曰：
"魂兮归来！
去君之恒干，
何为乎四方些？
舍君之乐处，
而离彼不祥些？

Hail Home the（Regal）Soul

From boyhood I have e'er been clean and pure,
Upright and resolutely pristine in grip.
Mine erst while master virtuous whom I served,
As solied by the filth of the world hast fall'n in his slip.
Good heavens, you have not his goodness fulfilled.
Long hath he suffered from his afflictions' whip.

The Deus Supreme to Yang the sorceress bade:
"There is someone down there on thy low earth,
To whom I think of giving timely aid.
His ghost hast left its frame corporeal;
Go thou to make his body with lift pervade."

Sorceress Yang replied, "I but divine;
My God, your words with hard ships full are fraught."
"Thou must make effort to have it done, or else,
When it decays, his ghost would fall to nought.

Then Yang the sorceress cried, when down she came,
"O soul, do come back soon to your late home;
You have now left your own used bodily frame;
Wherefore to mope about the quarters four;
Forsaking the goodly, old abode of yours,
To undergo the count less mishaps sore?

"魂兮归来！
东方不可以托些——
长人千仞，
惟魂是索些；

"十日代出，
流金铄石些；
彼皆习之，
魂往必释些！
归来兮，
不可以托些！

魂兮归来！
南方不可以止些——
雕题黑齿，
得人肉以祀，
以其骨为醢些；
蝮蛇蓁蓁，
封狐千里些；
雄虺九首，
往来倏忽，
吞人以益其心些。
归来兮，
不可以久淫些！

魂兮归来！
西方之害——
流沙千里些；

招魂

"O Soul, do come back home, return eftsoons!

The east, you should not bide there in a bower.

Arch giants are there seven thousand feet tall,

Intent on searching for human souls to devour.

"Ten suns there rise and blaze at the same time,

To burn hard rocks and melt sheen solid gold;

Those monsters are all used to that fierce clime,

Going there Soul, to ashes you would turn!

Come back, O Soul, for certain, come back home!

The East is not meet at all for you to sojourn.

O Soul, do come back home, return eftsoons!

The south, you should not there for long remain.

With forehead tatooed, black teethed, the savages south,

When they have seized as human booty sain,

To their fore fathers they mould offer as sacrifice,

And pound the bones of such into a thick paste.

There adders gather, wriggling quick with fright,

And foxes huge that range o'er wild plains waste.

Also there are the nine-headed pythons huge,

Rolling and sweeping, terror-strikingly swift,

Devouring men to accelerate its venom.

Come back, O soul, return,

The south you should relinquish for your kingdom.

O Soul, do come bak home, return eftsoons!

The perils and harms of the West are wild in excess.

Rolling sand dunes extend in wide expanse;

旋入雷渊，

糜散而不可止些；

幸而得脱，

其外旷宇些；

赤蚁若象，

玄蜂若壶些；

五谷不生，

丛菅是食些；

其土烂人，

求水无所得些；

彷徉无所倚，

广大无所极些。

归来兮，

恐自遗贼些！

魂兮归来，

北方不可以止些——

增冰峨峨，

飞雪千里些，

归来兮，

不可以久些！

魂兮归来，

君毋上天些——

虎豹九关，

啄害下人些；

一夫九首，

拔木九千些；

招魂

When whirled to the depth of Thunderous whirl pool,

You would be thrashed into partices sans recess.

Even if be freed from tortuous calamities.

You would find yourself in a boundless wild of despair.

Where crimson ants of elephantine size do crawl,

And jet black bees in shape like big gourd fly.

There not a sembrance of the grains ever grow.

You find but bunches of weeds to quell your hunger.

The soil there would corrode the flesh of men.

To quench your thirst, there is not a drop of water.

Suffering thirst and hunger, one could do nought;

Facing the boundless plain none could help aught.

Come back, O soul, return,

I fear calamity to yourself you've brought.

O Soul, do come back home, return eftsoons!

The north, you should not there for long detain.

Crystal line ice hath frozen into bergs bright,

And fluffy flakes of snow fly down amain,

Across the thousand *li* whole north demesne.

Come back, O Soul, do not long in the north remain.

O Soul, do come back home, return eftsoons!

Go not up high to the region empyrean,

There tigers and leopards watch o'er nine check points;

They prey on people lay of the world mundance.

There, a nine-headed monster up roots trees

By thousands at a stretch in his fit insane.

豺狼从目,
往来侁侁些;
悬人以嬉,
投之深渊些;
致帝于帝,
然后得瞑些;
归来归来,往恐危身些!

魂兮归来,
君无下此幽都些——
土伯九约,
其角觺觺些,
敦脄血拇,
逐人駓駓些;
参目虎首,
其身若牛些。
此皆甘人!
归来归来,恐自遗灾些。

魂兮归来,
入脩门些——
工祝招君,
背行先些;
秦篝齐缕,
郑绵络些;
招具该备,
永啸呼些:
魂兮归来,

Like wolves he darts his mad eyes to and fro,

And very swift in speed to come and go.

For fun he hangs his victims upside down,

And hath them plunged into unfathomed water

Only when he hath reported to Deus the matter,

A soul could have a wink of final rest.

Come back, O Soul, your flight is a mortal peril.

O Soul, do come back home, return eftsoons!

Descend you not to that infernal town, ——

Devilkins nine-tailed of the nether world

With horns protruding fiercely forward down,

And massive shoulders, backs and blood-stained daws,

At th' sight of living men would swiftly chase;

They have three eyes, with heads like those of tigers,

And bodies massive like those of fat oxen.

They are all a pack of men-eating monsters.

O come back home, bring not ill fate to yourself!

O Soul, do come back home, return eftsoons,

And enter please High Gate of Capital Ying.

Enchanters fair all beckon warmly before,

They guide by walking backward greeting you.

The perfumed wicker basket from the state Tzing,

Bedecked with multi-colour ribbons from Tsih,

Holding silk costumes fine imported from Tseng,

The articles of clothing for greeting you all set,

All welcomers do shout to cheer for joy.

544

544

反故居些!

天地四方，
多贼奸些。
像设君室，
静闲安些。
高堂邃宇，
槛层轩些。
层台累榭，
临高山些。
网户朱缀，
刻方连些。
冬有突厦，
夏室寒些。
川谷径复，
流潺湲些。
光风转蕙，
氾崇兰些。
经堂入奥，
朱尘筵些。
砥室翠翘，
挂曲琼些。
翡翠珠被，
烂齐光些。
蒻阿拂壁，
罗帱张些。
纂组绮缟，
结琦璜些。

招魂

O Soul, do come back home, return eftsoons!

All round the sky and about the earth,
You do find evil spirits rife.
Only in the room your portrait is hung,
There is found quiet, peaceful life.
High spacious halls and deep house rows
With balustrades to hallways conjoined,
And towers storied and kiosks doubled,
All piled up high on hilltops are adjoined.
Trellised doors cinnabar adorned,
With squares are all lined in ordered rule.
In winter, the mansions deep stay warm,
In summer, they remain quite cool.
The palace streams both large and small,
Are babbling forward slow or quick.
The fair days' breeze on coumarous wafts,
And blows on eupatories thick.
Through halls you enter chambers sung,
Vermeil ceilings span floor mat of bamboo.
In the bedroom of hone paved walls,
Halcyon tail plumes spread on hooks ormolu.
With emeralds and pearls on quilts decked,
Illume and sparkle the glossy and bright.
The folds of sheen are spread around,
And silken screens hung high upright,
Multi-coloured silk strands frill the fringes,
Tipped with gem pendants semi-round.

室中之观，

多珍怪些。

兰膏明烛，

华容备些。

二八侍宿，

夕递代些。

九侯淑女，

多迅众些。

盛鬋不同制，

实满宫些。

容态好比，

顺弥代些。

弱颜固植，

謇其有意些。

姱容脩态，

絙洞房些。

蛾眉曼睩，

目腾光些。

靡颜腻理，

遗视矊些。

离榭脩幕，

侍君之闲些。

翡帷翠帐，

饰高堂些。

红壁沙版，

玄玉梁些。

仰视刻桷，

画龙蛇些。

招魂

The interior of those rooms superb

Is full of objects rich and rare.

The tallow candles fragrance spread,

On prickets fine at night to flare.

Two octettes of beauties serve at night,

In daily shifts for timely change;

These maids in fealty offered aloft,

Far excel fairs of the common range.

Diversely are they all coiffured,

As they adorn your palace halls;

Their looks and miens are mild and suave,

Like those of a fay who one enthralls.

Though gentle without, yet firm at heart,

They cherish stead fast faith discreet.

Rows of bewitching belles in bloom

Do throng your night reposing suite.

With eye brows curved and slim and glints

Of pupils soft, angelic charm,

Glimpses they flash that captivate;

Of visage, tender, skin, like balm,

They glances cast with gleams that delight.

E'en though at your hunting tripina tent,

They'd all await on your short rest.

Curtains bedecked with halcyon plumes

Enliven the spacious hall room square.

Red mortared walls and cinnabar door

The beams that shine jet black upbear.

Glancing atop at the rafters carved,

One sees depicted snakes and dragons;

坐堂伏槛，

临曲池些。

芙蓉始发，

杂芰荷些。

紫茎屏风，

文缘波些。

文豹异饰，

侍陂陀些。

轩辌既低，

步骑罗些。

兰薄户树，

琼木篱些。

魂兮归来！

何远为些？

室家遂宗，

食多方些。

稻粢穱麦，

挐黄梁些。

大苦醎酸，

辛甘行些。

肥牛之腱，

臑若芳些。

和酸若苦，

陈吴羹些。

胹鳖炮羔，

有柘浆些。

酸鹄臇凫，

招魂

Sitting along side the balustrade,

One holds in sight the curved clear pond.

New lotus blooms begin to blush,

Amidst the leaves in folds and round.

Clusters of purple water althea

Are tossed in the stream to wave and bound.

The sentries clad in leopard skin

Their watches keep at the mount incline.

The nonce your chariot hath arrived,

Both foot and horse are set to align.

In frontal courts are orchids sweet,

Circling about trees noble abound,

Do come back home, O Soul, eftsoons!

Why do you wander far around?

Revered by members of your clan,

You'd receive victuals profuse from them all.

They'd offer rise, wheat, barley, oats,

To blend with the fragrant millet small.

Bitter and salty and sour in taste.

Pungent and sweet, to wit, as well.

The tendons of cows and oxen stout,

Well done as to be of savoury smell.

Fermented beans in vinegar seeped,

Produce the soup of Wu savour.

Turtle softly steamed, lamb roasted rare,

Each cooked in syrup with flavour.

Vinegar stewed swan, mallard with bean sauce,

煎鸿鸧些。

露鸡臛蠵,

厉而不爽些。

粔籹蜜饵,

有餦餭些。

瑶浆蜜勺,

实羽觞些。

挫糟冻饮,

酎清凉些。

华酌既陈,

有琼浆些。

归来反故室,

敬而无妨些。

肴羞未通,

女乐罗些。

陈钟按鼓,

造新歌些。

《涉江》、《采菱》,

发《扬荷》些。

美人既醉,

朱颜酡些。

娭光眇视,

目曾波些。

招魂

Wild goose, gray crane, well broiled to a yellow.

Salted chicken steamed, fat turtle stewed in pot,

In odour pungent, while tasty and mellow.

Fried frillings crisp, honey savoured cakes,

And high scorched malt fondant maltose.

Gem coloured liquor sweetened with honey

Fills the sparrow shaped beaker to its nose.

With dregs removed, the spirit iced and taken,

How the pure cool wine elates your spirit!

Finely carved goblets would be spread on your table,

Filled with long buried drinks divine.

O Soul, come back to your royal abode

We all hold you in awe no disaster would be thine!

Before the feast is full spread on the board,

The fair tuned chorus appears in the front.

Bells are then tinkled, tabours struck,

New songs are sung in chorus the moment.

Crossing the Stream, *The Lotus*, *Waved*,

*And Water Caltrop Picking Tune*①,

Would then be played and sweetly sung;

Court beauties drunk while hearing the croon

Look flushed and blooming in complexion.

Their flashing twinkles cherish smiles

From eyes that glint autumnal streams.

---

① Crossing the Stream (《涉江》) and Water Caltrop Picking Tune (《采菱》) were popular songs of the state Tsou and The Lotus Waved (《扬荷》) was a dance tune of Tsou.

被文服纤，

丽而不奇些。

长发曼鬋，

艳陆离些。

二八齐容，

起郑舞些。

衽若交竿，

抚案下些。

竽瑟狂会，

搷鸣鼓些。

宫庭震惊，

发《激楚》些。

吴歈蔡讴，

奏《大吕》些。

士女杂坐，

乱而不分些。

放陈组缨，

班其相纷些。

郑卫妖玩，

来杂陈些。

《激楚》之结，

招魂

Their raiments within are of silken lisles

Without, of gold-fibered brocade.

Elegant, lithe, but not bizzare,

Their raven locks are of glossy hair,

With jewelry that sparkles like star.

Octettes in pair like in mode and cheen

Commence their turns of Tseng State dance,

Their lifted sleeves like criss-cross poles,

All rise and fall in rhythmic prance.

With pipes and zithern① blown and plucked,

And drums to chords acclaim with hails,

The entire court is charmed in joy

While "Tsou O'erwhelmed" on the stage prevails;

Wu and Tsai② short tunes inter spersed 'twixt,

The old "Great Lü" is then the run;

Thus men and maids sit mixed together

In company for diversion or fun.

As hats and belts are laid to consort,

Agleam, reflexing, multifold,

While pretty girls of Tseng and Wei

With fancy items their turns hold.

"The heart astir" to wind up all

---

① These pipes(竽) were ancient tubalar wind instruments "four feet and two inches" long with thirty-six tongues or vibrating reeds. The zithern was a string musical instrument of twenty-five chords spread on a sounding board of five and a half ancient Chinese feet long, each of which measured about ten modern British or American inches in length.

② Wu and Tsai are names of ancient states and "Great Lü" is the names of an ancient melody.

独秀先些。

菎蔽象棋,
有六簙些——
分曹并进,
遒相迫些;
成枭而牟,
呼五白些。

Is leading other tunes manifold.[1]

Jade chips and chess men of ivory carved*,
Arrayed in battle state of six Po pairs,
Are engaged in fighting by throwing dice,
The intent is keyed up, the spirit dares.
To make "the owl" would tie in the risks,
To cry "Five Whites" is to triumph at last.

---

① These two lines mean that over and above all the other tunes mentioned before, the concluding chorus and concert exceed them all. The previous account of dancing and music has sometimes been regarded as rather exaggerated, but archeological findings have proved that this passage of music and dance con sists of much realistic elements. The excavation of Marquis Tsen Ĭ(曾侯乙)'s tomb in Sui hsien(随县), Hwu-pei(湖北) Province, in 1976 has unearthed bronze 16-bell affiliates(编钟), stone 16-piece affiliates(石编磬), together with drums, zithern(瑟), hepta-chords(琴), Pandean pipes(笙), linked bamboo piper(排箫) and flutes(横吹笛), 124 pieces in total. All these musical instruments had been exhibited in a very orderly array underground ever since the early days of the Warring State Period(战国,475 B.C. -221 B.C.), for the state Tsen(曾国) was only a small feudal dependency of the main state Tsou(楚), which must have more ground for the jubilant social activities briefly mentioned here above.

* This ancient game of "Jade chips and chessmen of ivory carved"(《菎蔽象棋》) had twelve chessmen made of ivory or animal bone, each of which cubic or rectangular in shape, six in white and six painted black, together with six chips made of jade and five dices each with one side white and other sides of dots numbered from one to five; it was played by two parties facing each other on an oblong wooden chess board of twelve rows of six squares divided in the middle by a "water belt" with three fish in it; the person throwing dice and moving his chessman forward with five whites facing upward was said to make "the owl" and win over-whelming victory. The specific rules of playing the game are lost through the centuries. The chessmen made of rhinoceros horn in the ancient state Tsin(晋), now in the south-western part of the province San-si(山西) in North China, was said to be notable.

晋制犀比，

费白日些。

铿钟摇簴，

揳梓瑟些。

娱酒不废，

沉日夜些。

兰膏明烛，

华灯错些。

结撰至思，

兰芳假些。

人有所极，

同心赋些。

酎饮尽欢，

乐先故些。

魂兮归来，

返故居些。

乱曰：

献岁发春兮，汨吾南征。

菉蘋齐叶兮白芷生。

路贯庐江兮左长薄，

倚沼畦瀛兮遥望博。

青骊结驷兮齐千乘，

悬火延起兮玄颜烝。

步及骤处兮诱骋先，

抑骛若通兮引车右还。

与王趋梦兮课后先，

君王亲发兮惮青兕。

招魂

While playing with the Tsin mode rhinoceros disks,

One seeth the sun reclining westwards fast.

Striking the bells hath shaken their frame,

Plucking the zithern touched chords of hearts.

Carousing day and night in revelry,

People steep themselves in joyance on their parts.

Alight are the boneset tallow candles,

On prickets gilt that sparkle full bright.

Some poets are tense with pressing thoughts;

The eupatory odour speedeth their flight.

The moment when people eject their feelings,

They would accord in writing peotry.

Let us raise a toast to all who are here,

You kins and friends, for your dear lodestar;

O Soul, please come back home in haste,

To your palatial abode from afar.

Envoi:

When the new year commenced springtide as I southwards hied,

The duck weeds burgeoned full and angelicas came to sprout,

Through Lu Stream lay my route, a wide spread bush on its left,

In the expanse how broad one viewed the far lookout!

Years ago fleet chariots drawn by steeds in number hundreds,

Aglow were the forest fires, to flush round the night azure,

I paused and sped, while leading hunt trains to forge ahead.

Then dashed right forward far across the hunt endosure.

I followed then my lord to Yün-moon to end the chase,

When he himself a rhinoceros had shot and slain.

朱明承夜兮时不可掩,**
皋兰被径兮斯路渐。
湛湛江水兮上有枫,
目极千里兮伤春心。
魂兮归来哀江南。**

** 这五行原稿缺佚

注　释
NOTES AND
COMMENTS

Lee Sao: Suffering Throes(离骚)

The title *Lee Sao*(《离骚》) of this great ode, a lament written by Chü Yuan after his expulsion from the capital Ying-*t'uh*(郢都) of the state Ts'ou(楚) during the Warring States Period(战国), is said by Sze-ma Tsien(司马迁) and P'an K'uh(班固) of Han(汉) to mean "suffering" or "undergoing" "sorrow" or "throes"(离忧,遭忧). Yen Sze-K'uh(颜师古) of Tdaung(唐) says, (emotional) disturbance or (mental) agitation is called sao(骚). Another explanation of these two characters by Wang Yi(王逸) of late Han, pronounced erroneous by Tsu Hsih(朱熹) of Soong(宋), gives out that they mean "the sorrow of departure or leaving" enforced on the poet by the king. The first interpretation supported by Yen's expounding gives the total sense of the subject much better and is therefore adopted here in this version of the poem.

The date of composition is uncertain in discussions of scholars. There has been much confusion among them from the start to this day because the poet's life in his clashes with the clandestine politics of Tsing(秦) and amidst the chaos of his times is far from being clearly unraveled, and the expressions 疏,绌,斥逐,放,放逐,弃逐,放流,迁 and 贬谪, some used by the poet himself in his works and most by our early scholars of his life and poetry, are somehow vaguely and loosely connoted at first and then dubiously understood and heedlessly contended by their successors.

In The *Life of Chü Yuan*(《屈原列传》) of *The Chronicle*(《史记》) by the great historian Sze-ma Tsien, it is only generally and laxly said that the plaint was written after the poet was repulsed with anger by the king("王怒而疏屈平") as a result of the calumniations of the envious adulator the Saun-quan courtier(上官大夫). Sez-ma's short biography is much too scrappy; it does not even give the semblance of a sketchy picture, though somewhat pieced out with certain facts in his *Annals of the State Ts'ou*(《楚世家》). The matter was not at all a simple one, as I have related in my account of Chü Yuan's repulse by King Hwai(怀王) and his expulsion from Ying-*t'uh* in regard to Tsing's(秦) strategy and Tsang Yih's(张仪) intrigues in section VI *Ts'ou and Chü Yuan of Introduction* (*vide pp.* 62 −67). After his repulse("疏") in the sixteenth year of Hwai *Wang's* reign, i. e., 313 B. C., he wrote his *Bitter Declarations*(《惜诵》) to affirm his innocence and loyalty. To be brief and explicit, the poet was called back to the court some two years later by the king for political necessity, and then, going to Tsih(齐) on a diplomatic mission and staying at the Ts'ou court thereafter for about a year, he was at loggerheads with the pro-Tsing faction once more, and this time was expelled(斥逐) from Ying-*t'uh* by his sovereign.

Judging from the internal evidence of the feelings expressed in the poems, I tentatively presume that *Suffering Throes* was composed in the fourth to fifth years after Chü Yuan's dismissal from office, compulsory leave(斥逐) from Ying-*t'uh* and residence at Han-pei(汉北), north of the Han Stream(汉水), late in the eighteenth year of King Hwai's reign, 311 B. C. In the first three years or more after the fell into disgrace the second time with his monarch, that is, in the nineteenth to twenty-first years of Hwai *Wang's* reign, he wrote *Drawing My Thoughts*(《抽思》), *Musing on the Beauteous One*(《思美人》), *Divining to Know Where I Should Stay*(《卜居》) and *Dis-*

tant Wanderings(《远游》). Then, in the twenty-second to twenty-third years, 307—306 B. C., he composed *Suffering Throes*, the greatest lyric poem and ode written by man, during his enforced sojourn at Han-pei. *Vide* section VII *Chü Yuan and His Works*, § 11 of *Introduction* and note 10, my comment on Pih(阰) and Pih(沘) on *p.* 473.

The original text of *Lee Sao* was written by the poet probably in the *Zûr* script(籀文) or great *tsuan*(大篆) originated by Sze Zûr(史籀), the grand curator of history (and astronomy) of King Hsuan of Tsur(周宣王太史). Chü Yuan's manuscripts, conceivably incised with a metal writing cutter(书刀) or prong(聿) on bamboo strips, conjoined together lengthwise in parallel rows and stringed up with tanned cords of hide(韦编), or better, brushed with a pointed tuft of deer's, rabbit's or weasal's soft hair on silk scrolls, must have vanished long, long ago, no one knows when and how. It was presumably copied by book-making scribes with the juice of the tree *Rhus vernicifera*(漆) on bamboo strips(简策), if not incised on them, existent in several copies hidden privately by Ts'ou subjects or buried in their tombs, so as to have escaped the ravages of Tsng's conquest, destruction and its extirpating fire by Ying Tsen(嬴政) and Lih Sze (李斯) to burn books in 213 B. C. Then, it was rendered into the more legible *lih* script(隶书), simplified from the small *tsuan*(小篆) by Tsen Meau(程邈), and transcribed on bamboo strips after the fourth year of Wei-*t'ih's*(惠帝) reign (191 B. C.) in West Han(西汉), when the criminal "statute" prohibiting the private possession of books, instituted by the bellowing tyrant and his valet, was publicly annulled(除"挟书律").

It is commonly known that in the reign of Yuan-*t'ih*(元帝) of

West Han, during the forties to thirties B. C., the celebrated scholar Liu Shan(刘向) compiled the works of Chü Yuan①, headed by *Lee Sao*, together with the *fuh*(赋) of his disciples Soong Yü(宋玉) and Chin Tsa(景差)②, followed by the works of Chü Yuan's admirers Chia Yieh(贾谊), Prince Hwai-nan(淮南小山), Tung-foun Suo(东方朔), etc. and Liu's own imitations, into an anthology entitled *Ts'ou "Tze"*(《楚辞》). That was the beginning of this *genre* of verse being called by this name, *tze* meaning poetry composed in a way radically different from the traditional type of ballads, songs lyrics and odes of *The Classic of Poetry*(《诗经》), in feelings and subject matter as well as in rhythmical form, and *Ts'ou "Tze"* meaning such poetry originated in the state Ts'ou by its great poet Chü Yuan. But Liu's anthology was lost through the centuries, most probably during the calamitous Five Hwu and Sixteen States Period(五胡十六国,304 -439), as were the books of Liu An(刘安), P'an K'uh(班固) and Chia Kwei(贾逵) of West and East Han(西汉,东汉), so mentioned by Tsu Hsih(朱熹) in his *Variorum Commentary on Ts'ou "Tze"*(《楚辞集注》) in the middle years of South Soong(南宋). Chü Yuan's extant works consist of twenty-five pieces in all, as counted from Liu's book, with *Lee Sao* leading, according to *The Roll of Arts and Letters* of P'an K'uh's *The Han Chronicle*(《汉书·艺文志》). However, the anthology of Liu is mainly preserved, minus its

---

① It has also been said that the compilation was made by some one else after him using his name as editor.

② The two poems *Hailing Back the Soul*(《招魂》) and *Great Hailing Back*(《大招》) formerly attributed to Soong Yü(宋玉) and Chin Tsa(景差) respectively by Wang Yi(玉逸), have been correctly restored to Chü Yuan's rightful authorship by Hwang Wen-ping(黄文炳) of the Ming Dynasty(明) and Lin Yün-ming(林云铭) of Tsing(清).

preface, in *Textual Critical Studies in Ts'ou "Tze"* (《楚辞章句》) by Wang Yi(王逸) of East Han, with P'an K'uh's preamble and terminal words to his collection, closely commented upon with annotations. Wang's commentary ranks as the first of well over a hundred critical studies of Chü Yuan's works from Han to today. Since paper was invented by Tsai Lun(蔡伦) of East Han in the reign Yuan-shin (元兴) of Her-*t'ih*(和帝), i. e., 105 A. D., which occurred earlier than when Wang wrote his book by some forty years; Wang, a scholar and a high courtier of rectitude, must have his book transcribed by copiers on paper and distributed among his friends to fight against the common practices of sycophancy and traducing under the dark predominancy of the nefarious "Great General"(大将军) Liang Ch'ih (梁冀).

Around the second year of Tsoon-ta-tung(中大通) of the reign of Wuh- *t'ih* of Liang(梁武帝), about 530 of the Christian era, *Lee Sao* was compiled, together with the poet's other extant works and his disciple Soong Yü's *fuh*, in the renowned *Literary Selections*(《文选》) of Siao Tung, Prince Royal Ts'au-ming of Liang(梁昭明太子萧统), which, thanks to it, has preserved a great many of our priceless ancient masterpieces. Then, Liu Shye (刘勰), a Buddhist bonze, the eminent literary critic of Liang and a cherished friend of the prince, wrote a glowing chapter on *Suffering Throes* in his noted book *Carving Dragons in the Heart of Literature*(《文心雕龙》), in which he discredits P'an K'uh's adverse criticism of the poet and his works. *Ts'en* script(真书) had become prevalent in the dynasties Gwei and Ts'in(魏,晋); so this ode and the poet's other works, as the rest of the selections, must have been copied with it. Afterwards, *Lee Sao's* text was many a time transcribed in this type of script brushed on silk and paper scrolls（帛书，卷子）in the Swei（隋）and Tdaung（唐）Dynasties，and especially twice annotated with comments by Lih Saen（李善）and later by five other courtier scholars（五臣）during Kao-*tsoon*（高宗）and Yüan-*tsoon's*（玄宗）reigns in early Tdaung，in Ts'au-ming's *Literary Selections*. The dynasty Tdaung is illustrious in the nation's history for its splendour in arts and letters. Its great poets Wang Wei（王维），Lih Bêh（李白），Yuan Ch'i（元结），Hang Yüe（韩愈）and Liu Tsoon-yuan（柳宗元）are among those influenced by Chü Yuan and handing down his poetic tradition to posterity.

Block-printing was innovated as early as in Swei（隋，589—618），was perpetuated in Tdaung（唐，618—907）and flourished in Soong（宋，960—1279）. A North Soong（北宋，960—1127）block-printing edition copy of Ts'au-ming's *Literary Selections* in the imperial collection of Chia-tsin（嘉靖）was said by the poet and critic Wang Sze-tsen（王世贞）in the middle of Ming（明）to be a delightful item. One wonders whether it still exists. In early Soong，Zau P'uh-tse（晁补之）gave the world his *Ts'ou "Tze" Recompiled*（《重编楚辞》）and his anthologies *Ts'ou "Tze" Continued*（《续楚辞》）and *"Lee Sao" Metamorphosed*（《变离骚》）. Later，Hoon Hsin-tsou（洪兴祖）of early South Soong published his *Supplemental Commentary on Ts'ou "Tze"*（《楚辞补注》）. Like Wang Yi，Hoon also had his personality lit up with fire by Chü Yuan's noble spirit. He led his upright life，wrote his volume and published it while the dynasty was sinking low in its cinders. Its two emperors Whei-*tsoon*（徽宗）and Ching-*tsoon*（钦宗）had become captives of its ferocious，marauding neighbour Ch'ih（金），and Soong's two big traitors，Tsang P'aun-tsoun（张邦昌）and Tsing Kwei（秦桧），the latter of whom defamed the national hero Yuo Fei(岳飞) with the crime "unnecessary to have existed"("莫须有") and fooled the doltish emperor to execute the ever-victorious general, were successively in power. For offending Tsing Kwei with fearless opinions, Hoon perished in his exile exacted on him by that treacherous monster for grudge and revenge. And then, in the middle of South Soong, the great scholar and Confucian philosopher Tsu Hsih(朱熹) gave us his invaluable *Variorum Commentary on Ts'ou "Tze"*(《楚辞集注》), *Dialectical Comments on Ts'ou "Tze"*(《楚辞辩证》) and *Hinder Words of Ts'ou "Tze"*(《楚辞后语》). The first volume contains a critical text of the poet's works with all the variant readings the editor could obtain then from bamboo strips and silk and paper scrolls of them of the past and a digest of preceeding interpretations and Tsu's own comments. The second volume contains the editor's opinions and his refutations of various mistaken comments by such as Wang Yi, Hoon Hsin-tsou and others. The third contains Zau P'uh-tse's two collections and Tsu's notes. Though not without slight errors occasionally, Tsu-tse(朱子) has done a comprehensive and lasting service to the greatest poet of the nation.

In the above, I have touched on the salient points of *Lee Sao's* composition, manuscript, transcription, commentary and publication from the start to the dynasty Soong. Poets and scholars like Chia Yieh, Liu Shan, Wang Yi, Lih Bêh, Hang Yüe, Liu Tsoon-yuan, Hoon Hsin-tsou, Suh Sêh(苏轼) and Tsu Hsih have all added lustre to their personalities and works by imbibing glory from Chü Yuan, though Yang Hsiung(扬雄), a turncoat, trying to teach the poet's spirit a shameful lesson of his own, only soils his foul name with more filth. It is not the purpose of this commentary to make a general survey of the bibliography of the critical studies of the poet. From Tsiang Ch'ih's（蒋骥, of Tsing，清）*Remaining Comments on Ts'ou "Tze"*（《楚辞余论》）of his *San-tai Pavilion Commentary on Ts'ou "Tze"*（《山带阁注楚辞》）, the second preface of which was written in the fifth year of Yun-ts'en's reign（雍正丁未）in Tsing，i. e.，1717，studies and commentations from Han to then are known to have had already numbered eighty-four，though most of them are not of very high calibre. Tsiang lists seventeen works after Tsu-tse in the bibliography of his excellent work. Critical studies of Tsing（清）from Tsiang，T'ai Ts'en（戴震）and Chü Fu（屈复）down amount to about thirty. Today，the number must have well exceeded a hundred.

As all my manuscripts and books，Chinese and English，were all pillaged of me in the so-called "Great Cultural Revolution" in August，1966，I have been deprived of all indispensable books of reference and the bare possibility to do any mental work or even to live on a single day. Without my rare Ming block-printing edition copy of Ts'au-ming's *Literary Selections*（80 *vols.*），a scarce facsimile reprint of a Solitary south soong edition copy of Tsu Hsih's three books（6 *vols.*），reprints of Wang Yi's book，Siao Yün-zone's（萧云从）*Pictures of "Lee Sao"*（《离骚图》）and others，and two copies of Sze-ma Tsien's（司马迁）*The Chronicle*（《史记》），one，a scarce fine facsimile reprint（40 *vols.*）of Wang Saen-fuh's（王善夫）solitary South Soong edition copy and the other，a rare Jien-lung（乾隆）block-printing edition copy（24 or 30 *vols.*），I am under insuperable handicap to have embarked on such an overwhelmingly hard task of rendering this most difficult poem into English，certain phrases or lines of which have been ceaselessly disputed upon between scholars these eighteen centuries，the date of composition of which is still contended among Chü Yuan students and even the years of birth and death of the poet are not yet agreed on by us all. So, I am doing this labour of love and defiance, including the writing of the *Introduction* and these notes and comments, doggedly these two and a half years, altogether unthinkable to myself more than two and a half years ago. For the original text, I depend upon a facsimile reprint of a rare Yuan (元) edition copy of Tsu-tse's three books in Lih Suh-tsoun's(黎庶昌) *Old Lost Books Library*(《古逸丛书》), carved on blocks, printed and published in Tokyo, Japan, in 1884 (光绪十年).

For commentary and materials in my *Introduction*, I rely on the above just mentioned, a reprint of Tsiang Ch'ih's *San-tai Pavilion Commentary on Ts'ou "Tze"*(《山带阁注楚辞》) and a few other books lent to me by my student Lin Ren(凌仁), *Reference Materials of Pre-Tsing Literary History*(《先秦文学史参考资料》) by the Study Section of the History of Chinese Literature of Peking University (北京大学中国文学史教研室), 1957 (in which is included Prof. Yer Koh-en's (游国恩) up-to-date variorum commentary on *Lee Sao*), a reprint of P'an K'uh's(班固) *The Fore-Han Chronicle*(《前汉书》), a *Kong-shih Dictionary*(《康熙字典》) reprint and two volumes of *The Sea of Phrases*(《辞海》) lent to me by Lin Ren; my own block-printing edition copy of Yau Nai's(姚鼐) *A Compilation of Types of Old Prose and "Tze"*(《古文辞类纂》) and a copy of Robert Bridges' *Miltion's Prosody*, Oxford, 1921, these two were thrown away as sweepings with a few others by the caitiff underlings. These are all the books I could lay my hands on under the Proletariat Cultural Great Revolution that has already lasted well-nigh ten years now.

For guiding the readers of this terse, intense, highly allusive ode

in its drift of thoughts and feelings, I translate Tsiang Ch'ih's close a-
nalysis of the text and his concise analytical synopsis which I find elucidating, as follows. Readers who may feel these two aids an encum-
brance or a superfluity could easily skip them as they please.

"From the beginning to the end, though there are whirling ed-
dies, immensities and thousands of perplexing wonders among the
thousands and hundreds of words, yet there is one dominant strain of
thought, continuous throughout like a string of pearls, whose orderly
progression from the forefront to the rear is plain like the stretch of a
broad way, capable of being illumined and counted, as it were, one
after another. The entire piece holds the love of goodness and virtues
（好脩）as the main theme and takes the following of Peng Yen as the
last resort（结穴）. From the start to line 58 （'But I do grieve the
scentful herbage rot and drop!'）, the poet speaks of how he offends
（his sovereign）for his love of goodness and virtues. Lines 59 （'The
rabble, greedy for gain and power, rusheth on'）to 106 （'That was
indeed esteemed by sages of renown!'）relate how in spite of his offense, he does not change his goodness and virtues. With line 77 （'I
wish to go after the example of Peng Yen'）as the high tone, the
main ideas converge on this swearing by his death. But the words are
orderly unfolded. From 'The rabble, … rusheth on' down, the beginning of his offense is touched upon, hence only '… in hunger I
long pine?' is said. From 'Heaving a prolonged sigh …' down, the
main trouble is spoken of, with manifold obstructions as details, so
'nine times dead' is flouted. From 'I repine at Ling-sieu's lack…'
down, the ultimate is forecast, with the king's final inadvertency as
the particular, so 'I would rather die quickly…' is affirmed. From
lines 107 to 108 （'… I regret mine incaution…'）down, because

his mere death would be of no avail, a thought occurred to him that he would seek an ideal master all over the four compasses, thus opening the horizon of the nether half of this ode, with his love of goodness and virtues not at all changed. The passage of Neü-siu, his sister, is closely introduced after line 124 ('... to command a grand sight the four wilds round'), with emphasis laid on line 141 ('The world with vines and tendrils climbeth to form factions'), meaning that if he wishes to find a sovereign, he must change his habitual way of doting on goodness and virtues, The passage beginning with lines 145 −146 ('Going southward, ... To present to divine Tsoon-hwah mine observings') is written in contrast to Neü-siu's words, with emphasis laid on the idea in lines 177 −178 ('Minding not the square peg ... , That is why our fair precursors suffered mincing'), meaning that he had only to choose the right King to serve, but his love of goodness and virtues should not be changed — this, in accord with that 'inner glory' of his. The two passages initiated by lines 193 − 194 ('My way layeth remote and so far, ... I shall go up and down to make my long search aye'), following in sequence line 177 ('Minding not the square peg to fit in a round hole'), give out that looking all over up and down, it seems to him indeed that his love of goodness and virtues is incompatible with circumstances everywhere, so they are concluded with lines 213 −214 ('The world is so confused, muddled and promiscuous, ... ') and. 253 −254 ('The times are muddled and jealous of the virtuous, ... '), to give credit to Neü-siu's words in line 141 ('The world with vines and tendrils climbeth to form factions'). But these are, in fact, only far-reaching estimations in the poet's mind, not incongruities from realities in his actual search. The four lines 255 −258 ('The maidens stay deep in their chambers and afar') tell how he looks back at his native state Ts'ou, for there is no one in the four compasses who cares for goodness and virtues, and feels he could neither depart nor stay, thus falling into a state of dubiousness. 'The Wise King' means King Hwai of Ts'ou. The passage of Ling-fung's words says, his love of goodness and virtues would certainly meet its match elsewhere; the enchantress urges him to leave Ts'ou to banish his doubt. From line 269 ('It is darkling here; …') down, his observation proves Ling-fung's words to be true that it is impossible for him to remain in Ts'ou. Sibyl Yen's words from lines 287 to 302 urge him to leave quickly by showing him how easily his love of goodness and virtues would find its compeer and co-operation abroad, but how dangerous it is for him to be enamoured of Ts'ou and not departing speedily. From line 303 ('… these garnishings, yet wan they look') down, the complexion of things gives evidence that his departure should no more be delayed to lend weight to Yen's assurance and pleading. From line 327 ('But these wearings of mine …') down, he has made up his mind to go far away, wavering no more as heretofore, with which the deliberation started in line 124 ('… to command a grand sight the four wilds round') draws to a conclusion. So, too, his love of goodness and virtues is to be put into accomplishment. The extensive whirling and eddying of his thoughts and feelings on half a piece of this canvas come to be fixed on this deed. But driving his magnificent chariot drawn by eight dragons, preceded and followed by other smaller ones a full thousand before and after, he advances in state across the western sky. Of a sudden, he stops, for he could not leave Ts'ou and go forward. The epiphonema says, he could not remain in Ts'ou, and so he ends by acting true to his words in swearing death to seek Peng Yen. Thus, the structure of the whole piece is inalterable like heaven-made and earth-fixed. "

The analytical synopsis goes like this. "From the inception to line 58, he begins by serving his sovereign with his goodness and virtues, which give rise to envious hatred of the rabble. From lines 59 to 106, it is said that his goodness and virtues, though besieged often on all sides, grow more dauntless and indomitable, but he is willing to become Peng Yen by swearing death in his fortitude. From lines 107 to 130, even though not dying Peng Yen's death, but looking for an ideal king around the four compasses, he would not ever change his devotion to goodness and virtues. In lines 131 to 142, Neü-siu says, as the world cares not to elect one who loves goodness and virtues, what is the benefit to seek such a king? From lines 143 to 182, when attested by Tsoon-hwah, it is known that his devotion to goodness and virtues is certainly not a waste of efforts, but it must depend on the choice of a right sovereign to serve. From lines 183 to 253, he tries to look round for such a master, but finds the envious hatred of the four compasses for the devotion to goodness and virtues indeed as Neü-siu has said. The four lines beginning from 255 recount his hesitation to remain or to go, and falling into dubiousness. From lines 259 to 268, he asks Ling-fung to divine and is told that if he leaves, he would certainly meet his ideal sovereign, but in Ts'ou he should definitely not remain. Lines 269 to 278 give his observation that the soothsayer's words are veritable indeed. From lines 279 to 302, he bids the sibyl Yen to inquire his proceedings of the gods; in reply, the oracle says, going abroad, he would find concord with an ideal master very easy, but delaying in Ts'ou, he is sure to encounter calamity. From lines 303 to 326, he surveys and finds the situation growing more threatening. From lines 327 to 370, he knows Neü-siu's words untrustworthy and Tsoon-hwah's catholic illumination(正果) dependable; making up his mind to go far away, he immediately sees his devotional love of goodness and virtues could serve him a long way; but then, could he really sally forth abroad and forget his Ts'ou? The epiphonema concludes with his swearing death to follow Peng Yen. This is the general outline of the whole ode."

Many Western critics and readers might find the whole theme "moralizing, abstract and dull". But that is because they are used to reading narrative, epic poetry such as Homer's *Iliad* and *Odyssey*, Virgil's *Aeneid*, Dante's *La Divina Commedia* and Milton's *Paradise Lost* for instance or the dramatic poetry of Aeschylus, Sophocles and Euripides of ancient Hellas, of Shakespeare, Corneille, Moliere and Racine of Renaissance and seventeenth century England and France, or else the literary extravaganzas *Gargantua and Pantagruel* and the mock romance *Don Quixote* down to our modern fictional works of Europe and America. In all these classical and popular works of general appeal, there is this common resort to he narration of a story or presenting a series of actions, which hold the interest of the readers and divert their minds from uninteresting affairs. Well and good; they should be thus esthetically occupied. But has it ever occurred to them that the contemplation of an ideal government and the appreciation of a personality who strives with his soul and body to realize that, whose every spiritual and moral effort and nerve fibre are strained to achieve peace, commonweal and public joy and to fight against fascisdom, tyranny and clandestime politics, are at least equally, if not more worth their interest and occupation in the realm of high poetry? Why is such a theme taboo to splendid poetry? There is no absolute necessity of falling into the accustomed rut of diverting the mind with narration and story-telling, or the presentation of actions only. A departure could be made, and that reasonably. So, here is Chü Yuan, with his wondrous ode, descriptively lyrical in nature, not a fresco of tales and stories for diversion, whose sole devotion is to goodness and virtues for the sake of the people. The matter of government and policies, though partially, only portially, basically solved in a number of countries, is still far from being settled in the greater part of our globe; the world today is in a State of chaos just like our Warring States more than two thousand years ago. If behooves us to understand such a poet and appreciate this masterpiece of his, to overcome our prejudice against the so-called "abstraction" and "moralization", and to fix our happy-go-lucky attention on humanity itself and its mortal questions.

Aristotle in his *Poetics* has already told us more than two thousand years ago, and we could not refute or improve on him today, that the modes of esthetic verbal imitation of life or the methods of poetical expression are divisible into three categories: the lyrical, the narrative and the dramatic. Odes, songs and lyrics belong to the first order, in which the impressions of reality produced on the poet as his feelings and sensations are directly presented by him to lit up the minds and personalities of his readers. Epic poetry belongs to the second order, in which the characters and incidents of the external world are portrayed to reflect objective happenings. Tragedies and comedies belong to the third order, in which the characters and incidents of life are pictured in actions and unfoldings to give semblance to real life. Of the three classes, the first is fraught with tensity because of its subjective nature, and for thorough transfiguration of the poet's empa-

thies and inscapes into his reader's feelings and sensations, it is sometimes, though not always, necessary to depict the intellectual, moral
and political temperament of the poet in advance in order to fully understand and appreciate him, as in our case. On account of their sub-
jectivity, odes must be shorter in compass or verbal dimensions, not
at all so sustained or liberal in length as to be commensurate with epics and dramas. This is my apology and answer to certain criticisms
of this ode's supposed short-comings and shortness.

In order not to disfigure the text with a host of Arabic figures, I
give, in the following, the numbers of the notes first, the line numbers next, and then the words, phrases or lines commented upon, followed by annotations. The greater part of this commentary is taken
from Tsu Hsih and Tsiang Ch'ih's books, though Wang Yi, Hoon
Hsin-tsou and others are also quoted and discussed. Good for close
reading and thorough understanding of the text, all these notes and
comments may be found cumbrous and burdensome by some readers.
If so, they can leave these alone.

1. *l.* 1, Emperor Kao-yang. See *Introduction*, *p.* 5.

2. *l.* 2, the whole line. Wang Yi(王逸) of East Han(东汉), the
first of over a hundred commentators of *Lee Sao*, explains the
character 考 as "the late father". On cast bronze bells(钟),
two-eared tripodal caldrons(鼎, *t'ing*) and vessels for daily or
sacrificial uses(彝器) of Saung and Tsur(商,周), 皇 means
"illustrious" or "excellent". Some commentators, past and recent, like Wang Kae-yün(王闿运) and Wen Ih-to(闻一多),
say, however, 皇考 means "forefather", and one of them, Rao
Tsoon-yieh(饶宗颐), identifies Pêh-yung(伯庸) with Tsuo
Yung(祝融), the official title given by *T'ih* Ko(帝喾) to his

Lord of Fire（火正）Lih（犁，according to the Tso *Commentary*
(《左传》) of *The Spring and Autumn Annals*）, the son, or
Tsoon Lih（重黎，according to *The Annals of the State Ts'ou*(《楚
世家》) of *The Chronicle*）, the great grandson, of Tsuan-shiuh
（颛顼）, Emperor Kao-yang（高阳氏）. But I uphold Wang Yi's
explanation here, for it is improper to speak of two remote ancestors not far apart, one after the other, while it is quite appropriate
to name a renowned ancestor first and then his "illustrious sire
deceased", in two contiguous lines at the start.

3. *l*. 3, *Kêng-yin*. See *Introduction*, *pp*. 6 −7. His date of birth is
called by the combination of a particular heavenly *kan*（天干）
with a particular earthly *tse*（地支）, viz., *Kêng-yin*（庚寅）.
Heaven opened up with *tse*（子）, the first symbol of twelve
earthly *tse*（地支）, earth was unraveled with *tser*（丑）, the second symbol, and man was born first with *yin*（寅）, the third
symbol, at the beginning of the universe, according to the cosmogony of *Lien-san*(《连山》), the earliest of the *Three Mutabilities*(《三易》), attributed to Hsla（夏）. Chü Yuan's date of birth
fell on *Kêng-yin*, as distinguished from the other one or two *yin*
days of the month.

4. *l*. 4, the whole line. Tsu Hsih（朱熹）, the great Soong（宋）
commentator, says the line means "When the star Sê-tih（摄提）
following the stem of the Dipper just pointed to the (north-)
north-east, the position of the first lunar month in the evening,
or, the stem of the Dipper, through the pair of triple stars of the
Sê-tih Constellation, pointed (north-) north-eastward to the position of the first moon of the year. " Sê-tih was the year star. It is
in fact a constellation of six stars, three on each side south of the

bright orange star Arcturus(大角). So, the month of the poet's birth was the first moon in early spring.

An earlier interpretation of these two lines by Wang Yi of Han has it that the year, month and day of his birth all pertained to the auspicious earthly *tse*(地支) of *yin*(寅). See my discussion of the poet's year of birth in section VII, §1 of *Introduction*, *pp*. 71 −80. Wang's interpretation is disputed by Tsu Hsih as unfounded; the year was not necessarily a *yin* one, says he, although the first moon, pointed at by the Dipper stem when he was born, showed his month of birth to be in the *yin* position. Wang Yi, Hoon Hsin-tson after him, and then Tsiang Ch'ih and their modern followers, are simply misled by the *yin* day and *yin* position of the lunar month to think the year also a *yin* year, and then imagine a rationalizing reason that "the three *yin*" "struck the very middle of the negative and positive laws"("得阴阳之正中").

5. *l*.7, the whole line. It is said in *The Tsur Rites*(《周礼》) that a boy is given his formal name three months after his birth, and when he has grown up to manhood at he age of twenty (counted on the lunar calendar), he is given his informal name for daily use. The poet's formal or ceremonious name is Tsen-tsê(正则), meaning the right, square, just, fair or even law. The ceremonious name(名) of a gentleman was used only on very formal, ceremonial occasions by his elders, superiors and himself. He was addressed by his relatives and friends only with his informal name for daily use(字). For the poet's other formal name Bing(平), other informal name Yuan(原) and their relevance to the condition of his birth and his carriage during boyhood as well as

to Tsen-tsê and Ling-chün, see section VII, §1 of *Introduction*.

6. *l.* 8, the whole line. His informal name for daily use is Ling-Chün(灵均) which means inspired harmony or intelligent and clear-sighted faculty conforming with justice and uprightness.

7. *l.* 11, the whole line. 芎䕅, the selinea, an aromatic herb, according to *The Native Medicinal herbal*(《本草》), is called 蘼芜 when tender, and 江离 when full-grown. It is an umbelliferous plant one to two feet tall with clusters of small white flowers in autumn. The original 辟芷 means 芷 or 白芷, the angelica which grows in secluded spots. It is an odoriferous herb over four feet tall, blowing small white flowers in clusters in summer. These and other aromatic plants said to be knit into apparels or braided as pendants by the poet for wearing, symbolize the fair, sweet qualities and attributes of the poet.

8. *l.* 12, eupatories autumnal. 秋兰 of the original is autumnal eupatories(兰草), not orchids(兰花). *The Herbal of Native Medicinal Plants*(《本草纲目》) by Lih Sze-tsen(李时珍) of the Ming (明) Dynasty says, "Eupatory has several species: eupatory(兰草) and arethusa(泽兰) grow by the water-side. Mountain eupatory(山兰) is eupatory growing on mountains. Orchid(兰花) also grows on mountains, but is distinctly different from mountain eupatory. Orchid which grows in this neighbourhood (Lih was a native of Chyih-tsur, 蕲州, Hu-pei, 湖北) has leaves like *Liriope graminifolia*(麦门冬) and blooms in autumn." Eupatory (also called hempagrimony) and arethusa, it should be kept in mind, belong to the class called *Compositae*(菊科), while orchid belongs to the class called *Orchidaceae*(兰科). Tsu Hsih, in his comments on the ode, says, "(Like selinea and angeli-

ca,) eupatory is also an aromatic herb. It blows in autumn. *The Native Medicinal Herbal*(《本草》) says, eupatory, looking like arethusa, also grows by the water-side, with purple stems, red at protuberant joints, four to five feet tall, with glossy green leaves which are long, pointed at end and saw-toothed on edges, luxuriant in summer." In his *Dialectical Comments on Ts'ou "Tze"* (《楚辞辩证》), after mentioning some mistakes and confusions, he says very plainly thus："Generally speaking, fragrant herbs of ancient times must have their flowers and leaves all sweet and must remain unchanged whether dry or moist, so that they could be mown and made into pendants. While what are called 兰 and 蕙 nowadays, although their flowers are sweet, have leaves that are odourless, their flowers are agreeably scentful, yet they are frail and easily withered; they could not be mown and braided into pendants. Very clearly they are not what were called by such names in olden days. But it is not known when the mistake set in." In short, eupatory, about four feet tall, blooming little flowers of light purple in autumn, is fragrant in stems and leaves as well as in flowers. It is also called 蕳,香,水,兰,兰泽草,都梁香. It has nothing to do, and should not be confused, with orchid(兰花).

Of orchid, Wuh Chih-jium(吴其浚) of Tsing(清) says, in his *Studies in Names and Realities of Plants with Illustrations*(《植物名实图考》), it "is what is called by Dao Ts'ien the recluse(陶隐居)'the swallow grass'(燕草) and in *Leisurely observations in 'Escape Study'*(《遯斋闲览》)'the secluded orchid'(幽兰). It has many varieties. On mountains in spring, orchids of a stalk with one flower and of a stalk with several flowers are to be found everywhere. Among those that grow in Fu-Kien, the plain-hearted ones(素心) are esteemed precious. " This "secluded orchid"(幽兰) , however, has nothing at all to do with the " secluded eupatories"(幽兰) of Chü Yuan's 结幽兰而延伫 and 谓幽兰其不可佩 in the latter part of the ode (*ll.* 212 and 274). Orchid, an evergreen graminifolious plant, has, as I know, the following sorts, 草兰 or 山兰; cymbidium is the most common variety; it has long slender leaves about a foot long, blooming one flower on each stalk in February, between the lightest of green and the white of a tooth in colour with deep purple spots and odourous in smell. 蕙兰, wei-orchid or wei-cymbidium, has more leaves and longer ones than the former kind, longer by about one foot; it blooms from six or seven to ten or eleven flowers on each stalk in April, same in colour and shape as the former but slightly smaller in size. 建兰, cymbidium ensifolium is the variety growing in Fu-kien (福建), with leaves middling in length between those of the former two, and five to seven flowers on each stalk, similar in shape and colour to, but more scentful than, the fomer's, blossoming in July. The plain-hearted(素心) kind of any one of the above varieties is celebrated for its rarity; it is cherished for its lack of deep purple spots on the flowers. And there is a rare species called ink-stick orchid(墨兰) from Fu-kien, with six or seven flowers of very deep mauve to each stalk as if dancing in joy, blowing in February with ethereal fragrance; it has broad leaves of about an inch wide of the most beautiful lustrous green. And there are the very precious kinds "plum of Soong"(宋梅) , "green lotus"(绿荷), etc. But all these — they are irrelevant here, I must apologize — have nothing whatsoever to do with Chü Yuan's 兰 or 秋兰 in *Lee Sao*, which is eupatory. Among modern students of Chü Yuan, there are Lim Boon-keng(林文庆) and Kou Mê-ruo(郭沫若) whom I know to have mistaken the second class for the first or to be confused about the two. Hence I make this digression on orchids to make the clear distinction between these two unrelated families of fragrant plants.

In Chü Yuan's *Nine Songs*(《九歌》), however, 石兰 in the *Hymn on the King of Hsiang*(《湘君》), *l.* 28, and in the *Hymn on the Mountain Sprite*(《山鬼》), *l.* 7, are, as Tsiang Ch'ih has pointed out in the first instance, mountain orchids (山兰).

"With natural endowments of inherent virtues within and further increased with acquired embellishments of eminent abilities, I am thus as if clothed with selineas and angelicas grown in secluded spots and, besides, wearing autumnal eupatories as my fragrant pendant on the girdle."

9. *l.* 15, magnolia. The magnolia(木兰) is said by *The Native Medicinal Herbal* to be an aromatic tree with barks like those of the cinnamon. It is of great height and beautiful foliage like the *Machilus Nanmu*(楠). It would not die when partly stripped of its bark. Twenty to thirty feet tall, it blooms large sweet flowers in late spring, darker purple outside the petals and light purple inside.

10. *l.* 15, big knoll. 阰, from Wang Yi(王逸) of East Han(东汉) down, has been said by commentators to be the name of a mountain, Mount Pih. The Tsing(清) scholars T'ai Ts'en(戴震) and Yü Yüeh(俞樾) propose "a big hill", "large clay knoll", "elevation", etc. It is attributed by a modern Chü Yuan student Rao

Tsoon-yieh(饶宗颐) to Mount Pih(沘山) of Luh-kiang *hsien* (庐江县), from which the Pih Stream(沘水, now called 淠水 or Bêh-sah River, 白沙河) flows, *vide* Rao's *Geographical Studies of Ts'ou "Tze"*(《楚辞地理考》), Commercial Press, Shanghai, 1946. Luh-kiang *hsien* is in An-whei(安徽), in the Ling-yang(陵阳) region where Chü Yuan was forced to stay for some nine years during the reign of King Hsiang(襄王). But according to Sze-ma Tsien's *The Life of Chü Yuan of The Chronicle* (《史记·屈原列传》), *Lee Sao* was composed after the poet was repulsed("疏") by King Hwai. And judging from the internal evidence of agonizing sorrow and despair for a long period in the poem as a result of his expulsion(斥逐) from Ying-t'uh to Han-pei by King Hwai from 311 B. C. onward, and the external circumstantial evidence that when he was banished(放,放逐,放流,迁) by Hsiang to Ling-yang in the south of the River, he had already said his say long before, his tears had gone dry and he was not in a mood to write a work needing such sustained effort as *Lee Sao*, we can reasonably make the conclusion that Mount Pih(沘山) of Luh-kiang has nothing to do with Chü Yuan's 阰 here. Rao's contention that Sze-ma Tsien's *Letter in Reply to Ren An*(《报任安书》) saying, "After his exile (放逐), Chü Yuan composed his *Lee Sao*", affords the proof that the ode was written in Hsiang's reign. But there is an incongruity between this statement and that one saying the ode was written after the poet's repulse("疏") by King Hwai. This incongruity serves to prove, I think, that the historian is lax in his vague reference to the occasion of the poem, but he is exact in his indication of the date of composition falling in the reign of Hwai. In conclusion, I would say that Yer Koh-en(游国恩), Kuo Mê-ruo(郭沫若) and Rao's conjectures that *Lee Sao* was composed in Hsiang's reign are all decidedly mistaken. As for the meaning of 阰, I adopt in my rendition T'ai Ts'en and Yü Yüeh's explanation.

11. *l*. 16, "herb evergreen" and these two lines. The original 宿莽 is an evergreen grass called *jüen-sze*(卷施草 or 卷葹), said to be able to stand having its heart plucked away without dying, according to *Erl Ya*(《尔雅》), commented by Kuo Po(郭璞) of Ts'ih(晋). These two lines mean to say that what he picked and collected were fall fragrant and durable things, just as his ways of life were all fidelity, goodness and permanence.

12. *l*. 20, the whole line. His sovereign King Hwai is idealized and metaphorically called the Beauteous One(美人), whom, beloved of himself, he had entertained the fond wishes of serving as aid to go straight the ways of *T'ih* Yao and *T'ih* Suen, but alas! Hindered by the clique maligners with foul vilifications, he has undergone rigorous trials, travails and tribulations. However, at the moment, he merely says here, in continuance with what is said before (he only knows how to devote himself to loyalty virtues and other intrinsic qualities), that he is now aware time is so fleeting and, thinking of the trees and herbage that fall sear, fears he would not be able to mate Her in time, that is, aid his lord in his prime of life to bring concord and bliss to his subjects.

13. *l*. 21, the whole line. The line means to say "Not holding on the prime of thy life and clearing away thy weedy practices, …"

14. *l*. 23, coursers. 骐骥, coursers or steeds that stand for fair virtues and wisdom.

15. *l*. 25, the whole line. 昔三后 of the original are said by Wang Yi

in *Textual Critical Studies in Ts'ou "Tze"*(《楚辞章句》) to mean "the three renowned kings of old", Yü of Hsia(夏禹), Taung of Saung(商汤) and Wen of Tsur(周文). In Tsu Hsih's *Dialectical Comments on Ts'ou "Tze"*(《楚辞辩证》), he attributes them to the three *Hwang*(三皇,*vide* section II of *Introduction*, *pp.* 4 −6) or to Sao-hao(少昊), Tsuan-shiuh(颛顼) and Kao-sing(高辛) (*ibid*, *pp.* 7 −8), for it is unlikely Yao and Suen(尧,舜) are mentioned after Yü, Taung and Wen in *line* 29; their purity means the beau-ideal and homogeneity contained in their polices. But Tsiang Ch'ih says, in his *San-tai Pavilion Commentary on Ts'ou "Tze"*(蒋骥:《山带阁注楚辞》), according to *The Penal Law of Leü of The Classic of History*(《尚书 · 吕刑》), 三后 here means not the three kings, but the three eminent lords or high officials Pêh-yih(伯夷), Yü(禹) and Ji(稷) at Yao and Suen's courts (*ibid.*, *p.* 9). The poet means to compare himself to these three virtuous aids to their masters, says Tsiang, and hopes his king to become Yao and Suen.

16. *l.* 26, the whole line. "The reason why the three renowned lords of old with their excellent colleagues had formed an assemblage of virtuous aids to their sovereigns was due to their purity of virtues."

17. *l.* 27, peppers of Sun with cinnamons. 申椒 means the Tsing peppers(秦椒,Chinese pepper) of the extirpated state Sun(申), a fief alloted to the progeny of Pêh-yih(伯夷) in early Tsur and annexed by Ts'ou during the Spring and Autumn Period. 菌桂 is cinnamon or cassia bark, used as spice and in medicine. *The Tseng-noon Classic of Native Medicinal Herbs*(《神农本草经》) says, "Cinnamon is produced in Cochin(交阯), round like the

tubular stem of bamboo. " It has white flowers and yellow pistils and stamens. Its tender bark rolls itself up like a bamboo shaft. It should be written as 筒桂, but was first corrupted into 箘桂 and again into 菌桂.

18. *l*. 28, coumarous and angelicas. Hoon Hsin-tsou(洪兴祖) in his *Supplemental Commentary on Ts'ou "Tze"*(《楚辞补注》)quotes *The Native Medicinal Herbal*(《本草》): "The coumarou(薰草) is also called tonka bean(蕙草). " *The West Mountain Classic* of *The Mountain and Sea Classic*(《山海经·西山经》) describes the plant thus: "On Mount Ver(浮山) grows an herb called coumarou, with leaves like hemp and square stems. red blooms and black seeds, smelling like the selinea(靡芜). Wearing it as pendant could cure plagues. " It is also called 零陵香 and 佩兰, growing in low damp spots and blowing in the middle of the seventh moon, very sweet in its flowers. 茝 is the same as 芷, angelica.

19. *l*. 31, Ghi and Zer. *Vide* section II of *Introduction*, *pp*. 10 −11, 13 −14.

20. *l*. 39, Queen Acorus. 荃, same as 荪, acorus or sweet-flag-sedge, flag-rush, is an aromatic herb that grows in crevices of rocks in small streams, nowadays commonly known as 石菖蒲, 白菖, 溪荪. Since it is figuratively used here to mean King Hwai of Ts'ou, it is personified and the word should be capitalized. As he is called the Beauteous One(美人) and Ling-sieu(灵脩) elsewhere in this ode. it is proper to give the name a feminine title Queen.

21. *l*. 40, slander. Slanderers of Chü Yuan of the pro-Tsing clique mentioned by Sze-ma Tsien in *The Life of Chü Yuan*(《屈原列

传》) and by Liu Shan (刘向) in his *New Relatings* (《新序》)
are the Soun-quan courtier (上官大夫, whose name is unknown), Jin Soun (靳尚). Tse-tsiao (子椒, Lord of War, 司
马), Tse-lan (子兰, King Hwai's younger son and Ching-
hsiang's brother and premier, 令尹) and Ts'eng Sieü (郑袖,
King Hwai's favourite concubine, 宠姬).

22. *l.* 41, the whole line. "I had known before, to speak faithfully is
my trouble, for it is hard for me to do so as it is difficult for my
sovereign to listen to me." — Tsu Hsih.

23. *l.* 43, nine-compassed Heaven. 九天 of the original gives rise to
abundant speculations about the structure of heaven. No one
knows for a certainty what the poet exactly mean by the expression. In his earlier poem *Sky-vaulting Queries* (《天问》), a host
of over a hundred and seventy perplexing questions, almost all
unanswerable at his time, he asks,

> 圜则九重
>
> 孰营度之?
>
> 维兹何功,
>
> 孰初作之?

> Ninefold is the rotund principle;
>
> Who was the planner of its make?
>
> Who the primordial effort
>
> At the beginning of time did take?

The question is whether "ninefold" means the vault of the sky
"is made up of nine compasses", "has nine layers" or amounts
to nine in some other respects. *The Book of Homage to Heaven
and Earth* (《封禅书》) of *The Chronicle* (《史记》) gives names
to the four cardinal quarters, the four intermediate ones between

any two of them in sequence and the central portion of heaven as the nine compasses. Yang Hsiung(扬雄) of Han, a zealous admirer of Chü Yuan's poetry, gives names to the nine heavens in *The Classic of Arch-mysticism*(《太玄经》), written by him in imitation of *The Classic of Mutability*(《易经》), but they are just empty names. Tsu Hsih's *Variorum Commentary on Ts'ou "Tze"* (《楚辞集注》) says of 九天 that, learning from Sao-tse (Sao Yung, Kong-tsi, 邵雍, 康节, the great authority on the three tomes of *Mutabilities*, 三"易", by Fwu-shih, 伏羲, Hwang-t'ih, 黄帝, and King Wen, 文王), that heaven rests on earth, earth is attached to heaven, they are mutually dependent and not supported by anything else, heaven rests on its own form and earth on air, and heaven's form is limited but earth's air is boundless, he comes to the conclusion that heaven, round like a ball, whirls round mornings and nights from left to right and from right to left, rolls back and forth, and forth and back, spinning to and fro and rising and dropping down endlessly, so that earth, the sediment of the whirling air, is able to float in the air without falling down. As to the epithet ninefold, it is simply the utmost quantity of positive numbers, connoting here the great speed and infinity of heaven's spinning and rolling. Next, Wuh Tsun(吴澄) of Yuan(元) puts forth the idea that the vault of the sky consists of nine layers in his writings, though he does not give any specific description. And finally, Tsiang Ch'ih(蒋骥) of Tsing(清), in his *San-tai Pavilion Commentary on Ts'ou "Tze"* (《山带阁注楚辞》), recommends the Roman Catholic conception of heaven brought to China in the eighties of the sixteenth century by the ltalian missionary Matteo Riccio(利玛窦), which was a fusion of Aristotelian logic and astronomy with medieval European cosmography, attributing nine layers to the vault of the sky, one wrapping over another like an onion. Of course, this is irrelevant here. We must presume that Chü Yuan means Sze-ma Tsien's nine compasses.

24. *l.* 44, the whole line and the next two lines. Ling-sieu(灵脩), Wang Yi says, means the wise and far-sighted, the king. The compliment turns out to be just the opposite of his character. "… For thy sake": "I have been struggling so hard with the sole purpose to conduct thee unto the kingly way." The next two lines are suspected by Hoon Hsin-tsou (洪兴祖), the early South Soong(南宋) commentator. to be an interpolation. They happen to be almost the same as two lines in *Drawing My Thoughts*(《抽思》) of the *Sylva of Nine Piece*(《九章》). Hoon points out that the character 羌 in the second of these two lines is not annotated by Wang Yi. till it appears again in line 61. But in Tsu-tse's text, these two lines are regarded as pertaining to *Lee Sao* here: he says, they might have already been lost (in some copies of the text) before Wang Yi.

25. *l.* 45, the whole line. In times of old. dusk was the set moment when the bridegroom, led by the matchmakers in a carriage, went to greet the bride in person at the door of her parents by riding a horse and taking along with him ceremonial followers, a band of instrumental music gaily dressed and a "flowery palanquin" well decked with embroidered and spangled silk and tiny lamps, borne by a group of bearers. After presenting a pair of wild-geese, a symbol of conjugal fidelity, the groom waited at the door for the bride's father to upbear his daughter to the palan-

quin, accompanied by her mother and an elderly maid. Coming to the groom's home, the bride was led down the palanquin by her elderly maid, the groom and the matchmakers to the hall of the groom's home where the couple performed the nuptial rites of doing obeisance to heaven and earth, to the ancestors of the groom, to themselves each other and to the parents of the groom, his brothers and sisters and all other relatives. That evening is called "the first evening" (初昏) in *The Ceremonial Rites*(《仪礼》), which devotes the whole of its second chapter to the gentleman's espousal rites(士昏礼).

26. *ll.* 51 −52, *woan* and *mou*. A *woan*(畹), a spacial measure of thirty *mou*(亩), is equivalent to 30 ×0. 1644 or 4. 932 acres. Nine *woan* amount to 4. 932 ×9 or 44. 388 acres. A *mou*(亩), a spacial measure of 0. 1644 acre, multiplied by 100 amount to 16. 44 acres. Fifty *mou* amount to 0. 1644 ×50 or 8. 22 acres.

27. *l.* 53, *liou-yih* and *chi-chü*. Both *liou-yih*(留夷) and *chi-chü*(揭车) are said to be aromatic herbs. The latter, also called 乞舆, 芎舆 and 藕车香, is described as spicy, growing at Peng-tsen (彭城, once the capital of King Hwai of Ts'ou, now Tung-san *hsieni*, 铜山县, Kiang-suh, 江苏), several feet tall. with white leaves and yellow flowers (or yellow leaves and white flowers).

28. *l.* 54, asarums. Asarum(杜蘅) is an evergreen aromatic herb growing on mountains, with heart-shaped leaves and small, dark purple flowers in winter; its tuber roots are for medicinal use.

29. *ll.* 57 −58, these two lines. These two lines are said by Tsiang Ch'ih to allude to the fine, capable men elected to office under the poet's recommendation. "What is the harm to him personally that they are trampled by his enemies? But what a great loss it is

to the state of Ts'ou!" Yer Koh-en says the second line alludes to the degradation of those who were formerly so line.

30. *l.* 68, the whole line. The epithet "autumn chrysanthemums" for 秋菊 is rather unwiedly in its length; so I prefer "asters" in its stead. Asters have several varieties, I learn, most of them bloom in autumn. and there is a sort called China asters(翠菊) which look like chrysanthemums and bloom purple, blue, red or white flowers in autumn. These, however, I understand, do not have deciduous petals. Here, it must be said, the expression 落英 is open to two differing explanations. In common usage, it means "dropt petals". We know Chü Yuan was not a botanist; he might not have actually dined on their petals, whether "dropt" or picked. He merely says here of drinking "the magnolia's falling dews" and eating "asters' dropt petals" to signify his poverty and purity. But the character 落 may mean 始, "beginning", "incipient" or "inchoate", as evidenced by the *Tsur Ode*(《周颂》) and *Plan the Beginning*(《访落》) of *The Classic of Poetry*(《诗经》). In this sense, the line should be "... asters' blooming petals ...", not "... asters' dropt petals ...", importing the poet's purity and high integrity.

31. *l.* 70, ... though in hunger I long pine. "... though in hunger I look sallow(癯颔) long!"

32. *l.* 72, pomelo figs. 薜荔(*ficus pumila*) is an evergreen vine with egg-shaped thick leaves two to three inches long, small white(？) flowers and fig-like fruits. It entwines on big trees or creeps on high walls, said to be luxuriant after a growth of thirty to fifty years. It is commented by Wang Yi to be an aromatic plant and quoted by Hoon Hsih-tsou from *Quanrse*(《管子》) and a Fore-

Han cantata(前汉乐章) to be also such. But as we know it, the plant is not fragrant and *Studies in Names and Realities of Plants with Illustrations*(《植物名实图考》) has already said so. Pomelo figs are popularly called "wood buns"(木馒头) or ghost buns (鬼馒头) south of the Yang-tse River; their seeds could be made into "cool size"(凉粉, an inspissated, gluey, curd, to be taken sweetened and with plum jam in summer). It is possible. I think, Chü Yuan had the false impression that the plant was a fragrant one, and the notion was perpetuated by Wang Yi. Tsu Tsiun-sun(朱骏声) of Tsing(清) says in his *Supplemental Commentary on "Lee Sao"*(《离骚补注》) that 薜荔 is 当归 (*ligusticum acutilobum*). also called 山蕲, 白蕲, which is a medicinal herb only two to three feet tall. with its stem. tuber roots and leaves all fragrant, blowing sweet white flowers in autumn. But in Chü Yuan's *Musing on the Beauteous One*(《思美人》), pomelo fig is described as such a tall plant that the poet has to clamber to reach it not as a small herb of two to three feet.

33. *l.*73, cassia barks. See note 17.

34. *l.*74, sweet ivies. 胡绳 is a sort of aromatic ivy, used as a string here to tie pieces of cinnamon barks and duds of coumarous.

35. *l.*77, Peng Yen. Peng Yen(彭咸) is said by Wang Yi to be a courtier of rectitudc of the dynasty Yin(殷) who drowned himself for his remonstrance to his king was refused. Hoom Hsintsou quotes Yen Sze-k'uh(颜师古) of Tdaung(唐) for saying that Peng Yen was an upright intellectual in the dynasty Yin who drowned himself in protest against the state of affairs under the rule of Zer(纣). Neither of these two sayings is known, says Tsu Hsih, to be based on any verifiable source.

36. *ll.* 81^1 −82^2, these two lines. He bends all his arduous efforts to serve the king, the head of the state, ultimately for the sake of the people who are now beset with distresses and afflictions.

37. *l.* 81^2, the whole line. His preceptive bridles are motivated by his will to do good to the people and his sense of honour.

38. *l.* 82^2, the whole line. He was dismissed from the offices of the Lord of Three Portals(三闾大夫) and Left Counsellor(左徒) to the king and expelled from the capital Ying-*t'uh* to Han-pei, but not exactly banished, late in the eighteenth year of Kings Hwai's reign, 311 B. C.

39. *l.* 88, the whole line. The king was totally ignorant of public opinion; he could not and did not even try to sound people's hearts.

40. *l.* 90, the whole line. The pro-Tsing rabble spreads the despicable slander, with Ts'eng Sieu's concurrence, that Chü Yuan had been trying to make love to her. It was incomprehensible to him that his enemies were so unscrupulously envious of his fair repute.

41. *ll.* 91 −92, these two lines. Literally, these two lines should be:
    It is the craftiness of the current times
    To shape things despite the compasses and the square.

42. *ll.* 93 −94, these two lines. Literally, these two lines should be:
    People flout the regular rules to pursue the crook,
    Vie in conspiring to form their law (perverse).

43. *ll.* 103 −106, these four lines. "As he could chew the cud of blame and the disgrace gulp down, now his anxiety at the absence of a fair name spoken of before (*ll.* 65, 66) has ceased to be his deep concern. Ever since ancient times, men of loyalty of

unimpeachable qualities, as a rule not fearful of death, all loved their fair repute jealously, while their villainous enemies invariably, blotted them with nasty concoctions. They had nothing to be framed up with, indeed; but their times were most often depraved. So, what was fair to them was usually foul to their age. If they did obeisance to their times, they could live in prosperity and honour. Otherwise, poverty and disgrace were their lot. Rather to bear the blot and die in order to be in accord with the virtuous of the past is therefore the utmost of purity. " — Tsiang Ch'ih.

This was truly Chü Yuan's invincible verity. But on the wide-open, inter-state political arena right then was exhibited the darkest forces of mankind just engaged in hot pursuit of facinorous power as represented by the Tsing of King Ts'au(秦昭王) and Tsang Yih(张仪)(See section VI of *Introduction*, *pp.* 89 – 103). Deception was one of the cardinal principles of Tsing. King Ts'au and Tsang Yih deceived King Hwai of Ts'ou repeatedly as regards the geo-politics of cross conjunction. Chü Yuan (by means of vilification), the 600 sq. *lih* of the Wuh-Saung region and the meeting at the Wuh Pass(武关), both directly through Tsang Yih and indirectly through the pro-Tsing ring. Viewed in such a perspective, Chü Yuan's struggles impart much significance even to us today.

"From lines 60 to 106, the growing calamity of the traducers is related, and his resolution to be good and virtuous becomes firmer every day, to show his will to become Peng Yen. " — Tsiang Ch'il.

44. *ll.* 109 – 110, these two lines. "Now that I have come to this

strait, I regret that I had not clearly seen my way with prevision so as to be at loggerheads with the world. I stand on tiptoe and strain my neck, ready to wheel round my car to retrace my way back. Thus, I may return to where I came from while I have gone astray not too far. " — Tsu Hsih.

45. *ll*. 111 −112, these two lines. "Whether making his horse amble slowly or gallop to his retirement, he is never forgetful of the fragrant herbs, that is, always keeps his purity intact. " — Tsu Hsih.

46. *l*. 115, nelumbo and trapa. Nelumbo or Chinese water-lily(荷, 莲) is an aquatic plant with large round leaves on tall stalks and large beautiful flowers called lotus(芙蓉,芙蕖) in summer, pink or white in colour and delicately scented. The lotus in bud(菡 萏) or in full bloom is celebrated for its elegance and beauty. Trapa(芰,薢 or 菱) is a floating water-plant with heart-shaped leaves and edible seeds of two, three or four prongs in autumn. Chü Yuan's fair repute is not at all contaminated by the foul traducings. On the contrary, his inviolate personality is etherealized by his fearless rejection of the rabble's rank impudence to a higher state of purity.

47. *l*. 118, the whole line. "So long as mine heart-felt feelings are truly sweet. "

48. *l*. 119, the whole line. The first four lines of *Over the Streans* (《涉江》), written during the poet's exile from Ling-yang(陵 阳) in going over the streams Kiang(江), Hsiang(湘), Yuan (沅), Waung(枉), Tsen(辰) and Süe(溆). are as follows:

From youthful days, I love this (novel) gown,

Now I am aging, but still do so as of auld;

> I bear by my side a sword of sheen blade long.
>
> And wear atop this tall, tall hat Cut-cloud.

A hat stood in those days for a man's dignity and personality.

49. *l*. 121, the whole line. The fair and sweet flowers that make his apparels and the gems and jades that form his pendants on the girdle — their fragrance and lustre are mixed up and spread all over his body. Tsu Hsih is perfectly correct in explaining these two lines thus. But Wang Fuh-tse(王夫之) of early Tsing(清) perversely gives the meaning "the fifth of soiled nether underwear" to the word 泽, thus destroying the whole sweet and beautiful atmosphere built up since line 115.

50. *l*. 122, the whole line. "My bright, pure qualities are as they use to be. " This was in the best tradition of the virtuous of this land. "These glittering qualities may recede and become self-contained, but not the least lessened or despoiled — if the Way could hold away through him. the world would be benefitted; if it were prevented from so doing, one should elevate oneself alone (道行则兼善天下，不用则独善其身). " — Tsu Hsih.

51. *l*. 130, the whole line. "In the above, he has sworn himself to death (*ll*. 77,103 −106). But thinking that his death would be of no avail to the world, he comes to realize that it is better to recede and preserve himself. And in so doing, he entertains the thought of getting a sight of the kings of the wide world. But his will to be virtous himself is never altered. ... The four lines 'In life, ... ' summarize the ideas from the beginning of the ode to this point; they are the joint or hinge of the whole poem. For at the start, he speaks of serving his sovereign with his inner virtues diverse and ' brave nurtures daedal '; when he is stricken with

traducings, he vows his goodness and honour; when he encounters dismissal, he swears he would stand on uprightness and die a straight death to follow the sages of the past; when he is ready to get a sight of the sages of the past; when he is ready to get a sight of the Kings of the wide world, he has donned his ‘old clothes that seem best’ — thus, he is throughout devoted to goodness and virtues. From these four lines onward, the drift of ideas follows from ‘to command a grand sight the four wides round’, turns on whether or not things are in harmony with his goodness and virtues, and ends at last in seeking Peng Yen at watery abode.” — Tsiang Ch'ih.

52. *l.* 131, My sister. “Neü-siu”(女嬃) is said by Wang Yi to mean Chü Yuan's elder sister. Hsüeh Tsun's *A Book of Etymology*(许慎:《说文解字》) says, Ts'ou people call elder sister “siu” (嬃). Tuan Yü-tsai(段玉裁) says, Wang Yi, Yuan San-soon (袁山松) and Lih Dao-yuan(郦道元) all say, Neü-siu was Chü Yuan's elder sister, but Ts'eng Yüen(郑玄) in his *Commentary on Universal Mutability*(《周易》) says, Chü Yuan's younger sister was called Neü-siu. Hoon Hsin-tsou's *Supplemental Commentary on Ts'ou “Tze”* quotes Lih's *Commentary on The Classic of Steams*(郦道元:《水经注》) for saying that “Chü Yuan had a good elder sister who, hearing of his banishment, came back to console him not to be distracted by it, so the village people called the place Tzi-kwei(秭归, meaning the elder sister comes back), which was later named Tzi-kwei *hsien*(秭归县). In the north of the *hsien*, there is Chü Yuan's previous residence, north-east of which lies Neü-siu's temple with a stone in it whereon she had washed and clubbed her clothes.” (See my remarks on the origin

of Ts'ou in section IV of *Introduction*, pp. 26 −27.)

53. *ll.* 133 −134, these two lines. Q'uen(鲧), great Yü's father, is said by Ma Chih-tsan(马季长) and Kung An-kuo(孔安国) of Han(汉), on the evidence of *The Canon of Suen of The Classic of History*(《书·舜典》), to be executed("殛鲧于羽山") by Suen for his blundering failure to drain the deluge during Yao's reign. But Soong(宋) scholars say he was merely banished to the plain of the Yeü Mountain(羽山) and imprisoned there. Chü Yuan, in his *Sky-vaulting Queries*(《天问》), asks:

永遏在羽,

夫何三年不施?

In his detention long at Yeü,

Why was he for three years not killed?

不施, says Tsu Hsih, means "not executed"; Suen's "Four Criminals"(四罪) were all not put to death, but exiled. Tsen Haw(程颢) also says, 殛 in *The Canon of Suen* means "died in banishment", not "executed" *The Great Chronile*(《路史》) by Lo Mih(罗泌) of Soong says, Q'uen, imprisoned at Mount Yeü, died after three years. There is a Mount Yeü in the south-west of Kan-yü *hsien*(赣榆县). Kiang-suh(江苏). The mountain is now identified with another one of the same name in the south-east of Pong-lai *hsien*(蓬莱县), San-tung(山东).

According to *The Grand Law of The Classic of History*(《书·洪范》), the difference between Q'uen's method and Yü's in draining the deluge is that the former built dams and banks to obstruct water from flowing, while the latter dredged streams, scooped earth on land and exeavated mountains and hills that blocked the ways of water. Q'uen was nick-named Taur Wu(梼杌), meaning he was atrocious. intractable and pernicious to the extreme, for 梼杌, the same as 梼柮, means shapeless chopped wood or splints, useless and hateful. There was a legendary monstrous beast called 梼杌, said to be looking like a tiger, having hair two feet long, with a human face, tiger's feet, swine's teeth, a tail eighteen feet long and able to fight on indefinitely.

54. *l.* 137, the whole line. Filthy-mouthed defamers and parasitic sycophants fill the court. They wear those rank and prickly weeds on their girdles.

55. *l.* 144, the whole line and above. "凭心: 'mine heart is so filled with anger'" — Tsu Hsih. But Tsiang Ch'ih says, 凭心, means formerly his heart was well satisfied with the king's trust in him. but it has turned out that he is in such a plight now. According to Tsiang, the line should be: Alas! my former content ends in such a plight.

56. *ll.* 145 – 146, these two lines. Tsoon-hwah (重华) was *T'ih* Suen's(舜) name, who died, while leading his troops to subdue the revolting Miao tribesmen, on the plain of Tsoung-ngou and was buried in the south of the Tsoung-ngou Mountains (苍梧山), also called Nine-Doubt Mounts (九嶷山), south of the Rivers Yuan and Hsiang(沅,湘). The Yuan Stream flows from Sze-tsur(思州), now called Sze *hsien*(思县) or Jin-k'ung (岑巩), in modern Kwei-tsur(贵州), north-eastward to Tsang-têh and Yuan-kiang *hsien*(常德,沅江县) into Doong-ding Lake(洞庭湖). The Hsiang Stream flows from Shin-an *hsien*(兴安县) in modern Kwang-sih (广西), northward to Tsang-sah and Hsiang-yin *hsien*(长沙,湘阴县) into Doong-ding Lake. These two rivers and their basins and tributaries are closely connected

with the life and works of Chü Yuan and later to the great Ts'ih（晋）poet Dao Tsien（陶潜）. Neü-siu's words above show that she was only a woman of the world, a realist. "IF the world were indeed as she said it is, that is, there is no one in it who loves goodness and virtues except himself, then his going 'to command a grand sight the four wilds round' would be painful labour lost after all. Shaken by doubts, he seeks instruction from a former sage. Since Q'uen was struck by Suen, and Nine-Doubt Mounts are near at hand in the south of Ts'ou, he crosses Yuan and Hsiang to present his case to him. " — Tsiang Chih.

57. *ll.* 147 −166, "For sixteen lines beginning from this. " says Yau Nai（姚鼐）of Tsing（清）, "the poet speaks of the kings who lost the Way coming to mishap, and the four lines beginning from 'Taung and Yü... ' speak of the kings who were on the way and were blessed by good fortune. Chih's losing the Way is recorded in the lost chapter *Wuh Quan of The Classic of History* （逸《书 • 武观》篇）, partially quoted in the chapter *Anti-gaiety of Mê-tse*（《墨子 • 非乐》）. Chü Yuan condemns Chih together with Ngaw（浇）for their addiction to pleasures（康娱）. Wang Yi and many other commentators mistake 夏康娱以自纵 as T'ai Kong of Hsia becoming pleasure loving and elate. "

58. *ll.* 147 −148, these two lines. Chih（启）, Yü's son and successor to the Hsia throne （*vide* section IV of *Introduction*, *p.* 33）, is said by Chü Yuan in *Sky-vaulting Queries*（《天问》）to have obtained the two cantatas *Nine Counts*（《九辩》）and *Nine Songs* （《九歌》）from heaven while he was a guest there in a dream of his：

启棘宾商，

九辩九歌。

In the transcription of written works and the rendition of different types of characters as from the *tsuan* script(篆) to *dih*(隶), mistakes were often unavoidable. *Lee Sao* was preserved to our West Han(西汉) days on bamboo strips probably in the *Zûr* script(籀文) or great *tsuan*(大篆) of Sze Zûr(史籀), the grand curator of history of King Hsuan of Tsur(周宣王太史). A fair specimen of this type of script is obtainable in a photographed reproduction of an authentic rubbing from *The Stone Drums Inscription*(石鼓文). Ts'eng Tsiao(郑樵) of Soong(宋) pronounces the *Inscription* carved in the state Tsing(秦) at the time of Sze Zûr. As to by whom its scripts were written, it is still not definitely known. In his *Variorum Commentary*, Tsu Hsih says, the characters 棘 and 商 in the first line above are mistaken renderings of 梦 (dream) and 天 (heaven) respectively because of their similarities in the *tsuan* script. What is more to the point is that the poet himself was mistaken in the first place, in the opinion of Tsu-tse (*see* his *Dialectical Comments on Tsou* "*Tze*",《楚辞辩证》), in giving credit to the story that Chih got *Nine Counts and Nine Songs* from heaven when he was a guest there in his dream. These two cantatas were actually musical pieces with verse recitatives composed during Yü's reign to celebrate his feat of draining the flood and restoring the soil to its productive use.《九辩》 (*Nine Counts*) means all the things of the Nine States(九州) could be enumerated and delineated, nine being the greatest number.《九歌》(*Nine Songs*) means the benefits of the nine achievements(九功之德) — the six stores of water, fire, metal, wood, clay and grain(水、火、金、木、土、谷六府), and the three principles of uprightness, utilization and common well-being(正德、利用、厚生三事) — are orderly shown and could be sung in songs. The title "*Nine Songs*" is mentioned in *The Neü Chronicle* (《虞书》)(the five chapters from *The Canon of Yao*,《尧典》, to *Ih and Ji*,《益稷》, of *The Classic of History*(《尚书》). *The Tsur Rites*(《周礼》) and the Tso *Commentary of The Spring and Autumn Annals*(《左氏春秋》) as a cantata of Yü. Although *Nine Counts* is not mentioned in any of the extant classics and their commentaries, yet named here in company with *Nine Songs* which is certainly a piece of Yü's music, it cannot be Chih's, but must be Yü's too. As Tsu Hsih has pointed out, after the poet himself. Wang Yi makes the further mistake of saying that Chih propagated Yü's two pieces of music in his *Textual Critical Studies in Ts'ou "Tze"*(《楚辞章句》), for he dared not say Chü Yuan was mistaken. And Hoon Hsin-tsou(洪兴祖) makes still furthermore the grave mistake of quoting "King Kai of Hsia(夏后开, the same as Chih) brought three ladies up to heaven and got *Nine Counts* and *Nine Songs* down"(夏后开上三嫔于天,得九辩与九歌以下) from *The Great Wild West Classic of The Classic of Mountains and Seas*(《山海经·大荒西经》) to prove the fictitious story, not knowing that this last portion of the book (five chapters) was fabricated by Liu Shin(刘歆) of East Han with materials indiscriminately taken from Chü Yuan and other early writers, In Yer Koh-en's(游国恩) discussions of these two lines in his volume. he confirms Tsu-tse's judgment on "*Nine Counts*" and "*Nine Songs*", but opines that the original 棘 is correct and 商 is a mistaken transcription of the character 帝, not of 天. 棘 is the same as 亟 or 急; he says: going up heaven three times to get these cantatas down shows that Chih was in great eagerness, and what *The Classic of Mother Ts'eng of Kwei Tsoun* (《归藏·郑母经》), the second of *The Three Mutabilities* (三易), says, "Chih, the king of Hsia, asked divination about his riding flying dragons up to heaven, the oracle said 'auspicious'" is just referring to this. Now, Mother Ts'eng, a sorceress of oneiromancy (梦卜女巫), being ordered by Chih to divine about his dream, exactly proves that 棘 is a mistaken transcription of 梦 and Tsu-tse is quite right in so saying.

This line in the original 夏康娱以自纵 is erroneously interpreted by a great many commentators from Wang Yi and Hoon Hsin-tsou down, including Tsu Hsih, Wang Fuh-tse (王夫之) and Tsiang Chih, because they all mistake 夏康 to be T'ai-kong (太康) of Hsia (夏), without noticing that what the poet means here is: the dynasty Hsia, impersonated by Chih, became pleasure loving and elated (康娱以自纵). In the original of lines 157 and 232, 日康娱以自忘兮 and 日康娱以淫游, the expression 康娱 occurs again and again. So, its first appearance here in this line should not be taken amiss. Although T'ai-kong, Chih's son, was a very much depraved king, even worse than Chih, for in the first year of his reign he indulged himself in hunting for a hundred days consecutively without returning to his court, so that King Yih of Yeou-chûn (有穷后羿) repelled him at the River Yau-jü (姚渠), wrested the sovereignty of his state from him and set up his own dictatorship for forty-nine years (from 太康元年, 2188 B. C., to 相八年, 2139 B. C.) till he was killed by Han Tso (寒浞), yet Chih was certainly the first one in Yü's line to degrade his house ultimately into utter dissolution.

59. *l*. 150，the whole line. This line in the original is beset with three difficulties. First，五子 has been mistaken by a great many commentators to be "the five sons" of Chih，whereas the lost chapter *Wuh Quan of The Classic of History*（逸《书·武观》篇），as quoted in the chapter *Anti-gaiety of Mê-tse*（《墨子·非乐》），bears evidence that 五子 was none other than Chih's young prince Wuh Quan（武观）。not "the five sons" of Chih. Second，the character 失 in 用失乎家巷 is a superfluous insertion surreptitiously introduced by mistake，according to Wang Nian-sun（王念孙）of Tsing（清）in his *Miscellaneous Notes in Reading — Extra Notings*（《读书杂志·志馀》）. Third，家巷 means 家哄 or 内讧，a noisy disturbance，big tumult or internal strife，and 用乎家巷 means "raised a royal row".

60. *l*. 153，the whole line. Yih，king of Chûn（有穷后羿），was a vassal of Hsia，noted for his archery. He usurped King Hsiang's （相）throne，gave himself to pleasures and hunting，and paid no heed to civil affairs. Tso（浞），chief of the tribe Hang（寒），whom Yih made his premier，became secretly enamoured of Yih's wife Tsun-wuh（纯狐），also called Tsang-ngou（嫦娥）. They planned together，and he told his reeve Voon Moon（逢蒙） to shoot and kill Yih while he was returning from one of his hunting trips. He then took his place as king and took his wife as his own wife. Yih came to power amidst the confusion of Hsia；he came to his untimely，wicked end deservedly on account of his reckless behavior. Hang Tso made his son Ngaw（浇）kill King Hsiang. Ngaw was later killed by Sao-kang（少康）. Hsiang's son.

61. *ll*. 155 −158，these four lines. Ngaw（浇，奡），Hang Tso's son

born by Yih's wife, was of great physical strength, said to be able to propel boat on land. He committed incest with his widowed sister-in-law Neü-gieh(女岐), Yie's(豷) wife, while asking her to sew some clothes of his, and then lived with her as a matter of course. Sao-kang(少康), Hsiang's son, setting his hounds in a hunting trip after some chase at night, came upon them unawares and beheaded him, or both of them. The anecdote is mentioned in *Sky-vaulting Queries*(《天问》).

62. *ll.* 159 −160, these two lines. Ghi of Hsia(夏桀) was exiled to Nan-tsiao(南巢) by Tseng Taung(成汤). See section II of *Introduction*, *pp.* 10 −11. The Hsia(夏) Dynasty, beginning from Great Yü's rule in 2205 B. C., lasted for seventeen reigns of 439 years till 1766 B. C., when it was ended by Ghi's exile to Nan-tsiao.

63. *ll.* 161 −162, these two lines. King Sing(后辛), the tyrant Zer (纣), pickled(菹), minced(醢) and parched(脯) his vassals and courtiers. Hearing that his lord inferior Marquis Chur(九侯) or Quai(鬼侯) had a pretty daughter, he demanded her of him. But the girl was not given to Iasciviousness. In anger, Zer killed her and minced the flesh of her father. Marquis Ngo(鄂侯), also called Count Mei(梅伯), remonstrated with him against the crime strongly. Zer had him parched. See section II of *Introduction*, *pp.* 17 −18. The Saung Dynasty, later called Yin(殷), beginning from Taung's rule in 1766 B. C., lasted for twenty-eight reigns of 644 years till 1122 B. C., when Zer killed himself by burning or hanging.

64. *l.* 163, Taung. See section II of *Introduction*, *pp.* 10 −11.

65. *l.* 163, Yü. See section II of *Introduction*, *pp.* 9 −10.

66. *l.* 164, early Tsur. For Wen and Wuh, see section II of *Introduction*, *pp.* 16 −21.

67. *ll.* 147 −166. In these lines, the poet speaks to Suen of things that happened after his reign. "Yü, Taung, Wen and Wuh, all blessed by heaven, held heaven in awe and the virtuous in reverence, kept to the Way and justice without faults, elected the good and the capable to office and observed laws and principles without deviations. Therefore, they could get the aid of gods and men, and their progenies were blessed in consequence." — Tsu Hsih.

68. *ll.* 171 −174, these four lines. "I have examined the rights and wrongs of the past and forecast the successes and failures of the future. Looking before and after, I have probed into the utmost possibilities of the changes of the people's affairs. And I have come to the conclusion that only the just could be intrusted and only good should be done." — Tsu Hsih.

69. *ll.* 177 −178, these two lines. "Although only good should be done, yet our fair precursors like Lung-boon(龙逢) and Count Mei(梅伯) were pickled and minced for their rectitude. Nevertheless. I do not repent for what I have done in despite of the risks I have undergone." — Tsu Hsih. "Minding the round peg to fit in the round hole means the virtuous choosing good sovereigns to serve. Those who are born with virtues should be the aids of kings. Only the sagacious rulers could really get the proper men to intrust. So, from ancient times down, to plan for the benefit of the people depends solely on good kings choosing right aids; besides this, nothing could be done. 'My coming to the brink of death is not the fault of my loving goodness and virtues,

but is due to my inability to choose the right sovereign. That is the reason why I come almost to being pickled and minced. Moreover, the world is not necessarily climbing with tendrils and vines to form factions and my uprightness and misfortune are not to be compared to Q'uen's obduracy.'" — Tsiang Ch'ih.

70. *l.* 180, the whole line. "I lament my time doth not occur when the virtuous are elected. but doth occur when pickling and mincing are the order of the day." — Tsu Hsih.

71. *ll.* 183 −184, these two lines. "While kneeling, I spread out my dress folds to free my mind to Suen, and I feel suddenly flushed with this inner glory of mine." — Tsu Hsih.

72. *l.* 185, a quadriga of jade-bitted dragonets. The original 驷 means a two-wheeled car drawn by four horses abreast, a quadriga. But 驷玉虬 here means a car drawn by four dragonets. A dragonet(虬、蚪) is said to be a young dragon with two horns on its head. And 玉虬 is a dragonet with a bit in its mouth decorated with jade on both ends that jut exposed outside its mouth.

73. *l.* 185, phoenix. 鹥 is another name for 凤皇, phoenix, a large fair bird (over six feet tall) of good augury with multicolour plumes. 鸾皇 in line 201 and 凤鸟 in line 203 all mean phoenix. Specifically, 鸾 is a sort of phoenix with a predominance of blue and green plumes, while red and orange prevail in the plumage of a 凤、皇 or 凰 is the female bird. Another explanation says the young bird is called 鸾鹥. These three names are used indiscriminately here to give variety. The chapter *lh and Ji of The Classic of History*(《书·益稷》) says, "When the nine tunes of *Great Continuance* were played with Pandean pipes, the phoenix flied hither to dance to pay tribute(箫韶九成, 凤凰来仪)." *Great*

Continuance was T'ih Suen's dance cantata. *The Book of Etymology* of Hsu Tsun(许慎) of Han says, "The phoenix is a divine bird. T'ien Lao(天老, Hwang-*t'ih's* liege lord inferior) said, the shape of the phoenix is *kilin*(麒麟) in front and deer in the rear, with a neck like a snake and the tail of a fish, having a back testudinated like a tortoise with dragon-like traceries, with cheeks like a swallow's and the beak of a cock. It is five-coloured. It comes from the Gentlemen's Country in the East(东方君子之国) and flies over the Four Seas. When it appears, there is great peace in the world."

74. *l.* 186, the whole line and what follows. "From the next line onward, for minding the round peg to fit in the round hole, he is going to have a sight round the four wilds, in order to seek a good sovereign. From lines 187 to 214, he ranges the heaven in his search." — Tsiang Ch'ih.

75. *l.* 187, Tsoung-ngou Mountains. Tsoung-ngou Mountains(苍梧山) or Nine-Doubt Mounts(九嶷山) are half in the Wilds or on the Plain of Tsoung-ngou(苍梧之野) and half in Ling-ling(零陵), in the south-east of the modern Ning-yuan *hsien*(宁远县). Hu-nan(湖南). They have nine peaks looking very much alike and are therefore called Nine Doubts. *T'ih* Suen of Neü(虞舜) is buried in the south of Suen-yuan where there was a temple to his memory. The nine peaks are called 舜源(Suen-yuan), 朱明, 石城, 石楼, 娥皇(Oer-hwang, the name of his queen), 女英(Neü-ying, his beebee), 箫韶, 桂林, 杞林, Suen-yuan, the highest peak, is also called the Ciborium(华盖).

76. *l.* 188, the mid cliffs of Quen-lung. Lih Dao-yuan's(郦道元) *Commentary* on *The Classic of Streams*(《水经注》) says, Quen-

lung Mountains(昆仑山) have three layers of cliffs, the lowest layer is called Van-doon(樊桐), the mid one is called Yuan-puh (县圃) and the highest. Ts'en-tsen(增城), where the god of heaven resides. Yuan-puh, seeming to be hanging down from the azure empyrean, is said to be the region of the fairies.

77. *l.* 189, these carved Heaven's gates. 灵琐, the carved Heaven's gates, nine pairs, covered with bas-relief designs on decorative panels decked with blue and gold, on the mid-top of Quen-lung, are said to form the portal of God's nether capital by *The Classic of Mountains and Seas*(《山海经》). They are there where the pantheon of Heaven is, hence called divine(灵).

78. *l.* 191, Shih-her. Shih-her(羲和) was the driver of Sun's car which was said to be drawn by six dragons.

79. *l.* 192, Yan-tze. Yan-tze(崦嵫) was the mountain or range of mountains into which the Suns were said to set.

80. *l.* 194, the whole line. He will go up and down to seek out his virtuous sovereign continually.

81. *l.* 195, Yen-tze. Yen-tze(咸池) was where the Suns took their baths.

82. *l.* 196, Fwuh-soung. Fwuh-soung(扶桑, 榑桑) was a great fairy tree over Taung Valley(汤谷, 汤 means hot like boiling water) or Yang Valley(旸谷, 旸 means "bright", it was the valley from which the Suns rose), on the branches of which ten Suns rose and swept away to the sky one after another after baching themselves in Yen-tze. according to *The Oversea East Classic of The Classic of Mountains and Seas*(《山海经·海外东经》). This part of the book was written by someone late in West Han. *Hwai-nan-tse*(《淮南子》) of early West Han, however, gives a simi-

lar account. Recent excavations, in the southern suburbs of Tsang-sah(长沙) in, 1972, of the Mah-wang Heap of early West Han tombs(马王堆西汉墓), unearthed a piece of silk-painting(帛画) on a large, T-shaped soul-summoning streamer (非衣,幠,复) of 6.7257 feet (2.05 metres) long covering the inner coffin of a Marchioness Dai(轪侯妃), on which is painted a Fwuh-soung tree with nine Suns, a big one high up above, eight small ones nestling below and the ninth hidden from sight behind the foliage.

83. *l*. 197, the whole line. According to Tuan Yü-tsai(段玉裁), *ruoh*-wood(若木) is another name for Fwuh-soung(扶桑), the fairy tree. A branch of this wood is torn off by the poet to detain the progress of Sun's car for some while.

84. *ll*. 197 −198, these two lines. "The poet means to say, 'Merely telling Shih-her to slow down. I am afraid, is not adequate to detain Sun and retard time's progress. So I go to where the Suns take their baths and rises, split a *ruoh*-wood branch and come back to brush his brilliance, telling him, thou wouldst better linger and loiter some while longer; speedest thou not so fast. ' So these words 聊须臾以相羊 are said to the Sun god to gain time. " — Tsiang Ch'ih.

85. *l*. 199, Wang-suh. Wang-suh(望舒), driver of Moon's chaise.

86. *l*. 200, Fei-lian. Fei-lian(飞廉,蜚廉), god of the winds.

87. *l*. 205, Whirlblasts. Whirlblasts(飘风), summoned by Fei-lian.

88. *l*. 209, Heaven's Porter. 帝阍 is God's gate-keeper or Heaven's Porter, whom "I call upon to open the Sky-gates(阊阖) and let me in to see God, but he refuses to undo the lock and leans on the gates, staring at me. " — Tsu Hsih. This is said by Tsu-tse

to be a figurative statement of the poet's seeking the "Great King" ("Heaven's Son") of Tsur in vain.

89. *ll.* 211 – 212, these two lines. By this time, twilight wraps around the vault of heaven. The poet, mentally and physically fatigued, keeps a standing vigil and braids a pendant of eupatory. Though his arduous efforts to search for a master in the empyrean region fail utterly, his steadfastness in upholding his goodness and virtues remains unchanged. While braiding his aromatic pendant, he muses on the thoughts in the two following lines and his repulse by Heaven's Porter a moment ago. It is inconceivable to him that even at the Sky-gates the situation is as bad as that. Then he turns away dejectedly.

90. *l.* 215, the whole line and following ones. "From lines 215 to 254, the poet speaks of his search in the world. 'Early at morn' here follows 'The time is gloaming' in line 211, for it is the morning after." — Tsiang Ch'ih.

91. *l.* 216, Mount Laun-feng. Tsu Hsih says, according to *Hwai-nan-tse*(《淮南子》, by Liu An, 刘安, Prince Hwai-nan, 淮南王, of Han), White Stream flows from Mount Laun-feng(阆风山) of the Quen-lung Mountains. *Kuan Ya*(《广雅》, by Tsang Ih, 张揖, of Gwei, 魏) says, Quen-lung Mountains have three strata of precipices: Laun-feng (阆风), P'an-doon (板桐) and Yuan-puh(玄圃,县圃). The *Commentary* on Soung Chin's(桑钦, of Han) *The Classic of Streams*(《水经注》, by Lih Dao-yuan of North Gwei, 北魏郦道元) says, "The Quen-lung Mountains have three layers of precipices, the lower one is called Van-doon (樊桐) or P'an-doon(板桐), the middle one Yuan-puh(玄圃) or Laun-feng (阆风) and the upper one T'sen-tsen (层城) or

T'ien-ding(天庭)."

92. *l.* 218, on this plateau no Lady Divine. "The Lady means saga-cious King. Here, he again does not meet his ideal, virtuous sovereign. In the next thirty odd lines, his visiting the vernal Pal-ace, search for Fwu-fei, catching a sight of the fair damosel of Yeou-soong and thinking of the two Yau sisters still unbound, all mean his yearning for a beneficent master." — Tsu Hsih. "This plateau" means Laun-feng, says Tsiang.

93. *l.* 219, Vernal Palace. Vernal Palace(春宫) is the palace of blue or Azure Heavenly *T'ih* of the East(东方青帝).

94. *l.* 220, the whole line. "With a pendant made of a furcate gem-tree twig laid on me — hanging on my girdle." For gem-tree, see note 137. The original 折琼枝以继佩 is literally "Plucking a furcate gem-tree twig to lengthen my pendant." My adopted ren-dering gives the idea that this furcate gem is a separate pendant by itself; so, I have to make "Untying my band of pendants" of line 225 "Untying my bands of pendants."

95. *l.* 222, the whole line. The original 相下女之可贻 means loo-king for her earthly maid through whom I could perhaps give this gift of courtship to her. Toward the end of *Hymn on the Lady of Hsiang*(《湘夫人》), the third poem of *Nine Hymns*(《九歌》), supposed to be a love song by the King of Hsiang(湘君) for his love of the Lady of Hsiang(湘夫人) before their espousal, Chü Yuan says,

捐余玦兮江中，

遗余佩兮沣浦，

采芳洲兮杜若，

将以遗兮下女。

Wishing to present his gifts of precious gems to the Lady of Hsiang, who cannot be seen, the King of Hsiang (湘君) lays them by the margin of the streams, as if left there unawares, hoping that she would pick them up and be touched by his heart-felt feelings for her. Yet he is anxious and afraid that these gifts of his could not convey his tender sentiments. So he picks bounteous bouquets of aromatic pollia (杜若) and gives them to her handmaids, asking them to tender his assiduities to the darling of his heart.

96. *l.* 223, the whole line. Wang Yi says, Feng-loon (丰隆) is the Chief of Clouds (云师). In *Hwai-nan-tse* (《淮南子》), Feng-loon is Thunder (雷). Tsu Hsih: "Feng-loon, the Lord of Thunder-claps, noted for his speed and power and getting whatever he is after, is asked to find out efficaciously the whereabouts of the Divine Lady, or of her earthly maid Fwu-fei first." At first sight, Tsu-tse's explanation seems almost infallible. But seeing that Thunder has already appeared above (*l.* 202) and comparing the lines "I summon Feng-loon (the Chief of Clouds) as my van-courier" (召丰隆使光导兮), "To lead me to where T'ai-wei's ten stars be" (问太微之所居), and thirty-six lines later. "On the left the Chief of Rain attendeth me. On the right the Lord of Thunder giveth guard" (左雨师使径侍兮, 右雷公以为卫) in our poet's another work *Distant Wanderings* (《远游》, *ll.* 89, 125 −126), I come to the conclusion that here Feng-loon is also the Chief of Clouds acting as a guide, not the terrible Lord of Thunder-claps, whose power is unnecessary. *Vide* notes 30 and 43 on *Distant Wanderings* below. For another proof, there are these two lines in *Musing on the Beauteous One* (《思美

人》）：

揭寄言于浮云兮，

遇丰隆而不将。

97. *l.* 224, Fwu-fei. Fwu-fei（虙妃，宓妃）was Fwu-shih's（伏羲，虙戏，宓牺）daughter, drowned in the Loh Stream（洛水）and being made its Spirit（洛神）.

98. *l.* 226, the whole line. Chien-sieu（蹇修）is asked to be the match-maker to mediate and bring the bands of pendants as gifts of courtship to the Divine Lady, says Tsu Hsih, so she seems to be an earthly maid apt to be a gobetween. But that is only a suggestion admittedly unfounded on any legendary tale, whereas Wang Yi's explanation that Chien-sieu was a courtier of Fwu-shih, Tsu says, is unwarranted.

Here, I must say that Tsu-tse is quite right in dismissing Wang Yi's attribution as his imagined fiction, but his own suggestion is also shaky. First of all, it may be pointed out that Wang Yi has made this mistake because the first earthly maid Fwu-fei（虙妃）approached by Chien-sieu was Fwu-shih's（伏羲）princes, therefore Wang erroneously thought that Chien-sieu might be Fwu-shih's courtier. Match-making is to mediate between the poet and his King, whom, if the union is achieved, he aims to make an ideal sovereign. Now, the two characters 蹇修 literally means lame or crippled virtue; the name is actually coined by Chü Yuan. I believe, to mean the type of person defective in virtue who cannot mediate between himself and his king. This Crippled Virtue, a personification, is in sharp contrast with Phoenix in line 245, Kao-sing's match-maker. In fact, Chien-sieu as a type represents two typical examples: Zûn（鸩）, who, a wrecker of the match, is poisonous and has already refused to do the job at the very beginning ("the thing should not be done". *l.* 240), and Treron(雄鸠), who, light-headed, sly, chattering, fickle and therefore unreliable, would not do at all too, though not so destructive as Zûn. While Zûn is a member of the pro-Tsing clique, Treron is a common courtier, though not a member of the gang, yet unable to perform the task taken up by him for his moral shortcomings. Phoenix(鸾皇), the foremost of his front guards (*l.* 201), unlike Chien-sieu, would do well to act as go-between, but Chü Yuan is afraid the time is already too late, for she would be anticipated by Kao-sing's Mystic Bird(凤凰) in winning Jien-di(简逖, *ll.* 245 −246). As for the poet's first seeking for the Maid Divine(高丘之女, *l.* 218) and then thinking of the union with Fwu-fei(虙妃), Jien-di(简逖, 有娀佚女) and the two Yau sisters(有虞之二姚), the Maid Divine's earthly handmaidens(下女), we must understand that any of these latter could be transformed into the Maid Divine (according to *ll.* 23 − 30) if she is joined with him — there is no feeling of inconstancy on his part, for the whole argument is a mere comparison, an imagined fiction. These notions set forth above are my own and, so far as I know, not thought of by scholars of Chü Yuan's poetry from Han to this day, but they are of key importance for elucidating the passage from *ll.* 215 −248. Tsaung P'in-lin(章炳麟), a modern etymologist, says that as the name 謇修 is not to be found in P'an K'uh's(班固) *Table of Notables, Ancient and Modern*(《古今名人表》), he has fished out from the section *Music Explained*(《释乐》) of *Erl Ya*(《尔雅》) that merely striking the bell was anciently called 修 and merely striking the *chin*

（磬, a ceremonial musical instrument of Hsia, Saung and Tsur, made of jet-black or dark green jade-stone or quartz in the form of a circumflex V, hung through a bore at the apex with a cord, from the middle of a horizontal ploe of a decorative shelf, just like a cast bronze bell was similarly hung on another shelf — they were striken with little wooden hammers at ritual occasions of doing homage to Heaven and Earth and the sovereign's ancestors in their temples) was called 蹇, and he concludes that music, the striking of bell and *chin*, was employed by Chü Yuan as a means to make the match ("吾令蹇修以为理"), just as Sze-ma Hsiang-rue(司马相如) played on the heptachord(琴) to tickle the heart of Tso Wen-chün(卓文君), the newly widowed daughter of the mercantile prince Tso Wang-sun(卓王孙) and make her elope with him. This is trifling, pedantic nonsense, for, in the first place, in ancient Chinese music, these two instruments are always named bell and *chin*, never *chin* and bell, unless when purposely inverted in verse, as once in *The Classic of Poetry*, for the sake of rhyme, so, if Tsaung's surmise is plausible, the name of the match-maker should be Sieu-chien, instead of Chien-sieu; secondly, playing on the strings of a heptachord might tickle the heart of a young widowed woman, but striking the bell and *chin* could not do so; thirdly, Sze-ma Hsiang-rue lived in the time of Wuh-*t'ih* of Han(汉武帝), more than two centuries after Chü Yuan, it is therefore inconceivable as it was impossible for Chü Yuan to tickle Fwu-fei, a Sprite, with the striking of *chin* and bell after the fashion of Sze-ma Hsiang-rue; and lastly, therefore, Tsaung's explanation is a forcedly fanciful and absurdly pedagogic vulgarization of Chü Yuan's poetry.

The idea of a young man of good breeding paying courtship to a girl of fair name and she accepting him without a third party mediating between the two families, no matter how poor the two families were, was sheerly unthinkable in China among the Han majority(汉族) from remote ancient times to the past two generations ago, say, till about from 1919 to 1930. The prevalence of such a social practice during the two scores of centuries was due to our ancient patriarchism in government, agricultural social structure and mode of living, and isolation from other major nationalities of high culture. The Revolution of 1911 in overthrowing the Manchu Dynasty left the convivial make of the nation practically untouched. It was the May, 4th Movement of 1919, the New Cultural Movement in China's modern history, that wrought thorough-going changes in the nation's nuptial system and family relations. Today, of course, in the humanity of 850 millions of the country, courtship and marriage are more or less the same as in Europe and America. But Western readers of this poem of Chü Yuan should certainly not think of Chien-sieu as a match-maker or go-between with undue associations. The culture of imagination makes people imaginative, tolerant and really civilized.

99. *l.* 228, the whole line. "Words in favour of the match and adverse criticisms by vilifiers become rife. Fwu-fei soon turns out to be stiff and stubborn." — Tsu Hsih.

100. *l.* 229, Chun-sze. Chun-sze(穷石) was a mountain in modern Tsang-yieh(张掖), Kan-su(甘肃); it was in the state Chun of King Yih(有穷后羿).

101. *l.* 230, Woei-pan. Woei-pan(洧盘) was a stream issuing from

Yan-tse Mountain(崦嵫山). See note 79.

102. *ll.* 231 − 232, these two lines and the next two. "These four lines speak of Fwu-fei as proud and given to pleasures in living. Although beautiful, she is unmannerly in her behaviour. So the poet gives her up and seeks his suit elsewhere." — Tsu Hsih.

103. *l.* 235, the four extreme expanses. 四极 are the four extremely distant quarters. The poet means to say that he has explored the four wilds spoken of in *l.* 124.

104. *l.* 237, the fair damsel of Yeou-soong. The fair damsel of Yeou-soong(有娀之佚女, the beautiful princess of the state Soong) means *T'ih* Ko's(帝喾, Emperor Kao-sing, 高辛氏) queen and Siue's(契) mother Jien-di(简逖). *Vide* section II of *Introduction*, *pp.* 7 −8,10. Siue(契, the same as 偰, 崇, 离), assisting Yü to drain the flood with merits and Lord of Public Instruction (司徒, 掌邦教, equivalent to the Premier) to Suen, was the progenitor of the dynasty Saung. The legend is alluded to in *The Mystic Bird*("玄鸟", traditionally explained as *The Ebon Bird*, the swallow, but the modern commentator Wen Ih-to, 闻一多, has proved with evidence from a note to *Notes of Rites*《礼记·月令》疏 *that* "玄鸟" means *The Mystic Bird*, the phoenix), *Ode of Saung*, Ⅲ(《商颂》三) of *The Classic of Poetry*(《诗经》). At the vernal equinox, the bird flies down to the ground. A legend has it that Kao-sing's queen, the beautiful princess of the king of Yeou-soong, in company with the emperor while he was doing homage to Heaven on a pavilion or steeple, picked up a mystic bird's egg and swallowed it; she became pregnant and later gave birth to Siue. This is according to Sze-ma Tsien's *The Chronicle*; we call it the first version of the legend. *The*

Lives of Illustrious Women(《列女传》) of Liu Shan of Han(汉代刘向) has the legend thus："In the times of Yao, Jien-di with her sister once bathed themselves in the Stream of Yüan-chiu(玄丘之水). There was a mystic bird with an egg in its mouth flying over them and dropping it, which was multi-colour and beautiful. Jien-di picked it up and swallowed it. She became pregnant and gave birth to Siue. Jien-di was capable at civil affairs, conversant with astronomical matters and glad of conferring benefits on others. Siue, being brought up by her, earned for himself a fair name." This we call the second version of the legend. *The Spring and Autumn Annals of Leü*(《吕氏春秋》) says, the king of Soong had a fair daughter, so he built a high steeple or spire(高台) for her to live in. This we call the third version of the legend; the *Leü Annals*, taking its early source of materials independent of Sze-ma and Liu's books, was written by the followers of Leü Puh-wei(吕不韦), premier of King Tsaung Hsiang of Tsing(秦庄襄王) and Ying Tsen(嬴政). Wang Yi mixed up the two versions of the legend by *The Chronicle* and the *Leü Annals*, and Tsu Hsih followed his suit. Tsiang Ch'ih, in his *Remaining Commentary on Ts'ou "Tze"* (《楚辞余论》), points out their mistakes by quoting Chü Yuan's two mentionings of what we call the third version of the legend in his *Sky-vaulting Queries*(《天问》) and *Musing on the Beauteous One*(《思美人》) to show that Jien-di, living in the high steeple or spire of Yeou-soong (*Leü Annals'* version), was heard by *T'ih* Ko to be beautiful and virtuous, so he sent the Mystic Bird as match-maker to pay courtship to her, to which her father and she agreed and thus she became *T'ih* Kao-sing's queen. The happy union gave birth to Siue and originated the Saung Dynasty.

105. *ll.* 239 −240, these two lines. Zûn（鴆）is a pernicious bird with plumes of deadly poison. The liquor with its feathers steeped in is said to be a sure fatal medicament. It is also called 运日. *Tsoong-san Classic of The Classic of Mountains and Seas* (《山海经·中山经》) says："On Mount Neü-wǔ（女兀之山）, there is zûn. " Kuo Po's（郭璞, of Ts'in, 晋）*Commentary* says, zûn is big like the buzzard, with purple and blue plumes, long neck and red beak, feeding on vipers. It is nominated here to stand for the traducers who fawned upon the king and backbit the good with poisonous fabrications. Instead of helping on his fair suit, it is always glad to be a destructive agent. Naturally, it "telleth me the thing should not be done. " *Vide* note 21.

106. *ll.* 241 −242, these two lines. Tsu-tse says, 雄鸠 is 鹘鸠, which is also called 鹘鸼, 鸥鸠. Its modern ornithological name is *Treron permagna*, said to be with dark blue plumes on the back and head, and white feathers on the breast and belly dotted with chestnut spots. The section *On Birds of Erl Ya*(《尔雅·释鸟》) says, it is like a mountain sparrow, but smaller, with a short tail, bluish black in colour on the upper part of the body, chattering. This bird is named here, because of its light-headedness（轻佻）, slyness for gain（巧利）and chattering fickleness（多语言而无要实, 不可信用）, as well expounded by Tsu-tse. It is therefore not to be relied on at all. The bird must allude to some of the courtiers. To render the name into turtle-dove, 雎鸠, as Lim Boon-keng has done in his version of the poem, is, however, quite improper, as that bird is celebrated

for the constancy of its affection and its tender plaintive note.

107. *ll.* 245 −246, these two lines. "As Zûn and Treron all could not be commissioned, he, 'hesitating and dubious', thinks of going himself. But that is contrary to the practice of good manners. …" — Tsu Hsih. The chief of his front guards, "phoenix … my van-courier" (*l.* 201), now he remembers, whom he has intrusted with the mission, may arrange the suit for him; but Kao-sing's Mystic Bird, he is afraid, would have anticipated him, so he gives up. There are two personified Phoenixes, one of whom (鸾皇, *l.* 201) is his van-courier, the chief of his front guards (凤鸟, sacred birds, *l.* 203), the other is Kao-sing's Mystic Bird (玄鸟, Phoenix, 凤皇, *ll.* 245 −246).

108. *ll.* 249 −250, these two lines. Sao-kang (少康) was the son of King Hsiang of Hsia(夏后相). When Hang Tso killed Hsiang and usurped his throne, Hsiang's queen Min (缗), already pregnant then, fled to her father's country Yeou-zen(有仍) and gave birth to her child the next year, 2118 B. C. The Hsia Dynasty was cut short in 2119 B. C. by Hang Tso's regicide and usurpation for forty years till 2079 B. C., when Hsia's old lord Mii(靡) put an end to Hang Tso and elected his master's son to restore the dynasty. Sao-kang as a lad, under the threat of being hunted out and killed in the land of his father's father-in-law, fled to Yeou-neü (有虞), the homeland of Suen's (舜) descendants. There, Neü Sze(虞思) gave him his two daughters to marry. Previously, *T'ih* Suen died in 2208 B. C., having nominated Yü to succeed himself. Out of cordiality for Suen's son Saung-chün, Yü waited for three years before he took his crown in 2205 B. C. He alloted the fief Neü(虞), the modern

Neü-tsen *hsien*(虞城县), to Saung-chün. So, at Neü there were Suen's clansmen, of whom Neü Sze was one. Suen was surnamed Yau(姚); thus, the two Neü daughters were his descendants.

"After the poet has lost his chance with Jien-di, he wants to go faraway but has no place to go to. So, he wishes to keep the two Yau sisters while they are not yet married to Sao-kong. " — Tsu Hsih.

We can see that in his hectic fit of seeking the ideal or beneficent sovereign — or rather, in the figurative shadowing forth of such a king in his successive mentionings of the renowned beauties one after another, the poet has annihilated the time element in his raving hallucinations and delirious utterances. In this very smithy of Hephaestus, Chü Yuan's imagination, those long dead and gone called upon by him come back from eternity one by one with flushing glows on their faces, vibrating breathings at their nostrils and palpitating pulses at their bosoms and wrists. They are more alive than many of the living we see and live with daily. In the same way, Yao, Suen, Yü, Tang, Wen, Wuh and Duke Tsur as well as Ghi, Zer, Lih, You, Yih, Tso and Ngaw are all summoned up with the highest of their spirits each at his appointed place in this ode or elsewhere in the poet's other works. The diction is anything but limpid and puristic; the imageries are rich and sprightly; the feelings are turbulent and fervid. These are as modern as any eminent modern poet could possibly be. There are people who cannot appreciate and exalt *Lee Sao* for its intensity and passion, its flight of empyreal imagination, its florescent symbolism, and can still less under-

stand such a confluence of high poetry and musics ways in presenting this state of craze and frenzy, for it is altogether beyond
them. Such a man is Hwu Sêh (胡适, "Hu Shih"), for instance, who even doubts whether there was ever a man named
Chü Yuan! But that is not Chü Yuan's fault.

109. *ll.* 253 −254, these two lines. "Fearing his cause for asking the
hands of the two Yau sisters is weaker than Sao-kang's, and his
own match-maker is awkward in presenting him to advantage,
he holds little hope for the outcome. So, grieving, he speaks
again of the times being muddled and envious of the virtuous.
For although he has been roving to the four distant quarters of
the world, the faults of their customs are just the same as in the
central state." — Tsu Hsih.

"As his cause is weak, his match-maker's words must be inef-
fectual and, as he is awkward in speech, his words must be unavailing. It is already known before Chien-sieu is sent out that
the issue would be disappointing, Tsu-tse has said that the
whole passage is a metaphorical account of the poet's looking
for a virtuous master. So, ranging the heavens to find an ideal
sovereign (lines 187 −214) and roving the world to search for a
perfect king (lines 215 −254), he has come to the conclusion
in giving credit to Neü-siu's words that the world is not what he
thought it is." — Tsiang Ch'ih.

110. *ll.* 255 −256, these two lines and the next two. "The last line
'The maidens... ' (闺中邃远) means Fwu-fei, etc. are inaccessible. This line, 哲王又不寤, means the King of Heaven
could not detect his porter's misdeed in beguiling and keeping
him in ignorance. (According to Tsu Hsih's interpretation, the

line may be rendered thus: The All-wise King is at a loss to show His will.) These two lines and the next two mean that 'There is no wise sovereign(明君) above, nor virtuous lord (贤伯) below. It makes me cherishing my loyal and faithful feelings incapable of being put to practice. How can I last forever with these dark, confused and envious customs?' He means to go away." — Tsu Hsih.

"The last line refers to his seekings above. The deep chambers of the maidens are inaccessible, because he has no good matchmaker. 'The wise king'(哲王) means King Hwai of Ts'ou. Looking over the world, he does not know what to do. Gazing at his native state, he is stupefied with grief. Thus, Neü-siu's words have sometimes proved to be true, and the fine sense of righteousness is not to be strictly followed all. So, the question is to be resolved in divination. Ranging the sky, he has not entered the portal of heaven. Fwu-fei — he takes no interest in her now. About Kao-sing's anticipating him and the words spoken for him being futile, he says 'I am afraid', and 'I fear', which are suppositions showing his lack of will to proceed. These are based upon to 'look about' and 'to command a grand sight the four wilds round' in lines 123 −124. It does not mean that there is really no virtuous king, or that he has actually sought any that turns out to be not fit. It only means that he has been trying to look around to see whether he could fix on an ideal king. But experience has taught him that jealous animosity against goodness and virtue is prevalent everywhere. Even if there be a gracious king, his getting himself as aid is not feasible. Thinking of resting his heart in Ts'ou, he is yet troubled by

King Hwai's not understanding his noble intentions. Wandering about and dubious, he is counselled by Ling Fung not to dote on his homeland. " — Tsiang Ch'ih.

111. *l.* 259, holy inula and bamboo splints. The original 薏茅 is, says Wang Yi, a divine herb(灵草). *The Native Medicinal Herbal*(《本草》) calls it 旋覆花, which is *Inula britanica*, of the genus called *Compositae*(菊科), two to three feet tall, blo-wing yellow flowers in summer. 筳 is bamboo splints. These were made use of to divine.

112. *l.* 260, Ling Fung. Ling Fung(灵氛) was an ancient soothsayer or sibyl noted for feeling people's fortunes by her divination. Her name has become the general namesake, especially when called by others, of the practitioners of her arts in posterity. The character 灵(*ling*) was used interchangebly with 巫(sibyl) in ancient days.

113. *ll.* 261 −262, these two lines. "Although the two fair parties, thou and thine ideal lady, would ultimately unite, yet who is it here in Ts'ou who could really admire thy fine qualities and vir-tues? None! Thou wouldst better be gone. "

114. *l.* 263, Nine States. The Middle Empire was divided into nine states (Nine *Tsur*,九州) as early as in the times of Hwang-*t'ih*. After the deluge during Yao's reign, Great Yü delineated them once more. This new draught is recorded in the chapter *Yü Trib-utes*(《禹贡》) of *The Classic of History*(《尚书》). Besides, there were the nine states of Saung-Yin, recorded in *Erl Ya*(《尔雅》), a modification of Yü's mapping. And again, in *Tsur Rites*(《周礼》), there is the Tsur variation of Yü's nine states. The Nine States or *Tsur*(九州) of *Yü Tributes* are, viz.,

Ch'ih, Yean, Tsing, Hsü, Yang, Ch'ih, Yüe, Liang and Yung(冀,兖,青,徐,扬,荆,豫,梁,雍). *Erl Ya's* Nine States combine *Yü Tributes'* Tsing with Hsü and its Liang with Yüe, and split its Ch'ih into Ch'ih and You(幽) and its Yean into Yean and Yin(营). The Nine States of *Tsur Rites* combine *Yü Tributes'* Hsü with Ch'ih and its Liang with Yung and split its Ch'ih into Ch'ih, You and P'ing(并).

115. *l.* 266, the whole line. "The fairs damsels are compared to the virtuous kings. The world of the Nine States is immense. Not only in Ts'ou are there fair damsels. Thou shouldst go far away without doubt. Among the fair who look for virtuous husbands, which one of them would reject thee from her candidates?" — Tsu Hsih.

116. *l.* 267, the whole line. Tsu-tse says, this line is a reiteration of line 264. Tsiang Ch'ih thinks it means "everywhere there are fine lords being elected as aids to wise sovereigns." "Ling Fung is made to speak these four lines 'again' as a reiterated counsel to the poet. His thought contained in line 255 is spoken of as dubiousness and his notion in line 256, showing he cannot forget Ts'ou, is shown to be his ever doting on his homeland. 'The good and virtuous would ultimately unite with their ideal sovereign, but here in Ts'ou, it is absolutely hopeless. '" — Tsiang Ch'ih.

117. *l.* 273, white artemisias. The original 艾 is 白蒿, botanically called *Artemisia stelleriana*. It is said to be "whiter than other artemisias from its first growth to autumn". It is of course not an aromatic herb.

118. *ll.* 269 −278. "The perverted caballers are proud of the rank

weeds they wear in big bunches on their girdles. They declare eupatory is not fragrant and should not be hung as pendants by others. Their obsession in depravity makes them incapable of even passing proper judgments on plants they see and prize or frown on. How can they tell what the gems of matchless beauty others suspend on their belts should be like? Inured to fetid things, they fill their perfume bags with muck. Yet they pronounce Sun peppers to be not aromatic and offensive. " Here, the poet's musings on the difference between himself and the pro-Tsing rabble end.

119. *l.* 281, The sibyl Yen. The sibyl Yen, 巫咸, was a soceress during the reign of King Tsoon(中宗) of Yin(殷).

120. *ll.* 283 −284, these two lines. For Nine Doubts, see note 74. "The sibyl Yen has asked the whole pantheon thronging across the sky to descend, and Suen makes the Spirits of the Nine Doubts also come to greet the poet. " — Tsu Hsih.

"From this, it can be seen that the thought contained in lines 177 −178 is the result of Suen's divine revelation. Nine Doubts are in the south of Ts'ou. They are like the hosts. The Spirits of the Mounts, ordered by Suen, greet the whole pantheon of heaven and come down with them to tell Chü Yuan through the medium of Sibyl Yen. " — Tsiang Ch'ih.

121. *l.* 288, the whole line. The original, 榘矱之所同, means figuratively what is measured and formed with the square and foot-rule of the joiner, common to his ideal king and himself. Hence, this expression means the moral standard of measure of ethical code.

122. *l.* 290, the whole line. Literally, this line should be: With

them, Tzeh and Kao Yau(挚, 咎繇) achieved harmony. Tzeh was Ih Yün's(伊尹) other name. Ih Yün, the great counsellor and premier of Tseng Taung, was picked up as an infant from a hollow trunk of a mulberry tree by the side of the Ih Stream(伊水) by a woman of the Sing tribe(有莘氏, 女). He was given the surname Ih from the stream. As a peasant tilling farms on the plain of Sing and as a cook, he was thrice sought for by Tseng Taung before his master acceded to the request. Taung started the world's first revolution mainly through his aid. He was called by his master his "Even Reliance"(阿衡). When Taung died, his grandson T'ai-ja (太甲) was wayward. Ih Yün banished him to Ton(桐) for three years. The young king repented and was welcomed back to Pûh(亳) to ascend the throne. Ih Yün lived to a hundred years. When he died, the new king, T'ai-ja's son Wau-ting(沃丁), mourned and buried him with the obit of a king. *Vide* Ih Yün's story in section II of *Introduction*, *pp.* 11 − 12. Kao Yau(咎繇, 皋陶, both pronounced the same, neither "Chiu Yu", nor "Kao Tau") was Lord of the Judiciary(士) at Suen's court. These two are mentioned here as virtuous aids to Taung and Yü. When Yü took his crown, he put Kao Yau in high office to execute his policies.

123. *l.* 292, the whole line. "If a good sovereign is eager to elect a virtuous aid, why is it necessary to have a go-between to mediate them? He can approach the man of his choice directly. There is no need for a third party to intermediate." — Tsu Hsih.

124. *ll.* 293 −294, these two lines. Fuh Yüeh(傅说) wrought at laying mud walls at Fuh-yan(傅岩) as a convict in penal servi-

tude, King Wuh-ting(武丁), Kao-*tsoon*(高宗) of Yin(殷), dreamt of him as an excellent man of virtue. Pictures were drawn of his likeness and sent all over the country to search for him. He was found out. Being talked to by the king, he was found to be virtuous indeed. Thereupon, he was made the premier in 1322 B.C. After his government of the country for some time, the dynasty Yin achieved great peace and prosperity. Wuh-ting's long reign of fifty-nine years marked a signal revival of Yin, chiefly on account of his getting the consummate aid of Fuh Yüeh.

125. *ll*. 295 −296, these two lines. Leü Wang(吕望) was Father Chiang Soun(太公姜尚), taking Leü, the name of his ancestral fief, as his adopted surname. He avoided the nefarious despot Zer(纣) and lived near the Eastern Sea(东海之滨). Hearing of Count West's coming to the fore, he attempted to reach him. When he arrived at Tsau-ge(朝歌), the capital of Yin, he became penniless. So he hired himself at a butchery, and at the moment he was angling on the bank of the Wei Stream(渭滨), Count West, dreaming the previous night that he would meet a sage, rode out hunting in a cabriolet and met him. *Vide* section II of *Introduction*, *p.* 13.

126. *ll*. 297 −298, these two lines and the previous four. Nien Ts'i (宁戚), a subject of the state Wei(卫), being engaged in a business of some sort for he had not met a master, put up one night outside the eastern gate of Tsih's capital and was feeding his cow and singing a song while striking its horn. His song runs like this:

南山粲;白石烂。
生不遭尧与舜禅。

短布单衣适至擊，

从昏饭牛薄夜半。

长夜漫漫何时旦？

The South Mountain is beaming bright;

Its rocks and stones all gliffer in white.

Not meeting the time when Yao handed Suen his crown,

With short frock barely to the skin hanging down,

I feed my cow from eve till midnight moon is on.

When would the livelong dark night

Gave place to dawn and daylight?

Marquis Hwan of Tsih(齐桓公), going out at night, overheard him and cried, "It's strange! The singer must be an unusual man." He ordered his followers to bear the man in a rear car back to his court and asked him to be his guest counsellor.

All these three instances show that there were no "match-makers" or go-betweens to intercede between the gracious masters and their virtuous aids.

127. *ll.* 301 −302, these two lines. 鹈鸠 of the original, the same as 鴺鶏, 鴺鸠 or 买鶏, was commonly taken to be the cuckoo(杜鹃，子鹃，子规). The cuckoo is a bird of the species *Cuculus poliocephalus*, which deposits its eggs in other bird's nests, so called from its note. Cuckoo begins to sing during vernal equinox(春分) when spring is in full swing. Wang Yi and Hoon Hsin-tsou think it means the cuckoo. Tsu Hsih in his *Dialectical Comments on Ts'ou "Tze"*(《楚辞辩证》) quotes Fwu Jien(服虔) and Loh Dien(陆佃) as saying, 鹈鸠 is 鴶 or 伯劳, which is the shrike or butcher-bird, singing in August. When the shrike sings, autumn would come soon after its announcement,

thus making all herbs lose their verdure.

"The sibyl Yen's words end here. He is counseling the poet to haste away while he is not yet old and time is not too late. Fearing the shrike would cry before its time means if the time is over, things would change more radically and there would be even less hope for doing anything." — Tsu Hsih.

"The cry of the shrike at the arrival of autumn makes grass wither. This alludes to the havoc of the traducers. The passage of musing (lines 269 −278) has shown that he knows very well Ts'ou world not do. But his ranging the heavens and roving the world without finding a good match-maker to intermediate have thrown him into a state of uncertainty and doubt. Here, the necromancer's words convince him of the easiness of co-operation between the two fair parties without relying on match-makers, and warn him that if he hesitates and loses the chance, harm would befall him. It is better for him to hasten his departure. Compared with Ling Fung's advice, this urging carries more pressure." — Tsiang Ch'ih.

128. *ll.* 303 −306, these four lines. "From these four lines onward to the end, Chü Yuan is again speaking of himself. 'These fair, rare wearings' means his intrinsic qualities and wholesome virtues." — Tsu Hsih.

129. *ll.* 307 −310, these four lines. "时缤纷", the times are troubled(乱也);不可淹留, could not long in such states remain, but must haste away (宜速去). Reeds (茅) are bad weeds, meaning the wicked elements. *The Supplemental Commentary* of Hoon Hsin-tsou(洪兴祖:《楚辞补注》) says: in the above, the caballers are quoted for saying that others should not eupatory

append, for it is different from their white artemisias, and that Sun peppers are not scentful, for these are different from their manured loam. Here, it is said eupatories and angelicas are scentful no more and queen sweet-flags and coumarous have changed into reeds; thus, sweet herbs of the past have turned rank and gross and gone the way of the fat weeds. At that time, keeping one's oath of purity unto death without change, there was only one man in Ts'ou — Chü-tse alone!" — Tsu Hsih.

130. *ll.*311 −314, these four lines. "Artemisias are also rank weeds meaning the madding crowd. The world is troubled and the customs (people's practices) become mean. The intellectuals(士) are loose in keeping their stringency, for the wicked mob has turned them into vile ones. It may be asked, why is it the good and virtuous of yesterday are turning awry and debased today? That is because the wicked are envious of them, making them unbearable to the world, so that those of them from the middling down have to change themselves to follow the vulgar multitude. And the basic cause why things have come to such a pass is that the good and virtuous of yesterday are to be blamed for their brittleness and lack of austerity. " — Tsu Hsih.

The above is as much as I can make out from Tsu-tse's commentary, the wording of which seems to me somewhat vague and slippery. The last line, as I translate it, means a condemnation of the crowd, the mob, the world, for their intolerance of the goodness and virtues of those from the middling down as to have forced them to undergo a debasing transformation and conform with the vulgar multitude. I think this is what Chü Yuan means by 莫好修之害也 and what Tsu-tse intends to expound.

In these two lines, the poet first blames the world, the society, for their intolerance of the good and virtuous, the great majority of whom are bound to be timid and weak. Then, in the next twelve lines, he examines the typical examples one by one and finds them indeed cheap and worthless.

131. *ll*. 315 − 318, these four lines. These lines are motivated in theme by *l*. 309.

132. *l*. 319, the whole line. 慆 is explained by Tsu-tse as "lazy, growing fat like weeds" (无即慆淫) from *The Enjoinment of Taung*(《汤诰》) of *The Classic of History*(《尚书》). A textual variant has 谣 instead, which means arrogant. Those who wheedle and fawn upon their superiors are as a rule arrogant towards their equals and inferiors.

133. *ll*. 319 −320, Sun Pepper in the first line and Cornus in the second. 椴 is 茱萸, the tree cornus, cornel, cornelian cherry or dogwood as well as its edible fruit, all called by such names. Both Sun Pepper(申椒, the Tsing pepper of the former state, Sun, 申) and Cornus are spices. Because they are unscrupulous in getting up and winning the king's favour, they have lost their former qualities and are aromatic no more.

134. *ll*. 325 − 326, these two lines. Even Sun Pepper and Eupatory could not weather the trial; how can *Chi Chü* and Selinea, which are an inferior sort of aromatic herbs, stand the test? When Sun Pepper is mentioned, Cornus is understood to be included.

135. *ll*. 327 −330, these four lines. "His fair and rare wearings keep their priceless, precious qualities intact. He had as lief see their beauty vilified and traduced as reach a compromise with the

world. But their fragrance could not be lessened or darkened the least bit. Eupatory, etc., have given up their beauties to follow the vulgar multitude. Though they keep their worldly positions at the moment, their foul names would spread far and wide. He is beaten and undone now, but the fragrance of his fair repute would last forever." — Tsu Hsih.

136. *ll.* 333 − 334, these two lines. Still in search of the heavenly maid, his ideal king, with his adornments of fair and rare wearings and rich vestures and noble, tall hat mentioned above full and lusty (as also said by the sibyl Yen in another way in *ll.* 299 − 300), he is going to roam up and down to conduct his survey (that is, "to go far away" — Ling Fung, and "go up and down as thou mightest rise and descend" — Yen). In the next line, when Ling Fung is mentioned, it is understood Sibyl Yen is included.

137. *l.* 337, gem tree. *The Gem Glossary* (《玉篇》) of K'uh Yê-wang(顾野王) of Liang (梁, one of the Southern Dynasties between Ts'in and Daung, 502 − 557) says: *Chung-tze* (琼枝) is a tree of jade, 840 feet (Tsur foot-rule) tall and 30 armful inclosures in perimeter, with *l'ong-kan* (琅玕, gem, jade, or pearly stone) as its fruit. Tsang Ih (张揖) says, Chung-tree grows in the west of Quen-lung Mountains on the bank of the Drifting Sands(流沙), 300 armful inclosures in perimeter and 70000 feet tall, with fruits, flowers and budding blooms which, when eaten, give immortality.

138. *l.* 343, the whole line. He is going up heaven by way of the Quen-lung Mountains once more. In *l.* 188, he has reached the mid cliffs of Quen-lung (*vide* note 76); in *l.* 216, he has gone

up Mount Laun-feng (*vide* note 91). This huge range of high mountains in the far west and north-west of the Nine States, inaccessibly far away and high, is regarded with awe and mysticism in Chü Yuan's poetry as in the works of other poets. Soung Chin's *The Classic of Streams*(桑钦:《水经》, of Han) says, Quen-lung Heights are in the north-west, 50,000 *lih* from the central Soong-kao(嵩高). The distance is exaggerated, as said by Tsu-tse.

139. *l.* 345, the rainbow-cloud flags raise their shadows. Shadows of flags and banners made of rainbows and clouds.

140. *l.* 346, the bells of the phoenix of chalcedony. 玉鸾(和鸾) of the original means the bells in the mouths of jade phoenixes fixed on the horizontal bars on the backs of the horses or on the front of cars of state drawn by them, said to be innovated in the times of Suen.

141. *l.* 347, Celestial Ferry. The Celestial Ferry(天津) of the "Silver River"(银河, the Milky Way) is the ford where the Chih Constellation(箕宿), the last one of the seven constellations of Blue Dragon(苍龙), lies adjacent to the Tur Constellation(斗宿), the first one of the seven constellations of Yuan-wuh(玄武), across the "River".

142. *l.* 351, the Drifting Sands. Both Tsu Hsih and Tsiang Ch'ih say, it is the Chüeh-yieu Salt Swamp of West Sea(西海居延泽). Tsu-tse quotes Sühn Kwa(沈括) of Soong(宋) for saying that he once waded through the quicksands of the Wuh-ding River(无定河); stepping on them made the morass perturbed a hundred steps around as if walking on an extended curtain; if sucked in, men, horses, carts and camels by hundreds and

thousands would be swallowed without a trace. "Drifting Sands" is also a common denomination given to the great desert from the far north-west across the vast north to the far north-east of the Middle Empire. In Mongolian dialect, it has been called Nga-lun(额伦); in Manchurian dialect, Go-pi(戈壁), from its south-western end to Sing-kiang(新疆), the great desert extends north-eastward to Hê-loong-kiang（黑龙江）for about 1200 miles.

143. *l.* 352, the Red Stream. The Red Stream(赤水) flows from the south-east of Quen-lung Mountains eastward into the Luteous River(黄河).

144. *l.* 354, Sao-hao, god of West Sky. Hwang-*t'ih's* son Sao-hao （少昊）had become the White God of Autumnal Sky in the west(西皇,白帝). *Vide* section II of *Introduction*, *p.* 7.

145. *ll.* 356 −357, these two lines. "I tell the host of cars to take a short straight way and wait for me at West Sea. I would go round Mount Pûh-tsur（不周山）and turn to the left to meet them there." — Tsu Hsih.

"That is because he wants to explore and search thoroughly the regions he would go over." — Tsiang Ch'ih.

146. *l.* 365, *Nine Songs* and *Sao.* For *Nine Songs*, see note 58. 韶 here is *Siao Sao*（箫"韶"）or *Great Continuance*, *T'ih* Suen's dance cantata, played with Pandean pipes. (See section Ⅲ of *Introduction*, *pp.* 16 −17 and note 73.) It is generally called *Great Continuance*（"大韶","大磬"）, meaning Yao's virtues are being continued by Suen（Ts'eng Yüen,郑玄）, and called in *The Classic of History* "*Siao Sao*"（箫韶）because the Pandean pipes（箫）, an excellent instrument, are used in the dance

cantata（Kung An-Kuo，孔安国）．

147. *l.* 366，the whole line. Tsu-tse quotes Yen Sze-k'uh（颜师古）：Suffering from deep calamity, he is thrown into bitter melancholy; so he whiles away time for temporary amusement.

148. *l.* 368，the whole line. "Rising up to a great height of the heavens where there is a torrential flush of light, I suddenly catch sight, in looking askance, of my homeland Ts'ou."

149. *l.* 370，the whole line. "Chü Yuan makes this hypothetic journey but has reached nowhere. He has gone up and down, and come back at last to Ts'ou. This is indeed the utmost of what is humanly possible and the extremity of eternal justice.（仁之至义尽也）" — Tsu Hsih.

"He wants at first to ramble all over up and down the sky. But having only roved over the western horizons, he cuts his journey short for cherishing Ts'ou and his inability to forego it! In the above, he has spoken of going up and down seeking his ideal Lady of Heaven. That is only said in expectation. Now, he has actually set forth. He must not remain in Ts'ou. Going abroad, he is sure to meet his destined Sweet. His manners at departing are bold; his will and wishes, firm and abundant. This man of goodness and virtues could now have his time. But, looking back at his native land on the sudden, he stops in spite of himself! Tsu-tse calls it the utmost of what is humanly possible and the extremity of eternal justice." — Tsiang Ch'ih.

150. *l.* 371，epiphonema. 乱 is originally the epilogue or final movement of a musical composition; here, I call it the epiphonema of the ode, an abrupt exclamatory ejaculation at the close.

151. *l.* 372，the whole line. "Let it be, then!"（已矣哉）is a cry of

despair. "No one" means no proper man at the helm of state. "The old capital" means the state of Ts'ou, with Ying-*t'uh* as its heart and mind.

Nine Songs (九歌)

1 Hymn on East Emperor Tai-ih (东皇太一)

1. East Emperor Tai-ih: Tai-ih was the name of the noblest god of Heaven. There are different opinions about which one of the two among the five stars of the Polaris is presided over by Tai-ih, the northern-most (天枢) or the second one counted from the south (北辰) which is the brightest of the five and casts a red brilliance. The traditional stand holds the second opinion, while Tsiang Ch'ih sides with the first, taking the fixed northern-most star as the seat of the Great *T'ih* of Heaven (天皇大帝). His temple is said by Wang Yi in his *Textual Critical Studies in Ts'ou "Tze"* (王逸:《楚辞章句》) to be in the east (suburbs) of Ts'ou ('s capital), hence called East Glitter. *The Book of Homage to Heaven and Earth* of Sze-ma Tsien's *The Chronicle* (《史记·封禅书》) also says, anciently homage was paid to Tai-ih in the south-eastern suburbs of the capital.

2. *l.* 5, saffron jades. This is used as a pressure gem (镇圭), which was a rare gem baton held by the king or laid before him on the table, signifying weight and steadiness of his rule, according to *Tsur Rites*, Spring Official, Master of Ceremony (《周礼·春官宗伯》), a foot and two inches long, with the symbolizing mountains of the four compasses carved on it.

3. *l.* 12, Pandean pipes and zithern. 竽 was a sort of Pandean pipes with thirty-six reeds circularly arranged. 瑟 was a zithern with

twenty-five chords, said to be simplified by Hwang-*t'ih*(黄帝) from Fwu-shih's(伏羲) first make of fifty chords.

2 Hymn on the King of Clouds(云中君)

"The first six lines describe the descending of the God of Clouds, the first two on His fragrance, cleanliness, fairness and beauty. In heaven, the clouds are floating and rushing about freely. Here, their King for a moment pauses and pores on the altar, meaning to enjoy the homage and oblation offered to Him. In lines 7 −8, He has disappeared in a flash. Line 11, ' Overseeing Ch'ih-tsur forever more' of the original — Ch'ih-tsur(冀州) means the Middle Empire." — Tsiang Ch'ih. The King of Clouds(云中君), also called the Chief of Clouds(云师), is named Feng-loon(丰隆) in *Lee Sao*, *l.* 223, in *Musing on the Beauteous One*(《思美人》), *ll.* 9 − 10, and in *Distant Wanderings*(《远游》), *l.* 89. See note 96 on *Lee Sao* above.

3 Hymn on the Lady of Hsiang(湘夫人)
4 Hymn on the King of Hsiang(湘君)

The third and fourth poems of *Nine Hymns* are supposed to be the love songs of two youthful deities, the King of Hsiang and the Lady of Hsiang respectively, in their first bewitchery for each other. Each of the enamoradoes has no knowledge whatsoever that the other party is equally over head and ears in love with himself or herself. The title of the first song should be *Hymn on the Lady of Hsiang*(《湘夫人》), instead of *Hymn on the King of Hsiang*(《湘君》), as it is supposed to be sung by the young god, and the title of the second song should be *Hymn on the King of Hsiang*(《湘君》), instead of

Hymn of the Lady of Hsiang(《湘夫人》), as it is supposed to be sung by the young goddess, at the beginning of their acquaintance and mutual attraction. As early as before Liu Shan(刘向) of West Han(西汉) perhaps, the two titles were mistakenly interchanged in transcription when incised on bamboo strips or brushed on silk scrolls. Or it was Liu as an editor or Wang Yi(玉逸) of East Han (东汉) as a commentator who erroneously inverted the original right order by interchanging the two titles, thinking laxly that the young god should be named before the young goddess in natural sequence, without noting that the first piece is supposed to be the love ditty of the young god for the young goddess and should therefore be entitled by the name of the Lady, and that the second piece is supposed to be that of the young goddess for the young god and should therefore be entitled by the name of the King. For twenty centuries, this error, seeming so obvious to me, has not been discovered and set right by editors, students and critics of Chü Yuan. This misplacing of titles has produced much confusion of thought and a medley of irrelevancies in the critical studies of these two poems from East Han to the present.

In the first song, being longingly charmed by the maiden goddess, the youthful god "With excellence fair by adornments graced," waiting for his beloved to appear, expecting her to come in vain but hearing in the distance she is playing on the Pandean pipes, perhaps thinking of someone meanwhile, rushes forth speedily in a cassia boat to seek her out. The addresses "君" and "夫君"(pronounced "vuh jün", not "fuh jün") in *ll.* 1,7 and 18 of the original are ancient terms of hail applicable to anyone to whom one is friendly, cordial, polite or respectful regardless of sex distinction. He finds her just plying her "dragon-winged boat to fleet north", and so conducts her by way of Doong-ding northward to some spot where he wishes to keep her company and pour out his feelings for her. But she seems to ignore him with cold nonchalance, running away with arch coyness, at the same time both surprised and glad at heart. For as soon as they have reached the northern middle part of the lake together, she left him shyly on a sudden and could be "Seen distantly at Jin-yang's water margin", shining her splendours over the River. He attempts eagerly to come near her without success, but could only pant out his complaint in *ll.* 19 −28. The sad disappointment of this first love tryst of the forlorn youthful god is thus expressed in *ll.* 29 − 30 and his lonely pensiveness in the next two lines. Then, the rest of the poem forms the wishful conclusion of the young god's monologue: he leaves his incised gem hoop(玦) and jade pendant(佩) by the watersides with the hope that she may pick them up, take pity on him and change her mind, and he culls

> "pollia bouquets from the green isle,
>
> To give as gifts to Her handmaids for the while."

expecting them to say a good word for him to his beloved. Anciently, gentlemen wore pendants(佩), rings(环) and incised hoops (or severed ringlets, 玦) of gem and jade; ladies wore pendants and rings, but not incised hoops. In the end, he cherishes the good hope of taking "time to wait as Her bonny swain." Eventually, this pair of natural spirits becomes happily espoused, he as the King of Hsiang and she the Lady of the stream, an ideal couple of eternal youth.

The second song which Chü Yuan entitled, I am confident as I do, but has been given the wrong appellation (*Hymn on*) *the Lady of Hsiang* since Liu Shan and Wang Yi of Han to Yer Koh-en today, is supposed to be a love strain of the goddess of that stream before her marriage with the King of Hsiang. In their passionate love at first sight (I suppose) "on the stream's north bank" (*l.* 1) for each other, neither of them is conscious of the other's ardent feelings for himself or herself at first. She yearns to attach herself to him and attract him; but without the chance or occasion of so doing, she could only vainly attempt to catch a distant sight of him and, hoping for the best imagine a dear, secret tryst with him, as stated in *ll.* 5 −6. The best, however, could not happen, she fears; the reason is implied in the obvious answer to the two questions asked by her of herself in the next two lines. "Yuan hath its angelicas and Lih, eupatories"; "but how could I belong to him and he to me?" There are scant means of such a delightful whim coming true. Her thought causing her to blush is made manifest in the bashful confession given in *l.* 10. Pining for him while looking at the rapid current flush and spout in the distance, she comes to senses that impossible things could not happen just as she reasons in *ll.* 13 −14. Yet, in her loneliness while galloping along the river bund at morn and rowing along the west water margin before eve, she simply could not resist the rapturous fancy that, were he to summon her, she would certainly fleet and "bound to the trysting nook with joy. " The expressions "佳" and "佳人" in *ll.* 6 and 17 of the original are not necessarily limited for usage to the fair sex in our ancient literature, especially poetry. Here, they mean the Prince Rare. Then, the next fourteen lines (*ll.* 19 −32) form a picturesque passage showing a lovely maiden goddess with her heart and soul deeply in love engaged in weaving in her weird imagination a minute fairy bower for her sweetheart to lead her to; it could not come from a bluff, high-spirited youthful god in his first love. But, very unfortunately for her, the darling of her heart is greeted away by Spirits of Nine Doubts who "come in company like clouds". Under the circumstances, she has to wait patiently for him to come back. Finally, she could only

> "cast my sleeve to float it in the River,
>
> And leave mine upper bodice by Lih Water"

to attract his attention and give hints to him "Forget me not!" when he comes back from the Nine Doubts, and in the last resort she culls

> "pollia bouquets from the level isle,
>
> To give as gifts to His handmaids for the while."

wishing them to remind him of her. Her best wishes are by no means hopeless; she would "take time to wait for the chance boon." And indeed, they are ultimately united as the King and Lady of Hsiang, blissful and bloomingly young, forever and aye.

In the above I have accounted for the veritable substance of these two songs of Chü Yuan, or rather the two hymns originally of rude feelings, uncouth language and ragged rhythm made by or for some witch or wizard of ancient Ts'ou, but recomposed by our poet into their present form. Later legendary developments have it that T'ih Yao's two daughter Erh-hwang(娥皇) and Neü-ying(女英) given in marriage by him to Suen as his two wives have been attributed to the Ladies of Hsiang(湘夫人) and T'ih Suen has been to the King of Hsiang(湘君), or that Erh-hwang has been identified with the Queen of Hsiang(湘君) and Neü-ying with the Lady of Hsiang(湘夫人). Liu Shan's(刘向) *The Lives of Illustrious Women*(《列女传》) says: When Suen ascended the throne as the Son of Heaven, Erh-hwang became his queen and Neü-ying his imperial concubine; in his inspection tour, he died on the Plain of Tsoung-ngou(苍梧), being given the laudatory title Tsoon-hwah(重华); his two queens died between the River and Hsiang and were buried there, being called the Queen of Hsiang(湘君) and the Lady of Hsiang(湘夫人). The chapter *Dan-k'ung of Notes of Rites*(《礼记·檀弓》) says, Suen was buried on the Plain of Tsoung-ngou(苍梧之野), unaccompanied by his two queens; the annotation on the chapter by T'seng-yüen(郑玄) says, the *Ladies of Hsiang* sung by Chü Yuan are Suen's queens. Tsang Hwa's(张华) *Record of Natural History*(《博物志》) says, the spirits of T'ih Yao's two daughters staying on Mount Chün(君山, the King's Mount) in Lake Doong-ding(洞庭) are called the Ladies of Hsiang; the islet is so called on account of the King of Hsiang; Yao's two daughters are Suen's two queens, the Ladies of Hsiang; when Suen died, his two queens mourned and their tears sprinkled on the bamboo stem shafts made them all spotted. Such spotted bamboos(斑竹) are also called Queens-of-Hsiang bamboo(湘妃竹). Lih Dao-yuan's(郦道元) *Commentary on the Classic of Streams*(《水经注》) says, when Great Suen died during his inspection tour, his two queens following him were drowned in the Hsiang Stream, their spirits wandering over Doong-ding Lake and appearing on the lee shore of Siao-hsiang(潇湘之浦). *The Life of Ying Tsen in The Chronicle* (《史记·秦始皇本纪》) says, he floated over the River and came to the temple on Mount Hsiang; caught in a wind storm, he almost failed to cross; he asked his attendant court doctors, "What deity is Hsiang Chün?" Whereat they replied, "It is known that Yao's daughter who was Suen's wife was buried here when she died"; hearing this, he fell into a rage and ordered three thousand of his convicts to cut down all the trees on the islet. However, Kuo Po(郭璞) of Ts'in (晋) in his annotations to *Tsoong-san Classic of The Classic of*

Mountains and Seas(《山海经·中山经》) is strongly of opinion that the Ladies of Hsiang of the temple on the Doong-ding islet were the two daughters of the *T'ih* of Heaven(天帝), not of *T'ih* Yao: to call them the queen and concubine of Suen is sheer confusion of pristine verity with later legendary tradition. And K'uh Yen-wuh(顾炎武) of Tsing(清) also stands firmly on the ground that they were daughters of God of Heaven, not of *T'ih* Yao; for evidence, he cites *ll.* 146 and 147 of *Distant Wanderings*(《远游》) of our poet to show that "Two Genii fair"(二女, Yao's daughters Erh-hwang and Neü-ying) are to be distinguished from the "Spirits of Hsiang"(湘灵). But Yer Koh-en(游国恩), our contemporary, while admitting the pristine King and Lady of Hsiang to be pantheistic natural deities, insists that as Chü Yuan wrote or recomposed these two hymns, the King of Hsiang is meant by him to be Suen, and the Ladies are understood to be Yao's daughters Erh-hwang and Neü-ying. The evidences given by him are: first, 参差(*l.* 8); second, 君 and 夫君(*ll.* 1,7 and 18) in the first hymn; third, 帝子(*l.* 1); fourth, 洞庭(*l.* 4); and fifth, 九嶷(*l.* 33) in the second hymn — to clinch his arguments that Chü Yuan, when he wrote these two hymns, had decidedly Suen and his two queens in mind. It seems to me however, there are obvious inconsistencies and mistakes in these instances. At rock-bottom, these two hymns should be entitled as I have done to theme in my text and translation, contrary to the practices of all the editions from those of Liu Shan and Wang Yi down to those of Wen Ih-to(闻一多) and Prof. Yer. My reasons for so saying are given in the analyses and expounding of these two hymns with relation to their titles in the first three paragraphs above. Now, let us proceed to discuss Yer's points in details. First, the Pandean pipes(参差, also called 洞箫, 排箫, 云

箫, 籁, said to be with sixteen reeds of a foot and two inches long or twenty-three ones of a foot and four inches long, arranged in a parallel row and partially incased) are indeed known to be originated by Suen, but here in the first hymn, they are played upon by the Lady of Hsiang and heard by the King, not otherwise; in their early first love for each other, it could not be that Suen had already given this wind instrument to his beloved and was hearing her pipe theme in the distance; furthermore, Suen had two wives as his queen and beebee, but here the love song sung by the King of Hsiang is certainly on only one Lady, not two Ladies. Secondly, Yer says, in the first hymn, the King of Hsiang is addressed by the Ladies as 君, for Suen was T'ih or King after Yao: this is mistaken, for the first hymn is a song sung by a youthful god on his love for a maiden goddess, whereas in history, Suen succeeded Yao three years after Yao's death, and during Yao's lifetime he was made Yao's Lord Protector (摄 政) for twenty-seven years (2285—2258 B. C.), in the early period of which Suen must have already married Yao's two daughters (he was crowned, or called T'ih or King, some thirty, or at least twenty-seven, years after his marriage with them), so this 君 cannot mean Suen being addressed as T'ih or King by his beloved ones in their early love for him, but should be explained as above by me. Thirdly, the title 帝子 in the second hymn (l. 1) is explained by Yer to mean "princesses" and to be applied to the two daughters of Yao: this, I believe, is also mistaken, for the song is a love chant sung by a maiden goddess on the cherished lover of her dreams, as I have analyzed and expounded above (not by a young god on his love for two youthful goddesses) ; and besides, nine lines later, the King of Hsiang is further called 公子 — both these appellatives simply mean "prince", a common denomination of respect, courtesy and good will spoken of or to a gentleman of good breeding. Fourthly and lastly, Yer says, according to numerous records from legendary tradition, Suen leading in person an expedition to put down the rebellious Miao tribesmen(有苗) died on the Plain of Tsoung-ngou(苍梧之野) and was buried at Nine Doubts(九嶷); his two queens following him failed to catch up with him and was drowned between Hsiang Stream and the River; and Lake Doong-ding was anciently also called Hsiang: thus, Chü Yuan must have Suen and his two queens in mind when he wrote these two hymns. Regarding this, I have to say that our poet might have such associations unconsciously in his mind while recomposing these two hymns, for one could not expect our poet to be strictly avoiding them, but consciously he rewrote these two songs only as the love chants of this couple of pantheistic natural spirits, and what is more, Doong-ding and Nine Doubts can exist as natural scenes and objects quite independent of their association of memories with Suen and his two queens. As to the young god's disappointment in his first love tryst and the young goddess's "Musing on Him the Rare, I dare not speak out"(思公子兮未敢言), Yer offers only a lame explanation to the former question by saying that, after Suen had died in his expedition, his two queens following him failed to catch up with him, but were drowned in Yuan and Hsiang(沅湘), as it was forcedly explained by Wang Yi and Hoon Hsin-tsou to mean that the King of Hsiang (Suen) failed to come because he was detained on the isle by his two queens (this is altogether incongruous with the total sense of the first hymn, it is senseless), while on the latter question, Yer could but be silent on the bashfulness of the young goddess, for after some twenty-seven or thirty years' marriage, Erh-hwang and Neü-ying could not be still shy of speaking of their thoughts of him.

3　Hymn on the Lady of Hsiang(湘夫人)

1. *ll.* 11 −12, these two lines. "Wearing a frock made of pomelo-fig's vine, tied with strings of coumarous, you hie on your acorus skiff which streams with buntings of eupatory. " — Tsiang Ch'ih.

2. *l.* 13, Jin-yang. A stream between Lake Doong-ding and the Great River.

3. *l.* 30, the north bank of the water. It is where the young god fell in love at first sight with the young goddess. See the first two lines of the next hymn.

4. *ll.* 31 −32, these two lines. These two lines describe the loneliness of the ardent lover.

4　Hymn on the King of Hsiang(湘君)

1. *ll.* 7 −8, these two lines. Birds would not perch on water plants and fish nets would not be cast on tree tops: there is therefore not much hope for her to make an eagerly wished for tryst with him.

2. *ll.* 13 −14, these two lines. The elk has nothing to do in the court-yard and a dragon would not come about the waterside: how could her dreams come true?

3. *l.* 21, purple grass. Purple grass'(紫,紫草,紫丹,紫茢,茈莀) full botanical name is called Lithospermum officinale, var. erythrorhi-ron.

4. *l.* 23, rafters of magnolia. 兰 of the original is 木兰(Magnolia obovata, see note 9 on *Lee Sao*) and 橑 is synonymous with 橼, 榱,桷, rafters.

5. *l*. 24, the whole line. The original 辛夷 (Magnolia kobus, also called 木笔 in Chinese) I take the liberty to change into aloes(沉香) to avoid repetition of the word "magnolia", and 楣 is "lin-tel"; 药, the same as 芷, is angelica, and 房 is either the right or left flank partition of the hall.

6. *ll*. 29 −30, these two lines. These two lines in the original mean "This chamber overlaid with lotus leafage and again covered with angelicas(芷葺) is bounded all over with asarums." For the sake of brevity and to avoid repetition of the word "angelica", something of the original is deleted in the rendition.

7. *l*. 38, His handmaids. 远者 of the original is explained by Tsu Hsih to mean the King of Hsiang's handmaids.

5   Hymn on the Major God of Life-ruling(大司命)

1. The Major God of Life-ruling presided over the star of the selfsame name, according to ancient astrology. Hoon Hsin-tsou(洪兴祖) quotes the Five Courtiers' *Commentary*(五臣注) on Tsau-ming's *Literary Selections*(昭明《文选》): "The Star Life −ruling takes charge of men's life and death, aids Heaven to direct His influence and obliterates the wicked while protecting the good." T'ai Ts'en (戴震): "The Upper *Dai*(上台) of the Three *Dai*(三台) is called the Star of Life-ruling, determining the duration of mundane lives, presided over by the Major God of Life-ruling in Chü Yuan's *Nine Hymns*."

2. *l*. 1, heaven's azure gates. They are the vast gates of Purple Deep Wall(紫微垣, formed by a row of stars, with eight as the east guard and seven as the west guard, each having a name of its own), also called Purple Deep Palace(紫微宫), in which God

of Heaven was supposed to reside. They are wide open now for the Major God of Life-ruling is going to descend.

3. *l.* 2,1. "I" is the homager or consecrator speaking of himself. He drives "multiplicate clouds dusky", for a tempest of violent wind and rain has been started.

4. *l.* 6, Koon-soung. The name of a mountain (空桑). Tsiang Ch'ih: "There are two mounts called by this name, one in the region between the ancient state Yeou-sinn(有莘) and Tsur's royal domain Sen(陝), the other in ancient Yean-tsur(兗州)." The former is in modern Sen-sih(陝西) and the latter includes the region south-west of modern Ho-pêh(河北) and north-west of San-tung(山东).

5. *ll.* 1 −8. "Seeing the gates of heaven wide open, the homager knows his God is going to descend; he rides the clouds to clear the ways for greeting Him. But the God's coming down is to perform the *T'ih* of Heaven's orders of overseeing the Nine States, not because He is bidden by the homager to descend. Therefore he dares not offer his greetings directly. Yet he fears to lose the chance of doing homage to Him; so he flits high and follows at a distance wherever He speeds. He sees that all the people of the Nine States are under His sway. At this, he is awe-struck with His authority." — Tsiang Ch'ih.

6. *l.* 12, Nine K'ong. "The present Soon-tze *hsien* of Ch'ih-tsur *fuh* (荆州府松滋县) and Ih-yang *hsien* of Tsang-sah *fuh*(长沙府益阳县) both have Nine K'ong Mounts(九岗山) and Tsang-teh *fuh* (常德府) has Nine K'ong-tsoon(九岗冲). All of these were in the domain of Ts'ou. It is not known which one of them is meant here." — Tsiang Ch'ih.

7. *l.* 16, I. "I" is the homager speaking of himself. "The Major God of Life-ruling, acting on His divinity, is quick in His motion without speeding, and His consecrator, following Him, fleets as quickly. In a few moments, He has already transmitted *T'ih's* decree and come to Nine K'ong. So, He is ushered to the place of homage. His august appearance, resplendent adornments and holy spirit are towering and sparkling there. People only know His Divinity has come down, without kenning His consecrator has done marvels to follow and then conduct Him to the place of homage." — Tsiang Ch'ih.

8. *ll.* 9 −16. These lines describe the descending of His Divinity.

9. *ll.* 17 −20, these four lines. "These four lines are addressed to His Divinity with regard to the homager himself. He comes for a moment in His inspection tour and cannot remain long. Fair blooms of sacred hemp are picked and given him as a farewell gift. He is getting old; if not favoured by His good wishes, his life would be terminated soon and with sorrow." — Tsiang Ch'ih.

"Hemp blooms white flowers like gem. It is known that eating them would give one longevity." — Wang Fuh-tse.

10. *ll.* 21 −28. "These are soliloquized on His departure. Line 26 is spoken because he is aging fast. Being old, he feels parting so easy and meeting very difficult; hence he begs that He would condescend to come down whenever consecration is performed. Life is such a great affair to men; it is He alone who destines it; therefore, how ineffably high and noble He is! Men have absolutely no say in the matter." — Tsiang Ch'ih.

The last two lines are freely rendered in my version.

6   Hymn on the Minor God of Life-ruling(少司命)

1. The Minor God of Life-ruling was the God of Fortune in charge of men's mishap and good luck. He presided over the star of His namesake, which is the fourth one of the cresent-outlined six stars forming the constellation Wen-tsoun(文昌) in front of the Great Dipper's ladle. Tsu Hish(朱熹) in his *Variorum Commentary on Ts'ou "Tze"*(《楚辞集注》) takes this hymn to be a song of forsaken love and dejection sung by the sorceress of the God on Him. In *Common Explications of Ts'ou "Tze"*(《楚辞通释》), Wang Fuh-tse(王夫之) says, one's having or having not offsprings was said to be destined by the deity; this hymn is explained by him thus to be a song sung to the God by a suppliant asking for an infant son. Our version of the hymn is rendered according to Tsiang Ch'ih's interpretation in his *San-tai Pavilion Commentary on Ts'ou "Tze"*(《山带阁注楚辞》), which varies from Tsu-tse's on certain details.

"The wording of *Hymn on the Major God of Life-ruling* is solemn and that of the one on the Minor God is familiar. The distinction is due to the dignified estate of the former God and the general station of the latter. The sense of tributary supplication is common to both hymns." The quoted comments above are given by Tsiang Ch'ih.

2. *ll.* 5 − 6, these two lines. "There are good elements among the people. You can bless them as you please. There is no need for you to be anxious that none or not enough a multitude could deserve your solicitude." — Tsiang Ch'ih.

3. *ll.* 9 − 10, these two lines. "The boon adorers are the homagers.

You fixing your eyes quickly on mine means the tacit affiance of love. From all the fragrant herbs, only the eupatory is selected; from all the beauteous ones, only I am chosen: this is alluding to King Hwai's intrusting him heartily as his Left Counsellor. " To the translator, there may not be such a political meaning.

4. *ll.* 11 −14, these four lines. "After the God's pledge of attachment, He comes in and goes out unexpectedly without a word or becking signal. The sadness of live parting and the gladness of new endearment have filled her heart and she is torn between conflicting emotions. " — Tsiang Ch'ih.

5. *ll.* 17 −18, these two lines. "Her God spends His night in the vicinity of *T'ih's* Heaven; He seems to linger in the clouds, reluctant to go farther away. The question shows what is envied and wished for by her. "

6. *ll.* 19 −22, these four lines. "Yen-tze(咸池) was the name of a triad of stars in the constellation Heaven's Water Expanse(天潢). 'Thee'(女), 'Thy'(女) and 'Beauty'(娥人) in the first three lines all mean the Minor God of Life-ruling. The sorceress is disheartened; for as her God still seems to be fascinated by her, she summons Him, meaning to say that they could fondle each other in their peregrination from earth to heaven to drink from the cup of their mutual blushing affection. But her God does not appear. Dejected, she sings a sad song to pine. "

7. *ll.* 23 −26, these four lines. "His mounting ninth Heaven shows that He is no more in Heaven's suburbs. The comet is a monstrous star, signifying calamity. It should be checked to protect humanity, the aged as well as the young. Her God has gone, but her feelings for Him are not ended, and so she ceases not to pour forth

her adorations. "

7　Hymn on East King(东君)

1. *The Classic of Rites*(《仪礼》)：The Son of Heaven doth obeisance to the Sun God outside the eastern gates of his capital.

2. *ll.* 1 −4, these four lines. "This is a hail to the Sun God. Dawn is the bright and warm phenomenon before the rise of Sun. The homager taps his horse as he mounts it to greet Him. All locutions of the first person in this hymn mean the homager. " For Fwuh-soung, see note 82 on *Lee Sao*.

3. *ll.* 5 −8, these four lines. In the first four lines of the second passage, the appearance of the Sun God and His approach and ascension on the altar are described.

4. *ll.* 11 −18. "After the Sun God has come down, a flush of music, sights, songs and dancing is exhibited to entertain Him. The flutes (篪) are made of bamboo pipes, a foot and two inches long and three inches round (with seven finger-holes and an aperture for) being played on horizontally. The circular reeds(竽) are Pandean pipes of different lengths with thirty-six reeds, bound round to form a collection. Line 18 is similar in sense to lines 33 −34 of *Hymn on the King of Hsiang*. Before the song and dances are over, his crowd of attendants gathers round and guards him up and away. "

5. *ll.* 19 −24. "In the last passage, the homager rises aloft to see the Sun God off. To be clothed in the upper garment of azure clouds and the nether dress of white she-rainbow means he has risen to the zenith of sky. *The Book of Heaven's Officials of The Chronicle* (《史记·天官书》) says：The nice stars of Bow and Arrow are in

the southeast of Wolf; they are Heaven's Bow and Arrow, point-ing towards the single star Wolf. Heaven's Wolf stands for the vil-lain, the marauder. It is shot at for being hated to be seen after dusk. He wields his bow to turn back sundown; failing that, he drinks the Sun God off with the Dipper's wine. After bidding fare-well to Him in the extreme west, he rides eastward in the profound night, for he is going to greet the rising Sun of the next day. How could the Lord of three Portals (三闾大夫) be without his king for a day? When the Sun God has risen, he greets Him by riding calmly an ambler. When He has gone down in the west, he rides aloft to greet Him in the east. The circumstances of slackness and stress are different." These annotations are quoted from Tsiang Ch'ih.

8   Hymn on the Count of Ho (河伯)

1. *Bao-po-tse* of Kê Hoon of Ts'in (晋·葛洪:《抱朴子》): Feng Yih (冯夷), drowned (in the Luteous River) in the eighth moon, was made Count of Ho (河伯) by *T'ih* of Heaven (天帝). Wang Yi: Count of Ho, turning himself into a white dragon and swim-ming by the water-side, was shot at by Yih (羿), Yao's lord of archery (according to *Hwai-nan-tse*《淮南子》, but *Tsao-sien Re-cords*,《朝鲜记》, says he was Tsuen, 夋, *T'ih* Ko's, 帝喾, lord) hurting his left eye. Such legendary tradition, too remote and shadowy, is pronounced untraceable and untrustworthy by Tsu Hsih. Only it is certain He was the God of Luteous River (黄河之神).

2. *ll.* 1 −4, these four lines. Tsu Hsih: "These are also words of the sorceress; by 'Thee', the Count of Ho is meant. Ho was the eld-

est of four Rivers（四渎之长）. Its Nine Streams were Duh-shai（徒骇）, Tai-sze（太史）, Ma-cha（马颊）, Fu-vuh（复釜）, Fwu-suh（胡苏）, Jien（简）, Ji（洁）, K'ur-ban（钩磐） and K'ê-tsin（鬲津）. They were conducted by Great Yü（大禹） into the sea; the first one was the northern-most stream and the last one the southern-most." In the Spring and Autumn Period, some of them dried up and others changed their courses. They were in the several hundred square *lih* of lands from the north of today's Têh-*hsien*（德县）, San-tung（山东）, to T'ien-tsin（天津） and Ho-jien（河间） of He-pêh（河北）. Tsiang Ch'ih: "These lines express the homager's first wishes, saying that she would like to ride against dashing winds, driving dragons and dragonets on the upheaving waves. The water cars are those that run against the currents. Hsu Yü-jien's（徐云虔） *Records of South King*（《南诏录》）: Dragonet fish（螭鱼） has four feet and a long tail, with multi-colour scales; its head is like that of a dragon, but without horn."

3. *ll.* 5 −8, these four lines. Quen-lung Mountains are where Ho flows out from. The elucidations by Tsu Hsih, Wang Fuh-tse and Tsiang Ch'ih on these lines are either too scrappy or noncommittal. Wang thinks they are spoken by the Count of Ho. Conjoining them in sense with the previous four lines, I understand them to be sung by the sorceress to mean that, expecting and wishing longingly to see Him and ride in water cars with Him on the Nine Streams, she mounts Quen-lung cliffs to look for His advent; without His sight, her heart feels "flighty and unsound"（飞扬兮浩荡）; dusk falling, she feels like lost and forgetting to go home; but thinking of the far water-sides at the Nine Streams（惟极浦兮）, she recovers her calmness of mind（寤怀）.

4. *ll.* 9 −11, these three lines. In the first two lines, she thinks of His palace under water. Then, all of a sudden He appears; so in the third line, she asks Him "What doest Thou down there under water?" Line 10 is rendered according to Tsiang Ch'ih's explanation. Wang Fuh-tse has "Palace of pearl with hawkbill portal."

5. *ll.* 12 −14, these three lines. 鼋 are large sea turtles or tortoises (蠵龟). White ones of them are rare. Tsiang Ch'ih: "The sorceress meeting the Count of Ho late in the afternoon does not drive water cars with Him, but rides large white turtles in His company, not on the Nine Streams down in the east, but near by a River isle. Just then 'waves drift down in torrential swish' and they could not remain long together. It is so difficult for them to see each other and so easy to be parted."

6. *ll.* 15 −18, these four lines. "They grasp each other's hands to say good-bye. The Count fares eastward in the direction of the torrential stream. Fishes swimming against the waves follow the sorceress to bid farewell to the Count, while the multitudinous waves rolling in the same direction the Count fares to seem to greet Him." — Tsiang Ch'ih.

9 Hymn on the Mountain Sprite(山鬼)

1. Tsu Hsih takes the whole poem to be but an allegorical lyric of our poet's unhappy relations with his sovereign King Hwai of Ts'ou. Judging from the objective nature of all the other pieces of this collection of hymns, I consider Tsu-tse's submitting this love song of the Mountain Sprite's homager for her to be merely the subjective reflections and pinings of Chü Yuan unwarranted. We must keep in mind that this piece, like the others, is also a recasting by our

poet of the original hymn of valid feelings and coarse mould infused and fashioned by some village enchantress or conjurer.
Wang Yi has pointed this out from the correct tradition, but he has
meantime confused it with his own ideas that all these songs have
been deeply tinged with the poet's personal feelings and allusions
to his own life. Tsu-tse has set to rights many a similar distortion
by Wang on *Lee Sao* in his *Dialectical Commentary on Ts'ou
"Tze"*(《楚辞辩证》), but here he appears to be nodding. There
are variant names for this sort of bizzare beings 山鬼 in Chinese,
such as 怪夔,罔雨,猥,魖,枭,山精. *Bao-po-tse*(《抱朴子》) of
Ts'in calls them 跂,超空,貚,飞龙. They were supposed to be
fantastic spirits of wood or stones. Actually, some of them must
be quite different from others, and all are beasts instead of being
fairies, elves, sprites or manitoes. But here, the beloved being is
supposed in make-believe to be a fairy-like beautiful sprite or manito capable of loving and love-making. Tsiang Ch'ih attributes the
date of composition of this hymn to after that of *Over the Streams*
(《涉江》), on account of the similarity of certain descriptive details in some lines of both poems. His conclusion is misguided, I
think, by the reflections of similar natured phenomena.

2. *ll.* 1 −8. "This piece is also the locution of the homager or adorer,
here a sorcerer. The manito, 'Thou'(*l.* 4), resides in a seques-
tered mountain recess. Lines 5 −7 describe her accoutrements and
retinue. Red panther is a leopard with a red tail and black spots.
Brindled wildcats are those marked with streaks of mottled yellow
and black. Pomelo-figs(薜荔) and usnea(女罗) are both their
climbing plants with vines and tendrils winding round upright tree
trunks and branches to support themselves; so they are made use

of here to serve as vestures of the manito. Orchids and asarum blossoms are plaited and wound round the Sprite's chaise and its pennants; she plucks these from wreathes of them to present to her love. This passage describes the bewildering weird beauties of the Mountain Sprite and her trappings as well as her bewitching affection for her adorer; hence she is called Ling-sieu(灵脩) in line 15 (of the original), meaning inspiring goodness and virtue." — Tsiang Ch'ih.

3. *ll.* 9 −16. "In these lines, the homager is speaking of himself. Biding in deep bamboo groves, he could not see the sky; besides, the way is difficult. Paying homage to spirits and deities should be done when the sky is just turning bright. Seeing not the sky makes him arise rather late, and the way being difficult retards his movements; that is why he comes so late, as it is already broad daylight. He stands erect high up on a mountain where homage is to be paid, so that the Sprite could easily find him. Clouds are floating about below. East winds sprinkle magic rains as the manito appears. *The Classic of Mountains and Seas* says, 'The mountain beast is called *Kuai*(夒), like an ox, blue in its hide, without horn, with one hoof; its coming and going always bring along wind and rain.' Again, 'Kuan Mount(光山) is full of wood godlings, with human body and dragon head; their coming and going are marked by whirlwind and gushing showers.' This charming manito belongs to such kind of beings. 'in mine eve of life' means the homager is getting old. Being aged and solitary, with his mind severed from pomps and vanities, he wishes to be attached to the Mountain Sprite." — Tsiang Ch'ih.

4. *ll.* 17 −20, these four lines. Tsiang Ch'ih explains the first two

and a half lines as the homager "picking fairy fungi…" and seeing the Sprite has vanished quickly. I think it should be the Sprite "picking fairy fungi…" who has vanished quickly. The rest half and one lines are rendered according to Tsiang. Tsu Hsih explains these four lines as the Sprite "picking fairy fungi…" thinks of her homager, who does not come; she thinks of him and repines at his not coming, but knows that he is also thinking of her. Wang Fuh-tse interprets the text quite differently. For instance, here he regards 灵脩 (Ling-sieu) and 公子 (Prince) of the original addressed by the Sprite, a female, to her homager and host. According to Wang, the Mountain Sprite says, she, biding in bamboo groves and roving about the cliffs, rides gusts of wind by chance to come down to the world; "because of your admiration, I stay with you and forget to return to my accustomed haunt; but I fear my sojourn would be too long, for the year is coming to its end; the host's earnestness is wearing thin, I am afraid he would treat me with pomp and honour no more; so I better go to pick fairy fungi on mountain heights; I repine at my host's not inviting me to remain long rather sadly; fearing that I may forget to return, I hurry back; but after having gone back, although you would think of me later on, I would not find time to return and see you again."

5. *ll.* 21 −23, these three lines. "'The mountaineer' is the homager speaking of himself. Drinking rock spring and shading from cypress and pine mean he is waiting for her. The mountaineer, so fair and pure — the one he waits for, does not come after all; it shows how distrusted he is by the Mountain Sprite." — Tsiang Ch'ih.

6. *ll.* 24 − 27, these four lines. "This passage describes the

homager's going his way back home. He retires sadly for the departure. It is night now. Being waited for long now, she does not come. He could only chew his sadness and go home alone." — Tsiang Ch'ih.

10 Hymn on Spirits of State Warriors Slayed in War(国殇)

1. *ll.* 1 −4, these four lines. The first four lines relate the beginning of a battle, an instance of many a one. Long arms like tridents, halberds and spears are used together with short ones such as swords, daggers and poniards, while axle-barrels of chariots clash one another, pennants, banners and streamers shade the sun and hostile hosts fly against the sky like clouds.

2. *ll.* 5 −10. The next six lines describe the defeat. Two wheels of our chariots are "buried", that is, halted; four of our horses held by the enemy. "Although there are casualties, the drum is beaten and our morale is high. Corpses strew the plain in the fury of the battle. This is because Heaven is wroth, His ires run high; a multitude of warriors are mowed down on the plain unburied." — Tsu Hsih.

3. *ll.* 11 −14, these four lines. "Having trodden the battle-field, the warriors could not have their spirits return home, for it is too far away. Yet they bear tall swords and strong bows of Tsing even after death; beheaded, their hearts are unhurt, that is, regretting not." — Tsu Hsih.

4. *ll.* 15 −18, these four lines. They are brave and heroic during lifetime while fighting on the field. Even after death they are still strong and inviolable. What great spirits they are!

11 Epode to All the Hymns Above(礼魂)

The rite is rounded off and drums are rapidly beaten. The bouquets held by the sibyls while they are dancing are exchanged between them, and another round of dance is begun. Fair chorus girls' songs and chantings are gracefully sung. When homage is paid in spring, the bouquets are culled from mountain orchids. In autumn, they are made of fresh and pure asters. Rites will go on forever, year after year.

Sylva of Nine Pieces (Six Selected) (九章(选六篇))

1 Over the Streams(涉江)

1. "*Over the Streams*(《涉江》) and *Plaint on Ying*(《哀郢》) were both composed during Ching-hsiang's reign when the poet was exiled to south of the River. But *Plaint on Ying* was written on his leaving Ying-*t'uh* for Ling-yang from the west to the east. *Over the Streams* relates (in advance) his route from Ngo-tsu(鄂渚) to Süe-puh(溆浦), from the north-east to south-west, after his exile to Ling-yang. Old comments distinguishing them are not mistaken. The feelings expressed herein are forthright and quite contrary to those that are mournful and hesitant, wanting to proceed yet halting, in *Plaint on Ying*, for those were enforced from severe condemnation and thus carry the sorrow of banishment, while these were dashed from indignation and show the resolve of parting, the sources from which they issue being different. As *Pining My Past Days* has said,

> Wishing to lay mine heart ope and mine acts make clear,
> I got unexpectedly into fault instead.

Perhaps, being unable to return after nine years' exile, he again encountered his King's wrath for his petitioning and was further banished to Tsen-yang, so his words are resolute and undaunted. It is said in the poem that he 'would sail', 'would fleet away' and again he 'will stay long afflicted in hapless plight and keep to my repulsion without dismay'. Thus the poem was composed before he embarked for his exile. " — Tsiang Ch'ih.

2. *ll.* 1 −12. " ' Novel gown' means the dress that was different from those worn by the general run of people, implying that his intents and deeds were above the ordinary. 'Cut-cloud' was the name of the tall hat. 'Night Glow' (明月) was a matchless orient pearl (夜光珠). 'This gem nonpareil' (宝璐) was a peerless gem. Gem sprouts (玉英) were said to be eaten by fairies to give them immortality. In these incipient lines, his sublime intents and deeds, going after those of *T'ih* Suen the sage and capable of brightening the four compasses and lasting through ten thousand generations, are borne forth to bring out the ignorance of the south barbarians spoken of below. " — Tsiang Ch'ih.

3. *ll.* 13 −34. " ' South barbarians' (南夷) is a term of censure for the Ts'ou rabble. ' I would sail the Hsiang and River' means in his journey from Ling-yang to Tsen and Süe (辰溆), he must sail the River and steer through Doong-ding. Hsiang Stream is the main current of Lake Doong-ding; hence *The Classic of Streams* (《水经》) calls Doong-ding Hsiang Stream. Crossing Doong-ding is therefore sailing the Hsiang. Ngo-tsu (鄂渚) is the present Wuh-tsoon *fuh* (武昌府). Sailing the River westward by Wuh-tsoon, he must proceed from Ling-yang. Line 16 means it is going to be in early spring, when the residual cold of winter would not be over yet. Leaving his boat and taking to land traveling, he would reach Foun-lin (方林). Therefrom he would put off on the Hsiang for Yuan. The Yuan flows north-eastward into Doong-ding with its source in the south-west. So, the trip is to be continued by ' Rowing upstream in a windowed boat on Yuan'. Waung-tsu (枉陼), Tsen-yang (辰阳) and Süe-puh (溆浦) are all place names. *The*

Classic of Streams says, the Yuan flows north-eastward by Tsen-yang *hsien*, confluent with the Tsen Stream(辰水) and then absorbing the Waung(枉水) at Waung-tsu(枉陼), to pour into Hsiang; it is also said that the Süe(溆水) flows from the Great Süe Mount(大溆山) north-westward into Yuan. To take the water route from the Great River, through Hsiang, Yuan, Waung, Tsen to Süe is to journey from the north-east to the south-west. Süe-puh is in the midst of a sea of mountains; the haze of clouds and rains there is canopied by mountain vapours and fog screens. Tsen-yang and Süe-puh were the south-western extremity of Ts'ou, the region of Miao and Yau tribes(苗瑶), uninhabited by civilized people. Chü Yuan's going there — was it his wish to get away from the mob, as the Sage had declared before him to float into the seas to live among barbarians?" — Tsiang Ch'ih.

4. *ll.* 35 −48. "Tsi-eü(接舆), a recluse of Ts'ou, letting loose his tresses undressed, pretended to be mad. Later, he had his hair shaven. His name was Loh Ton(陆通); Tsi-eü was his informal name. He was a contemporary of Confucius. When the latter visited Ts'ou, he called on him and cried, 'Phoenix! Phoenix! Why dost thou come to inhabit a dearth of virtue!' Confucius was going to speak to him, but he went away. King Tsau of Ts'ou(楚昭王), hearing of his being virtuous, sent messengers with twenty-four hundred taels of 'gold' (at that age meaning bronze) and two quadrigae to invite him, but he declined the offer. His wife coming back from the village extolled his decision of refusal, and they changed their names and escaped to the O-mei Mountains(峨眉山) in Zho(蜀, now Sze-tsuan, 四川) to be eremites. They lived to be hundreds of years old and were said to have turned into

fairies, according to Hwang-fuh Mi's(皇甫谧, of Ts'in, 晋) *Lives of Elevated Men*(《高士传》). Soun-wuh(桑扈) was also called Tse-soun Pêh-tse(子桑伯子); 赢行 is what *The Ceremonials of Confucius*(《孔子家语》) calls to live or abide naked. Oo Yuan (伍员), lord premier of the state Wuh(吴), met disaster by being killed for remonstrating his king Vuh-tsah(夫差). 'Ride on high unheedful of the world' means to keep to the right way. 'Keeping to my repulsion without dismay' is to go to the barbarian region. In so doing, he seemed apparently to be incapable of 'Enjoying longevity with Heaven and Earth' and vying 'in glory with the moon and sun', but since he had laid such a burden on his own shoulders, his fated future could only bear causal relations to his past noble deeds, and their meanings are thus not incompatible." —— Tsiang Ch'ih.

5. *ll.* 49 −54. "The first line means he was first exiled to Ling-yang and now come to Süe-puh, getting farther away from his King. 'Fair and foul ones change places' means villains are at the court, while virtuous people are in the wilderness." —— Tsiang Ch'ih.

2 Plaint on Ying(哀郢)

1. "Old accounts of Ching-hsiang's exile of Chü Yuan to the south of the River(江南) give no name of specific locality. Now it is certain that after leaving Ying, he went directly to Ling-yang(陵阳). From indications in the *Rolls of Arts and Letters of The Fore-Han and Hind-Han Chronicles*(《前后汉志》) and *Commentary on the Classic of Streams*(《水经注》), it is very clear: the approximate spot was between the present Sher-nin(休宁) and Tze-tsur (池州). As it was near the margin of Ts'ou's eastern-most border

and he was ordered to reside there by regal mandate, so he laments 'Being exiled nine years, I can return not！' But in his last years, he sailed on Luh-kiang(泸江) and by Ngo-tsu(鄂渚), navigated Hsiang and Yuan, passed the Mon Swamp(梦泽) and reached Tsen-yang(辰阳), and then again went from Loon-yang(龙阳) to Tsang-sah(长沙) to drown himself in Mi-lo(汨罗), wandering and roving almost all over the south of the Great River. We can draw the conclusion then that though he was made to stay at Ling-yang, he was allowed to move about rather freely；'How Shiah and the River could not crossed be' means that he was forbidden to boat across the waters and land on the north banks. There are some students who say that Chü Yuan's wandering all about the south of the River was due to his traducers' maligning him to have him banished to many a place；so, although being exiled nine years and unable to return, he still yearned to go back to Ying without meaning to end his life；but when he was condemned and exiled again and again, beyond all reasons, foolings and forbearance, he could only end his life in Mi-lo. This view is noted herewith to register a doubting difference." — Tsiang Ch'ih.

2. *ll*. 1 −8. "These lines relate the beginning of his exile. It has been Heaven's constant law that the good are blessed and the wicked are punished, but now a deviation occurs — the good are stricken. By 'the people' and 'they', the poet himself is meant in his complaint. He is condemned by his monarch for his fidelity, the blame to which is imputed by him to Heaven, for he dares not lay the charge to Ching-hsiang. The people are said to have suffered from the injury as an understatement. 'Scattered are they, missing one another' means himself departing from relatives and friends.

'Wandering eastward' means being banished eastward south of the River to Ling-yang, in the far east of Ying-tuh. Shiah（夏, meaning summer）is the stream flowing from the River in summer into Han（汉）, but is dried up in winter, hence so named. *Ja*（甲）day is the date of departure named according to heavenly *kan*（天干）." — Tsiang Ch'ih.

Tsu Hsih explains "the people", "they" and "their" literally. "In this mid-spring, the second moon, amidst the harmony of the negative and positive 'airs', the people should live in a buoyant, happy atmosphere. But when Chü Yuan was exiled from Ying-t'uh, there happened to be a dearth of crops. The famine-stricken people scattered from the capital and he was among the crowd drifting towards the east. He took pity on their enforced migrating while grieving his own misfortune. For lack of an object to direct his murmurs, he wails in these lines that 'Heaven hath miscarried from its constant law', blessing not the innocent and punishing not the evil, but making the refugees throng to the east during this calm season of the year, in all their sufferings." Tsu-tse's comments on these lines are denied by Tsiang for being stuck in literality. At the same time, Wang Fuh-tse's explanation of this passage （he considers it to be descriptive of Hsiang's flight from Ying-t'uh to Tsen, 陈）is aptly controverted to be utterly mistaken, and therefore also his attribution of the date of composition of this poem to the capital's surrender to the Tsing general Bai Chih（秦将白起）in the 21st year of Hsiang's reign. Tsiang's arguments against Wang are well supported by Yer Koh-en（游国恩）in modern times in his *On the Superexcellences* from *Studies in "Sao"*, first series（《读骚论微》初集）.

3. *ll.* 9 −24. "These lines record the realities of the poet's exile to the east. Ying-*t'uh* was the capital of Ts'ou, at the present Kiang-ling *hsien*(江陵县) of Ch'in-tsur *fuh*(荆州府). 闾 means family lane portal. The Mallotus(楸), a tall tree of the homeland, was looked upon lovingly without wishing to shift one's eyes from. Shiah's mouth(夏口): Shiah Stream issues from the River and flows into Han(汉) at its mouth. Dragon Gate(龙门) was the eastern gate of Ying. *The Classic of Streams*(《水经》) says, Shiah Stream flowing from the River winds in the south-east of Kiang-ling *hsien*; so Shiah's mouth must be in the near vicinity of Ying. But the capital's citadel is already out of sight, which makes his 'heart pulsating and full of laments'. Marquis Yang(阳侯) was Fwuh-shih's(伏羲) lord inferior. *Hwai-nan-tse*(《淮南子》): he was marquis of the ancient state Ling-yang(陵阳国侯), which was by the River and he was drowned in it: thus his Spirit could heave big waves. " — Tsiang Ch'ih.

4. *ll.* 25 −26, these two lines. "'To float downstream' is to sail eastward. The mouth of Doong-ding pouring into the River is in Pa-ling *hsien*(巴陵县) of Yuo-tsur(岳州) today. To sail from Ch'in-tsur to Yuo-tsur by going eastward. Doong-ding flowing from the south is upstream and the River going easterly is downstream. When Shiah Stream flows into Han, Han is also called Shiah; and when the poet has his back against this Shiah as he sails in the River, he is farther east away from Ying, but still pining westward for it. Grieving the wide domain as a rich terrain of habitation in the past, he mourns for the residuary customs of the riverside: all these are what his forefathers brought up and reared to leave to their descendants; therefore, thinking of them increases

his sad thoughts. " — Tsiang Ch'ih.

5. *ll.* 37 −48. "Ling-yang, a *hsien* in the county Tan-yang(丹阳郡) according to the *Han Chronicle*, is between Ning-kuo(宁国) and Tze-tsur(池州) at present, known on account of the Ling-yang Mounts in its northwest. Coming to Ling-yang, seeing waves of Luh-kiang(庐江) stretch to the sky southward of the Great River, the poet has now arrived at his destination of exile; he asks, where he will stray. " Here, Tsiang Ch'ih explains 夏 as the Shiah Stream, saying that "even if it becomes a hilly plain(丘陵), he would be incapable of knowing (for he is forbidden to go north of the River and besides he is now exiled a thousand and several hundred *lih* eastward), so how could he know what would happen to the two eastern gates of Ying, even if they were fallen to ruins?" Tsu Hsih explains the word 夏 here correctly, I think, as "great mansions"(大屋) and 丘 as "ruins"(丘墟), and I translate accordingly: the poet is thinking of (though he says he cannot conceive) the great mansions of Ying-*t'uh* fallen to ruins when it would be sacked by the Tsing cohorts some day. The poem goes on to say that he has now stayed far many years at Ling-yang, far away and isolated from Ying-*t'uh*. It seems to him that he left it on the sudden but continued to cherish it and so disbelieved his own act. Hoon Hsin-tsou's note says that Chü Yuan's first expulsion was in the 16th year of King Hwai, two years later he was recalled and given the mission to visit Tsih as special envoy, in the 30th year he remonstrated against the meeting at Wuh Pass (武关), which Hwai refused and so died as a kidnapped hostage. When Ching-hsiang was enthroned, the poet was again exiled. So, he had been expelled and then recalled formerly by Hwai. But

now his exile to the south of the River for nine years without returning must be in the reign of Hsiang. Hence lines 47 −48. — Tsiang Ch'ih.

6. *ll.* 49 −60. "Hard struck with bitter throes, he cannot help hating the caballers. The wicked cringelings fawned on the King, making him 'pliantly weak within', so that the faithful, wishing to serve royally, were segregated by them. Yao and Suen, handing not their crowns to their sons, are charged by the evil-doers with 'foul unnatural faults'. The virtuous, anxious to do good to the state and far-sighted, are disliked by the King. The villains full of raving flatteries, are cherished with trust. So the sycophants become daily dearer to the monarch and the upright get ever farther away from him; thus, the maligners being intrusted wreak damage to the sovereign's heart." — Tsiang Ch'ih.

7. *ll.* 61 −66. "'Die on the knolls' is to have their necks lie on their native knolls as on pillows." — Tsiang Ch'ih.

3　Thinking of Sah(怀沙)

1. "*The Life of Chü Yuan of The Chronicle*, after relating the dialogue between the fisherman and the poet, says directly that Chü Yuan then composed *Thinking of Sah*. We find *The Fisherman's* Tsoung-long(沧浪) is in the present Loon-yang *hsien* of Tsangtêh *fuh*(常德府龙阳县). So we know this piece was written when he was setting out from Loon-yang. *Thinking of Sah* is entitled in the same way as *Plaint on Ying* and *Over the Streams*. Sah was originally a place name. Lo Mih's(罗泌,of Soong) *Great Chronicle*(《路史》) says, Sao-hao(少昊) and Tsen-noon(神农) both founded their capitals at Sah. Tsang-sah is its remaining site to-

day, where Mi-lo River(汨罗) is. *Thinking of Sah* means thinking of the place where he was going to end himself. Chü Yuan had come from Ling-yang, through the River and Hsiang to Tsen and Süe, with the intent to live there for good. But he returned ultimately to drown himself, being dashed to it by raging sorrow or being unwittingly enforced to the water by Hsiang, as said by *Strange Tales*(《述异记》, by Ren Foun, 任昉, of the South Dynasties, 南朝) and *The Extra-biographical Life of Chü Yuan*(《屈原外传》, by Suin Ya-tse,沈亚之, of Tdaung,唐). But why did he not die at Tsen or Süe? The answer is that he wanted to stress his intents to waken up his king; to die unheard of and unknown was not his wish. Tsang-sah was a big south-east city of Ts'ou, not far away from Ying and entirely different from wild outlying borderlands. Furthermore, Hsiung Yih's (熊绎) first fief was here. As Chü Yuan was exiled, he dared not cross the Great River, but going back to die at his ancestral place of residence was in accord with the idea of foxes dying on the knolls of their birth. Hence his thinking longingly of Sah. The poem first dwells on his going south, and then clinches his final vow of death. For from then on he did not go elsewhere; his resolve to plunge into the stream was made up herein. Therefore, *The Chronicle* expressly records it to note Chü Yuan's death. But to say, as *The Chronicle* does, that the title 怀沙 means 'bosoming stone' (to jump into water), is to miss the intended sense. The tone of the poem, although more akin to the note nearing death than *Over the Streams* and *Plaint on Ying*, is yet sorely entwined but not knotted, forthright but not dashing, and so should be dated before *Lamenting on Whirl-blasts* and *Pining My Past Days*. How could it be regarded at haphazard as the final work before death?" — Tsiang Ch'ih.

2. *ll.* 1 −10. "This poem was composed by Chü Yuan when he, having met the fisherman and made up his mind to drown himself in Hsiang, was going from Yuan by way of the Lake southward. 'South land' of line 4 means Sah he was thinking of, at present Hsiang-yin *hsien*(湘阴县) of Tsang-sah *fuh*(长沙府), where Mi-lo River(汨罗江) is, in the south of the Lake. The last four lines mean to say that examining his own feelings and testing his intent, although being repressed, yet restraining himself, he dares not blame others, but furbishes his own virtues." — Tsiang Ch'ih.

3. *ll.* 11 −20. "In the first two lines, it is asked, 'will he shift his stand to follow the times?', and the answer is, the constant law is there, it is inalterable and he has no wish to step aside. Tsuai(倕) was *T'ih* Suen's Lord of Arts(共工), noted for his skillfulness. To keep to one's good first plan and rules and to value one's upright, noble feelings are held in high esteem by the sagacious. But to have one's virtue untried is like unto not letting skillful Tsuai try his axe and chisel. How, then, could the world appreciate his dexterous parts?" — Tsiang Ch'ih.

4. *ll.* 21 −32. Lih-lur(离娄) was notable in ancient times for his quick-sightedness. According to *Mencius*(《孟子》), *Tsaung-tse*(《庄子》) and annotations on them, Lih-lur, also called Lih-tsu(离朱), was a subject of Hwang-*t'ih*(黄帝). When that ancient emperor lost his 'Mystical Orient'(玄珠), that is, his Way(道), on ascending the Quen-lung Cliffs, he sent Lih-tsu to search for it. The man was said to be capable of seeing the tip of an autumn hair a hundred steps away. 矇 of the original means those who have pupils but are sightless and 瞍 and 瞽 both mean

those who have no pupils. "This passage is a furtherance of lines 19 −20. Black tracery in twilight shadows seems hazy and almost invisible. To the blind, it is even more than being not clear. Lih-lur cast but a glance and he caught sight of everything with ease. But the stone-blind of course could not see things, no matter how hard they try. The virtuous being given no chance to test their gifts seem to be without capabilities. To the doltish caballers, they appear to be quite unworthy and not at all preferable. So, they are turned upside down or mixed up and adulterated with the naught. That is why the virtuous are grossly wronged. " — Tsiang Ch'ih.

5. *ll.* 33 −52. "This passage illustrates line 32. The first two lines say that he is capable of bearing heavy burden, but is so utterly depressed as to be of no use. Endowed with stirling qualities, but downtrod and unknown to people, he could do nothing to recommend himself. ' Heavy burden' speaks of the greatness of his power, ' jades' and ' gems' speak of the excellence of his qualities, ' affluent art' speaks of the learning concealed in him, ' gifts hidden' speaks of his latent capabilities, ' kindness and its deeds apt' and ' caution and earnestness' speak of his all-round virtues and ' noble law' speaks of the genuineness of his self-possession: it would take Tsoon-hwah, or Yü Taung to apprehend all these — what have they to do with the caballers' stupidity?" — Tsiang Ch'ih.

6. *ll.* 53 −60. "Changing not his stand means he would persist in his virtuous devotion. Clinging to his ' brave fortitude bright' means that he would follow Peng Yen as his example. By this time, his voyage still has not yet reached the south land. So he says that he would be glad to wind his way up northward to Ying to act his

Way. But as the world is muddled and promiscuous, like unto the day's falling to the dusk, it is hopeless after all. To ease his dole and cheer his sorrow, he could only expect these after his death, following the quietus that would put an end to his consciousness. That is why he is thinking of Sah, being resolved to die there. These are said to give stress to his wish for faring to the south. "
— Tsiang Ch'ih.

7. *ll.* 61 −80. "The epilogue concludes what goes before and amplifies it. At the moment, the poet was going from Yuan to Hsiang in his water route, so he speaks of both here. The waters of these two streams flow severally into the Lake with turbulent dash. Pêh-loh(伯乐) was reputed to be well versed in discerning the choice equestrian blood among horses. Here, he is compared to Suen, Yü and Taung, and by the steed he himself is meant. With heart fixed, one would not be shaken by mishaps, and with intents extensively focused, one would not be harassed by the darts and arrows of fortune. These concluding lines wind up with the idea that, sailing on the rapid currents, he has been going over a distant, tortuous way; as no sagacious sovereign has risen, he is thus enforced to be in such straits; one's fortunes and mishaps are destined and he is of course not to be easily flushed or frightened by any of them; but to be not understood by the whole wide world is indeed to be mightily grieved; so that bearing the colossal burden all by himself alone, he is going to embrace death undauntedly, taking Peng Yen for his company. " — Tsiang Ch'ih.

4　Pining My Past Days(惜往日)

1. "Be this the final work of Ling-chün? It was in vain during his li-

fetime to awaken his King, so he did it at last by means of his death: this is what the world calls the last throw. To die silently was not his wish. Thus he hallooed, pointing his finger to the crimes of maligning cringelings for befooling their kings, and emphasizing the catastrophic crash that would surely happen as a result of the demolition of law and rectitude. Locution of perilous consequence is used here to move his present King, so that he might not but be roused to conscience and action. If that could be accomplished, his own death would be lighter to him than a feather of the wildgoose. That is why Chiêh Tse-tuai's death is briefly spoken of and Marquis Wen's regretful awakening is amply dwelt upon, showing urgently his expectations after death. Of the *Sylva of Nine Pieces*, only this one is most plain reading, not only because this is his utterance nearing death, in which he had no time for verbal flush, but also with the purpose that it could be readily read and easily comprehended by the mediocre King. Alas, who knows that the dunce pretended to be deaf and refused to listen at all!" — Tsiang Ch'ih.

2. *ll*. 1 −8. "'Having ta'en decrees to make policies clear' means having received regal mandates to make clear to the people the current policies of the state. Lines 3 and 4 mean upholding ancestral institutions (or rather uses, practices) and enlightening the people why they were so and explaining the similarities and differences of cases applicable to existent statutes not clearly specified. Ancestral institutions were observed without infringement and state laws were appropriately executed in their detailed application: such was the foundation of properly conducting state affairs, being different from the personal rule motivated from subjective likes and dis-

likes. 'Trustworthy hands' means the poet himself. The last line shows King Hwai's trust in and favour with him, quite contrary to the blames later on founded on no faults of his. These are what Chü Yuan pines for and could not forget." — Tsiang Ch'ih.

3. *ll.* 9 −18. "Close in confidence" means keeping state secrets fast. For line 10, see note 21 on *Lee Sao*. "My masters sovereign" and "my lords" refer to Hwai and Hsiang. "His kings, giving credit to the maligners' scandals, became wroth at him, and the calumni-ators went further in misgiving, puzzling and cheating them, so that he was expelled and exiled again and again, and then asper-sions and sawders became more rife and mudding, and his kings persisted in tipping over to stupidity." — Tsiang Ch'ih.

4. *ll.* 19 −26. "Faultless on his own part but befouled; he is shy to see the passage of time and the kaleidoscopic sights of the macro-cosm. His kings' ire is all along unstinted. Although expelled and exiled and having become an eremite, he still guards his fair repute day by day. That is why he will depress himself to plunge into the waves. From this it can be seen that Chü Yuan's death was very much enforced on him. The last line says, after he has drowned himself, his life and name are not to be sorrowed for, but it must be pined that his duped kings knew and know not their villains."
— Tsiang Ch'ih.

5. *ll.* 27 −46. "My lords superior having no knowledge of the lengths and breadths of things have been ignorant of the state of affairs around them. 'Do make fair herbs darkened around the swamp tract evolve' means (our Kings' ignorance) has disabled the virtu-ous and sagacious of the state into nonentities. (For Pêh-lih Yih, 百里奚, see section IV of *Introduction*, *pp.* 25 −26 above. For Ih

Yün, 伊尹, see section II of *Introduction*, *pp*. 11 −12 above. For Leü Wang, 吕望, see section II of *Introduction*, *p*. 13 above. For Nien Tsi, 宁戚, see note 126 on *Lee Sao*. For Tse-süe, 子胥, Oo Yuan, 伍员, see section IV of *Introduction*, *pp*. 27 −28 above, For Chiêh Tse-tuai, 介之推, see section IV of *Introduction*, *pp*. 24 − 25 above.) The kings being dullards, the sagacious are bound to be repelled; they could go nowhere to present their cases, but have to run their course of death: that is because the traducers isolate and shadow their kings, so as to make access to them impossible. If it happened that good fortune favoured the virtuous and wise, the world had Pêh-lih Yih, Ih Yün, etc.; if otherwise, Oo Tse-süe paid with his life and the state Wuh(吴) was blotted out of existence. In the case of Chiêh Tse-tuai, his death wakened Marquis Wen of Ts'in(晋文公) to penitence for his ungrateful negligence of his old-time benefactor: this was a solitary instance of equity realized, though it came too late. Our poet's reiteration of the event shows that he has much to expect with fidelity after his death. " — Tsiang Ch'ih.

6. *ll*. 47 −56. "This passage says, from old times the untimely death of faithful lords was never not due to their kings' credit in calumniations. " — Tsiang Ch'ih. "Green herbs" of *l*. 53 means the good and wise.

7. *ll*. 57 −66. "'Former days' refers to King Hwai's reign. See-sze (西施) was a noted ancient beauty of the state Yüeh(越). The last two lines allude to the poet's pleas for himself from Hwai's reign to that of Hsiang. The more he pleaded, the more he was found to be at fault. " — Tsiang Ch'ih.

8. *ll*. 67 −76. "The run of fleeting coursers is swift, but using no bri-

dle nor bit to harness them would only court overthrow. Hitched-up log timbers floating on drifting streams are buoyant, but having no rudder nor oars to steer or propel with would only cause drowning. Flouting laws and ruling by flighty fancies and frivolous likes and dislikes would only result in catastrophic crash. 'Calamities twain' means extirpation of the state and captivity of his body. His duped sovereigns giving credit to scandal-mongers and scrapping catholic laws and order are all due to their ignorance and heeding not his counsels and appeals. Therefore, on the eve of his death he raises a clamour on the crimes of the vilifiers and the stupidities of his Kings. Chü Yuan's death happened about in the fifteenth year of Hsiang's reign. In the twenty-first year, Tsing took Yan (鄢) and Ying-*tuh*, annexed Doong-ding, the Five Lakes(五湖) and all Ts'ou's domain south of the River(江南). 'Calamities twain' soon proved to be true.''— Tsiang Ch'ih.

5 Ode to the Orange(橘颂)

1. *l.* 3, the whole line. "Line 3 受命不迁 was explicated of old as a faithful liege vassal given orders by one King should not serve a sovereign of another state. But it must be understood that line 5 深固难徙 (Steadfast and withal immovable), meaning changing not one's heart to follow vulgar practices, is even more the fundamental of self-enjoinment. For 'not to be moved' and 'immovable' are differently explained; so, they are rendered conspicuous with line 6 更壹志兮 (In purpose and intent fixed through). The date of composition of this ode is not ascertainable. But reading the last lines, one feels there is a grieving sense of the shortness of natural life. Thus, the poem is perhaps a work nearing death.''— Tsiang

Ch'ih. The translator, however, thinks otherwise of its date on the evidences of its verse form and the fact that the poet did not die young. It is definitely the earliest of Chü Yuan's extant works, composed during his middle twenties. *Vide* section VII of *Introduction*, *pp.*80 −81 above.

2. *ll.* 1 −16. "Heaven and Earth give growth to this fair tree Orange which is habituated here to the water and soil of Ts'ou, as *The Chronicle* has said, ' There are thousands of orange trees in Kiang-Iing(江陵). ' It is given the trait of being not to be moved and is steadfast in its roots. About its being not to be moved, *Li-tse*(《列子》) says, orange planted north of Hwai River(淮) becomes citrus(枳). It is hard to be moved or immovable, for when it bears fruits, replanting it would make it fruitless. That is to say, it is accustomed to the domain of Ts'ou and not to be moved elsewhere; furthermore, its roots are so steadfast, that even moving it a little distance off would make it barren of fruits, which shows how determined its purposes and intents are. ' Triple snowlike interior' means the inside of its peels, its pulp and its seeds. The orbicular fruits of Orange are externally green first and then yellow while mellow, its beaming alternately coloured lustrous exterior lined with pure white within, like unto those full of virtues and untainted by the muck and slime of the world. The Orange should be pruned yearly and rived of its moths, unlike other trees, so as to be ' kept trim, chaste and demure'. In this first portion of the ode, the merits of the Orange are enumerated to compare to the poet's own qualities: ' not to be moved' (不迁) means he is unfit to go to other states; ' immovable' (难徙) means he does not throng with the madding crowd; by ' leaves' and ' blossoms' (花叶) his arts

and letters are meant; by 'brambles' and 'twigs'（枝棘）his square conduct and firm intents are meant; by 'fruits globular and rotund'（圆果）his virtues in practices are meant; by 'foliage'（文章）his practical virtues originated from the warp and woof of the Way are meant; by snowlike interior（内白）his practice virtues nestling in his deep solitariness are meant; and by the qualities 'trim, chaste and demure'（宜脩）his fair deeds are meant — the subtlety of analysis and the aptitude of implication are both exhibited here." — Tsiang Ch'ih.

3. *ll.* 17 −36. "This second portion of the ode expands the ideas of the Orange's being 'not to be moved' and 'immovable', and dwells on them with singing interjections, for these are the subject of the poem. 苏世 means awaking the world. Since the inception of its growth, the intents of Orange have been different from those of all other trees; therefore, it could stand upright and be distinguished among all others. Its bearing the trait of 'being not to be moved' is verily delightful. Its roots being 'steadfast and immovable' is due to its not longing for foreign states. It could stir up the world to awakening, and its independent intents are not to be stopped or turned aside from their marks by buffets and blows (of the weather). Thus, pondering on benefits and harms and paying good heed to its upright stand, it could be free from faults, and keeping its independent virtues selflessly, it could match heaven and earth. The above is an expansion of its being 'not to be moved' and 'immovable', though an encomium of the Orange, but not exclusively singing of it. Wishing it to last with the livelong year and befriend him is the poet's wishing to be its friend all his life. 'Beautiful'（淑离）is speaking of its flowers, leaves,

twigs and fruits; with such beauties added to its chief qualities of being 'not to be moved' and 'immovable', the Orange is beautiful and temperate (not excessive), both rigorous and gracefully adorned. It has no the longevity of pines and arbor-vitaes, hence said to be 'youthful'. Its purity is compared to Pêh-yieh's; so, it is taken as his image." — Tsiang Ch'ih.

6　Lamenting on Whirlblasts(悲回风)

1. "This piece was written after *Thinking of Sah* reiterating his intent of following Peng Yen. In it he is on the brink of death, but not yet quite set for it, for he fears his death could not awake his king and thus it would be of no avail to the state. With the bare hope that his monarch would waken up before his death, he still thinks it is better not to die. So Chü Yuan has cogitated deliberately and intensively of death. He died on the fifth day of the fifth moon. This poem was perchance composed in the autumn of the previous year." — Tsiang Ch'ih.

2. *ll.* 1 − 4, these four lines. " 'The thing' means the coumarou; 'marking the first signal' means it is being shaken by the whirlblasts. The incipient sound signifies the approach of the rigorous fury of autumn. The mournful exile, stricken with sorrow in autumn, is touched by the signal sound on the coumarou to hie to his death. Here he sings his strain to begin with." — Tsiang Ch'ih.

3. *ll.* 5 − 20. "Seeing the autumn wind blasts would reduce all things low, the poet is stirred up in intent to follow Peng Yen in drowning himself. Years ago, he had made up his mind to end himself as Peng Yen did. How is it that he keeps this resolve till now and has never forgotten it? It is because his earnest is not false. For

though his feelings are ever changing, their verity, his aim, cannot be concealed. How could fickleness last long? Wild birds and beasts cry for the sake of aggregating severally in their own flocks and herds. Rushes and weeds growing together luxuriantly are all not fair and sweet. Fishes differ in their species because the scales of each of their sorts are not the same as those of the others. Dragons and dragonets not commonly seen have their stripes and textures different from those of fishes. Sonchus(荼) and *Capsella bursa pastoris*(荠) grow not on the same plot of ground because they taste differently — one is bitter, the other sweet. Eupatory and angelica, deeply odorous, are distinguished from weeds and rushes each for their particular individual fragrance. As things all have their respective kinds, so his aim, the verity of his feelings, cannot be covered up. Thus, what Peng Yen, the Beauteous One, whose 'example will remain fore'er fair', has done in ancient days, with his feelings and veritable aim in good accordance, is taken by him as his bona fide model with far-stretched thoughts. 佳人 (the Beauteous One) in line 15 of the original is taken by Tsu Hsih to mean the poet himself, by Wang Fuh-tse to mean the virtuous man and by Tsiang Ch'ih to mean Pen Yen, whose 'example will remain fore'er fair'. I prefer Tsiang's interpretation. The loftiness and far-reaching nature of his intent are like the floating clouds rushing about in heaven. For fear lest his intent might be shaken or confused, he had long ago composed poems to fasten it permanently. With a fixed purpose of mind unforgettable like such, how could one with the least bit of counterfeiting hold himself so? Composing poems refers to *Suffering Throes*, *Drawing My Thoughts*(《抽思》) and *Musing on the Beauteous One*(《思美

人》）, all of which were written in King Hwai's reign, declaring his aim to become Peng Yen." — Tsiang Ch'ih.

4. *ll.* 21 −52. "This passage resounds the topical motif of the beginning although cherishing the intent of Peng Yen, yet he has not done what Peng Yen had when he sees autumn blasts shaking the coumarou, he resolves to put that into practice. Peppers are spicy, aromatic things, signifying upright tenets or principles of integrity. Line 22 means he behaves himself in conformity with the rules of the moral law or tenets of rectitude. 膺 is explained as breastchief or bosom covercloth(络胸者也, 心衣, 兜肚). Line 44, 'Their aromata have become spent' alludes to his setting forth his purpose in some poems above (line 20). 'The orphaned one' and 'The exiled one' mean the poet himself. Being both orphaned and exiled, he bears his afflictions acutely, which means after King Hwai's death, he has been twice banished by Hsiang. Fixing his thoughts on Peng Yen's deed, he persists in his principles against the pusillanimous ways of the world. He is often beset with repinings, remaining awake all night long. When dawn comes, he is about to wander along to dissipate his sorrow. But he soon finds excruciating ruminations gather thickly and press hard on his breast like the wearing of a prickly bosom covercloth, without his being able to set out for rambling. He tries to flee away in fancy and be gone from his misfortune with his corporeal existence blown off like the night by gusts of wind, so that his pangs could be dispersed into nothingness. But (while indulging in such a fancy), he cannot help feeling his heart pulsate like boiling water. So then, he strokes his bandages and lapels to calm the throbbing, in order that he might airily go on with his imagined wandering. But as he

proceeds, he sees with the rise of autumn blasts, 'Cyperus and asarum are withered and fallen'; thus, then, his anguishing ruminations cannot even more be suppressed. So he would rather carry out his resolve to die. The reasons are that the orphaned liege vassal is stricken by the pangs for his old master who came not back from the Tsing Pass, and the exiled one, roving in the southern wilderness, could not expect the return to his native soil. With these thoughts wringing his heart ceaselessly, how could he refrain from doing as Peng Yen had done?" — Tsiang Ch'ih.

5. *ll.* 53 −70. "These lines relate the poet's insufferable passion in vowing death after his exile. 眇眇 and 默默 mean to be 'void of human shapes and sounds'. 景响 is 'influence' and 闻, 'voice' or 'sound'. Ascending a mountain cliff to look back at his mother-country, he imagines his King's voice and appearance without being able to hear and see them, for the graciousness between the sovereign and his liege vassal is effaced now and the safety or peril of the native land is unknowable, so that his melancholy and pangs become the more intolerable. The deep silence being overwhelming and profound, his spirit seems to be floating about in its vastness unattached to anything. (Line 62 is rendered by the translator according to its obvious sense as he understands it, whereas Wang explains it to mean 'the infinite expanse I am unaware of in my confusion'. Lines 63 −64 seem to me to allude to the four intial lines of this poem; they are forcedly explained by Tsu-tse, Wang and Tsiang; I render them in the light of my version.)... The above describes the state of mind of unrelievable profound sorrow. By exhausting the saddest thoughts of pensive poets and plaintive singers of ancient times and modern days, nothing can match this

passage. The inscape of emotion is delineated and etched with fineness and to perfection. Could such heart-eating anguish be put off with neglect? That is why plunging over waves and following wind gusts, he would drown himself in the stream. " — Wang Fuh-tse.

This supreme passage is a lyrical, picturesque depiction of the emotional state of the poet's throes. Having fixed his resolution on death, he is in a delirious state of high passion. He is raving in his imaginative world, seeing no human shapes nor sounds, remembering nothing of the past; melancholic woes throng in his mind; dolorous moments press on his head and shoulders; and then he feels himself like a speck of white ashes floating in the profound silence and infinite space. Suddenly the signal sound shaking the coumarou remembered reminds him that he would die before long at last. Thus, from his harrowing hallucination he is called back to his inflexible aim to die. Tsiang Ch'ih's interpretation of this passage, especially of lines 61 −62 and 65 −66, closely relates the sublime, sometimes shadowy, images therein with the poet's remembrance of Hsiang's sound, look and bearing by minimizing their extent, seeming to me to spoil the poetical effect of the passage with too much far-fetched literality. In the same way I take Wang's statement "he imagines his king's voice and appearance without being able to hear and see them". Although Chü Yuan's determination to kill himself was motivated by his warning protests to his kings for the sake of the state, yet here, making up his mind to put that into practice, he is in a raving state of emotional stress far removed from the remembrance of sense impressions of the voices, looks and bearings of either Hwai or Hsiang. Our predecessors are too much the traditional Confucian in their thoughts in trying to link every poetical image they find here with the conception of feudal loyalty.

6. *ll.* 71 −78. "From this passage onward, the scope of spiritual peregrination is offered. These lines speak of his rising from water to heaven. The aperture of winds(风穴) is said to be on the heights of Quen-lung Mountains. *Hwai-nan-tse*(《淮南子》): 'The north portal of Quen-lung is opened to receive Buh-tsur Winds(不周之风)', i. e., north-west winds. Going up heaven and mounting Quen-lung, he reclines by the aperture of winds and dozes off. Shifting and waking up, he is drawn by downward sights of Ts'ou and becomes homesick." — Tsiang Ch'ih.

7. *ll.* 79 −94. "In these lines he describes his descent from heaven to the River. 'Mountains Quen-lung' refers to his reclinling by the aperture of winds. Ming Mountain is in Mer-*tsur*(茂州) of Tseng-tuh *fuh*(成都府), where by the Ming River(汶江,岷江), the main upper stream of the Great River flows. The River is originally Ts'ou's stream. On account of his love for the land of Ts'ou, though he could not set it to rights in his lifetime, he yet aims to clear its stream before his death. Again, the aperture of winds on Quen-lung is folded high up in mountain mists; so he clears away their opacity, and then sees the Ming Mountain, from which the River issues froth. Whereupon, he rises on it to clear the stream, only to find its torrential waves heave and roll, its roaring currents flow and flush, and he has to overcome the violently rushing flood singly — no matter how hard he strives, how could he clear its luteous quality? All he could do is to follow the currents, let the waves have their way, observe the morning and evening tides and

notice the manifold changes of the seasons. " — Tsiang Ch'ih.

8. *ll.* 95 −102. "These lines recount his landing from the River. To use a crooked and prickly twig as a whip to lash a horse is to speed its race. Time is so whipt in order that he could rush along like lightning flashes to visit Chiêh-tse's and Pêh-yih's memorial places. He says that extirpation of the state will surely come and is to be looked forward to with terror, and that he yearns toward their modes of conduct and calibres of mind with admiration. So he tells them, 'The reason why I would rather die here in Ts'ou than go elsewhere is that I cannot help pining at my past expectations and cannot bear to see the future excision of the state.' Indeed, a man would gladly show his heart-felt feelings to his kindred souls." — Tsiang Ch'ih.

9. *ll.* 103 −110. "These lines tell of Chü Yuan's return to the River from its valleys and then his ventures into other streams. Sun-duh Di(申徒狄) remonstrated Zer without avail and drowned himself in Ho(河); the account is given in *Tsaung-tse*(《庄子》). From the River, the poet goes up north to Hwai(淮) and down eastward into the sea, then again going up north he enters Ho(河) and traces upstream to see the spirits of Tse-süe(子胥) and Sun-duh, both his own kinds. Suddenly he feels their deaths could not save Saung and Wuh's excisions. So he wavers and hesitates, refraining from immediate death, with his doleful thoughts whirling the more inextricably." — Tsiang Ch'ih.

Distant Wanderings(远游)

This poem was composed by Chü Yuan after he was vilified and insulated by the Saun-quan courtier, Jin Soun and their caballers(上官大夫,靳尚等), and, what was more insufferable to him, as a result of their further traducings with the concurrence of Ts'eng Sieü(郑袖), the favourite royal concubine of King Hwai, he was expelled from Ying-*t'uh* to Han-pei, where he wrote this poem before *Suffering Throes*. For the details of its political *milieu* and emotive background, readers are referred to section VI, *pp.* 62 −71, and section VII, § 11, *pp.* 84 −91 respectively of *Introduction*. Of the authenticity of Chü Yuan's authorship of this poem and the inferiority of Sze-ma Hsiang-rue's(司马相如) A "*Fuh*" *on the Magister*(《大人赋》), of which Kuo Mê-ro ludicrously affirms it as Hsiang-rue's first draft, Tsu Hsih(朱熹) in his *Variorum Commentary on Ts'ou* "*Tze*" (《楚辞集注》) has pronounced most aptly that Sze-ma's *fuh* often pilfers expressions of Chü Yuan's poem, but the plagiarist cannot hope to peep at one ten-thousandth of what our poet has reached. We have passed our critical judgment on the *Dao Têh* school, its philosophy and literary properties (*vide* section V of *Introduction*, *pp.* 41 −46). Chü Yuan, we know, was a younger contemporary of Tsaung Tsur(庄周) by twenty odd years. He has taken a fancy to the quietude and inertness(清静,无为), the "utter purity" and "Original Prime"(至清,泰初), of *Dao Têh* in this fantasia as a balsamic unguent to his tormented feelings at the time when he wrote the poem. But we can be definitely sure he was not the least a convinced believ-

屈原诗选英译

er in "Lao" and Tsaung's philosophy, just as his divining to know where he should stay casts no doubt on his standpoint of sober earnest and high seriousness in matters of political ideal and practices as well as personal veracity and conduct. Some people, like Kuo, has been misguided by the poet's momentary fantasy to conclude with *naiveté* that since Chü Yuan was not an adherent of *Dao Têh*, the poem *Distant Wanderings* cannot be his work. Meantime, we have ample proof from all his other works and his deeds that he was decidedly not a disciple of "Lao" and Tsaung. Keeping this understanding in mind, a reader of this poem would not fall into any misconceit of our poet's thought and personality. In the following, the elucidations and comments are mainly adopted from Tsiang Ch'ih's book, some of which are held in common by Tsu-tse and him.

"*Distant Wanderings* was composed by Chü Yuan. After his rejection by the king, the poet, commanding a remote view of the universe after grieving and sighing, repined on the meanness and narrowness of the world and mourned the transience of mortality, thus having this piece written with the idea of chastening his body and soul in order to rise aloft and soar in the empyrean, so that he could be coeternal with heaven to see the multiversant, changes in mundane affairs. Although this is a fable, yet if his assumed locution of the fairy prince could be fulfilled, it would indeed be the secret to immortality." — Tsu Hsih.

1. *ll*. 1 − 4, these four lines. "The incipient four periods form the theme of the whole piece. Chü Yuan, because of affliction and melancholy, is stirred up for a distant peregrination to give vehemence to his spirit. But without lightening himself to rise aloft, he could not journey far, and as he is no fairy nor sage in agile

quality, he aims ardently at imperishableness and transformation. These are, therefore, of course enlivened words, not to be taken as originally intended. " — Tsiang Ch'ih.

2. *l*. 5, the taint of mud and slime. "This expression refers to ' the wringing and blockade of the crowd ' in line 1. " — Tsiang Ch'ih.

3. *l*. 6, Depressed and lorn, and *l*. 7, Awake and restless. "These two expressions(耿耿,营营) show his sad, distressed feelings. " — Tsiang Ch'ih.

4. *l*. 20, loftiness. "Loftiness(正气) is the quality of being elevated in character, sentiment and demeanour, in another word, uprightness and greatness of soul. With grieving thoughts, he dwells on how man lives between heaven and earth ever with sorrow and pain for just a trice and soon it is ended. So, the further he thinks, the more dolorous his heart becomes. His spirit flits away, but his body still stagnates here, simply because he is ' Weak in agility and without the means ' to uprise. How could he then not turn inward to chasten himself for upheaving his loftiness to achieve metamorphosis? Gathering loftiness means to purify one's form or stuff and to focus the spirit; it is the occult secret of becoming a fairy. " — Tsiang Ch'ih.

5. *ll*. 21 −22, these two lines. " ' And placid, vacant, free from likes and dislikes, … to be quiescently inert ' is just the high sereneness of Tsê-soon. It would be diametrically different from his being ' Sad for the wringing and blockade of the crowd. ' That is why the poet wishes to go after him. " — Tsiang Ch'ih.

6. *l*. 23, Tsê-soon. Tsê-soon-tse(赤松子), an ancient fairy, was known as the Chief of Rain(雨师) during the prehistoric reign of Emperor Tseng-noon(神农). It is said in *The Lives of Fairies*

(《列仙传》) questionably attributed to Liu Shan (刘向) but probably written by someone in Eas Han, that he ate water gems, was Tseng-noon's teacher, could enter a big fullblazing flame to burn himself without being hurt, stopped on the Quen-lung Mountains(昆仑山), often visited the stone chambers of Mother West-Wang(西王母), and flitted up and down in wind and rain. The young princess of the Emperor chased him, was turned into a fairy and went away with him.

7. *l.*25, the supreme men's fine virtues. The rare qualities of those (至人) who turned to be fairies in the past.

8. *l.*29, Fuh Yüeh who rideth the Tsen star. Fuh Yüeh(傅说), a convict of penal servitude shaping mud walls at Fuh-yan(傅岩), the site of which is at present in the east of Bing-lo *hsien*(平陆县), San-sih(山西) Province, was dreamt of by Wuh-ting(武丁), King of Yin(殷), as a man of virtue and sagacity. He was sought for in the Kingdom and found. Wuh-ting, conversed with him who showed himself true to the king's dream. Thereupon he was made the premier of the state and in a few years the declining dynasty was revived by him. After his natural term of life, as the legend has it, he was raised to ride at the eastern side of the Milky Way the Tsen constellation(大辰,辰星), the middle one between the three constellations Sing(心), Yeh(尾) and Chih(箕), which are the fifth, sixth and last in order respectively of the seven constellations of the Blue Dragon(苍龙七宿).

9. *l.*30, Hang Ts'oon. Hang Ts'oon(韩众,韩终), before he was transformed into a fairy, is said to have eaten the sweet-flag for thirteen years, then long hairs grew all over his body and he was able to recite ten thousand words a day. Soon he flitted away.

10. *l.* 35, the whole line. "Often vaguely and distantly seen on tops of mountains or in the clouds, they, with their corporeal matter dissolved and sublimated, have their spirits flashing about without restraint and so coming to and going away from the earth freely." — Tsiang Ch'ih.

11. *l.* 44, the herbage fresh declining early, and *l.* 47, these residues green. "These two expressions both allude to the poet himself." — Tsiang Ch'ih.

12. *l.* 49, *T'ih* Kao-yang, and *l.* 53, Hsien-yuan. See section Ⅱ, *pp.* 6 −7 and 7 respectively of *Introduction. The Chronicle*(《史记》) says, Hwang-*t'ih*(黄帝) became a fairy and ascended to Heaven.

13. *l.* 50, the whole line. "With *T'ih* Kao-yang too remotely gone, for whom should I strive to show my virtues and capabilities, or who is going to appreciate my sterling qualities?"

14. *l.* 51, the whole line. The extra-metrical statement 重曰 means, according to Hoon Hsin-tsou's *Supplemental Commentary on Ts'ou "Tze"*, the feelings and intents of the poet are not yet fully expressed, so he continues to write his *fuh*. It is evident that the following lines are a furtherance of the preceding, for in line 49, we are told "Old *T'ih* Kao-yang hath too remotely gone", but in line 158 near the end of this poem, he has already "come to Tsuan-shiuh the old *t'ih* at Tsen-p'ing", as a sequel to his continual efforts at distant peregrination. Tsuan-shiuh was Emperor Kao-yang's name.

15. *l.* 53, the whole line. "This is because Hsien-yuan was too noble and remote." — Tsiang Ch'ih.

16. *l.* 54, Wang Jao. Prince royal Jao(王子乔), also called Ts'in

（晋）, eldest son of King Lin of Tsur（周灵王, 571—545 B.
C.）, turned to be a fairy. He liked to play on the circular Pandean pipes（笙）in imitation of the chantings of phoenixes. Rambling between the Ih and Lau（伊, 洛）Streams, he met the fairy
Fwuh-cher the Elder（浮丘公）, who led him up the Soong
Mountains（嵩山）. There he disciplined himself with rigour for
twenty years and rode away from the peak of Kou-tse Mountain
（缑氏山）on the back of a white crane to the fairyland.

17. *l.* 55, the "six airs". There are several different explanations to
the "six airs". According to *The Primal Questions*（《素问》）, a
book recording the questions asked by Hwang-*t'ih* and answers
given by Gieh Pêh（岐伯）regarding diseases and medicines and
therefore the earliest authority on human sicknesses and their
cures in China, the "six airs" are specified as "wind, heat,
moisture, fire, dryness and cold"（风, 热, 湿, 火, 燥, 寒）. In
The Classic of Stars（《星经》）by Sibyl Yen of kan-szê（甘石巫
咸氏）, said to be *T'ih* Yao's physician, they are "the sun, the
moon, stars, time periods, shade and brightness"（日, 月, 星,
辰, 晦, 明）. In Tso's *Commentary on The Spring and Autumn
Annals*（《左氏春秋传》）, they are "Shade, Light, wind, rain,
obscurity and brightness"（阴, 阳, 风, 雨, 晦, 明）. Chü Yuan obviously has his own idea of the "six airs"; here he mentions only
three of them, namely, the midnight "air" of the North（沆瀣）,
the noon "air" of the South（正阳）and the orange "air" or glow
of dawn（朝霞）.

18. *ll.* 57 −58, these two lines. "A man's soul is originally pure, but
cannot help being adulterated by his post-natal foul airs. Therefore, one must absorb the quintessential 'airs' of heaven and

earth — that is to say, according to a note(疏) by Kung Yin-dah
(孔颖达) of Tdaung on the *Commentary*(《系辞》) of Confucius
on *The Universal Mutability*(《周易》) by King Wen(文王),
these are 'the pithy airs of Shade and Light(阴阳精灵之气) of
the universe thickly gathered together to form all things(氤氲积
聚而为万物也)' — to benefit oneself, and then the dross is
purged out and the soul's purity could be kept intact. This is the
initial step of courting loftiness(正气)." — Tsiang Ch'ih.

In another word, the pithy or quintessential airs of Shade and
Light, the two primordial elements of the universe and human affairs — when these get into the human system, the dross is
purged away, according to the mystic and occult philosophy of
Dao Têh.

19. *l.* 60, Nan-ts'iao. Nan-ts'iao(南巢), an ancient site, is now five
lih north-east of Ts'iao *hsien*(巢县), An-whei(安徽) Province.
There is the Wang Jao Cave(王乔洞) on Mount Chin-ding(金庭
山), where the prince was said to rise aloft to become a fairy.

20. *ll.* 63 −68, the quotation. Such is the daoist counsel given by the
fairy prince Jao to the poet, a quick outline or the simple essence
of *The Dao-têh Classic*(《道德经》). Keep thy mind vacant, he
says, and wait for inertness(无为); it would come of itself.
"When the external 'airs' have penetrated the body, the internal
virtue would be synthesized: the six 'airs' could be combined
into one 'air'. But the union would come only after his efforts
to intermingle them up. That is why he makes his inquiry of the
prince. The 'way' is the method of admixture, which could only be apprehended, but not told. 'Minute, it is without an in'
signifies its occult secret; 'grand sans bound', its boundlessness

to fill heaven and earth and the four expanses. But as the soul is not confounded with confusion, the union of the 'airs' would become natural, so that, mysterious and superexcellent as it is, at midnight some day in tranquility, it would not leave him any more. When this union is complete, he would achieve complete freedom. This is the middle part of courting loftiness." — Tsi-ang Ch'ih.

21. *l.* 71, nightless T'an-chiu. T'an-chiu (丹邱) means Minium Mountain, so called because the forests and cliffs of the mountain is often canopied with a haze of minium colour. Legendary lore invests it with the repute of being nightless and the etherealized clime of flying fairies. Having apprehended the way, Chü Yuan now fares straight to T'an-chiu.

22. *l.* 73, Taung Vale, and *l.* 74, nine Suns' shine. Taung Valley (汤谷), also known as Yang Valley (旸谷), was in folklore the eastern valley where the Sun rises in the morning and there water is hot like boiling. There is a great fairy tree Fwuh-soung (扶桑) in the Vale, on the branches of which nestle the nine Suns while the tenth is in the sky. See note 82 on *Lee Sao*.

23. *l.* 75, Jetting Vale. Fei-ts'ui (飞泉), Jetting Vale, in the south-west of the Quen-lung Mountains (昆仑), is said to hold a spring jetting vital elixir which gives immortality to its drinkers.

24. *l.* 76, nonpareil gems twain. These two pieces of big peerless gems are called Woan gem (琬圭, nine inches tall and oblong in shape, with an heaving curve on the top) and Yean gem (琰圭, also nine inches tall, acutely triangular on the top), both radiant-ly lustrous in sheen. "What the fairy prince has taught him in the above is concerned with self-chastening within. Here he speaks

of the things he imbibes and keeps in his breast. When he listened to the instructions, he already understood and was putting to practice the union of the 'six airs' into one. But if the one 'air' is not animated or fervent, it is not potent and vibrant. So he takes in the pith and marrow of all things to make it profound and vehement. This is the last step of courting loftiness." — Tsiang Ch'ih.

25. *ll.* 77 −80, these four lines. "The colour that is beauteous without is most lustrous and translucent; the essence that is purified within is most quickened and potent; the dross is daily purged away; and the soul becomes daily more vivacious: such are because he could truly chasten his body and sublimate his spirit, so that transformation has been achieved herein indeed — what is the anxiety, then, of being 'Weak in agility and without the means'?" — Tsiang Ch'ih.

26. *ll.* 81 −82, these two lines. "Here we know he has already turned a fairy and so can rise aloft and be buoyant. The South State(南州) is his old homeland. 'The cinnamon in winter verdant' is quite different from 'the herbage fresh declining early'; the landscape offers a contrast to his former feelings." — Tsiang Ch'ih.

27. *l.* 85, the whole line. In the original, there is the expression 载营魄, which means "bearing the transparent 魄", a piece of dull matter inseparable from the spirit(魂) in a living person, that is dragged down to earth because of its weight in ordinary cases after one's decease and the spirit flies away alone but in the case of a man changed into a fairy, this piece of dull matter is purified and lightened to accompany the spirit, so that they could freely

fly away together.

28. *l.* 88, Sky-gates. Tsoun-uh(阊阖), the gates of God's Tse-wei Palace(紫微宫) or Purple Palace(紫宫). They are a constellation of fifteen stars(紫微垣), in the north-east of the Dipper, with eight on the east and seven on the west side, standing in guard of the North Polar Constellation(北极五星) and Ker-tsen Constellation(钩陈六星).

29. *ll.* 87 −88, these two lines. "The following is a description of his sights in his distant wanderings. In these two lines, he first speaks of the visit to Heaven's portal. His asking Heaven's Porter to 'wait for me' is quite different from 'He leaneth on the Gates, staring me fore the sill' of *Lee Sao* (line 210). " — Tsiang Ch'ih.

30. *l.* 89, Feng-loon, and *l.* 90, T'ai-wei's ten stars. Tsu-tse in his *Variorum Commentary on Ts'ou "Tze"*(《楚辞集注》) mistakes Feng-loon(丰隆) here, as in line 223 of *Suffering Throes*, to be the Lord of Thunder(雷师). *Vide* note 96 on line 223 of that ode and note 43 below. The constellation T'ai-wei(太微) consists of ten stars, all with individual names which we need not specify here, situated in the south of the Dipper. It was known to be the southern palace of Heaven's God(天帝).

31. *l.* 91[1], twice bright Heaven. A note on the line "Stopping in the double sheen of empyrean briliance"(集重阳之清征) in Tsauming's *Literary Selections*(《昭明文选》) says, "the empyrean region is light and its brilliance is twice light, hence the double sheen. " Hoon Hsin-tsou (洪兴祖) says in his *Supplemental Commentary on Ts'ou "Tze"*(《楚辞补注》) that Heaven is the accumulation of light, it is ninefold, therefore it is many times

bright.

32. *l.* 92[1], Tsin-sze. It（旬始）is God's name，also the name of a star by the side of the Dipper. Its other name is T'ai-ih（太一，太乙）.

33. *l.* 92[2], the sacred place. Tsing-*t'uh*（清都）is where God resides. *The Classic of Stars*（《星经》）："The star T'ai-ih（太一），the spirit of God，is half a degree south of the star T'ien-ih（天一），presiding over sixteen gods."

34. *l.* 93，His palatial court. "T'ai-yih（太仪）is the court of God's palace where the rites of awe（威仪）are practiced." — Tsiang Ch'ih.

35. *l.* 94，Mount Ee-vei-lü. This mountain（于微间，医无间）was anciently known as the chief borough（镇）of the state *You-tsur*（幽州），the north-eastern division of the Central Empire. After his peregrination of the sky，he comes down from the north-east.

36. *l.* 95，chariots ten thousand. See my discussion on this phrase in comparison with "my chariots a full thousand" in *l.* 359 of *Suffering Throes*，section Ⅶ，§ 11 of *Introduction*，*pp.* 84 −91.

37. *l.* 106，Kur-moun. Beginning from line 95，these eleven lines give an account of his journey in the east. God T'ai-hao（太皞），the Great Light，was the spirit of Fwu-shih（伏羲）；he ruled in his lifetime by virtue of the Virtue of Wood（木德）and died in the east as the god of Wood Virtue. His subordinate Kur-moun（句芒）was the Lord of Wood（木正）.

38. *l.* 107，and then turn right. This is to journey in the west. To pass by God T'ai-hao and turn right is to go from east to west.

39. *l.* 108，Fei-Iian. Fei-Iian（飞廉）was the Principal of Winds（风伯）.

40. *l.* 114, the whole line. Ruo-sur(蓐收), the lord of God, was the son of Sao-hao(少昊), the Golden God of the Western Sky(西皇), Ruo-sur means that in the autumnal eighth moon, plant life fades and droops; he is therefore the elemental astringent force of nature.

41. *ll.* 119 −120, these two lines. "From these two lines to line 154, an account of his travels in the south is given." The God of Grand Shadow(太阴神), also called Yuan-wuh(玄武), stands for the seven constellations of the North(斗,牛,女,虚,危,室,壁). His symbols are the emyd and the serpent(龟,蛇), "Just then, he goes from the west to the south, and Yuan-wuh is in the north; so he summons him." — Tsiang Ch'ih.

42. *l.* 122, Wen-tsoun. *The Classic of Stars*(《星经》): the six stars of the Wen-tsoun(文昌) Constellation form the outline of a half crescent, in the front of the quadrilateral ladle of the Great Dipper, each having its own name.

43. *l.* 125, the Chief of Rain, and *l.* 126, the Lord of Thunder. They (雨师,雷公) are mentioned together here. So, Feng-loon(丰隆) in line 89 must be the Chief of Clouds(云师); the swift conductor or guide of the poet; he cannot be Thunderor Thunderclaps, else the Lord of Thunder here would be rhetorically redundant with him. See note 96 of *Lee Sao* and note 30 above.

44. *l.* 139, divine Yen, God of Fiery Virtue. He(炎神) was Tsengnoon(神农), in his lifetime the second of the earliest three *hwang*(三皇) or emperors of the nation. His subordinate lord was Tsuo-yung(祝融).

45. *ll.* 140 −142, these three lines. Literally, the original 南疑 should be "the southern Doubts", that is, the Nine Doubts(九

嶷）in the south. "From lines 119 to 142, the poet says, going from the west to the south, he passes above over his homeland Ts'ou, feeling sadly touched at heart, but he makes up his mind not to recede, checks his thoughts of kings and friends and cuts short his sorrow. Then he flits further southward, passes over the Nine Doubts(九嶷）, covers the strange domains and soars above the expanse of the South Sea." — Tsiang Ch'ih.

46. *l.* 143, Tsuo-yung the Lord of Fire. He(祝融）, also the Spirit of the South Sea, comes toward and keep off on-lookers.

47. *l.* 144, Fwu-fei. She(宓妃）, Fwu-shih's daughter, was drowned in the Lo Stream(洛水）and being made its Spirit(洛神）.

48. *l.* 145, *Yen-tze* and *Tsen-yün*. The former(咸池）is a dance-cantata, Hwang-*t'ih*, revised by Yao(尧）, also called *Great Harmony*(大咸）; the latter(承云）, a piece of music of Hwang-*t'ih* or of Tsuan-shiuh(颛顼）, meaning *Sustaining Clouds*.

49. *l.* 146, the whole line. "Two Genii fair" are Erh-hwang(娥皇）and Neü-ying(女英）, Suen's queen and beebee. They come hither to attend on the poet, to play, dance and sing the nine airs of *Great Continuance*(九"韶"歌）.

50. *l.* 147, the whole line. The Spirit of Hsiang(湘灵）is the fair Lady of Hsiang. The ancient zithern(颂瑟）is an instrument seven feet and two inches long, a foot and eight inches wide, with twenty-five chords.

51. *l.* 148, the Gods of Sea and the River. The God of North Sea, named Hai-ruo(海若）or North Hai-ruo(北海若）, and the God of luteous River(河伯）, named Feng-yih(冯夷）.

52. *l.* 153, the whole line. "Without this abundance of music, his grief could not be ended; so, this account of music in the south

is alone full of details. It must be noted that in all these delights in music, there is a strain of afflicting sorrow. " — Tsiang Ch'ih.

53. *ll.* 155 −156, these two lines. "Now he travels to the north and has at last reached the Arctic Gate at the horizon. " — Tsiang Ch'ih.

54. *ll.* 157, Tsing-yuan. This 清源 is the source of water, the North Sea. The God of the north is Tsuan-shiuh(颛顼); his spirit, Yuan-ming(玄冥), meaning the quality of being distant, obscure and lonely, or Darkness. Here he finds towering, mountainous ice and ever-falling snow.

55. *l.* 161, Jê-lê, the God of Nature himself. Jê-lê(黔嬴), so pronounced according to Tsu-tse's note on this name, was the God of Nature(造化) in Heaven. "From line 159 onward, he ranges up and down to the zenith, the nadir and the four extremities of the universe. The Sky has six spaces(六间) and earth has four margins(四维). " — Tsiang Ch'ih.

56. *l.* 166, the unfathomed deep. This 大壑 means the Eastern Sea.

57. *l.* 167, sans the ground, and *l.* 168, sans the sky. Deep and profound far beyond the earth and heaven, the state of occultness and purity.

58. *l.* 169, without sight, and *l.* 170, without sound. "To be without sight and without sound is to be in the state of quietude and purity. "

59. *ll.* 171^1 −172^2, these four lines. Here, having undergone a complete metamorphosis, he has attained "utter purity"(至清) and come next to "Primitive Prime"(泰初) at long last. *Li-tse*(《列子》) says, "Primitive Prime is the beginning of 'airs'. "

Tsaung-tse(《庄子》) says, "In the state of Primitive Prime, there are quiescence and namelessness." "'Having gone through the infinite deep' and via a by-way to the six spaces of heaven (六间) and four corners(四维) of earth, he finds himself in the company of Jê-lê, the God of Nature, visiting what is above and below and the four spaces, and vast shadowiness and profound silence. He has indeed gone through all boundlessness now." — Tsiang Ch'ih.

Divining to Know Where I Should Stay(卜居)

"This poem was composed by Chü Yuan. Taking pity on people of his time for getting used to the crooked practices of fawning and sophistry and their contrariety to uprightness, the poet feigns ignorance of the right or wrong of these two things and would rather ask divination from the achilleas and emyd shell to decide for him. So he wrote this poem to lay open his choice between the two for warning and quickening the common run of men. Some said that Chü Yuan could not be without doubt on the question, hence his inquiry of the soothsayer. This is mistaken. " — Tsu Hsih.

"Chü Yuan composed this poem to show his solitary intent. Where to stay means how to behave — the way for the virtuous man to bear himself. With confidence at heart and divergent from the world, he has his distinction between purity and foulness clear like diverse streams and his consideration of good hap and ill fortune light like a wind-swept feather. Others could not plan for him; deities and spirits could not alter his stand. Apprehensive that the coming generations might regard him as too turgid and know not how to demean themselves fairly, he affects to ask divination of the achilleas and emyd shell which Tsan-yün dares not decide, to express his intent. So he exhausts the harms done to the state in wavering, to show his resentment. But Wang Yi(王逸) says Chü Yuan's heart was confused and his mind perplexed, knowing not what to do and hoping to hear of strange measures: how foolish this is!" — Wang Fuh-tse.

"Where to stay means the way to demean oneself. Having offended because of loyalty, the poet could appeal nowhere, so howling his sorrow by means of divination. To say that he does not know what to do is simply an expression of indignation." — Tsiang Ch'ih.

1. *l.* 1, for three years. "These three years are not exactly known when. Tracing the sense of the context, I suspect it was at the time when the poet was expelled to Han-pei(汉北) by King Hwai(怀王)." — Tsiang Ch'ih. *Vide* section Ⅷ, §10 of *Introduction* (*pp.* 82 −84), for my conjecture of the poem's date.

2. *l.* 3 −4, the Grand Soothsayer Ts'eng Tsan-yün. He(太卜郑詹尹) was the high official in charge of divination in Ts'ou. The Grand Soothsayer(太卜,大卜), also called the Chief Soothsayer (卜正), was the official head priest to prognosticate or interpret oracular divinations on momentous events. According to the *Tsur Rites*(《周礼》), the Grand Soothsayer officiated in interpreting "the three auguries(三兆), the three *Mutabilities*(三'易') and the three oneiromancies(三梦)". In the Saung and Tsur Dynasties, this was one of the six "Great" posts installed by the sons of Heaven(天子), the kings, to take care of main state matters. There were two such heads in the department, of the rank of lower courtiers(下大夫), under whom were the master soothsayers, the soothsayers, the emyd men and the achilleas men(卜师,卜人,龟人,筮人).

3. *l.* 6, adjusted his achilleas and rubbed his emyd shell. The original 策 means 蓍, the achilleas. Botanically, the plant is called *Achillea sibirica*, an herb of many years' growth, two to three feet tall, blowing white or pink flowers in autumn. Confucius has been quoted for saying that it "is like men of venerable age; old men, having lived through long years and come across plenty of

things, know better. " It was said that the herb, growing for a thousand years, would yield three hundred stems. Its stems were collected by ancient soothsayers for drawing lots in testing muta-bility(拈筮占卦). *The Book of Homage to Heaven and Earth* in Sze-ma Tsien's *The Chronicle*(司马迁:《史记·封禅书》) has it that Hwang-*t'ih*(黄帝), having obtained the precious *t'ing*(宝鼎,a two-eared tripodal vessel cast in bronze, later kept to signi-fy the political sovereignty of a state) and the divine achilleas, used the latter to calculate the twenty-four sectional divisions of the seasons(二十四节气) and the twelve time periods of the day (日辰). The nether shells of the emyd(龟底壳) were used for scorching in fire and detecting people's lots therefrom(龟卜). Here, "The achilleas were adjusted for lot-drawing and the emyd shell was rubbed for being parched and lot-finding. " — Tsiang Ch'ih.

4. *ll.* 11 −12, these two lines. "The original 送往劳来(literally 'in seeing people off and cheering those who come') means to please and flatter all people indiscriminately. " — Tsiang Ch'ih.

5. *l.* 14, toil with labour. "… 'toil with labour', etc. means to be a recluse. " — Tsiang Ch'ih.

6. *l.* 15, the whole line. "It means to seek elevation to a high offi-cial post by associating with magnificence. " — Tsiang Ch'ih.

7. *ll.* 17 −18, these two lines. "These allude to his going after Peng Yen(彭咸). " — Tsiang Ch'ih.

8. *l.* 21, soar aloft and over all. "This also means to be a hermit. " — Tsiang Ch'ih.

9. *l.* 25, a woman. "This is a hidden thrust at Ts'eng Sieü(郑袖). To speak of attending upon a woman side by side with soaring

aloft is because the whole court got advancement by serving her, without doing which one could only retire to be a hermit. " — Tsiang Ch'ih.

10. *ll.* 26 −27, these two lines. "This is to stand upright singly at the court. " — Tsiang Ch'ih.

11. *l.* 37, the yellow cygnus. The yellow cygnus(黄鹄) was a fabulous bird of huge size; in one flight, it covered a thousand *lih*. Fairies rode on its back. It was not the common cygnus.

12. *l.* 41, the whole line. "The above are the poet's questions to the divination. " — Tsiang Ch'ih.

13. *ll.* 42 −43, these two lines. "The indiscrimination of right and wrong. " — Tsiang Ch'ih.

14. *ll.* 44 −45, these two lines. The earthen *phu*(釜) was an ancient vessel for measuring grain. Opinions vary on its capacity: some sayings had it that it held 6. 4 *t'ur*(斗) , the modern namesake of which is about 4. 54 cubic feet (English measure); another saying was not sure whether it held 20 *t'ur* or 30 *t'ur*, the modern namesakes of which are about 14. 18 cubic feet or 21. 27 cubic feet respectively (English measure).

"The ringing golden bell is shattered and trashed. The earthen *phu*, with sound not resonant but rather displeasing, as the multitude strikes it hard, roars like thunder-claps. These two statements show the mis-use of proper things. " — Tsiang Ch'ih.

15. *ll.* 46 −47, these two lines. The wicked are all the rage now, while the man of virtue is openly brow-beaten. That is the reason why he wants to learn through divination how he should bear himself. All such are words of indignation.

16. *ll.* 51 −59. "The foot is much longer than the inch. But when a

foot is sometimes inadequate in length, it is shorter than it ought to be. The inch is much shorter than a foot. But when an inch happens to be a little too long, it is longer than it should be. Things natural may fall too short of their use, such as the sky is vacant in the north-west and the earth is scant in the south-east. The intellect of man cannot always con, such as Yao and Suen did not know all things and Confucius fell short of an old farmer in knowledge of cultivating corn and raising cabbages. The sun and moon run according to their respective definite laws, but there is the difference between waxings and wanings. The depth of wisdom he fails to fathom is illustrated by Pêh-yih(伯夷) being starved to death at Mount Ser-yang(首阳) and the brigand Tsê(盗跖) ending his natural years beside his home window. What one should rid oneself of proves sometimes unfortunately to be auspicious. What one should pursue turns out sometimes to be ill-starred. Deities and spirits do not tell people of ills beforehand, but especially would not induce people to do unrighteous things. So, how could the emyd shell and the achilleas take part in the affair?" — Tsiang Ch'ih.

The Fisherman (渔父)

"*The Fisherman* was written by Chü Yuan. The man was a recluse of that time. Some say these are the poet's assumed words. " — Tsu Hsih.

"In *The Fisherman*, Chü Yuan relates what occurred to him by writing this *fuh* poem. Between the River(江) and the Han Stream (汉), there were in ancient days high hermits secluded in farming and angling, like Tsi-eü(接舆) and Tsaung Tsur(庄周), to fend their lives and be removed from harms. This fisherman is of their kind. Compassionating Chü Yuan for his loyalty and firmness that would lead him to disaster, he wishes to turn him to his own way. Thankful of the man's kindness, the poet relates the happening to show that he is not unaware of this, but his good hap and ill luck are closely linked with those of the king, his feelings for him could not be contained, his daedal attainments are not of just these latter days and his spotless integrity could not be soiled, and that he is not ignorant that those who dart to the azure in ideals but shrink back in the face of realities are laughing at him for his vain endeavours, but he simply could not follow their counsel. The Stream of Tsoung-loung (沧浪之水) is in the east of the Han River(汉水), in the south-east of Mount Wuh-taung(武当山) of Chün-*tsur*(均州) today. *The Fisherman* was written to express his feelings on the encounter. Thus, this piece was plainly composed at Han-pei(汉北) in King Hwai's(怀王) reign. *Mencius*(《孟子》) also contains this song of Tsoung-loung. It was the same folk strain heard by Confucius on the

Han when he went to Ts'ou from Yi(叶) and Dun(邓). " — Wang Fuh-tse.

"Some say this is also Chü Yuan's assumed piece of work. But as the Grand Curator of History has quoted it in the *Life* of the poet, it is not impossible that it is a veritable record. It cannot be known, however, whether the fisherman did really exist. But the River depths and Tsoung-loung were actually passed by and over by the poet, it could be readily imagined. " — Tsiang Ch'ih.

For the date of composition of this short piece and its other relevancies, see section VII, §17 of *Introduction*, *p.* 137.

1. *l.* 1, River depths. "The River was the Yuan Stream(沅江). At Tsang-têh *fuh*(常德府) by the side of the Yuan River today, there are the Nine Depths(九潭). " — Tsiang Ch'ih.

2. *ll.* 3 −4, the Lord of the Tri-Lane Portals. The Lord of the Trio of (family lane) Portals(三闾大夫) was the title of a noble official post at the court of King Hwai of Ts'ou(楚怀王). "Chü Yuan shared the surnames of the triad of royal families — Tsau, Chü and Chin(昭,屈,景). He took charge of the heraldry of these, leading their choice elements to heighten the flowers of the state. " Thus, he might be called the Lord Chancellor of the Heralds College of Ts'ou. Lane-portals were gates of lanes, each leading to twenty-five households; so each of the triad of royal families consisted of about as many households. You Hsiung(鬻熊), the lineal descendant of Hwang-*t'ih's*(黄帝) grandson Tsuan-shiuh(颛顼), Emperor Kao-yang(帝高阳), was King Wen's(文王) teacher. During King Tseng's(成王) reign, his great-great-grandson Hsiung Yi(熊绎) was allotted the fief of Ts'ou(楚) as a viscount(子).

3. *ll.* 30 − 33, the song. This short song is also quoted in *Mencius* (《孟子》). Old commentators from Wang Yi, Tsu Hsih to Wang Fuh-tse attribute the Stream of Tsoung-loung(沧浪) to the lower tributary of the Han River. Tsiang Ch'ih points out that this Tsoung-loung is the confluent stream of the rivulets Tsoung and Loung issuing forth from Mounts Tsoung and Loung(沧山, 浪山) in the north-east of Süe-puh(溆浦) and flows into Yuan Stream (沅水). The region was later named Wuh-ling(武陵) and Loon-yang(龙阳). It has several remains reminiscent of Chü Yuan. The attribution of Tsoung-loung to the lower tributary of Han River would be incompatible with the "River depths" in *l.* 1.

图书在版编目（CIP）数据

屈原诗选英译:英文/孙大雨译.
—上海:上海三联书店,2022.8
（国学经典外译丛书.第一辑）
ISBN 978 - 7 - 5426 - 7801 - 0

Ⅰ.①屈… Ⅱ.①孙… Ⅲ.①古典诗歌—诗集—中国
—战国时代—英文②楚辞—英文 Ⅳ.①I222.3

中国版本图书馆 CIP 数据核字（2022）第 142535 号

国学经典外译丛书·第一辑

屈原诗选英译

译　者　孙大雨

责任编辑　钱震华
装帧设计　徐　徐

出版发行　上海三联书店
　　　　　（200030）中国上海市漕溪北路331号A座6楼
印　　刷　上海颛辉印刷厂有限公司

版　次　2022年8月第1版
印　次　2022年8月第1次印刷
开　本　700mm×1000mm　1/16
字　数　640千字
印　张　45
书　号　ISBN 978 -7 -5426 -7801 -0/I·1779
定　价　99.00元